R R I I V V E E R R R R U U N N .

R
I
V
E
R
R
U
N

A
R
M
O
R
I
C
A

Y
E
S
T
E
R
N

BY S.P. SOMTOW

Riverrun Trilogy
Riverrun Copyright © 1991 by S.P. Somtow
Armorica Copyright © 1992 by S.P. Somtow
Yestern Copyright © 1996 by S.P. Somtow

ISBN: 1-56865-194-5

Borealis is an imprint of White Wolf Publishing.

White Wolf Publishing
780 Park North Boulevard, Suite 100
Clarkston, GA 30021

Cover and Interior Illustration by Troy Eittreim
Cover and Interior Design by Michelle Prahler

Contents

Contents

Contents

RIVERRUN

for
my friends in Baud Town,
whose private universes intersect with mine
by way of
an electronic metaphor:
I wonder sometimes if you are real.

Row, row, row your boat
Gently down the stream;
Merrily, merrily, merrily, merrily,
Life is but a dream.

BOOK **ONE**

ALPH, THE SACRED RIVER

". . . *sad and weary I go to you, my cold father,*
my cold mad father, my cold mad
feary father . . ."

—*Finnegans Wake*

To My Sons

They are standing at the river's edge; sometimes
I watch them, sometimes
I cannot bear to watch, sometimes
I wish for the river to run upstream, back to the mountains,
Blue as the sky, as grief, as delusion.

They are playing by the river's edge; sometimes
Long past sunset, I hear them in the wind that shakes
The cottonwoods. I cannot bear to listen.
In my heart I know sometimes
That the river has reversed its course; I know sometimes
That the river will not turn back till its watery end,
Black as the sky, as grief, as disillusion.

They have walked away from the river's edge; I have named them
After the gods. Sometimes
I do not think they are coming home. Sometimes, not daring to look,
I say when I open my eyes they will be long gone, not gone;
That the river will run upstream, downstream.
Better not to look at all; for in the momentary closure,
The blink's breadth between two truths is what I feel for them; sometimes
I know it to be love.
Red as the sky, as grief, as joy.

CHAPTER ONE

THE DREAM BOOK OF THEO ETCHISON

T h e o   E t c h i s o n

It was the nineties, the time before the mad millennium. I was young and puffed up with shiny new epiphanies. A dollar could still buy a Coke and a candy bar and telephones were disembodied voices that left everything to the imagination. And some people still chose to die at home.

Oh God, I really want to remember it all. I want to see, taste, feel my family's journey across the Arizona desert then down the dark river that leads every place. So much of it seems dreamlike now, fabricless, fantastical. It's so easy to think I made it up. I have too much imagination anyway. They always used to tell me that. Too much imagination. Especially when I would tell the truth. Too much, too much.

How much is a universe? A thousand universes?

I was young.

When I try to recall that time, it's not the air conditioner spluttering dust into the old station wagon that I remember first. Not the shimmering sand. Not my father's eyes, hypnotized by the road, not my brother Joshua cussing out that eighteen-wheeler zipping past us in the right lane. No. It's a smell I remember first, a smell hanging in the air like stale orange juice, the smell of my mother dying.

I'm young. Bursting with hormones and ideas, on the brink of simply everything, and here I am sucking in death with every breath as we drive across the desert on our way to Mexico and the Laetrile clinic.

It's suffocating. I climb over the back seat so I can lie in the back, propping my head with a Stephen King novel. My mother stirs. I hear the rustle of her blankets but I don't look back at her. I'm afraid to look.

A country and western song is blaring. We haven't been able to get any other station since we left Buckeye. Dad and Joshua are fighting.

"Dude, Dad, it was a stupid idea for you to leave the 10. At least we could have found ourselves a truck stop by now."

Dad sighs.

"I'm hungier'n shit," Josh says.

My mother stirs. I do not look back because I know how her eyes will be—sad and sunken, the color of pea soup. She'll be sitting with her head quashed against the window and the blanket wrapped tight round and round her like a winding-sheet. And she'll be shivering. Even though the air is stifling and the sweat is pouring down onto my T-shirt. I want it to end, I'm thinking. I want her to die.

"Hungrier'n shit," Josh says. I hate him.

Phil, my dad, says, "Look, Mary. Dust storm up there. Whirling against the blue mountain."

"It's beautiful, dear." Her voice is tiny and feelingless. "I'm cold."

"Look at that sucker, kids," Phil says.

"Dude," says Josh.

I want her to die. I don't look. I don't turn around, don't even acknowledge with a grunt. After a while the Stephen King book starts bruising my neck as I lie back. I root around for my knapsack and try to scrunch my head up against that instead. My own book is inside, a three ring binder where I've written down all the brightly colored dreams I've been having since we left Virginia. The dreams have been much more vivid than this journey. Outside my dreams, the smell seeps into everything and fogs up the whole world.

I want it to be over.

I close my eyes for a while, hoping somehow to shut out the smell. The perspiration penetrates my closed lids and I wonder if I'm crying. My father says, "Is Theo asleep?"

Josh says, "Wake up, shitface. You won't see anything that lies ahead."

"Perhaps he prefers looking back," my father says.

"Sometimes the past is all we have," says my mother, almost inaudibly. Sullenly I look at the highway we've been traveling. The road shimmers. On either side are mountains, blue-gray and twisted. The road climbs and the car groans even though we're nowhere near sixty-five miles per hour. My head slams against the back seat and I grimace from the pain as we lurch toward the crest of the mountain.

"Hungrier'n shit," says Joshua.

That's when we see the billboard for the Chinese restaurant.

It's framed in the dip between two jags of sandstone, Day-Glo pink letters against a green background. It's twenty-five miles down the road and it features Charlie Chan's World-Famous Peking Pizza.

"Talk about nouvelle cuisine," my dad says.

"Feed me already," says Joshua.

"Feed your fucking zits, you mean," I say. I'm craning to see the billboard, cradling the side of my head in my crooked elbow so I won't have to look at her.

"I have no zits, little brother," says Joshua, "not since I started eating—"

"Organic," I say, sneering.

"Lay off each other," Dad says. I can tell he's not paying any attention to the road; I keep thinking he's going to have an accident any minute. Veer off the embankment. Like Wile E. Coyote. We might as well all die, I think. "We've got more important things to think about than—"

"I'm cold," says Mary. The heat is intolerable.

"I'll eat Chinese," Josh says. "I'll eat anything as long as the place is air conditioned."

The road is level now. Another billboard tells us that we can also expect Szechuan burgers topped with sizzling spicy shrimp.

"You find culture in the strangest places," says Dad.

I want us all to die. That's the first feeling that comes back to me when I force myself to think about those times.

I've seen those movies where some pretty pasty-faced girl is riddled with cancer and she lies there dying for the whole movie while the others recite strings of platitudes and the girl stays pretty until the very end when they close her eyes and the credits start to roll over the sappy love theme. There'd just been a slew of those movies, last summer back in Virginia, before we knew the truth about our own family. Joshua and his girlfriend Serena used to go to the drive-in a lot, and sometimes they would take me. Sluglike Serena would always bring three handkerchiefs (because she'd seen one of those TV critics refer to them as three-hanky movies) and she'd lay them out on the dashboard. Then she and Joshua would retire to the back seat so I was always the only one who got to endure the movie. I would sit, arms folded, with my head jammed between the two bucket seats, and sometimes my back would get clawed up some, especially in the drawn-out death scenes which seemed to get them pretty worked up. Serena had this morbid sex thing with death (she talked about the sick-dying scenes in the soaps a lot) but when she learned about Mom she never set foot in our house again. She could tell reality from fantasy all right.

Movies can show you everything about death except the smell. Death isn't beautiful. It's humiliating and gross and embarrassing and when you know it's about to happen it tears you apart in ways you never dreamed of.

The third billboard shows Dr. Fu Manchu waggishly waving a chopstick. Even the country and western song has turned to crackling. I slump back down against the knapsack. The three-ring binder protrudes and I feel hot plastic on my ear. I take out the book. There's a purple felt tip in it and I start hunting for the last page I was working on.

"What's the boy doing?" my father says.

"Scrawling in that notebook of his," says Josh. "The one he won't let any of us look at."

It's the book I've been writing down all my nightmares in. All those bad dreams that have been coming at me since our journey began.

The car rattles and my felt tip does a spider dance along the faint blue lines. I close my eyes. I try to remember my last dream, the dream about the burning world.

This is how it goes:

It's pitch-black. All I can hear is the sound of a battle, something like one of the battle scenes in Ivan the Terrible which Dad makes us watch on PBS a lot when he gets into his really down-on-sitcoms mood. A lot of screaming and rifle reports and weird flashes and people crying out in a language I can't understand. Now and then there's lightning and there's someone's face . . . a skull . . . a man with slate-colored eyes who stares at the carnage.

He has a thin smile on his lips and a droplet of blood at the corner of his mouth. He's staring straight at me out of the darkness. He knows my name. The lightning flash fades and the battle rages on in the dark.

I hear the sound of water.

I hear the man with slate-colored eyes say, "Truthsayer . . . truthsayer . . . truthsayer." I do not know whom he is speaking to.

Somehow I know he's on another world. I know that the world is burning and he has to reach the water.

The water roars.

I see a woman riding in a chariot drawn by animals with antlers. Smoke streams all around her and her cloak flaps over her face and her face is covered with serpent scales. She looks at me across the void between the worlds. There's water running between us. A creek maybe, a lake, a river.

Suddenly I know her name: Katastrofa Darkling.

I feel Joshua breathing down my neck. I try to wrestle the book away from him. "This is private, Josh."

He climbs over the back seat. He sits down next to me. He won't let go of the book. He's trembling. Suddenly I realize that he's scared.

"Where did you get that name from?"

He looks at me. For the first time in several days I feel the bond between us and I know that I love him. It hurts me and it makes me angry.

"You shouldn't read my book of dreams," I say. "It's private. I'm entitled."

He wipes the cold sweat from his forehead, sweeps back his long dark hair. "I dreamed that dream," he says. "I heard that name." Something in his eyes . . . something to do with sex, I think.

"She's an ugly bitch. A scaly woman, an evil woman. Her eyes are red and empty."

"She's beautiful," he says softly.

"Then you didn't dream my dream, bro," I say, furious because I desperately need to have a place inside my brain that doesn't belong to anyone else in my family.

"I dream about Katastrofa Darkling a lot," my brother says. "You plucked her out of my mind somehow. You always do things like that. You're one of those ESP freaks . . . you fucking ought to be on talk shows."

I realize that he fears me.

Arrogantly, Katastrofa Darkling gestures. . . . The soldiers' tusks glimmer in the light of many moons.

"No magic about the kid," my father says, almost missing the turnoff to the Chinese restaurant. "Too much imagination is all." I have been hearing this all my life.

"Give me back my book," I say. My brother is about to turn the page. He is engrossed. I can tell he is aroused somehow. His cheeks are flushed and he won't look at me.

None of us are looking at each other.

⑤

"Get to the river! Before the whole world blows!"

The man with the slate-colored eyes is listening to the voice of a dying man. I can't see the dying man's face at all. But now I see that the man with the slate-colored eyes is wounded. He's crawling toward the river and—

I feel betrayed when my brother says, "I never saw any of it this clearly, Theo. But I saw something."

The dying man is a magician, I think. He cries out: "Get to the river! Find a new truthsayer!"

The man with the slate-colored eyes sees the water. I see the water through his eyes. The water is a gateway. The water gushes as the earth rumbles. Behind us, the whinnying of alien beasts of burden over the death-rattles of men.

He can't see clearly. Tears sting his eyes and fumes choke him. The water rushes down a precipice toward a vague mist fringed with rainbow steam.

"Sometimes when I dream of Katastrofa she is like a dragon and she sucks me into herself and folds her wings around me—"

"Like Serena," I say. We're carrying on this conversation in a whisper because we sense that it has something to do with sex. Our parents are pretty liberal, I mean they really don't mind when we say *fuck* and like that, but we both get pretty self-conscious when it comes to discussing . . . well, if we didn't have ourselves as evidence, we'd wonder if Phil and Mary knew anything at all about the birds and bees.

"Serena was a slug," I say.

"You asshole," says my brother, but he's not angry about it. I can tell that he's thinking about the other woman, the woman in my dream. Somehow the same name has cropped up in both our dreams. It's happened before. We are close, Joshua and I, although I do hate him most of the time. He is more handsome than I, when he's relatively zitless as he is right now, and he knows how to talk to people, and he's good at bullshitting, which has always been totally difficult for me. And he drives, which I can't yet for another two years at least.

In the dream I am swallowed up in the water, dark and warm and full of promises.

There's a game my dad and I once used to play. It goes like this:

Sit on my lap and I will close my eyes. Sit on my lap and steer and say, "Trust me." We'll be like a single person, father and son, a team, each one of us holding the life of the other in his hand.

We have not played this game for seven years.

The station wagon stops. The air conditioning stops. The air stops moving and the dust settles on me and my brother.

"I suppose we should get out of the car now," my father says.

"I'll help Mom," Joshua says, and bounds over the seat to open the door and to let me slither out of the back into the sunlight, still clutching my binder under my arm, trying to soothe my rumpled Redskins T-shirt.

"Jesus! What kind of a place is this?" I hear Joshua say.

"In the middle of nowhere . . ." my dad says, "as if we've somehow stumbled into another country."

There are no cars in the parking lot. There's nothing all around us, no gas stations, no Circle K convenience stores . . . nothing but this thing that looks like a palace out of a 1950s spectacle. It's got fifteen-foot-tall portals with gold-colored plastic bas-reliefs. It's got a roof with pointed eaves and murals with long bearded men in faded robes. Everything's caked with dust, and the lettering over the cracked façade reads:

IN XAN D D KUBL KH
A ST PLEASURE D DE

There's a smile in my dad's voice as he says, very softly, behind me, "Where Alph, the sacred river, ran . . ."

And Joshua says, "Through caverns measureless to man . . ."

And my mother says, "Down to a sunless sea." And begins to cry. Bitterly, so bitterly.

My Dad has resigned from the poetry chair of a small university in Northern Virginia so we can make this trip together. Before all this happened we lived in Alexandria in a small house by the Potomac and I went to GW Junior High, and on Sundays, when other families went to church, we read poetry together. "Poetry *is* religion," my dad used to tell us. I know a lot of weird words (and even now some line comes clanging in my head like a cracked church bell) but I am young so the lines all jangle inside me and I don't know what they mean but I don't care because they sound awesome.

The sun burns us. But there's a gritty wind that bears away some of the fragrance of death.

"Shall we go in?" It's my mother talking.

At last I turn to look at her. The Navajo blanket she's been draping herself with slips down to her shoulders. She is almost bald from the chemotherapy. Her hollow cheeks are soaked. She draws the blanket tight around herself and wipes at her tears with a frayed corner.

"Maybe it's closed . . . maybe it's . . ." Joshua starts to hum the Twilight Zone theme in an ominous falsetto.

A tiny placard is taped to the door. It says WELCOME. Funny how we haven't noticed it till now.

I hear the roar of water . . . as if we were standing by the sea. But it's the middle of the desert, I tell myself, the middle of nowhere.

CHAPTER TWO

IN A CHINESE RESTAURANT

J o s h u a   E t c h i s o n

I had always known that my brother did not live in quite the same universe as other people. You and I and everyone we know, we go from *A* to *B*, from morning to night, from six in the morning to six oh one. But to Theo everything always seemed to be eternally in the present. We see the world as a series of discrete entities, but to Theo they were always connected. Sometimes I swear he could see the future. And he was bad at lying. That's what drove me crazy the most.

Before we got to the Chinese restaurant, we'd been on the road for weeks. My mother had been sick for almost two years, and this journey was supposed to bring us all together, as well as maybe cure her, if we made it as far as Mexico and the macrobiotic Laetrile clinic of the notorious Dr. Isabella de la Verdád. I don't know if anyone really believed that part of it would work, although reading the brochures had set me off on an organic food kick that I've been trying to stay on even now.

My brother stood apart from the three of us, hearing something we didn't hear, an alien music. He was a malnourished-looking boy, and my Redskins T-shirt hung all the way down to his knees on him, past his shorts. He had big eyes, the color of the creek in back of our grandmother's house in Spotsylvania County, and he was looking shiftily around, like there was someone watching him. It was a make-believe cloak-and-dagger game I'd often seen him play when he thought he wasn't being watched.

My stomach was growling and so I pushed open the door into the gaudy restaurant. In the hall there were three funhouse mirrors. Beyond the inner door, a ceiling fan turned, squeaking, and there were some dilapidated tables set with candles. Tourist posters of the Great Wall and the Forbidden City hung on the walls. No air conditioning, I thought bitterly.

I led my mom inside by the hand and helped her into a chair. It was one of her good days today. Dad sat down next to her and helped her with her medication. Theo was off by himself, peering into every booth.

"Some place, huh, Josh," said Dad.

"Yeah."

"I wonder why they built a place like this in the middle of no-where. . . . I wonder how they can make a living. . . ."

"Maybe some people just too rich to think of being practical, sir." A sort of Chinese Peter Cushing loomed above us. His shadow crossed my mother's face. She looked down at the table. "Twenty years ago, a man misread a map, thought the freeway would pass through here, buy up all the land . . . make Xanadu at the center of the wilderness."

"A poet," Dad said, smiling a little . . . only the second time that day. I knew my dad was only forty but for a year now he had seemed as old as King Lear.

"It take one to know one," Peter Cushing said, arching one eyebrow. "My name is Cornelius Huang."

"And I am Philip Etchison."

"Ah, but I know your work. I thought *The Embrasure of Parched Lips* particular fine. Bittersweet, autumnal, almost like death-drinking songs of Li Po."

"Mr. Huang—"

"Please do me singular honor of calling me Corny. All my friends do."

I could tell that my dad couldn't quite believe his ears. It's the kind of coincidence that only happens in a Victorian novel or a Woody Allen movie. He blushed all the way up to his receding hairline. When Mr. Huang told us he was going to make us his ten-course Peking banquet— no charge—and began shouting orders at the kitchen—and his whole staff started lining up at our table, tallest to smallest, bowing to us smartly one by one—my dad just started laughing and laughing. He didn't look like King Lear anymore . . . more like Old King Cole.

I was happy for him, and even Mom managed a wan laugh.

Then we started eating.

Around the third course, Theo came and sat down next to me. We were never a family for all sitting down together and making small talk through a meal, and Theo was always too hyper to sit through dinner, so no one much minded.

"Had any more weird dreams, little brother?" I said. The incident in the car still disturbed me, wouldn't let go of me.

"Shh," he says to me over the sweet-and-sour fish. "Shh. Don't you hear it? Don't you hear anything?"

"Hear what?"

"The water roaring."

I listened. Somewhere in the distance I could hear something that sounded like Chinese heavy metal. But behind that noise was there something . . . something like the trickle of water? Chinese water torture? I dismissed it. "Don't hear it. It's just your—"

"Imagination," my brother said, and sulked for a few moments over the beef in oyster sauce, which I only picked at for fear of MSG.

We ate in silence. The waiters—members of Corny Huang's family—slithered about, noiselessly replacing our dishes. The Chinese heavy metal music segued into lush strings. I ate a lot, not because I was hungry, but so that I wouldn't have to think.

"Enjoying the meal?" It was Cornelius Huang, towering over my mother and scrutinizing me and Theo.

Theo looked up, saw him clearly for the first time. I'd never seen him look so panic-stricken.

"Corny Huang," said my dad. "You missed it when he introduced himself to us, Theo. He's . . . a fan of mine."

Theo's eyes widened. He got up.

"The next course is conch," said Mr. Huang.

"I know you." Theo began backing away. His chair thudded on the linoleum tiles.

Suddenly an image burst over me—

He's standing beside the river. His plumage is the color of alien suns. He lifts the conch to his lips. The river parts and the dragon comes forth—

"I know you. You're the gatekeeper. The herald. The servant of—"

My Dad was laughing. "So much imagination," he said. "He'll be twice the poet I was when he's older, when he starts bombarding the *New Yorker* with—"

I know Theo when he's like this. He's dead serious. This was one of the times when he was seeing all those interconnections that go right over us normal people's heads.

"Dad"—I said it even though I knew it would be futile—" listen to Theo. . . . When he feels that something's wrong, it always is." I got up too. There was something going on between my brother and the Chinese dude. They were gazing into each other's eyes and Theo was still backing away, right into the window against the view of endless desert.

"Truthsayer," said Mr. Huang. He began muttering to himself in Chinese, and his relations looked at each other in consternation.

Truthsayer? I thought. That's a word from Theo's notebook . . . a word out of one of his dreams. For a few seconds I thought I could hear the rushing of a mighty flood. And the screams of a dying world.

Can't be, I thought, shrugging. Probably just someone flushing a toilet back there.

Our family had a game we play with fortune cookies. This is how it went:

No one reads their fortunes. The first player picks someone at the dinner table and asks him a question—*any* question—and the person he picks has to open the cookie and read whatever it says. Then the *second* person picks another person, and so on, all the way back to the original person. It always works. You always get a viable answer. Doesn't matter what the questions are.

Mr. Huang knew about our game. "Ah, Mr. Etchison," he said, "you explain about it at length in your immortal *Sonnets about Chinese Cooking*, a nineteen seventy-nine chapbook I believe—"

My father beamed.

"For this, you must get special cookies. I have these printed specially in San Francisco." He clapped his hands and one of his daughters brought in a silver tray with four oversized cookies. "These are very special fortune cookies, you like, I know."

"Theo, come back to the table," my dad said, as Mr. Huang discreetly withdrew. When Theo saw that only the four of us were left he sat down sullenly.

I whispered in his ear, "Theo, your dreams're leaking into your real world again. . . . Get a grip on yourself, dude."

"You heard what he called me," Theo said softly, intensely.

"Mary, ask the first question," my dad said, and he pointed his finger at her. She looked at me. I tried to meet her gaze.

She asked me: "Will Joshua Etchison get into an Ivy League college next fall?" And they smiled at each other a little, to show us that they were still in love, despite everything.

I opened my fortune cookie, and read, " '*You will receive an unexpected award.*' "

Dad laughed. "The question is, Josh, whether you're *expecting* to get into an Ivy League school or not." He took a bite of the green tea ice cream and he squeezed my mother's hand. I knew he was on the verge of cracking but he was trying to hard to be strong.

It was my turn, and I said to my dad, "Is Phil Etchison's poetry going to be quoted a hundred years from now? Like Keats, Byron, all that crowd?"

He chuckled and opened his cookie. "Poetry! How appropriate!" And he read these words to us in stentorian tones:

> " 'The sky will be blue forever, and forever
> The earth will stand and every spring will blossom
> Till the end of time. But you, O Man,
> How long do you live?'
> —Li Po

"I wonder what this fortune cookie is trying to tell us. Perhaps," he mused, "I should desist from the hubris of seeking immortality. Perhaps I should sell out, pursue the vulgar taste . . . perhaps . . ."

"Oh, Dad," I said, "I don't see you turning into a Rod McKuen type—not with all those $64 words."

"I guess not." He waved a chopstick at Theo and said, "Tell me, son, that book of yours that you've been writing in all the way from Alexandria . . . the one you're so secretive about . . ."

Theo looked around nervously. For some reason he seemed to be afraid of Mr. Huang, who was nowhere to be seen.

"Will I ever get to read it?"

"That's your question?" I said. I didn't want to get Theo all worked up, because he was liable to blurt out things that people didn't want to hear.

"Sure," Dad said. "I'm allowed to ask anything I want, aren't I?"

"There are things you just shouldn't ask, Dad," Theo said. He feigned a laugh, but I could tell he was much more unnerved than he looked. He opened his cookie and read: " *'It is often a mistake to pry into the mysteries of nature, as witness the predicament of Dr. Frankenstein. And yet, there is little one can do to prevent it.'* "

"These are the weirdest fortune cookies I've ever encountered," Dad said.

There was a long silence.

I watched my brother. I could see that he was falling into that inner world of his. "Go on, Theo," I said, "ask Mom a question."

He looked straight at my mother and said, "When are you going to die?"

His words died away in the wheezing of the overhead fan.

My Dad was absolutely white. He was clenching and unclenching his fists. My mom seemed strangely calm.

"Let him say it, Phil," she said. "We have to come to terms with it; we've never really talked it over as a family before. . . ."

It was appalling. I could feel my rage uncoiling inside me.

Trying to control himself, Dad said, "Theo, learn some tact."

Theo turned to me. He had this blank possessed look and he made me so mad that I just couldn't stand him, I really hated him for always putting his foot in his mouth like that and I grabbed him by the neck and I just started punching him again and again.

"You tell the fucking truth too fucking often," I said and I shoved him hard against the next table and I could see blood pouring from his nose.

"You're hurting me," he said.

I stood there breathing heavily, sweating. I had all this fury and I didn't know what to do. I heard my mother weeping quietly to herself. I couldn't hit him anymore.

He looked at me with that same blank look. What was wrong with him? I heard the roaring of distant water. I knew he could hear it too, more clearly than I, and I knew that my parents heard nothing.

Slowly he turned from me and began walking toward a door marked RESTROOMS.

"Don't go after him," Dad said. "He didn't mean to—"

"I'm sorry," I said.

"We're all upset," my mother said. Then, "Do you have any more of those painkillers?"

Only then did I notice the fortune from her cookie, lying half-crumpled on top of a half-eaten piece of shrimp.

It said:

"Dark is life, dark is death."
—Li Po

CHAPTER THREE

THE SUNLESS SEA

Theo Etchison

I always ask the one question everyone wants answered and doesn't dare ask. I don't know why I said that. I feel like I'm about to cry but the tears don't come. I'm not surprised Joshua punched me out. I hate myself. Why am I like this, why do I always blurt out things that are true that no one wants to hear?

I can taste blood. I have to find the bathroom and wash it off my face. I have to get away from all of them.

I go down the corridor. An arrow points toward the men's. The corridor slopes down and the walls are damp. Where's the moisture coming from? I think. We're in the middle of the desert, aren't we?

I hear someone call my name. It's my brother. He's coming after me. The corridor slopes downward, downward. There are mirrors against the walls, funhouse mirrors and normal mirrors and mirrors I don't dare look at because I think they show my nightmares. What kind of a place is this? I'm in a tunnel. I come to a neon arrow that points further ahead and it still says RESTROOMS. I guess I'm getting too imaginative again. Like in school sometimes during finals when I drift away for what seems like a ninety-minute action-adventure-comedy-drama but when I drift back again only a minute has passed and I'm still trying to answer the same true or false question.

I can hear someone breathing. Footsteps behind me. The sound carries along the walls of the chamber. I feel like I'm in a cave. I can hear water lapping against stone. I stop. Behind me, the footsteps stop too. A metallic echo. I feel cold suddenly. Scared.

I turn a corner.

Truthsayer.

I think about the bad dreams I've been having. I've been standing on the edges of other times, other worlds. They've been consumed by fire. One by one. The universe is like my mother's body, slowly being eaten away by something dark and malevolent. Maybe that's all the dreams mean . . . they're all about her, about how scared I am she's going to die.

Suddenly there's the bathroom. I'm not quite sure how I got there. It's a big clean place, with flower tiles, smelling faintly of lemon. I take a leak, then go to the sink and start to swab at the blood with a hand towel. It doesn't hurt anymore but I feel pretty fucking humiliated.

I hear a voice. My name. Startled, I turn around. It's only Joshua, leaning against the door. I think he's trying to make peace.

"Look, I didn't mean—"

"It's okay."

"I'll make it up to you."

"All right." The blood and water are draining down the sink. "So make it up to me."

"What do you want me to do?"

"Well," I say, "you're bigger and stronger than me. Give me something to hold over you. Something that'll even up the odds."

"You want me to tell you one of my secrets."

"Yeah."

"I'll kill you for this."

"You offered."

"All right." He thinks about it for a long time. I tap my fingers on the sink. At last he says, "You remember Serena Somers?"

"God, do I. Sluglike Serena," I say, "how could I ever forget her. I guess you're going to tell me how you made it with her in the back seat . . . but you forget that I was there. What kind of a secret is that?"

"I never fucked her," he says, kind of shy.

"What?"

"I told you! We were just making a lot of noise to give you . . . ideas."

"Gross me out!" I was looking at him with a newfound admiration. I mean, Sluglike Serena had been had by half of GW, let alone the high school. "Well," I say, "no need to stoop to Serena when you had the buxom Beatrice Pfeffer."

"Didn't fuck her either," my brother says, which is a truly astounding revelation, because I can't think of anyone else he's even claimed to, and that leads me to the inescapable conclusion that he must be a . . .

"You guessed it, dude," he says. "I'm a v-v—"

This is a totally heavy secret. He must really feel bad about hitting me. "C'mon, bro," I say, "you didn't hurt me *that* bad. Like, you didn't have to tell me that big of a secret."

"Fuckin' Jesus, Theo," my brother says, "when *is* she going to die?"

And he starts to cry. I mean really cry, like a kid. And I feel terrible because I don't remember ever seeing him cry even though he is the closest person in the whole world to me. I don't know what to do.

Just then, I hear a toilet flush and the door to one of the stalls opens. Shit! I think. Someone's been in here all this time, and me and Josh've been spilling our guts.

Now I hear water. A lot of water. Water cascading down cataracts, racing toward the sea. The roaring numbs me. I know that Joshua can hear at least a faint echo of what I'm hearing, because he looks where I'm looking . . . the toilet stall.

"Something wrong with the plumbing around here?" he asks.

"Nothing wrong with plumbing." It's Peter Cushing Cornelius Huang himself, standing by the swinging door, peering at me from beady eyes set in a cadaver's face . . . except that he's wearing these weird robes, an iron collar studded with diamonds, and he has sort of a mohawk and a cape that billows all about in the wind that has suddenly sprung up, and he has a jeweled conch shell in his hand that he's about to lift to his lips . . . and there's smoke all over the restroom, and dust, and there's the smell of my mother dying that I've known so well these past weeks. . . .

"I know you," says my brother. "I saw you. For a moment. I think Theo put the image in my head."

"The herald," I said.

"Truthsayer," says Cornelius Huang. "I've been sent to fetch you . . . by the man with the slate-colored eyes."

And suddenly the wall behind him bursts asunder and I see a river so wide I can barely make out the far shore, where a castle perches on a crystal mountain girt with rainbow fire. . . . I know this place so well, it's the place I go to every time I close my eyes at night in motel room after sleazy motel room, the place I've been going to to get away from the nightmare of reality. . . . The water is pouring into the room now, pounding savagely at me, but I don't feel any wetness. . . . One world is melding into the next.

"What's going on?" Josh says. "Let him go!"

Tongues of blue flame spew from the herald's eyes. I'm rooted to the cold white tiles as the water that I can't feel swirls and churns and crashes around me. The lines of fire wrap themselves around me and I can't move. My brother reaches for me. He grabs the sleeve of my T-shirt. My shirt tears. "Theo!" he screams. The fire burns me with its searing cold.

"The man with the slate-colored eyes," says Mr. Huang, "he been waiting for you for long long time. He been waiting for his own personal truthsayer." He never speaks above a whisper but his voice cuts through the thunder of the river.

"Where are you taking me?" I scream.

"To the Land of Nod," he says, "the Desert of Dreaming . . . beyond the Sunless Sea."

"But those are just dreams," I say.

I flail against the ropes of icy flame. I try to grab my brother's arm, but the herald turns his head and Joshua is thrown against the sink by an invisible force. The mirror shatters against his face and I see splinters in his cheeks and see his forehead speckled with crimson. Behind him, the water rises. It is dark and warm.

"Dark is life," says Mr. Huang. "Dark is death. You should have read that fortune cookie, Theo Etchison."

In the dream I cannot help being drawn toward the water, dark and warm and full of promises. . . .

But it's not like the dream! I fight the water. I can't leave my family like this, my mother dying, my last words to her full of bitterness and frustration. The water wells up. The restroom is engulfed in Spielbergian mist. Lights flash. Water in my eyes, water in my nose, pouring into my lungs, and Mr. Huang still standing there with the conch to his lips, blaring out an irresistible summoning. . . . His hair is the color of sea-weed.

There is a ghostly outline of a boat. The prow is carved into a gargoyle gushing blood that trails into the water. . . . A man stands with his hand resting over the gargoyle's eyes. He wears a cloak and all I can see are his eyes . . . slate-colored, lifeless. He looks at me and suddenly I am in the grip of the summoning and I am so far away from my old anger and from my strife-torn family and I feel the tug of a distant universe and I want to give myself to the rhythmic swell of the dark dark waters.

I hear Joshua's voice: "Theo, Theo . . ." but it is dying away. . . . My brother is fading like an old pair of jeans. . . . The wind is rising over the waters. . . . Another voice calls my name, "Theo, Theo, Theo." A rich voice, murmurous and echoing like the voice of the very river. I feel more than myself, I remember all the weird words from family poetry evenings by the fireplace; I feel them jangling inside my mind and I feel like all at once I know what they all mean.

I know that my brother is watching me fade away like some hokey special effect. Deep inside I am still calling out to him but I do not think he can hear me. I wonder whether he will ever hear me again. I can often see true things about other people that they don't want me to see, but I can't see anything about myself, I just see blank when I try. . . . I have no reassuring words for Josh, I can't tell him that I will ever return.

CHAPTER FOUR

LETHE-WARDS

J o s h u a   E t c h i s o n

What was happening to us? One moment Theo and I were just carrying on a regular convo in the men's room, the next a kind of a Viking ship was bursting through the toilet stall and Mr. Huang had turned into some kind of space ninja with superpowers and he was sucking my brother into a watery vortex. . . .

I couldn't see what Theo was seeing. The boat, the man with the slate-colored eyes, the swirling water . . . all these things were blurry, dream-like. I could hear him cry out to me and I tried to grab him but the first time I tore off a piece of his shirt and the next time my hand went right through him and then he wasn't there at all, none of it was there, it was just a squeaky-clean restroom in a Chinese restaurant in the middle of the Arizona desert.

Maybe I was dreaming, I thought. Maybe Theo's just taking a shit in one of these stalls. I knocked on the only one that was closed. A hollow echo. Wildly I looked around. I started to panic.

Then I pushed open the door of the stall and saw—

Churning water! And Theo being pulled up into that Viking ship, spectral now, fading from view, and—

Nothing.

I turned and ran.

The restaurant. My parents sitting where I'd left them. My mother staring off into space, my father shaking his head, Theo's knapsack leaning against the upturned chair.

"Something terrible's just happened," I said. "Theo—Theo's—"

It seemed almost too absurd to tell them.

"What is it, dear?" my mother said faintly.

"He's gone . . . something happened in the bathroom."

"Did he trip?" my father said.

"No, goddamn it, he's . . . gone, vanished. I saw something. . . . I don't believe what I saw." How could I explain ships from other universes, old Chinese guys shooting blue sparks from their eyes? "I think Mr. Huang knows . . . but I don't think he'll tell us."

"If this is one of you guys' pranks—" said Dad.

"No, Dad."

Something in my manner must've convinced him I wasn't totally bull-shitting, because he whispered a few words in my mother's ear and got up to follow me.

"In the bathroom, Dad. Look, I know this sounds ridiculous, but I think Mr. Huang kind of . . . kidnapped him."

My mother started at this. Maybe she had felt something when it was all happening. Dying people are psychic, I've heard.

"Where is that man anyway?" Dad said. "We haven't even paid him anything." He wasn't quite grasping the gravity of all this. "Oh, Mr. Huang!" He stood straightening his glasses for a moment. None of the employees were in sight—no Mr. Huang and not one of his sisters, cousins and aunts. "C'mon, Josh, we'd better get Theo out of wherever he's hiding."

We followed the sign to the restroom. I could have sworn the corridor wasn't the same. It sloped gently downward and the walls were almost like the walls of a cave, and they were covered with picture writing . . . not hieroglyphics exactly, because the letters seemed squatter and there were more colors and some of the characters looked like aliens from a space opera. I remembered the funhouse mirrors, but this time there were more of them and they seemed to distort more.

"It's taking a long time to get there," I said. "And it feels different somehow."

"To paraphrase Lewis Carroll," my dad said, "sometimes it takes all the running you can do to stay in the same place."

We kept walking. I don't think we were getting anywhere.

"Theo!" I kept shouting. My voice echoed and I could swear I heard water rippling.

Then the corridor turned sharply and we were in a kind of grotto. There was an underground stream that gushed down from a hole in the rock, ran for about twenty feet, and disappeared down a shallow tunnel to our right. A shaft of blue light played over the water. Dust motes danced.

"We must have taken a wrong turn," said Dad.

"Look!" I said, pointing to a little shrine in a niche in the rock. A jade figurine sat on a gilded throne. There was so much incense that I couldn't see its face. Beneath it was a bronze plaque with the legend:

Where Alph, the sacred river, ran
Through caverns measureless to man
Down to a Sunless Sea.

CORNELIUS HUANG, A LOVER OF FINE POEMS, EXPLORER OF SUBTERRANEAN CAVERNS, FOUND THIS STREAM BENEATH THE EARTH AND ERECTED THIS MODEST LITTLE XANADU ABOVE IT . . . ANNO DOMINI MDCCCLXXXVI

"Well, that's a hoax for sure," Dad said. "Get a load of that date—eighteen eighty-six! Corny's not that old—I don't care how many ancient Chinese secrets he knows."

I was nervous. This place wasn't here the last time. Something was terribly wrong. The incense smoke cleared from the figurine's face and my heart started beating even faster. I knew that face. . . . I'd seen that face in my dreams and in my sleepless nights, I'd been so turned on by that face that I hadn't been able to get it on with Serena Somers or any other girl . . . that face, part woman, part serpent, so sexual that even now I could feel my penis stiffening. . . .

I felt hot all over. I know I was blushing.

She says to me: "My name is Katastrofa Darkling. I am the woman in the dragon, the woman in the dragon's breath, the breath of the dragon . . . I am Katastrofa Darkling." She bares her breasts to me and—

"Joshua," my father said.

I must have been staring at the statuette like an idiot.

"Looking for the bathroom?" No mistaking that voice. I whirled around. Mr. Huang was standing at the only exit from the grotto. I started to shake.

"What have you done to my brother?" I screamed.

"Josh, your manners," said Dad.

"There is no bathroom down here," said Cornelius Huang. "I am sorry, but the signs are misleading. But I see you have discovered my little secret . . . my elfin grot. The water comes from a spring far beneath the earth. Allow me to . . . show you the way."

"You were standing there when Theo disappeared," I said. I was angry now, I didn't care if my dad thought I had gone crazy. "You were standing there with weird lights in your eyes and wearing some kind of wizard robes."

Mr. Huang laughed, very softly. Even my dad seemed unnerved. "Don't you stand there looking all innocent," I said. "I saw you . . . I *saw* you! Maybe you've got some kind of child-sacrificing cult or maybe you're one of those psycho sex killers. . . . Maybe you've got a big battery of machines with sound effects and images and smoke and lightning. . . . I don't know, I don't care. You've done something to Theo."

"Wizard robes? Child sacrifice?" said my father. "Really, Joshua . . . some of Theo's flights of fancy must be rubbing off on you. . . . Mr. Huang, you'll excuse—"

"Call me Corny." And he gazed at me, all snake-eyed, and chilled me. I didn't want to admit how much he scared me, especially since Dad was acting like it was somehow all my fault.

The three of us walked back. There were no cavernous corridors, no stalactites. Only the funhouse mirrors were the same. We climbed some steps covered with thick shag. There had been no steps coming down. And then we were suddenly walking into the main hall, and my mother was where we left her, propped against her pillow and wrapped in her Indian blanket, looking out of the window at the setting sun.

I half expected to see Theo sitting beside her. But he wasn't there. She looked up at us. "Where's Theo?" she said.

Dad shrugged. "I expect he's just fooling around somewhere—you know how he gets," he said.

We waited for one hour. It grew dark.

"He knows better than to go out in the desert," Dad said.

"It's fucking freezing," I said. There was dust in our eyes, and the temperature had dropped to 29°, and the wind was howling. Three beams of light from our three flashlights crisscrossed over a desolate vista: stones, sand, many-armed cactuses.

We had gone outside with Mr. Huang. My mother had been put to bed on a couch in the restaurant's lobby, and one of the innumerable relatives was tending her. I felt queasy leaving her with them. My mind was fogging up. I wasn't sure I could remember what happened anymore. Something watery. There had been a ship . . . a man with gray eyes . . . another man in robes whose eyes sparked laser lightning. I couldn't have seen those things. My Dad had to be right.

The heat of the day . . . the oppressive closeness of the car . . .

stepping outside had made me lightheaded, prone to suggestion . . . that's all it was. Maybe the MSG did something too. MSG always fucked with my brain cells. Yes. Theo had gone outside to play by himself, the way he always did. He'd wandered off somewhere.

It was easy to believe that.

We stumbled about in the darkness, shrieking out Theo's name. We looked for footsteps but soon we were treading in our own. And always Mr. Huang talked, calming us, regaling us with arcane fragments of poetry. And I could see that my father was bewitched by him, and that even I was beginning to feel the strange seduction of his soft-spoken words, and there was a kind of despair in me too, because under his spell I was rapidly forgetting the things I knew to be true.

Inside, past midnight, we sipped tea in dainty cloisonné cups and my father brought up the police for the first time.

"There are no police here," said Mr. Huang. "Tucson, perhaps . . . a hundred miles, no freeway. Your son is not that far away. They will not come."

"Telephone?" Dad said.

He chuckled. "I have, of course, no telephone," said Mr. Huang.

Of course not, I thought.

On the sofa, my mother moaned.

"I have to wake her up and give her her medication," said my dad.

"A beautiful woman, even in death," said Mr. Huang.

"She's not dead yet," I said.

"Ah, but I was merely speaking in a metaphysical sense. She is, as Wagner put it in *Tristan and Isolde*, already *'todgeweihte'* . . . consecrated to death."

"And Theo? I suppose you consider him dead already."

"If he is out there," said Mr. Huang, "the desert is harsh."

"There's got to be someone you can contact."

"Ask your father."

I looked at my father. He had my mother cradled in his arms. Her gaze darted fearfully from side to side and he was whispering to her. He waited.

Another hour passed. I could see that my parents were both drifting off. I was struggling to fight off this unnatural weariness. . . . My eyelids were fighting me; my limbs were leaden. I kept seeing Katastrofa Darkling whenever I closed my eyes.

I could almost hear her voice. She was saying something like: *"There are some things you were never meant to remember, Joshua. . . . It were best if you forgot them."* I tried to open my eyes. It was dark. A single candle flickered from the nearest dining table. There was some kind of incense, too, drenching my lungs in a suffocating odor. I looked around. My mother was fast asleep . . . my father stirred a little. Mr. Huang was hovering over him, moving his hands back and forth over his scalp like a conjurer about to pull a rabbit from a hat. Dad's eyes were open but glazed. The incense burner was right next to the couch on an ornate marble end table.

Then Mr. Huang took out a silver bowl of water, dipped a handful of twigs in it, and started to sprinkle my dad with it.

I said, "Dad? What's happening? What are we going to do about Theo?"

"Theo?" my father said, in utmost bewilderment.

"Theo . . . your son . . . remember?" I said. "A kid who tells the truth too much . . . a dirty-blond kid with eyes like—" I blinked. I couldn't remember Theo's eyes. Had I said blond?

I couldn't remember his face.

My father looked at me blankly.

I felt cold water droplets on my face. Mr. Huang smiled.

Jesus! I thought. They're fucking with my mind. Suddenly I knew we couldn't allow ourselves to fall asleep here. Maybe it was the incense. Maybe it was Mr. Huang's mystic passes in the air or his weird water. But they—whoever *they* were—were stealing memories from our heads, and I knew that when we woke up we would be a family of three, with no recollection of poor crazy Theo at all. . . .

I forced myself to get up, tried to hold my breath . . . I went over to my dad. Angrily I elbowed Mr. Huang aside. "We've got to leave!" I said.

He just looked at me. Then he began reciting in a high-pitched sing-song:

> " 'As though of hemlock I had drunk,
> Or emptied some dull opiate to the drains . . .
> And Lethe-wards had sunk . . .' "

A dim memory from a mythology lesson. Lethe . . . the river of forgetfulness . . .

"Very fine poet, Keats," said Mr. Huang, and sprinkled more water on my father.

I looked around. There was Theo's knapsack, still leaning against the chair! I seized it. The dream book tumbled out. I took the book and shoved it under his nose, turning the pages. "Look, Dad . . . these dreams . . . Theo's dreams . . ."

In her sleep, my mother mumbled, "Theo? Theo?"

"*She* hasn't forgotten!" I shouted.

"She's delirious," my father said, but I thought I saw uncertainty in his eyes.

"Let's go . . ." I said.

"We're tired. Your mother needs to rest. Mr. Huang has kindly offered to let us stay here as long as we want. . . . He's so lonely without human company," he said.

In the candlelight Mr. Huang's face, etched with shadows, looked like a bird of prey.

"The Laetrile clinic!" I said. "They can only hold her reservation until next week. . . ."

"Mexico's less than a day away," my father said.

The voice of reason. I knew I had to trick them somehow. I saw the bottle of Mom's medication beside the couch. I leaned down, knocked it to the floor. "I didn't mean to—" I said. The bottle shattered.

"You clumsy—" said Dad. He started to go after the pills.

"It was an accident!" I felt like a little kid saying that, but I was desperate. I spun around as if to avoid a blow, karate-chopped the incense burner so that it flew across the floor and—

Clang! Ashes and pills strewn across the floor . . . the little capsules charring, giving off a foul vapor . . . "Goddamn it, Joshua, where are we going to get more pills. . . . She'll be writhing in agony if she doesn't get her next painkiller in four hours. . . ."

"Tucson," I said. "We're getting out of this place, Dad."

I turned to Mr. Huang. He glared at me. There was defeat in his eyes. I gathered up my brother's secret notebook, slung the knapsack over my shoulder, started resolutely for the door, pausing only to grind the crushed painkillers into the ashes with my foot.

I could hear my father lifting Mom to her feet. I could hear him shuffling behind me. I opened the door and breathed in the sweet frigid desert air.

"I'll drive," I said quickly, before he changed his mind.

Half an hour later we switched off. My Dad seemed energized again and I was getting drowsier and drowsier. I climbed into the back of the station wagon.

This is what I read by flashlight in my brother's dream book as the car strained up curvy mountain roads toward Route 10.

*I remember the first dream really well and that's why I'm going to write
them all down. The first dream is more than a year ago so it really isn't
supposed to be in this book which is a book of what I am dreaming about
on this journey. But I think it is important because it is the first time I see the
man with the slate-colored eyes and it is only a day after Dad has told us
that her cancer is fatal. That was also the day our family went to see King
Lear at the Wolf Trap Festival so some of it is probably mixed up into the
dream.*

I see a desolate landscape with ice and snow everywhere and mists
tendriling out of caverns and frozen lakes and waterfalls.

I see a castle.

I see a King. He is about to divide his kingdom up between three
children . . . not daughters like in the play but a man and a woman and
I'm not sure about the third one. The throne is surrounded by a river that
leads everywhere. I am walking toward the throne. They're all talking
softly in kind of Shakespearean English and I can only make out a few
words.

*The king has a scepter in his hand and there is a jewel that contains men's
souls.*

I'm standing at the river's edge now. The smell is so familiar . . . I
know that it's the smell of my grandma's house in Spotsylvania County.

I know that the king is dividing his kingdom and that something bad is
going to happen. A blood-tinged mist rises out of the river.

*The king's son turns to me. He smiles. He is cruel. He has slate-colored
eyes. He loves to destroy. He has smashed whole planets just to see sparks
spiral in the starstream. There is a void in his heart and yet I feel . . .
drawn to him.*

A man stands next to him . . . a tall Chinese-looking man with a
mohawk. . . . He raises a conch to his lips and blows an ear-splitting
note and the king looks up. I see the king's hands, palsied as he feebly
tries to grip the scepter.

The jewel in the scepter: lights dancing. Men's souls.

I'm afraid. The man with the slate-colored eyes is coming to me and I
want to run but I can't, I'm rooted to the riverbank like the trees by my
grandma's house, I'm powerless, and there's a part of me that wants me
to like him, empty eyed, soulless.

Now I wake up.

I remember this dream for the first time today, the day after Easter,
1990. It's the day we're packing to go to Mexico. That's when I decide to

go down to the 7-Eleven and buy this three-ring binder to record my dreams. It's got to mean something.

I think the sun was rising when I finally dozed off. I was trying to remember little things about Theo, those details that make someone a real person to you. Theo and I were close, I knew that . . . but where were the things I should have remembered vividly?

. . . a baseball flying past the sun . . . stubby fingers clutching a stolen beer can . . . trying to beat the high score in Gauntlet . . . what else, what else? . . . I still couldn't remember his eyes.

I concentrated. The sun was in my eyes. I tried to picture him. The sandy hair . . . a slender body, almost shadowlike . . . a mole on the back of his left hand that he was too sensitive about . . . the eyes! I could see his face in my mind, but it had someone else's eyes. Slate-colored eyes.

As I finally drifted into fitful sleep, I wondered if I would be the same person when I woke up . . . whether all of us were somehow being transformed into other people, people from a world not quite our own.

BOOK TWO

THE RIVER LETHE

"—Et le rêve fraîchit."
"—And the dream grew cold."

—Illuminations

To My Son

He is standing at the river's edge; sometimes
I watch him, sometimes
I cannot bear to watch, sometimes
I wish for the river to run upstream, back to the mountains,
Blue as the sky, as grief, as desolation.

He is playing by the river's edge; sometimes
I feel he is not alone, I hear a second laugh in the wind that shakes
The cottonwoods. I cannot bear to listen,
Knowing as I know the one unborn, the one I have named
God, because he is my son's dark elder self.
If the river had run backward my other son would not
Cry out to me from the depths. In my heart I know sometimes
That the river has reversed its course; I know sometimes
That the river will not turn back till its watery end,
Black as the sky, as grief, as disillusion.

He is walking away from the river's edge;
I think he will never come home.
Better I do not look at all; for in the momentary closure,
The blink's breadth between two truths, two truths can both be true.
When I close my eyes I have two sons, and each
Is the others shadow. Surely he would not play alone,
Or stand alone at the river's edge, or walk away
And leave behind his shadow,
Gray as the sky, as loneliness, as love.

CHAPTER FIVE

THORNSTONE SLAUGHT

Theo   Etchison

He has thrown his cloak over me and I can taste blood and darkness. We're rocking and I hear planks creaking and rope squeaking and a howling wind but I can't smell the salt sea . . . it's another odor, a stench of something putrefying. I want to puke into the cloak but I'm so choked my vomit can't make it up my throat. "Jesus Christ, get me out of here!" I try to scream but all that comes out is a strangled whisper.

I try to tear at the cloak but the fabric is too tightly woven . . . it's almost like polythene . . . and I'm sweating. At last I manage to claw my way through its folds and I poke my head out at the ship.

The deck of the ship is slick with thick red fluid. Blood is soaking into my T-shirt and seeping up my shorts. Where I am is close to the ship's edge and I see the water. It's black and it smells of stale meat. It's flecked with bloody foam. The wind is howling.

The man with the slate-colored eyes stands at the prow, one hand on the head of the gargoyle, looking out over the water. He doesn't seem to notice that I've crawled out of his cloak. The only light on the ship comes from lanterns that dangle on wooden posts and give off a sulfurous smoke as well as light. I can't tell how the ship moves. There are others on board, but they shy away from me. I see someone at the stern, pulling on something—maybe a rudder, maybe a punting pole. Maybe he'll tell me what's going on.

I make my way across to him. He leans into his pole, away from me. "Where am I?" I say.

He laughs. I touch him on the shoulder. He's made of bone. He turns around and his face is a skull.

He says, "The River Styx." And laughs again. "Surely, truthsayer," he says, "you knew that already."

I've heard of that place. It's the river in the underworld, the river that the dead have to cross to get to the kingdom of Hades. It's just a myth, I tell myself, and this is one of those dreams, only it's more real than ever before. I start to shiver. My breath hangs in the air, but the skeleton has no breath at all.

"So," says a new voice, "he has regained consciousness."

I can smell his breath. It's like meat that's been left out overnight. I can't let him scare me, I think. It's a dream. A dream. I'm really back in that old Chinese restaurant with that Mr. Huang dude hovering over me waiting for my brother to finish taking his leak.

"Come to me, my child," he says.

I am suspicious. "You shouldn't have grabbed me out of where I was."

"Why not? You were not happy in your world."

"People are dying. Not just Mom, I mean . . . my whole family's dying, one way or another. They—"

"Need you . . . yes, yes, yes." He looks into my eyes. I feel what he's feeling . . . the hatred, yes, but beneath it a kind of sorrow, a kind of bereavement. "My kingdom needs you . . . needs a truthsayer."

The wind springs up and his cloak spreads out like the wings of a pterodactyl. I can't look away. I'm fascinated by him. There is a kind of longing in the way he looks at me. There's something I have that he can never have. I don't know what it is. "You don't need me," I say. "I don't even know who you are; I don't understand what I'm doing here except dreaming up a storm." Usually when I start dreaming like this there's a surefire way I can force myself to wake up. I start thinking about how badly I have to pee . . . I think over and over, I'm going to wet the bed, I'm going to wet the bed. I used to do that a lot all the way into puberty.

I try that now . . . over and over—*wake up you're going to wet the bed wake up wake up. . . .* His gaze never leaves me. It's not working, I realize. In fact, I've just pissed all over my shorts. Oh God, I'm terrified. I'm so fucking terrified I could—

He reaches out and squeezes my shoulder. "We're going to be friends, Theo Etchison."

"Jesus Christ! What gives you the right to know my name? Who the fuck are you, anyway?" I scream. My voice dies away in the wind's howling. The skeleton man has let go of his pole and he's chuckling . . . his teeth chattering like one of those windup skulls you buy in joke shops.

"Oh, didn't I introduce myself?" says the man with the slate-colored eyes. "I am Thorn. Prince," he adds, "Thorn. And you are Theo Truthsayer."

I twist free of his grasp. My shoulder aches. "No I'm not," I say.

"Don't fight it, my child. Being a truthsayer isn't easy, but you can't help what you are. None of us can. For example . . ."

He looks out toward the water. I see a woman with seaweed hair, floating on the water. She's naked. Her skin is pale, iridescent like a seal's. The skeleton man beckons to her and helps her on board. She walks toward Thorn, mesmerized.

He grabs her by the shoulder just like he grabbed me. Then he snaps her neck like a dry twig. Blood comes spurting out of her mouth. He kisses her. Slurping up the blood. Hungrily. It's the first time I've seen him show any kind of passion. He covers her neck with kisses and blood oozes from each kiss and he laps it up and I can hear his heavy breathing above the squall.

At last he seems satiated. He casually drops the woman onto the deck. The corpse slides back and forth on the blood-slick wood in an eerie counterpoint to the pitch and yaw of the ship. Casually, Thorn finishes his sentence. "For example, I am a vampire." He kicks the body out the way and it sort of rolls all the way up to the prow. I hear dogs howling. They've come loping out of the hold and they're tearing her apart. No, there's only one dog, and it has three heads. We pass through a cloud of mist. "Want to make something of it?" says Thorn.

"But . . . that girl . . . did she just let you suck her . . ."

"Why shouldn't they? They're my subjects. . . . I own them. Duty to the empire and all that."

"You killed her!" I scream, forgetting to be scared for a moment because he makes me so angry.

Thorn begins pacing the deck. It's very misty and I can only hear the creaking of the planks and glimpse his cloak now and then flapping through gusts of fog.

I'm scared of him but I still think I've got to be dreaming. So even though I'm standing there with piss on my underpants I tell myself to get it together, force myself to wake up. If you concentrate hard enough you can wrench control of your dreams into your own hands and you can turn dark things to light. So I just stand there hollering for him to take me home and telling him to get the fuck out of my dream, and finally he just says, very softly, "You have nowhere to return to, my friend. Just make the best of it."

"My family."

"They're dead by now. My herald was under orders to leave no traces. . . . They will have been erased from your world completely. . . ."

"Killed!"

"No . . . erased. No one will remember them. . . . They will never have existed . . . excised from the fabric of your universe like a malignant cancer." Water laps against the side of the boat and I feel sick to my stomach from the pitch and yaw and the wind that smells of dead people. "Oh," and he laughs a little, "perhaps I should not have used the cancer simile; how thoughtless of me."

"They're not dead." And as I say it I know it is true. And I look him right in the eye with all the rage I've carried with me on this trip.

For the first time I think he seems uneasy, shaken.

"Why wouldn't they be dead?" he says.

I close my eyes. I see an image of our station wagon straining to climb a mountain road. I'm looking down at it, like from an airplane, and it's blurry. . . . The road is shimmering in the sun.

"They're alive," I tell him, "so that means you don't know everything."

He looks away. He is angry. I think he's going to strike me, but instead he stalks away. "Truthsayers," he mutters as he strides into the mist that masks the prow. There is something about me he doesn't like, that much is certain, but he needs me. I can feel that.

"Truthsayers," he says again. I am just standing there and now he won't look into my eyes again and I think he is afraid.

No one has ever been afraid of me before, not like that.

I close my eyes. This isn't the real world. The real world is that mountain threaded by the thin gray road and the groaning station wagon. I'm far from it, so far away . . . but there's a way there, a way through the stream that tunnels through the basement of the Chinese restaurant. The stream is part of a river that twines around everything and holds the universe together, and when I concentrate I can almost see the pattern, link by link; I can trace the convolutions as the streams fork and unfork.

Mom! Dad! Joshua! I'm crying out with my mind. The car has reached the top of the mountain and now it's careening downhill. Dad's absent-mindedly riding the brakes and I hear Josh saying my name and suddenly it occurs to me that Dad doesn't know who he's talking about.

He doesn't know who I am.

Abruptly I snap out of the vision and now all I can see is the swirling dark water and the ship and the bloodless corpse and my host, striding back and forth, and the ferryman whose face is a skull. I stare past the gargoyle prow and see the mist parting. There's land, I think; a dark rock jutting from the water like a leaping whale. I can't tell how far it is, but closer to us there are drowned obelisks thrusting out of the water, their hieroglyphs caked with algae, half-submerged sphinxes with insectoid eyes. We are moving toward the whale-rock. Navigating between the heads of sunken statues. Thorn summons me. I go and stand beside him. There is a bond between us because of my nightmares. Sometimes I feel this way about my father.

"Thornstone Slaught," he says, and points to something that looks like a barnacle on the top of the whale-rock. I squint. That's when I realize the scale of this thing. The barnacle is a castle. I can make out eaves, towers, crenellated walls, a statue of a woman with a flaming torch and the face of a demon, a Statue of Liberty gone wrong. The castle is perched on a mountain and the mountain is wreathed in mist and around me the wind howls ceaselessly.

"Thornstone Slaught?" I say. "What are you talking about?"

"It's the name of my castle, stupid," says Thorn. "It's the largest, darkest, most terrifying castle in the universe. It's where you're going to be living."

"Look, we're not communicating or something," I say, knowing that there's a little part of him that is afraid of me. "You kidnapped me. I intend to go home. You need me for something, but I have a hunch it's nothing that's gonna benefit the human race or any other race. I won't do it."

"Saving the universe, Theo Etchison, is hardly what I'd consider detrimental to the human race. Or—" he looks away, his eyes gray, distant "—any other race, for that matter."

"Saving the universe! Easy on the high fantasy, dude."

He looks out over the water. He's calling out—with his eyes, I think—calling to someone. Soon another of those people with seaweed hair is rising out of the water; a boy this time. Casually Thorn pulls him up onto the deck, draws him into his arms, punctures his jugular with a quick bite, slurps down the spurting blood.

"Yes, boy, there is a universe out there to be saved all right," he says softly. "And soon it will be too late. Unless you help me. But people like you have no conception of these things. You cannot imagine anything outside that tiny circle of family, friends, country, planet. . . . What if I told you you could save your mother?"

"Why should I believe you?" I say. "You told me five minutes ago that you'd ordered her killed. You were pissed when I said she was still alive."

"I can show you how to reach the source of the river that flows between the worlds," he said, "the place where times and spaces merge . . . where you can catch a moment in your past, like a fish, before it can wriggle downstream toward reality. . . ."

I don't trust him. But I see hope. I think. That's why I decide to stay on for a while, watch, learn. Not that there's anything I can do right now anyways. We're pulling in toward Thornstone Slaught now and the sea is strewn with sunken monuments.

I try to see my parents and my brother in that station wagon. They're very faint. They're on the 10 now, heading toward Tucson. Dad has already forgotten me. Maybe Mom remembers, but she is too delirious to speak. Even her pain seems faint to me.

Joshua is thumbing through my dream book and Dad is driving with his eyes fixed on nowhere, on nothing.

CHAPTER SIX

FIRST AND ORACLE

P h i l   E t c h i s o n

There we were at a cheap motel on First and Oracle, me, a middle-aged academic whom some called a poet, my wife, sick in body, my son, sick in the head.

I left them in the room. I sat at the bar beside the pool, watching bloated women with crimson faces bobbing up and down in the Jacuzzi under the blazing sun. I sat nursing an exotic drink, looking past the pool, past the desert palms, to the corner of First and Oracle, trying to sort out the patterns in my disordered existence—for was that not what poets were supposed to do?—and finding only more and more bewilderment.

Mary's illness was chemical, easy to understand in a way. We both knew she was going to die. We always knew that. We are not stupid. We know that Laetrile does not work. That was not what the journey was about. The journey was a symbol. The journey was to bring our fractured family together before it came apart forever. The journey was to end in death for Mary; we were resigned to that. But perhaps there would be life for Joshua, life free from delusion.

A neatly gift-wrapped ontological metaphor—that was what the journey meant to me. My wife would give up her life and Joshua would finally stop imagining he had a younger brother named Theo.

Theo!

He always wanted a younger brother. I remembered how he cried when Mary had the miscarriage. I stirred my Blue Hawaiian and thought about that awful day, thirteen, fourteen years ago. Strange. I couldn't see it very clearly. It had been snowing. We were living in Indiana then. Or was it high summer in Montana? Mary slipped in the shower. On the stairs. The image just wouldn't come to me. I could see Josh crying though, bitterly, not understanding at all. In my arms. Our house was a brick house with crawling ivy—no, a ranch-style wooden house—no, colonial—no . . . I drained the glass, asked the bartender for something else. "Something strangely colored," I said. "Green?"

"Grasshopper maybe."

"Sure."

Waiting for the next drink I suddenly knew that the memory was completely gone. It must have been truly traumatic, I thought. Poor Joshua. A few years later and the imaginary companion started to appear . . . then the notebooks in an alien hand . . . little things, nothing that would put the boy in a padded cell, just . . . unnerving things.

What sort of things? I couldn't remember.

I hated myself for being a terrible father.

My brother Theo . . . he'd say. And fret about Theo's bad jokes or Theo not flushing the toilet . . . little things . . . what little things exactly? Memory like a sieve. Stop drinking! Stop!

A truck squealed to a stop at the traffic light at First and Oracle. The fat women slithered from the hot tub like the Slugs That Ate Texas. A jock dove into the pool. I downed my grasshopper and asked the bartender for something else . . . red maybe. Something red. Campari? No, redder, blood-red.

"Sir, I'm afraid I'm going to have to refuse to serve you. You're getting a little—"

The bartender stopped. A hand on his shoulder. A towering Chinese man stood behind him. I half recognized him. Where from? Memory like a sieve . . .

"Serve him." The man winked at me. He was tall. He was terrifying. His eyes were a window to the next world.

"Are you Death?" I said.

"Hardly, Mr. Etchison," said the Chinaman, "nor do I play chess! I fear you have seen too many Bergman films. My name is Cornelius Huang, and I am proprietor of this place. A *red* drink I believe you asked for, Mr. Etchison."

I mumbled something.

He poured a shot of vodka into a tall glass. Then he took a sharp instrument out of his shirt pocket—a sort of cross between a hypodermic and an astrolabe—and he jabbed himself in the finger with it. Casually, he let three drops of blood fall into the vodka. With the first drop the

drink turned pink. With the second it became a milky maroon. With the
third, the liquid was crimson and ringed with froth. He handed me the
glass. I shrank. "Drink, drink," he said, nodding encouragement. "It is a
fine drink for the composing of great poetry . . . for it dissolves boundary between reality and illusion."

I took the glass. I drained it in one gulp.

Theo . . .

Did Joshua realize the symbolism of that name? *ho theós* . . . God?
Did he know that the illusion of a younger brother who always spoke the
truth no matter how great the pain, no matter what the cost—was a mad
messianic metaphor right out of some nineteenth century novel? Joshua
wasn't just waiting for Godot . . . he was waiting for God . . . and I
had no God to give him, I with my hopelessly humanist sensibilities and
my incurable distrust of higher authority.

I set the glass down on the counter. A dusty wind blew across the pool
and burned my eyes with chlorine and grit. "A fine drink, Mr. Huang," I
said. But he was gone, and the bartender looked at me blankly, as though
Cornelius Huang had never been there.

I found Joshua in the hotel suite, poring through that book of dreams.
Mary was in the next room asleep and drugged to the gills.

He looked up. The television was blaring. It was one of those *Friday
the Thirteenth* movies. "Dad, you've been drinking," he said. And turned
his attention back to the book.

I said, "Son, I want to play a new game."

He said, "I don't know what to do! You're slipping away from me, the
whole world is sliding away from the truth, what I know is the
truth. . . ."

"Son, let's pretend—"

"He's gone. Sucked into a toilet bowl by an ocean tempest. And that
Chinese dude made you forget everything. Somehow."

"What Chinese—"

"Mr. Huang."

"You've never even met Mr. Huang. He's the manager of the motel or
something. I only just saw him today for the first time—"

"Then how come I know his name?"

"Son—"

"I know what you're going to say. Schizophrenics are devilishly smart.
They'll do all sorts of secret research to feed their delusions. You'll tell
me I've been snooping around looking for facts to trip you up, Dad . . .
but it's you who's losing his mind . . . look how drunk you are. Jesus

fucking Christ." He looked at me with a kind of terrible pity and I was afraid for a moment, afraid that he was right, afraid that *I* was the one who had lost touch with reality. . . .

I had to be strong. Behind that mask of certitude was confusion and illusion. I had to be his anchor, to be strong for him. "Let's pretend it's all true, son . . . let's pretend. For the sake of pretending." There was a part of me that didn't want to play this game. For a moment I thought of the alcohol dyed crimson with the Chinaman's blood. "I'll try to believe I have another son who vanished mysteriously when we were wandering in the desert. I'll try to believe that black is white, son," I said, "because I love you."

Behind us, the hockey-masked killer sliced another woman to ribbons. The music welled up, distorted into bursts of static.

Joshua wept.

"We'll start with the dream book," he said. "And we'll go to the police. And track down the Chinese restaurant with the river in the cave." I didn't know what he was talking about but I played along. If I humored him, perhaps he would let slip some clue, some key that I could use to set him free. Or I could learn what I had done wrong . . . some scene of primal child abuse we might have both repressed. . . .

"There's not much time," Joshua said. "Mom's due at the clinic . . . when? next week?"

"We'll take all the time you need," I said, feeling my whole past oozing through my fingers. Jesus, I wanted another drink.

I wanted the Chinaman's blood.

CHAPTER SEVEN

KING LEAR

Theo Etchison

The whale-rock is deceptively close. It takes a good part of another day to reach it. I can't tell how far anything is, I don't know what size it's supposed to be, and the horizon is too close . . . that's how I know we're not on Earth anymore.

I sleep and dream a dream within a dream.

It's spring break I guess. We drive down to Virginia Beach. Everyone went to the putt-putt golf course and I'm standing alone at the balcony of our room in the Sheraton listening to the seagulls. It's unseasonably hot. I taste the salt air and the gulls clamor and drive me crazy like a heavy metal concert I can hear the seawaves pounding and then I'm not dreaming anymore. The seagulls are warcries. Smoke in my nostrils.

But I *am* dreaming. . . . I remember the dream . . . war . . . dust of a burning planet . . .

The ship collides with the beach. I look up. The whale mountain fills the whole sky haloed with soft sunless light. The craft moves in sharp spasms and I realize that we're going onto the beach with some kind of pseudopods. The next spasm hurls me against the side and I see the battle raging at the foot of the mountain. I can make out figures in the blood-tinged sand-dust thrown up by their chariot wheels.

Elephant men in punk helmets. Glistening lizards with swords that glitter with laser light. Elves with pointy ears. Amazons mounted on robot horses. There's a mound of corpses sliding into the sea and a flock of carnivorous insects feeding. There's a smell of burning blood. The smoke makes me cough. It's a little bit like incense.

"Get a move on, truthsayer." It's Thorn, pulling me up by my T-shirt. "We're home now."

He throws his cloak around me and we kind of leap into the air. I'm holding on for dear life as we like hover a moment and then take off and soar over the battle toward the mountain.

"Afraid of heights?" Thorn whispers.

I open my eyes. We're descending. In the midst of the battle there is an old man sitting on a palanquin on the shoulders of about fifty dudes with reptile faces. I know the old man from one of my dreams. He is King Lear. He has long white hair and a face crosshatched with wrinkles and ice-blue eyes. He surveys the carnage. There is no feeling in his eyes. He is a madman. But we're alike. We are both lost. Adrift among the dimensions. Somehow I know we're in the same position, me and him.

He doesn't see us yet. The beach is on fire.

The old man clasps a scepter in his bosom. He stares wildly about, mutters to himself, and the reptile litter bearers stand, impassive, indifferent to the fire that sweeps along the sand and the cries of dying creatures.

Rolling toward us come gargantuan war machines, catapults that spew fire mounted on turrets. I try to look away, I bury my face in Thorn's cloak and choke on the smell of blood and brimstone. And suddenly we've landed. My feet hit something solid. Pain shoots through my ankle. I yelp. Rudely I am thrown aside. We're on the palanquin. I've been kicked onto the floor and my arm is dangling between two litter-poles and I feel cold lizard breath on my fingers.

I pull myself up. I'm crouching now, staying out of their line of sight. My eye is level with the hem of the king's garment. It's the kind of thing a Roman emperor wears in old spectacles, but there seem to be people woven into the cloth, shadowy people that you can only see out of the corner of your eye, when you try to look at them they kind of get siphoned into the folds of the robe . . . yeah, the cloth is kind of woven out of human souls I guess. It flutters and flaps and throws grit in my face.

"Father," Thorn says softly.

"Call them off," says the king. "Don't they recognize me? Don't they know who I am? Don't they realize I'm the master around here?"

Thorn laughs. Very softly. When I look in his face I see a little fear—not the fear of something he cannot understand, as he felt with me, but the thrill that goes through you when you are about to defy your parents.

"Call the buggers off, Thorn," says the old king.

Thorn looks around. A decapitated head lands at his feet. He kicks it off the palanquin. There's a glint of triumph in his eye maybe. "Herald," he says. He's never raised his voice above a whisper, but I can always hear him above the roar of the sea and the screams of dying creatures.

Mr. Huang is standing beside him suddenly, Mr. Huang in a business suit, dusting himself off with a handkerchief.

"Where were you?" says Thorn. "I need you to sound a cease-action."

"I was pouring a man a drink," Mr. Huang says. "It's what you ordered me to do, sire. Surely you don't expect me to be in two places at once." He plucks the conch-trumpet out of the churning air. He blows an eerie blast that echoes and reechoes against the mountain that fills the sky.

Suddenly the conflict ceases. The dust settles. A war-tower tumbles onto the sand and crushes some of the soldiers. The soldiers assemble in small groups, the lizard warriors gathering behind the palanquin of the old king.

The king stands up. He is every bit as tall as Thorn, though his white beard roils about his face like a cloud bank. I'm a little bolder now and I sit up.

"Father," says Thorn, "King Strang."

King Strang's face is like the mountain itself, furrowed and craggy. There is a wound on his forehead, and something wriggles in and out of it . . . a maggot perhaps. I stare at him. He exudes nobility even though his forehead festers.

"Welcome to my castle, Father," says Thorn, but there's a hint of menace in what he says.

"Welcome? You call this a welcome?" Strang says. His voice is hoarse, almost inaudible. "A couple of hundred soldiers, war-towers, big guns?"

"Dark times, Father. You'd have done the same thing. A man can't be too careful."

"But I'm your king!"

"That's where you're wrong."

I'm piecing the story together in my mind from scraps of dreams. The king is the old man who was trying to give away his kingdom to his three children . . . that was in the dream. There were three children: a daughter, a son, and one I wasn't sure of. The son was Thorn and the daughter was Katastrofa Darkling.

"You may recall, Father, that you gave up the throne."

"On condition," says King Strang, his voice trembling, "that I retain the title and the style of king—"

"Poor fool; you should have listened to my brother, Ash."

"I have disinherited him. As you know." So Ash was the third child— the one who wouldn't flatter. That was kind of like in the play we saw at Wolf Trap.

"Poor Father. Ash was the only one who ever gave you good advice."

I sat all the way up now.

"I bid you welcome, Father," Thorn says, and smiles a fake smile. Then he turns toward the mountain and claps his hands. "Open the damn gate, herald," he says. I hear three blasts on the conch.

Three times and three times again and the wall of rock like *dissolves* somehow. I gasp. But why should it surprise me? Nothing in this place is what it seems. The rock has become a kind of veil or force-field shot through with veins of colored light. Behind it I see level upon level of Thornstone Slaught . . . staircases that spiral up forever like the model DNA molecule in Mrs. Carter's biology lab. . . . It's like you took about fifty shopping malls and smashed them all together. As I look up and up the decor gets more and more Medieval-looking. I get the feeling that there was once this old castle on top and like they kept burrowing down into the mountain and here at the base it's more high-tech.

I feel movement; the litterbearers hoisting the palanquin high over their shoulders . . . turning.

"South wing all right for you, Father?" says Thorn. His voice is as sweet as a sugar-coated cyanide pill.

"Don't make jokes, son," says the old man. "I've already lost a dozen guards because of your security system. And I can't replace them, you know . . . not since the power failure at the clone plant." He's just mumbling really; I'm the only one who hears him. Suddenly he reminds me of my father for a moment. I start crying. I don't know why.

"South wing it is."

"I am still King Strang! You must house me in the Imperial Suite, as is my right!"

"You don't need all those rooms, Father . . . what are you going to do, call a transdimensional summit meeting? Who'd come?"

I see the rage flare up in King Strang's eyes. He raises that scepter of his, the scepter I have seen in my dreams that can suck a man's soul right out of his body. He doesn't strike his son . . . he's looking around for someone to lash out at. That's when he notices me for the first time. I'm wiping my eyes with a fold of my T-shirt. I must look pretty fucking pathetic. His anger dims a little.

"Imperial Suite," he murmurs.

"Papa," Thorn says, shrugging, "this isn't a hotel, you know. And your credit cards have all been canceled." He winks at me. I don't think they use credit cards here—the joke must have been for my benefit. It occurs to me that Thorn is actually showing off in front of me, that he actually has this need to impress me. "You're just a useless old man, Father . . . might as well get used to it."

"Useless . . . old . . ."

I look around. The lizard warriors have all stiffened. They stand ready to spring, their javelins poised. The light from the burning beach makes the shadows dance on their faces. I see now that they all look exactly alike. . . . They've been manufactured somehow. The clone plant. That must be what Strang meant.

A moment of tension. I don't know if they are going to attack.

"Call off your clockwork dinosaurs, Father," Thorn says.

"My Imperial Guard . . . my most faithful retainers—"

"You never could get much loyalty, Father," says Thorn, "unless it was from some preprogrammed device."

Strang lifts up his scepter . . . makes as though to strike his son.

"Treason," Thorn whispers.

And clicks his fingers.

All at once the battle starts up again! Fireballs whiz through the sky! Chariots charge! The lizard warriors are flinging their spears, which turn into shafts of laser light that set the war-turrets aflame. The litterbearers are still standing, ready to carry their master into the castle. The battle rages around us.

"You can't do this to him, Thorn," I say very softly. I don't know why.

He looks at me. Picks me up by the scruff of my T-shirt. Stares into my eyes. "What are you talking about?" he screams.

I realize suddenly that what I've just said is part of my knack . . . my truthsaying gift . . . if you can call it a gift. "You can't treat your father this way," I say, "or things'll go bad for you, Thorn."

"What are you speaking up for him for, weasel?" says Thorn. He slaps my face. I taste blood. "Don't you know how many people he's killed, how many worlds he's destroyed? Look at him, boy . . . he's the enemy . . . he's the corrupt heart of everything . . . the one we're going to have to save the universe from. He's mad, boy, and when he's mad the cosmos goes insane and it's up to us to clean it up."

"He's mad because you drove him mad," I say.

He slaps me again, I go sprawling, my head smashes into the old king's knee . . . I feel his whole body give a little, like there's nothing inside. He feels like my mother, desiccated, empty.

Then I feel the old man's hand on my head.

I look up. I can't understand what I see in his face. It is not tenderness. I am too far beneath him for him to feel anything like that. "Who is this child," he says, "who speaks the truth however great the pain?"

I turn. Father and son glare at each other with the utmost hatred in their eyes.

"I have my own truthsayer now," Thorn says.

The king says to me, "I suppose you know why I can't set foot in Thornstone Slaught again."

"Your honor's at stake," I say.

"Goodbye, truthsayer," he says, and runs his bony fingers through my hair and makes me think of Dad for a moment. And I start crying again without knowing why.

CHAPTER EIGHT

THE UNCERTAINTY PRINCIPLE

Joshua   Etchison

A few hours after Dad's about-face, my mother's condition got really bad and we had to check her into the university hospital. There was a chance we weren't even going to make it to the Laetrile clinic after all. But we'd always known that.

I didn't want her out of my sight. Maybe they'd come and take her away too and then Dad would forget she ever existed too. He was always drunk now and when he slipped away to drink he would come back remembering even less of our family's past. I struggled with the orderly because I wanted them to put a cot in her bedroom so I can watch over her all the time, but they gave me an injection and I woke up in the motel room in time to see my dad feverishly throwing a few clothes into an overnight bag.

"Come on, son," he said. "We're going to get to the bottom of this."

"Humoring me again, Dad?" I said.

He looked around crazily, like a madman in a B horror movie. Then he went over to his big suitcase and pulled out a few books.

I recognized his latest poetry book, *The Embrasure of Parched Lips*. I've got you! I thought, and I sprang off the couch and wrested it from his hand.

"What are you—"

I turned it to the dedication page. Triumphantly waved it in Dad's face. "Wake up, Dad! Who'd you dedicate this book to? Don't you remember?"

He took it from me. A puzzled look crossed his face. "Dedication page's been ripped out," he said. "Did you do it?" And he showed it to me. It was gone.

He slammed the book shut. A Polaroid snapshot flew out of it and landed on the floor. "Look, Dad—it's us!"

We both looked at it as it lay on a heap of underwear above the tawdry polka-dotted shag. Me and Mom and Dad and Theo. Smiling stupidly. Uncle Tim had taken that picture.

We knelt down on either side of the dirty clothes. My father smiled. "Who's your friend?" he said. He really didn't know.

"Friend, Dad? You know I wouldn't hang out with any freshmen. . . ."

He took the picture. We peered at it. Slowly, like a mirage, Theo's image faded from the photograph. Dad laughed. He was uncomfortable. "There isn't another kid in the photo . . . trick of the light or something I guess," he mumbled.

God, I hated Theo. For making my dad think I'm insane . . . for going away and leaving me to deal with all this bullshit . . . someone, some force was erasing all traces of Theo from the world, but it was taking time. Like with the snapshot. Reality was probably pretty resistant to change. . . . Whatever was "fixing" the world was changing as little as possible, and only at the moment when change was needed. If Dad and I had never looked at the Polaroid, Theo's face would always have been on it. That's how it worked. I once read an article in *Discover* magazine that said the whole universe works this way . . . that the act of observing the cosmos changes it.

Sometimes it wasn't quick enough.

Sometimes you could catch it just before it changed.

They called this the uncertainty principle.

Thoughts raced. If I could figure out the sort of things that would have to be changed and *catch* them a split second before they changed and arrange for Dad to see them too . . . but I knew that if I even *thought* about them too much they would start to want to change. . . . The reason for the Polaroid was that no one had been thinking about it, it had just slipped out of the book—had to figure out a way of focusing my thoughts on something else, on *tricking* whatever this reality-changing phenomenon was. . . .

"Hurry up, son. Stop daydreaming." He'd always talked to Theo in that tone.

My Dad stood at the door with two overnight bags full of clothes. "We're going to do some investigating . . . you and me . . . get to the bottom of this. Missing persons bureau—we'll go back to that Chinese restaurant you keep talking about . . . anywhere you want." I got up. Got a whiff of his breath. He'd already been drinking, and his lips were stained red as though with pomegranate juice . . . or blood. "Let's get us some cholesterol burgers before we go down to the police station."

"Dad, you know I only eat health food now."

"Bullshit, kiddo! You love Burger King more than life itself."

What other things did my father no longer know?

That clinched it. There were bugs in this alternate universe business. Leaks. They were trying to rub out Theo from the world, but sometimes they would miss and rub out something else.

For instance, how come I hadn't forgotten anything?

Or had I?

Phil Etchison

I drove my mad son down to the police station. There was a man named Milt Stone, a tall man of Indian descent. He knew who I was; apparently there'd been an article in the *Star* that mentioned my arrival in town. Apparently a Mr. Huang, proprietor of our motel, had told them that Phil Etchison, the world famous poet, was passing through, and . . .

"Matter of fact, Mr. Etchison," said Detective Stone, waving us to a sofa piled high with papers in his over-air conditioned cubbyhole of an office, "the wife, she's really looking forward to going to your autograph party. Reads a lot, you know. She likes Stephen King and Rod McKuen." I suppressed my impulse to throw up and smiled at him, wondering what on earth he meant by my autograph party . . . I didn't remember agreeing to one.

"Do you have . . . any alcohol?" I asked him. My son turned away from me.

"Don't you go blaming your father, now," Stone said to Joshua, not unkindly. "He's going through a lot." He rummaged in the little refrigerator behind his desk and pulled out a battered can of generic beer. "You say your boy run off?"

I looked at Joshua. Took a swig of the beer. It was still warm and burned my throat but it felt good. "Joshua will tell you about it," I said. "He's the one who . . . remembers it best."

"Well, I can surely understand how you wouldn't want to talk about it, sir," said Stone. "The wife told me how much you loved that boy. . . . She showed me what you wrote about it on that there dedication page."

Joshua tensed. What had he been trying to show me back there in the room? The dedication page and then the photograph that for a split second seemed to show an image of another boy . . . what did all that mean?

I'd dedicated *The Embrasure of Parched Lips* to Mary, hadn't I? And there was a little poem about . . . about her miscarriage, about Joshua's rage . . .

I didn't want to tell him he was mistaken, didn't want to embarrass Joshua, so I only said, "Joshua will tell you about it."

"We have a computer, Mr. Etchison, that links up all the missing person reports with all the information we can lay our hands on. But I imagine your boy'll turn up. Was there any . . . trouble between you?"

Joshua said, "He was kidnapped. By a man named Huang. The man who owns the Chinese restaurant on Route 10."

Stone looked up sharply. "The big restaurant with the façade that makes it look like the set of *The Last Emperor*?" he said.

A thin smile on Joshua's lips. "That's the one."

"Why, son, that restaurant's just an idea in the mind of a mad old Chinaman that came breezing through Arizona a hundred years ago. Go down to the county museum, there's an artist's impression of what it would have been like. Impressive as shit. But there ain't no restaurant like that on Route 10. Hell, there ain't no Route 10 no more; they turned that into an interstate."

Joshua was trembling. He got up and asked for the bathroom. I took the opportunity to tell Detective Stone about his problem. "Just humor him," I said. "Please."

"Strange," he said, "I don't see as how you folks could have known about the old Chinese restaurant, not unless you were experts on our local history. . . ."

I took another swig of my beer. Stale tobacco smoke lingered in the air. A spider crawled up the frame of a frayed college diploma.

"Detective Stone—"

"Call me Milt. Please."

"Milt, Joshua will go to any lengths in order to suck us into his private reality."

"Seems like a normal enough kid."

"He scares me."

And then Joshua stood in the doorway, wiping his hands on his hair.

"Want to see the computer now, kid?" said Milt. Josh nodded. "They always brighten up when I mention that computer. If you gentlemen would care to come with me . . ." He got up, straightened his shirt against his massive body, and motioned me toward the doorway.

"I'll handle the case now, Milt, if you don't mind." A woman's voice. Very low . . . with the velvet smoothness of a viola. Joshua paled, moved toward me. It was then that I saw her framed in the sodium yellow of the light from the hall beyond: a delicate-featured woman with long red hair. Even the unflattering police uniform she wore became her somehow. There was something reptilian about her face.

Milt Stone did a sort of double take. When he answered it was in a
different voice; he sounded almost hypnotized.

"Of course," he said. Blinked a couple of times. Then turned to me
and said, "Forgot to introduce you. Superintendent Darkling . . . Kathy
Darkling."

"Katastrofa," said Joshua softly.

The woman laughed, a silvery laugh with a mocking edge. "It's an
honor," she said, "to meet the celebrated poet." And inclined her head
toward me, though she managed to make it seem condescending. "Many
of my . . . people have enjoyed your verses, Mr. Etchison."

"I know you," said Joshua.

The woman seemed to notice him for the first time. Her demeanor
darkened. "The young are such dreamers," she murmured. That's what I
thought I heard her say.

"We'll find your brother for you," said Kathy Darkling. "I promise."
Joshua's face was soaked with sweat, even though the air conditioning
was on full blast. She took him by the hand. Like the detective, my son
seemed mesmerized. "Our computers know *everything*."

We followed her down the hall. She didn't so much walk as glide. We
lagged by the water cooler; she turned to look back at us. Her eyes had a
yellowish cast. Somehow she didn't seem entirely human.

I caught up with her. I wanted to whisper a word or two to her about
Joshua's madness. She merely said, "Reality is a shifty thing, Mr. Etchison. I've had a lot of experience with disturbed teenagers; let me talk to
him for a while."

"Be my guest."

"Alone, if you don't mind."

She opened the door marked with her name, ushered my trembling
son inside, stepped in after him. It slammed in my face.

"Women detectives," said Milt, shaking his head. "She's new; just got
assigned here yesterday; women like that, they always gotta prove they're
ten times more hard-assed than us men."

CHAPTER NINE

INSIDE THE MOUNTAIN

Theo Etchison

I blink and we're inside the mountain.

Thorn and I and the three-headed dog from the boat and Mr. Huang. Walking across a hall that just went on and on, granite columns stretching up out of sight, intertwining, statues, flashing lights; people hurrying, eyes downcast when they catch sight of us, creatures scurrying by, robots, little globes that flit through the air squealing and squeaking to one another, weaving in and out of the throngs of people. We're in the space I glimpsed before that I said looked like a fifty shopping mall pileup. It also looks like a mishmash of a dozen science fiction movies, except it's a whole lot more lived-in. The robots look battered, the people look dowdy, the columns are peeling, half the flashing lights are out of sync. There are a lot of sphinxes like the ones half-submerged in the bay. Little sphinxes lining the walls, a huge one poking up out of the floor that has about a dozen cleaning ladies swabbing at one of its paws with mops.

"Not quite what you expected, is it, Theo Truthsayer," Thorn says. He continues striding ahead. It's hard to keep up with him.

"Well . . . it was high fantasy when you abducted me, and now it's kind of a hokey space epic," I say. "Or the cover of one of those old pulp magazines."

"Or like the dreams of a lonely, over-imaginative teenage boy," Thorn says, reviving, for a moment, my flagging hope that this is all some wild nightmare that just won't end.

"You're right," I say. "Look—a bit of *Star Wars* here, a touch of *Blade Runner,* even a few decorations lifted out of *Land of the Pharaohs.* Sure I'm dreaming."

"You do not like my taste?"

"I don't like *you.*"

"And I thought it would make you feel more at home to be surrounded by images from your personal mythos," says Thorn.

"Don't do me any favors."

"Very well then." He shakes his head and suddenly it's all gone . . .

all of it . . . and instead we're inside the ultimate vampire castle. Cobwebs stretching up as far as I can see. Sweeping staircases coated with dust. Mist roiling about our knees. There are people here too . . . gibbering corpses . . . misshapen mutants shambling through the mist.

"It's all mutable, you see," Thorn says, gesticulating grandly. "All the elements, all the beings we perceive . . . the fabric of the universe is the fabric of dreams . . . starstuff is the stuff of fantasy. . . ."

Is he trying to tell me that I'm dreaming? Maybe I'll wake up soon, but I'm not going to hold my breath waiting anymore.

"But you're different. You have no imagination, Theo Truthsayer."

We have reached a stairway that just goes up and up and up, but I know it's not to heaven. The air we breathe is foul and the steps are piled high with human skulls. Thorn kicks them out of the way and I hear them clatter, clatter, clatter down the steps, the echoes blending with distant cries of pain.

"No imagination?" I say. "No one's ever accused me of that before."

"I dare say they've been telling you you've too much of it, my boy. But that's not it at all. . . . You're a truthsayer. Every person, every object, every event in the universe spins a cocoon of fantasy around itself, but you, you see the inner truth of things. You hear the inner music. That is your gift, your curse. You have no aura. You are transparent. You are—if I may use so corny an expression—pure of heart. That's why I've hunted you out . . . laid traps for one such as you in a dozen worlds . . . sent the one you call Mr. Huang to fetch you to me. . . ."

He takes the steps two, three at a time. It's hard to keep up. I don't know how may steps it's been . . . a hundred, five hundred. But it doesn't seem to tire him. He talks the whole time, obsessively, but I'm hardly listening because the last couple of hundred steps are so exhausting. The familiar dog is bounding beside us with the drool dripping from his three mouths.

"I, of course, I . . . being a ruler . . . am not pure of heart. But you will already have understood that. Power corrupts, you know. Yes."

In some inchoate way, I sense he is actually trying to apologize to me for slapping me around in front of his father. It was a matter of face, I suppose, having a truthsayer to kick around. Or more than face.

"I didn't appreciate being treated that way in front of him," I say, "and I didn't appreciate the way you treated *him,* either." I keep thinking about my own family and how fractured it's become, and I wonder whether I would ever treat my dad that way even though I know he doesn't understand anything about me.

"Keep your eyes and ears open, boy, but don't try to change the way things are. You're needed here, I tell you." The staircase turns, narrows, I see a vague light above.

"You wouldn't need me if you were so damned important."

"I'll have you thrown in irons."

"Big deal." Bondage is big with these people, I decide.

He's about to hit me again but thinks better of it maybe. He continues: "Things were good once, you see. My father ruled wisely. The three of us—Ash, Katastrofa, and I—we lived in a kind of paradise, isolated from everything ugly. The River flowed near my father's castle and through the River came travelers from distant worlds and my father too became a traveler. . . . He roamed the many universes with an old man who always knew the true paths from the false. . . . He reached the River's end, the ocean of oblivion. . . . He came back with the scepter that feeds on souls. . . . He grew dark in his heart."

"You think you're not, Thorn?" I say.

"I'm a lesser evil!" he says. There is a despair in him, the same despair I have seen in the face of his father. "It's all a consequence of my father's act, don't you see? It's a disease that's infected us all . . . turned me against my family. . . . It's a cancer eating away at the entire cosmos. . . ."

"Sounds kind of melodramatic," I say. I don't want to believe him. But it's so like what's been happening to my own family. I can't help feeling something for him.

"So will you help me, Theo Truthsayer? And perhaps, if you are really good at what you do—"

"I'm not sure what it is I do yet!"

"—we can bring back your mother. That's right, little one. A little wrinkle in the transdimensional probability nexus . . . we can iron that sucker right out."

⑸

I don't know how much longer we climb those stairs. I think there must be some kind of shortcut—they're just doing it this way so they can impress the shit out of me—it's working.

At last we reach Thorn's throne room. It isn't so much a room as a desolate heath, with the wind howling and with twisted rocks jutting from the purple-gray wild grass. There is a kind of sky overhead although I know we are still somewhere within the castle. Alien moons shine down from behind shifting wisps of mist.

A dining table appears. We have lunch. While Thorn drains blood from the veins of a beautiful woman who lies, naked, on the table in front of him, servants in black serve me, on a gold platter, something that looks like a Big Mac, fries and a chocolate shake. But it all tastes like blood. I think they've just disguised it to look like things I'm familiar with. Make me feel at home. As if I could. But when I really concentrate I can feel the seething life force in the chocolate shake and I don't want to drink it.

"You're not hungry?" Thorn asks me.

"I can't help thinking that if I eat the food around here I'll be forced to stay here forever."

"Ah, how very mythic," Thorn says, laughing. Then, winking, he adds, "Go on, eat, it's harmless. I won't give you food that'll blind your mind. You're too important for that."

I believe him. I eat the food hungrily. It seems that I haven't eaten in a very long time.

"In any case, boy," Thorn says, "I should think you'd best get some rest now. We'll start in the morning."

"Start what?" I say.

"As if you didn't know!" Thorn says. "Why, the destinies of a million worlds rest on your slender shoulders, and you sit around playing this game of childish naïveté as though—"

I try to blot him out. I think about my parents and my brother. They are fading . . . or are they? I see my brother sitting in a little room. Talking to a woman. A snake-woman! I've seen her in my dreams. Her name is Katastrofa Darkling.

Later they take me to my room. It's like the throne room, an endless field of tall gray grass, shrouded in slow mist. The sky is the color of Thorn's eyes and illumined with the same dull sourceless light. Here and there are weathered gravestones. In the middle of it all there's a bed, a desk, a color TV, all the stuff from my room back home in Alexandria. There's my favorite comforter on the bed, the almost threadbare one that has a bunch of Ewoks on it. The mist curls in and out. I sit down on the bed and point the remote at the TV, but all the channels are showing *The Twilight Zone*.

They've left me alone now. I know everything in the room's an illusion. When I really concentrate I get a sense of its real size. And all those objects I'm familiar with are fake too. The TV turns out to be hollow. When I lie back on the bed it kind of stretches out and envelops me and suddenly I'm floating in utter soundless darkness. When I sit up again it's the old bed shaped like a racing car and kind of too short for me.

I look in the drawers in the desk and sure enough the desk is just a façade and inside it are alien objects . . . something that looks like a cross between a sea-urchin and a stethoscope, a couple of spiny purple fruits, a kind of a laptop computer, a . . . fountain pen. I take the pen and touch it to the TV screen and *The Twilight Zone* disappears and instead there's like this map . . . in three dimensions . . . a mass of threads of light, like a Tesla coil, hanging in the air. I peer at the light-strands. Forking and unforking . . . I see that it's all one thread of light, weaving, winding, spiraling, doubling back on itself. And I get the feeling that the map is why I'm here . . . that somehow I'm the only one who can read it.

I stare into the map for a long time. The map rotates; I see it from many angles. As I follow the twisting strands I realize that the map is in more than three dimensions. I seize upon one strand and trace it with my finger and I feel my whole hand being sucked into somewhere else, fading out of the real world. . . . It must be the river they're always talking about, I think. The river that is the path between all the different realities.

My concentration breaks; the map shrinks and drops into my palm . . . a marble.

Rod Serling reappears on the TV screen. I stick the marble in the pocket of my shorts. Then I start to get ready for bed. I'm filthy and there's nowhere to take a shower until . . .

I look up. There's a door standing in the middle of the field. It's like the door to the bathroom at the top of the stairs at my house. I get up and step inside. It's exactly like back home. A couple of fresh towels, my Alvin and the Chipmunks electric toothbrush with its batteries dead, my sci-fi trivia toilet paper and a poster on the wall of Traci Lords in *Not of this Earth* with a big brown mustache that my friend Tommy drew in anger the day we all piled in the car to leave for Mexico.

I draw the blinds and I can see all the way down Quantico to the corner with the condos the next block down and the snow melting and Tommy waving at me from across the street.

I take off my clothes and wash them in the sink. I put the marble next to my toothbrush. The clothes are matted with blood and green scum. It takes a long time to get it all off. I hang them on the towel rack, take a shower . . . as I'm drying myself I take another look through the window. . . . It's summer now and Tommy is older, taller, and he has another friend, a girl.

I close the blinds.

I clutch the marble and step through the door into the heather and the howling wind and the gray light filtering through shifting mist. I'm naked but I can't feel the wind. I get into bed and I fall asleep, gazing into the marble with its microscopic filaments of light, staring at worlds within worlds.

In the real world I always dreamt of this place, but here I dream of the place I left behind:

Joshua is sitting in a small room across from Katastrofa Darkling. She wears a policewoman's uniform. Above their heads, a naked bulb swings. Behind her face is a poster for a death rock band. She holds a marble between her thumb and forefinger and forces Joshua to look deep into it. I can't tell what he's thinking.

"Stare into it! Stare into it! Tell me what you see! And it better be right, or you'll never see him again. . . ."

I see my brother through the eyes of an insect. His face repeated endlessly in the facets of my compound eyes. I hear the snake-woman laughing. I see sweat on my brother's forehead and I'm beginning to feel what he feels . . . not the passing lust he felt for pudgy Serena, but the real thing . . . love maybe . . . an emotion so powerful he doesn't have room for Mom and Dad . . . or me.

My insect-consciousness flits past them, shoots across the room to the door and the keyhole through which I see my father pacing back and forth, back and forth. . . . He's reading and rereading my dream book, trying to puzzle it out.

A detective is with him. They are waiting.

I turn around to see the fire glittering in the woman's eyes. She is too beautiful to be human.

"Come on," she says. "You are his closest relation. Surely you must have a bit of the ability."

"What ability?"

"You know."

"I don't know."

"Fool . . . when he drifts away from you, when it seems to you that he's gazing into some fantasy universe, where do you think your brother is? Hasn't it occurred to you that you might have the power to follow him, to see what he sees . . . if only a shadow of what he sees? Your brother is already taken, and I must settle for what I can get . . . though half-truths can be more dangerous than lies."

My brother looks blankly at her.

"What's in the marble?" she says.

My brother shakes his head. Then, "The River," he says softly, with a kind of vague recognition.

"What is the meaning of the River?" she says. And touches his hand.

"The meaning of the River is . . . fuck fuck fuck oh fuck oh fuck," he says and he can't control himself and I know this is what he's like when I peer into his room in the middle of the night and he has a big boner in his sleep and comes all over the sheets and wakes up, gets all embarrassed about it, and won't look me in the eye.

She holds his hand tight now, tight, and forces him to look into her eyes. . . .

Now we're in the throne room again . . . me and Thorn and the herald and some of Thorn's followers, with the dog clawing at dirt at the foot of the throne. I'm wearing these death rock kind of clothes they left out for me with a silver skull in my ear and a black cape.

"I see you've found the map of the River," says Thorn.

I hold up the marble.

"Good," he says. "Let's see if you can read it!"

All at once I see that the throne is at the edge of a brook that winds across his field of vision. I wonder why I haven't seen it before. The sound of trickling gets louder.

"Feel the River . . . feel it run from the beginning to the end of space-time. . . ." Thorn says, and already I can hear the rushing of the waters, a timeless tuneless music. With my mind I reach into the marble and grab hold of the fragment of light that is the point we're standing at. . . . I step forward. . . . I feel the water lapping at my feet.

"We're in your hands," Thorn says. I can tell he's not happy with this arrangement.

"Where are we going?" I ask him. But already I know, already I am plunging into the water, already it's up to my waist and I still go on, following the thread, like Theseus in the labyrinth, finding the safe stones to stand on as the current begins to surge and—

We're hurled into the vortex now. . . . We're standing in a bubble of silence as the water churns around us . . . storms of colored light burst over us . . . mists whirl madly . . . translucent creatures with gargoyle faces fly at us . . . on either shore time races while in our pocket universe time stands still. Vistas of alien worlds blur into one another.

Slowly I see that we're on board a vessel, all glass and metal, that I am standing by the prow with the marble in my hand . . . that I'm thinking the ship into moving. . . . I'm stilling the water. . . . I'm thinking easy now, easy, as though I'm petting a frightened animal, and I'm calming the turbulence.

The water becomes gentle. We are borne by the downstream current. The raging light does not touch us. I know it is illusory . . . that each person sees something different . . . that what I see reflects my own confusion.

"Having a good time, boy? Navigating becomes you." Thorn looks at the vortex. I think that the river he sees is a river of blood. He smiles grimly.

"You're just testing me," I say. "This is a well-mapped part of the River. . . . You come this way all the time. You didn't bring me here for this."

"Little by little, Theo Truthsayer," he says. "There are places where my father has destroyed the gateways. The worlds we rule are linked together by a thread. Easily snapped. Easily cut off."

The River passes through an area where light does not rage. There is nothing beyond the riverbank. Not even blackness. There is a sense of utter desolation. Like seeing my father forget I ever existed. These are dead places. I see what Thorn means about whole worlds being cut off from the River. Perhaps these places can be reached again. The River's always doubling back on itself. But the way isn't on my map. That's why they need me.

The River forks again and I will the skiff down the right fork. Just as we are turning I see the dragon.

At first it's just a chain of gold-scaled rocks that stretches upriver. Then the rocks lengthen, link up, and the dragon's head thrusts out of the water, confronting us head-on.

"Katastrofa!" Thorn exclaims in disgust.

The dragon's eyes are the eyes of a beautiful woman. The scales iridesce in the cascading water, clanking like bronze plates. Clinging to the dragon's neck is a young man. Joshua.

We see each other for only a second before the skiff plows on. His eyes don't give anything away. I don't know if he was kidnapped or if he came of his own free will.

"This ruins everything," Thorn says, shaking his head. "I wish I had some blood."

CHAPTER TEN

KATASTROFA DARKLING

J o s h u a   E t c h i s o n

I was face-to-face with her at last. I couldn't control myself. She held my hands in hers across the desk in that shabby windowless room with the naked light bulb swinging back and forth, back and forth, like a torture scene in a Nazi war movie. She was everything I remembered from my dreams. Her long red hair streamed behind her although I could feel no wind and the air conditioning was off. She had almond-shaped eyes the color of summer grass, and her features were perfectly symmetrical. My hands sweated at the touch of her lizardskin gloves. I was trembling. I was having kind of a waking wet dream. I was full of desire and embarrassment and I couldn't look her in the eye.

My throat was dry and I kept staring at the water cooler. DRAGON-SPRING WATER, said the logo, and it showed a coiled-up crimson dragon breathing fire, but the fire was misted from the condensation. She kept asking me questions. How long I'd had those dreams. Detailed questions about Theo's dream book that made me suspect that her knowledge of it was sketchy.

I told her what I could remember. The bit about the king and the three children—the King Lear part—made her tense. Her lips tightened. "It's not true," she said. "Not the way he tells it. It's too complicated. . . ."

"Where's my brother . . . Jesus Christ, what have you fucking done to him?"

She knew who Theo was all right. But not as much as she let on. She had nothing to do with his abduction. I could tell that right away because when she let go of me, when I slipped from her spell for a moment, I screamed at her, "I want him back—I want him back—I want everything to be the way it used to be."

And she looked at me blankly for a moment, then said, "Of course. Everything will be the way it was. If you come with me for now."

The room was filling up with smoke. The bulb swung back and forth and I could feel myself being hypnotized.

"You can't take me anywhere. . . . We're not connected to the River

here. . . ." I whispered. What river? How had I known there was supposed to be a river?

She merely smiled and got up.

"Would you like a drink?" she said, and got a paper cup and went to
the water cooler.

Dragon Spring Water . . .

She handed me the cup. I lifted it to my lips. The water was cool, so
cool . . . and her hands burning hot as they brushed my cheek. She
leaned over and pushed the water button again and let the water spill
onto the floor and the water was gushing now, the water was spiraling
round and round me like a lariat. . . .

"Can you become a truthsayer?" she said. "You have it in your
blood. . . ."

"I'm not a truthsayer!" I shouted. "I don't even know what one is!"

"What a paradox!" she said. "When you say that you are not a truthsayer, it has the unmistakable ring of truth and makes you into a truthsayer anyway, which means you were lying which means you can't be a
truthsayer. . . ."

She wasn't joking. The paradox was driving her crazy. *I* was driving her
crazy because I wasn't Theo. But she still had to have me. I was the next
best thing. I didn't know what it was for . . . she'd mumbled something
about saving the universe, but, Jesus, give me a break.

"Come on," she said, "let's test the current."

Then she enveloped me in her arms and I guess I kind of came in my
pants but before the embarrassment hit me I was being sucked into a
whirlpool and the water was changing colors and Katastrofa was changing . . . bursting out of her cop's uniform, scales slicing up through her
skin, her fingernails thrusting, curving into claws. . . . Still she held me
tight in her embrace though I could feel the talons ripping my shirt and
she kissed me and I could taste her tongue taste the brimstone and the
myrrh in her breath sweet and bitter and sour and she whispered "Not so
fast little boy slower slower slower there go go go slower slower you want
to give me pleasure don't you taste me taste me" and she was hot to the
touch, hot as the foam churned around us and we stood at the eye of the
tempest and behind her the pendulum light bulb swung and I could feel
her nails shred at my jeans now and feel the sharp tingle of her brush
against my hair down there and I winced from shame but I was aroused
again bursting again and still she whispered "slower slower do you want
to rush headlong into hell boy? slower slower" and it was like those
sleepless nights I had alone with my burgeoning new body sleepless
thinking alone when the summer moonlight streamed into my bedroom

in Virginia and the shadows on the walls embraced made love while the wind blew sticky through the open window hot and pregnant with impending rain, she—

Enveloped me in her arms like the sticky wet wind of summer as the water swirled around us—

P h i l   E t c h i s o n

—and I stood at the doorway listening. Pacing. I could hear nothing of what went on inside. Until suddenly there was a cry, an animal cry, like a prisoner being interrogated in a war movie. I looked down. My shoes . . . my socks were soaked. A pool of water had formed at the threshold of the inner room. More water was seeping out. Behind the door I could hear a rushing sound . . . a sound I used to hear a long time ago when Mary and I were newlyweds and I taught Eng. Lit. in Buffalo . . . when we would go to Niagara Falls for the weekend.

The sound lasted a split second. I blinked.

There was a brief discontinuity of some kind . . . a quantum shift. At that moment, the fellow I had met in the bar at the hotel came down the hallway.

"It's good of you," I said, "to let me tour the police station. I never know when I might need to use a bit of . . . atmosphere . . . a twinge of memory."

He looked a little perplexed for a moment, as though something I said didn't make sense.

"It's kind of you to offer to escort me to the autograph party, too."

"Think nothing of it. . . ."

Again, the bewildered look.

"What about Joshua?" said Detective Stone, and looked at the doorway the water had been spilling from. A Hispanic woman with a mop elbowed past me, swabbing at the floor.

"Joshua?"

J o s h u a   E t c h i s o n

—and then we were racing downstream and she was changing into a dragon and I was riding the dragon as the colors of the vortex whirled around me—

Theo Etchison

—and the dragon sinks under the surface of the River and I scream my brother's name but I know he doesn't hear me and it's because the snake woman's holding him close—

"Concentrate, boy!" Thorn says. He grasps my shoulder and I bark in pain. "You must concentrate on your truthsaying. . . . My father has been diverting the River. . . . The maps aren't that good any-more. . . ."

"Joshua!" I shriek it at the top of my lungs. His name echoes along the banks of the River, bounds and rebounds over the twisted mountains of a thousand alien landscapes—

Phil Etchison

"Joshua?" I asked again, as I got into the front seat of the police car.

And again Milt Stone looked quizzically at me, and consulted the three-ring binder, with its notes written in some childish handwriting. And he said to me, "Tell me, who did you dedicate that chapbook to, I mean that *Embrasure* thing?"

"My wife. It was when we first found out about her illness."

"I suppose you know that Laetrile isn't going to work?" he said, with infinite sadness in his eyes, as he started down Speedway, heading toward an exit to the 10. "I don't mean to be cruel," he said, "but we see our share of cancer patients in this town, heading down Todos Santos way, toward that clinic of Dr. de la Verdád's. They come back with nothing but memories and hefty invoices their insurance won't cover. I don't want to hurt you, Phil, but I hate to see you go through—"

"It's okay, Milt," I said. "She doesn't have cancer. It's worse than that."

I know he was waiting for me to say something like AIDS, something fashionable. Cancer is often a cover-up these days. But I trusted him. I couldn't help myself. "There's nothing wrong with her . . . not physi-cally. . . . They thought it would be a good idea if I humored her . . . told her I was taking her over the border for a cure. . . ."

He looked at me expectantly. I started to weep a little. It was the first time I'd wept, really wept, since we set out from Alexandria, she and I, a desolate couple, each of us in his private bubble of reality. God, things would have been better if we'd had children. Maybe she wouldn't have gone all the way over then. But she had made herself barren.

The car moved swiftly past a shopping mall, a chorus line of service stations, a burnt-out hulk of a McDonald's.

"Mary's a paranoid schizophrenic," I said. "She hears voices. She believes she has been impregnated by the Holy Ghost. She believes she is about to give birth to God." I started to sob.

Strange, I thought . . . every time I tell someone about Mary, it seems like I'm telling it for the first time. It never gets any better.

"What about Joshua?" Milt Stone said.

I didn't want to talk to him suddenly. Even though he'd been such a friend to me the previous day, in the bar, coming up to me when I was on the verge of drinking myself into a stupor, letting me talk about my poems. When people see me the way I really am, it's an ugly thing, and I feel much better hiding my face behind the printed page. I didn't want to think about that scene in the bar. In fact, I discovered to my surprise, I had repressed it utterly. . . . I couldn't remember anything at all except that jarring moment, that disjunction, and the water seeping out under the doorway of the inner room in the police station.

I started to panic. "Mary . . . I've left Mary. . . . Where is she? She could have wandered off anywhere, God knows what she might have said to someone—"

"She's at the hospital. We're on our way to pick her up. Remember? To go to your autograph party."

I couldn't for the life of me remember when I'd agreed to that autograph party. My mind was overwhelmed by a single memory, a memory so sharply etched that it seemed to me almost like a scene from a play, something starkly artificial. . . .

I remembered the first time Mary had started to go off the deep end. At the maternity ward, holding our second son in her arms, trying to breast feed him . . . stillborn. Squeezing the milk from her as though it would bring him back to life. And the nurse standing by, wringing her hands and looking from me to her and back again.

God, sometimes I wished that she were really dying.

I wished for the cancer to come down and eat her away . . . anything rather than the mad delusions that consumed her soul.

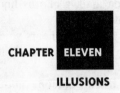

CHAPTER ELEVEN

ILLUSIONS

Theo Etchison

Something has happened, something has changed . . . back there, in the real world, my world. The dragon sinks into the stream and I start to realize there may not be a world to go back to. Not the same world anyway.

"Soon," Thorn tells me as the River rages around us all, "we'll have a big test of your truthsaying abilities . . . and we'll all know whether my investment in you was in vain."

"What happens if—"

"I don't know! One thing at a time!" he says, and the three-headed dog yaps viciously and runs in circles around our feet. There's an ominous tone in his voice and I get the distinct feeling that if I don't pass this test I'm totally history.

Phil Etchison

We went to the hospital; Mary had been sedated; apparently she'd had some kind of outburst. Every now and then her mind completely reedits her vision of reality, and she has a seizure. Millions of bits of information fly madly around in her head and then they all fall into place at once and there's a cogent universe, with its own rules . . . but not *our* universe. They wouldn't let me see her. Sighing, Milt Stone drove me to the bookstore.

It was a kind of mom-and-pop—or rather, a pop-and-pop place in a small shopping plaza on an endless main drag that traverses all of Tucson. I usually don't agree to signings. They are mostly exercises in humiliation, unless you are someone like Stephen King. I didn't even remember agreeing to this one. But I was surprised to see a dramatic banner outside the store, with my name in pseudo-Medieval lettering, and that the window was piled high with a display of my latest poetry book . . . with a cardboard cutout figure of myself skulking professorially behind them. No wonder Milt Stone had recognized me. I peered inside, where I could see a wine and cheese table and the store's proprietors bustling about. Although we were early, there was already a big crowd, and I ducked to one side, into the doorway of a McDonald's, so that I could continue to look at the window display without being seen. Milt followed me.

A huge poster showed the book's cover painting, a lurid thing that looked like a composite of every B-grade movie I'd ever longed to see during my deprived Calvinist childhood. A spaceship soared over a tropical landscape where a dragon was breathing fire over an exotic alien princess chained to a throne. There were quotes from Gene Wolfe, Isaac Asimov, and Philip K. Dick, each one more fulsome than the last.

"Phil Etchison's latest sci-fi classic . . ." it said over the title of the novel. I began to feel . . . not quite myself. Possessed by someone else, some malevolent spirit. "There can't be a quote from Philip K. Dick on my book," I said. "Philip K. Dick has been dead for eight or nine years. And besides. . . ." There was something else wrong too. Something I couldn't quite put my finger on.

"Dead?" said Stone. "Why, he was just on Larry King last night . . . that fourth book in the *Blade Runner* series . . ."

"There's no such . . ." I stopped.

Blinked. The poster was still there, but the Dick quote wasn't. I wanted another drink. My mind was playing tricks . . . or someone was playing tricks on my mind.

"Yeah," Stone was saying, "I seem to remember hearing he'd died. My wife reads a lot, she's the one who tells me these things. Come to think of it, Larry King wasn't even on last night. Because of the riots, you know. In China."

But that wasn't the worst of it. I knew who Dick was and I was pretty sure he had died, but I was also absolutely certain that the newly published novel I had come to sign was not my own.

I mean . . . seriously . . . *The Pterodactyls of Eternity*? Surely that wasn't something that could have been penned by the author of . . . of . . . I drew a blank. My own book.

Besides, I've never liked science fiction.

I stepped into the bookstore. Detective Stone followed me in. He was staring strangely at me, as though I had become a different person before his very eyes. Fans can be very tiresome sometimes, but I did not want to be rude; he had, after all, given up a day's work just so he could chauffeur me around Tucson.

"Would you care for a drink?" A Chinese accent; a tall cadaverous man in a dark suit, holding out a squat glass with a frothing red liquid. Smiling, I took it from him. I took a few sips.

It was as though I had awoken from a dream. The crowds were gone. The spread of canapés and expensive wines had vanished; in their place was a silver platter of wilted lettuce topped with a few forlorn chunks of American cheddar; the wine came in those milk carton things. The stacks of science fiction books had shriveled to a desultory pile of copies of *Songs about Embalming*, my latest chapbook from that university press somewhere in the Dakotas. A few of my other books lay next to them; there were a couple of *Embrasures* that were probably survivors of a Waldenbooks remainder table. I swiftly downed the rest of my drink. The Chinaman, too, had vanished. The drink had been sickly sweet, with an almost sanguinary flavor to it; it tasted familiar, but I hadn't been able to place it. I wanted more, but I couldn't see the bottle it had come from.

"I've just had the strangest dream," I said to Milt.

"So have I," he said softly.

"What's happening to us?" I said. Before he could say anything, a young man had thrust a copy of the book into my hand, and was brandishing a ball-point pen. I asked the man's name, turned to the dedication page, and signed right underneath the inscription to my wife. There was, I noticed with some satisfaction, a line forming. Only two or three people, to be sure, but attention was attention. I forgot about searching for the mysterious blood-colored drink.

"Mr. Etchison!" It was a teenage girl, a little on the chubby side, with oversize mirror shades and a neon pink T-shirt. "Like, how amazing you're here and everything and I can get this book signed. . . ."

I looked at her blankly. She did a quick double take. Our eyes met and I saw that she expected me to know who she was. When I didn't react, she said, in a sullen tone, "A couple months on the road, he sees me in my awesome new hairdo, and he doesn't even know who I am. . . . I sat up with your wife all night one time, remember, when she was like, puking a lot."

My astonishment must have been plain. "Look, Mr. Etchison, don't worry. I didn't run away or anything. I'm in town with my mom, I'm like, doing this tour of the college, you know, I don't know if I'm going to go to U of A, or ASU, but my mom totally agrees that I need to be out of Virginia 'cause, you remember, I quit that congressional page job because you know what a lewd old man Congressman Karpovsky is, with that scandal and everything, and him living two blocks away on Kirby. Jeez, Mr. Etchison, you still don't know who I am, do you?"

Some of the customers had gathered around. She pulled a copy of *The Embrasure of Parched Lips* from her satchel and presented it to me along with a gold Cross pen.

"I'm Serena Somers." She opened the book to the dedication page, which read:

To Joshua and Theo

She added, "I used to go out with your son, remember?"

"Sluglike," I said. I did not know what it meant or why the word had slipped out.

Serena laughed. "I guess that nickname's always gonna stick," she said, "even though I like, lost 17 lbs. on that Walter Hudson diet they show on late-night TV."

"Who are you? Why do I seem to know these things about you?" The situation was becoming steadily more Kafkaesque.

"What do you mean, Mr. Etchison? Oh, I guess you're in one of those moods of yours, where you like, seem to slip into another universe or something." She winked at Milt Stone, who shook his head ruefully. "Sometimes, when he's writing poetry, he disappears for like weeks! And he doesn't even know his own name."

"You don't understand," I said. "I'm not the one who goes away. It's not me, it's—it's—everyone else, what can I say? Slippage. Yes. The universe is like an infinite mosaic of tectonic plates and they rub up against each other and wear away at the edges of reality and—"

I looked around, realizing that I had raised my voice several decibels above the acceptable level of rational discourse. Why did everything around me seem so *wrong*? I looked at the book I had just autographed for Serena Somers. Everything about it seemed wrong; the heft, the off-white of its binding, the point size of the typeface. Yet the words inside were unmistakably mine. Unless my whole life up to that moment had been a dream. Which did not seem unlikely.

"What a coincidence," said the girl I'd never laid eyes on before. "Us meeting like this, three thousand miles from Alexandria. The kind of thing you'd find in one of those, like, Dickens books Mrs. Pritchard keeps making us read." Nervously, she ran her fingers through her spiked blond hair.

"What a coincidence," I repeated. I signed one or two more books and downed a glass of the flat Asti Spumante one of the store owners had thrust into my hand.

"Do you think I could go and see Mrs. Etchison?" she said. "I know Joshua probably doesn't want to talk to me anymore, but I still think he's cute."

"Joshua?"

"Oh, Mr. Etchison, you really can be such a dweeb sometimes."

Milt was beckoning to me urgently. I felt as though I was drowning. He grabbed my sleeve and led me to another part of the store, behind a display of the latest Stephen King titles.

"Repeat after me," Milt said. *"I am not going mad."*

"I'm not," I said.

"Think back. Two or three hours ago. In the police station. You and me. Sitting across from each other. Were we just shooting the shit, was I just an admiring fan who volunteered to give you a tour of the station? Wasn't there something else?"

Yes. At the edge of my consciousness. Something else.

My consciousness. Streaming past me. You never step twice into the same river. Facts beneath the surface. And every time I bent down to grasp them they'd swim away. Taunting.

"If you won't admit there's something fishy going on," said Stone, "at least tell me *I* ain't going crazy. I don't want to lose my job yet. I'm the only one of my people on the force here, you know. Affirmative action's a load of bullshit." I saw bitterness in his face for the first time, sensed that he was a man who did not easily reveal himself.

"You're not going crazy," I said, though I was starting to have serious doubts about both that proposition and the preceding one.

Theo Etchison

—surging around me. I stop. I hold the marble in my fist and feel it sucking all the warmth from my body. I close my eyes. Something's happening, something's shifting. Every time I use my power the universe buckles and I can change the course of the River. That's what it's all about.

Thorn is speaking. I can hear him above the roar although he never raises his voice. He says, "We're getting to a place, my boy, where the River goes mad. That's because my father's been storming around, sealing up the gateways between the worlds, doing everything he can to smash the links that hold the universe together. Don't ask me why. Perhaps he just regrets giving up all that power. But I don't have to tell you that without communication, there's no community. There's no family. The universe shatters into a million pieces and they all go sliding into their own private pockets of barbarism, their own private hells. I guess you understand why you're needed."

"I guess." But I am thinking of my own family and how Thorn and his herald have severed the links between us and how each of us is sliding into his own personal darkness.

"Don't think of them. Think of the gateway."

I clench the marble tightly. I can see it even with my eyes closed. I can see the filaments of light, twisting, untwisting. The threads are spun by my own thoughts. Am I a truthsayer because I can always know the truth, or because I *make* the truth happen by what I say? When I blurt those things out does it make me responsible for them coming true? This is a majorly horrifying concept and I don't want to accept it either way.

There's only one thing I know for sure. There isn't any River and there isn't any vampire named Thorn or any of those other things I've seen since I zoned into this parallel universe. These things are all metaphors. They're half-familiar things plucked out of the junk heap of my mind, out of the sci-fi movies and the Stephen King books and the gore magazines and my dad's awesome poetry readings. They're familiar things because they keep me sane. There isn't any fantasy world. Maybe there isn't any real world either. Maybe every man is an island after all. This is the most totally frightening thing of all.

Maybe I'm the only person in the universe and maybe I'm just imagining everything—

"And maybe you're God, Theo," Thorn says, and I can hear the smirk in his voice, "just like your name says."

"Can you read my mind?"

"No. But I've burned up a dozen like you. I know the stages you people go through. First the bewilderment, then the solipsism, then, maybe . . . enlightenment. But usually not."

I don't want to understand him. Instead I concentrate hard on what's in the marble. One of the strands of light needs mending. It's writhing like a snake, sparking, shorting out the threads that lie alongside. I know I can mend it. I can reknit the filaments and make the paths run straight again. I'm not sure how yet. It's something to do with vibrations or wormholes or . . . the fabric of space-time. I feel the River flowing all around me. My hair's standing on end and there's a coldness seeping into my bones and my hands are clammy from gripping the marble.

"The gateway that's been sealed off," I ask, "where does it lead?"

"Earth," Thorn says.

I open my eyes. "Earth."

"My father dogs our footsteps," Thorn says, "and tries to lock the gates behind us. He does it for spite, perhaps."

The ship that isn't really a ship pitches against the wind that isn't a wind. "I'll have to make a new gateway," I find myself saying. And thinking: Or I'll never see them again and it'll be my own fucking fault.

But how? "Say the words," Thorn says.

"What do you mean, say the words?" The three-headed dog is barking somewhere far away.

"I don't know! Who am I, a truthsayer? There's some kind of mumbo-jumbo you people do, and then we have a new fork in the River that links two more regions of space-time. Speaking a thing's true name, I suppose."

"That doesn't sound very scientific," I say. No, more like a fairy tale, where a wizard can call something by its true name and gain power over it.

"You need long Latin words before you can believe in it?" says Thorn. "Very typical of you people. All right. Here are some polysyllabic utterances that will get you in the mood. *Transdimensional disjunctive node. Hypercosmic transsonic digital-to-analog superspatial simulations. Hocus-pocus.*"

I don't need the pseudoscience. It's all becoming clear to me. Kind of. I can't explain it except with cumbersome metaphors, but I know it's true: I just know.

Every man *is* an island. The universe splits off a million million times each millisecond, and each of us carries a private universe around with him wherever he goes. Where the universes intersect, that's when we think we encounter other people and we think they are our friends and our parents and the people we love. But we never really know them because we never cross from our little bubble of reality into theirs. When we part company with a friend, we can never know how alien the world he inhabits is from ours. We can never know. That's not quite true. *You* can never know. I can. I can cross over. It's a special talent.

There was one true world once, at the beginning of time. In the infinitesimal moment before the big bang, when the universes began to peel off, one by one, like the skins of an onion. They keep splitting off, each one one quantum different from the last, but they all contain within them an echo of the one true world. That's what my talent is. I can hear the echo. I can tune my mind to that echo the way a piano tuner tightens a string. Because I can hear it, I can also speak its language. Because it's a living thing, I can make it understand me.

Thorn is rambling on now, he's talking about the Uncertainty Principle or something, but I don't have any need for explanations. I can feel everything all at once. I'm at the center of the storm, the storm is me, I'm making it happen, I'm alone speaking with the heart of the one true world.

King Strang has left the shore where his son spoke treasonous words and where he looked into the truthsayer's eyes. He lifts his scepter and leads his lizard warriors into darkness. Rage goads him, blind rage with leathern wings and the face of a skull.

Time is running out for him. The dark thing that has pursued him since he snatched the scepter from the source of the River pursues him still.

He must dam up the River. Cauterize the pathways. He follows the trail of his son, skimming the stream on a lightning-wheeled chariot. Seal the gateways! Randomize the currents so that no one will ever know whither they flow!

Strang—the king who looked into my eyes and whispered, "Truth-sayer . . ." It's him I'm fighting. He's old and he knows many secrets of the River, many hidden twists and bends and subterfuges. But he is not a truth-sayer. He is only a king.

"Tell me what you see!" says Thorn.

I see King Strang, a hundred times human size, defending the great gates of a city. I am the giant killer. I wield a sword of light.

Behind the gateway come the cries of a besieged people, hungry, hope-less, out of control. Strang moves, jerkily, a massive stop-motion ani-mated monster. His arms and legs are of clay.

I leap from the prow and my sword streaks behind me into the sun-light. My sword is a rainbow blur. I thrust. The Strang-monster shifts, gazes down at me, his feet pounding the rocky shore. He roars. "De-spair!" he screams. Behind the gate, the crowd takes up his cry. I can taste the desolation in the wind. I feel like I'm going to piss myself again. Strang has four arms, and his nose has thrust upward into the horn of a rhinoceros.

Earth is behind the gate.

"Strang!" I shriek. My voice is tiny. The wind shrills. Salt fills my nose, my eyes. I run toward him with my sword held high, a tiny figure against a man-mountain, and all the while I hear Thorn's laughter in my ear. And all the time the landscape shifts. Mountains rise up behind the citadel. A waterfall gushes. I'm running uphill toward the portals that seem to recede the more I run. And still there's the giant, and the ground quaking with every footfall.

And suddenly I'm much younger and I'm swinging a plastic sword and

wearing the Viking helmet that I bought from Toys 'R' Us and I'm running alongside the brook in back of my grandmother's house in Spotsylvania County and the monster is my grandma's fifteen-year-old cat Pizzi-
cato who's dying of feline leukemia although no one knows it yet. I'm
thrusting at the air and shouting imaginary Nordic curses. I'm maybe six
years old and it's one of the summers that stretches forever. My Dad has
been reading the *Völsunga Saga* to us every night before we go to sleep in
the attic among the antique chests and the broken dolls and the bundles
of faded love letters.

"You're nothing,"—I yell at the Strang-monster—"You're just a
scrawny old feline riddled with cancer!" And I see an image of my mom
fresh out of the chemotherapy and I'm charging her with like this big old
hypodermic needle and all the images are fusing and melding and shifting in and out of each other and I know it's Strang, trying to make me
weak. But I can see through him.

I lunge at him. Suddenly he's small and shriveling fast. I slice his head
off with a single blow and it flies upward, shrinking still, buzzing, until it's
no bigger than a fly.

"You're not really King Strang," I say to the head that's circling my
head, spattering my cheeks with blood, "you're just a kind of afterimage
that's trying to block the path of the River . . ."

And the gates burst into flame and I see people rushing out, calling my
name, falling to their knees in front of me and acclaiming me as their
savior. I'm starting to feel like a superhero in a comic book saving the
universe and I'm scared because I know that's not me that's just a dream
play—

I hear Thorn say, "You did it! You *do* have the ability." And I hear the
dog yapping, barking and howling at the same time from his three
throats.

And I squeeze my eyes tight shut and I'm standing at the prow of the
vampire's ship, and when I open my eyes I see the water gathering into a
funnel, and at the end of the tunnel I see . . . this is what I see.

My father, bewildered, autographing copies of his book.

My mother, sitting in a chair, rocking herself back and forth.

My mother's not dying anymore. But she's not cured either. Something
has taken the place of the cancer. That's why I'm trapped. Forever.

They think she's mad but that's not what it is. She's been stranded in
the universe the way it was before . . . many universes ago. The universe where there were two sons and my mother wasn't sick yet. Every
man is a island. A desert island. They think she's mad but she's a universe unto herself. And I'm the only one who knows.

"You asshole," I say to Thorn. I'm so angry I can hardly feel it at all. I try to strike him, to punch him out, to kick him in the balls, but I just go right through him like he's not there. Which he's not, of course. "You've made it impossible for me to go back."

"I need you," Thorn says. He touches my cheek. I feel his weariness, his sadness . . . and his shame at having to beg for help from a lowly kid like me. His cloak flutters in the imaginary wind and I hear the creak of imaginary planking. "I suppose you know now that I can't stop you from returning. I can't keep you here. You're a truthsayer. One way or another, you could find your way home."

"If I go back, my mother will be dying again," I say. "As long as I stay here—"

He shakes his head. I get the feeling he almost regrets putting me through hell. But then again, maybe he's just manipulating me.

I say, "Why couldn't you have given me a better deal? Okay, let's say I agree to give up my freedom so my mother won't die. But did you have to make her into a madwoman? Couldn't you have just wiped me out of all their minds . . . remade their universes so that I never existed for any of them . . . so they could at least be happy without me? And what about Joshua? Why did your sister Katastrofa have to kidnap *him*? And isn't there a third child of your father? What about him? Nothing's guaranteed, nothing's safe. . . . We're pawns in a three-way chess match."

"Now wait a minute," Thorn says. "I can't edit reality that much. I did what I could. Some people can be shunted from reality to reality—as you say, just like moving a pawn from square to square. Some people cling to their private universes and won't budge. I can't just say, hey, Zap, the world is another world. I'm not God." He looks me in the eye and adds, in all seriousness, "Are you?"

BOOK THREE

THE RIVER STYX

"It doesn't take long for the experience of the numinous to unhinge the mind."

—Umberto Eco

To My Wife's Sons

When she stands at the river's edge, sometimes
I watch her; sometimes
Knowing the things she sees, unknowable to me,
I cannot bear to watch; sometimes
I wish for the river to run upstream, back to the mountains,
Blue as the sky, as grief, as desolation.

She sees them playing by the river's edge; sometimes
I think I hear their laughter in the wind that shakes
The cottonwoods. I cannot bear to listen,
Knowing she suckles the stillborn, unborn
Gods, her dream-selves, drawn from the secret river
Inside. Oh, turn the tide, push back the waterfall, make her no longer
Cry out to me from the depths. In my heart I know sometimes
That the river has reversed its course; I know sometimes
That the river will not turn back till its watery end,
Black as the sky, as grief, as disillusion.

She is walking away from the river's edge; sometimes
I know she will never come home.
Better I do not look at all; for in the momentary closure,
The blink's breadth between two truths, two truths can both be true.
When I close my eyes I have two sons, and each
Is the other's shadow; she is the two-breasted Madonna
Who suckles the dark and light, the quick and lifeless;
Red as blood, as desire, as disenchantment.

CHAPTER TWELVE

THE THIRD DARKLING

<u>S e r e n a   S o m e r s</u>

Actually, I had lied to Mr. Etchison. It wasn't, like, a total accident that we happened to be in Tucson at the same time. And I wasn't with my mother. I was with Ash. My mother didn't know where I was. Ash had taken care of her. He had put her in the state where she was constantly expecting me to come back from the mall at any time, but it didn't bother her that I had been gone for days. It was strange because in a way this was what I'd always like wanted.

I had already been to see Mrs. Etchison in the madhouse and talked to her. She was the only sane person on the entire planet, as far as I could tell. Apart from me, of course. I knew that the whole world was going to blow if I didn't do anything. It was that serious, but nobody knew, nobody would believe me, maybe nobody even cared.

I planted myself in the bookstore just so I could catch Mr. E. and maybe force reality on him. The book I thrust in his face wasn't part of his world at all; it was trapped inside a bubble of the old, true universe that Ash had conjured up somehow.

"Couldn't you just have put a bubble around the whole world?" I asked him, standing by the young adult rack, watching Mr. E. pull into the parking lot in a cop car.

Ash muttered something about the energy expenditure and quantum mechanics and Schrödinger's cat—a bunch of sci-fi clichés that didn't really satisfy me one bit. But there was nothing I could do. There was something about him that made me trust him. I *had* to trust him. He was the only one who believed me about the way things used to be. Him and old Mrs. E., but she was too doped up to notice much anymore.

Ash took me in to see Mrs. E. and it was strange to know that the three of us, two visitors and a madwoman, were the only ones who knew what was literally the secret of the universe. Of like, one universe in particular.

We sat across from her, talking in whispers, with a nurse hovering in the background with a little tray of hypodermics and mega-shiny electronic gadgets. Mrs. E. looked better than she had in a long long time. She didn't have the cancer anymore, you see. Schizophrenics do not smell like they're rotting away on the hoof—that's how she used to smell, the whole house reeked of it so that all I wanted to do was get Joshua out of there. Theo never forgave me because I never set foot in their house after I found out. I didn't mean to be cruel but death is just too much for me to take.

She wasn't dying anymore. Schizophrenics smell sweet. Ash told me that this is sometimes known as the odor of sanctity and that saints used to be schizophrenics oftentimes. Ash tells me many things.

Ash used to be my imaginary friend when I was little.

Now he's real.

That's the one piece of reality that Mrs. E. and I don't share.

She can't see Ash. When I told her about him she smiled indulgently, shook her head; I knew she half-suspected I was another inmate and only play-acting about being a visitor from Virginia.

"Couldn't you . . . you know, like leave us alone for a while?" I asked the nurse.

"Regulations," she said. And sat down sullenly in the corner. "I'm surprised they let you in at all . . . not being a relation, you know." I had had Ash to thank for that. I don't know what he did, but somehow he had enchanted the secretary, the head nurse, one of the psychiatrists . . . and here we were. Sipping tea together in a madhouse in Arizona.

I just couldn't get used to seeing Mrs. E. with hair again. She lost all her hair from the chemotherapy; that's how I pictured her all the time, even after it changed. Her hair was beautiful. It was like Josh's hair. She was beautiful too. With Josh's eyes.

We sipped tea together and I told her, "I've come to make it better for you, Mrs. E. Everything is mutable. That's what Ash says."

She only smiled and nodded her head. "We can bring them back, make the world the way it was before," I said. "We can, Mrs. E. Somehow I don't know how but somehow somehow I—" Oh Jesus, I totally wanted to cry and puke at the same time.

"And make me sick again," she said.

I couldn't answer her. I knew that would happen if we turned time back to the very moment reality had branched off. Wasn't there any other solution? Only Theo would know. I'd already learned from Ash about Theo's mondo superpowers. I half-expected him to burst through the window at any moment with a purple cape billowing behind him and lightning flashing out of his goofy grin.

"Get me out of this place," said Mrs. Etchison.

The smell of her madness . . . even above the medicine smells of the hospital . . . I turned to Ash.

He shook his head. "I can't leave her here!" I whispered to him. Mrs. Etchison was weeping quietly to herself.

"Reality . . . too much shifting . . . unstable," he said.

"How about," I said, "if we took her back to where it first happened . . . to that Chinese restaurant?"

"If the gateway is still there," Ash said.

He stood in the doorway's shadow. No one could see him but me. Oh, but he was beautiful. There was this unearthly light about him and his face was really pale and there were a few faint freckles on his cheeks and his hair was long and totally black, like a night in the country. This was how he had always appeared to me when I was a kid. I never knew that he was there to plant the memories in me so I wouldn't be afraid when he started coming back soon after I had my first period. He was preparing me for all these changes. Soothing me so I wouldn't go crazy.

Or maybe he had only just appeared to me last week for the first time but he'd edited my past so that I had always known him. What difference did it make? No one can be more than one version of herself at any one time, right? Except Theo. Always except Theo.

Thank God we're normal, me and Joshua and Mary and everyone else.

"Listen, Ash," I said, softly so no one could hear, "maybe we could help her escape. We can all go to the gateway and bring back Theo and change reality back to the way it was but maybe have Mrs. Etchison not be sick anymore, you know? And we could—"

The nurse was standing over me, staring strangely at me; I guess she saw me talking to myself and wondered why I wasn't an inmate myself. "Mrs. Etchison has to have her pills now," she said. "I'm afraid you'll have to come back tomorrow."

"Bye, Mrs. E.," I said, and kissed her on the cheek.

"Give the boys my love," she said. The nurse shrugged, not bothering to hide her contempt.

After that I saw Mr. Etchison in the bookstore, and I saw how he looked at the book I wanted him to autograph . . . not recognizing what he had written many worlds ago . . . and I knew something had to be done. I had to get Mrs. E. out of the loony bin and we had to go back, find the gateway, cross over to where the boys were, get Theo to do something.

I guess I must have been crying my guts out when Ash led me out of the bookstore. The old Nova was parked on Speedway. We'd stolen it from a used car lot. Ash put his hand on my shoulder and it was almost like he could read my mind, because he said, "He won't necessarily be able to fix things, you know. He's not God."

"But you say he's the only one who knows the true nature of things," I said, though it was hard for me to believe that Josh's kid brother, that introverted, moody boy, was in fact the physical center of the universe which was one way Ash had been trying to explain it to me on the flight down from Washington.

We got into the car. The seat was boiling hot. I couldn't touch the steering wheel. The sun was in my eyes. I hate Tucson, I thought, I'll never go to college here, no, I want to go to New Hampshire or somewhere like that and ski my way to a bachelor's.

"The asylum's closed to visitors now," said Ash, "but Mary Etchison is not considered dangerous; there aren't any bars on her room or anything like that. We should be able to get her out quickly."

I pulled out. Ash couldn't drive, but he looked old enough to be in charge of me and maybe with my learner's permit we'd be able to bluff our way if we were stopped—assuming he could make himself visible.

We were about to be stopped now.

Siren. Blue and red flashing lights. I lurched, slammed on the brakes, pulled over. I was really nervous. This had never happened to me. Oh God I thought they've already reported the stolen car, I'm ruined for life they'll send me to juvie and I won't be able to get my license for sure let alone save the universe or whatever it was I was supposed to be doing. I looked at Ash, but his expression was hard to read. You really knew he was from another world at times like this.

I turned off the engine and the air conditioning went off right away and I was just burning up. I forgot to roll down the window for a moment. I just sat there. I couldn't breathe.

"What's the matter?" Ash said. "Is there something I can do?"

"I don't know what I did wrong—I don't think it was that left turn, and I'm not speeding."

Finally I rolled down the window. There was a tall Indian policeman standing there. I looked up at the rearview mirror and saw Mr. Etchison sitting in the passenger seat of the police car.

"You're not in trouble, honey," the policeman said, although he didn't seem pleased. "Even though you look a little young to be driving."

"You'd never have thought that last year, officer," I said, "but with the Walter Hudson diet, and me losing all my chunkiness, I turned out to be only a wisp of a human being, really and—" Running off at the mouth. Because I was nervous. "Oh, Ash, say something, please!"

Ash sat immobile, face like an ancient Greek statue, staring.

"Just who are you talking to, Miss?" said the policeman.

"Can't you see him?"

He scratched his head. For a split second, I knew that he could see *something* in the passenger seat . . . perhaps a blur, a mist, a flash of rainbow-colored light. Whatever he saw was beautiful. Ash is always beautiful, no matter how he is perceived. He has a softening effect on people. The policeman smiled.

"The name's Stone, dear, Officer Milt Stone." He showed me his badge. "I wouldn't have stopped you, but you see, Mr. Etchison, the famous poet—oh, I know you, you were at the signing—he suddenly thought you were someone else, it seemed so important for him to talk to you—but—"

"He's right," I said. "I *am* someone else."

I think he saw Ash again, because he looked nervously at the seat next to me, then grinned again, showing a mouthful of uneven teeth. At that moment, Mr. Etchison came up behind him. Over and over he said one word: "Sluglike."

It seems that when one is crossing from reality to reality, fading in and out of existing and having-existed and about-to-exist, it really helps to be easily remembered for some undesirable physical trait. I started to mention the Walter Hudson diet, but Mr. E. was so weirded out I knew we didn't have time to discuss eating disorders.

"Disjunctive fugue," Ash whispered in my ear.

Mr. Etchison stared wildly, walked around the car in a steady clockwise motion muttering "sluglike" every few paces. It would have been funny if it weren't—

"Disjunctive fugue occurs because reality doesn't just shift all at once," Ash said, "it kind of snaps, like elastic, and some people have a slower rate of reality inertia. Of course, Theo's rate is zero. He's a constant, like the speed of light. Mr. E.'s his father and he must have the truthsaying genes in him so maybe he does have a little of the talent . . . if we could only open his eyes . . .

"Oh my God," said Officer Stone. "Oh my God, I do see someone there . . . someone shimmering a little . . . half man, half kachina."

"Welcome, Mr. Stone," Ash said. "I'm generating a small bubble of our reality so that you'll see me and you won't think Serena's gone insane. Please take Mr. Etchison by the hand and we'll see if we can't bring him out of disjunctive fugue."

His eyes glowed. He was totally beautiful, like one of those teen idol stars. I felt safe with him because he didn't seem quite a man . . . that's why I started dreaming about him at night, the night I had my first period and my parents had gone to the store and I was so alone. God I loved him, not the way I loved Josh, which was always thinking oh my God is he going to touch me how am I going to feel if he touches me is he going to kiss me will his breath be bad how will his lips feel Chapstick against the purple passion flame lipstick from Dart Drug and then pulling away, stopping before he can touch, so deathly afraid of being loved by him because he's all boy, all hormones, raging. Not Ash.

I was safe with Ash.

So safe. It was even okay to stop being fat.

CHAPTER THIRTEEN

THE HARVESTER OF TEARS

Theo Etchison

And so Thorn has challenged me to be God, like my name says. I hate my name. I wish they'd named me Chris or Mike or David. Names do make a difference. I know things by their true names. I *know*.

It scares me.

I've changed my room—my prison—about twenty times now. Sometimes I make it exactly like I remember from when I was real little. I make the bed a giant crib, I make the doors gargantuan, I make every sound that steals in through the window seem never-heard-before. Other times I give it a far future flavor like in a *Star Wars* sequel or rig it up like the cave of a fearsome dragon, but I know it's all one featureless place, the reality of my room is a kind of psychic playdough that they've given me to mess around with. To shield me from the truth. The one thing they can never hide from me.

After my big test, Thorn is anxious for me to start work, as he calls it. He calls me to his throne room where I watch him drinking blood from jeweled chalices. I tell him I'm tired from that test and he threatens me but I can tell that I have the upper hand in a way. I start making demands. He tells me that planets are being blown up and whole societies are falling into oblivion just because I'm sitting around acting like a spoiled child. I can't really grasp what he's saying and I just tell him over and over that I want to return home. It's been like that for days or what passes for days in this buttfuck Egypt of a universe.

I tell him I need more freedom.

I want to be able to travel around without being watched all the time by the herald who is also Mr. Huang who is the man who will blow the conch and summon all the storm troopers if I just try to look at something I'm not supposed to.

I need to see, hear, feel what my parents are doing. . . . Yeah I can feel them all right, I can know things that are going on but it's way at the edge of my perception, like hearing the CNN Headline News from a television set in your parents' bedroom while you've got a heavy metal band blasting from the boombox on your desk.

That's what I tell him, and I can see him squirming, but eventually he relents and he lets me roam unguarded through the palace. That's how I learn so many new things.

I'm getting used to the way the images shift around—in my own room I can control it completely now. I keep the marble that's really a map of the universe in a little pouch that hangs around my neck. Usually I still wear the clothes I'm used to but some days I try on their clothes—cloaks that flutter without wind, high pointed collars that swell up behind your head, halos, spiked breastplates, glow-in-the-dark ear cuffs. Or sometimes they seem to wear nothing at all. You have to stare at them for a long time to see the wisps of iridescent smoke that curl around them and slowly change color according to their moods. It's kind of a bracelet thing that generates the smoke.

The third day of my freedom is when I see the harvester of tears.

I'm all wandering through the castle. People don't notice me much or when they do they won't look at me, they just shuffle past me with their eyes downcast, not making a sound because mostly the castle is carpeted with thick rich muffling tapestries. One day I did a hundred rooms, I counted them one by one, one room with a hundred stringed instruments built in the shapes of outlandish animals all covered with cobwebs, one room with vases, thousands, laid out in rows, chipped, dusty vases, one room with music copyists dipping their quill pens in inkwells made from the skulls of whales and dinosaurs, one room all black, featureless, one room where women danced naked through fire . . . I counted them and forgot them except for quick impressions . . . like when I was a kid leafing through one of Dad's poetry books and letting the images tumble through my head like the leaves in autumn. That was the first day. The second and third I'm more selective. I don't go into every room anymore, just the ones where the doors seem somehow more inviting.

Jesus but I feel alone, I wake up wetting the bed sometimes and I think that this is kind of an embarrassing thing to do considering I'm supposed to be like the messiah or something. I want my family. I even want Josh to beat me up or something. Jesus I'm lonely. He's counting on that, Thorn I mean, counting on me wanting someone to talk to, anyone, even a prince of darkness. But I don't want to give in yet.

I wander.

Around the two or three hundredth level of the castle I find like these parapets that open out into gardens. The gardens seem to just hang in the air; you can't see what holds them up. I step out into thin air. I'm thinking, so what if I fall to my death . . . it's so far down anyway I won't feel a thing. But no, I'm walking on air.

Many of the plants are what I'm used to. There is a row of cottonwoods that remind me of the time we were staying in Colorado at our cousins' place next to the Arkansas River and my dad wrote a poem about us, a sad poem about how we were going to grow up and leave him.

Well we didn't really grow up that much but we did leave him.

I'm walking on thin air breathing in the fresh scent of the foliage that weaves in and out of the cloud banks, while far below me the sea beats against the rocks, the sea that leads to the Chinese restaurant back in the other world, my world. Jesus I'm alone.

I try to feel my family. I feel Josh least of all. He's like completely drowning in these sex emotions that I really don't quite know how to deal with. I kind of see my mother sitting at the edge of a hospital bed. My dad is in a car. A police car I think. I hope he hasn't done something foolish. Mr. Huang is dogging him. Keeping him drunk so he won't see the world change shape. They all seem so vague, so many realities ago. To feel them I not only have to reach across space and time but also across alternate worlds, alternate spaces and times. I feel tired, so tired. I'm burning up from the effort. I lean against what seems to be the trunk of an oak tree.

"If only plants could talk," I say under my breath, wiping my brow with a fold of my T-shirt. "I'd at least have someone to talk to besides mad princes and their minions." I'm talking to myself. It's come to this.

All at once I'm conscious of the grass whispering. I think it's calling my name. I crouch down. The grass rustles. Clouds stream through me. I hear it for sure now: *Theo, Theo, Theo.*

I think about the talking flowers in *Alice in Wonderland* or was it

Through the Looking Glass, the flowers that get pissed off and ask Alice "What makes you think we *can't* talk?" and speak in conundrums like everyone else in the Alice books, like everyone here too.

I put my ear to the grass. I hear voices. Rustling. Tinkling. A kind of lullaby. My name, over and over.

What makes you think we can't talk?

Theo, Theo, Theo.

"Why are you whispering my name?" I ask them.

Vanity, vanity, comes the surf-shatter whisper of the grass. *Not any name of mortal being. We call on God. God. Theo, Theo, Theo.*

I tell them I am Theo.

They are singing to me now.

I hear my name in the ceaseless rhythm that is the grass the desert the station wagon moving inexorably toward my mother dying.

"The flowers lie too much, Theo Truthsayer."

I look up. It is Thorn. I haven't seen him coming; he doesn't come and go like ordinary men.

Thorn stands beside me on his own little cloud that tendrils around his ankles. He stands in a private wind that blows his cloak away from where the wind I feel is blowing.

"Are you ready to come with me now?" Thorn asks me. "There is so little time. If only you knew, if only you understood how troubling the affairs of the universe are. . . ."

I know that he will say anything and do anything to get me to cooperate. I flinch from him.

"You're going to tell me you're not ready to start work yet," he says. "But my patience is wearing a little thin. We've worlds to conquer . . . lives to save . . . madmen to catch before they destroy the universe . . . all the things heroes are supposed to enjoy. And let's face it . . . you're starting to like it here. You're even warming to me a bit."

"It's the kidnapping syndrome I guess," I say. "You know, the one where the victim starts to feel sympathy for the abductors."

"Very good." Thorn laughs, a dry, uncomfortable laugh. "You're the kind that follows the TV news, you're up on the latest psychobabble."

I don't look at him.

I only hear the grass, which whispers always, *You are God, Theo, you, you, you. And you alone. Alone. Alone.*

"Come on, Theo," says Thorn, "let's see how you cope with the real world. The world as it is. The thousand worlds. The world of which all you've left behind is so infinitesimal a part that it saddens me to think you want to cling to it. . . ."

He takes me by the hand. We step from cloud to cloud, upward toward the sun. The ocean stretches toward the horizon that's far too near to be the earth's, and the water is far too gray, like dull steel.

"I want you to know that I am not that bad," Thorn tells me. He sounds to me as though he's trying to convince himself . . . or perhaps his father, who isn't here but who I know obsesses him. "Hold my hand tight. It will help you to see. Look! Into the face of the sun."

I stare upward at the sky. "Time for a ride, Theo Truthsayer," Thorn says. "Let's go, little one. Stare into the sun."

I stare. Pain makes me want to squeeze my eyes shut and draws tears. When Thorn throws his cloak over my face I feel relief and blessed coolness. We are moving. The wind is rushing at my feet and the cry of the grass becomes more and more faint. Darkness is moist and cold; the cloak keeps off the sun so I'm feeling it only as a vague tingling in my face.

I can hear Thorn's voice: "You think I enjoy drinking the blood of my subjects, little boy? How little you understand."

"Of course you enjoy it!" I've seen that look of lascivious pleasure, I've seen his lips twist into the special smile of the paingiver.

He doesn't answer me. I think about Thorn's father. I know Thorn is thinking about him too, and that he's already starting to regret that confrontation beneath the cliffs of the gray sea.

We're moving. Not across the desert with the thunk-thunk of broken air conditioning and the smell of death. I can hardly feel movement. I'm wrapped up in Thorn's cloak. I'm his creature, clinging to the cool fabric.

Presently I try to peer through a fold of his cloak. The wind blasts me. It's already sunset. I don't understand how the day and night work in this world, so I don't know how long we've been in flight. But we're still over ocean. The air hums. It's hot, with a sweet smell, something like chrysanthemum tea.

I flinch from the wind, but soon I bunch up the fabric so as to make a peephole for myself. The wind makes my eyes smart and at first I can only see vague shapes. They're ice-trolls rearing up from black waves. They're statues of moon-pierced marble, smashed pyramids, megalithic faces half submerged, staring at the moon with eyes that are crystal mountains or lakes of still water. Jesus this is beautiful, I'm thinking, but part of me knows I've made this world myself, out of bits and pieces of my dad's Sunday poetry readings, and that what I see may have nothing to do with what *is* at all. They have been telling me that I'm the truthsayer, the only one who can see the one true world behind the quadrillions of phantom universes, who can know the true names of all things and control their very existences; but how can this be? I ask myself. How? When everything I've seen, touched, smelled, has been dredged up from things I've dreamt?

From the dream book:
I'm in the forest and I see the Red King, sleeping against the trunk of a tree. I know that the tree is Yggdrasil, the tree of the universe. My guide is Alice, and I know I've somehow been transported to the set of a movie version of Through the Looking Glass. Among the trees I can see cameras moving over well-greased dollies and lizard men making notes and pulling foci. I watch but I'm not quite there, because I'm somehow in the cameras as they slither around the periphery of the clearing.

"Silly Alice!" says someone. It's the voice of the Vampire King. "You're only a sort of thing in the Red King's dream."

Another voice: the voice of the dragon princess: "You wouldn't want him to wake up now, would you?"

A third voice: "If he wakes up, we'll all disappear."

The cameras titter among themselves like seventh grade girls in the school cafeteria.

I walk over to the Red King. He's snoring. He's a giant red chess piece with diamonds for eyes. As I walk toward him I realize that I can go right into him. I can fuse with him, become him . . . and if I do he will regain his soul and awaken.

I'm being pulled into him.

I'm not even real, I'm more like an astral projection or something, a kind of a hokey New Age thing people like to talk about on late night TV shows.

I'm swirling into the Red King . . . swirling . . . swirling . . . and so I scream and scream to make myself wake up . . . but if I wake up and I am not inside the king will he wake up too? I don't think about these things I just stand there and scream and scream but no one can hear me and . . .

"We've arrived," Thorn tells me.

I feel soft grass against my ankles. I twist free from his cloak. We're standing in a courtyard. And there are like these gargantuan columns covered in hieroglyphics all around us, so tall that their tops disappear into mist. You can hear wailing in the distance. I can't tell if it's birds or women. They sound lost. Another sound too, a whip cracking perhaps. I'm scared. I want to leave.

"You can't," says Thorn, reading my mind. He must have seen the cosmic marble clenched between my fingers, flashing, as I stand there thinking to myself *If I run down to the river I can find my own way home.* Roughly he grabs me by the arm and pushes me forward. The hall is huge, like the Roman Forum in *Fall of the Roman Empire* and the Forbidden Palace from *The Last Emperor* and the Ishtar Gate from *Intolerance* all rolled into one. I stumble forward. The air smells like salt, like the sea, like women's tears. I pause to look at the hieroglyphics on the columns. They are the usual Egyptian sort of things, with vultures and reeds and hippopotamuses and ankhs . . . and also my face. A thousand times my face staring down at me from sandstone columns. The sighing comes closer now. It's definitely human . . . a mob of humans, maddened by grief.

A creek runs alongside us, bordered with mosaic tiles. It's the creek that smells of the sea, of human pity. He pushes me along the edge of it. I look away from the glyphs.

"Good," says Thorn, "no need to read the inscriptions that foretell your coming to salve the world's suffering. Don't want to give you a swelled head or worse, some kind of a Jesus complex. Come on."

Our footsteps barely skim the stone floor, but already the columns are rushing by on either side like the palms along the avenues of Beverly Hills that you always see in movies when you're driving through Lalaland.

The creek gets narrow. We come to a wall that seems to have condensed out of the sky of Thorn's gray world.

The creek flows from an opening in the wall. The opening is encircled by a stone dragon that swallows its own tail.

In my fist, the marble flashes. I'm very scared now but Thorn pushes me along the tile bank, through the opening, into a chamber hollowed out of rock. The water splashes me. It is salt. There is a smell of lemon freshener. Suddenly I realize that we have come, by a curious circumnavigation of dimensions, to the bathroom under Mr. Huang's restaurant in Arizona. I can see myself and Joshua fighting . . . I'm leaning over the sink, bleeding into the running water. It's me and not me, another me, and behind me there's a shadow-me and another and another. . . .

"Too many realities . . . I can't see," I say softly.

"Look harder, Theo Truthsayer," says Thorn.

My other selves begin to melt. I'm focusing hard now. The other times and places that are in this room start to dissolve, and now I can't hold on to them, they're like a dream that slips away when the sunlight comes on you suddenly in the morning.

That's when I see the altar and the woman.

She's the mermaid I saw on the open sea, the one Thorn drained of life and flung back into the water. She's lying on a black altar cloth with candles at her head and feet and incense burning from braziers at the four corners. Behind her I can see women with bare breasts, wailing, pounding their fists against their hearts, weeping. I can't tell how many women there are because it's dark. Their tears are dripping onto the dead mermaid and a little rivulet of tears trickles down the side of the altar, down seven stone steps, becomes the creek that flows out of the room into the grand temple into the courtyard into the stream that joins with the gray sea.

Now and then, behind the weeping women, a tall man lashes at them with a whip. I wince. Their tears are wrung from them. How can their grief be real? But I know it is. I know their pain because I see what is in their hearts.

"Go up the steps," Thorn says. He gives me a little push. "I'll be right behind you."

I walk up to the altar.

Where the tears drip down onto the stone, there are flowers and strands of grass that spring up from cracks and crevices.

I'm standing over the dead girl, gazing into her eyes. She doesn't seem dead to me. The greenish hue of her skin is like new grass peering out of the snow.

I know that she died willingly. That these women's lamentation is a willing thing, not wrung from them with threat of torture. It is how the world works. The living fling themselves into the death-giving embrace of their king and their death gives birth to the grief from which spring the tears that make up the water that girds the kingdom and gives life to the earth. It's all one process: the love, the kiss of death, the sorrow of the sisterhood, the water of life.

So I know something more about Thorn now.

I know that he's unhappy.

"In this place, they call me the harvester of tears," Thorn says.

I know now that Thorn has done a very difficult thing by kidnapping me and exposing to me his need for me, his vulnerability. I can't see him as evil anymore. He's arrogant and spiteful and full of cold asides, but it's because he has to live with himself all the time, and I know that he hates himself.

It's because I know all this about Thorn that I finally say to him, "I'll help you if I can, Thorn. You didn't choose to be who you are or how the universe works. I want to get home to my family. But maybe the reality I came from will never come back. Until I find my way home, I'll stop struggling against what you've shown me to be. I am a truthsayer. I know it's true and there's nothing I can do to make my powers go away. I'll help you if you'll help me. We have to establish some kind of a working relationship."

He turns away from me. Perhaps he is weeping. But I know he is too proud to show it to me, a precocious little shit from Virginia.

CHAPTER FOURTEEN

SEEKING ASYLUM

Phil Etchison

So there we were: a policeman, a teenage girl who seemed to know everything about me and whose image in my mind seemed inextricably linked with that of a slug . . . and a supernatural being I couldn't even see at all except, now and then, as a kind of dappled light against the torn red vinyl of Milt Stone's police car.

We were going to rescue my wife from the madhouse.

Once I had accepted the idea of my own insanity, I was able to enjoy myself after a fashion. The girl spoke to me often of disjunctive fugue, a concept even the deconstructionists and semioticians might have had trouble defining. She was being prompted by the invisible companion. I had yet to see this Ash, but Milt claimed to be convinced. Maybe it was just that he was a Navajo and lived closer to the spirit world than us chairs of poetry from Northern Virginia.

Serena and I were in the back seat peering through the security glass at the back of Milt's head as he drove. We had abandoned the other car. It had been stolen, but Milt was curiously unmoved by this. As we turned onto Speedway he merely called it in and turned it over to someone else to pick up, identify, retrieve.

"Can you show me that book again?" I asked Serena. I meant the book that was mine and not mine, the book with the wrong dedication and the wrong binding. She held it out. There was something fluid about the book, something shifting.

"I can't let you touch it. Do you understand why?"

I played along. "Reality contamination," I suggested. "Particles of my reality infecting it, converting it . . . reality as virus." What a great metaphor; maybe even the title of my next chapbook.

This is what I read:

> *They are standing at the river's edge; sometimes*
> *I watch them, sometimes*
> *I cannot bear to watch. . . .*

"What is this?" I said. "It seems almost like a kind of parody of my poem. . . ."

"It's not a parody, Mr. E.," Serena Somers said gravely, "I remember when you wrote it. You had just come back from Colorado . . . a holiday in the country. I saw it on your desk."

I reached out to touch it.

"Oh no, you don't," said Serena.

"One home for the perpetually confused, coming right up," said Milt Stone, and we pulled in.

The sun was setting, suddenly, as it always does in Arizona.

Joshua Etchison

I flew on the back of the dragon woman, through clouds of fire, following the course of a sulfurous river.

"How far are we going?" I shouted.

She didn't answer me. We flew on.

The vortex swirled. The fire filled the sky. The fumes choked me. The wind was hot, searing. I felt like I was going through a kind of death. But when I couldn't take it anymore there was suddenly a chilled glass of ice water in my hand, and the glass bore the logo of the Dragon Spring Water Company and the face of Katastrofa Darkling smiled up at me from the water and I drank and drank and the goblet never seemed to empty, I drank death and oblivion and Katastrofa, and with each gulp I thought less and less of the other world. . . .

Phil Etchison

. . . and then it was dark. I longed for a drink and I knew I couldn't have one, especially fizzy red drinks prepared by overbearing Chinamen. There was a soft breeze and the oleander bushes swayed. The oleanders were what stood between me and Mary, Mary who stood at the window of her prison looking out at the wrong universe.

I could see her framed in the window. The window was open; she stood with parted lips and the wind made her hair move, strand by strand. "Mary," I said, "Mary, look down at me."

She said: "Phil. Serena, you brought Phil with you."

Joshua Etchison

I kissed the dragon, I was inside the whirlwind dragon. She was all woman and all dragon and one by one she plucked the memories from me:

Mother Mary in the woods smelling of death by the stream with no hair and three blankets shivering in the summer and—

Phil scribbling in his notebook, never looking at us kids, and—

Theo, his back to me, biking down the dirt road in Spotsylvania County away from me away from Grandma's house and—

She kissed away the memories. And I said, "I can't live without the memories, without the memories I'm just a sort of a thing in someone else's dream."

And she said, "You don't have to live. You're already dead. That's what the crossing did to you. You're not the real truthsayer and to you the gateways are dim and dangerous. You've crossed the boundary and it's killed you. But I will love, dead or alive. It doesn't matter to me. Half-truths are better than no truths at all."

It made no sense but it didn't matter because I was kissing her inside the whirlwind inside the dragon.

Phil Etchison

I said, "We're taking you away. Because somehow . . . everything's changed. Maybe you're not crazy."

"Of course I'm not."

Serena said: "I'm going to create a diversion."

She began running toward the front entrance, screaming. Milt turned on the siren. He ran after her. I saw the two of them on the steps. She was doing a very convincing job of struggling hysterically. I heard an alarm go off and I saw a couple of orderlies running out of the front entrance.

"Open the window all the way," I said. It had gotten cold along with the vanished sun. Mary struggled with the window. She reached for the bushes, slid down. She was in my arms. I tasted bitter poison, the sap of the oleander, spat it out. "Come on," I said. I held her hand and steadied her. Her hospital gown billowed and when she looked back at me her eyes seemed focused on another world. A faint sweet smell came from her; behind the sweet smell another odor, like a stale locker room. I remembered that it was the smell of schizophrenia that I had grown used to in the long years of marriage—

—but then I remembered another smell too, a smell of dying, and I knew that *that* was the smell I had grown used to, not this, and I teetered on the brink of two realities, thinking this is not my wife and where have the children gone and why are we in Tucson not in Mexico heading toward the Laetrile clinic at the speed of light and—

Tire squeal. Milt backed up the police car. Serena leaped up on the hood. The orderlies tripped down the steps in front of the hospital's baroque façade, bathed in yellow radiance from floodlights mounted on cactuses that lined the driveway.

I opened the door, shoved Mary onto the back seat, followed. The police car backed up all the way down the drive, then stopped so that Serena could climb in the front. There was someone else with her. I could see him clearly now.

"Is that Ash?" I said.

No one answered me.

The car careened up the avenue. I thought someone would be pursuing us, but we were not even noticed. Ash became clearer. He looked to me like a boy barely past puberty, delicate-featured, a mischievous smile, and the same unfocused gaze that Mary had.

The other cars in the streets become blurred. Street lights were streaks of rainbow-fringed light. The road turned, twisted, knotted itself into ribbons. The weirder the landscape, the clearer Ash became to me. Suddenly I intuited that we too were a blur, a thing seen from the corner of the eye, quickly dismissed as a trick of the light.

Ash spoke to us. He had the power to make us calm. His voice was a quiet music that stilled my unease and filled me with the sense that I stood at the edge of something huge and wonderful and ungraspable; you get that feeling sometimes when you go to the symphony and you arrive there late and you have to stand outside until the first intermission and from the foyer you hear a huge mysterious music muted by distance, muffled by velvet and marble. Yes, that's what he sounded like to me, though all he said was "Phil, Phil, Phil, be still, be still."

I was sandwiched in between Ash and Mary. In front, Serena clutched the book with my wrong poems to her chest. Milt Stone drove on; we took the 10 I think, because I saw the freeway sign float past, unless it was a sphinx or a brontosaurus.

I said, "Why are we here? Where are we going? Milt, you're a policeman, aren't you? . . . Don't you have a job to do?"

"Not anymore," he said. "I've heard a voice that's calling me to an ancient place. I've called in at the office and they all understand. I'm on vision quest leave, that's what you could call it. Where there's a lot of Indians, the white men's rules gotta give a little."

He began to sing. Ash kept time by slapping his thigh, but soon the slapping sounded like the pounding of a drum, and when he began whistling it was like one of those wooden flutes, shrill and haunting as the wind on the high mesa.

I squeezed my wife's hand and she squeezed back, tentatively at first, and then with a whole lot of pent-up passion. "I thought you'd never come," she said. I thought she meant coming and rescuing her from the madhouse, but suddenly I knew she also meant come inside her universe, step away from the world I still believed to be the real, sane world, into the cosmos of her lunacy and my two lost sons.

"I love you," I said. I wondered how long it had been since I had told her that.

The street lights whirled. The headlights of oncoming eighteen-wheelers stretched and stretched until they lassoed us with ropes of yellow radiance. Cactuses danced in the air.

"Where are we going?" I shouted.

Ash said, "Back to where the realities first diverged. It's the best way to get our bearings."

I kissed my wife with a passion I had not felt since the birth of my lastborn. . . .

What lastborn? Were not our sons illusions, creatures of her madness? Yet now I was being pulled into her dream world, now I felt as though it were I who had been mad, I whose body reeked of schizophrenia. But the passion that swept over me was not insanity. I kissed Mary and she kissed me back and it seemed that the whole world whirled with us at the whirlwind's center.

J o s h u a   E t c h i s o n

And she said to me, "How does it feel to be dead," and I said, "It doesn't matter if we can be together, like this, at the eye of the storm,"

and I was thinking fuck Theo fuck my parents fuck all of them because
I've gone beyond where they are, I'm dead but it's as if they were dead
and I was alive for the first time. And kissed her.

<u>P h i l   E t c h i s o n</u>

As we broke away I saw the outline of the Chinese restaurant against
the kaleidoscoping desert. What Chinese restaurant? Yes, there had to
have been a Chinese restaurant. Where we opened up fortune cookies
and Joshua had punched out—

Joshua. *Joshua.*

"How did we get here so soon?" I said.

We were in a howling dust storm. Dust pelted the windshield, pebbles
clanked against the fenders and the hood. The wind screamed. In the
middle of it all stood the Chinese restaurant, like a Medieval castle on a
cliff jutting from a storm-tossed sea. I saw the castle too. I saw the
clashing rocks and heard the song of the mermaids. I knew we were
driving through universes in collision.

Suddenly the storm ended.

The Chinese restaurant melted into sunrise.

We were parked atop a mesa. There was no visible roadway down to
the 10, which snaked below us. One by one we got out of the car.

"This isn't the place," I said.

But I knew that it really was the place after all. The same coordinates
at any rate. The identical spot in an unidentical world.

Mary smiled.

"Jesus, I wish I could have a drink," I said.

Ash said, "It's the drinks that have addled your mind. Drinks in fantastical colors, weren't they, drinks served by a tall man with a jaundiced
complexion." I could see Ash almost clearly now, the way you see a
ghost; he was translucent; he refracted the dawn so that he seemed
haloed in a rose-tinted iridescence.

"Yes," I said, "I seem to remember that there were always these
drinks, and that they were brought to me by—Cornelius Huang, he called
himself." Every time I had had one of those drinks, hadn't I felt somehow more comfortable with the way things were?

"He calls himself Corny," said Ash, "because he is a herald. He works
for my brother Thorn. My brother is a vampire. My sister, Katastrofa, is a
weredragon. You understand, they were not always this way. They be-

came worse, you see, after my father divided his kingdom—each became an outward image of his inner self."

If this was how things really were, was it all that surprising that I found the drink-induced realities more credible?

"No more drinks," Serena said, "please, Mr. E. Even if you go into withdrawal or worse."

As though I were emerging from a dream state, I found my vision clearing. The wind was brisk and cold. There was no Chinese restaurant at all here. No gilt pavilions lined with gaudy dragons. No tall Chinese man in a mandarin's costume.

There was, improbably, a well.

Around the well was a circle of stones, each one as tall as a man, each one covered with faded pictographs.

I saw Serena conferring with Ash. I saw Milt Stone go off toward the cliff's edge and stare into the rising sun.

Mary said, "Is it all coming back to you now? The Chinese restaurant? I was dying of cancer then; do you remember?"

An image: Mary wrapped in a Navajo blanket, bald from chemotherapy, her eyes sunk, always cold even in the blazing desert daylight—

Theo who always spoke the truth—

"But these are your fantasies. . . . I've seen the drawings you did in the asylum, I've seen the transcripts of the stories you told the analyst back in Virginia. . . ."

"Then why have they become so vivid, Phil? You never shared my fantasies before, did you?"

"I've always wanted to have children. The children you spoke about so often . . . acquired an inner reality for me." That was the explanation I had set forth in the dedication poem to *The Embrasure of Parched Lips.*

Mary laughed and suddenly I remembered the smell of her dying.

And knew that it was a true memory. Because eyes can deceive you; but smells never lie. I was coming to terms with disjunctive fugue, I supposed.

We followed Milt Stone as he strode toward the well. He seemed to know what he was doing. As he walked he seemed to shed everything that bound him to the white men's world—his walk became more measured, more in time with the timeless music of the wind; he sang a wordless melody; his hair streamed, his arms moved in an arrhythmic flapping, like the wings of a circling bird of prey.

"What are you doing, Milt?" I shouted to him.

His walk took him perilously close to the edge of the precipice. He did not stumble. He did not look down at his feet. His gaze was fixed on the well.

"Hey, policeman, you're gonna like fall off," Serena said. "This is no time to practice your Wile E. Coyote imitation."

Milt began to sing. I know the words of the song by heart now, because whenever I relive these moments the words come to me, alien and jagged as the desert rocks:

Piki yo-ye	Dsichl-nantai
Piki yo-ye	Saa-narai
Piki yo-ye	Bike hozhoni
Piki yo-ye	Tsoya-shich ni-la
Piki yo-ye!	

It was a joyous song, and though the sand seared my eyes I knew that the mountain was my friend. I wanted to dance as he was dancing, to give in to the wind's music, but I was afraid. I did not think I could give up so much of myself. I was fearful of every footstep. Far below us, along the 10, cars drifted like dead leaves in a stream.

At length he stopped. We others went up to him. We didn't want to get too close to him. It felt as though if we breathed on him he would topple to his death.

He said, "This is one of the openings through which the first men came up into the Fourth World, the world of sorrow in which we now live. This is the entrance to the underworld which is also the labyrinth of dreams. The people were driven out of the underworld by a great flood. Once upon a time, when I went to Arizona State and took the courses that would help me live in the white men's world, I would have called the place the Unconscious. Dr. Freud would say the Unconscious is like a vast and sunless ocean. Dr. Jung, more to the point, would probably agree, though he would be less likely to see a sexual connotation in every large body of water. Perhaps that is why we are all experiencing this gateway in the form of a well."

I am not a fan of New Age blandishments, and I didn't particularly enjoy Milt's speech. As an undergraduate, I had sat through a whole series of Joseph Campbell lectures, so I was familiar with the mythic underpinnings of psychoanalysis.

So I was a little annoyed when the creature Ash nodded knowingly. Of course, Ash was quite probably a figment of someone's Unconscious himself, and, with archetypes, it takes one to know one.

And as for Serena and my wife—they were as rapt and glassy-eyed as Catholics at mass. I was alone in my doubt.

I elbowed them all aside and stood at the edge of the well. I leaned down. The shaft went down, down, down. It was like Alice's tunnel to Wonderland. I could hear the ripple of moving water. It was the echo of the flood that had driven Milt Stone's people up from the ancient void. I heard it the way astronomers hear the Big Bang echoing still on their radio telescopes eons after it happened.

I could hear the sea. I could see lights: the gold vermilion of a seaside sunset, the silver glitter of a moonlit lake. I thought I could see a face.

More than a face. I could see a teenage boy enveloped in the embrace of a fire-breathing dragon.

The boy was dead. I knew he was dead because of his eyes. They stared up at me without recognition, though I knew that he ought to know my name, that I belonged to him.

I whispered, "Joshua."

Mary gasped. She stood next to me now, and I felt her cold fingers skimming the hand that clutched the edge of the well.

"All right, Mrs. E.! You see, he *is* starting to come back now!"

"Do you see anyone else?" Mary said.

"Not yet."

J o s h u a   E t c h i s o n

—and kissed her, and turned away from the memory of my father's eyes—

P h i l   E t c h i s o n

"Not yet," I said. Because I had not yet given in to the wind's music. Because I still felt impelled to anchor myself in a single reality. Because I did not easily trust my emotions. Because it was hard for me to acknowledge the truth of elemental feelings: grief, faith, love, disillusion.

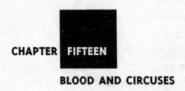

CHAPTER FIFTEEN

BLOOD AND CIRCUSES

Theo Etchison

My first day at work: there's a whole fleet of Thorn's ships, triremes, longboats, galleons, all of them with gargoyle prows and black sails and ghoulish crews, but I'm riding in the flagship of them all, sitting at the right hand of Mr. Death himself, with a three-headed dog yapping at my heels and Cornelius Huang making his conch sing somber music.

I'm standing right by the prow with the marble in my hand and I guess I'm kind of piloting, even though this path is so well worn that the fleet meets no resistance from the reality stream. We move through a thousand universes in a thousand seconds. I scarcely feel them blipping by.

The fleet puts in at like this island that's in the middle of a lake where lots of streams converge. It's neutral territory. I can feel it. The dog has stopped barking and Thorn paces about the deck unconfident of his authority. A harbor comes into view and Mr. Huang blows seven earsplitting blasts in seven directions.

I can see a city. A *Blade Runner* city gone cancerous, skyscrapers piled on skyscrapers, smokestacks belching, pillars of fire, traffic on the ground and in the air. We've stepped from fantasy into science fiction. I've left the Medieval kingdom of vampires and mermaids and arrived at another world.

I don't get a chance to look at the city for long. It hurts me to look. The city seems to be breathing, writhing, spewing out people who scurry through streets and skyways and slidewalks like hive insects.

We stand by the prow of the ship but no shuttle comes to pick us up and we make no move to go ashore. The timbers creak and ooze dark blood.

"Let the map guide you," Thorn says. I hold up the marble. It catches the light of an alien sun. "Do you know where we are going?"

"I think it's something like an arena or conference room," I say. Although what I'm seeing in my mind's eye is more like a kind of mega-Nintendo game. But that's ridiculous, isn't it?

"Yes, something like that."

I close my eyes. Seize the pathway with my mind. Call out its name in the secret language of truthsaying. And we are there, all at once, Thorn and I and a couple of hangers-on. Once again I should have believed my instincts. The place we're in is kind of like the Coliseum in Rome, with tier upon tier upon tier enclosing a kind of arena. But what's in the arena—except that it's in 3-D or maybe even 4-D and surround-sound, *is* a lot like a Nintendo. Well, that's all right. I'm not intimidated by video games, even ones as big as a thirty-story building. After all, I'm a kid. I haven't yet traded in my lightning reflexes for the hormonal imbalances of adolescence, not like my brother Josh.

"Well," says Thorn, "we're all waiting."

"Lemme get this straight," I say. "You tore me away from my family, dragged me across a jillion space-timelines, fed me a bunch of bullshit about compassion and saving the universe like we were in some third-rate Dungeons and Dragons game . . . just so I could set a new high score on—on—"

"It's the fate of the universe all right," Thorn says. "Remember, boy, you may be the messiah or whatever, but you're still filtering the wonders of these myriad worlds of ours through that pubescent little brain—you see what you know."

So what do I know today, my first day on the job?

The herald blasts away on his conch. They announce my name. I look around at the tiers of guests and I see all kinds of species. There are humans in outlandish costumes with their hair piled into pyramids and obelisks. There are these giant calamari-creatures flopping around in glass tanks, staring down with unblinking eyes. There are aliens of every description, reclining on couches, drinking, gobbling up little rodents that scurry back and forth under the furniture. There are bipedal vultures in ecclesiastical robes and there are hive-beings that look like baskets of flowers. As Mr. Huang announces my name to the four directions I can feel them all tense up. My coming here has changed everything.

"Maybe you'd better watch for a while, sit the first couple of matches out." Thorn gestures and we're suddenly on a balcony that juts out from the first tier.

There are four of these balconies protruding from different parts of the amphitheater. Ours is packed with sycophants. It's cold here. Fumes rise out of clefts, and the walls drip with blood that coagulates into squishy stalagmites. A stream flows down the center aisle. I know that it's fed from the same source as the stream in the place where the tears are harvested.

Thorn ascends his throne, sits down and points to a cushion at the bottom of the steps where he wants me to sit. I can hear them whispering all over the hall but I can't catch the words. The brook's murmuring covers up their voices. I shiver.

"Watch carefully," Thorn tells me.

I concentrate on the swirling 3-D video game thing that right now looks like a swirling mass of stars and planets and comets. Everything in it symbolizes something in the real worlds. Each twinkling speck of dust is a real place—a star system, a pocket universe, a chain of dimensional gateways that must be controlled. As I watch, I see people swimming through the simulacrum. This part's a little bit like lasertag I guess, because I think the people are blasting away at each other with like toy weapons. As they do so, some of the stars change color. They're falling into different spheres of influence.

"It's all really happening," I say. "It's not a game at all."

"A very astute observation," Thorn says. "Keep watching. You have to learn the rules."

I watch. It's a real power trip, I can see, for the contestants. They dart in and out of the starfield. They grab planets and hurl them at each other. One of the players is better than all the others. He moves like a robot. He has lightning in his eyes. He somersaults through the vortex, dodging comets and spitting out stars and moons. There's something about him that really frightens me. He can't be human. He's too swift, too mechanical, too perfect.

I can't help staring at him. The way he arcs up. Like a high diver in reverse. His leaping leaves faint light-trails and makes the audience sigh. He's a beautiful thing but there's death in him somehow.

I'm jealous of him the way I'm jealous of Josh, who's always handsomer and more self-assured and who always says the right thing and never shows me any weaknesses except maybe for the time he told me he had never had sex with Serena Somers.

Someone comes spiraling out of the starfield. It's a blur of flesh and glitter and it tumbles to the distant ground and hits it with a thud. The audience jumps to its feet—those that have feet—and a throaty roar echoes through the amphitheater. A bloodthirsty sound. They're hungry for death. The sound goes on and on until it about shakes the walls and I look away from the arena for the first time.

"A casualty," Thorn says. "They are rare, but it does happen when a combatant of unusual skill comes into play. It's probably my sister's doing."

A distant fanfare from all the way across the amphitheater.

"They're calling for time out, I imagine," Thorn says. "How about some popcorn?"

J o s h u a   E t c h i s o n

I think I *killed* someone.

I closed my eyes. The screaming went on and on. My blood was racing. I didn't know how I could have killed him. I hadn't even touched him. That wasn't how the game was played.

I blinked. I was floating in a huge black void. I was seeing stars. Maybe it was from the pain behind my eyes. No. It was a miniature cosmos and I was in the middle of a *shenjesh* game and I'd just killed someone just by thinking at him.

The roaring was beginning to subside. I closed my eyes and I was transported back to the pavilion of Katastrofa Darkling.

She was leaning over the edge of the balcony, her hair billowing in an artificial wind. She was a shadow against the streaming starlight. Her eyelids were dragonscales, but otherwise she seemed to be all woman.

She smiled because I'd defeated the last opponent, but her eyes didn't smile at all. All at once I felt exhausted. I sank down on the nearest couch. An attendant immediately started to rub me down with an oily, pungent fluid.

"It smells disgusting," I said. "What is it?"

"It's like, embalming fluid," the attendant said. She went on working me over while others loosened my tunic and brushed my hair. A slave girl—the kind you see in Biblical spectacles, wearing nothing but chains and tattoo—was rubbing my feet. Now and then she squeezed out a maggot and tossed it into a silver bucket.

Katastrofa sat beside me. "You really made the last one fly," she said. "You're not afraid of anything."

"No," I said.

She kissed me. Abraded my lips with her scaly tongue. I felt a piece of skin tear loose. I didn't care. She spat it out into the bucket of maggots.

"You're really coming apart," she said. "But on the whole, I love you better this way."

She kissed me again and I felt desire stirring but it was more like the memory of desire, a ghost of what I felt when I was still alive. She kissed harder and I opened my mouth and it was like a transfusion. I felt the animation. I felt my limbs twitching. It was all dim. But I knew I was dead and I should be grateful to have any feelings at all.

She bit me gently on the cheek. I felt a twinge of remembered pain. Enough to know that I still wanted to be able to feel those things. And then the pain was gone.

"You're strange," I said. "I feel your arms and I don't feel them. I think I'm dreaming but I never seem to wake up."

I heard a distant fanfare. The game would start again soon. I did not know how long I had been playing. It was a game of life and death, a game that maintained the balance between the many worlds over which the Darklings ruled, but it never occurred to me to care about what the game meant. I knew I was good. I knew that when I played I was rewarded with a few moments of remembrance. Each time the high was less and less and each time I became more desperate. I wondered if all dead people feel that way. Maybe when you're lying there all dead and a second lasts a hundred years and then a few drops of blood seep into the earth and touch your lips and you go insane with remembering how it used to feel when the blood rushed recklessly through your veins.

Katastrofa had enslaved me. Death had not released me; it had only tightened her control.

She embraced me and I felt her dragonfire through the chill of my dead flesh.

"Only a minute or two until the next match," she said softly. "You have to win this one for me. Something has changed. There's a new factor. My brother Thorn has found another champion. He's going to be hard to defeat."

"I can kill anything," I said.

"We have visitors," she said. "Be careful. Remember what you have become, and don't think about turning back time. Can't be done."

"Whatever you say," I said. I was a lifeless puppet and she held all the strings.

There was a thunderclap and a cloud of smoke, as if someone had let off about a dozen of those extra-strength Hong Kong firecrackers. Then I saw the tall mohawked Chinese dude in the weird robes, the one who had abducted my brother. He had a conch shell in his hand and he lifted it to his lips.

He blew three blasts. On number three my brother came through the puff of smoke. We saw each other at the same time.

Suddenly I felt frighteningly, overwhelmingly alive. I was bursting with hate and grief and the smell of Katastrofa confused my nostrils with nausea and desire and I could feel my family's love wrenching me apart ten different ways and I knew that all these feelings came out of Theo, that he too could make me dance at the end of his string and make me forget I was dead. And while Katastrofa was good at creating the illusion of power, Theo was the power itself.

And I saw that Katastrofa was afraid of him.

Theo Etchison

We're on the balcony of the dragon-woman and there I am staring at someone who seems to be Joshua yet doesn't give off any of Joshua's vibes. I know the woman; I've seen her in my vision interrogating Josh at the police station. She's the one who brought him here. She's the enemy of Thorn, and she's his sister.

She's slowly turning into a dragon as she argues with Thorn, her voice becoming more metallic, her wings unfurling. I'm burning up and the sweat is pouring down my back.

"Stay away from my turf," she says. She doesn't so much say it as belch it out with accompanying smoke rings and sulfur-smelling fire. Her wings snap open with a steel-factory kind of clanging.

Thorn says, "This is neutral territory, sister, you know that. This is where we learn to sublimate our destructive passions."

"Get away." Her breath hangs in the air.

"Who's your new boyfriend?"

"Someone important."

"I know you have kinky tastes, sister, but I didn't know you were into dead people."

"You didn't? But you were the one who taught me." Her wings flap. The floor of the pavilion shakes. The heat penetrates the soles of my feet and I stand there hopping from one foot to the other and it's like dancing on live coals.

"I'm not . . . dead. . . ." Josh says softly. I think that's what he's saying.

I look into Josh's eyes and I think, he's beyond salvation, I can't reach him. I go toward him, I go on tiptoe because the floor is glowing from dragonfire. I touch him on the cheek and his cheek peels off in my hand.

"Joshua," I say.

I don't know if he recognizes me.

He's trying to say something. It sounds like *I'm not dead*, repeated over and over. It's the dragonwind whistling through snapped vocal cords.

"Pay no attention to him," Thorn says. "We've a mission to accomplish. We've a vision to fulfill. He's no one anymore, he's just a shadow of what you are."

But I'm a truthsayer and I know better. I know that everything that made him alive is squeezed into a tiny ball inside him no bigger than the marble that holds the key to all the universes. I'm the only person who knows his true name and his true self and I'm the only person who can lead him back out to the world of the living and I can only do it if I plunge my mind into the hell he's hidden in to pull him out.

Trumpets are sounding again. An alien with a Howard Cosell-like voice is floating through the amphitheater on like this big flying disk. He declaims and his words are punctuated by brassy discords.

"Gentlecreatures! Generals! Ambassadors! Delegates, Senators, Neutralities, Principalities, Angels and Arch-angels!"

A hush falls. I can hear the dragonwoman breathing. I know that to Joshua she appears simply as a beautiful woman. He can't tell the beast from the woman. It's something to do with sex I guess. Also something to do with our mother. He sees her through the blur of mixed up emotions through the tangle of conflicting realities through the one-way mirror of death.

"The Princess Katastrofa has graciously consented to sponsor the next challenge," the announcer says. There are scattered titters. The starfield whirls. "Who will take it up? Who will answer the challenge of the champion of the Princess of Fire?"

Joshua stands up. He's glowing. Katastrofa breathes on him and he's on fire and he's forgotten who he is. "No!" I scream and I try to grab his arm and pull him toward me but his arm comes off in my hand and blood sprays my face and he looks at me with unseeing eyes and I know that all he can see is the woman in the dragon darkness.

The emcee goes on: "The Duke of Shendering has formed an alliance with the Queen of the Stone Lizards. The Empress of the East has unveiled the spear-tips of the stars and smashed the nebulas of night." And all kinds of bullshit like you might hear if you were eavesdropping on a table of young nerds majorly caught up in a fantasy roleplaying game.

Katastrofa (she is suddenly a woman again) scoops up Joshua's arm from the smoking floor and snaps it back into its socket like a Lego piece. The skin knits together and the blood and pus are slurped back into the flesh. "I can keep you together for a long long time," she says as she embraces him. She blocks him from seeing me and I scream out to him with my mind but he has closed himself off to me even though I know there's a part of him deep down inside that knows me and wants to hear me.

My brother is bathed in crimson light. The crowd is shrieking out his name and his name is a warcry. My brother turns away from me completely and disappears in a cloud of smoke and the next thing I know he's walking slowly toward the heart of the churning starfield across the sky to the accompaniment of drums and blaring trumpets.

He stops for just a moment. Perhaps he's heard my silent cry. He's listening for something. He's a tiny figure poised at the edge of the Nintendo of death.

"Who will take up the challenge?" says Howard Cosell, his tentacles trailing from his hovering platform.

Thorn says to me, "This is the moment, Theo Truthsayer. This is why I've brought you here."

And I'm thinking: In the heart of the simulacrum it'll just be me and him and who's to know what passes between us?

If I can get him alone . . .

"At stake! The seventeen worlds of the Westerly Riff, once allied with the kingdom of Ash, now fallen into obscurity with the damming of the River!"

"I will be your challenger," I say.

A dead silence falls.

Then I hear Katastrofa wailing—it's a sound like a mountain wind and like a police siren—and I hear her wings slapping the dense air. Thorn laughs. I do not think he will be laughing long. Maybe their game is to control the universe, but I have my own game and the stakes are the lives of the people I love.

"You are not . . . ashamed . . . to be making war on your own flesh and blood?" Thorn asks me softly.

"Isn't that what you're doing?" I say. "Anyways, me and my brother're always fighting."

I think about the time Josh bloodied my nose and we're in the bathroom of the Chinese restaurant and he told me the truth about Serena Somers.

CHAPTER SIXTEEN

MESA OF LOST WOMEN

S e r e n a   S o m e r s

Mr. Stone made a fire beside the well, in the shade of one of the standing stones. He brought out this three-ring binder from the police car. It was full of notes in a kid's handwriting, tiny disjointed letters.

Evening was falling. Soon it would be below freezing.

Mr. E. and Mr. Stone pored over the notebook by flashlight. I knew what it was, of course. It was one of Theo's dream books. Theo always kept some kind of notebook where he'd write down his secret thoughts. I'd snuck a look at it once when I came over to study with Josh when Theo was out there somewhere communing with nature or whatever it was that he always did all by himself in the woods by their house. It was full of stories that Theo would write down after he woke up every morning. I think the two men were trying to find clues in Theo's notes: clues about how to get from world to world. They squatted in the shelter of the stone with their heads touching.

"I could hear someone in the well," Mr. Etchison kept saying.

"The well is the key," said Milt Stone, "the passage through the labyrinth of dreams." Mr. Stone is strange because sometimes he talks like a redneck and sometimes he talks like a college professor. I think that the way he talks is a kind of camouflage. I know all about that because all through junior high I hid my intelligence behind layers of blubber and geekishkeit. So I understood him. That's why I never called him "chief."

Mr. Stone had blankets and sleeping bags in the trunk of his police car. Mr. Stone had everything in that trunk, I mean he must have been a boy scout or something once because he was more prepared than anyone had a right to be. I mean, getting blown into another universe isn't like your everyday crisis, but he had that trunk crammed: tools, food, butane tanks, even a spare car battery and a couple of Stephen King books.

Mrs. E. and I lay down to sleep next to the well and were lulled to sleep by the water's whispering and the wind's wuthering. There was no sign of Ash, but that didn't surprise me; he had a way of coming and going and blending with the scenery until he felt like showing up again.

When I woke up it was still night. I could hear the men snoring. Mrs. E. wasn't lying beside me. I saw her silhouetted against the full moon, looking skyward at the stars, so many stars, so many more than I'd ever dreamed you could see. I picked up the blanket I'd been lying under and wrapped myself up snug and made my way toward her through the ice-cold wind.

"There's really just you and me," said Mrs. E. softly, "because Phil doesn't really remember. And Milt is in it because of some spiritual need that doesn't have anything to do with us."

I stood there and listened. Mrs. E. always used to talk to herself a lot in the days when she was dying of cancer.

"In the end," she told me, "it always comes down to us women. We're the anchors. We're strong, we can hold on to reality while for them it just keeps slipping through their fingers. That's the real difference between men and women. They *want* to know but we just *know.*"

"But Theo knows," I said, "if you believe the things Ash has been telling me, I mean about his superpowers or whatever they are. According to Ash, everything we see or think we see is just a shadow of what he sees."

"When he grows older he'll probably lose it," she said. "The truth will become a dream to him. And he'll be just like the rest of the men, hopelessly trying to grasp something that's always out of reach." It didn't seem at all strange to me that a woman fresh out of the loony bin should know about truth and reality and the things that separate men from women.

I could see that she had been crying. I didn't want her to stand out here in the cold. I said, "The fire's still warm, Mrs. E."

"Won't you call me Mary now, Serena?"

"Sure," I said. We were, like, fellow journeyers now.

"I seem to remember," she said, "you used to be kind of fat once."

"A regular Pillsbury doughgirl," I said. "And you were kind of thin." She smiled.

"If we come out of all of this with our family intact," she said, "I'm going to be getting thin again, real thin."

"I guess so," I said. This was what was hanging over her. She could have her family back maybe, we could turn back the wheel of the worlds, and she'd be dying once more and maybe I'd be fat again. I guess we both had something to sacrifice to bring back Josh and Theo, but for me it wasn't anything like slow painful death. I marveled at how strong she was.

She turned her back on the moon. The wind whistled. I could feel my cheeks flaking.

"Do you know what Phil said to me this evening?"

"What, Mrs. E?" I couldn't quite bring myself to call her Mary yet.

"He said he loved me."

I knew that Mr. E. hadn't said that to her in a long time. Maybe not since the illness set in. Oh, he'd shown her time and time again—this whole cross-country journey was a kind of proof of his love, since they all knew that the Laetrile treatment was just a bunch of bullshit—but I never remembered him ever telling her. Not that I'd been around much after she started to, you know, smell bad. Jesus, I love those death scenes in hospital soap operas, but they don't make TV in smell-o-vision.

I envied her too because Joshua had never said anything like that to me. I dreamed about him in secret.

"There's a kind of magic on this mesa," said Mary Etchison. "We're stuck between worlds and anything can happen. I feel almost like we're in the middle of *A Midsummer Night's Dream.* And we can sleep and wake up to find ourselves different people. We can lose our own names. We can fall in love with—"

"Dudes with donkey's heads," I said, remembering the movie we saw in Mrs. Lackland's Shakespeare class. "I'm not surprised you can't sleep."

"Yeah. The wind has this haunting music to it. Can you hear it? Listen, listen."

What I heard in the wind was Ash's voice, the voice I always heard when I was a little girl tossing and turning and being afraid of the pattern of leafy moonlight through the Venetian blinds in the steamy summer Virginia nights. A voice that tickled me, you know, down there, before I'd learned the words for desire, before I'd learned to touch myself and rock myself to sleep against the rolled-up comforter with the smell of sweat and goosedown in my nostrils and the image of Joshua dancing in my squeezed-tight eyelids. That's what I heard in the roaring of the wind. "Yes," I told her, "it *is* magic."

"The first time I made love with Phil," she said, and she wasn't really talking to me anymore, although she was pressing her hand against my cold hand, "was in a barn at his parents' country place."

"That's intensely romantic," I said, thinking about the drive-in and the one time I'd gotten close to relieving Josh of his uptightness.

"Not that romantic." She laughed. "Horseshit you know. But there was something magical, like tonight. I think there was someone else with us. I think he was standing over us or maybe sitting beside the bed. He was my guardian angel. I never saw him but when I dreamed of him he was a slender boyish creature, not quite a man or a woman. I think I've seen that person again. He came with you to the psychiatric ward, I think. That *was* him, wasn't it? I think he's with us now but I can never be sure whether he's really there."

"Ash?"

"His name doesn't matter."

In a way I was even a little jealous. Ash was my childhood secret. But it was exciting too, knowing that we'd shared this experience. Maybe all of us women have someone like Ash in our lives and we spend all our time repressing the memory.

"It's because of him that we haven't slid from universe to universe like the guys have," I said. "He told me that. How he even went back in time to whisper in my ear when I was four years old, so I'd recognize him and not be afraid when I saw him again."

"I think it was when I stopped seeing him that I started to die," Mary said. She wiped her eyes. "Jesus God Serena I don't want to die. But it has to happen for things to come out right."

"Maybe not. Maybe Theo knows something we don't know."

"No. There's no magic really," she said. "It's just wishful thinking."

"No magic?" I said. "But you said so yourself! Listen to the music of the wind, you said! You even made me hear it—you made me hear—oh, so much awesomeness!"

The wind howled. The moon was radiant, wreathed with a wisp of cloud. I could hear coyotes, I thought. The magic was still there.

"Come on, Serena," she said. "Maybe we can toast some marshmallows or something while the others search for the truth."

"Yeah, Mary, yeah." A satisfying moment of female bonding.

"Did you know you're getting beautiful?"

But to me I'm still sluglike Serena, I thought.

A helicopter crossed the moon. Abruptly the spell was broken. We both looked back at the standing stones. Mr. E. was waving at the helicopter with a big white cloud tied to a branch.

"Does this mean we're being rescued?" I shouted.

We ran toward him. He was gesturing wildly at the sky. Mr. Stone was squatting on a blanket in some kind of loincloth. He didn't seem to notice the cold at all. He was a little withered-looking but beautiful, like one of those sepiatone postcards of olden time Indians that they sell in souvenir stores along the Arizona highways.

"No, no, not rescued," he said excitedly, "not rescued at all—*we're* going to be doing the rescuing."

"I radioed for supplies," Mr. Stone said. "Tents, pickaxes, canned food, portable generator, you know, stuff."

"You must have a lot of clout," I said. "I don't quite swallow the business about, like, vision quest leave."

"Sometimes I surprise myself. We're going to be here for a while. We have to get the rituals right. I'm having a few anthropology books delivered along with our canned corned beef." He pronged a marshmallow with a twig and brandished it at Ash.

Ash was back. I could see him in the flickering firelight. Meanwhile the chopper was landing about a hundred yards from us. Mr. Stone got up and sprinted toward it, yelling for help carrying the supplies. Mr. E. followed him. I crouched down by the fire while Mary tended to the half-cooked marshmallow.

I found Theo's notebook lying half open next to the fire. I leafed through it. I read about dispossessed kings and rivers guarded by lizard warriors. I read about a building-sized video game that controlled the fate of the universe. There were a lot of pages crammed in that three-ring binder and it seemed to me that even while I was reading the number of pages got bigger. When I turned to the end I saw the words forming one by one on the last sheet. As each word formed it seemed as though it had always been there. The universe was in flux and editing itself the whole time I was watching.

The pieces were starting to make sense for me: the river linking the known worlds, the old king, Strang, who had divided his kingdom, the siblings squabbling over spoils, King Strang haunted by a dark bargain he'd made so he could control the river, Ash dispossessed for speaking the truth. In his dream book Theo compared it to *King Lear,* but I had to admit I'd never seen it—I had a hard enough time with *A Midsummer Night's Dream.*

The chopper moved off. Mr. Stone and Mr. Etchison were jabbering away to each other about ancient Native American peyote cults. Mary was asleep, wrapped in a blanket. I grabbed the marshmallow before it burned and handed it to Ash. He munched it very slowly. The light danced in his eyes and the shadows striped his face and he looked kind of like a lurking tiger.

"Talk to me, Ash," I said. "Tell me the things you used to tell me."

He whispered to me in the secret language of my childhood.

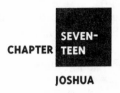

CHAPTER SEVEN-TEEN

JOSHUA

Theo   Etchison

The emcee has a glowing baseball in his hand. The ball is one of the worlds they're fighting over. He hurls it into the spinning void. The cheering crescendos.

My brother has already dived after it.

"Go on then," says Thorn. Katastrofa glares at him. She has become a woman again. She's only all the way dragon when she's near Joshua. He excites her somehow and she changes.

I take the marble out of my pocket. Concentrate on it and through it into the heart of the simulated cosmos. I clamber up onto the edge of the balcony, on tiptoe, right on the railing. I sway. I can hear the crowd catch its breath. I close my eyes and I can still see the marble with my inner eye, even more clearly than before. I keep my eyes closed and I leap. It is a leap of faith. And before I know it I am caught up inside the game and I can feel the starwind and the stars themselves hurtling past on pathways within pathways.

I'm flying. The game has become huge. I can't see the crowd. The outside world is meaningless. But in the distance I see Josh. He's good. He flits about, rolling his body up into a ball and catapulting himself forward by sliding through the gravity wells of the heaviest stars.

At first I don't do anything because I'm totally overwhelmed by what I'm seeing and feeling. This mega-video game is an analog of reality but it also *is* reality. I know this because I can zero in on any part of it with like a zoom lens in my mind, and the more I zoom the more I see, there's never a moment where I realize that it's all just dots like it would be if it were a computer screen. I turn up the amplification on one cold blue dot and find myself shrinking until I'm a dot floating high above the atmosphere of a windy planet where the ice mountains spurt blue liquid fire and in a detached kind of way I feel the searing cold of it too.

I look at another dot and it becomes a crowded world—a world of countries and wars and—zooming closer—alien creatures thronging the streets and—closer—a furry mammal being sacrificed to a fire-breathing

god. Priests with demon masks and acolytes with censers standing all
around. I think I'm in one of my dreams because the outlines are all
blurry but it could be from the incense that burns my eyes. And I can feel
the animal's deathscream, so quickly—

I unzoom myself because the long view is more detached and less full
of pain.

I watch Joshua in pursuit of the glowing baseball. There are other
players too but he's better than all of them. Well, he's good at sports and
shit. He zeroes in on the ball as it spirals through octopoid nebulas and
careening star systems. No one can keep up with him. They are shadows
dancing against the starstream.

I follow him. I cloak myself in clouds of galactic dust. I shadow him as
he chases the ball and dodges his opponents. I'm close to him but he
doesn't see me.

I stretch myself out so that I'm huger than a star system and more
attenuated even than the emptiness of space. I stretch out. I tuck myself
into the curvature of the universe and thread myself through the wormholes that interconnect the spaces between spaces. I can do all this because I can see the essences of things and to see truth is to become one
with it. I am the web and the worlds warp through me as the cosmos
weaves itself into a tapestry of seamless becoming.

This is no video game. The Nintendo of death is just another metaphor
that my mind has been using to screen out the flood of data. Everything
is a metaphor. Reality is a metaphor for a deeper reality that's a metaphor for a deeper reality. I wrap myself around the cosmic egg. I'm the
incubator of all life. I'm God.

Just when the megalomania is getting to be too enjoyable, I hear a
gnat-voice buzzing in my ear.

"You're drifting, boy! Your mind is wandering!"

It's a little Thorn-thing, flitting in and out of my ear. He's in here with
me, riding me. I try to throw him off but I can't dislodge him. "Leave me
alone!" I scream. But I'm so spread out that my screaming has little
effect—a few more subatomic particles collide at the hearts of a few
stars, a backwater planet experiences an unseasonable rainstorm.

Thorn laughs. "Stop bucking and start saving the universe," he says.

He goes on talking—it's dull stuff about maintaining the illusion of
control and the integrity of the body politic—it makes no sense to me. I
grit my teeth. Jesus! I've got my own agenda, even if it means saving a
few universes on the side.

I can see Joshua now. He's outstripped his opponents. I'm right behind him but he can't see me because he's concentrating so hard on catching the runaway planet.

Suddenly I sprint ahead, ricocheting off the gravity of the black hole at the heart of a nearby galaxy. I stand in the path of the fireball. I reach out my hand to catch it. It grows into a baseball glove. The planet smacks into my hand and I stagger back for a moment. It's like a live coal. The glove is gone suddenly and I'm treading water in mid-space and juggling the world like a hot potato.

Josh rears up in front of me. He rushes at the planet. His eyes are lifeless. "Oh no, you don't," I say. We fight like this all the time, over a baseball, over a game cartridge, over the last slice of pizza. But I've never seen him so vicious except for the time he punched me out over what I said in the Chinese restaurant. I see that he's wearing a dragon in his ear. It looks like a little silver earring but I know it's part of Katastrofa that's along for the ride.

I keep dodging his punches. He hurls a white dwarf star at me and it grazes my cheek. It's not like Josh to play dirty.

"Don't you know me?" I cry out. Thorn laughs in my ear. Maybe there's a glimmer of recognition in Josh's eyes, maybe not. He pauses. I compress myself tighter and project myself at him and butt him in the stomach and then, as he folds back on himself, I stretch myself wide, wide, wide, until I'm like a cloak wrapping him up in myself like a wind seeping into every pore and before he can react I rip the dragon earring from his ear and throw it into the nearest star . . . then I start shrinking with Joshua inside me, and the planet that was in my hand starts to balloon and balloon and . . . I orbit the planet like a crazed comet until I can feel Thorn losing his grip on me and then I swoop down onto the surface of the world. . . . The black sky turns to brilliant blue and there's a yellow sun glaring at us and we're falling, falling toward the desert below, our arms and legs in a tangle. . . . We're falling toward what looks like Route 10 and Arizona. . . . I spread my arms out and my arms sprout wings held together by wax that's starting to run in the searing sun. . . . Josh! I cry out to him with my mind and he clings to me, dead weight that's making me plummet toward the sand and . . .

I open my wings. I catch the wind. I remember how Thorn carried me through the cloudbanks of the vampire planet and right away my wings become leathern batwings. I slow down. We're circling a mesa. In the center of the mesa is a well and around it there are people. My father! and my mom and a girl who looks like Serena but can't be because Serena was fat. And an Indian dude in a loincloth who's dancing up a storm around the well. And a police car parked beside standing stones.

Is the baseball we've been chasing after Earth?

How did the police car get up on the mesa? There's no road. Below it I see the traffic on the 10. I see that the well is a gateway. It's the same gateway that I came through the first time. Only the world has changed. It's not the same world and they're not the same parents I had before. Those parents are lost in a far-off branching-off of space-time.

I'm circling closer. My Dad is waving a branch with a shirt tied to it. The wind is roaring but I can hear the Indian guy singing in a wheezing falsetto. Mom and the girl who looks like Serena are talking, waiting. Mom looks different too. I've seen pictures of her in my mind before, I know she's exchanged cancer for madness, but actually seeing it in the flesh makes it come home to me.

Joshua stirs. His skin is blue. He smells of dead things, of meat left out too long. Three digits are missing from his left hand and chunks of flesh from his cheek. He's trying to speak to me. A maggot crawls out of his mouth.

I realize that Dad is trying to attract my attention.

"I'm here, Dad!" I shriek. "I'm still alive, I'm still your son—and I've got Josh here too—"

He waves frantically.

Suddenly, seeing through his eyes, I know that he can't see me at all. What he is seeing is a helicopter. When I cry out to him he hears the rattle of a chopper's engine. They're waiting for supplies. I hover right over their heads. Josh flails a little and another of his fingers breaks off. I see where the other digits land and are transformed into sleeping bags, piles of food, a cooking stove and a generator. Pieces of their dead son are sustaining my parents and they don't even know.

At last I reach the ground. My brother's still holding on tight. I call out to my parents a couple more times and then I realize that we're not stopping at the ground—the ground has no substance—we're falling right through the fabric of the mesa. We go on falling. With my head still poking above the rock I shriek out, "Mom! Dad! Serena!" over and over. But they just keep on gathering up the provisions and piling them up beside the well, and when I look up I see the helicopter that was me streaking up into the sky and I know that for them it is night. So I know that although our worlds are intersecting they aren't the same world. And then I sink into the rock with my brother in my arms. He's dead weight, pulling me through the soupy stone like a ball and chain.

We're falling softly down an endless tunnel. I'm not scared. Our fall is just fast enough that I can't really see what we're passing. The walls are covered with graffiti kind of like the New York subway. Now and then I think I see things half-buried in the rock. Skulls. Zombies. A condom dispenser. There's music in the distance, just a buzz, as though from a pair of abandoned earphones. It sounds a bit like a heavenly choir and a bit like heavy metal. We keep falling. Joshua never speaks but just goes on staring at me with empty eyes that are starting to weep a thick and bloody pus.

The tunnel becomes dark. I can hear water. The music echoes up the stone well. We're still falling slowly. I look up and there's a tiny pinhole of light at the top and I think I can make out my dad's face peering down.

I think I hear Josh murmur something. Yeah. Something about "falling to Australia." When I look down at him his lips are frozen half-opened in an unformed syllable.

Suddenly we hit the ground and we're running.

Joshua's running with easy smooth steps. I've always hated how he can run. There's nobody home inside his head and still he leaps across boulders and dodges stalactites with the grace and strength of a wildebeest while I sprint and huff to catch up with him. The cave slopes downhill. Along the walls there're like old Egyptian tomb paintings but they show people we know—Mom wearing the moon on her horns, Dad dressed like Osiris. Some of the pictures are kind of pornographic. It smells of sex and death in here. I'm choking as I run.

Josh turns a corner. I make a superhuman effort and sort of tackle him and we go sprawling against a pillar of salt.

"Don't run away from me; don't you know me, me, me?" Something is oozing from a wound in his scalp. I shake him. I don't care if I hurt him because I don't even think he's inside. I slap his face and slick my hands with his thick cold blood. My hand stings with the ice of his cheeks. The caves grow darker. "I know you're in there somewhere. Wake up. Come back from the dark place you've run away to!" But I'm thinking, only God can raise the dead.

Then, abruptly, there's a flicker in his eyes.

J o s h u a   E t c h i s o n

I woke slowly. I had been far away. From the moment Katastrofa slaked my thirst with dragon spit I had been in another country, a gray country where shadow was substance and substance was decaying memory. I had been dead.

I thought I would be dead forever. I'd been playing the game for a long time. I had become a robot, living only for the times when Katastrofa would touch me, waken me a little . . . and then Theo had been there in the balcony and the spark of me that was still alive inside my body was suddenly kicking and screaming in my mind. Theo had called me by my true name, the name that held my essence before I was even an idea in the minds of my parents. . . . He had summoned me from the dark country . . . though I had forgotten my name or that I even had a name.

I woke in a cold cave looking into my brother's eyes. He was all shaking me and slapping me and finally I said, "Stop it already, I'm here, I'm here, Theo," but what came out was a parched murmur. I looked down and saw that I was still coming apart and there were pieces missing and what was left wasn't pretty to look at.

"Fucking Jesus, Joshua, what's happened to us?" I could see he'd been crying.

"There's no time," I said. I could hear the beating of dragon wings. I knew that as soon as I saw Katastrofa I would fall under her spell again. "When they find us it'll all be over. They'll control us again."

Theo said, "We can get home."

"I don't even know where we are," I said. Everything had been hazy since the police station in Tucson. I had made love to Katastrofa and then I started playing the game and the universes kept changing.

"A while ago we were on Earth, I think," Theo said, "because I saw Mom and Dad and maybe Serena Somers and this Indian dude. Jesus, Serena looks totally different if it *is* her. I mean she's rad-looking now, like thin."

I listened to the water dripping down the stalactites, pinging on the damp stone floor. Our voices echoed. I was reminded of the last time I had seen Theo—I mean, before we came here—somehow I didn't think we were that far from the marble bathroom beneath the Chinese restaurant. But we hadn't passed through any Chinese restaurant to get here this time. "So where are we now?"

"We're on an alternate Earth I guess," said Theo. "The Earth that came into being when we vanished. Earth is a pawn in their power struggle. Something to do with controlling the gateways that lead to the River."

"Yeah, the River that connects all the known worlds," I said. "And it's not a real river, it's a metaphor within a metaphor. . . . Sounds like bullshit to me but I guess it's true. Even if it all came out of your dream book."

"I just wrote down my dreams. . . . I didn't *make* any of this happen," Theo said. But I could tell that he wasn't sure about that. He was kind of enjoying the notion that he *did* dream all these universes into being somehow. It's good to be God; I know; Katastrofa had shown me that I had a little bit of the talent too—well, about as much talent as Theo had in his little finger anyways.

"How did I die?" I was certain of my death at least. It was an effort to animate my arms, my legs. I couldn't feel the maggots slithering. My body and I weren't part of the same entity at all. Getting it to move and talk was like trying to make a hand puppet do Shakespeare.

"It was something in the water," Theo said. "You drank water out of the cooler . . . Dragon Spring Water . . . maybe eating and drinking their food and water is bad. . . ." He didn't sound too sure of this part.

lc1d,4] There was some kind of myth, I seemed to remember . . . a beautiful goddess abducted into Hades by the king of the Underworld. . . . She ate six pomegranate seeds and so was doomed to spend six months of the year as Queen of the Dead. *"You've* been eating and drinking," I said, "and you don't seem to be dead."

"I don't have all the answers. . . . I see things, that's all. I see them without understanding them. That's why I always blurt out the truth and fuck up everyone's life for them. I'm kind of an idiot savant, I guess. I catch reality and hold it in my hand and then it's up to *them* what they want to do with it."

I felt it again—the overwhelming memory of having once been alive—I wanted so much to flow into every cell of that cadaver and start pumping the lungs and pushing the dead air out. . . .

"Save me, little brother."

"I saw what she did to you. I saw it all the way from beyond the gateway. Hell of a way to lose your virginity."

"I should punch you out for that."

"You can't. You told me your heavy secret, remember? I know all about what you didn't do with Serena Somers. But you'd change your mind if you saw her now."

"Listen." The wind in the cavern died, rose, died, rose, and I knew it came from the flapping of leathern wings.

"She's coming. And Thorn can't be far behind."

I was scared shitless. I knew that only my little brother could bring me back to life—my brilliant, socially challenged, ratfaced little brother with the attention span of a gibbon on speed and the power to see through bullshit. I held on to him. He was the only thing that anchored me to my past and kept me from sliding still farther into the abyss. Jesus I hated him sometimes, like now when he was flaunting his knowledge of my sexual secrets, which were deep and dark to no one but myself. "You know how to get us out of here, don't you?" I said.

"Kind of." He pulled out a marble. "This is it, I guess." It kind of glittered and I could see that it wasn't a marble at all but a round thing woven from a million strands of light. "Look, you know there are three of them—Thorn's the oldest. Katastrofa's the middle child. Both of them want it all for themselves. That's what the game is really about. We play at hurling toy planets around but what we play is what really happens. Worlds blow up. Fleets of starships crash into the hearts of suns. You know—real *Star Trek* kind of shit. And we're making it happen. Well there's a third one too. His name is Ash, but no one ever talks about him. He was disinherited. He seems to have vanished. He's the only one who refused to flatter his father. That's Strang, the king. I met him once. He's mad. He goes from world to world trying to undo what's done. He has a scepter that can catch people's souls and in it are the souls of trillions of beings—everyone who's fallen victim to his hunger for power. He pulled this scepter out of the source of the River. Every moment of every day it tortures him, but he can't give it up. The scepter is the thing the others want; without it it's really all video games—cosmic video games—not absolute power. But to have it is to go insane, I guess."

"Am I in the scepter too?" I said. I didn't know how I could be in more than one place at the same time, but then that was what the River was all about—it was *everywhere* and *everywhen* at the same time.

"I think you are, Josh," Theo said.

I could see that he knew of a way to make me whole again . . . to bring us all home . . . maybe even to cure Mom . . . but that it was something fraught with dangers, something he didn't want to contemplate.

"I've faced King Strang before," he said. He didn't look at me. He sounded so frail, so vulnerable. Painstakingly I unclenched one hand and stroked the nape of his neck. I couldn't feel the sweat. I couldn't feel him at all. But I knew he was struggling not to recoil from my dead flesh. "He's haunted but he's not really . . . evil. Maybe we can deal with him somehow. If I can find him."

He got up. Held the marble in his palm, gazed into it until he seemed to be hypnotized. The threads of light coiled and uncoiled and the marble started to unravel and soon there were strands of light spinning all over the cavern, lassoing the stalagmites, spiraling, corkscrewing, twisting, lancing the darkness . . . and I realized it was all a single connected thread that reached back all the way to the primordial moment a split nanosecond before the Big Bang was scheduled to go off. . . . The light spun around and around us until we were cocooned in it. . . . Theo held out his hand to me. I made my fingers close around his. . . . He pulled me up. The light circled us and filled me with painful memories. . . .

—We were standing at the river's edge beneath the shade of the cottonwoods. It was autumn. My father was inside writing a poem—

Theo twisted a strand of light around his right hand. "Hold on tight, Brother!" he said. I felt the light tugging at us, then suddenly we were moving so quickly that caves were blurring, the cave paintings animating themselves like a gigantic flipbook against the stone formations—home movies of our early childhood played as I was pulled along. My gut churned with the acceleration but at least I was feeling something, knowing some part of me still lived . . .

Then I became aware of the River. We were moving upstream. The River was the strand of light and Theo was reeling it in so we could fight the current. Cities flashed past us, cathedrals of ice, jungles where dinosaurs battled, futuristic wastelands, walls with Babylonian bas-reliefs. We were sitting in a rail woven from the threads of light from Theo's marble.

"How did we get here?" I said.

"We're like *inside* the marble, I guess, and the marble is inside the baseball and the baseball is inside the video game that's inside the City that's beside the River that's the strand of light inside the marble."

It wasn't too comforting to know that we were riding a kind of Möbius strip, shuttling endlessly between truth and metaphor. I guess it was just one of those concepts that only Theo could grasp, him being a truthsayer and all.

"Where are we going now?"

"To find Strang! Who's wandering up and down the River, closing off gateways . . . before he permanently closes off the way home."

"What about the game?" Wasn't I supposed to be in some kind of competition to catch a baseball that was really a planet?

"We're still inside the game," Theo said. "It's just, like, a higher screen of it that you never reached before."

And I was feeling more and more alive. I could feel the wet wind whipping against my arms and face. I could taste the wind, salt and sugary and bitter. We raced, churning up the water on either side as if we were water-skiing.

Theo Etchison

But I know that we're not going to escape that easily, because from behind I can hear the beating of great wings and I can feel the distant fire against the back of my neck. And I know Thorn can't be far behind. They're following my trail even while they're still up there in their balconies overlooking the arena, sipping their blood cocktails and feeding on the frenzy of the audience.

CHAPTER EIGHTEEN

PICTURES IN THE SAND

Phil Etchison

After we had brooded over the dream book all night, Milt Stone got up at the crack of dawn and went over to the edge of the mesa. He started to sing. I was wrapped in a sleeping bag and had three blankets wound around my head because of the cold. I made a slit to watch him out of. Mary and Serena were awake too, piling brushwood on the fire.

Milt wore a loincloth and he had bells on his wrists and ankles and when he danced they tinkled. He pounded his feet on the rock and sang—it was all in Navajo I supposed—and it seemed as though he were addressing his words to the mountains, the sun, and the well. I wondered how he could do all this seminude dancing when the temperature had to be no more than about 35°. Sometimes I saw Ash—a ripple in the sunlight, a wavering shape—who appeared to be pounding on a drum. Sometimes there was the sound of a flute, unmistakable even above the whistling wind. Sometimes there were other voices, harshly warbling, coming out of the very air. There was magic in this place, no doubt about it. Reality itself seemed tenuous, stretched thin like the skin of a burgeoning balloon, perhaps on the verge of bursting.

Why was Milt dancing? Why didn't it seem to matter that we had gone off in a police vehicle and I never saw him report back to any superior? I just couldn't buy the idea of vision quest leave, not even here in Indian country. I guess I was just too whitebread a kind of person.

Milt Stone was beautiful against the rising sun with his hair flying and his jowls quivering with every stamp of his feet. But after a few hours I was beginning to wonder when it would stop and what relevance it had to our predicament.

Mary and Serena stuck by each other. They made coffee and fried up a batch of bacon and eggs and did other stereotypically female things; it was a moving sight to me, because Mary hadn't done anything simple and domestic since our second child was stillborn and she had retreated into her schizophrenia . . . no! . . . since the cancer . . . no . . . I was deluged by warring sets of memories.

It got warm . . . the wind burned us and the sun scoured our faces. Milt Stone danced. Mary and Serena brought me breakfast and we sat around the dying fire, not speaking to each other.

Until I couldn't stand it anymore and I said, "There's something really fishy about Detective Stone." And I told Mary about my doubts. (Serena I didn't really talk to that much, because though she seemed to remember me perfectly, my recollection of her was still more or less confined to the inappropriate adjective 'sluglike.')

Mary said, "Maybe you should call the police station yourself."

"Yeah," Serena said. "Mr. Stone looks like he's barely halfway through his dance routine."

The women were right. I was going to fuss until I knew for sure. I went over to the police car, which was parked about two hundred yards from the edge. There were still bundles of supplies from the chopper visit last night. I looked inside the car, expecting one of those car radios—they always have them in cop movies—but instead found a futuristic looking cellular phone, the kind that looks like a Japanese robot toy. It had flashing LEDs and a backlit LCD screen that displayed rows of arcane symbols which, on closer examination, turned out to be the alien starships of Space Invaders, moving back and forth in orderly ranks, tentacles twitching.

There were other things about the car that seemed not quite right either. For example, the gearshift wasn't your usual PRNDLL but read something like PRNDBQZLL—the "Q" seemed a little bent out of shape. Also, the steering wheel was on the left, which indicated that it was the kind of car that you drove on the right side of the road—but in America we drive on the left, don't we? Did we? I panicked. It had always been left. No, no, it shifted to left during one of those crazy reality shifts when everything became a mirror image of the last world and we all wrote backward and got younger. Younger? How could that be?

Left or right? Why couldn't I remember something as simple as that? I stared at the dashboard and its crazy hieroglyphics, and I realized I was having a full-blown attack of disjunctive fugue. And that phrase hadn't even been in my vocabulary two days ago.

I gulped. Took a few deep breaths. Listening to Milt's falsetto wheezing faintly over the wind seemed to calm me down a little. I picked up the phone and saw, to my relief, that the handset sported the usual Day-Glo green lighting and the familiar digits as well as the # and the *. I dialed 911 and asked for the Tucson police.

"Detective Stone, please," I said. "There *is* a Detective Stone there, isn't there?"

Static.

"S-t-o-n-e," I said, spelling it several times for an air-headed-sounding receptionist.

"Stone? Sir, we have no Detective Stone here. You wouldn't mean Stein, would you? There's an Angela Stein in homicide."

So on our way to the top of this mesa to which no roads led, we must have been treated to yet another shift in reality. This world contained no Milt Stone; Milt Stone was not what he appeared to be; perhaps he was, like so much else I'd been experiencing, a figment of someone's imagination . . . my own, perhaps.

Fucking wonderful, I thought. Maybe when I go to sleep tonight I'll wake up in the body of Stephen King. I could sure use a $15 million advance for *my* laundry lists.

I had a wild hunch. I picked up the phone again and dialed home.

A teenage boy answered. "Who's this?" I said. I was terribly afraid of what he'd say.

"Josh, of course," said the boy. "I didn't realize you were out, Dad. You need me to pick you up or something?"

"I need to speak to your mother," I said.

There was no answer for a few beats. Then the boy said, "Look, Dad, where are you? I'd better pick you up. You know you're not supposed to be wandering too far from the institute."

"Where's your mother, damn it?"

"Stop ragging on me, Dad . . . Dad?" I heard someone talking in the background. "Dad? It's some kind of fucking crank, Dad!" Josh said. But he wasn't talking to me. Someone else came on the line.

"Philip Etchison," said the voice.

"Philip Etchison," I said.

"I got an echo," I said.

"Who the hell are you?" I said. "Is this some kind of prank call?"

"Jesus Christ, you sound just like . . ." I said.

I couldn't be talking to myself. Surely not. I realized I'd broken out in a sweat. Someone touched me on the shoulder and I just spazzed. It was Mary. "Jesus Christ, Mary, talk to this man," I said, "tell me I haven't gone over the edge."

"I would hardly be a good judge of that now, would I?" she said. She looked at the phone—she didn't seem at all fazed by its futuristic design—and twiddled with a lever. It turned into a speaker phone and she put the hand-set back down. "Hello?"

"Mary?" I said on the speakerphone. "Oh my God, it can't really be you . . . oh God, oh God . . ."

"He's crying," I said.

Then I heard Joshua's voice again. "Listen," he said, "I don't know who the fuck you prankers are, but leave us alone. My Dad's been in therapy since Mom died. . . . He's been hearing her voice. . . . He can't sleep, he can't write. . . . You're fucking perverts to call us. . . . Just get out of our lives—leave us the hell alone."

"Put Theo on," Mary said.

"Who's Theo?" Josh said. And hung up.

I started to dial back but Mary put her hand on mine to stop me. "This isn't our world," she said. "We're trespassers. They've a right to be the way they are just as we've a right to go back to our own reality."

It made me uncomfortable to know that there were two of me here and that I was the one who didn't belong, who'd vanish in a puff of smoke as soon as the world was restored.

"Let's go back," Mary said gently.

It was past noon and the sun was blazing. Milt was still singing and the drums were still pounding out of the empty air.

S e r e n a   S o m e r s

At around one or two in the afternoon Mr. Stone stopped as suddenly as he'd begun. He went back to his car and got out a kind of a tarp from the trunk and started to drape it over the standing stones, across the well. Mr. and Mrs. E. got back from their phone calls. And we just stood there, not knowing what he was going to do next. I tried to ask Ash about it but he was nowhere to be seen.

In about fifteen minutes he had turned the circle of stones into like this tent, maybe the size of our family room. The tent-flap faced the cliff edge. Mr. Stone looked carefully in the four directions, mumbled a few words to the tent-flap, then he slithered in and sealed himself off. I heard banging and crashing noises, like a dog shambling through a junkyard at midnight.

The three of us from Northern Virginia, we just kind of stood there looking at each other and looking totally stupid. I guess you don't run into many weird Indian rituals in Fairfax County. Last year I'd been to a Thanksgiving powwow in a church hall in Bethesda, but it hadn't been anything like this. Mostly they sat around selling like all this junk jewelry.

We stood a while longer. No more banging noises, but I could hear a flute playing softly. The flute reminded me of Ash. Ash was in there. He was responsible for all this somehow.

The tent-flap opened a crack. Light flickered inside. "You can come in now," said a voice. It didn't belong to anyone I knew.

We filed in one at a time. Mr. Stone was in the shadows, his back to us. A fire burned in a crescent-shaped hearth he'd put together from a pile of stones. The front end of the police car poked into the tent through tarp walls. He motioned us to sit in a semicircle. There were places for each of us, little pillows. We squatted and waited.

"He's made this place into a *kiva*," Mr. E. said with an air of academic authority, "a Navajo sacred place." The well murmured and made his words all blurry and echoey.

Mr. Stone emerged from the darkness. But it wasn't Mr. Stone exactly. It was a woman.

Mr. Stone was wearing a buckskin dress with fringed edges. It was covered with beadwork. He had let his hair down. His face was painted white, and he had on bright red lipstick and heavy mascara. He walked toward us. Even the way he walked was different. He swayed back and forth. This wasn't like a scene from *The Rocky Horror Picture Show*. Mr. Stone didn't look like a guy dressed up as a woman. He *was* a woman. Well, maybe his tits weren't that developed, but Jesus, I could empathize with that. This was getting intense.

"Well," he said. That voice! It was pitched an octave higher, it had the lilt of a woman's voice, but it was kind of unearthly too. Like one of those disembodied spirit voices they have in old black-and-white horror movies. "You may have noticed that I'm not quite the man you thought I was."

"My God," Mr. Etchison said, "you're a *berdache*."

"You ain't ignorant, that's for sure," said Mr. Stone. "You've taken some of the same anthropology courses I did when I was in white people's college." He sat down across from us, on the other side of the fire. "Yes. I am a *nadlé*, a sacred man-woman, and a powerful shaman. My pueblo sent me to the white people's college so that I would absorb as much knowledge of alien worlds as I could. After all, my job is to commune with alien worlds, so it's only right I should be sent to live among aliens. Would you care for tea?"

"With pleasure," Mary said. I could tell that Mary trusted him completely. I'm not sure where the teakettle appeared from, but what Mr. Stone was pouring into these Japanese teabowls was a greenish fluid that didn't look much like tea.

"Don't drink it!" said Mr. E., but Mary had already drained the entire bowl.

I looked at the man-woman, like totally confused, and he said gently, "I suppose I should give you the condensed version of Anthropology 101, since you haven't been to college yet. . . . When I was little older than you, Serena, I went up to the high mesa to seek a vision. When I came back I told my parents, 'I am a woman.' That's what the vision told me. When a boy has a vision like that, the parents celebrate with a feast, because the parents of a *nadlé* are always blessed with good fortune. Their son will be able to talk to the gods. I have been doing that since childhood, and yes, it's a living."

"What's in the tea?" I said, staring deep into the bowl and seeing . . . I don't know what . . . someone else's eyes stare back at me.

"Peyote!" said Mr. E. "Drugs! Be careful!"

"Oh come on, give me a break, Mr. E.! You went through the sixties, you can't tell me you never tripped, I mean, you used to go to those parties with Andy Warhol for God's sake . . . like, don't be such a tight-ass."

Mr. E. looked really pissed off, but when Mary started to laugh he couldn't help laughing a little too.

"Listen. This is a sacred thing we are doing now, my children," said Mr. Stone, "but laughter too is sacred . . . something that you white people have forgotten with your crystal cathedrals and your televangelists. Laugh, children, laugh. . . ."

And we did. We laughed ourselves helpless. And suddenly I noticed the sandpainting. How had it gotten there? We had been sitting around it the whole time. It was drawn in brilliant colors and the smoky firelight dappled the ochers and turquoises so that it seemed alive. The painting showed all of us . . . Mr. and Mrs. E. and the two boys and me . . . very stylized . . . standing in line. There were gods with frogs' heads holding our hands and leading us toward a well. Ash was standing in the well. His eyes glittered. As I stared at the sandpainting, I could have sworn that he winked at me. I thought I was going to shit myself. Music filled the *kiva*—the wind was like children laughing and gnarled wooden flutes and drums made of human skin and—my flesh was crawling, I was thinking Jesus, I really want to go home, there's a sale at Garfinckel's this Saturday.

"Drink the tea," Mr. Stone said. His eyes were big and empty like the sockets of a skull. He was crying into the fire and each drop made the fire sizzle and sent up a cloud of blood-tinged mist. I took a sip. It was bitter and I made a face. Mr. Stone's eyes grew wider and I felt that I was going to slide right into them, into the well that led into the country of dreams. I looked back at the sandpainting and Ash was beckoning to me. His fingers were definitely moving. No, it wasn't just the flames.

"What's the plan then?" Mr. Etchison said slowly. He lifted the bowl to his lips. But he didn't drink, not yet.

"Well . . . I have made a study of Theo's dream book," said Mr. Stone. "He talks about another country . . . a kingdom inside his dreams that's in some ways more real than this one we're in now. He's in that dream country, Phil, and so's your son Josh. There's a war going on there. He's got it all explained away in sci-fi terms—planets and lizard warriors and starships—but I have to use the metaphors I know, and I have to explain it by saying that the forces of the universe are in conflict—that it has lost its *hozhoni*—that is, its harmony is broken. And it is because the eternal order of things has been disrupted."

"Oh," said Mr. Etchison, and then, as he always does at moments of totally intense epiphany, he began to quote Shakespeare: "You mean:

> *'Take but degree away, untune that string,*
> *And hark what discord follows.' "*

"Well, yes, something like that," said Mr. Stone. "We must come to a state of *hozhoni* ourselves before we can resolve this problem. We must feel love for one another. We must drink the peyote tea together. There are many ways of traveling to the shadow world. Some, like Theo, have never left it. He is the lucky one. Others, like this *nadlé* who speaks to you in the words of Yeibichai, grandfather of all the gods, can journey to the shadow world by sending forth our spirits from our bodies. But that takes training, and you people have no time. You must find the two boys before the universe is torn asunder by disharmony. Or else . . . we may find ourselves in a world cut adrift, spiritually barren, the gateways to the other worlds sealed off forever."

"Come on, Mr. Stone," I said. "You're not telling us that if we sit here and guzzle hallucinogens and like do a bit of transcendental meditation, then Josh and Theo will just come floating up to us through the well?"

There's only so much New Age jargon you can swallow at one time. I tried to blink the soot out of my eyes.

"I'm afraid it won't be that easy." Mr. Stone fluttered his eyelashes at me. God he was beautiful! He made me feel queasy, and I quickly downed the rest of my peyote tea. "We will have to find them. So drink up, and I've got a whole kettle brewing so you'll get plenty of it . . . because when we're through drinking and meditating we're gonna pile into my police car and just drive ourselves on down into the well."

I saw the car's front end aimed right at the well and realized that Mr. Stone was dead serious.

BOOK FOUR

AMA NO GAWA:

THE STAR RIVER

"Drunken, I walked to the edge of the moonlit stream."

—Li Po

From My Sons

When I stand at the river's edge, sometimes
I feel you are watching me; sometimes
I think you cannot bear to watch me,
Knowing the things you know, unknowable to me.
I can only know the things I have touched and seen,
Not rivers that run upstream, back to the mountains,
Not truths within truths or dreams within dreams,
Gray as the sky, as loneliness, as love.

But you can know the laughter of the wind that shakes
The cottonwoods; and you can know
The milk that suckles the unborn, stillborn gods,
Your dream-selves; you can drink from the secret river
Inside. Oh, turn the tide, push back the waterfall, let me hear for
        once
The voices from the depths; for in my heart I know
These things are real; the river has turned backward;
The river will not turn backward till its watery end;
Black as the sky, as night, as self-destruction.

Don't let me walk away from the river's edge. I know
I will have to enter the water to come home. I know
That in the blink's breath between two truths, that I must grasp
Both truths and make them one. I have two sons. I have heard
        them.
I have seeded the two-breasted Madonna who suckles the dark
And light; the quick and lifeless; the transient, the eternal,
Red as the sky, as desire, as death.

CHAPTER NINE-
TEEN

DEATH AND TRANSFIGURATION

Phil Etchison

I drank deep. My mind began to unclog. I knew now that my memories had been drowned in drink. Those strangely colored drinks, so often handed to me at just the right moment by a tall Chinaman who had professed to be a fan of my poetry. . . .

We all drank deep. With each draught I found another memory. Like Theseus in the labyrinth, I had found the end of the ball of yarn and was stepping backward through the convolutions of my past.

I saw Milt Stone sitting with his eyes closed, murmuring softly. He was entering a trance I supposed. We all were.

Mary said softly, "Where are we going?"

And Milt said, "We are going to die."

I knew what he meant immediately. He was talking about the shamanistic experience—the loosening of the soul from the body—to travel into the spirit world. It was a familiar idea but not one that I had ever thought I would experience. I said, "We can't go . . . where Theo is . . . because we don't have the power that he has. We can only go by dying."

"I don't care," Mary said. "I've been close before."

"I'm afraid," Serena said, and Mary comforted her. "Why do we have to die? Ash doesn't die when he comes to see me. Thorn didn't die when he stole Theo."

Milt said: "I don't know who these people are. Perhaps they are a kind of kachina then. But I haven't heard of them. Even though I am a shaman, and a sacred man-woman, you can't expect me to have heard of everybody in the world beyond."

We drank. I felt myself sinking, sinking.

I began to dream with my eyes wide open. In the dream I saw myself standing at the edge of a stream fringed with cottonwoods. It was like a place in Colorado I used to visit, where the Arkansas dwindles to a creek; like my parents' place in Spotsylvania County too. I was squatting under a tarp beside a fire guzzling hallucinogens in a slo mo replay of my college days, but across the fire I could see the river clearly. I was alone.

The sky was brilliant blue and I knew it was summer, the eternal summer that belongs to boys who are out of school, the summer of sneakers and swimming holes, Ray Bradbury summer; standing outside myself, seeing myself look soulfully at the trickling water, shying a flat stone at the stream and unable to make it skip . . . conscious of a terrible aloneness.

Then Mary was beside me at the river's edge. I looked at the Mary sitting on the ground of the *kiva*. I squeezed her hand. She smiled at me. The man-woman who was our guide and shaman threw a handful of herbs and sweet-smelling dry grasses onto the fire. Through the incense smoke I saw the other Mary, healed and free of madness. She raised her hand toward me in benediction. Water gushed from her palms. The odor of sanctity filled the *kiva;* I almost choked on its sour sweetness.

"Mary," I said softly. And the Mary beside me held my hand tightly, and the Mary beside the river kissed me and with each kiss—just as with each swallow of the peyote tea—I regained a lost piece of myself.

Serena was lost in her own dreams. She was crying out "Ash, oh Ash," and giggling like a little girl. Perhaps she was seeing a scene from her childhood. At one point she cried out in pain.

I heard the laughter of young boys. They were playing in the shallow water. Leaping the stepping stones. Little children. I had been told their names many times since suffering the selective amnesia of shifting worlds, but now, when the littlest one looked at me from the far bank, and I saw his eyes—Mary's eyes—the color of the sky flecked with the murk of the river, I called out his name: "Theo, Theo."

"Be calm. Be still." It was Milt. "I know you want to burst with the joy of rediscovering yourself. But you must hold it all inside."

We drank again. "I'm afraid it's time now," Milt said at last. I don't know where the bow and arrows had appeared from but suddenly he was standing next to the well, wrapped in a blanket of many colors, and he was drawing an arrow from this quiver. He licked the point of the arrow and nocked his bow and took aim at me. "Do you wish to make the spirit journey with me?" he said to me. I hesitated. "You have to say yes! Quickly! I can't kill you without your permission!"

The youngest boy looked at me from the far side of the river. I knew I belonged to him. He raised his arm toward the sunset in a manner reminiscent of the last lines of Thomas Mann's *Death in Venice,* and I cursed myself for the over-intellectualizing fool that I was. "I do," I said very softly.

He asked the same question of the women and one by one they nodded their assent.

The arrow flew straight and true. The pain seized me all over. I was on

fire. I was shaking, sweating, weeping tears of blood. I clutched my heart
and found it in my hand and it was a rose whose thorns stabbed deep into
my palms, my scalp, my side. I stared and saw the women writhing on
either side of me. In the corner of my eye I saw Milt fastening a rope
around his neck and thrusting one end up at the sky, saw him kicking,
saw his tongue loll from his parched blue lips, saw him fall lifeless to the
floor of the *kiva,* saw him sprawl over the center of the sandpainting.

It was then that I died.

I knew it was death because I had become quite still, quite feelingless.
Darkness blanketed me, and a cold beyond coldness. In that darkness I
glimpsed the light that hides itself in the thickest darkness, and I knew
that the dark and the light were one. I was on the verge of becoming part
of the flame, part of the prime mover of the universe. It is not something
that can be explained, only intuited; and I, who had spent my adulthood
far from intuition, even though I professed to be a poet—I who had hid
behind the walls of the university rather than live and love and swallow
fire, as poets must—I was ashamed of the sham my life had been. I
wanted to dive into the source of the river and forget everything.

Now I knew why, when I'd looked into the well and seen the half-
remembered image of my son Joshua, I had thought him dead. If he had
been pulled across without warning, without the shamanistic ritual . . .
it would have been hard to resist the seduction of the light.

God! I wanted to give myself to it completely! To become a drop in the
eternal ocean . . . God!

But then I heard a voice. Theo's voice. Calling me from the brink. I
felt his hand on my shoulder, pulling me away from the light. And saw
him—yes, in that *Death-in-Venice* pose, poised at the river's edge, at the
boundary of life and death . . . and he only said, "Dad, not yet."

And then it seemed that I saw him walk toward the well across the
glassy sea . . . turning back now and then to look back, wistfully, at the
reality we were leaving behind. And I started to follow.

He stepped into the well and disappeared.

Then Milt rose from the ground—with infinite slowness it seemed—
and walked toward the driver's side of his police car . . . which was
somehow more than a police car . . . it was wreathed with strands of
laser light. The others were rising too. A soft blue radiance haloed Milt's
face. Mary followed him to the car, swimming through air thick as water.
Serena walked shyly behind her. The car was glowing. Shafts of golden
light pierced the incense clouds. When I looked up I saw that a full moon
was shining even though the sky was a black tarpaulin. There was flute

music in the air. The women were seated in the back now, and Milt went around to open up the passenger door for me.

I got in. Milt was already sitting beside me. The gearshift still had all those unfamiliar letters. He saw me staring at it and said, "You'll see what they're for soon."

The inside of the car was awash with light. I realized that the light was Ash; that Ash was with us, that he had never left us. In fact, I distinctly remembered Ash . . . a young man who'd stopped by and given me a jump-start one morning when I was stalled in the winter snow . . . one of my poetry students who had dropped out after one class although he'd written the most brilliant poem I'd ever seen, scrawled it on scratch paper and made it into a paper airplane and sent it zinging toward my desk my lectern my pulpit and the airplane hovered above my head like the proverbial paraclete before nose-diving for the trash can. Oh I knew Ash all right. Why had those memories never surfaced before? There was a mythic polish to them that made them seem almost planted . . . but I had no time to worry about it anymore. Milt had put the car into Q—whatever that was—and he was concentrating so hard that the sweat from his forehead was making his mascara run.

I could hear something revving up. The car was shaking. The light was deafening. The car's vibrations filled me with warmth and assailed my nostrils with the fragrance of musk and civet.

I looked out of the window. I saw myself then, and Serena and Mary, still sitting there in our trances . . . we had left ourselves behind. I looked away. It is not good to gaze on yourself without a soul.

The well was ahead. The well was the mouth of a serpent. I could see down the gullet . . . down to the bubbling lava. . . . Milt Stone pumped the accelerator and the engine pounded like a human skin drum and screeched like a bird of prey and we were on fire and . . .

The car spurted! Swelled! Was propelled toward the well and the well threw itself wide open to receive us and . . .

"Make sure your seatbelts are fastened!" Milt shouted urgently. I scrambled for the strap. Serena screamed.

I could feel Mary touching my neck. Her hand was sweating.

We were spinning! Falling! Down the esophagus of the dragon! Milt shifted gears. We were in Z now. It was a gut-wrenching sensation.

As we plummeted I saw that the car we were in was . . . unfolding itself . . . turrets were unfurling, antennae pushing up from the hood, the hood ornament ballooning into a pagoda . . . with terraces of hanging gardens. . . . The seat belt was writhing as it snapped away from me and became a tower of light reaching up into the height and crowned with circling stars. . . . The front telescoped out into a throne . . . The interior of the car became huge and numinous, vaulted like a Gothic cathedral, with stained glass panoramas depicting mythological scenes of war and ravishment. . . . The incense came from braziers set against Ionian columns . . . from somewhere in the distance came the soaring melismas of a boys' choir, arcing across vast smoky spaces, canyons in marble, mosaic-stone skies inlaid with jewels and dusted with gold. . . . The figure of Milt was changing too, growing. . . . His fingers shortening into talons . . . his aquiline nose becoming even more hawklike . . . quetzal plumes sprouting from his scalp and the nape of his neck. . . .

And still we were falling, falling, still I could see, through gaps in the cathedral walls, the well-wall glistening with wetness as we plummeted. . . .

And then I heard—it seemed to be a wind at first, before I started to make out solo voices—a huge collective roar as from a crowd at a political rally, a crowd at a rock concert. . . . What was it? The hall we sat in—was it cathedral or throne room? At the far end a curtain was whisked aside and sunlight streamed in and the roar of the crowd became deafening. . . . Serena took the lead, clambering over the back seat—which had become a long velvet couch with gilded human feet—and running across the smoking marble floor to what seemed to be a huge bay window opening onto a parapet that overlooked a city. . . .

I looked down and saw myself transformed. I had been rather conservatively dressed before—having come more or less straight from my autograph party—but now I found myself wearing some kind of chain mail—it looked like chain mail at least, but it hugged my body like tight sweats. Mary's getup was not unlike that of the goddess Isis, while Serena resembled a Salvador Dali interpretation of a Valley girl, complete with earrings that appeared to represent a pair of golden phalluses.

Where Milt had been driving appeared now to be the bridge of a starship which occupied what could be construed as the antechapel of the vast chamber, at the opposite end from the terrace where the sound of screaming multitudes had crescendoed so that I had to shout to hear myself talk.

"Serena, hold on a moment. . . . Where do you think you're going? Don't you think we should be a little more careful? . . ."

It was useless. She stood at the edge of the bay window and turned to me and shouted, "Hurry up, Mr. E.! The whole city's turned out to see us! And now you'll get to meet Ash at last—all of him—not some half-real projection into our dimension. . . ."

I hesitated. Detective Stone now seemed far from human as he super-
vised a dozen crew members in garish trekkie-clone uniforms. He was
pacing up and down, a flask of bubbling blue liquid in one hand, back
and forth along something that looked like a cross between the bridge of
a starship and a Medieval torture chamber.

When he saw me move toward the terrace he levitated toward me,
flapping his wings now and then and squawking. Mary cried out with
pleasure, for though he had changed his shape he still moved with the
same strange grace he had exhibited while dancing on the mesa's edge,
while pouring peyote tea in the garb of the man-woman.

"My memory has come back now," said Milt.

"You're not a Navajo shaman anymore? You were just faking, I suppose," I said. But the memory of death and transfiguration would not be
dismissed. I knew it would never leave me and that I was forever
changed.

"A shaman? Why, sure enough." He punctuated his statements with
chirps. "But that was in your world. Here, you see, I am someone else. I
am Corvus Ariano, High Pilot of the flying citadel of Ash. My duties
consist mostly of conserving our supply of the water of transformation."
He indicated the flask of blue liquid. A similar blue liquid seethed along
a creek which seemed to run down the middle of the chamber. "When
Prince Ash sends me to other worlds to perform diplomatic missions on
his behalf—helping you to stay in touch with reality was one such mission, I might add—when I leave the homeworld, I have a lot of trouble
remembering who I am. With some people, universe-hopping is second
nature; with people like me it's a necessary evil, and when you do hop the
results seem more or less unpredictable."

"Come on, Mr. E.!" Serena shouted. "It's time for you all to meet
someone in the flesh—someone you've seen only as a shadow before."

We stepped out through the curtains. We were on a parapet overlooking a city. The place I had thought of as the cathedral was perched on a
huge structure, perhaps a pyramid. I took Mary's hand. It was cold. I
turned to look and saw that she was moving slowly, ever more slowly
. . . and that her eyes had stopped blinking.

She was turning to stone.

I didn't have time for the crowds gathered in the plaza below, who
were shouting out our names and calling for Prince Ash to appear. Serena was leaning over the balcony, waving frantically and blowing kisses.
Milt—or Corvus, as we were now to call him—was standing rigidly at
attention, and Ash, his master and our host, was slowly taking shape on a
dais overlooking us all, an androgynous youth of surpassing beauty. . . .

The crowd prostrated itself as one man and whispered the name of Ash. . . . I could not enjoy the spectacle, because my wife was hardening in my arms, and as I kissed her lips I tasted marble.

Wildly I tried to call for help. No one was paying any attention to me. They stood at the edge of the parapet acknowledging the cheers of the crowd. Milt—Corvus—held up something at the sky which looked like a TV remote controller. He pushed a button and the sky dimmed. Another and the fireworks began. The light rained down and colored my Mary's whitened face with garish greens, harsh blues, flashing vermilions. Only her eyes remained alive. They stared, time-frozen, with an expression of timeless compassion, like the eyes of a Madonna. Her hands were outstretched and her Isislike headdress displayed an image of the moon between the horns of a cow.

I stayed, clasping the image to me, until the cheering had subsided, the fireworks had quieted, and a soft music began to play from, I supposed, concealed speakers somewhere on the veranda. Servants had brought in a table and chairs and it seemed that we were about to be served a traditional English tea. The situation was so incongruous that I began to laugh. . . . I laughed until, without warning, I found myself in tears.

Ash touched me on the shoulder.

"You must be done with grieving now," he said. "We have a lot to do."

"What's happened to her?"

I looked at Ash. Ash was not tall, but an aura emanated from him. He looked at the statue that had been Mary. Then, beckoning to two of the servants clad in black who always seemed to appear when he needed them, he said, "Place the image of the Mother of Waters back in her votive niche." They carried my wife away. "The people are happy," Ash said—his eyes danced in the light of the now-silent fireworks—"because she has been restored to them; they are always sad when she is forced to leave us."

"Leave you?—But she's my wife," I said.

"She has always been much more than that," Ash said. "You will see, Truthmaker."

"Truthmaker?"

"It is our name for you; it has been, since the most ancient stories were told about how you fathered Theo Truthsayer on the Mother of Waters, who caused herself to be born in the world of humans. . . ."

"I don't understand."

"Surely you of all people should, Philip Truthmaker. You've spent your entire life mythologizing the mundane. . . . Is that not the function of poetry?"

I bowed my head in shame. "Ash, I've betrayed the very idea of poetry. . . . I've settled for a cushy chair of poetry at a second-rate university. . . . How can you expect me to understand about Mary?"

But wait, I thought. In different worlds, we sometimes took different forms. . . . I knew that. Corvus Ariano was some kind of pilot in this universe, while in ours he was a transvestite witch doctor. Could it be that Mary, the madwoman (or cancer victim, depending on which set of memories I trusted) was some kind of godlike being here? But she was also a statue.

"Not a statue," Ash said, reading my mind, it seemed, "but a creature who lives in a time frame so dilated that a single breath she takes can start with the birth of a sentient race and end with the fall of its last civilization. Later, tonight, we will worship her together. But first, let's have tea. Corvus!"

"My Lord," said Milt Stone.

"Open up the sky."

We sat down. The tea was peyote tea, brought to us in a silver service and cut with milk and sugar. There were cucumber sandwiches, and I half expected the March Hare to come leaping over the balcony and the Dormouse to be found snoring among the sugar lumps.

Presently the sky folded up like the roof of a convertible, and beyond it I saw a glittering starscape—comets, planets hurtling, nebulas, constellation on constellation, constantly shifting. Serena had hurled herself upon the cucumber sandwiches. . . . I think that she probably felt long overdue for a break from that Walter Hudson diet . . . and Corvus was doing things to his TV remote. I didn't feel at all hungry, but I didn't dare ask any questions for fear of having my mind blown beyond repair. The sandwiches tasted more like seaweed than cucumber, with perhaps a hint of chocolate.

"You want to know what's going on," Ash said, "and you're too polite to ask." I nodded. "Corvus, what's our position?" Corvus murmured a string of coordinates; Ash smiled. "We are on our way to rescue your sons," he told me at last.

"Yes." I thought I must have sounded stupid.

"I'm sure you know the general situation from Theo's dream book: Theo and Katastrofa are quarreling over my father's kingdom. I'm in disgrace, and my father is doing his King Lear thing, wandering around a blasted heath somewhere, doing a passable imitation of Paul Scofield on acid." Behind his flippant tone I had a sense of relentless tragedy playing itself through to its preordained dénouement. "Theo has found Josh and they are traveling upriver together. Perhaps they are looking for my fa-

ther. Perhaps Theo will be able to reach him; everyone else has tried and
failed. My father's pride is a terrible thing and, since the demons in the
scepter of life and death have begun to possess him . . ."

Downing more tea seemed to make this outlandish universe more and
more credible. Only the idea that I had been married to some kind of
mother goddess for the past eighteen years seemed hard to swallow, but
even that was not too bad after the fifth cup.

"By the way, in case you hadn't noticed, this city is also a gigantic
spaceship. We had to do a lot of fantasy transdimensional space folding
to get the city to look like that police car, let me tell you . . . but I think
you'll agree that it was the only possible getaway vehicle."

I wasn't counting, but it was at about that moment that I think I
surpassed the White Queen's record of believing six impossible things
before breakfast. I was rapidly coming to the conclusion that Charles
Lutwidge Dodgson—Lewis Carroll to the uninitiated—must have been
responsible for designing this universe. He was as believable a demiurge
as my boy Theo.

"We are now closing in on where I think your sons have gone to, at a
sizable fraction of the speed of light . . . which is why the sky seems
restless," Ash went on.

"And as soon as we find them we'll scoop them up, bring them home,
sweep my wife off her pedestal and live happily ever after?" I said.

"Intense!" Serena said, awed.

"It sounds like a plan and a half," I said.

"It's the only course of action left to us," Ash said, "if we are to
preserve the integrity of the universe." And again I felt the sense from
him of hurtling toward inevitable doom.

"Jesus," I said. "And until a few days ago I didn't even know I had any
sons."

"You know it now," Ash said. "It is as though you had awakened from
blindness."

"Yeah, Mr. E.," Serena said between mouthfuls, "you *know* it."

"Do I?" It occurred to me that, in my entire life, I had never taken
anything on faith before. What kind of a poet was I? "Why should I risk
my sanity to save people whose existence I'm not sure of?"

"Because you love your wife," Ash said.

Later that evening, as I lit incense sticks in front of her shrine, watching the stars streak by through the observation window set into the dome
of her cathedral, I realized that Ash was right. Choristers mounted on
mechanical clouds flew overhead, eulogizing her with spirited anthems;

thousands of the city's inhabitants lay prostrate on the floor of the cathedral, their palms pressed together, now and then murmuring their private prayers to her so that their voices melded with the mushy resonance of marble; children strewed flowers and lit candles; widows beat their breasts and pleaded for their husbands' resurrection; Ash, too, prayed, kneeling in a private pew, with four acolytes wielding censers and a fifth to asperge him with water to which a drop of the Water of Transformation had been added, sanctifying it. But I alone loved her as a man loves a woman. I alone was the consort of the goddess.

I placed a wreath in Mary's hand and kissed her on the cheek. I backed down the thousand steps, thronged with worshipers. I entered something that looked like a confessional booth, to be magically transported to the bridge of the starship, where Corvus was directing his staff, striding about and flapping.

Serena looked up from a terminal where she'd been doing her Lieutenant Uhura thing. "Mr. E.!" she said. "It's awesome—Big Bird here has located them."

Corvus didn't seem too affronted at this nickname. Perhaps he was not a big fan of children's television. Personally, I did not see the resemblance. Most of his feathers were blue-black, and there was still enough of the sacred *nadlé* about him for me to feel a little . . . well, sexually uncomfortable in his presence. "Put them on the screen," he said to Serena, who began pushing buttons in earnest.

Corvus whipped out his remote, pointed it at the air, and clicked. All at once I saw them. They were life-size and three-dimensional; it was almost as though I were standing between them. They were riding a raft of light, and Theo was standing just as I'd seen him in my peyote vision, with his arm upraised. Joshua was a decaying corpse, moving jerkily as though by stop-motion animation. Around them was the River; I knew what the River was by now.

"It's like a scene from *Huckleberry Finn,*" I said.

"Oh, come on, Mr. E.," said Serena, "these boys are going upriver, not down. . . ."

A shadow fell over them. There was a dragon overhead, about to swoop down. "Don't you panic now, Phil," Corvus said. "We'll be there any minute."

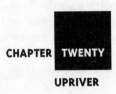

CHAPTER TWENTY

UPRIVER

Theo Etchison

The dragon's getting closer. Thorn's closing in. We're straining to go upriver. The river slopes upward and it takes all my strength to keep on the path. We're cocooned in our million strands of light and anyone who pursues us can see us, burning on the water like a captive sun. I can tell that Josh is still in Katastrofa's power. She's close. He can feel her. He has enough of my ability to be touched by her across this distance. She's making him uncomfortable, she's stirring up all those adolescent emotions he has—the only feelings she allowed him to keep when she killed him so she could bring him across to her side of the river.

We're shining so brilliantly I have to close my eyes. And still the light streams in through the closed lids, a lake of crimson fire. I have to move forward on instinct alone. Maybe—

Joshua screams. It's too bright for him. The fire is raging and his body, drained of the water of life, is starting to char. I can smell singed hair. I don't know what to do except . . . maybe . . . I start to think about safe places, places where I used to hide from everyone when I was little . . . the attic at our grandparents' house in Spotsylvania County. . . . One time when I was maybe six and Josh was eight and we hid inside the great oak chest all night, popping up now and then to surface and breathe the moist mosquito night . . . rummaging through old love letters by flashlight. . . . The chest was like a doorway to another world. . . . "Josh," I say softly, "think about the old oak chest. Think hard. Think security. Think how safe we are, just you and me, alone with our grandparents' past. Can you see it?" I hope against hope that I can force this old memory out of him. If we're thinking the same thing, focusing on the same moment in our common past, maybe I can move into his thoughts, amplify, breathe life. Maybe.

"Yeah," Josh says slowly. The fire is cooling. I can feel a veil of darkness dropping over us. I open my eyes. Yes. We're still on the raft woven from light but we're also together in the wooden chest bobbing up and down on a sea where the cockroaches are pirates and the mosquitoes are circling albatrosses . . . and there's a salt breeze fragrant with the scent of crushed pineapple and banana and coconut. "You still remember that?" he says. "Jesus."

"You rang?"

He laughs—a feeble laugh, but enough for me to know he is still there, trapped somewhere inside his own dead animated flesh.

We move on. High in the air, flashes of lightning from cloud to cloud show that we're still inside the light-cocoon inside the river inside the marble inside the video game inside the inside out. "Ahoy," I say, and wave the marble like a cutlass. "Ahoy, ahoy," and "great white to star-board" and "south-south-west" and "fifty lashes, then keelhaul him!" and other stock phrases out of late-late-night pirate movies. Joshua smiles.

"Shiver me timbers," he says weakly.

I can feel the planks groan from the weight of our cargo . . . bread-fruit trees . . . gold . . . ivory . . . tawny slave women . . . yeah. I wrap the illusion more tightly around us like a down comforter on a winter night. I pull together the pieces of the sky so it is one seamless blue and you can't see the lightning of the paths of light. For a few moments Joshua seems almost human. I do love him a lot really, even now when he's not really here at all.

"Hey, little brother . . . an island."

"A whale maybe." That's what always happens in cartoons.

"No, an island, really an island, palm trees bending, monkeys dancing on the beach, girls with nothin' on under their grass skirts." And he points. I see something else. I see a tall round glittery mound burst from the ocean . . . covered with like thousands on thousands of gold-green-fire-red tiles. Yeah. And the water starting to seethe around the island like there's a volcano about to erupt out of the depths. They're not tiles, I'm thinking, they're scales.

"It's no island, Josh," I say. "She's tracking us. The dragon woman."

He's starting to shake now. All over, like someone about to have an epileptic seizure. His eyes go all glazed. She's touched him. Grabbed him where he feels it. Jesus it pisses me off. I'm just standing here on top of an old chest bobbing up and down in the ocean facing maybe two hun-dred tons of fire-breathing lizard and I don't know what to do.

And then she rears up out of the water and the illusion splits in two and the sky is sheared and crashes down like a tarp and she's ripping the sky apart with her fangs and—

"Give me what's mine," she says. It's a tiny voice for me alone, a whisper in the wind that whips us as she lashes the water with her tail and—

I have to sustain the illusion. I reach back into our past again. Try to conjure up the smell of the dust as it dances in the moonbeams that slide down the chinks of the roof. . . . "Go away now," I whisper in a six-year-old's voice, "go away now, monsters." But the dragon doesn't hear me. She plunges and breaches again and her screech tears open the sky. Josh is still shaking. . . . She has a hold of him.

"Don't listen to her!" I say.

But he says, "There's something else . . . you wouldn't understand."

And then, all at once, the illusion shatters. We're on the river and cocooned in light. The dragon's circling us. She's coiling around and around and squeezing us back into the marble. And Joshua is giving in to her. I can feel him slipping from me, feel the life go out of him. . . . I've got to do something. I shake him.

"No . . ." he says. "Don't worry about me. . . . You're dead to me now . . . they're all dead to me, Mom and Dad and everyone else in the old universe. . . . This is the thing I belong to . . . when you grow up and your hormones kick in you'll understand . . . yeah. . . ."

There's only one thing to do. I've got the marble gripped tightly and I hold it up over our heads. "I am the truthsayer," I scream. "I'll forge a new pathway. I'll bend the course of the River—I'll go where you can't follow."

I hear the dragon screeching. Behind the dragon comes Thorn, his cloak flapping as he rides the thundercloud, his three-headed hound growling at his heels. He calls to me and I feel drawn, seduced . . . but I can't give in to him.

"They're mine!" the dragon shrieks. "Stay away, Thorn!"

Suns and moons crash into each other above our heads as we race upriver and our gaze windows in on a hundred disparate universes. Thorn has plucked a burning sword from the air and hurls it into the dragon's mouth. She bucks and we go under a wave, we go crashing through a wall of water.

"Hold on," I say to Josh. I grip his hand. My nails dig into his wrist. Instinctively I understand what I have to do now. I'm still holding the marble aloft and my fist is sparking and flaming like a catherine wheel. I've got to thrust out into the space between worlds, pulling the river along with me, forcing a new gateway open.

I whisper a word that cannot be spoken, a word that has come to me suddenly, as in a dream. It is the True Name of a thing that has never, until this moment, existed.

Then I swallow the marble again.

Katastrofa shrieks—a sound of timeless despair.

There's a sudden disjunction. I feel inside me all the pathways that have ever been, that might have been, that never were. I can hear the beating of great wings and smell the fetor of Thorn's breath and feel the wind of Katastrofa's passing all at once . . . but I no longer see them. There's nothing. The world has gone black. A tiny moment of stillness now. All I am conscious of is Joshua's wrist. Warm blood trickling against my fingers.

"Listen," I say, "listen."

Out of the silence comes the sound of water.

Then light.

Joshua Etchison

I'm not really sure how it happened. I wasn't conscious a lot of the time. Theo had rescued me and we were fleeing somewhere. We were trying to find the old king who was going to restore me to life except life was such a radical concept by then that I wasn't sure I wanted it. There were two things pulling at me. There was Theo and whenever he touched me or even looked at me I could sense the past inside, animating my corpse . . . making me move of my own free will . . . and then there was Katastrofa who was jerking my corpse up and down on a string. You'd think I would want to be free but there were advantages to being a puppet too. I mean when Katastrofa touched me I wanted to be dead forever, I wanted to be led around on her leash, I wanted to like melt right into her as though she were mother earth folding me up between her breasts soft as warm sod ready for ploughing.

I was ready to run back to her when Theo dredged up one of our shared memories and got me all confused. We were in our light-raft and then we were in a chest in our grandma's attic and then we were like on a big pirate ship and being menaced by a monster or maybe like Moby Dick . . . and when the monster called out to me it was *her* voice. And then Theo did something and we were sucked back into the whirlwind.

We emerged out of darkness into a place awash with light, soft, like an overexposed photograph. We hit the ground running but we weren't so much running as kind of floating along. I guess the world we had reached must have had a lower gravity or something.

"Stop, Theo, stop," I said.

We kind of slowly braked ourselves. Skidded against a charred tree stump.

"Where are we?" I said.

"I don't know. Do you feel . . . do you hear her calling you?"

"Not at the moment." Maybe I did feel something—but it was only a faint echo of the force that had yanked me out of my universe—and I felt less dead somehow.

"We don't have much time," Theo said. "I used my truthsaying to blast open a new channel. But now that it's open they can follow us. It'll slow them down but they'll be able to pick up the trail."

"What place is this?" I asked him.

"I don't know what it's called," he said. He was breathing hard. The air was different too—it smelled of fresh flowers and pollution.

We heard something in the distance. Explosions. Very far away. We stood next to the stream we'd emerged from. The landscape was smoky. Trees with gnarled arms swayed back and forth though there was no wind, and the creak of their branches made a kind of music, the kind you always hear in those African jungle movies on those xylophone things. There were three round things in the sky but I couldn't tell if they were faint suns or brilliant moons. They seemed to give no heat. The trees cast shadows within shadows, fringed with purple and indigo. The air was soggy. We walked on. The forest thinned and there was an open area. The grass was all gray. Here and there was a charred shrub or cactus. There was a burning smell that made us want to stop breathing.

Theo screamed and pointed. There was a naked man impaled on a cactus. He'd been dead a few days I guessed. Not as long as me. But he was in worse shape. Since I'd been with Theo I'd felt my body regenerating a little. I'd had to start biting my fingernails again. There were more bodies scattered about. Some were eviscerated. Others had burned to death.

"Jesus," Theo said, "I hate death, I hate the idea of dying."

"What about me?" I said.

He didn't say anything. He just went right on walking. He wasn't looking at the dead people anymore. He was walking fast, maybe so I wouldn't see him cry. I could barely keep up even though I wasn't falling apart anymore. But I could see where he was going. There was a city in the distance, a mass of spires and emerald towers nestled beneath a snowcapped volcano.

At last we reached a highway.

It was full of people and they were all making toward the city. They had carts drawn by weird beasts of burden. They were in rags mostly.

They had banners and placards. I couldn't read them. It looked like Russian or maybe Greek. Many of them were carrying babies in their arms. There were thousands of them. Some had dead people with them, stacked in wheelbarrows, carried on stretchers. A lot of them were maimed. We couldn't see any end to the procession. The road snaked from the city on the horizon way across the plain until it vanished into another forest.

They didn't say anything as they walked but there was a kind of murmuring chant. Now and then there were like these high priest types in flowing robes that were swinging these incense burners. That was how the smell of flowers came to be mingling with the stench of spilled gasoline and stale vomit. I had a hard time keeping up with Theo.

"I guess they're refugees."

"Who are they? Where are they going?" I said.

"We did this," Theo said. "We're the assholes who—"

Then I understood. It was the game that was causing this. We played at tossing video images through a simulated universe but somewhere it was all really happening. The children of Strang were all at war and burning up star systems and making people die. The games we played were real.

"Let's join them," Theo said.

"How can we face them?—"

"We're refugees, too," he said.

He led me by the hand. We kind of blended in with the group. The priests were pounding drums and blowing on conches. There was mud on their faces. They trudged forward in a weary, steady rhythm. Now and then a car moved slowly through them packed with people, with kids riding on the hood, their horns honking out a lugubrious melody. In this world the cars looked sort of like '57 Chevys except for the psychedelic body paint.

We didn't know what language people'd be speaking here but it seemed like English more or less although sometimes the way their mouths moved didn't seem to match the sounds that were coming out. I guess they weren't really speaking English at all—Theo was kind of "dubbing" it with his mind. I wondered if the picture was "dubbed" too . . . whether the half-familiar images in this world had just been put there to give me a point of reference.

Like that city up ahead—looking like a cross between the Emerald City and a fortress from a samurai movie—why did it seem like I'd seen it before? In a dream maybe. Or perhaps I had somehow eavesdropped on Theo's dreams.

We were walking beside an old couple. He had his arm in a sling and she had burn marks all over her face. They were walking with canes, easy to catch up to. I said to the woman, "What are you running from?"

She said, "There's a war. And a dragon that's burning down the villages."

"Hurry up," Theo said. He tugged me onward. "We have to get inside the city. Katastrofa has found the new course in the River. Fucking Jesus, run, Josh!" He yanked me ahead by the elbow. We overtook the old couple.

Sprinted past women who were singing a whining song and making their tongues dart in and out—*lululululu*—while slapping their breasts with an open palm and tearing out their hair.

"Look," said Theo, "there's a pickup truck that's moving faster."

I saw it. Weaving in and out. A group of men pounding on drums sat on the back and there was something—a statue maybe—covered with kind of a Navajo blanket. A couple of kids were holding the corners of the blanket tight so it wouldn't flap. There were other kids with warpaint sitting with their legs dangling from the back. It looked like they were flicking spitwads down at the pedestrians.

"I'm too fucking tired to go on, little brother," I said. I could feel her, far away, could feel her stirring in my loins. I think she was making my dick tingle a little. I could feel the life oozing from me and I didn't even mind.

"She's here," he whispered. He ran up to the pickup truck. "Hey," he shouted to the kids, "my brother's tired and like he needs a ride."

"Come on up!" said one of them. A spitwad sailed past my ear. A second kid, with a mohawk a foot high, cackled. "If you can catch up!" He slammed the side of the pickup. "Giddyup!" It wheezed and started to move a little faster.

"We can make it!" Theo said. He came back to me and started to pull me forward. We ran. We elbowed people out of the way.

"Whoa!" the kid screamed and the truck halted momentarily. A dozen pairs of arms reached out to us. They pulled us aboard. I scraped my skin. It hurt, so I knew there was still some life left in me.

We slumped with a thud onto the back of the truck. I looked up and saw the covered-up statue shaking.

"Shit—it's the Mother—get her!" one of the kids bawled out. All at once they dived. Too late. The blanket slid off and I saw the statue's face.

"Jesus," Theo said, "it's Mom."

Silence. I got up and so did Theo. Everyone on the truck was flat on their face. I looked around. The procession was jerking to a halt. I could hear people whispering: *The Mother, the Mother.*

The statue had our Mom's face. It was made of marble. Except for the eyes, which seemed to be alive. She was in there somewhere.

Slowly . . . agonizingly slowly . . . the statue began to topple. The people on the truck were too petrified to do anything. Only Theo could act.

He stepped forward. Held out his hand. Propped up the statue and pushed it back into a precarious upright position.

The statue smiled.

"Y-you touched the Mother," said one of the kids. I guess curiosity had gotten the better of him and he'd sneaked a peek. "And you didn't—shrivel up and die."

They scrambled up and threw the blanket over her again.

"She smiled," said one of the drum-toting dudes.

Somebody whispered "Truthsayer." Then I heard the word ripple through the crowd . . . could see the reaction work its way down the highway like a mouse down a snake's gullet.

"It's gonna be hard to stay anonymous around here, Theo," I said.

"Shh! Listen!"

Other noises were working their way up the highway toward us. Screams. Explosions. Someone was attacking. People started pointing at the sky. I looked up and saw them. Metalskinned vultures. Swooping down with the three suns at their back. Lines of liquid fire were spurting over the landscape. The pickup revved up. People began stampeding toward the city, trampling over each other. Babies were screaming. The boys on the pickup started to stamp their feet and chant and clap their hands while the older men banged their drums and danced.

The vultures made another pass. People sizzled and charred. A banner collapsed on a troop of drummers. The priests began to whirl and shriek and the women's ululation went up a couple of octaves. Why were they strafing us? And what was our Mom doing here, frozen into a marble Madonna?

The pickup was moving faster. We ran over something squishy. "It's not human," Theo said, but I don't think he was convinced. There were hundreds of vultures now and the sky had gone black.

Then, bursting out from behind the wall of deathbirds, came Katastrofa. She was a dragon all in crystal, writhing against the vultures and knocking them out of the sky. People screamed. They left the highway and moved in a mass across the landscape toward the city. Cars exploded. Body parts rained down on us and still the kids did their ceremonial dance and the men drummed. People were really dying and I had done it—I had caused it to happen by diving into the Nintendo of death.

"She's only after you," Theo said. "She wouldn't have come herself otherwise."

"I—"

"Come on."

I could feel Katastrofa now. I wanted to die again. I didn't want to run from her. I wanted to wrap myself in dragonflesh and forget how many people I had killed.

He grabbed hold of me. Pushed me forward until we were crouching at the feet of the statue. "Quick," he said, "under the blanket."

We crawled inside. We huddled under the blanket, clinging to Mom's image. There was a familiar smell under the blanket—the smell of our mother dying. We drew the past around us and tried to ignore the sounds that burst over us, the screams of the dying and the roar of the angry dragon. The pickup lurched and bounced and skidded. We weren't driving on the highway. We could hear the kids' bare feet tramping on metal. One of them was crying instead of chanting. Maybe he was hurt.

I held on to the statue and tried to shut out Katastrofa.

CHAPTER TWENTY ONE

THE KING IS MAD

Serena Somers

Night fell and the city shifted into high gear. Me and Mr. E., we stayed in the chapel where they were worshipping Mrs. E. for a while. We knew the city was navigating through Theo's River because there was this humming and because, if you looked out over the balcony of the palace, there were streaks in the sky where the stars should be. Mr. E. smiled when he saw it and quoted a Japanese haiku by some dude named Basho:

" 'Over the sea, a tempest!
Over the Island of Sado, flung out—
The river of stars.' "

I guess it must have been profound because he was like weeping and all. Poets get that way I guess, it's their job to like launch into this heightened emotion thing. He was pacing up and down and murmuring to himself and you could tell that there was something inside him about ready to burst, a new poem. I think maybe he saw himself as the island with the tempest raging around him and the stars all swirling in the night sky. Mr. E. can be beautiful sometimes, when he doesn't get too pretentious.

I wasn't feeling pretentious. No, I had like this gnawing emptiness inside me. I get this way when the old eating disorders kick in. I think it was because I knew that Joshua wasn't really alive anymore. I'd overheard them talking. It was always Theo Truthsayer this, Theo Truthsayer that . . . and Josh wasn't really in this cosmic equation of theirs, he was just one of the little people like me and maybe Mr. E., crushed between the millstones of destiny.

All I wanted to do was eat. That's how I found myself slipping out of the palace, leaving Mr. E. to his Byronic posturings, wandering down a dark alley in an alien city that just happened to be hurtling from dimension to dimension at the speed of thought.

Phil Etchison

We were moving closer and closer to our moment of truth. I was in the control room of the flying city. It was fascinating to watch Corvus at work. Ash I saw less of; he had withdrawn to some private room. We were getting closer to Josh and Theo; but we were also getting closer to Ash's father, and that put him into a state of melancholy from which neither food nor conversation could retrieve him.

But Corvus had become positively loquacious.

In the observatory at the very summit of the flying city—which was as unlike Jonathan Swift's Laputa as could be imagined—we watched the universes rush by. Although the city was enclosed within a sphere of force, which was able to contain an artificial environment and project a simulated sky overhead, Corvus showed me that we were actually engulfed by the River itself, and that we were racing against the stream, toward its source. We sat in a domelike structure from which Corvus could send messages to his control room. On the screens that surrounded us I saw only water—water of many colors, water that dashed against the portals of the city, water that frothed, seethed, bubbled.

In the center of the chamber was what Corvus referred to as a map—a continually shifting hologram of a single strand of light, folded over and over on itself, continually writhing and changing direction and thickness. At Corvus' command the view would zoom or telescope, so that now and then we could see little blips moving up and down the light thread, and Corvus would say: "There they are! Let me get a fix on them!"

In a little niche on one wall was another statue of Mary. This one was only about a foot tall, but the eyes were the same—unmistakably alive. I asked Corvus about it.

"They are all fragments of the same Mother," he said, "all of them equal, all of them containing her whole essence, although the one you have restored to the Cathedral is, of course, the *original*."

"Let me get this right—my wife is worshipped here as a goddess of some kind?"

"No, she *is* a goddess of some kind . . . *the* goddess. And you, while not a god as such, Phil, you have a certain status in the universe, since you're the Truthmaker—the father of Theo."

I watched the patterns change in the map; I watched the waters surge against the viewscreens; now and then the city surfaced, and we were momentarily touched by the light of alien suns and moons; I listened to Corvus discourse learnedly about the place of the *nadlé* in Navajo society. "I play the ambiguous shaman in countless universes," he said, "but only in this one, the universe of my birth, am I aware of all my secret selves. . . . Sometimes, as a shaman, I have an inkling of them . . . some unborn memory stirs. . . ."

I wanted to know the rules by which these parallel worlds operated. Surely there were paradoxes to be encountered. I recounted the unnerving incident in which I had found myself speaking to myself on Milt Stone's cellular police phone.

"Each one is a continuum," said Corvus, "across a number of dimensions. Sometimes one changes little from world to world; sometimes the changes come in discrete, disjunctive quanta. We are all Heisenbergian to one degree or another. If philosophers were cats, they'd think of us as Schrödinger's catnip. Why, even the map of the River resembles nothing so much as a ball of yarn sometimes, the very ball that Theseus used to scry his way to the monster at the heart of the labyrinth."

"Your conversation works on so many levels," I said, "that I can't decide whether you're brilliant or you're mad. . . ."

"The shaman as paranoid schizophrenic . . . surely you've heard that thesis before," said Corvus. Flapping his wings, he began to sing.

Serena Somers

Okay. I had to find food, but I doubted whether there was going to be a McDonald's in the area. We were in sci-fi land here, so I imagined there'd be one of those dingy taverns full of geeky aliens guzzling smoking blue drinks and robots with enormous breasts. But I didn't see anything. Where the palace was, the highest level of the city, was mostly monumental buildings; the big square I'd seen from the pavilion was a long way down, and could only be reached by winding pathways with steep steps.

Finally I found a street vendor who was selling something that looked like barbecued chicken livers on skewers. I didn't have any money but when I told her I was from the palace she let me have all I wanted. I bolted down a couple of the sticks and washed it down with like this fermented grape Kool-Aid stuff.

I walked downhill a little more and then I saw—a phone booth. Yeah, they had phones here and somewhere in this town, maybe, there was a phone with my number. I remembered how Mr. E. had been able to call places on the police car phone back in the last universe. What'll happen if I call home? I did. Collect. Yeah, our calling card number worked here.

I heard myself answer. Maybe I wasn't so far away from the real world. Maybe we were separated from each other by the mere width of a single electron.

"Is Mom home?" I asked myself.

"Are you still at the mall?" said the other Serena. Who did she think I was?

"Yeah, the mall," I said. Back home, that's where my mom still thought I was. "Like, aren't you surprised to hear from me?"

"Why should I be?" I guess in this universe Serena was a girl who talked to herself a lot. I wondered if she was fat. Maybe she was anorexic in this universe—that'd be cool.

"What'd you have for dinner?" I said. "I'm starved. I haven't had anything to eat in about the last six universes."

"Oh come on, Serena, you know I don't eat." Bingo!

"Where I come from," I said, "I always eat. But lately, with the Walter Hudson diet—"

"You really can be full of bullshit. All this nonsense you start spouting sometimes." She chuckled. "Thank God this is only a dream," she said wistfully.

"Thank God," I said. Then I suddenly thought of something. "Hey, Serena," I said, "you think we could like . . . meet somewhere? I mean, if you're only dreaming, I guess it won't matter if Mom catches you sneaking out of the house, right?"

"Sure. Be right over."

"But you don't know where I—"

And then she was there. Popped into existence right next to the phone booth. I stared at her. And at the phone. Funny how I hadn't noticed the extra buttons it had—the % and the & and the @ beneath where the * 0 # is on a regular stateside phone. We *were* in sci-fi territory after all. Jeez!

"Serena!"

"Serena!"

Hey, wait a minute, I thought. "Isn't it supposed to drive you crazy if you meet yourself face-to-face in an alternate universe? Anyone who's seen *Back to the Future* knows that!"

"Alternate universe? What are you talking about? Besides, you're not me, you're *fat.* And you're here because I always wanted to have a twin and I was lonely and I started to hear you talking to me in the middle of the night somehow, like tonight. I prayed for one who'd be fat because I wanted someone just like me but who wouldn't, like, eclipse me on Mother's Parade."

"I'm not fat—" It was useless. Why had I tried to kid myself? Pretending I'd been dieting. I was the same as I always was. The difference was that I knew it was okay to be myself. And yeah, I wasn't sluglike anymore if that was what one meant by fat. But it was half cholesterol, half attitude. "You could learn a thing or two from me," I said. "Before I saw you I thought it'd be cool if you were an anorexic, but now I know better. You hate yourself, just the way I used to."

"You bitch! Get out of my life! Who needs fantasies anyway—I should have outgrown them a long time back. Now if you'll excuse me, I think I'll get back to dreamland."

She punched a few buttons on her phone and disappeared. I looked at the phone for a moment, wondering which one the beam-me-up button was. It stood to reason that I wouldn't get along with myself.

I guess I'd better get back, I told myself, and started trudging up the hill. I stopped at the sidewalk vendor for a few more skewers first.

Phil Etchison

After a while things became less ludic in the observation chamber. The city was having a hard time negotiating the current. The map was changing faster than we could follow it.

"It's the boy," Corvus said. "He's making it up as he goes along!"

"My son?" I said, still getting used to the idea I *had* sons.

Serena popped into the chamber out of thin air. "I see you've figured out how to use the phone," said Corvus.

"I went outside—Mr. E., I met myself—it was awesome, it was horrible at the same time!"

"We were just discussing that possibility," Corvus said, turning his attention quickly back to a Frankensteinian control panel with flashing lights, bubbling retorts, Tesla coils, twittering electronic noises, and keyboards full of hieroglyphs. "Oh . . . the boy is really something, let me tell you . . . blasted a new path, he has."

A puff of blue smoke and a burst of static on the console.

"Brace yourselves!" Corvus shouted.

I clung to the nearest chair. On the viewscreens we could see a lightning montage of a city in panic—earthquakes, traffic jams, swaying pylons, people running in the streets. I could see Serena sliding down the floor.

"Another jolt!" said Corvus. I squeezed my eyes tight shut . . . and then it was over. We were stable again. "Screens on the River," Corvus said softly.

Serena and I looked around. The River ran black here, battering against the shields of the city. On each of the screens there formed the image of an old man, haloed in a diffuse blue light, white-maned, white-bearded, with a scepter in his hand.

"It's the king," said Corvus. "He's blocking the new fork in the River."

The image became more focused. His robes billowed in the wind. His eyes burned. What I saw in his eyes was arrogance, power, and a terrible desolation. He stood, his feet skimming the water, his arms in the air, in the kind of pose one always associates with King Lear. The tempest raged about him. It seemed to emanate from him. He was at its center.

"The king is mad," said Corvus.

"How are we going to get past him?" Serena said.

"I don't know."

Images of King Strang on every side. Closeup of his eyes. He was a king from an antique tragedy, going through the motions of pity and terror, and yet there was also in him a quality of soullessness; the carbuncle on his scepter seemed to have more life than was in his eyes. It glittered and showered the air with sparks, and every spark was human. I had read enough of Theo's dream book to know that the sparks were the lives that the scepter had stolen—that the gem in the scepter was the visible metaphor of the corruption of absolute power.

"There is only one person who has remained loyal to him," Corvus said, and once again I recognized the archetypal matrix around which our adventures were woven, "and that is Ash; and King Strang will not see him. But Ash could move the king to compassion, away from the darkness. If only the king would—"

I said, "How far are we from Theo and from Joshua?"

"They're very close. The city can feel them." He indicated the map with its fibrillating strands of light. "Thorn and Katastrofa are also there. Everyone is converging on a single world, a single city. . . ."

"Which city?"

"This one," said Corvus. "For, you see, our flying city is only the top half of the great city of Caliosper; the rest of the city is anchored to the planet Sharán, which was once the third capital of the empire, and the home of my prince and my commander, Ash."

"But," said Ash, emerging out of the empty air so that it seemed he had been with us all along, "I have been banished from the world. It is my punishment for telling my father things he did not want to hear."

"Surely there is someone who can talk the king into listening to us," I said. And even as I spoke, I felt myself being sucked into their world, their mythos.

"Couldn't you?" said Ash.

But it was Serena who answered him while I hesitated. "Come on, I'll go," she said. "Me and Corvus'll go and see the mad king. Something has to be done."

"Yes," I said. "If he could just lower his guard for a few minutes, we could sneak into the city past him and his henchmen—" Amazingly, the plan sounded sensible even to me. Which showed how deeply this universe with its fluctuating realities had seeped into my consciousness. Perhaps I was starting to be a real poet after all. Realities are infinite, I told myself, but there is only one truth.

It wasn't fair! I told myself. I was a father who desperately wanted to see his children—even though my memories of them were confused— and the king who thwarted me was a madman who never wanted to see his children again. That was, I realized, the very essence of his madness; that he had cut himself off from a part of himself, willfully refusing to be healed. It was the essence of my madness too. I was sure that I was mad at least some of the time.

I wanted to see the king, to come face-to-face with my own dark secret self, to face my fear of becoming whole.

"Yes, Serena," I said, "we'll all go."

"I cannot," said Ash. "This reality is foreordained and cannot change."

We left Caliosper in a shuttlecraft shaped like a golden swan. Presently we came to the fork in the River. A wall of water climbed halfway up the sky. Beyond the wall, I knew, were my sons. On an island in the center of the interchange stood the old king, much as we had seen him in the viewscreens of the observation deck.

Serena Somers

We touched down on the island and there were these lizard soldiers who took us into custody and took us to the king, me and Corvus and Mr. E., who when he saw the king went white, as though he had seen his own ghost. And I knew what that was like, since I'd just done the same thing in a back alley in Caliosper.

We parked the swan just inside the eye of the storm. The whole island was the center of a whirlwind but around the king the air was perfectly still and stifling as a closet. We knelt down in the presence of the king but it was like he didn't even see us.

King Strang stood there staring at something beyond the tempest. I couldn't take my eyes off his scepter. I was scared and awed at the same time. The king had Ash's eyes, the eyes that had haunted me since I was a little girl. But his face was half eaten away by rot. It was like he was the kingdom and the kingdom was him, and whatever happened to the cosmos could also be seen on his face. It was being consumed by death. This was the person who was preventing us from reaching Josh, but I couldn't feel anything but pity for him.

At last Corvus said softly, "Your Majesty."

The king didn't look at him. He tilted his head slightly and said, "Corvus?"

"Yes. I am your old retainer, the one who followed your son into exile."

"Get out," the king said.

"Thorn and Katastrofa are burning down the universe," Corvus said. "Right now they're on the other side of that wall of water. . . . The world they are fighting over is Sharán. You used to love that place. You called it the treasure of your old age. You used to walk through its silent forests. They are desolate now. You willed the planet to your favorite son, but now you have dispossessed him."

"Who are you?" said the king. "Why are you telling me these terrible, terrible things?"

"I am, O King, your servant," said Corvus. "And this is the father of the truthsayer. And this is the woman who loves the truthsayer's brother."

I didn't know what to say so I kind of curtsied, like in an old movie. I looked from Corvus to Mr. E. The medicine man-astrogator was speaking in I guess a ceremonial way, sometimes flapping his wings to point up his words, and hopping back and forth in a semicircle. It reminded me of the minuet from Mrs. Mueller's ballet class, which I stopped taking when I started to bloat.

Mr. E. started babbling. "Jesus," he said, "a complex, recursive, solipsistic metaphor—the endlessly replicating self—"

What was he talking about? Mr. E. always withdrew into a fog of philosophy when he couldn't cope. I'd seen it before.

"Corvus? Is it really you? Have you come back to me, abandoning my faithless son?" King Strang spoke very softly, but his words had an echoey quality, as though you were in a cathedral.

"I haven't abandoned him, King; I haven't abandoned you. He is the only hope for conciliation between your children. You have to let us through."

"I don't care about the universe anymore," said the king. "I don't care about conciliation. Can't you see that I'm angry, that I'm disintegrating?"

"But you must remember how it used to be . . . before you plucked the scepter from the source of the River. . . ."

"What I have spoken I have spoken," said the king. "It cannot be unspoken. To unspeak the words of the king would undo the fabric of the universe."

I just couldn't help myself anymore. "What bullshit," I blurted out.

Suddenly everyone was staring at me. The wind was dropping. I could see chinks in the wall of water. The king's face darkened. But I didn't care anymore. The silence was appalling and I had to fill it. "Ash is like the only one who's ever loved you. If you can't understand that, you shouldn't be standing around hurling the whirlwind at people—who do you think you are? If you can't even do the right thing anymore, you're not even a real king! Mr. E. and me, we came a long way to save the people we care about. I don't know why you're trying to stop us but I'm not going to let you stand in my way, you, you, you mega-dweeb!"

It was an intense moment. Mr. E. and the king were facing each other off, having a staring contest. The lizard soldiers were so shocked they were actually tripping over each other.

"I—" said the king. His soldiers leaned forward to listen.

At that moment the wall of water kind of shimmered and started to fade.

"Command—" said the king. He gritted his teeth. His scepter began to sparkle, and I knew that it meant he was thinking about killing people.

"Quick!" said Corvus. "Into the swan!"

Something snapped. We sprinted into the swan and Corvus aimed it right at the disintegrating wall of water.

"Death!" the king screamed.

The spears started flying.

I don't think that Strang could control the tempest and order his lizards around at the same time. At that moment the storm fizzled out and the city of Caliosper rose up behind us out of the mist-covered water. We streaked up into the sky and swan-dove at the wall of water with the city on our back. I shrieked. We hit the wall of water with a thundering slap and then we were somewhere else altogether.

CHAPTER **TWENTY TWO**

CALIOSPER

J o s h u a   E t c h i s o n

So my brother and I didn't sneak into the city after all. We were brought through the city gates in triumph. We stood on the back of the pickup truck on the shoulders of shamans and were drummed and chanted and gonged and fluted all the way in. They were all chanting "Truthsayer, Truthsayer," and the more they chanted the more I felt that I was finally leaving death behind.

Of course, you never really leave death behind. I'd learned that since crossing over into this other world. I'd learned that death is always with you, that it's as much a part of you as your shadow, lengthening as the sun begins to set. Even now I knew that Katastrofa was outside the city and moving in fast.

The walls of the city were so high that they muffled the shrieks of the dying outside. The metal vultures dashed themselves to pieces against titanium bricks or against the forceshield that extended above the walls high into the stratosphere of the planet. I learned these things from picking up bits of people's conversations as the procession moved uphill along steep narrow streets and the mood became less fearful and more festive.

It seemed Theo was the only one who wasn't getting a high off the sense of rejoicing. He stood beside me—well, we were both standing on this kind of platform that rested on the shamans' shoulders—and stared off into space the way he does when he's in his private universe. (Of course we were *all* in his private universe in a way, but I guess he had found a private universe within this private universe . . . the way he'd found this planet inside a river inside a marble.) Looking at him made me afraid. I said, "C'mon, little brother. Look at all this fucking spectacle, dude!" Dancing girls were just running out of the houses and thrashing and writhing and stripping right there on the street. Trumpeters were playing wild riffs as they skate boarded up the pavement.

"Something's going to happen," Theo said. "It's Mom and Dad . . . they're coming to rescue us. But . . . but . . ."

I thought of the shadow death. Suddenly I could feel Katastrofa outside the walls, I could feel her tugging at me. I remembered the way she smelled—of musk and lizard and a grown woman's thighs. God I started shaking then, and just like that I couldn't hear the music, couldn't hear the cheering of the crowd.

Theo   Etchison

We're at a high point. I've almost managed to bring Joshua back into the real world. The walls are blocking out the dragon woman. And also the people. I can feel them, thousands and thousands of consciousnesses, flitting like fireflies through the darkness of the inanimate. They've set up a wall that blocks off Katastrofa's influence even more effectively than the city does.

But I'm really scared now.

Scared because I can feel Mom and Dad coming toward us, and

Thorn, and Ash, and Katastrofa, and even Strang, yanking at their frayed puppetstrings.

The thing is, Joshua has started to breathe again. When I first saw him in this country, he didn't breathe at all. When he spoke those few words to me he would suck in the air and kind of bend it past his vocal cords and back out again but you couldn't really call that breathing. That's the thing about Joshua that I've been least willing to see, but now that he has started to take slow gasping breaths now and then, I understood what it was about him that made me *know* he was dead—not the dripping wounds, not the pallor, not the maggots crawling out of the gashes in his arms—it was the breathing. Now he's halfway between death and life and it makes me even more afraid of him.

Even though there doesn't seem to be anything to fear for now. There's music in the streets and dancing girls and laughter. The pickup strains and groans its way uphill and Joshua's even smiling a little. Jesus I'm scared. Even the smile scares me.

Suddenly there's like a loud blast from a dozen trumpets and the music stops. Everyone stops in midstream. They turn their faces skyward. A shout goes up: "The citadel! The citadel!" I follow the line of their gaze . . . up the hillside where the streets converge upon a plateau where it seems the rock has been sheared flat . . . upward to the sky where two suns blaze while a third is in eclipse . . . and I see another city descending on this city, a city like a cluster of lights, like a gemstone with a thousand facets, and I see that the mesa is designed to nestle the citadel, that the diamond in the sky is made to fit the greater city like the jewel in the scepter of King Strang.

Joyful chaos in the streets! Children are scrambling over the roofs of cars, the drumbeats are coming thick and fast and rhythmless no . . . oh Jesus, I'm thinking, it's awesome, it's intense, it makes me tremble. . . . We're racing up the mountain now, cutting through kidney-shaped parking lots and zipping through tunnels painted with garish abstracts. . . . I know who's in the citadel. We're getting closer and closer to the moment when things will all come together, the Rome all roads lead to. I'm scared and elated and . . . I turn to look at Joshua. He's still smiling. He can't see the way I see.

Oh what a citadel it is. I mean like it's Xanadu and Oz and the Forbidden City of Peking all rolled into one. A cathedral rises out of a faery mist, and on its topmost spire is perched an image of my mother with outstretched arms and wings, and out of the cathedral comes a strange celestial music, like windchimes, whale songs, and the roaring sea all blended into one massive surfer wave of sound. Beside the cathedral there's this palace with a parapet that soars across the town square. That's where we're headed now, me and my brother and a million other people, oozing up the side of the mountain.

Then I see them standing up there at the edge of the veranda. I see Dad and I see Serena Somers—I think it's her, although she seems to have fleshed out a little bit once more from the last time I saw her—and next to them I see someone I recognize only from my dreams: Ash, the third child of the old king. Next to him is this bird-man. I think he's like the exalted grand vizier or chief minister of Ash's kingdom. They're all tiny figures, up there, waving and nodding their heads.

I know that Ash isn't supposed to be here; that he's been dispossessed and driven away, with only the immediate world of the floating citadel to call his own. But you couldn't tell that from the way the people are reacting. They've stopped yelling out my name now and they're calling for their prince. They just keep cramming into the town square and I can see banners being erected and lasers zapping patterns into the sky. They've started a rhythmic chant of Ashhhhhh, ~~Ashhhhhh, and every~~ time they say the *shhhhh* of Ashhhhhh it sets up a whooshing in the air as if a tornado was brewing.

Josh is shouting it too. Good, I'm thinking, it'll stop him from feeling the deathspell of the dragon woman. And pretty soon I'm screaming out Ash's name too, screaming my throat raw.

The crowd parts to let the pickup through. A crystal staircase unfurls from the parapet. The steps are as wide as one whole side of the square and they come down to just where the pickup is parked. They're made of some kind of forcefield material because you can see right through them, they're like a rainbow-fringed hologram-looking mirage just hanging in the air.

The shamans who've been carrying us on their shoulders let us down. The statue of the One Mother is hefted onto a litter. The Navajo blanket is removed and we see her dazzling eyes, shining with the light of all the world's suns. A gasp goes up from the crowd. There is a moment's silence before the hubbub starts again.

The head shaman calls to us. We board the litter. Twenty men raise us up as we stand on either side of the statue. Twenty boys and girls swinging incense burners walk ahead of us up the steps, and chanting priests walk behind us with their eyes downcast, holding their palms in front of their faces.

So there we are being carried up the crystal steps amid a crowd gone crazy with weird music blasting us from every side and it's a freaky feeling because I want it to go on and on, my heart's pumping like mad and I'm on top of the world, the local god or something like in those movies where this majorly smart white hunter dude stumbles into a lost civilization somewhere in Africa and they mistake him for the Mega-Juju. It's fantasy and it's my own and I remind myself that it's just a metaphor like everything else in this country on the other side of death, but you know how caught up I can be in my own fantasy, and how other people can be caught up in it too, and it just replicates itself over and over like the shouts of the crowd that echo from the spires and towers and parapets of Caliosper. Jesus fucking Christ. That's who they think I am. Kind of.

The drums get faster now. The litterbearers are huffing and puffing their way to the top. We are being carried up the sky. The crowd sounds distant now, one mass of indistinguishable sounds.

Finally we're on the terrace. The light is so brilliant that I can't help crying. They let us down slowly. Someone bangs on a big old gong and the incense-swingers start swinging insanely, so that the smoke blocks out some of the suns' light and engulfs us in a fragrant haze.

Joshua looks afraid suddenly. I touch him on the shoulder. He has seen Serena Somers. Dad has seen me.

He says, "I seem to know you now. It's like taking off a pair of dark glasses. Theo. Theo."

And embraces me. I start to cry. But he doesn't embrace Josh, who has the stink of death still on him and whose skin is still blue. And yes . . . I think maybe he's stopped breathing again. Sometimes like in a low budget horror movie you see the corpse lying there and you think it's some actor desperately trying not to move, not to breathe, until they cut away. . . . It seems like this for Joshua only it's life he's imitating . . . waiting for my dad to look away so he can be dead again.

Dad says softly, just for me, " 'Who knows if in the land of the dead they think that *we* are dead and that it is they who are living?' " It's a quote from Euripides or one of those ancient Greek dudes; my dad's brain is like a giant CD-ROM, and when he's at a loss for words he has the whole of Western literature stored in neat little packets of gray matter, stacks upon stacks. I love him for it though. I love him fiercely even though he only half knows me.

"Dad," I say, "it *is* Joshua. That's what they've done to him for not being me. Dad, there's still life in him, I can feel it, and you know I can't help feeling what's true, it's the way you made me."

"We're going to take you back," my dad says. "We're going to be together, you and Joshua and Mary and me, all together, like this never happened, I swear it." He hugs me again and he is crying too.

Joshua Etchison

Serena Somers. Sluglike Serena. She stood there like a butterfly just popped from her chrysalis, and she kissed me, even with the skin peeling from my blue-gray face. She had come a long way to find me. A long way from the safe world of Twinkies and soap opera death scenes. I kissed her back and life flooded me. . . . It was like getting a blood transfusion . . . or like a dead man, a vampire, drinking the warm blood of a living person and raging because what he feels is only a shadow of what he remembers.

Then there was Dad. But he wasn't sure about me. He was confused. He didn't have a single strand of yarn to cling to like Serena had. Serena loved me, had always loved me. It was an obsessive thing, a thing only teenagers can know, because when you're Dad's age you're past the idea that there's only one thing in the whole universe that matters. Serena's single-mindedness had been so overpowering that she was able to cling to her memory of me even while the universe changed around her, even while it tried to obliterate my existence and wipe out the paradoxes of our transdimensional journey.

I could feel that intensity. It wasn't comforting, not like the embrace of Katastrofa which made me forget everything because I knew I was dead and death was the end the solution orgasm without end amen. No she was like my brother—even more so because she found the part of me that refused to know that it was dead and wanted her bad even though it was true what I'd told Theo, we'd never really done it but we'd come pretty close sometimes, especially that one night at *Friday the Thirteenth Part Umpteenth* when Theo was snoring in the front seat covered in popcorn.

"Kiss me back, Josh," Serena said. "I didn't come all this way to star in *I Walked with a Zombie.*" I looked over to where Theo and Dad were, they were all crying and hugging each other but I thought, I'm too old for that now and too young to be like Dad.

Philip Etchison

—and I saw my two sons and knew them for what they were, and knew that we were participants in a timeless drama on a stage free from the constraints of day-to-day logic; another logic ruled here—the logic of myth, the semiotics of dreaming, the labyrinthine symbolism of Messrs. Jung, Frazer, and Campbell. We had our masks to wear and our selves were subordinate to our mythic roles.

But under the masks we were also ourselves, worrying about the mortgage and the IRS. I remembered it all now. My wife falling ill. My two sons: Joshua with all his friends, Theo the inward-looking one. I remembered, too, how the world had shifted back and forth. The peyote juice had annulled the drugs that Cornelius Huang had given me. It was one of those *Alice in Wonderland* situations with all the bottles marked "Drink Me" that turned you into someone else and the mushroom antidote that the caterpillar prescribed. I was myself now. The son who had always seemed devoid of feeling to me was bursting with emotions; the son who had been full of vitality had become one of the living dead.

And of course, my wife was a self-replicating statue of whom each part was the whole.

"All right," I said. "I am nothing if not the head of this family. I came here to fetch you all and I'll do it even if the world comes to an end. Goddamn it, let's get out of here, let's pile into the station wagon and get back on Route 10."

"Easier said than done, Mr. E.," said Serena.

I could hear the beating of mighty wings. I could feel the heat in the air and knew that it was the breath of a distant dragon. Some of the incense wavers had dropped their censers. The priests were no longer chanting. Something had come over them.

Prince Ash looked at the four of us and the statue. He had not said a word during the reunion scene, but had stood afar off, fearful, perhaps, of intruding. Perhaps, not being a human being, he didn't even really understand the way we humans love each other, which is a beautiful and terrible thing and not easily comprehended by aliens.

He gazed at me now, saddened, I think; he said, "Our problems are not your problems. Your Earth is only at the periphery of all this. Perhaps, as a consequence of the power struggles that are going on in our kingdoms, it will even cease to exist, but it will be as though it had never existed, so you would not be there to suffer the loss of its never having been. We had no right to pluck Theo Truthsayer from the world. He should have gone on living there, shedding his own kind of light on his own community of humans. I have no right to keep you here."

He waved his hand. The family station wagon rolled onto the pavilion, somewhat in the manner of *The Price is Right* or one of those other game shows. With the crowd cheering in the distance, there was a distinct ambiance of television.

"I didn't bring you here, Theo," said Ash, "but I am glad you came. You gave us hope. For a brief while at least."

I looked at Theo.

"I know the way home, Dad," he said. "Or if I don't, I can blast our way home, I can cut a new canyon for the River to follow."

He pulled a marble out of his pocket. He held it in his fist, held it to his forehead. We waited, the five of us: a dilapidated poet, a teenage zombie, a boy messiah, a girl with an eating disorder, and a statue.

We waited.

"I don't think we can leave yet," Theo said at last.

"Why not, son?"

"Listen!"

The beating of mighty wings. Fire in the sky. Dragon's breath. The crowd in the square in panic now. I couldn't read Ash's expression; he had hidden his sorrow behind a mask of civility.

"What is it, son?" I said. "Is it the end of the world?"

"Maybe," Theo said.

A fireball struck the station wagon. It exploded. Serena began screaming. Joshua looked at the sky. His eyes were full of terror and of lust.

And Mary's eyes too had changed. The statue of the One Mother was weeping.

CHAPTER **TWENTY THREE**

LOSING OUR MARBLES

<u>P h i l   E t c h i s o n</u>

To say then that all hell had broken loose would be to succumb to the cliché and belabor the obvious. Hell was the most obvious image that came to mind at first. Fire ripping down from the sky, fire threading its way up the streets toward the citadel, fire crackling along the walls of Caliosper. There was also something of the quality of the climaxes of the *Alice* books—playing cards with truculent expressions flying in our faces, roast legs of lamb and suet puddings stalking around in a rage, lizards and flowers running in circles. There was also, at first, the feeling that we—my family, the prince Corvus—were enclosed in an inviolate faery circle that the fire could not touch. As I watched the conflagration spread, I couldn't quite grasp that it was really happening. I was still seeing it all as metaphor, as bits and pieces of someone's—perhaps Theo's—dream. The extravagance and extremity of these visions suggested the febrile fecundity of a child's imagination. Truthsaying and mythmaking are, in essence, the same thing.

That's why, as I watched more and more truckloads of refugees cram into the town square, as I observed, in the distance, beyond the city walls, forests flare up, villages explode, exaltations of metallic vultures smashing themselves to bits as they tore at each other amid clouds of flame, I felt no panic. I had begun this adventure as a poet without a soul, but now I had something I had never had before—I had faith in the power of my son's imagination, which was fueled by his love for me, for Mary, for his brother. Theo's imagination was born from love and sustained by grace. We had recognized each other, embraced, forgiven; in understanding him, I was also coming to grips with a kind of theology. Epiphanies blossomed into new epiphanies. I was drunk on epiphanies.

Therefore—as the palace began to shake—as gargoyles tumbled from the cathedral's topmost spire—as clefts opened up in the floor of the pavilion and sulfurous fumes began to pour from them—I was untouched by any sense of alarm.

Corvus was relaying orders to some of his helpers.

"If we get as many people as possible into the citadel," Ash was saying, "maybe we can save them—make it to the River before the world blows—" I saw the desperation on his face and felt for him a sublime compassion.

Calmly I walked up to the family station wagon, which was still smoking from the exploded fireball. It no longer had a roof, and one of the tires was flat, and the trunk seemed to be on fire.

"Kids," I said, "let's get in the car. Enough bullshit now."

S e r e n a   S o m e r s

So like, there we were: Mr. E. charging toward the car, Joshua wresting himself from my arms and shambling distractedly around the parapet, Theo waving the marble at the sky, the marble that was sizzling with lines of laser light . . . and we were under attack.

So maybe this planet was going to blow up or something, but I really only cared about what happened to the people I loved. And Joshua was going berserk now—deader than ever—I thought he was going to lose more pieces of himself.

Fire was in the sky. I ran after him and shouted, "The car's that way, Josh! Mr. E.'s planning to leave now!"

When I caught up he twisted free again, saying over and over, "It's no use, Serena, everything's changed, I can never come back . . . I drank the water, I ate the food, I fucked the girl—I belong here now."

"Fat lot of good it was saving myself for you," I said.

"Look! In the sky!"

The fire parted. There came a dragon with black leathern wings and scales like polished copper and eyes like suns. The dragon—

J o s h u a   E t c h i s o n

—came toward me. The dragon had been calling me all along. My penis strained against my underpants. I remembered the water from the cooler flooding the office in the police station and the face of the woman detective and her voice and her soft hands that gripped so hard, like lizard claws, and her eyes burning—

Phil Etchison

I was trying to get the car door open. When I saw the dragon I suddenly didn't feel so detached anymore. The door was jammed or something, maybe from the explosion. I tried the handle again and again.

Theo Etchison

I am holding the marble high in the air. Thousands of true names whir through my mind. I'm holding up the marble and trying to see into it with my inner vision—

Everything's on fire. They're going to blast away the world, they're going to rip the fabric of the universe to shreds so they can pull me out and use me. The flames are everywhere but instead of fire I think of water. . . . I think of the River. . . . I think of the source. . . . I think of the stream that once flowed through all things and now has been bent and twisted and dammed up so many times that it's forgotten its true course. . . . I think of water, cool, healing, life-giving water . . . water . . . the fountain . . . the source . . . the spring . . . the beginning and the end . . . water . . . water water. . . .

The dragon wheels overhead. She screams and the towers begin to topple. Then from the opposite side of the sky comes the ship of Thorn . . . the ship at the head of a fleet of ships, bursting through the clouds and the flames. . . . There's Thorn, there's Cornelius blowing on his conch, the blasts of trumpet music harsh against the dragon's screeching. . . .

Philip Etchison

I couldn't get the door to open. I stood openmouthed on the parapet watching the dragon and its attendant vultures and the fleet of ships with death's head prows. . . . I saw the dragon with a ship in her talons, tearing it apart, saw the ship's crew spiraling toward the ground, each with a trail of smoke and flame. . . .

Serena Somers

I saw Joshua and like he couldn't take his eyes off that dragon and he had gone all cold and his eyes had gone dead and I shook him and all I did was gouge the flesh from his shoulders and—

And then there were two colossal shapes in the sky, one like a dragon and the other like a bat and they were clawing and shrieking and it was like something out of *King Kong,* the pterodactyls rushing at one another ripping out flesh with their beaks—

"Ash!" I turned to look for him. But he wasn't there anymore. He had deserted me.

Phil Etchison

Two monsters battling in the sky. They were locked together, plummeting now, unable to stay aloft anymore . . . and they were transforming—the bat-thing into a tall man with a dark cloak that trailed up into the fiery mist, the dragon into a woman with blazing red hair—and still they fought. . . . I knew then they must be siblings . . . only siblings fight that way.

But where was Ash, the third sibling? I saw him now, standing on a hovering platform with Corvus by his side, flitting above the crowd, trying to allay the panic. The throng jammed the square, people piled on people, screams upon screams. They must have been suffocating. I kept banging on the door. At last it came open.

"Get in!" I shouted. "Serena! Joshua! Theo—"

The man and the woman were still falling out of the sky. The man radiated an utter darkness, the woman an overpowering sensuality. My son Joshua was staring at the woman and turning more and more corpse-like.

"Get in the car!" I shouted. I slid into the driver's seat. Screamed through the open window at the three kids. Joshua seemed not to hear me.

Theo said, "I have to find the way," and slipped even further into his somnambulistic state.

Only Serena heard me. "He won't come, Mr. E.!" she said. "He's totally under her spell."

I started the car, gunned the engine. A lightning bolt struck the car. I was shaking. But I had to control myself. I was still their father. I had to be strong.

"Get Theo!" Serena screamed.

I saw Theo bolt. The man in black was gaining on him. I had to do something. I released the brake and sputtered forward. They ran into the palace and I crashed through a window in pursuit of them.

Theo Etchison

Thorn is coming down toward me out of the sky! I clutch the marble tight. That's what he's after, I know it. I run from the veranda, run into the great hall of the palace. People are scurrying around inside. They all seem lost. A child is sitting in a corner drooling and playing with a yo-yo.

I run. Down corridors, down caverns, down, down, down. . . . I think I'm running down to the heart of hell . . . and he's following me. Never more than a few steps behind. The dog growls, yelps, snaps at my heels. There's nowhere to run, but still I run.

I run.

The flames are gaining on me, hissing down the corridors of the palace that is also a starship and a cavern and a maze and the inside of my mind. I run through a knot garden, where the paths transform into new shapes even while I'm running, where the hedges touch the sun and stone sileni stare and grimace. . . . Thorn is right behind me. I can hear the yapping of the three-headed dog. I don't know where to go. There are doors and doors behind doors. I open one randomly and see an old woman wrapped in a Navajo blanket look up at me with sunken eyes and I know it's Mom a long way in the future in some other future dying and I slam the door and try another and another and there are mirrors behind mirrors and doors behind doors and—

Somehow I'm on the street now. People are jostling me. I can smell Thorn and the dog at his heels. Thorn tackles me. The marble slips from my fist and rolls away . . . somewhere . . . where? There are people everywhere, running into each other, trampling over each other, wailing . . . people on fire, people tearing their hair and their clothes, people packed into sobbing heaps, people walking in circles—

"The marble!" Thorn says.

There's no sign of it. It's somewhere under all those people. I feel it, because the thread that connects me to it is not the kind of thread you can cut; I am made of what the marble is; I can't help being the truth-sayer.

But Thorn can't feel what I feel. He lets out a cry of despair that seems even to out-thunder the clamoring sky.

He doesn't let go of me. He holds me tight. Pins me to the ground. His fingernails dig into my back and he's foaming at the mouth and his fangs glint in the light of the burning sky.

"Let me go," I say. "I can't belong to you. A truthsayer is just a truthsayer. A truthsayer can't be bent. You have to understand that, Thorn."

His grip loosens a little. In the pandemonium the two of us seem enclosed in a private bubble of silence.

"But I showed you my innermost torment!" he says. "I showed you the harvester of tears. Theo, Theo, do you think I enjoy being the Prince of Darkness? Together we could have conquered the terrible destiny that corrupted my father. I cared for you, Theo. Perhaps I even loved you."

"Perhaps you did," I say. But still he won't let go of me. "But you're never going to own me, and until you understand that you'll never be ruler of yourself, let alone your father's kingdom."

"I need you," he says at last. "You're right, it's because I can't own you that I'm obsessed with possessing you . . . but the kingdom's mine by right, I am the oldest. . . . You know that my father shouldn't have divided it up . . . he sowed the seeds of chaos and I can't reap alone. . . ."

I know he'll say anything to make me stay with him. And I know that, in his own way, he does love me. I know that this pleading is the most difficult thing he has ever done. He weeps. His tears are tears of blood. We look into each other's eyes for a long moment and I start to feel as though it's my duty to heal the universe . . . that there's a kernel of truth in what he says.

But at that moment the bubble of silence bursts and the hubbub breaks out all around us again.

"Help!" I scream at the top of my voice. "Help!"

A battered station wagon screeches to a halt alongside us. Dad! Somehow Thorn seems to lose all his strength. I twist free of him. Dad gets out of the car. I run to him.

"Stay the fuck away from my kid," Dad says. Very softly. I almost have to read his lips.

Thorn stands there, his cloak flying. He seems very frail suddenly. Behind him is his ship, plowing through the mass of people as though they were the sea, lopping off heads and arms and churning up blood as it comes to a stop behind the vampire prince.

"Let's go get the others," Dad says. I climb into the front seat next to him. He starts the car again. The crowd parts. "Do you know where we're going?"

"I think so."

"All right then, you steer. Scrunch up real close to me. Remember when you were seven years old and we used to do this?" I know what he's thinking. I'm too big to get into his lap but I kind of lean over and put both hands on the steering wheel.

"You trust me, Dad?" I say.

"Yup."

"Prove it."

He closes his eyes and slams his foot down on the accelerator.

CHAPTER TWENTY FOUR

TRUST ME

Theo   Etchison

I concentrate. I don't want anyone to die. I can't just steer the car through people the way Thorn's ship moves, killing as it rives the human sea. I think: Part the sea. Like the Red Sea in that old movie, the one with the Egyptians in their cool chariots. I concentrate hard. The crowd begins to shift to either side of us. It's good because my dad is flooring all the way.

His eyes are still closed. That was the game we used to play when I was little sitting on his lap and sliding with agonizing slowness from the gate to the driveway to the open garage. The name of the game was "trust me." One time I missed the fencepost by like a quarter of an inch, but Dad never said a word about it to me even though I guess it was like questionable if insurance would have covered it if I'd let him get it dented. I was seven years old. Dad never let me play "trust me" again until this moment.

How could Dad have known that of all the times we ever spent together—reading poetry—going to ball games and movies—fishing—sitting by the fire, him talking a mile a minute about some philosophy thing I couldn't understand, me crouching against the warmth and drinking in the awesome words, smooth words, words with shiny edges, words that hovered on the brink of understandability—of all the moments he and I were father and son, the times we played the "trust me" game were the times I truly loved him?

Because he's chosen to play the game now, while the world is collapsing around us, because of this, I know that the choice I've made is a true choice. Because of this I know I must go home with him, I must dream the true path that will take us to the true world. . . . I can't stay here with Thorn and become the instrument of his greed.

Because I've made this choice Thorn is enraged. He's called down his whole fleet out of the sky and they're slaughtering everyone they can. We're being pelted with body parts as explosions rock the town square. I turn on the windshield wipers and squirt the cleaning stuff on it so's the blood won't stay.

I steer into the path the crowd has made for me and now and then I feel a crunch of bone as we run over someone who I hope is dead already. My Dad doesn't know where we're going. He still hasn't opened his eyes.

"Trust me," I whisper, very very softly.

We lurch through the square. I spin the wheel like crazy. The ships of Thorn are chasing after me. I see the cathedral. There's a ramp leading up to the great open gates, guarded on either side by thirty-foot-tall stone demons. "Step on it, Dad," I say. "Open your eyes—"

I dodge the nearest ship. It crashes into the steps. People are scurrying out of the way as I turn the car up the ramp. My Dad still hasn't opened his eyes. "I trust you," he says. Now I start to think maybe he's right not to look, because I'm linking up with the marble which is rolling around somewhere in the plaza. As I link up, reality begins to shift, and we're in more than one place at the same time—the cathedral ramp, the men's room of the Chinese restaurant in Arizona, the madhouse where they've been keeping Mom—all these places are here and now as I start to search for the way home.

The gates swing open like the swinging doors to the toilet like the tollgate on the airport access highway like the gate between worlds—

"Don't look!" I cry out. Because I've seen the ships of Thornstone Slaught as they slam into the sides of the cathedral, seen the gargoyles tumble and the mermaids gasping for sea water, seen Thorn's minions crush themselves between the prow and the limestone facing. . . .

"Don't look, Dad!" I say, and he doesn't look. He's just sitting with both feet jamming down the gas. I think maybe he's asleep, dreaming. As we all are, all the time, reality or no.

Joshua Etchison

Serena was trying to push me toward the station wagon but suddenly it had zoomed off after Theo. She was shaking me and trying to put life back into me, but I didn't want life anymore because I could see Katastrofa coming down from the sky.

She was changing as she descended. Claws retracting. Her body collapsing in on itself. She danced on a cloud of fire. Her eyes flashed. She was becoming a woman.

The bat-thing was transformed too but I could see that it was after Theo, not me. I smelled Katastrofa's breath on the wind and it was like the burning world wasn't there almost—almost, it had backed off, the sounds of the desperate dying were faint, almost like surf beating against some seashore far away, and the fire in the sky seemed cool. That was because I was beginning to die again and to die means not to feel to sleep without dreaming to dissolve out of the matrix of the world; but dying for me was to be able to feel only one thing, Katastrofa and her embrace of darkness.

"Don't look at her," Serena said. She was tugging at my arm. "She wants to drive you out of your body, she wants to make you into a shell and fill you with herself—" And she pushed me away from the parapet, through the great French doors with their billowing drapes that had caught the fire from the sky and she pulled me into the great hall of the palace, pulling with all her might because I was dead weight, not helping her at all.

She dragged me across the hallway. A chandelier crashed onto the mirror-marble. A throne crumbled and crushed a fleeing man. I couldn't feel the palace shaking or the rubble smashing into my face or the dust I was breathing in. I was dead. I went whatever way I was pushed. We reached a staircase and I tumbled down it with Serena leaping after me two and three steps at a time. After a while we seemed to be in a cavern. Or a well. We were still running. Katastrofa was behind us. Gaining. I could feel her in my mind, the slimmest sliver of heat and arousal, the only sensation I could feel at all.

We were running across bare desert now. Mesas reared up against the horizon. The scorching sand was like snow to my feet, numbing. I saw Serena sweating, crying out because of the pain, and still she was dragging me, pushing, pulling, shoving me away from Katastrofa. Sometimes Katastrofa seemed to be a woman and sometimes she was like a dragon and filled the whole sky with her eyes as twin suns beating down on an alien landscape.

"Oh Jesus, I can't go on, I can't, I can't," Serena said at last. Her hands, slick with sweat, slipped from my arms. She sank down on the sand. I crumpled down beside her. There was no shade. The eyes of the sky shrank into the eyes of the dragon. Katastrofa stood above us. Her shadow fell on me, wavering, dancing.

"Give him to me now," Katastrofa said to Serena. And she knelt down and touched me . . . and I felt the woman-warmth flooding me. . . . I felt myself getting sucked in. . . . She licked her lips. . . . Her saliva dripped onto my side and where it struck my skin it burned me and it was all I could feel even in the streaming sunlight. . . . "Death," she said, "death, death, death . . . you have been consecrated to death . . . you don't want to go back . . . you want to stay in the safe dark cold numb stillness where only one mind can touch yours. . . . oh, Joshua, Joshua, listen to me, listen to me because I'm the only one who has really loved you, I'm the one who will make you king of the infinite gray spaces, king of the dark kingdom, king of the dead."

And she flung her arms wide and blocked out the sun. And she bent down to kiss me and I knew that there was nothing I could do except return to darkness. . . . It's only when she'd blocked out the light completely that I felt warmth at last, the warmth I'd always craved, the warmth of womb and woman.

Serena Somers

I knew I was losing him. He was lying on the sand like a sacrificial victim and she was swooping down on him like a scavenger bird. There was only one thing left for me to do. I threw myself between them.

"Get away from him, bitch!" I yelled at her.

She raked at my eyes. Her fingernails were pushing into claws. She couldn't stay human that long because she wasn't really human at all. I punched her in the face as hard as I could. She recoiled. I guess nobody had ever fought back before because she seemed like majorly surprised.

"I knew him long before you did," I said. I was surprising myself. I mean, when I was facing the mad king, I'd been so much at a loss for words that I'd ended up calling him a *mega-dweeb,* which must have made me sound pretty stupid, I mean, you summon up the courage to sass the king of the universe or whatever he was and then you find that you're stuck with the vocabulary of an eighth-grade Valley girl. I didn't think I'd ever live that down, but I was angrier now than I ever was then, because I knew now for a fact that this rotting corpse flailing away in the desert sand was the man I loved.

How many times had I eaten an extra pound of M & Ms just because I thought Joshua wasn't going to speak to me anymore? How many times had I sat beside him at the drive-in, talking too much because I wanted him to touch me so so bad but I was afraid so I would flinch away even before his hand started to inch across the frayed green vinyl? Too late to regret it. I had to fight to keep my man.

Katastrofa . . . the scales kept rising up to the surface of her skin . . . her cheeks undulated and I could tell that she was barely keeping her shape. "What can you give him?" she said derisively. "I was the one who embraced him when you wouldn't. I have power. I am a queen and you're nobody at all. I can give him the world. Many worlds. Maybe he's not the great one, the Truthsayer—but he's got the talent and he can win the kingdom back for me, he can glue back the pieces of the shattered empire. What can *you* do for him? You're a fat little slug who never even let him fuck you."

"I'm not a slug anymore," I said. "And as for not fucking, I'm going to fix that right now, right here."

Slowly I started to wriggle out of my clothes.

"You can give him the world," I said. "I can't argue with you there. But I can give him my chastity. To heal him, I can sacrifice a virgin—me. That's more than you can do, because you've never loved the way I've loved, in secret, hiding myself inside my walls of lard."

I could tell that what I was saying hit home. She started to back away. And then she began to howl. Not like a human being at all, but like a wolf in the forest on a freezing winter night.

I knelt down beside Joshua and I kissed him. I kissed the scars on his cheeks that crawled with maggots. The scars began to knit together. The gray started to leave his face. I kissed his mouth and felt the lips turn warm. And I started to remember those summers when I had lain awake half the humid night thinking about him not daring to call him because I was afraid he wouldn't answer, stuffing the warm sticky chocolate bars from under my pillow into my mouth so I wouldn't have to think about him. . . . There was no chocolate here. Only his parched lips.

I devoured his lips. I breathed the moisture back into them. I shielded him from the dragon's breath with my body. I wrapped my legs around his thighs and felt him become aroused and wasn't scared anymore. And all the while Katastrofa screeched and beat her wings and stirred up the sand to sting my eyes and irritate my tissues but I wouldn't let her hurt me. I thought of water, cool spring water . . . I dreamed my most private dreams . . . at last I kindled fire in Joshua and he began to move, slowly at first, and to breathe in piping arrhythmic breaths, and then I felt his hands clench my buttocks, my thighs, smelled sweat as it burst out from newly opened pores. . . . I teased his penis free from whatever it was he was wearing, some futuristic-looking tunic kind of thing, I held it between my palms like a votive candle and then I kissed it again and again, watching it grow hard, watching with wonder because it was something I'd only ever imagined before. Then I let him plunge it slowly into me and at first it didn't feel that good because maybe I wasn't moist down there, it wasn't simple to get moist the way it was when I used to do it alone in the dark, but suddenly there came a moment when it all seemed to fit perfectly together and I hugged him hard to me and his eyes were right over my eyes and there was so much joy in them that I knew he was coming back to me out of the dark country and that the dragon couldn't hold him after all. . . .

And with a terrible cry, Katastrofa spread her wings wide and soared up toward the sun, and . . .

The desert dissolved. We seemed to be in another place altogether . . . a cathedral with brilliant abstract stained glass windows. . . . We were making love on the altar of the one Mother . . . the shrine was the *kiva* and the stained glass was the sand painting and we were thrusting hard now, our two rhythms melding into one into the heartbeat of the world and the drumbeats of the shamans as they danced and our breaths were the sacred incense rising up to smell fragrant in the nostrils of the Gods and we clung closer and closer now laughing and warm in the glow from the fire and the magic potion of life and death. . . .

Phil Etchison

We pulled up beside the altar. The image of Mary stood watch over them. Incense burned in a brazier next to them and smoke filled the cathedral so we could not see the ceiling. Here and there shafts of light pierced the gloom, light in the vivid colors of the stained glass windows. The cries of the dying could be heard, and the explosions in the burning city, but in this cathedral the sounds were muted, cushioned with stone upon stone.

Ash was seated on a throne at the Mother's feet, and Corvus beside him. Corvus was manipulating some kind of hand controller; Ash was deep in contemplation. He had isolated himself somehow; though he was close to us, he had surrounded himself with a circle of impenetrable loneliness.

Theo got out of the car first. I followed. He began to walk up the steps toward the statue of the One Mother. He was communicating with her somehow, I think, although she did not show any signs of change, except for the one tear that glistened on her left cheek and her lips, half-parted, as though on the verge of speech.

Joshua and Serena climbed down from the altar.

"He's on his way back," Serena said. "I showed that dragon woman what it's like to be young and human and in love." And she led Josh to the station wagon and they sat down in the back seat, and they started to kiss; and I was so reminded of me and Mary and the first time we kissed because in that kiss came the potentiality of Joshua and Theo and all these worlds we had traversed. . . .

"Let's go, Theo," I said.

He stood in front of the image.

"Theo," I said.

"Not without her," Theo said.

Only then, it seemed, did Ash dissolve the circle of silence around himself. He got up from his throne and faced us. He seemed frail and lost. He said, "Don't take the Mother. . . . We will all be lost without her. . . ."

I followed Theo up the steps. He put his hand to Mary's lips. The marble fell into his hand. Light wove spiral patterns around them both. I heard celestial music above the distant screams.

Theo said to Ash, "My friend . . . the doom of the world was spoken when Joshua and I played for possession of it as puppets of your brother and sister. What we're seeing now is only the doom fulfilling itself. There's nothing I can do. That's the truth, Prince Ash, my friend."

Ash said, "I know you're right, Theo."

Theo said, "Fold up the city and everyone in it. When I open the gate, perhaps you can take a lot of the people with you—perhaps you can save some of them—but you know that your father will be on the other side waiting to slam the gate shut forever. I can't change that."

He lifted the marble to his lips. Placed it on his tongue and then, closing his eyes in a kind of private ecstasy, swallowed it like a communion wafer.

For a few seconds the strands of light danced around him, weaving, gyring, circling, zagging. Then they joined into one funnel of dazzling brilliance and Theo swallowed all the light into himself. He began to glow all over. He was the brightest thing in the cathedral. Gravely he said to me—with every word the light from within him flashed all over the cathedral, driving away the shadows from its darkest interstices—he said, "Dad, Joshua, Serena, Ash, Corvus. You all have to trust me now. I don't know if I can get us home, I don't know if I can even trust myself. Only Mom knows. Only the dying and the mad can see to the heart of things."

His brightness forced me to shut my eyes tight. I could feel hot tears. I did not know if they were from the brilliance or from the intensity of love that I felt for him and from him, or from my knowledge that I had, in my middle age, finally put myself back on the path that leads to illumination and redemption.

Reality wavered. For a moment Corvus became the sacred *nadlé* and the police detective and other figures I didn't recognize from other universes. The cathedral's vague loftiness transmuted into the tarp-topped kiva and its dancing firelight.

Mary wept. And Theo, a shining figure, stood under the effigy, and the tears rained down and became a torrent, and the water ran down the steps. . . . I stood ankle deep in water. . . . The floor was thick with foam and I could hear the roar of the River. . . .

Mary softened. Still weeping the river from her eyes, she descended the steps with her hands upraised in benediction.

"Hi, Mom," Theo said, and kissed her on the cheek.

The cathedral . . . the world . . . rumbled. "Hurry up," I said. The screams were closer now, more real. I could hear the columns of the palace snapping one by one, the rubble tumbling as the roof crumpled. "Into the car!"

Mary started running now. In three or four steps she had become all human. I opened the door and threw a Navajo blanket over her. She sank down in the seat. Water was gushing down from smashed stained glass windows, erupting from cracks in the walls. "Follow me!" Theo shouted. I got in and started to drive. Water engulfed us but Theo ran ahead, a smear of dazzling light against the wall of darkness. I floored it. I could feel us moving but I didn't know where. I knew I just had to keep my son in sight.

We breached the water. We were skimming the surface of the River. How were we managing to drive on the water? I didn't stop to think, although I noticed that we had somehow acquired these extra gears that we had seen on Milt Stone's police vehicle.

Something streaking overhead—a bird, a plane—Theo landed on the hood, climbed over the roof and in through the back window. Then he sat down beside me. He was a small, wet boy, and the glow was fast fading, but only because it had become a part of him, inside him always. "Which way do I go?" I said.

"It doesn't matter, Dad," he said. "As long as you never lose me again."

The station wagon rose into the air. Beneath us, I saw the spires of the cathedral jutting from the water. Then, abruptly, the city seemed to fold up on itself and vanished beneath the water. . . . In a second I saw Milt Stone's police car soaring up above the water.

Serena said, from the back, "Neat! We're flying!"

"We're not flying . . . we're not even really moving," Theo said. "The universes are moving and we're staying still."

And then, rising out of the water, came Strang. A giant Strang, a thousand feet of Strang, breasting the current like a classical Neptune, wielding the scepter. He was scooping up the water, making it play tricks, sculpting it into the image of a gate.

I looked into Strang's eyes and saw my own eyes stare back at me. I saw my own past failure. I had called myself a poet but I had not listened to the truth. Strang had wrested his power from the source of all power, but he had refused to hear the truth about the nature of his power. We were each other's shadow. I could not conquer the mysterious lord of some extradimensional empire, but I could conquer myself. If I had the will for it, and the heart.

"Ram it, Dad!" Theo said.

Behind us, the police car's siren came on.

Strang smiled at me. I knew that he recognized me too. But he was not yet ready to accept himself. We are all fools; one day we will all die. I wanted to tell him that. I wanted to embrace him.

I rammed the gate. We could see nothing but water on every side. Then we burst through—

The gate sluiced shut behind us—the Red Sea closed up—the way between the worlds was lost to oblivion—

A starfield, perhaps a computer simulacrum, where suns and planets whizzed past and nebulas swam through emptiness and here and there shadowy entities, thinner than vacuum, flitted past playing at being gods—

An arena where lordlings watched games of life and death and languidly placed bets on the fate of worlds—

An ocean of tears—

We fell from the sky onto the tabletop rock that was already beginning to crumble—

A stone room where a hanged shaman is tearing away the rope that hangs down from the sky and is leaping down onto the sandpainting singing a wild song and asperging us with peyote tea—

We saw our own lifeless bodies frozen in a weird anthropology tableau around the fire, pierced with arrows, leaning against the standing stones, and as the drumbeats pounded we slipped back into them—

And fell with the shards of rock that dissolved into desert sand, and then—

An ocean of sand—

We were racing down Route 10. They were giving us a police escort toward the border, toward Mexico and the Laetrile clinic, and—

T h e o   E t c h i s o n

—and the air conditioner is sputtering dust into the old station wagon as we rattle southward alongside the shimmering sand, and my father's eyes are hypnotized by the road, and my brother Josh and his girlfriend are in each other's arms where they've been, sucking face, since Phoenix if not Albuquerque, and there's a smell in the air like stale orange juice, the smell of my mother dying.

OCEANUS, THE RIVER THAT SURROUNDS THE COSMOS

"KaiuouriouV topouV deu qa brhV,
deu qa brhV alleV qalajjeV."

"*You will not find new places;
You will not find other oceans.*"

—Cavafy

To Myself

I have come back from the river's edge; sometimes
I wish I had never gone, sometimes
I know I cannot stem the stream of time, however hard
I long for the river to run backward to the mountains,
Blue as the sky, as grief, as delusion.

They have stopped playing by the river's edge; but sometimes
Long past sunset, I still hear them in the wind that shakes
The cottonwoods. I cannot bear to listen.
In my heart I know sometimes
That the river has reversed its course; I know sometimes
That the river will not turn back till its watery end,
Black as the sky, as grief, as disillusion.

I will not follow them back from the river's edge; sometimes
I do not think they are coming home. Sometimes, not daring to
    look,
I say when I open my eyes they will be long gone, not gone;
That the river will run upstream, downstream.
I have named them after the gods, hoping to become one myself.
Better not to look at all; for in the momentary closure,
The blink's breadth between two truths, two truths can both be true.
The tension between two truths is what I feel for them; sometimes
I know it to be love,
Red as the sky, as grief, as joy.

EPILOGUE

THE RIVER OF NO RETURN

T h e o   E t c h i s o n

We've been in Mexico a week now. The Laetrile clinic is by the sea, in a small resort town that's crawling with Americans and has so many Burger Kings and McDonald's that you'd never know it was another country. They even have Taco Bell—can you imagine that?

Oh, but it is different though. Our hotel is by the beach and although it's hot there's always a breeze. It doesn't feel like an American hotel though it is really. We have like our own adobe cottage and there's a cliff nearby and steps down to the sea.

It's like nothing happened. Mom is still dying and I'm still having these dreams. I can't sleep. Joshua spends a lot of time alone now that Serena flew back to Virginia. Without Ash there to keep the illusion going she couldn't keep her Mom thinking she was still at the mall.

Josh goes down to the sea every day and stares at the sunset or the yachts or at nothing in particular. Every day he says less and less. He is waiting for something to happen.

I've made friends with a Mexican boy who hangs around outside our bungalow. The only English phrase he knows is "teenage mutant ninja turtle," and he repeats it over and over, kind of like a ritual incantation. We talk at each other in the evenings when it's cool. I tell him all about my adventures in the other kingdoms. I don't know what he's telling me about. His name is Jesus.

This particular evening, Mom has come back from a bunch of tests. We're sitting outside, by our little pool, in the place where the cliff-top overhangs the ocean. We've ordered Chinese food. Jesus and I eat our sweet and sour pork off the same plate. Only Mom isn't eating with us, because she has a special diet they make her stick to.

Mom has never talked about it. As far as outward appearances go, she acts like she believes we drove straight down from Alexandria and there never was a Chinese restaurant or a transdimensional empire linked by a river that flows through every place in the cosmos. She's dying, she's always been dying.

But I know that she knows everything. Because of what she was in the other world. I know that when she was standing in the cathedral and I was like praying to her almost, I know that she held one end of the marble just as I held the other end of the endless strand of light. I know that her tears are the source of the River. I know that her cancer is the same cancer that is eating away Strang's kingdom. I know that to heal her is to heal the other world.

I know the journey has only just begun.

Dad has started a new poem. It's different from what he wrote before. It's full of images from the other world. I know he remembers. He was always the one who remembered the least before, but now he has changed. It's because of that game of "trust me" that we played over the dying city.

The sun is setting. The wind stirs. My mom is getting cold.

"Maybe I should be getting inside," she says.

"Yeah, Mom," I say. I go to get her blanket and I throw it around her shoulder. Jesus I love her I'm thinking and the wind is so strong it blows away the smell of stalking death and masks it with the moist salt tang of the Pacific. Dad takes her by the hand and the wind becomes stronger now.

Jesus mutters something and Dad says, "What do you mean, a hurricane? There's no hurricane." But the little kid just points at the sunset and at something whirling above the water far out to sea. Something is churning up the waves, something big and vaguely dragon-shaped.

I hear a distant horn call. Is it a conch? And the wind gets stronger now and it's wet like someone breathing down on you from the sky, maybe a fifty-foot woman.

"Don't look at it, Josh!" I say. Because I'm getting a sinking feeling. Once they'd just have brushed off what I said with the old crack about too much imagination but this time they don't—not after all we've been through.

But Josh looks, of course. He looks out to sea because he's always looked out to sea every day and every night we've been in this town. And suddenly I know he's been waiting for someone to appear, and that the person he's been waiting for has arrived.

Josh says, "I can't help myself, Theo. I'm still dead. We never captured my soul back from the scepter of the king, did we?"

He strides away from me. He stands at the edge of the cliff. I don't know what he sees exactly. Maybe it's Katastrofa rising from the foam cupping one breast and lifting the other arm in a gesture of summoning.

"Don't go after her, Josh!" I shout.

"I can't help it, little brother. . . . I don't belong here yet. . . . I don't—"

Dad's risen from his chair and is standing beside us. And Mom is here too, shivering, while the wind rises. Yes. I can smell the incense in the wind. We are only a blink's breadth away from the other kingdom. I carry the way inside me always.

"You can't go back," I say. "Strang closed the gateway. The worlds will never intersect again." But I am protesting in vain because I know that there is always a way to the other country.

And before I can stop him, Josh takes the way out.

"Katastrofa!" he screams at the top of his lungs.

He leaps.

He is a blur. The wind brings to our ears a ghostly mariachi music. We don't hear Joshua thudding against the rocks below. We don't see him anymore. By the time he should have reached bottom he isn't there anymore.

Only the three of us are left. We all know where he has gone.

"We have to go back," I say. Very softly.

"Yes," my dad says.

"There's so much to be done. We've got to stop the war. We've got to reconcile Ash with his father. We've got to find Josh's soul in the king's scepter and maybe take the scepter to the source of the River and lose it forever." I'm saying aloud what we all know, because I can't bear us not communicating, because that would be like the old days before we went through all these things together when we first knew that Mom was going to die and no one could say what they really felt. There is one thing I'm not saying though because I can hardly dare to hope it. I think Mom can be healed. If we can heal the madness in the other kingdom. Yeah.

The three of us hug each other very close. We haven't done that in a long time. The sun sets and in the darkness we can hear the horn of Cornelius Huang, a strident note across the gathering storm.

"Let's all get some sleep," Mom says. "We've got a long journey ahead of us."

Mom and Dad go inside the house. They leave me alone on the cliff overlooking the sea.

I look around for Jesus. He's not here either. He must have panicked when Joshua jumped into the sea. Oh, now I see him. He's running on the beach, playing tag with the wind. He's a tiny figure. Otherwise the beach is deserted. Everyone's down at the local club where all the Americans hang out, getting drunk and brooding about the imminent death of their loved ones; because, beautiful as this place is, it's one long premortuary wake as we wait for Laetrile and miracles.

I feel the wind on my face. I feel my brother's spirit in the wind's breath. I feel everyone who has crossed over. Oh fucking Jesus I feel so much I want to burst because I can't even name one of my feelings.

And I'm thinking: Jesus I'm young even though I think I've lived a dozen lifetimes and I've seen, touched, tasted the dark river that leads every place, the river that you're only supposed to cross one time, the river of dying and never coming back, and it's going to be easy for people to say I made it up and blame my imagination even though I always tell the truth, too much, too much; I'm young and I feel a quintillion years old with the tangled strands of the River inside me that stretch from the big bang birth of the universe to the cold death far in the far far future; it's only because I'm young that I can feel this old; because to grasp eternity is a gift of youth.

One day I won't be a truthsayer anymore. Only then will I be able to say it was "just" a dream. For now, my dreams are the world.

Los Angeles, 1988–90

ARMORICA

Row, row, row your boat
Underneath the stream,
Ha, ha, fooled you all!
I'm a submarine.

BOOK **ONE**

<u>T H E   F O R E S T   W H E R E   T H I N G S   H A V E   N O   N A M E S</u>

"I'll tell you, if you'll come a little further on,"
the Fawn said. "I can't remember here."

—Through the Looking Glass

PHILIP ETCHISON: *Tales of the Wandering Hero*

1: In the Forest Where Things have No Names

When I was old enough to leave the womb
And seek adventure in the world beyond,
My mother gave me an old iron sword
A loaf of bread, a condom, and a kiss
And told me, "I've just one piece of advice
For you, young Theseus: don't forget your name."

I journeyed far and wide. I forded rivers
And entered the dark forest. I slew all sorts
Of monsters: trolls and harpies, snarks and serpents,
Boars, bears, and dragons; wizards, manticores,
Though they would plead: "Oh, spare me, Gilgamesh!"
"Ulysses, let me live, and I'll vouchsafe you
Three wishes, maybe four." I killed them all,
And each, in dying, apostrophizing me,
Rebounded to the glory of my name.
I ravished maidens, too, and heard them cry,
"Ah, Krishna, you have barbecued my heart,"
Or, "Romeo, Romeo . . ." and my name waxed mighty.
Till one night, sitting beneath the tree of knowledge,
The Bodhi Tree, or Tum-tum, as some call it,
I felt an apple land upon my head,
And realized I no longer knew my name.

I went home to my mother. She embraced me,
Heard me recount my stirring tales of conquest,
Loves lost and won, beasts slain, and castles stormed.
But though I had no doubt of her affection,
Nor of the hearth's warmth, nor the people's love,
I never could be sure this was my home,
Or this the mother I remembered, or the hearth
Where as a child I warmed myself. Perhaps

I never had a name, and all those names
The beasts cried out were merely myths, dreams, eldritch
Fantasies. Perhaps not. Or perhaps
My name was a yet undiscovered thing,
Hiding behind some shadowy bourne, and I
Had really not yet left my mother's side,
Nor wandered in the forest, vanquished beasts,
Loved princesses and warred with wily wizards.

At last, I begged my mother to reveal
The secret of my birth, my one true name.
She gave me a well-rusted iron sword
A kiss, a condom, and a loaf of bread,
And said, "It's time for you to leave the womb.
But this time, Perseus, don't forget your name."

You see:
It is a question of identity.

CHAPTER ONE

IN A LAETRILE CLINIC

Phil   Etchison

It was the Nineties, the time before the mad millennium. I was not old then as I am now, but a few weeks had aged me beyond all understanding. I had driven three thousand miles and in that blink's breadth between two points in space-time I had seen worlds born and unborn; I had seen empires made and unmade; I had sailed the river that spans the universes, from what-has-been to what-will-be to what-could-be to what-might-have-been to what-ought-never-have-been. God, what a journey it had been.

And this is how I came to feel so old: By the end of that journey I knew it was no longer I who was driving the beat-up station wagon of my life across the Arizona desert—not I who had the power to pilot the ship of the river between worlds—not I who controlled my destiny, but my son Theo: Theo whose life was an eternal present, Theo who saw past the accumulated bullshit of our old minds straight through to the heart, who called all things by their true names because he knew no other names for them, Theo whom myriad creatures of other dimensions worshipped as Theo Truthsayer, but who was to me my son, young, tousle-towheaded, blurter of unfaced truths, stripper of illusions.

I loved my son, but it was he who had made me old.

On the second day of November, at the Laetrile clinic by the sea, I remembered nothing of our odyssey. My wife was riddled with cancer and my son sulked and did not speak to me, and I had not written a poem in nine months. Our recession-proof money market funds had been trickling away as we whiled away the evenings watching cable television and waiting for my wife to die. We were in a kind of premourning mode.

On the second day of November, at the Laetrile clinic by the sea, in a Mexican town manufactured and peopled by gringos, my son and I sat on the veranda of our bungalow and waited for my wife to come back from treatment. We did not speak, but listened to the rhythm of wind and sea and ate our prefabricated pizzas with indifference. We'd been at the clinic for three months and the Laetrile wasn't working. No one had expected it to, but we'd thought that maybe the journey would heal all of us, three people who once loved each other but who now stood always apart and alienated.

On the second day of November, the city of Oaxaca celebrates the Day of the Dead—a Zapotec ceremony with a thin veneer of Catholicism—and the people dress up as skeletons, feast over the graves of their ancestors, go on candlelit processions bearing coffins of the living dead, set up *papier-mâché* altars with images of departed ones and sculptures of skeletons engaged in the myriad acts of daily life. It is a Divine Comedy—festive and tragic—and a very big deal.

Oaxaca was a continent away, and there were more Americans than Zapotecs in this Baja town. Doubtless it was for the tourists that the town was doing its own version of the Day of the Dead. I have been speaking of destiny and the control of destiny; yet often what appears to be a serendipitous predestination is only the accidental confluence of the streams of probability.

Perhaps it was only fitting that this Day of the Dead, which was to the genuine Day of the Dead in distant Oaxaca as a Barbie doll is to a beautiful woman, this plastic reconstruction of an authentic darkness, should be the setting for the beginning of our second journey into the world my son made, the world that made my son.

For most of my life I have eked out a living as a second-rate poet, the chair of poetry at a second-string university, handing out second-hand epiphanies to second-class students. I too have been a plastic shell of an authentic poet. I've touched my own reflection in the mirror and wondered which was more real, my face or its imitation. I am my self's own Memorex. The shadow's shadow.

A year, more or less, had passed since we first came to the Laetrile clinic. My wife's condition was a little worse than before. I was a year older, but I felt infinitely old. But my son Theo was just the same. For a year he had teetered on the brink of adolescence; but he was no taller now, and his voice had not deepened. It was as if he had chosen not to grow. A late bloomer, he would have been called at school in the States, but here at the clinic there was no school as such, only a recreation room with a library where those of us, patients or spouses, our minds on other things, sometimes saw fit to hold impromptu classes for the dozen or so children imprisoned here with us. (I myself had been known to speak on Keats and Whitman.) And so it was that no one really noticed Theo's refusal to participate in the passing of time.

I, it must be said, had not noticed it until that very moment.

Theo wiped the pizza sauce from his lips. The afternoon sun was behind him, over the sea. God he looks young, I thought, younger than when we first came here. I wondered whether I could broach the subject without embarrassing him. With his mother not due back for a half hour, there was a window of opportunity for us to do some male bonding.

"Theo," I began.

He looked at me. He smiled a little.

"What are you thinking, Dad?"

"I'm thinking that we haven't had a real conversation in about a year."

"If this is some kind of warm-up to a birds-and-bees lecture, Dad, I think I should warn you that I already know everything."

"No jokes, Theo. Let's be serious."

"But I *do* know everything, Dad. And you've forgotten everything."

"What do you mean?"

"Does the name Joshua Etchison mean anything to you?"

This is what I saw in my mind's eye: a flaming angel leaping into the sea. It seemed to be a memory, but how could it be? A second-rate poet does not see angels, does not have visions of paradise and inferno. I took a sip of Diet Pepsi—the clinic permitted no alcohol on the premises—and I looked my son in the eye and said, "No."

Theo said, "I want you to listen to this poem, Dad—" and he began to recite, in a dreamy treble, words that were not quite my own:

They are standing at the river's edge; sometimes
I watch them, sometimes
I cannot bear to watch, sometimes
I wish for the river to run upstream, back to the mountains,
Blue as the sky, as grief, as delusion.

But I said, "No, no, that's not how it goes at all." I remembered writing that poem. It was at my parents' summer place. By chance, at sunset, I caught Theo standing at the edge of the creek that borders their property. And I started thinking about how much I loved him. This poem had no "they" in it. It was all "you"—"you" by the river's edge, "you" whom I named God. The "they" was a travesty of what I felt for him, the love so big and deep I dared not express it save by hints and misdirection.

"You're thinking that you only have one son."

—a flaming angel leaping into the sea—

"I know I only have one son. If I had more than one," I said, "I'd go insane."

"You *are* insane," Theo said.

And suddenly I knew that he was telling the truth. For months now I had been plagued with the notion that the life I was living was somehow not my life. There were the missing pieces in the puzzle of memory—the entire journey between Virginia and Mexico had been reduced to disconnected fragments: a desert highway and a Chinese restaurant that rose out of the sand like a disjunctive Xanadu; a police car that could fly to the top of a mesa; peyote tea and blood-tinged cocktails; and yes, a flaming angel leaping into the sea. All images as real to me as countless other mundane memories, yet images that logically could not be true, even if I could somehow connect the dots into some chimerical hyperimage. "Am I insane?" I asked my son.

"Well, like, if you aren't, you ought to be," he said. "That's why I decided we should have this talk. I mean, since Mom's going to be in treatment for a few hours yet, and we never seem to get a chance to talk. I mean alone. I mean man to man. Man to boy. Whatever."

"Weird," I said. "I thought I was manipulating you into having this conversation, but it turns out you were manipulating me."

"No jokes, Dad," said Theo. "Let's be serious."

This had to be some kind of Möbius-stripping timeloop. We were back at the beginning of the dialogue, but somehow our lines had gotten switched.

"All right," I said. "Assume that I've forgotten everything. Speak to me. Tell me."

"All right. To start off with, how much do you remember about the trip down here? Do you remember the Chinese restaurant?"

"I think so."

"We took a detour. Across a hundred dimensions. And we had a run-in with the Darklings. They're the family that rules the thousand worlds connected by the River. They're what you might call dysfunctional. Like us. They're fighting over the kingdom, you know, like King Lear's three daughters, and I was captured by Thorn, the vampire, because I'm a truthsayer and I can navigate between worlds; and then Katastrofa— she's a weredragon, kidnapped Josh because she thought he'd kind of be able to do what I do—and Mr. Stone, that Navajo policeman, he led you to us through a sandpainting—and Mom's really an aspect of the One Mother—are you following me?"

I was confused. More than confused. Sullenly, I bit off another piece of pepperoni pizza and wished in vain for a tall, stiff drink. My son was narrating all this very matter-of-factly, the way one might discuss the weather, and every one of the outlandish things he said rang true. But none of it made sense.

"If I really have another son," I said, "where is he now?"

"He's dead," said Theo. "He jumped into the sea. We don't have much time. We may still be able to save him."

I saw the face of the flaming angel. For a moment I almost grasped the truth. Then it slipped away again. I looked at my watch.

"She's not due back for a while yet," Theo said. They were trying out a new procedure on her. "Let's go for a walk."

"You want to go and see the festival?" I said, though the prospect did not fill me with glee.

"Sure." He got up. We didn't clear away our plates—the domestics at the clinic were relentlessly efficient—but started working our way to the edge of the cliff, where a stairway wound precipitously downward to the beach. It was windy and my son moved swiftly, leaping the steps two, three at a time, his hands barely skimming the rickety banister. Now and then, at a landing, he would wait for me. Below, a boardwalk snaked along the shore, from the edge of town, past the clinic and the clustered bungalows, toward the cliffs just north of us, where there was a sacred cave, dedicated to Our Lady of the Sluggish Tears, a limestone statue of the Virgin that, the tourist brochure told us, weeps "so gently that only a few tears may be collected each year, and these precious drops are of miraculous abilities, being imbued with curative powers." (When we first came to the clinic, we'd done the obligatory visit to this tawdry shrine and bought the obligatory postcards and bottles of holy water spiked with a few molecules of those sacred tears.)

As we descended, the wind brought the fish-salt smell of the sea and the sizzle of salsa music and the crowds and the surf. A black-clad procession moved along the boardwalk, accompanied by a funereal and out-of-tune brass band, punctured and punctuated by the flatus of a bass drum. It was a sorry excuse for a festival. Though I had not, admittedly, ever seen a better one. Except—

Moving toward the citadel of Caliosper, a million times a million, human and monstrous, a throng more multitudinous than the extras in a 50s spectacle—

Another misplaced memory.

We had reached the boardwalk. There were stalls that sold candles shaped like skulls, marzipan rotting corpses, skeleton costumes, clay and *papier-mâché* tableaux of skeletons engaged in such pursuits as golfing, skin diving, driving limousines, and giving one another enemas; there were *mestizos* hawking fake Rolexes; and everywhere the American families—the children in strident skater pants and the parents with strident voices—strutting about with stereotypical American arrogance. Yet I knew that these families were largely like mine: each had a loved one dying of cancer; each had come to the Laetrile clinic in a final, forlorn hope. Perhaps that was why they acted with such exaggerated good cheer, and clung so fiercely to the archetype of the American.

We stopped at a candy stall and I bought Theo a sugared skull with glittering ruby eyes. An old woman begged and a New Yorker with a blue beehive hairdo complained noisily about the poverty and the filth. In the procession, dwarfs with whited faces swallowed fire, and a coffin was borne on the shoulders of masked youths.

In the midst of all this there came a procession of another kind. A cadaverous bald man in an Armani suit was striding through the throng, advancing on each obvious American, shaking hands vigorously, kissing the odd baby. Behind him were a dozen secret servicemen (one can always tell from the suits) and half a dozen flamboyantly pneumatic young women, passing out stickers, buttons, and autographed pictures.

"It's Congressman Karpovsky," I said, suddenly aware that there was a world outside the Laetrile clinic—and that back in the States there was an election going on. "Isn't he running for president or something?"

Theo laughed. "But why would he be doing that here? Unless Mexico's like, become the fifty-first state while we weren't looking."

Karpovsky loomed over us suddenly. "Gotta cater to the special interests, my boy," he roared above the pandemonium. "It's a good question, lad, glad ya asked it. I'm getting in a photo-op here because of my national health plan. We're gonna have a tax credit for alternative medicine—ya know, acupuncture, voodoo, hoodoo, faith healers. Gotta break the backs of the medical establishment before they break ours, eh? Ho, ho, ho."

At that moment, one of the attractive women handing out bumper stickers broke ranks and ran up to us. A child-woman, really; she could have been as young as seventeen, except that her suit, her heels, and her sophisticated makeup had metamorphosed her into an ageless *Vogue* cover.

"Hey, Mr. E.! Theo!" she cried, and she and Theo hugged each other as though they were the closest of siblings. I sort of resented it a little. My son had not hugged me in six months. Nor I him. In fact, as I was to learn later, we had not even been inhabiting the same universe.

The woman turned her attention to me, catching me in an almost torrid embrace, while Congressman Karpovsky looked on with a raised eyebrow. I didn't have the slightest notion who she was.

"Just go along with it for now, Mr. E.," she whispered in my ear. "I'll totally explain everything later."

Theo was smiling broadly for the first time in maybe two weeks. He yanked at my sleeve and then whispered, "It's Serena Somers, Josh's old girlfriend. You don't remember her because you don't remember Josh. It's okay. It's all gonna come back to you soon."

"Congressman," said Serena, "this man's a famous poet—from inside the beltway, no less. Philip Etchison."

"No, really? Met you at the *Washington Post* cafeteria one time. I was giving an interview and you were having lunch with that Dirda fellow. An editor at *Book World*. You remember?"

I didn't remember him.

"Congressman," Serena said, "look, I'm about up for my break and—"

"Sure, dear," said the congressman, "see you back at HQ." He saw a demographically photogenic family and loped off to shake their hands.

Theo said, "I thought you said you were never going to work for him again—that he like sexually harassed you or something."

"Oh, he's in therapy," Serena said. "Keeps his hands to himself now. Chews nicotine whenever his hormones rage too much."

"How's ASU?"

"Oh, I'm not going to ASU at all now . . . I'm taking a year off . . . transferring to Dartmouth . . . well, you know, Arizona . . . I don't like the memories."

"I know what you mean." Theo's eyes darted, as though some ancient enemy stood in the shadows, though the sun had not yet set.

I stood there in a crowd of dancing skeletons. My son and this woman were clearly on terms of the utmost intimacy. They jabbered on, their hands constantly touching, like people who have harrowed hell together and are continually surprised by the miracle of still being alive. I stood in utmost bewilderment. Serena Somers . . . somehow the epithet *sluglike* came to mind, but it was not an adjective that could easily be applied to this poised young woman.

When she was sure the congressman was out of earshot, Serena said, "Actually, the real reason I came down here was to see you. I hitched a ride on the Karpovsky bandwagon because I couldn't talk my mother into springing for a ticket to Mexico. And it's true he's in counseling, otherwise none of the girls would be working for him—they all know his reputation. But look, there's not much time. Everything's shifting again. We've had a reprieve, but the war's not over."

"Uh huh," said Theo. "I've been feeling it too, I guess."

"What war?" I said. "What reprieve?"

"I've been getting like weird vibes for about six months now. Like one day last week, I knew for a fact that Ronald Reagan was president of the U.S., not Mondale."

"He *is,* isn't he?" I said.

"And then there's the right-left thing. One day I wake up and we're driving on the left, and we've always driven on the left, and we've always had a bay window that faces the sunset and a dog named Buffy, but then other days it's the cat who's named Buffy and there's no bay window."

"It's the Darklings," Theo said. "They're sifting through reality again. They want me back. Or maybe it's Josh, trying to claw his way back to the land of the living. But he can't because we've all turned away from him, because he doesn't exist here, never has, never will."

"I haven't turned my back on Joshua," I said. "I'm not even sure who he is supposed to be."

"You really have forgotten everything, haven't you, Mr. E.?" asked Serena.

"He sure has," said my son. "I've been trying to break it to him gently all day, but he's not really grasping it."

"Mr. E., you have to think about Joshua."

—a flaming angel—

"All right. I'm thinking. I'm thinking."

—a flaming—

"Come on, Dad, this won't wait, stop playing mindgames."

—flaming—

Dark angels roared past us, their black robes flapping in the wind. The sun was setting at last and they were breaking out the candles for the vigil of the dead. I bought a Corona from a passing vendor and slugged it down. I *was* starting to remember. Didn't want to remember. The pain. Better to block it out. (That's why I will always be a second-rate poet. I don't have the guts to face my pain. I have the words, but I have nothing to say.)

"He was your son, Mr. E. He flew away on the wings of a gold-scaled dragon woman."

—a shadowy figure stood behind Theo, his face mottled by the cotton-wood leaves as they speckled the sunset, and—

Flaming.

Serena took my hand. And Theo took my other hand. I shrank back from his touch, which had become unfamiliar over the past months. But he gripped me hard, demanding. Perhaps it was I who had withdrawn from him, I who had failed to give. Serena's hand was warm, Theo's cold and uncompromising.

"We're gonna fucking *make* you remember, Dad. Come on. We're taking you to Mom."

"But the clinic's south of here," I said, for I saw that they were leading me north, along the wooden path that led past the makeshift bazaar toward the grotto of the limestone Madonna.

"We know where we're going," said Serena softly. "It's you who are lost."

CHAPTER TWO

STEALING THE MADONNA

Theo Etchison

When I see Serena Somers elbowing her way through the crowd toward us, I know it's finally time to get back to the River. Because if Serena has somehow contrived to come here, then she must know about Joshua. Which means I'm not the only one who's managed to keep sane while the universe tries to boomerang back on itself and to unchange the changes in reality.

"Go easy on my dad," I tell Serena. "He's old. It's hard for him to leap tall universes in a single bound."

"Weren't you fat once?" Dad says. I can tell that another image has surfaced in his mind.

"Yeah, I guess," says Serena. "But I like myself now."

"Dad, they're coming back for us. They can't play their game without me, and . . . if I get sucked in, you will too. And there's Josh, floating around in limbo, not dead, not alive."

My father looks terrible. Before Mom got sick, before I began having the dreams that all turned out to be true, Dad used to charm us with words . . . not charm as in flirting or being cute but charm as in what you do with a snake; he'd make words dance around you till you were dizzy. Since Mom was diagnosed . . . well, kind of since the chemotherapy started I guess . . . he's been losing the gift. Now's another time when words fail him. He looks around and I bet anything the one thought that's racing through his mind is like, I want a drink. I don't want these memories to breach the placid surface of my mind. Because each one hurts.

Dad says, "I see a flaming angel. He is leaping into the sea."

"Come on, Serena," I say. We still haven't loosened our grip on his hands because we feel he's going to slip into what Ash calls disjunctive fugue, when the universe *twangs* back and forth on itself like a guitar string and your brain can't keep up with the changes.

We lead him gently north toward the cave. And as we move, we're kind of like a magnet moving through a pile of iron filings. I mean, the crowd begins to align itself, begins to get a direction. It's darkening and they are lighting candles and falling in with the procession. Over the ocean's tangy smell there's a hint of incense.

Dad says, "Let's start with an hour ago, when Theo and I were sitting on the veranda waiting for Mary to come back from treatment."

"Dad, you've been waiting for her to come back for three days now. Maybe it was only a few minutes for you, but the world has shifted like half a dozen times and you've just been sitting there, in a little puddle of your own private time. We had a nuclear holocaust yesterday and all life was destroyed. You don't remember that, of course. The world was wrenched back on course and everyone's memories have been erased. Except mine, because I'm a truthsayer. I had to twist back the course of the River so that the war never happened. It's okay. Some of the more sensitive people in the world will have a vague feeling that it happened . . . like they've woken from a nightmare but they can't remember the details."

Serena says, "Wow. I dreamed I was in a forest fire. The trees were crashing all around me and I was all, No! No! but no one could hear me screaming."

"That wasn't a dream," I tell her. I know that she believes me. She's been able to swallow a lot of inconceivable truths. It's because she loves Josh so much; this love has clung to her like the strand of wool that showed Theseus the way out of the labyrinth.

God I envy people their dreams. Recently I came to the realization that I've never really had a dream. I can't dream because I'm a truthsayer. For me the very act of dreaming makes it true.

"Anyway," I tell Dad, "it's all over now, and it's not even that important. The main thing is us. We're at the center of this storm. The Darklings are trying to throw our world out of phase, but it's only because they want *us*. They couldn't give a shit about one tenth-rate planet in a distant corner of a Z-grade galaxy. You'd better start remembering soon, Dad, because they're chasing us down."

As I'm saying this, darkness is falling—wham!—like a fade-out in a movie. And the candles are everywhere—tall candles, short candles, scented candles, and the special Day of the Dead candles shaped like human skulls—most of them in like these glass holders to keep the wind from blowing them out. I suck my sugar skull. The sugar tastes bitter. Maybe it's my mood and maybe it's another reality shift. I throw the skull into a trash can heaped with Corona bottles. And suddenly the night is scary. The crowd's pressing on us. It's carrying us toward the shrine whether we want to go or not. Dwarfs and mutants and skeletons dance past us and the candlelight flickers so their white-faced features seem to bob up and down in the sea of night. Musics clash: salsa music, funereal brass music, and in the distance a church choir singing words in Latin that sound like *libera me, domine, libera me, domine.* And the wind is roaring now, though we can't feel it much because there's this line of market stalls with canvas awnings shielding us from the sea.

There were like a whole bunch of American tourists out, but they all seem to have melted into the shadows. I don't know . . . this afternoon the festival seemed all fake and plasticky and now it's starting to feel real. I can smell death. I'm scared. Even more than when I reversed the holocaust, because that was an impersonal kind of thing, feeling the glitch in the flow of the river and steering hard to starboard to get the world back on course—truthsayers do things like that all the time, they nudge the universe and mostly the universe snaps back by itself, like a rubber band.

So here we are being sucked into the flow of a human river. And it reminds me of the trek to Caliosper . . . it's easy to imagine in the pandemonium the beating of aliens' wings. I wonder when the Darklings will start to appear.

"Why don't we walk by the beach?" Dad says. "We'll get there quicker."

"No, Dad. Don't you remember? Water could be a gateway."

"Yeah. Right." I think he sees, or is starting to see at least. We move swiftly, the three of us, threading our way through the throng. Pallbearers dance and the coffin lid goes *bang bang bang* as the cadaver within pops up to crack jokes and strum his guitar. Flamenco dancers leap and twirl. The air is a collage of gasoline and incense and fish and tamales and old puke.

"Hurry, hurry," I tell him. But there can't be any hurry, really. The whole crowd is headed the same way. Up ahead is the Madonna's grotto, its entrance glittering with thousands of twinkling Christmas-type lights. Of course the Madonna has nothing to do with the Day of the Dead, but here in this Disney-style Mexicoland all the traditions are tossed together like a Waldorf salad. There are the black-robed women mourning the tears of the world . . . they don't belong here at all . . . I last saw them on Thorn's world . . . in another cave next to a different sea. But

they are here, palms folded, floating alongside the parade. And there
. . . whirling through the skeleton celebrants . . . isn't that Cornelius
Huang, towering Fu-Manchuishly over the dancers? He lifts his conch to
his lips . . . I hear its savage blast rip through the salsa cacophony. "Oh,
Jesus, hurry, hurry."

There's the entrance to the cave. All of sudden, inexplicably, there's
silence. The crowd has fallen reverently to its knees. Not a whimper
except the battering of the surf against the shore. The three of us are the
only ones standing. The lights around the entrance shimmer and then
they're all like the lights in Times Square in New York where they have
the newspaper headlines scrolling across, and the lights flash:

WELCOME THEO TRUTHSAYER BACK TO THE FRAY
and
ONLY YOU CAN SAVE THE UNIVERSE
and
THOUGHT YOU COULD ESCAPE, EH? MUAHAHAHAHA!!!

which prompts my dad to say, "Hm. I suppose this might be considered sort of the comic-book interpretation of the cosmos."

"Yeah, Dad, but . . . in a way . . . the cosmos is what I dream. And
maybe I'm bright, because you always read poetry to me and make me
watch foreign movies on PBS and shit, but . . . I'm still a kid underneath and I still have a comic book kind of a mind."

"My son, the solipsist!"

"Better pay attention to what he's saying, Mr. E.," Serena says. "The
weirder it gets, the truer it is."

The three of us are the only ones standing. Half the town is prostrate
around us. The sea of backs stretches all the way to the sea of water.

"Come on, Dad, hurry the fuck up," I say. I'm really scared now. I've
seen a shadow flitting at the periphery of my vision.

And then we're at the entrance to the cave.

And then we're inside. There's so much incense that we seem to be
standing in the clouds. Serena coughs. Through the mist we see the
pinprick flames of a thousand candles. A choir is singing. It's those same
words: *libera me, domine, libera me, domine . . . free me, lord.* Could
they be addressing themselves to me? Oh shit I hope not. In this world
I'm just a kid, frail and powerless. Sure, I wrench the course of time back
on track once in a while but hey, it's all in the dreaming, it's not supposed
to leak out into the real world. I can't free anyone. Not here. Not yet.

I feel in the pocket of my shorts. I'm looking for the plain glass marble
that is actually a schematic chart of the entire River. I touch something
cold. That's probably it, but in this world it's probably only a marble.

There's an altar rail, but there's too much smoke to see what's behind it. We only see the tall man with the Chinese features and the Mandarin hat, with the conch tucked under one arm. Apart from the hat, he is clothed in the vestments of a priest.

"Cornelius," I say softly.

"You," he says to me, "I expect you to know my name. But these others . . . they shouldn't remember anything. They're not part of this scenario. You'd better get rid of them before we're forced to eliminate them completely."

My father lets go of my hand suddenly. "I remember now! There was a Chinese restaurant . . . you said you were a fan of my poetry . . . you kidnapped my son." There's so much anger in him. It's all coming back at once. The hurt. The grief. The fury. "You took him away and you and that . . . that vampire master of yours . . . and you were using him for . . . for something."

Cornelius Huang smiles.

". . . and my other son . . . you've done something to him."

"Not my department," says Huang.

Behind the wind and the surf we hear another sound . . . yes . . . the beating of mighty wings and the hollow roar of a dragon's breath. So I know Katastrofa is in the vicinity too, circling above the cliffs maybe, waiting to pounce.

Huang holds out his hand and a crystal goblet materializes in it. It fills with a frothy red liquid.

"You're just in time for communion," he says.

Oremus, the choir thunders.

Huang raises up the goblet. "The Holy Grail," he says. "But are you worthy of it?"

The grail sparkles in the candlelight.

Ave verum corpus, shrieks the choir.

My father is staring at the chalice. He's hypnotized by it. I know the power it has over him. "Don't take the wine, Dad!" I scream. "It's gonna make you blind again, you'll forget everything—" But Dad's moving toward the altar rail and he genuflects in front of Cornelius Huang as his lips widen in an orca smile. Serena runs forward and dashes the goblet out of Huang's hand and it crashes somewhere, we hear the tinkle and the long long echo of it through the cavern as above our heads the stalactites seem to whirl and Huang's standing there, looking at his bleeding hand, still clutching a shard of glass that has sliced into his palm, and the blood is spurting up, spritzing my father, moistening his lips, and my father's all, "Howl, howl, howl," like he was wandering through a high school production of *King Lear*. And Cornelius Huang says, "Children, children; you force me to take dire measures."

He blows one shattering blast on that conch of his and that's when the cave kind of splits apart like an egg. The tide must have been rising or something because now seawater's sluicing in through the cracks in the cave wall. People are screaming. I think we're having a flood. I can hear the ocean battering at the cliffs. And all of a sudden we're moving . . . I mean we're still in the cave but the cave has been unmoored from the world and the cave's become part of a big old ship and I *know* that ship . . . it's Thorn's ship, and I know we're adrift once more on the great River that runs between the worlds, and that the cave is nothing more than another inlet of that River . . . and there's Dad, still kneeling at the altar, baptized in the blood from the herald's hand. Oh fucking Jesus I am scared because I hadn't wanted it to happen that way. I didn't want to see Thorn again, to fall into his power. I don't see him now but I know he's got to be close.

Just then Serena tugs at me and yes, we're still enveloped in mist, but through a break above our heads we can see Thorn and Katastrofa, brother and sister, battling in the sky. Thorn is a monstrous bat and Katastrofa a crystal dragon coiling and uncoiling around the bat's torso. Blood rains from Thorn's lips. "You don't have me yet," I cry to Cornelius Huang. "And you don't have Dad or Serena. Your master's desperately fighting for control of me."

"But it is I who have custody," Cornelius says, without unclenching his teeth.

"Not yet. I appeal to the Madonna for protection," I say, and I leapfrog over my dad and into the outstretched arms of the Madonna.

The mist around her clears. Mom's face looks down on me. A single tear has been moving down her cheek for many months. She is pale and veined in pink; she is stone and flesh at the same time. She used to have a stone child in her arms, but now she has only me.

Dad looks up. "Oh, my God," he whispers. "It's Mary."

Serena says, "That's what we've been trying to tell you, Mr. E. On Earth, which is like only a shadow of the greater world, Mrs. E.'s a middle-aged woman with cancer, but like in the *real* universe your wife is like the great mother goddess of everything. She only seems to be a statue because time moves so slowly for her that sometimes she doesn't take a breath in a thousand years. And your wife has cancer because, in the *real* universe, everything's falling apart because of the war between the Darklings."

I don't think Dad really has time to assimilate this because the battle in the sky seems to have finished in a draw and both bat and dragon are plummeting toward us, talons outstretched, and we're like three blind mice, or maybe sitting ducks, nowhere to run or hide . . . so I put my arms around the statue and I say softly, "Help me . . . Mom . . . wherever you are . . . if you can hear me . . ." as Huang advances toward me with a butterfly net in his hands. . . .

Something happens to the statue. The tear, which was glistening on her cheek, begins to race down it, and more tears come welling up, and the stone heats up so it almost burns me. And what happens next is incredible because her arm comes flying up and it sort of hits Huang in the face and he goes flying into a wall of candles. It's a supreme effort of her will to condense time like that. Somewhere in the universe a sun has died to fuel her gesture. Then, well, the statue like freezes up again, this time in the new posture with its arm upraised, and the brother and sister Darkling are still hurtling down toward us, but the statue's movements bought me maybe a split second to act.

I pull the marble out of my pocket. I home in on our location inside the twisted strands of the River which are all folded up inside the marble. I forge a new rivulet. Not for me, because I know I must stay and fight and maybe bring my brother home. But Dad and Serena have to go home. They're not involved. They shouldn't get stuck here. They're not truthsayers. No one has the right to make them pawns in all this. It was selfish of me to try to drag Dad into this, I realize. Better to leave him back on earth, to have him lose all memory of me or Joshua . . . for then, if we don't return, he will never know how he once loved us, or the pain of losing us. Oh, God, why did I have to remind him about Josh? How could I have wished the pain of remembrance on him? No. No. I summon the wall of water and it rises from the sea.

"Don't fight it, Dad . . . Serena . . ." I say. "Go with it. It'll take you back to where you started from."

I force the water in over Dad and Serena and watch the current carrying them away, toward home.

Then I wait for the shadows to swoop down and carry me away.

But that doesn't happen. Instead, I feel the statue heave, uproot itself, and me along with it, raising itself slowly into the air. Bat and dragon plunge into the water. The salt spray soaks me. I look around. The statue, the altar, the railing, the limestone floor of the cavern, all these things are hovering above the sea. We're cupped in the palm of a hand a hundred feet wide, and the palm is attached to a gigantic elbow which is connected to a monstrous arm which is bending as the hand rises up toward a human face which is gradually blotting out the entire sky. . . .

It's a weatherbeaten face, with long white wind-whipped hair and now I see the lips parting and the stench of the giant's breath billows around us. I know the face. It's Strang, the mad king, the one whose kingdom the three children are battling over, the one who once caged the darkness in a crystal scepter and was given dominion over all the worlds fed by the River that leads every place.

"Mom . . ." I say. "It's Strang."

The jaws gape, snap shut. With us inside, coasting on a stream of saliva. The statue of the One Mother and I are rolling down the king's esophagus. *Dad! Serena! Joshua!* I try to cling to their memories as we slide down the monster's gullet. I'm choking on the fetor. I don't think I'll ever see them again. At least I've saved Dad and Serena, I think. The universe can wait for someone better than me, stronger, more compassionate. Blackness engulfs me, and I'm full of despair.

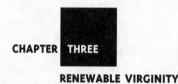

CHAPTER THREE

RENEWABLE VIRGINITY

S e r e n a   S o m e r s

We broke through the wall of water. Me and Mr. E., that is. I knew that Theo had done it. He probably thought he was saving our lives. If you can call it living.

We were back in the cave, but there was no statue behind the altar rail.

About a dozen choirboys were chanting listlessly, and censers were being swung. An old Indian woman prayed beside the rows of candles. From outside came the sounds of the festival. There had never been a flood. The Darklings had never come.

"Where's—" said Mr. E., rubbing his eyes as though wakening from a nightmare. "Where's—" I suddenly realized that he couldn't remember Theo's name.

Theo had never existed.

Even I, who loved Theo like a brother, couldn't remember the color of his eyes. That's the remarkable thing about all these reality shifts. They edit the whole past as well as the present. A universe vanishes and another replaces it. In the world where I used to go out with Joshua Etchison and he had this weird, introverted brother who had an uncanny habit of blurting out the truth at the wrong moment, where he lived with his poet father and his dying mother in a Virginia suburb of Washington . . . in that world I'd been a virgin. Not that I'd wanted to be. I was too scared not to be. I made myself fat so that I could stay a virgin. In the minutes between wakefulness and sleep I'd fantasize about Joshua.

Then I learned that this whole universe was a backwater tributary of the River that flows from universe to universe, and that Theo was a truthsayer, one of the few beings with the ability to navigate from world to world . . . and that his services were being fought over by the Darkling siblings as they battled each other for control of a mega-universe, a cosmic egg that was rapidly splintering into pieces that King Strang's horses and men couldn't put together again, not without Theo's ability always to see the truth, and to know the true names of things. He alone could hear the original music of the universe, of which every other universe is only an echo. Oh, yeah, Theo was special. Some might even call him God, since it couldn't really be determined whether it was him dreaming the universe into being or just him seeing the truth at the center of the infinite onion skins of illusion. He was the key to everything. The still point of the turning world, Mr. E. would probably say, since he always quotes other people's poetry in moments of confusion. Theo the God. Theo $= mc^2$. And all this time we'd just thought he was weird.

They came and took Theo away, and the world, rushing in to fill the vacuum of his absence, made it so that he never existed. And Phil, his father, had no memory of him at all. Mr. E.'s a poet, and poets are supposed to be truthsayers in a way, but Philip Etchison would've been the first to admit that he wasn't that kind of poet. He was always down on his own poetry, ever since he got passed over for the Pulitzer. But Joshua remembered. Because he had a piece of Theo's talent, a watered-down version of it.

So they took Joshua away. But the journey into other worlds is a kind of death, and Joshua wasn't properly prepared for it, and by the time Mr. E. and I found him, he was already dead. But he was also undead.

I sacrificed my virginity to save his life.

I guess I have a bit of the talent too, though not as much as Joshua and certainly not like Theo, who's like a totally different kind of being; I mean, he doesn't even *think* in past and present, everything's always present to him, and every possibility is equally real, equally unreal. Yeah.

Well, we all came back from the River. Me and Mr. E. and Theo and Joshua, and Mrs. E., who had gone from a terminal cancer patient to a hallucinating schizophrenic to the goddess of the universe and back again to a dying woman. But see, Joshua had kind of gotten used to being dead.

That's why he leaped into the sea.

Joshua had never existed. Which meant I had never made love to him to save him from the dragon woman Katastrofa, second child of the mad King Strang. Which made me a virgin again. Reconstituted my hymen and everything. I hadn't had a physical examination, but I was sure of it. That was something that made me different from my other friends in school. I never really went out with anyone. I just radiated this hands off thing, I guess. Which was strange since the boy I loved had never existed.

Okay. I was thinking all this out, trying to get it all straight because I was giving it all to Mr. E., in chronological order, as we walked along the boardwalk in Baja down to the asylum. Theo and I *had* been trying to explain it all to him before, but it always came out jumbled because we never knew how much he could actually remember or how much he could take before his mind would go off into a labyrinth of disjunctive fugue.

Did I say the asylum?

"I thought we were at a Laetrile clinic," Mr. E. said.

We'd walked about half a mile and I had already eaten three of those sugar skulls they were selling in every stall. That meant I was scared, so scared I'd forgotten my pledge—I'd stuck to it for a year now—no more eating disorders. I knew I was going to chomp down enough candy skulls so I'd be up half the night puking in the hotel room.

"You don't understand, Mr. E. There *is* no Laetrile clinic, because Mrs. E.'s not dying of cancer anymore. Don't you remember? I told you five minutes ago . . . when you lose your sons, your wife's disease usually changes to something else. Last time it was schizophrenia."

"This is madness."

"Yeah. It is."

At least it was still November 2nd, in the last decade of the twentieth century, on a beach in Baja. I was pretty sure of that. When reality changes it takes the path of least resistance. So I was probably still here working for Congressman Karpovsky and all that. I wasn't certain of that, but I told Mr. E. that even though the clinic was gone, the Hyatt would still be there.

We worked our way through the crowd of celebrants. There were a lot of tourists. Even though they were wearing the skeleton outfits too (they were selling them in the hotel for $5, one size fits all) the tourists had like this corn-fed look about them, you know, you can take the boy out of Idaho but you can't take the Idaho out of the boy, that kind of thing? And that was different. Because when we were walking toward the shrine the tourists had like all faded away and there was this sense of menace . . . maybe because the minions of Thorn and Katastrofa had infiltrated the festival. Okay. It was back to normal now. Muzak and fakery. Popped another candied skull. Sucked another soul. It was hot and sticky on my tongue.

We walked on without talking for a while. A sandy street led away from the boardwalk, into town. Just a few feet from the festival and there wasn't a living soul. I guess the whole town was out there playing "puttin' on the tourists." We walked uphill. The street wound a lot, hugging the contour of the landscape, I guess. The music was faint now.

"I don't remember this cemetery," Mr. E. said. "In fact. . . ."

I could tell that the disjunction was hitting him hard. I guessed that the Laetrile clinic must have been here last time he looked. Now, instead, there was an adobe-walled church, a graveyard . . . with a great view of the sea and the fireworks display, far away, over the water, strangely quiet.

"Remember," I said, holding his hand. "You never came to any clinic."

"Then what am I doing here?"

"Reality takes the path of least resistance. Theo explained it to me once. It's like the way matter curves the fabric of space, making a big gravity well around itself, you know? Well, you and I, Mr. E., with our sentient souls, we curve the fabric of perception around us. So even though there may be no logical reason for you to be in Mexico anymore, it's easier for it to give you some wild serendipitous excuse for occupying this bit of space here than it is to send you careening across to Virginia. Know what I mean?"

We found ourselves opening the wrought-iron gates and entering the churchyard. The place was full of people . . . it would be, being the Day of the Dead . . . and many of the graves were brightly lit with candles. There were like clusters of people around each of the candlelit graves, and they were eating and drinking . . . the air smelled of flowers and corn tortillas. This was a lot closer to the real thing than the revelry by the beach. A solemn-eyed kid sat on a tombstone, chugging a Corona and puffing on a cigarette. There was a subtle war of musics . . . three or four ghettoblasters playing everything from Menudo to Metallica . . . but softly, unobtrusively. Each of the families was doing its own thing, whether it was weeping over the dead relatives' photographs or leaving offerings of tamales and even, on one grave, a neatly stacked pyramid of unopened Big Macs . . . or just sitting around catching some rays . . . moon rays, that is . . . there was a full moon in a cloudless sky.

"But Serena . . ." said Mr. E. "Our bungalow used to be over there. This wasn't a cemetery at all, it was where our family was staying, you know, during the treatment." He pointed to a patch almost flush with the cliff edge. Now there were only grave markers. "My car was right there. If that's disappeared, and never existed, how the hell am I supposed to have gotten here in the first place?"

"How should I know?" I said. "Let's check it out."

We walked through knee-high grass. The grass tickled the holes in my jeans. It suddenly occurred to me that I hadn't been wearing jeans before—I'd been in my designer uniform, the one all of Congressman Karpovsky's campaign flunkies wore—relentlessly yuppie-looking. Did this mean I wasn't with Karpovsky? Was there a new set of memories that I hadn't cottoned on to yet, a whole 'nother reason why I happened to be in Mexico and not in Tucson studying for a Literature test?

At the cliff's edge, a low wooden railing was all that stood between us and a sheer drop into the ocean. We could see the parade going on far below, an undulating snake of candlelight from the town to the Virgin's shrine.

There weren't a whole lot of graves on this end of the cemetery and none of them were decorated with flowers, lights, and foodstuffs. In fact, Mr. E. and I seemed isolated from the others all of a sudden.

"This is where we were sitting, on white chairs with wrought-iron backs," Mr. E. said. "I and . . . someone. You're telling me it was my son."

"Your son Theo."

"I think I see him in my mind's eye. He's slender and small for his age, almost as though he'd willed himself not to cross into puberty country. His hair's a mess and . . . dirty blond and . . . I think . . . a Redskins T-shirt. Too long. Hugging his knees almost. I wish I'd picked up a Corona down there at one of the food stalls."

"No, no! No alcohol. Hang *on* to that memory, Mr. E.! Sometimes, when these disjunctions happen, the only thing left to anchor you to the last reality is . . . you know . . . a face, a landscape, maybe even just a smell."

"God! I just remembered how Theo smelled."

"Yeah. Smells don't lie."

"He wasn't grubby. His T-shirt was always soaked in sweat but it had a kind of sweet smell. A residue of the Teenage Mutant Ninja Turtles bubble bath that kid Jesus gave him for Christmas."

"Jesus?"

"Yeah . . . a scrawny little Mexican kid who used to hang out by the veranda. He and Theo ran around together a lot. I mean, they didn't exactly *communicate,* because he didn't speak a word of English. Maybe Theo taught him a few words. I don't know. Jesus Ortega. Yes."

"You sure remember a lot, Mr. E., considering the evidence of your eyes, which totally contradicts everything you're saying. I think you must have a little bit of the talent after all. Well, it's not surprising that it'd be in the genes, is it, now?" But I was pretty frustrated because I knew there was so much more that he *couldn't* remember. What is it about people when they hit middle age? Memory becomes slippery. Images slide away like eels.

"I remember that I'm supposed to be waiting for my wife. And we have a car, a battered old gas guzzler, and it's parked about there . . . by that headstone."

A firework went off overhead. It lit up the headstone and we both read the name at the same time:

Mary Etchison

"Oh, God," said Mr. Etchison. "Oh, God, she's dead."

CHAPTER FOUR

FREE FALLING

<u>T h e o   E t c h i s o n</u>

So it's like I'm plunging down this well. I think it's a well because of the way it echoes. But it's dark and I've lost my hold on the Madonna. I fall and fall. Eventually . . . though I know I'm still falling . . . I get a grip on myself . . . it's free fall. There's no gravity. I'm weightless. Maybe I can maneuver a little bit if only I can get rid of the notion that my feet are *down* and my head is *up.*

The way I figure it, Thorn and Katastrofa were both trying to kidnap me and the One Mother. Strang intercepted them and swallowed me up.

I'm inside him in a way. But that's an illusion, like everything else in all the universes, and I know that I can see through it if I use my gift. I fumble in my pocket for the marble. This is hard because of course I'm still falling . . . probably somewhere near the velocity of light by now . . . and I have to make myself perfectly still inside before I can reach for it.

But it's there. It's cold and my hand is clammy as it wraps around it and pulls it out. There's a faint blue glow about it, and that's how I see the walls of the well for the first time. It's all massive blocks of odd-shaped stone cunningly fitted together like the cyclopean walls of Troy and Mycenae. Here and there is a niche in the wall or a shelf, and each one is crammed with an entire world. But I'm falling too fast to recognize them. I hold the marble up to my face. Inside are the million strands of light that chart the course of the River. And the filaments are twisting, writhing, weaving in and out, changing color . . . I can see that the whole structure of the universe is spinning out of control. Worlds are leaking into other worlds so fast that the cracks don't have time to heal.

I can't fix it all by myself. I'm just one of me. But I know that if the streams all fuse into one, there's not going to *be* a universe. Every world will be every other world all at the same time. It's a chain reaction. Disjunctive fugue will hit everything that has consciousness. Every reality will be true at the same time. We can't survive that. Don't the Darklings understand that they're fucking up the whole cosmos?

And I'm still falling. Falling. Falling.

Somehow I'm going to have to reach my dad . . . to call to him across the chasm that separates our worlds. I've got to find him first. It's hard because when I try to focus on him, to think myself deep into the heart of the marble, the image shifts and shimmers and won't stay still. It's because Dad's becoming a different person with every split second that passes, because he's at the intersection of a dozen lifelines and he has a dozen pasts and he doesn't have the gift of picking among them. I see him now. He's standing at the edge of the cliff. That's just where he was earlier today when I started trying to explain everything to him . . . and when the worlds started leaking out all over each other.

They're in a cemetery with low adobe walls. It's party time there. There's people feasting, praying, decorating the headstones, and some of them have fallen asleep in the tall soft grass. It's a little windy up there. There's kids running around like crazy in their little skeleton costumes. I don't see any of this that clearly . . . it's more like a kind of radar . . . the people are like little blips against a 3-D screen, and my dad and

Serena are big blips, because to them I still exist, and they're thinking of me.

That's when I notice that Jesus Ortega's one of the kids who are playing tag, weaving in and out of the headstones, sucking on corpsicles, laughing as the fireworks go off. I wonder if he's thinking about me. He's a kid and sometimes it's easier to talk to them because their world view isn't set hard, like concrete, it's still kind of fluid, and I know he probably felt the glitch when the world shifted course. But he doesn't speak a word of English. Well, he can sing the *Teenage Mutant Ninja Turtles* theme song. Big deal. But he's like five years old, so his mind is wide open, he doesn't wear the blinkers of adulthood or even of first-gradehood. Maybe I can use him as a conduit to my father.

Yeah. And as these thoughts are racing through my mind I'm still plummeting down the dream-esophagus of King Strang . . . whizzing past suns and moons and gods and goddesses and through the hearts of dusty nebulae. But I have to concentrate on the universe inside my marble . . . the microcosm. I close my eyes tight but I can still see the strands of the River . . . or rather I can feel them, I can reach my hand inside and grasp them, squeeze them, the way you might put your hand into a nest of wriggling snakes. It's got to be done though. Yeah.

—*Jesus*—

Can he hear me?

—*Hay-fucking-soooos!*—*Listen to me, you dadburned varmint!* (he hears me as a kind of spectral Yosemite Sam)—*Jesus!*

I think he hears something. He looks up. A firework bursts out up there, green, red, and white, the colors of Mexico.

"*¿Teodoro?*" he whispers. It's like he's seen a ghost. My image flickers in the candlelight. Shit, I *am* a ghost to him. I'm dead in this new version of reality. Figures. Should've known. "*¡Pero eres muerto!*"

"I know I'm dead," I tell him. He hears me in the whine of the wind. He shivers. I speak to him in images, not words. Today is the Day of the Dead and it's all right for you to hear me. I'm not going to hurt you. I need your help. Go to my father. I know you can't understand the words, but I will whisper the sounds in your ears and you'll be able to make him listen. Go, Jesus. A plan is forming in my mind. I've got to communicate with them or we'll never see each other again, and Joshua will be dead forever.

Jesus looks for his mother at first. He's frightened now. He sees his mother by the grave of his little sister. She's rocking another little sister—the twin that lived—in her arms. I guess he realizes that she's preoccupied because he looks away now, looks at where my dad and Serena are sitting, staring out to sea. I try to touch across the gulf. All he feels is a chill nothingness that creeps up his spine. "It's okay, Jesus," I say, and I start humming the *Turtles* theme song to him. And he's not scared anymore when he hears that silly ditty in the air, because I guess he realizes it's actually me and not some evil demon released by the dark magic of the *Día de los Muertos*.

Laughing, he toddles over to where my father is sitting . . . and I go on falling, falling, falling into an emptiness I dare not name.

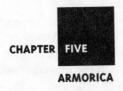

CHAPTER FIVE

ARMORICA

P h i l   E t c h i s o n

And that, to me, was the moment of epiphany.

At once I remembered it all with the crystalline immediacy of an MTV montage: the brochures about the Day of the Dead. The cross-country drive, down the 79 through West Virginia and Kentucky, then cutting a swath west, a piece of Louisiana, a chunk of Texas, New Mexico, the Arizona desert, then turning south . . . I remembered it all. The dust. The bus popping up at the hillcrest, the station wagon huffing and puffing, the big blue crowded bus with flying streamers and horn playing the opening of Beethoven's Fifth Symphony again and again, tatata-TAH, tatata-TAH, as it caromed off the side rail and into us and then Mary's frayed seatbelt breaking and the windshield shattering and the two boys bouncing downhill like bloody logs, rolling into oncoming traffic and—

The bus bursting into flames. The Mexican police. The hospital. The morgue. A town called Todos Santos. It was as though I'd dammed up the memories and the sight of the headstone had broken the wall and now I was experiencing this collage of pain for the first time.

And then there was the other set of memories. The Chinese restaurant on Route 10 just outside Tucson. The man with the slate-colored eyes. My wife dying of cancer. The smell of a dying woman couldn't easily be dislodged. Mystic journeys and fantastical beasts and flying cities—memories that could not, logically, have any truth to them—memories that warred with these new memories of terror and loss—and clamored to be recognized as truths.

There were more fireworks. I read the two smaller headstones that flanked my wife's. I understood now why this section of the graveyard wasn't decorated with flowers and candles. The markers read:

In memoriam
Joshua Etchison
and:
In loving memory of
Theo Etchison

It was the gringo section of the cemetery.

"Why aren't they buried back home, in Virginia?" Serena said. "And how did they die?"

"There was an accident. It happened . . . um . . . a year ago," I said, seeing images of the funeral for the first time. "I couldn't face going back. I was . . . on the verge of bankruptcy. I wouldn't have been able to afford the funerals back in the States. And anyway I didn't want to see any of our old friends. I didn't know how I could face *you.*" Suddenly I realized that, in *this* universe, I knew exactly who Serena was. But why couldn't I go back and face her? Oh yes. I had let Josh drive. Impetuous Josh, Josh-without-a-license. I had done it because I was all wrapped up in the opening lines of a new poem I was writing.

In the poem, a young man in a fantasy kingdom takes leave of his mother to go out into the world and seek his fortune. She admonishes him never to forget his name. But that is the first thing he forgets, and his adventures turn out to have been illusions. In the forest where things have no names, only illusions can exist. I was working on the poem or I could have warned Joshua or grabbed the steering wheel or . . . (no! screamed another part of my mind. You yourself have wandered into the forest where things have no names . . . you yourself have fallen prey to illusion. . . .)

I could tell that Serena had not known that, in this world, her boyfriend and his brother and my wife were all dead. She'd been relatively calm up to that point, methodically explicating the implausible sequence of events that had brought us to this juncture, but now she was starting to cry. "Mrs. E. wasn't supposed to be *dead,*" she said. "Just—you know, like in a psychiatric ward or something—so we could rescue her like we did before. I can't take this, I can't see a way out of this mess."

"There now," I said. "There now."

I embraced her. We sat down at the edge of the cliff. We looked out over the sea. I thought of the flaming angel. Serena sobbed like a child. I remembered how plucky she had been when she rescued Mary from the asylum and—

But that was another memory, from another universe.

We sat for a long time, not talking. In the cemetery, a strolling band strummed and sang love songs to the dead. A kid—it was one I'd noticed earlier, belting down a bottle of beer—came up to us and offered us some tamales from a basket.

"Thanks a lot, kid," I said, and fished in my wallet for a couple of bucks.

"Hey, no money, Felipe," he said. And when I looked at him blankly, he said, "You don't recognize me? You think we all looking alike, maybe? I'm Jesus Ortega, you know, the one who play with your son."

"But my son is dead."

Jesus laughed. "You silly man," he said, "your son dead, yes. I play with him." He cackled and did a little dance around Theo's gravestone. Chasing the wind. "Cowabunga, dude!" he shrieked. He listened to the wind and answered it with a string of lilting Spanglish.

"Theo . . . he's your imaginary companion?" I asked him. I had to shout because the wind had begun to whine as soon as Jesus started dancing . . . almost as though it were reacting to the boy.

"You silly old man," said the boy, "you know Theo he is the wind. He is the wind and he talk to me, very clear, in the laughing."

For a moment I heard the laughter of my son. Serena must have heard it too because she stiffened in shock. She was shaking. I could feel the warmth drain from her hands, her cheeks.

"Theo's talking to us," she said. "That's *his* voice. Listen."

I hear the clink of beer bottles, the silvery tinkle of children's laughter.

"It *is* Theo," Serena said. "The kid, he's like *channeling* him or something. I bet Jesus doesn't even speak English. He looks . . . um, the way I look when I'm in Spanish class and Professor Schmitz makes me read aloud from, you know, *Don Quijote* or something—and I'm just sounding it out, one syllable at a time, not getting any of it."

There he was, holding out his basket of tamales and smiling. He had the kind of large, liquidescing eyes that you see on those Sally Struthers late night sponsor-a-starving-child telethons. I took a tamale and peeled the husk and wolfed it down even though it was really drink I craved, not food.

"Stone," said the boy.

I looked around. He's talking about the headstones maybe.

In memory of my beloved son
JOSHUA EMERSON ETCHISON
1975-1992

But wait a minute . . . hadn't it said "In memoriam" before? And "Emerson" wasn't my son's middle name. I was certain of that, as certain as I'd been only a few hours before that I had no son named Joshua at all.

"Stone," the boy said.

What went through my mind was a welter of free association: stone stone stone we are all stone *tu es petrus* and here was Jesus telling me *stone stone stone* and what kind of rock am I to build on when the foundations of the world are sinking sinking like a stone stone?

But it was Serena who said, "He's talking about *Milt* Stone, you know, Detective Stone, back in Tucson . . . the Navajo guy who took us across the River last time?—we have to go to him and—"

All I remembered was a man who could turn into a woman at will, who danced on the mesa in the sunset, who made us a big pot of peyote tea and shot us full of arrows and—

(Jesus is Greek for Joshua, I remembered suddenly.)

"Thank God. You *are* remembering," said Serena. "The kid's telling us we have to find Mr. Stone. In Tucson, I guess. We're going to have to make the crossing again. Theo pushed us back into the world so that we wouldn't have to get involved, but now he realizes this isn't the right world . . . that there's no turning back. Maybe the right world doesn't exist at all anymore. Or it's about ready to get zapped into the phantom zone."

"How can we get to Tucson?" I said. A vivid memory came to me: I'd sold my car to pay for the funerals. I wasn't due to get a royalty check from my agent for another three months. The university had fired me. I'd been living a hand to mouth existence, giving poetry readings on the beach to aging hippies passing through Baja, gathering a few pesos here and there, getting smashed every night . . . what a tawdry lifeline, I thought. I was glad I hadn't physically lived through it. But *someone* had. Whenever reality did one of these elastic snaps, it always seemed to invent the most cliché-ridden of possible pasts. Perhaps there was some kind of law of conservation of banality at work. Musing over these philosophical complexities, I found I had consumed two tamales, and Jesus' basket was empty.

"You go stone," he said, "you go stone, you go through stone, make stone flesh, make stoned flesh live." Which was about as clear as the Book of Revelation.

"Don't worry, Mr. E.," Serena said. "We can hitch a ride on Congressman Karpovsky's campaign bus. We're leaving here at midnight . . . he was really only down here for the Day of the Dead photo-op, and he's due to speak at the Phoenix Convention Center tomorrow night . . . come on, the congressman won't mind; he wants to be seen with poets, you know; it boosts his image with the space cadet contingent. Come on, Mr. E., we gotta get on the road!"

"Maybe the congressman won't even *be* here in this reality."

"We won't know until we walk down to the Hyatt, will we?" She was jumpy now, pulling me up from the graveside, dancing around me. "Come *on!*"

"Hasta la vista, Señor Etchison," said Jesus, waving, as Serena yanked me by the hand and we made our way out of the cemetery . . . we ran downhill toward where the Hyatt stood, gleaming against the cliffscape like a glass cathedral.

Inside the lobby, a couple of young women, college age like Serena, manned a reception desk beneath a huge *Karpovsky* banner. There were plenty of tourists still awake, and a twenty-foot ice sculpture in the shape of a skeleton—the Hyatt's contribution to the festive atmosphere—dominated the bar area. Serena went over to the desk and returned with a badge imprinted with the legend PRESS CORPS. "It's totally easy to get things done," she said, "when you're a jeans and lumberjack shirts type of campaign. No paperwork. No bodyguards. No fear of assassination." She pinned the badge on me. "Just look as though you belong," she said. "After all, Karpovsky will probably vouch for you anyway . . . he doesn't have any idea who's on the staff and who's not . . . you know how congressmen are." She smiled wryly and pointed with her chin.

Karpovsky was seated at a Steinway grand in the middle of the lobby bar, pounding away at the keys and singing a Tom Lehrer song—*The Masochism Tango*—at the top of his lungs. Tourists were laughing and singing and thrusting little pieces of paper toward him to autograph.

"You don't have a prayer," one of the tourists was shouting, as he took a deep slug from a coconut that had been sculpted into a crude skull. "And I ain't just saying that because I'm a libertarian."

At the word prayer, Karpovsky changed key abruptly and switched to a rousing rendition of *The Vatican Rag.*

"Congressman, Congressman . . ." Serena was leading me toward him by the hand. "Isn't it just wonderful that Phil Etchison has joined us?"

The congressman stopped singing, but so many people were singing along that it made little difference.

"Hi, Phil," he said, and Serena mouthed the word *poet* to him. "You're the poet, aren't you?" he said, not at all fazed at her ersatz teleprompter. She mouthed something else to him—I had the presence of mind to pretend not to notice—and then he added, "Oh, yeah . . . the *Washington Post* cafeteria . . . met you there. Your assistance to my campaign is something to be treasured, Phil, profoundly treasured."

I said, "Aren't you worried about the Catholic vote? I mean, singing that Tom Lehrer song in public."

"Catholics?" he said blankly. The room became fuzzy. The piano changed color . . . going from black to white to crystal to a wild spectrum of color. The crowd was swimming before my eyes, faces melting, merging, melding . . . suddenly I realized that I was being hit by a bad case of disjunctive fugue. The piano was metamorphosing into the snout of a whale. The people were like barnacles. The air reeked of salt and seaweed.

"Where am I? . . . Where am I going to? . . ." I said. "Serena!" And Serena extended her arms to me, but her arms were the fins of a leaping marlin . . . a kingfisher hovered in the air above her head. Serena's hair was changing into a shock of wind-whipped kelp . . . and her tongue flicked in and out like an eel . . . and then, at the far end of the atrium, where the scenic elevator once was, there was a huge tree that had thrust through the floor of the hotel and burst through the glass roof toward the sun.

"Run to the joshua tree," Serena cried, in a voice that sounded like the shattering sea, and in the background a band of angels sang *The Vatican Rag,* kicking their legs like Vegas showgirls.

I ran—leaped through a hoop of fire—faded out.

—and—in a dream I suppose—I was falling falling falling down the well, down the wrong end of a telescope, with the tangled skein of the River twisting and turning around me and I was falling falling falling until I saw the eyes of a flaming angel leaping in the sea and I cried out *no no no* and tried to grasp a thread of the River but the water slipped through my hands and—

—flaming—

When I woke up I was on a bus and we were pulling up to a border crossing. It didn't look familiar, but there was the Rio Grande and a narrow bridge and, here and there, barbed wire.

"Need a shower," I groaned. I had no idea how I had gotten onto this bus or whether I even had my passport and my credit cards on me anymore. I suppose that it was silly to worry about passports when I had already leaped several tall universes in a single bound, but there are times when a little anal-retentiveness can get one through a lot of chaos.

"Wake up, Mr. E.," Serena was saying, shaking me as I wiped the crusts from my eyes. "World's gone haywire."

I found my wallet and my passport. I pulled them out and rubbed my eyes. Something didn't look right about the passport. I looked out at where the immigration officer stood and I saw a great blue sign above the road:

WELCOME
TO THE UNITED STATES OF
ARMORICA

I looked down at my passport. It read:
Passport
United States of Armorica
And between the two legends was blazoned a dragon swallowing its own tail, crushing a griffin in its coils; the griffin, facing left, gripped three broken arrows in its claws. "This isn't home," I said. I looked around me and saw the congressman at the back of the bus, orating enthusiastically while a news team videotaped.

"I know," Serena said. "This time the world has *totally* shifted . . . but I don't think anyone knows about it except us." She pulled me to my feet. "Let's get off the bus and look around. These immigration formalities always take hours. In fact, they seem to be searching one of our buses for illegals; it's like they've never heard of congressional privilege."

I staggered after her and she led me down the two steps to terra firma. I ached all over. I had no memory of the ride, but it must have been a bumpy one. The world must have shifted while I slept. And yet my memories hadn't changed . . . they were there, all of them and all the alternate memories also.

Outside, a desertscape stretched out in every direction, broken only by the river. The sky was a deep blue, almost indigo, and the river—the merest trickle—was the color of mud. The bank was steep and shored up with concrete in places. We walked along the edge for about a quarter of a mile, not talking, each of us no doubt wondering how we had managed to lose ourselves in this no man's universe. Here we were, crossing the river into America to find a shaman to lead us to Theo . . . and it wasn't even America anymore. Although some things were still the same. For instance, we could make out a stream of people in the distance, running across the stream toward a barbed-wire barricade on the other side. A patrol car raced alongside the fence, lights flashing.

El Norte was still the land of opportunity, to be attained by stealth and conquered by cunning. We watched the line of immigrants. Sometimes they popped out of bushes or crawled out from behind rocks . . . sometimes a pickup truck would drive up, disgorge a load of people, then roar away. The border patrol didn't seem to be catching anyone.

Then, suddenly, we heard machine gun fire.

I whipped around to see that Congressman Karpovsky's entire retinue had come out of the buses, and that men in neo-Nazi uniforms were mowing them down. No, they were not even men; the soldiers had the faces of pigs and lizards. It was shocking, unconscionable, but I had no sense of reality. I felt no outrage and no terror. I could only feel despair. Not only because I no longer knew what or where anything was; it was because I no longer knew myself. I turned my gaze away from the massacre, but I could still hear the rat-tat-tat of the guns and the thud of flesh on sand.

"Jesus," Serena said. "Let's make a run for it."

"What's the point?" I said. "What can we achieve? We're not truth-sayers . . . we have no role to play in these wars . . . we don't even really exist here . . . isn't that true, Serena? The only reason we're still here at all is to balance a few cosmic equations. . . ."

"Come on, Mr. E., it's lame of you to philosophize now, this is a crisis." She started down the riverbank. I followed her. The machine gun fire continued. I realized that no one on that bus belonged to this universe and that the massacre was some kind of nightmarish attempt on the part of nature to straighten out the paradoxes. The bank was steep and I stumbled and finally our descent was more like a crawl. There was mud in my clothes, in my hair. I was breathing mud. But Serena was ahead of me. She was already into the water and running. I dragged myself to the edge. Though the water was barely ankle deep, the current was swift. I tried to stand up and it knocked me face down into the water. I coughed up mud and phlegm. I looked up at the sun through the watery blur and saw Jesus.

Haysoos, that is. He was hovering in the air above me. "Come on, Señor Etchison!" he was shrieking. His hands were folded in prayer and he was nude, like a Renaissance *putto*. I heard the flutter of his wings.

"What are you doing here, Jesus?" I said.

"In Armorica, anything can happen," he said. He giggled. The sun streamed from his eyes. Serena was already racing to the other side, her feet barely skimming the water. The *putto* did a somersault and laughed, hung downward by his knees from an imaginary bar. "Run, Señor Etchison." And in the rustle of his feathers there was the voice of my son crying out, "Cling to the truth, Dad."

"Theo!" I screamed. Because I could see him suddenly, pulling the puppet strings of this angelic apparition, his puffed cheeks whistling the desert wind, the gold dust falling from his fingertips. In this universe my son was God, but he was still my son.

And so, clinging to Theo's image in my heart, I sprinted across the water to Armorica.

BOOK TWO

THE FOREST OF ARDEN

". . . these trees shall be my books,
And in their barks my thoughts I'll character
That every eye which in this forest looks
Shall see thy virtue witnessed everywhere."

—As You Like It

2: In the Forest of Sexual Ambiguity

Sometimes (my mother told me as I lay
Encradled, swaddled, diapered and squalling)
You'll only think you've reached the Tum-Tum tree
(Or Bodhi tree, depending on your mythos);
For there are other arbors of enlightenment.
Sometimes you'd think that all trees came equipped
With gateways into other worlds; that you,
Observing each new-minted microcosm,
Could always know the difference between lost
And found. But that, my child, ain't so.

Imprimis: found: the ancient Aztec priest
Who, flaying a virgin, honored mother earth
By dancing in her skin. Next: witness: lost:
Ed Gein, alone in the Wisconsin forest,
Straps on the mounted breasts of a dead woman
And dances, also honoring the mother.
Both celebrate the mysteries. Both elevate
The hostess-flesh, Jocasta, and transform.
Odin and Oedipus both traded eyes for knowledge.

One day, my son:
I'll send you forth into the wide wide world
With nothing save a loaf of bread, a sword,
A condom, and a kiss. So listen well,
As you lie cradled, squalling, diapered.
You don't need speech to know these truths are true.
I made you. One day you will kill me,
Flay me, wear my skin. And I shall speak
Anew through my insensate sluicing wounds,
And speaking, live. The river of life is blood.

O my son:
A lullaby I sing, knowing you too
Shall one day dance in the forest of transforming;
You too shall lose and find yourself; you too
Shall wear an alien skin. The shaman and the madman
Are the same person; only the watchers' eyes
Are different. So if thine eye offend thee,
Pluck it out. Blinded, you still shall dance.
The hungry mother shall devour her sons.
Within each tree there beats a human heart.
Don't be afraid, son. Dance. Dance. Dance
Till the heart grows still, and the river runs aground.

CHAPTER SIX

IN A DESERTED GAS STATION

<u>P h i l   E t c h i s o n</u>

And as we reached the far shore, Jesus the Cupid darted up—the wings invisible-fast, like hummingbirds'—into the sunlight, and was lost to view.

"Don't look back!" came the *putto's* voice in the shimmering air.

I knew that he wanted to spare me the sight of any more carnage. I could still hear it though . . . tinny thudlets over the ripple of the river, video game rifle reports. I wanted to thank him, but all that was left of him was a shower of tinkerbell sparks. I decided to obey his admonition, especially since, being an educated man, I knew what had happened to Orpheus. It was just as well, for I heard a final, earth-shattering blast, smelled burning flesh in the air, felt the heat wave, saw the sky go blinding-bright for a moment before I closed my eyes.

And when I opened them again, it was as if none of it had happened. The air was clean and dry. The desert vista stretched into the distance, where, at the horizon, a jagged band of mountains divided the blue from the yellow.

"Are you all right, Mr. E.?" Serena said. She held out a can of diet soda. I touched it; jabbed my fingers into cold. "Piece of the Arctic," she said, laughing.

"Where'd it come from?"

"Machine," she said, pointing up ahead with her thumb. "Our money still works here."

There was a gas station where she pointed. I was sure I hadn't seen it before. It was as though it came into existence at the very moment I chose to perceive it. It was a rather literary sort of a gas station . . . the pumps half buried in sand, the mangy dog coiled by the garage door, the soda machine sweating fresh dew . . . the weatherbeaten old man on the rocking chair, shotgun in one hand, Stetson over his eyes . . . a battered Cadillac with its hood popped . . . an old newspaper blowing in the wind.

By literary, I mean that this was a gas-station-in-the-desert of the Ray Bradbury school of writing, poetic and atmospheric and yet somehow a plot device. Especially since there was no road, and even the rust on the pumps and the sores on the dog looked freshly minted.

Still, I wanted to know where we were, and to have some general notion of what kind of universe we were trapped in. Serena had already tested out the coinage, and I still had money and credit cards. We couldn't get far without a car, but perhaps the old man had a phone. With a phone, I could rent a car. We could get to civilization. Maybe.

"Sir? Sir?"

I tapped the old man on the shoulder. As he leaned back, the Stetson slowly slid up to his forehead. He peered at me and said, "Howdy, pardner. Welcome to the gas station of no return."

Serena and I looked at each other in alarm.

"Don't you worry, mister!" said the old man. "Had you right scared, didn't I? Some folks think I'm some kind of psychotic or even"—he rolled his eyes and raised his eyebrows so taut the Stetson popped right off his head—"some kind of serial killer!" He guffawed. "You'll never get out of here alive," he added. "*The Texas Chainsaw Massacre* don't got nothing on this place."

"I see," I said. "But would you mind telling me exactly where this *place* is?"

He only laughed. "This place," he said, "is what you make of it. It ain't nothing but what you see in it. Most people, they only see sand and cactus and the old gas station and the dog, and me, sitting here, born old. But then there's some that look out over that sand and they see, oh, wonderful things. To everything there is a season, you know. Pity that season's always dry around here."

"My name is Phil," I said, offering to shake his hand.

"Caleb Cadwallader," said the old man. The name, like his manner of speaking, had a rough poetry to it. I found him engaging, though I could not quite dispel the notion that he was somehow artificial, put on this desert to complete the fantastical illusion, like Adam's navel.

"Caleb," I said. His handshake was as salt-of-the-earth as I imagined it would be.

"Mr. E.!" Serena was saying. She'd gathered up the flying newspapers and was waving the front page at me. I took it from her and read:

Two Sun Gazette
KARPOVSKY IMPOSTOR SLAIN IN SHOOTOUT

A con artist purporting to be Congressman Oren Karpovsky (D-Philanderphia), together with an entourage of androids, was the victim of a terrorist bomb attack intended for the congressman himself. The man has been identified as Laurence Tremaine, sometime freak show impresario and snake oil vendor, who, disguising himself as the presidential candidate, had been stealing money from American tourists under the guise of taking campaign contributions. The shootout occurred just a few feet from the Armorican border, and Azteca patrolmen watched helplessly as the bomb, an Atlantean model, went off. The real Karpovsky will speak this evening at a fundraiser at the Goldwater Auditorium at the University of Two Sun. Once derided as a "New Age monstrosity" by William F. Buckley, it is now thought that Karpovsky has a strong chance of an upset in the Platinum State primaries on Super Baldursday.

At first I was convinced the whole thing was a hoax—right down to the dangling modifier in the last sentence. I had seen Karpovsky, seen the campaign workers, watched him work the tourists. Then it occurred to me that the universe into which we had now been catapulted was certainly bizarre enough to encompass such a scenario, even though it didn't jibe with many of the details I remembered. There'd never been anything like this in any other reality shift; generally the world had been the same, and only one or two details altered—big details as far as my life was concerned, to be sure, but of little consequence to most other people.

This new shift was of several orders of magnitude. It's not just a bunch of weird spellings, I thought, as a second sun, small and reddish, began to rise in what appeared to be the northeast. Conflicting theories jostled in my mind. Perhaps there was another Karpovsky in this universe—somehow we had all gone through the interface together—and the resultant paradox was so untenable that nature had contrived this esoteric plot development to eliminate the redundancy—and so, zap!—Karpovsky had become an impostor, and his entire retinue a passel of androids, and as for Serena and me—nature had contrived to have us slip quietly away. This was an impressive theory, except that it endowed nature with purpose, foresight, and an understanding of television-style plotting. And I did not believe in nature as a sentient force. It was not my style.

I read the article over once more. Then I let it drop, and it was carried away by the wind.

"Is there somewhere we can rent a car around here?" I asked the old man.

"You're welcome to take the Cadillac," Caleb said. "It was left here by the last people who stopped here, ooh, five, ten years ago. Name of Etchison. Soft-spoken, all-Armorican family. Liked them a lot. The lady was dying of cancer, as I recall; she had them chemotherapy bald patches. Ain't nobody been here since. I've been a-sitting here and a-rocking back and forth for all this time, waiting for someone to give it to. I say, you look a lot like him. Don't recognize the young lady though."

"We had a station wagon before," I said, wondering what had happened to these other-worldly analogues of my family.

"Oh, that's here too," he said, pointing vaguely toward the mountains. I thought I could make out a car's hood, complete with hood ornament, poking up out of the sand. "That's always been there, long as I've been. At first it was just a smudge, but the outline of the car gets more and more clear every year. I'd give it another couple of years before it pops."

"Pops?" I said.

"Things is always popping in this desert," Caleb said. "It's because it ain't real."

"What's not real?"

"Why, all of it, of course," said the old man. "You must not be from around these parts."

"We're from Virginia," Serena said, and the man nodded as though that explained everything. "I don't think 'popping' has reached our neck of the woods yet." She was as mystified as I, but she was a lot smoother about demystifying herself. "Could you, I mean, like explain it to us?"

"Sure. I ain't got nothing better to do." He settled back in the rocking chair, which launched into a brief flurry of rocking, offered us both a chaw of tobacco, which we declined, and said, "Oftentimes, the future haunts the past. Around here, if something is for sure going to happen some day, we sees an afterimage of it . . . okay, a *before*image is more like it . . . in the sand, you see. Now sometimes the future ain't so certain, and the beforeimage is nothing more than a bit of a glow, or what they calls an aura. Other times, this beforeimage, it just gets clearer and clearer, until, in the end, it *is* reality. You follering me?"

"I think so," I said.

"Sometimes this beforeimage is so powerful, it's even realer than the image which it's *before*. Like the Etchisons, for instance—"

"You met us before," I said, "and they gave you a message for ourselves? They projected themselves into the past, something like that?"

"Nah, you ain't the Etchisons," said Caleb, "because there was four of them. You look like him, though. I'd know him anywhere. He's a famous poet."

That was good to know. In the world I came from, I was, to be sure, a poet of sorts, but I could hardly be considered famous . . . not in a world where kitsch was king . . . but if Phil Etchison was a famous poet here, how could I be sure that he and I were the same person? Perhaps I was like the pseudo-Karpovsky, an impostor, soon to be mowed down by Mexican machine guns.

"Like I was saying," Caleb said, "the Etchisons came here once. Or they will come. I forget. Things haven't been the same since time went through that Möbius strip . . . you know, after the big recession set in. And they said, if a middle-aged man with a sad face and a pretty college girl was to come for help, looking lost and forlorn, I was to give them the Cadillac. You see, everything works out in the end. Or beginning. I forget which."

"Is there a yellow brick road?" Serena said, only half joking.

"There used to be," said Caleb. "They tore it up when they extended Route 10."

"So this *is* Arizona?" I asked. I was suffering from déjà vu, even though it was clear that the events I was living through had never happened before, although they might conceivably happen in the future, whereas, in the cyclical view of time, they might already have happened anyway, except that, if there really had been a Möbius strip that time had twisted through, then we were all inside out, although since existence is subjective there would be no way of verifying our inside-out-ness, and—

"Mr. E.?" Serena was saying. She touched me lightly on the elbow. "You're totally zoning out."

I blinked. The Cadillac had been moved. It gleamed in the harsh light of the two suns. It was no longer a wreck; it had been waxed, polished, burnished until it shone like bronze. How long had my mind been going around in circles? Long enough for them to have fixed up the car? Or had I been the victim of a bait-and-switch routine?

Caleb Cadwallader was handing me the keys. Abstractedly I took them. "I was trying to think all of this through. I mean, the philosophical implications," I said, though attempts to think things through had succeeded only in entangling me further. I was a mouse in an n-dimensional maze.

"Maybe I should drive," Serena said.

Gently, she pried the keys from my hand. She climbed in and I got in beside her. The car purred. The air conditioning cut on and blasted my face. I realized that I had been sweating like a pig. I probably smelled like one too. The last time I'd shaved had been about twenty-nine universes back, and I'd spent the night on a moving bus. I sank back into the leather upholstery . . . it was soft and smelled brand new.

"Let's go," Serena said.

"Where?" I murmured.

"Oh, you're hopeless, Mr. E.," she said. "We'll go to Tucson, or Two Sun, as they call it here. That's where Mr. Stone was when we left him."

"Mr. Stone? Oh, the Indian shaman, right?"

"Really, Mr. E.," she said. "You're not seeing things *mythically,* that's your problem."

"You, my dear, are scolding me with the self-righteousness of a coed who's just had her first encounter with Joseph Campbell 101. I know all that stuff. I had *lunch* with Campbell, for god's sake!" Suddenly I wondered whether that was true.

"Okay. Well, maybe you're not seeing them *trilogistically,*" she said, "or you'd know that we've reached Stage Two of the hero's quest—where the plot thickens, where everything seems hopeless—where the grail is impossibly out of reach . . . where the lady is unattainable—and we're proceeding right on course toward the encounter with the Ultimate Darkness, after which—if we win—we go on to the Ultimate Redemption."

"I see. But we might *not* win."

"In which case we'll all go home with the board game, the T-shirts, and the gift certificates, but someone else will go on to the grand prize."

If this was a hero's quest, I thought—but did not dare say it aloud, because Serena seemed so delighted with her specious undergrad conceit—there was something dreadfully wrong with the picture: me. I'm not a hero, I thought. Everyone in my family is more heroic than I. Joshua, with his raging hormones, charging into the void on the back of the dragon lady. Theo, uttering the truth no matter what the pain. And Mary, who is pain personified.

Oh yes. I knew who my family was now. The fact that the world had dissolved into a maelstrom of unreality had sharpened the focus on those whom I loved. I had plucked the images of my wife and sons out of the thousands of convergent memory lines, and I saw them clearly for the first time.

We drove on. There was, indeed, a yellow brick road; here and there, you could see a stretch of it alongside the freeway, threading through the thickening saguaro forest. Both suns had climbed up to the zenith, and the air conditioning was beginning to wheeze. Serena drove on. The signs were in a kind of dream-English—they said things a preliterate child might think a grownup was saying:

JILTED ONCOMING TERRIFIC

PEDESTRIAN CRUCIFIXION

SPEED CRAP

I wondered whether God was a child in this universe.

It was at that moment that the air freshener spoke to me.

"We meet again, Señor Etchison," it said.

It was one of those dangling air fresheners. It gave off a nostril-clenching scent of baby powder. It was, indeed, in the shape of a baby, or rather a young boy, with delicately fluttering eyelashes and wings.

"Jesus," I said.

Jesus the Mexican street kid—first transmogrified into a Renaissance *putto,* then into this cardboard Cupid—was once more leading the way. "Did you hear what the air freshener just said to me?" I said to Serena, but her eyes were on the freeway and she didn't turn to look at me. In fact, it seemed that I had been plucked out of the timestream altogether. Because the car had slowed down to an infinitesimal crawl . . . and it wasn't that we were moving slowly, it was that I was caught up in some real-life video effect. The vision was for me alone, I realized; yet another solipsistic experience I would never be able to share.

"Do you have a message from Theo?" I said.

In the wind from the air conditioner, the air freshener flapped back and forth against the rear view mirror.

"Si, señor." Then came a second voice, the voice of my son. . . . "Dad, come quickly. I'm afraid."

"But I don't know where you are. We're probably not even in the same—reality, universe, whatever." Again, the inadequacy of my role as hero was hammered home to me.

"Doesn't matter anymore. They're all starting to run together. The universes. The walls are breaking down. If I don't fix it, there's gonna be like one big goulash. The Great Unmaking. Chaos. Oh God, Dad, I'm so scared."

"Where are you, son?"

"A dark place."

"Tell me how to find you."

"I don't know, I don't know! The darkest place there is. The bottom of the abyss. Shit, shit, shit I'm scared and I just want to cry."

"Don't be scared. I'm coming. It's going to be all right." Jesus, I was weeping as I spoke those words of comfort to a fragrant piece of cardboard.

"Hasta la vista, Señor Etchison," said Jesus, and then the air freshener was just an air freshener again. Time sped up and the car was racing down the freeway.

A sign read:

TWO SUN—SMILES

Saguaros everywhere. Jagged mountains in the distance. A dust storm whirled, far off, against the deep blue sky. Oh, the place had an aching familiarity to it, though it was light years from the world I knew. I'd been through an entire *Twilight Zone* season's worth of weirdness in the past twenty-four hours. I was worn out. I started to drift off again.

Time for dreamland.

Time to prepare myself for another day of fantasy and dark magic in the good old U.S. of Armorica.

CHAPTER SEVEN

THE BOTTOMLESS PIT

Theo Etchison

I've reached the bottom of the bottomless pit. I can tell because I'm not moving anymore. I don't know if I'm still in the belly of King Strang. I guess not. That was just an illusion.

The only light is the vague blue glowing from the cosmic marble in my hand. I'm walking now, one palm up with the pale blue radiance streaming. I can make out shapes: here a statue with three eyes, there a stalactite. I can hear water dripping. I'm near one of the tributaries of the River.

I've just lost contact with Dad. He's on a freeway somewhere heading toward Tucson. I can almost hear the air conditioner squeal as he strains uphill. I'm almost there with him, but he can't feel my presence anymore.

Even while I'm standing in the darkness gazing in the marble I can see the filaments of the River coil and uncoil and I know what's happening and I know time is running out. The barriers between the worlds are all dissolving and pretty soon there's only going to be one big crazy goulash of a universe where everything is true at the same time, which means chaos. It's all I can do to hold back the waters . . . and I can't really do it all because my mind can't process all of it at once. I can carve out a kingdom where things aren't going crazy quite as fast. I can center that island of stability around where my dad's car is hurtling up the freeway toward Tucson. But I don't know how long it will last.

I reach out with my mind and wrench the rivulets apart as best I can.

I'm not able to reach my dad anymore but I can still feel him and he's like a pinprick of consciousness battling upstream against the flow of reality . . . the freeway itself is a kind of river . . . no, a thread . . . suturing the wounded world. I hope. God, I hope.

So I close my eyes and drift into an amniotic sleep. I don't dream because I can't.

It's morning and I'm in a forest.

I know it's a forest even before I'm awake. I've been in a forest before, at my grandparents' place in Spotsylvania County. A forest at dawn is all dampness and birdcalls and leafy-earth-sweet-rotten-smelling. I can hear the ripple of a nearby brook. It must be part of the River because beneath the babbling I hear the echo of the music of the dawn time.

I rub my eyes. I've been sleeping against the trunk of a joshua tree. Two squirrels skitter up my arm and disappear. I listen for the ancient music which only I can hear. It's faint, but it's still here. I sit up and that's when I hear the bells. I reach up and touch my head and I pull down a jester's cap; you know, the kind the Joker wears . . . not the *Batman* Joker, the one in the pack of cards. I look down at myself and I see that my clothes are gone and I'm clutching a kind of a baton in my hand. It's a stick with a Joker's head on the head and the same kind of cap and bells. There's clothes hanging on a line that goes from the nearest branch of the tree across to somewhere near where the water's whispering to me. They're pied clothes, half green, half red. If I put them on, I'm going to look like the court jester. Not cool.

But the morning air is nippy. I'm shivering. I spring up, jump up and down a couple of times to like get the circulation going, then I get into the dweebish threads. They're warm, but the sleeves are all big and they swish around when I move my arms. I stick the cap back on my head. I feel like a fool. Well, I guess that only makes sense.

I shake the stick. Somewhere, a cuckoo cuckoos.

"Okay," I say to no one, "someone's decided to make me the court jester. But I don't know any jokes. I mean, why did the dead baby cross the road? Because it was stapled to the chicken."

I think I hear a laugh, but maybe it's the chittering of some forest animal.

I work my way toward the brook. It's farther than I realize, but that only makes sense, too. We're in topsy-turvy country and nothing feels right. In fact, it's only when I stop listening to the rippling, when I close my eyes completely and make myself still, and then I take one step forward, that I discover that I'm suddenly there. By the water's edge. I've almost stepped too far, down among the rushes. I squat at the bank. I can see myself in the water. Underneath the circus outfit it's still me, Theo Etchison, a sad case of delayed puberty. I've got the same dirty blond hair and blue-green eyes. I shake the stick and try to think of a joke.

What happens next is that this little reed basket floats by, and there's a baby inside, and it's coughing and sneezing. I'm all, "Holy Moses!" and I reach out to maybe grab the basket, but I can't get it in time, I mean it slips from my fingers before I can get a grip on it. I wonder if it really *is* Moses, because, since the universe has just been radically reshuffled, almost any fragment of our history or mythology could be thrown up against any other fragment. Okay, so I don't want it to just drift out of sight, I mean the baby's squalling now, and maybe someone should be taking care of it. So I get up and I start following alongside the bank. The current's amazingly fast and next to the brook is all brambles and maybe even poison ivy because it only takes a few minutes before I feel itchy all over and I have to stop. There's a bend in the stream . . . it's wider now . . . and the baby in the basket rounds the corner and vanishes from my sight. But then I see that there's something else coming my way, bobbing up and down in the current, and it's like a big wooden chest, painted in blue and gold with a design of waves and dolphins . . . the lid's wide open and I see there's a baby there too, with a circlet of gold leaves around its head . . . one of those Greek hero dudes, Perseus maybe . . . wasn't he sent out to sea in a wooden chest? . . . and no sooner does that chest go sailing around the bend than there's something else . . . it looks kind of like half of a giant peach, and there's a baby all curled up inside the peach, too, swimming in peach juice. Not a clue who it might be, but it's oriental-looking I guess. It must be some other classic hero from some culture I'm not familiar with. I don't know what to make of it, especially when more baby containers come drifting past me . . . there's a miniature Viking ship . . . there's a humongous lotus pad and the baby is sitting upright, cross-legged, meditating, with a pale yellow halo around his head . . . it's getting weird, I tell myself.

There's a lot of rushes now and I have to half wade out to follow where the babies are floating to. The water gets surprisingly deep all of a sudden and I see that, upstream, there's a lot more objects floating toward the bend in the creek. On the other bank, the trees go on and on, so dark and thick that there's barely any light except for the rising sun skimming the water. Well, I think to myself, this must be the place where heroes come from. Dad's always telling me about how in mythology the hero tends to have an unknown origin . . . some king or princess finds him floating down the stream in a little raft made of rushes . . . and he turns out to be the child of a god. I've stumbled on Hero Central here, the lost and found department for the dudes who are going to save the universe. I guess it makes sense that this place would be at the bottom of the bottomless pit, the beginning at the ending.

But what am I doing here? I'm not really here to save universes, only to find my brother and bring him back to the world, my world. I don't really give a flying fuck about the rest of the world. I just want my family back and I don't want my mother to be dying of cancer anymore.

Well, so anyway I'm standing knee-deep in water watching the future saviors of the world go past in a solemn procession of miniature boats, rafts, treasure chests, and vehicles of the future. And then I see one that's not on a boat or a lotus pad or anything like that. There's like this three-ring binder, open to about halfway through, drifting downstream alongside the other mythology paraphernalia, and on it there's a baby with closed eyes, and he's not screaming or whimpering like the other babies, he's just lying there, and he's all purple-blue, like he's having trouble staying alive.

Somehow this has got something to do with me. It's the three-ring binder. I'd know it anywhere. I try to wade out farther but all of a sudden there's like this gully in the stream bed and I'm way in, up to my neck, and the water's ice-cold and soaking into my Joker threads. I'm not that great at swimming and the current's pretty strong but I push back against the riverbed and try to propel myself toward the binder and the baby. And all the while I'm remembering what's in the binder, the words I wrote myself, scribbling down my crazy dreams all the way from Virginia to Mexico not knowing that they weren't dreams at all . . . I can see the writing, uneven felt-tip scrawlings, the immature handwriting of a four-teen-year-old kid, and I know that if I don't catch the book soon the water's going to seep into those cheap college ruled pages and the writing's not waterproof and even if it were how could it withstand the water of making and unmaking? . . . and I know I've got to save the note-book, save the child too, or the things in the notebook are going to be flushed down the toilet bowl of eternity.

So I try to grab hold of the book and I try to hold it and the baby above the water. I can see words here and there like *the king sitting on the* and *lizard skittering up the limbs of the joshua tree* and *dragon woman screech-ing in the sky.* But the sentences are dissolving. Changing. The baby's not completely dead but I don't know how to wake it up. I know the baby's not me but I have a feeling it's part of me, that I'm responsible for it. The pages are getting soggy. I can't do any more than steer the book and the child toward a shallower part of the shore and so that's what I do. I give it a little push and there it goes. I can't tread water anymore and I feel myself submerging and the icy water floods my nostrils. I grab on to some rushes and drag myself toward the bank. When I pull myself out, the book and its cargo are already rounding the bend. I can't lose that book! My whole world is in that book. I'm pretty frantic I guess and I'm thrashing around, not really getting anywhere. I make it back to shore, but it's not the same shore I left behind . . . because here there are these twisted rocks that jag up out of the soil and they're shaped almost like beasts . . . and then I see an old man, leaning against one of the rocks, fishing.

"Help me," I gasp.

He doesn't look up and I'm crawling and staggering toward him, shaking the wet from my carnival costume like a dog.

"You gotta help me, dude," I say. "Out there . . . there's something that belongs to me. If I don't fish it out of the water—"

He doesn't say much. But he casts his line way out over the stream with a sudden flick of his wrist and then he starts reeling like crazy. And pretty soon there's my dream book, hooked by one of the rings, zeroing in on us. And the baby along with it. He pulls it in and I pick the binder gingerly out of the water. I don't really know what to do with the baby. It seems smaller than it was before . . . and dry, like a mummy almost.

"Is it dead?" I ask the old man.

He snorts.

I cradle the child in the crook of my arm and it seems to stir a little, but it's even smaller than it was before. It's shrinking . . . shrinking . . . presently it's almost like a little axolotl, wriggling in the palm of my hand.

"Quick!" the old man says. "Swallow it before it regresses into nothingness! Or else it'll never be reborn."

He turns to me and looks at me with such commanding urgency that I believe him. I open my mouth and gulp it down. It's the size of a tadpole but it burns the roof of my mouth and it sears my throat as it goes down, like acid.

The old man looks at me, nods curtly. "Good."

"What was it I just did?"

"Not for you to know yet. But you're going to be glad you did it. When the right time comes, that is." He throws the fishing line out once more, and stares at the water dourly. There are no more babies floating by. The forest has thickened still more. The air is misty and still.

I take my notebook and leaf through it. Most of it still seems to be there. "You can dry the pages over yonder fire," the old man says, "and your clothes too, I dare say." He points behind with his thumb, and, creeping behind the massive rock he's leaning against, I see there's a fire—the wood is damp and green and there's a lot of smoke—and an unidentifiable animal, a rabbit or lizard, spitted above it. I place the open book against some warm stones and I shuck my jester's outfit and spread it out on the rocks. There's a pile of blankets, and I wrap myself in one of them and try to warm myself. My stomach is still queasy from swallowing whatever it was, the distilled quintessence of hero I guess. I keep thinking a monster's going to burst out of my stomach like in the movie *Alien*. Presently I hear the old man cry out: "Boy! Boy!" and I scurry to his side. I get the distinct impression that he's used to being obeyed.

I just sit there, watching him as he fishes. I've got the blanket wound round and round my thin shoulders. I'm holding on to the jester-headed stick, listening to the wind toy with the bells on its hat.

Now and then the old man turns to look at me. His eyes are sunken in a field of cross-hatched wrinkles. He wants to say something, I'm sure, but he can't get it all out for some reason. So he turns back and stares at the tip of his fishing pole.

"Who are you?" I ask him at last.

"It is not for you to question," the old man says. But I don't feel I'm in danger, so I know he's not working for Thorn or Katastrofa. "Perhaps I should start by testing you, child. Do you know what this place is?"

"The bottom of the abyss," I say. "And I guess right here is like, the birthplace of heroes, judging by the little boats that go floating by. I've recognized Moses, and Perseus, and the little dude in the peach, he's from some Japanese fairy tale, isn't he?"

"Momotaro," says the old man. "There is also Karna, son of the sun. And half a dozen others you can look up in any good dictionary of mythology."

"But what about the hero I—I swallowed?"

"Oh, that's the best one of all . . . the hero with no name . . . the one who is to come." And the old man smiles for a moment before the sadness sucks him up again. "Do you know who I am, boy? Perhaps we have met before."

"I think you are a king," I say, "even though you're not dressed like one. I mean, you're not wearing a crown or any of that shit."

"So you can identify me even through my disguise. Wait! I think there's a nibble."

The fishing line snaps.

"Got away," the king says sadly.

I know where I've seen him before now. "You have my father's eyes," I say, "but you're not my dad. The last time I saw you was beside another shore, and you were at the head of an army, and you were all covered in gold and jewels. Today you're dressed in rags, but I still know that you're King Strang."

"Good for you. A good fool always tells the truth. He is the only person at court who can get away with it. Know any good jokes?"

"Well, I *do* know a few dead baby jokes, but maybe this isn't the right time to tell them."

The king laughs. "A nibble!"

"You're not using any bait."

He laughs again. Then he reels in the line, peers at the hook, and murmurs, "You're right." He pulls up his tunic. There's a wound in his side that oozes pus and dark rheum. There's like worms crawling in and out of it. It's totally gross looking but I can't help staring at it. They're not maggots; these worms are *big* motherfuckers, with armored segments and fangs, and they're all dripping slime, and they're a silvery-black color. Vomitous. I wonder why someone like King Strang would have a festering wound and not get it treated. After all, even though he's precipitated the present cosmic crisis by stupidly dividing up his kingdom between his quarreling offspring, he's got to have *some* resources. I mean, he's an ex-emperor of the universe for God's sake.

"Are you okay?" I say. "That thing looks like it needs stitches."

"Oh, it's not a wound that can be healed by any ordinary means," says the king. "In fact, you're the only one who is even capable of seeing it." He picks out a nice fat worm and threads it carefully onto his fishhook.

"Why?" But I already know the answer to that question. I am Theo Truthsayer, and I see the truth however great the pain. That's the job description. That's what I do. The wound in the king's side is an old wound and there is no mortal means of healing it. I feel the pain too. I can't help feeling it, it's almost as though it belongs to me too, to everyone. He doesn't answer me but as he pulls his tunic back over the wound the pain recedes into a dull ache, just gnawing at the threshold of pain.

"So, fool," the king says, "make me laugh."

"Why did the dead baby cross the road?" I say.

"It was stapled to the chicken," says old King Strang. He laughs again. "No, child, you don't need to tell me jokes. Your very presence lightens the sadness in my heart. I once had children of my own."

"And they are all betraying you. All except Ash."

"Don't mention Ash to me!" says the king, and he stares steadfastly at the stream.

The day goes on; my clothes dry; my notebook remains more or less intact; I get over my nausea at having swallowed the future savior of the universe. I eat the tender flesh of a brook trout. The king holds court in the ballroom of the forest, in a clearing in the light of the rising moon. The constellations are all new, and they dance across the sky. I'm the king's fool, and I dance and sing in front of him and sometimes I elicit a faint smile, as when I attempt to act out the music videos of Right Said Fred and Nirvana, music from a lost world.

Then, as the moon begins to set, as the fire dies down, I tell King Strang this isn't where I belong. "I didn't come here to make you laugh," I say, "although God knows you need someone to cheer you up after all that you've suffered. I didn't come here to heal your wound—you've told me it can't be healed. I came to find my brother. I've gotta bring him back to my world before it's too late, because I think he's got this love-death thing real bad."

King Strang has started to snore, his hands folded across his lap, leaning against a rock that's shaped like a human face. He doesn't seem to be listening to me. I think, well, shit, I guess I should start on my quest now. I know that Joshua has to be with Katastrofa, because that's where he was bound when he leaped into the sea.

I get up and get ready to steal away.

But King Strang tugs at my elbow and whispers to me, "You're wrong. You *are* here to heal and to make laughter." I jerk my arm away and look down at him. He's been talking in his sleep, I'm sure of it, because his eyes are still closed and he's started to snore again.

I move away. Twigs snap on my sneakers.

The king stirs again, and he cries out, "My son! My son!" in a voice so hurting that I'm tempted to stay with him after all. But I can't.

I want to say to the unhearing air, "I'm *not* your son, I'm Theo Etchison and my real Dad is a middle-aged poet from planet Earth." Somehow it won't come out. I'm a truthsayer and it feels untrue to say that I am not his son.

So I just slip from the clearing and move deeper into the darkness. I keep within earshot of the sound of the River. I stare into the marble, trying to get a fix on Katastrofa.

King Strang may be right about a lot of what he's telling me. I mean, he's been around. He's ruled the universe before, even though now he's an old mad king who only wants to go fishing. But even if he *is* right about my real purpose, I still have to find it out for myself. I'm young, but not too young to have a sense of destiny.

CHAPTER EIGHT

IN A LOVE MOTEL

<u>S e r e n a   S o m e r s</u>

TWO SUN—SMILES

was what the sign had said, and it wasn't kidding. *Smiles,* as every second-grader knows, is the longest word in the dictionary because there's a whole mile in between—yeah. We'd been driving down that freeway and every road sign had this quality of being plucked from the mind of a kindergarten prankster. From where we were into Tucson was about longest mile I've ever driven. It took like *hours.* But the universe sort of "grew up" as we drove; after a few hours there were fewer and fewer of the signs with stupid puns, and it was almost as if the cosmos had like lost consciousness or something and it was rapidly clawing its way up through the chaos of infancy and settling down into the world we all knew. In fact, about early evening there was only one sun setting behind the jagged blue mountains, and the forest of saguaro that stretched out on either side of the highway seemed almost the way I remembered it.

"I think things are getting, you know, more normal, Mr. E.," I said. Mr. E. kept on driving silently, but at least he wasn't talking to the air freshener anymore. "Look!"

I pointed to a sign that read: *Tucson—25 miles.* The spelling, along with the number of suns, was back to the old way. "Theo's been working on the universe," I said. "Pounding in a few nails, plugging up the leaks."

"My son is an unlikely demiurge," said Mr. E., "but better him than me."

I thought of the massacre on the Mexican border and shuddered. "We're not home yet, are we?" I said. That would be too much to hope for. "Maybe Theo's patched up the whole works, and Josh and Mrs. E. are waiting for you back in Virginia."

"No," said Mr. E., sighing. "My passport still says *Armorica.*"

We pulled into Tucson long after midnight and there wasn't anywhere else to go. Chowed down at the Pack-'em-Inn Steak House—no kidding! the place was still there even though we'd shifted sidewise down a zillion universes—and ended up sleeping in a cheap motel on Oracle, one of those $22 a night places where the cowboys go to cheat on their wives. It was a dingy fleabag and there was only one queen sized bed in the room, but I really didn't think Mr. E. was about to molest me, so I just fell asleep on the window side of the bed, fully clothed, watching Mr. E. pacing back and forth, fiddling with the TV, which only had like two channels—CNN and a hardcore porno channel. On CNN, Congressman Karpovsky was being creamed on *Crossfire*, and on the porno station two lesbians were eating each other out and looking so bored doing it that I wondered how anyone could get excited watching it.

Drifting off, I heard the congressman say: "And I think it's about time all these *National Enquirer*-type scandals were laid to rest. Yes, I've had my share of amours, but you know, nobody's perfect . . . give me a break, Jack Kennedy used to have women delivered to the Oval Office by a secret back door, at least so the rumor goes . . . why don't you guys stop policing my bedroom and start examining my policies?"

I drifted and dreamed.

First off, in the dream, there was Joshua and the sea. A shimmering Joshua, walking to me across the water. I guess I was maybe on a boat. I could feel the rocking, hear the creaking of rope and wood, taste the salt water on my lips. The Joshua I remembered so vividly even though I was in a world where he had never existed. Sullen Joshua, glaring slitty-eyed at the sea, avoiding my gaze, Joshua whose proximate maleness was so threatening I'd hidden my real self behind folds of lard, Joshua whom I'd loved in secret until, grudgingly, we'd sought each other out; Joshua of the excruciating wordless evenings at the drive-in with his little brother as our reluctant chaperone; so what if he didn't say anything, I could always fantasize about him being the strong, silent type, couldn't I, and not face the fact that his silence was his own way of hiding from himself, as palpable as my obesity? And this was all racing through my mind as I watched him walk toward me on the water with his hands outstretched like one of those kitschy paintings of Jesus and all of a sudden I realize this is going to be one of those sex dreams or maybe a religious dream I'm not sure, sex and religion all squished together like one of those Madonna music videos I guess but that's like totally trivial and so fucking adolescent turning your innermost longing and anguish into images from MTV damn it Serena, you're a college girl now, this is bullshit, bullshit, but (I love the way Joshua smells, not a harsh male odor = malodor [did God intend that pun?] but kind of a faint muskiness lacing the tang of the salt sea) there's something about MTV, when you grow up on it you can't stop seeing the world that way, a jigsaw of bit-sized images set to the pounding beat of teenaged loins, oh *Josh Josh Josh* was what I—

—cried out, woke up a little I think, thought I still smelled that fragrance of his in the air above the Pine-sol rodent-dropping blend of the motel room. Then I heard Mr. E. snoring beside me. He was cocooned in the bedspread. The television was still on and the moonlight was streaming in through the open window, and I was shivering because like, in Tucson, the nights can be freezing sometimes. I staggered out of the bed so I could shut the window.

At the window:

A lone neon sign flickered, on-off, on-off, an electric pink wolf next to a cactus. I lowered the shades. Now the only light was from the television set. I sat against the headboard and stared at the screen thinking maybe I could hypnotize myself back to sleep. I wondered what was going on at Karpovsky headquarters and whether—since this Karpovsky was not the same Karpovsky I'd left Mexico with—I'd even be expected to turn up for work there—or whether I'd find another Serena Somers.

On TV, Larry King was interviewing Congressman Karpovsky.

"Congressman—I know you probably don't want to hear this, but all the pundits are saying you don't have a chance. Why?"

"Well, Larry, I think that people need a little dose of reality now and then. The world needs a truthsayer. Only a truthsayer can show people the way toward healing. Only a truthsayer can save the universe."

"But how are you going to answer the charges of sexual harassment that the young woman has brought forward?"

Congressman Karpovsky looked straight out of the television set, straight into my eyes. I knew I wasn't just watching television anymore. Shit, maybe this was still part of the dream. I almost got the feeling that his hands were going to reach right out of the CRT and touch my face. "Serena," said Karpovsky in a husky parody of a sexy voice, "if you're out there listening, remember that I still love you."

"You're lying!" I said, thinking, I'm talking back to the television, this is like, stage one of paranoid schizophrenia, maybe it's time to see a shrink and have him write up a prescription.

"Oh, Serena," and his face *is* coming out of the screen now, it's a big distended face with a slobbering tongue, "it wasn't rape! You asked for it! You were wearing that titillating halter top—and I'm just your average red-blooded American male with a libido the size of Vesuvius—oh, don't worry, I'm not saying any of this on national television, it's just our minds talking, telepathically linking through the crystal energy of the television set, bet you didn't realize there was anything to all that New Age bullshit, did you?—oh, I'm here on Larry King mouthing an endless string of platitudes but my soul, my soul is in that fleabag with you and your boyfriend's father, maybe we should wake him up for a threesome, eh, wouldn't you like to get it up the ass as well as in the moist and quivering mouth of yours, baby, yeah."

And I suddenly had a memory, fleeting but crystal-clear—the memory unraveled and it was like watching a fast-forward videotape and I was watching it like it hadn't really happened to me and maybe it *really* hadn't happened to me, maybe it was a memory from some other reality, some other me, but if it hadn't really happened why was it so vivid, so compelling?

I think it's the congressman's office. It's a cluttered place—books, papers, a great bronze eagle perched on the desk peering at a crystal whale, a trophy from an environmental organization. And it's me, seventeen, a summer or two back, an age ago.

I'm shaking Karpovsky's hand across the wide mahogany desk (how many acres of obliterated rain forest goes to find one mahogany tree, one desk? but I live with the contradiction, tell myself Karpovsky didn't buy that desk, it was always there, like the glass-eyed eagle and the Colonial style filing cabinet and the sofas upholstered red leather). *Why do you want to work for me, Serena?* His eyes are fixed, hard, emotionless. *I believe in your message. And anyway, Congressman, you're kind of cute.* Why had I said that? I don't know why, it's like the time I played with matches when I was little right after they told me not to and I made the big bonfire in the back yard and the neighbors' treehouse caught fire but it served them right too because they wouldn't let me up in there because there was a big sign that said NO GIRLS ALLOWED and that was B.J., you know, Before Joshua. But the words had come out and what happened next was like, you slip at the top of the stairwell and in the split second before you fall you see the whole thing, your mind draws a chart of your trajectory, and it's all cold and logical and scientific and then, well, you fall (the plush pile carpeting and row upon row of leatherbound tomes all meticulously dusted but never opened) *I'm glad you believe in my message, Serena. Love one another. Would you care for a joint?* (I don't do anything like that, sir.) *You don't do* anything *like that?* but my eyes betray me because in a moment his hands have reached for me across the burnt-out rain forest and pulled me between the eagle and the leaping whale and all I can think about is Joshua, if you could only see me now, my blubber cushioning me against the bronze beak and the crystal snout and the congressman's breath smells of old wine and tobacco.

No! No! I don't remember this, it's false, it's invasive, it's been planted here, it never happened to *me*, not, not, not *me*.

Then why am I crying?

CNN cut to a commercial now. It was a personal injury lawyer telling me I could sue, put a dollar value on pain and suffering. Mr. E. continued to snore.

I've got to know if this is all true. Even if it's a false memory that's been tacked onto my mind because of one of the laws of conservation of reality, it hurts too much. I get up. Somewhere in one of my pockets there's a phone number. A secret number.

You see, Serena, I'm a very big man. An important man. A man who's going to change the way the world thinks. I have inside me this huge and overwhelming compassion for all who suffer. But I also have a tragic flaw, oh, can you understand that, Serena? I'm a lonely man, and I never had a childhood . . . and here we are, you and me, you're so fresh and young, like an unplucked flower, and I am old and weary and withered, a great man with a tragic flaw, an uncontrollable libido.

Yeah. Scrawled on the back of my driver's license. The secret number of the cellular phone that rings everywhere the congressman is, because the little sucker is always tucked in the back pocket of his pants and he *always* answers it.

I looked back at Mr. E., who's moaning a little in his sleep. Maybe he's dreaming about his sons. I hope so. Our dreams are the only things that keep everything real sometimes. I picked up the phone, dialed the number, charged it to my parents' credit card.

Déjà vu. The last time I tried the phone in an alternate universe I'd ended up talking to myself.

"Serena!"

"Serena. I figured you'd call."

"Serena, what are you doing over there? You're here, not there."

"Aren't you the least bit surprised there's two of you?"

"No." There was a lot of giggling in the background. I heard a man snoring. "Why should I be? I always have these dreams. You're my shadow or my alter ego or something. You're always flitting through my life and you're always on some life-and-death mission and shit."

"Karpovsky's asleep? And you're—"

"In bed with him. Along with half the staff!" Serena's laugh was as familiar to me as my own. "Our beloved idol's just getting a little relaxation in—you know he has a big press conference tomorrow, and Larry King really raked him over the coals this evening. It wouldn't have been so bad *in person,* but this interview by remote business sucks, like, it's totally hard to act like a human being when all you have to react to is a talking head on a monitor upbraiding you from Washington."

"You gotta help me, Serena," I said.

"No problemo, sis," she said. "I know why you're here. You're looking for Mrs. E. and for that Navajo police detective."

"How'd you—"

"You leave clues. I leave clues to myself maybe. I find them scribbled on post-its and while-you-were-outs. They're in my own handwriting. Maybe I'm one of those automatic writing people, they had a bunch of them on Oprah last month."

"Well, so what do I do next?" It looked like I'd been through this universe many times before. Maybe I'd planted clues on every pass.

"I'm not sure, but I'd recommend the madhouse first. According to these notes, you busted Mary Etchison from there once. Maybe, now that you've jumped worlds again, she's back inside and hallucinating up a storm."

"How much do you know about all this?" I said.

"As little as I can help. Do you think it's fun having a multiple personality? Only reason Karpovsky keeps me on staff is to fend off the folks from the equal-opportunity-for-the-handicapped league. Yeah, and I keep my mouth shut about the orgies. Unlike some other people I could name." I'd gathered that some tabloid sex scandal thing was in the works, but I knew no more about it than I'd glimpsed on CNN just now. I was more interested in whether I'd actually . . . well, how true that memory was. I owed it to Joshua to have been faithful to him, I guess. A strange feeling to have about someone who didn't exist. I didn't want it to be true. Yet, if it wasn't true, how come I had the secret phone number?

"I want to know something, Serena," I said. "I just arrived here. I was watching TV . . . and I had like, this flashback. About Congressman Karpovsky in his office and, you know, doing things to me."

She laughed. "Oh, he's in therapy now."

"But did it happen?"

"Oh, Serena, why torture yourself over it?" Serena said. "Getting thin, getting fat, yo-yoing back and forth, you and Oprah have a lot in common. At least you have someone to love, you and your Joshua. There's no Joshua here. All I know about him is from the little notes. I envy you, crossing from world to world chasing after him, I mean it's like, so romantic. My therapist says that's why I made you up, because there's a big yawning hole in my life because of, you know, the congressman, robbing me of my youth or something . . . these therapists, they're so anxious to have you fit into their theory they like mythologize the shit out of everything you tell them. Fucking idiots."

"Did I or didn't I?—"

"Funny, I was dreaming about Joshua just before you called. About him walking on the water."

The Serena on the phone was me all right. No question about it. She understood me to the core and I understood her. But Joshua to her was just a dream-companion, a mirage. This Serena had missed the boat. I knew how she'd lain awake nights, thinking vague thoughts about sex, something that only happened to other people, or woke up in the middle of a thunderstorm with a gnawing and unnamable ache inside about something she only half understood. I'd lain awake like that too. But of course I also had Ash, my imaginary companion . . . the third Darkling.

"You're just a shell of a Serena," I said softly.

"You always end up telling me the same thing," she replied. "I don't know how you can like say that, seeing as you're nothing but a phantom, a secret shadow of myself."

"Bullshit!" I said. "I dare you to come and meet me, and then you'll know."

"I'd rather hear voices than see hallucinations. I mean like, you can be a little bit crazy, and then you can be totally lock-'em-up-and-throw-away-the-key psychotic. I don't mind having an imagination, but I don't want my imagination to run my life."

"You're *not* imagining me!"

"Sure. Say hi to Joshua for me." Serena hung up on me.

It was maybe three in the morning or so, I guessed.

I switched channels. The hardcore channel was going full steam. I watched three people grunting and heaving to a New Age score for a while, hunched up in the sofa because Mr. E., sensing my absence, had spread out all over the bed and I didn't want to move him.

I'd go to the asylum tomorrow and see if Mary Etchison was there and if she remembered her two sons. I'd go to the police station and look for Officer Stone. But first I wanted to go down to Karpovsky HQ and give my alter ego the surprise of her life.

CHAPTER NINE

ANOTHER SERENA SOMERS

A n o t h e r   S e r e n a   S o m e r s

My therapist always told me not to block out these . . . imaginary friends. These voices that claimed to come from alternate realities and talked about things that were like just different enough from the real world to make me think I was going crazy.

When I was younger, I mean, the day I had my first period, I saw this man-woman hovering over my pillow and I couldn't exactly hear what he was whispering in my ear but anyway I got the feeling that his words weren't really for me, they were for another me that somehow occupied the same space and time as I did but wasn't the same person. Does this sound like multiple personality disorder? But no, I wasn't all the way crazy like that. My therapist called it a borderline case. She said, well, it could have gone all the way to dissociation if the trauma had been really bad, I mean like if my dad had raped me when I was three and shut me up in a cage and stuff like that. Lots of people, their minds fragment because the things that happen to them are so intolerable they create other personalities . . . buffers between them and the pain of it. Luckily, nothing like that had ever happened to me.

Maybe to another me, but not *me* me.

I used to daydream a lot though. About the not-me mes. There was a me who lived on another planet, a kind of cosmic shopping mall where the meaning of life was for sale in every major department store. There was a me who was abused and abandoned and chained up inside a coffin by sadistic Satanist parents, forced to participate in weird ritual sacrifices and yes, that me was an all-the-way multiple personality, naturally. There was a me who wasn't the slut of GW Junior High, but who kept herself pure and had been in love with one boy all her life, since childhood, a boy named Joshua, but that love was such a big and scary thing that she shielded herself from it by becoming a fat slob. This particular me was often visited by a creature from another dimension named Ash, a imaginary playmate who was sublimely beautiful and sexually nonthreatening. The man-woman hovering by my pillow. Yes, the things Ash whispered in my ear were intended for this particular me, a me who was intensely vivid to me, who was in many ways my ideal picture of myself, and yet was alien to me because she wasn't me.

One time I told all this to my therapist—well, she's not really *my* therapist, but you understand, we are in family therapy because of my parents not getting along and fucking up each other's personal space— and she said, "Honey," which I hate being called, "you are going through your changeling period."—"What's that?" I said, and she's all, "Why, everyone goes through that in their adolescence sometimes. You think that you're really someone else—maybe a faery child—come floating downstream in a basket—magically conceived, yes?"—and I'm, "I just wish I wasn't such a slut,"—and she sighed and said, "You need to get a firmer grip on your femininity, and that doesn't mean squatting on mirrors and fingering yourself; so maybe you are screwing around a lot, which is not a good thing and I hope at least you're practicing safe sex when it comes to that, but you see you're not giving your *self* away in those sex acts, you're not yielding your true self at all, because your true self belongs to this fantasy lover, this Joshua, you see; and I know you've thought this fantasy through thoroughly because the name you picked for your secret lover, Joshua, you know that was the given name of Jesus, and so you know that you are looking for redemption by saving your true self for this fantasy lover, that you can lose your virginity a million times but you become a born-again virgin in your imaginary landscape, you follow what I'm saying? and there's not much I can recommend for that except I could give you a pyramid to put under your bed."

"Sure," I said, "like, a pyramid. Totally fucking phallic." My therapist always made perfect sense up to a point, and then she'd spring some New Age bullshit on me like a pyramid or some crystal. It always amazed me that our insurance condescended to cover these wacky voodoo sessions.

That day in November, I still had the pyramid with me, and before I slid into Karpovsky's bed I also took the pyramid out of my sleeve and chucked it underneath the mattress. Another of the girls saw me do it and laughed. There were three of us who did these special "night duties" with the congressman—none of us really minded, you know, because we did really believe his message, and we did really believe him when he said that this thing of his was an addiction, he was in therapy, and that we weren't bimbos, we were his special girls. We believed he was a great man with a fatal flaw and that we were there to assuage that flaw so he could be great for the rest of the world. Tonight, it was me and Janelle Silverman on duty. She was a nice Jewish girl from North Arlington, ex-Yorktown High School, sophomore at Smith now, taking a year off, writing a children's book on her laptop PC in between the congressional perquisites.

The congressman was tired after his big speech. The university audience really used to get him fired up—those rows and rows of coeds with their ill-concealed beavers beckoning to him as he stood on the pulpit and rhapsodized about his shining vision of a future where poverty would be defeated, where the old would live out their years with dignity and health benefits, where the young would be better educated and know about safe sex (for some reason he was particularly insistent, some might even say strident, about this issue, and those of the retinue who knew the dark secrets would glance demurely at the floor whenever he touched on it), where women and children and minorities were empowered (my parents used to shudder whenever they heard that word uttered; you'd think it spelled the end of civilization; they were, of course, Republicans), where, where, where—and he always did a Jimmy Stewartlike stammer here as his passions hit fever pitch (he practiced the stammer daily after brushing, before flossing)—the human spirit could soar once again—like the great eagle that once soared above the fruited plains, before We came to dispossess Nature and Ourselves. God it was moving. God I loved a good cry, and this audience loved the speech. Truth, Justice, and the Armorican Way. Yeah, okay, so he's tired, and he nods off after a single perfunctory handjob from Janelle, while I watch television.

CNN—human interest story—*today marks the tenth anniversary of the suicide of Phil Etchison, the poet who was to become the guru of the Me Generation.* (Sort of a masturbatory Rod McKuen.) Never read him, but I don't know, I felt some kind of frisson watching a bunch of ha-ha-twenty-nine-year-olds, wearing nouveau New Wave duds—Jesus, I barely remembered those Michael Jackson zippers—laying a wreath at his tomb because it was back in Alexandria and against the backdrop of Virginia green that I'd missed out here in desert country. Cut to Tucson, where apparently his wife, in a loonie bin here, has come out of her padded cell for her one day a year of semilucidity; she speaks to a group of earnest-looking students, ironically enough, in the same building where else-where my lord and master was addressing a packed hall.

Oh yeah. The frisson. There'd been a post-it note stuck to my wallet earlier today. Found it when I was fishing out the credit card to pay for lunch. *Find Mrs. E.* Well, that was this woman, wasn't it? Of course.

Last month, in the toilet, scribbled on a tissue box: *bust her out of the madhouse.* In my handwriting, always in my handwriting.

I watched for a moment, and then there came a phone call on the secret number. Janelle giggled and I answered it.

It was one of the other Serenas, so I assumed that what was happening now had subsequently sprang out of my own imagination . . . my not-quite-insanity.

"Karpovsky's asleep?" she said. "And you're—"

"In bed with him. Along with half the staff!" This wasn't true, but I'm sure my alter ego got her kicks that way. After all, since she was only a figment, she couldn't know the reality of a man's tongue, slithering down your midriff like a prehensile snail. I cackled. (I can be wicked when I'm talking to my other selves, much more wicked than I ever am in my plain jane reality.) Then I told her about looking for Mrs. E.—why not? I'd just seen that nut case on television. And the Navajo police detective was in another note to myself. Scrawled in lipstick in an old address book. (Actually, one time the congressman had us tie him to the bedpost, and we, in full warpaint and loincloths, danced around him shaking baby rattles.)

Was I leading her on? What difference did it make? I looked around and now both Janelle and the congressman were fast asleep even though the lights were all on and the television and there was even music, a Tori Amos song leaking from the abandoned headphones of Janelle's Discman. Whenever I'd talked to myself in the past like this, I always ended up alone somehow, so I could never prove anything to anyone afterward. There'd be like this bubble of unreality that would descend on me. God it was weird.

So this alternate Serena seemed very concerned about whether I'd fucked the congressman or not. You know, the real answer to that was no, not exactly, not all the way, you could sort of sense the final scruples clattering around in his head like jawbreakers in a gumball machine. Congressman Karpovsky had, for reasons I couldn't totally fathom, stopped a couple of centimeters shy of the final insertion. Don't ask me why. I wouldn't have cared. I had been round the block a whole lot of times. In his own way, I guess, the congressman respected us. A complicated man. He wanted to *not* have his cake and *not* eat it too. Denial was fulfillment. Well, you know what they say—brought up by Jesuits.

Shit.

So I was talking to myself on the phone, making up some line about having dreamed about Joshua because I wanted to share some part of what I'd never experienced. But she knew I was lying. Because she said to me, "You're just a shell of a Serena," and she dared me to come and meet her.

How could I meet her, how could I like face myself and *know* that I was crazy, like that poor Mrs. Etchison? I suddenly remembered once, in Modern American Literature 101, they made us read one of Etchison's poems, one about his wife's madness and how she believed she had two sons.

> *She is walking away from the river's edge, sometimes*
> *I know she will never come home,*
> *Better I do not look at all; for in the momentary closure,*
> *The blink's breadth between two truths, two truths can both be true.*
> *When I close my eyes I have two sons, and each*
> *Is the other's shadow; she is the two-breasted Madonna*
> *Who suckles the dark and light, the quick and lifeless,*
> *Red as blood, as desire, as disenchantment.*

The oddest part was how these lines all came to me at once, a crystal-perfect memory, even though I was sure I had dozed through the class and I probably thought it was a total crock at the time. Now I remembered not only the poem but Professor Martindale's tortuous exegesis—myth and archetype, illusion and reality, love-death, madness, the Manichaean duality of existence, Etchison's obsession with the Gnostics, the place of neo-Hellenism in the classical revival of the early 1980s, oh, yeah, the whole lecture unfolded in my mind like the fucking Bayeux Tapestry.

There was a knock on the door.

A secret knock: three shorts and a long—Beethoven's "knock of fate." I was too scared to answer the door. I knew what was behind it and that it was now or never; either I was crazy or I was crazy.

Another knock: the old shave-and-a-hair-cut.

An agonizing wait for the "two bits" that never came.

Then Congressman Karpovsky murmured in his sleep: "The damn door. Shit. Didn't anyone do the damn Do Not Disturb sign?"

I had to open it, but I made sure the chain was latched. Cautiously, I cracked it, just wide enough to prove to myself that I was looking straight into my own face. But thinner. I mean, this was a me that looked *good* when I knew I only looked average. Even though she clearly hadn't showered in a couple of days and her hair was all stringy.

"Can we talk?" she said.

"You can't come in," I said, panicking.

"Yeah, I know. Come down to the lobby or something."

"Okay." I didn't know why I was so quick to agree, but, now that I was certifiable, I guess I didn't like have much to lose. I went back inside and slipped into some clothes—actually it was one of the uniforms of us Karpovsky's cheerleaders—short but unscandalworthy gray skirt, any color blouse, UAW jacket, little green button to show solidarity with the Greens. I went out into the hallway.

"You won't need that," Serena said, and I realized I was still clutching the secret number cellular phone. "We're talking face-to-face now."

The lobby was a forbidding place at night. This was a faceless name-brand hotel with a lot of mirrors and a scenic elevator and a lot of fountains, conspicuous consumption in the middle of the desert. Tall columns of circular mirrors dwarfed us. They were hung with ferns. It was a kind of techno-redwood forest. A stream ran through the middle of the lobby and it was stocked with koi. There was no one else around. Once more, no alibis for my insanity.

"We don't have much time," Serena said, and she pushed me into the nearest sofa—plush, southwestern, pink and beige—"because one of us is going to cease to exist any minute."

"What are you talking about? Is this fusion?" Which was what was supposed to happen when multiple personalities started getting to know each other and the barriers broke down and they could become absorbed into one another.

"No, Serena. It's like, not what you think. You're not crazy."

"I'm glad we agree about *that*," I said, and neither of us laughed.

"This isn't the America you know anymore."

"America? What's that?"

"I mean, Armorica."

"Okay, so *I'm* not crazy, just everybody else in the world."

"Okay, this is gonna be hard to swallow, Serena, but you and I are equivalent people from like these parallel worlds, okay? And all the worlds are smooshing into each other, as in a multi-universe pileup, because the River that connects all the universes is going through major turbulence because Josh went back through the barrier and Theo went after him and the Darklings are battling each other and . . ."

She looked at me in frustration. "I'll take that part as read," I said. "But what about us?"

"Well, I think there's really only supposed to be *one* of us here. When we crossed over, the universe did radical surgery on itself to eliminate all the paradoxes as quickly as it could. It killed off one complete busload of Karpovsky followers and convinced everyone they were all impostors. Then it shifted Mr. E. so that he's been dead for ten years, so the Mr. E. I'm traveling with could be the only one. Josh and Theo are gone anyway, so that just leaves you and me, and one of us has got to go."

"So you're gonna blow me away with a .357 Magnum now?"

"Oh, get real, girl." She gripped both of my hands in hers and I saw, suddenly, that she really *was* me. The me that would have been if I hadn't given up on myself when I reached puberty. The me that had been kept strong, and innocent, and wise, by a deep, unselfconscious love. Oh, God, I envied her. Me. And when I looked into her eyes I saw that this was a chance to become that me. To wash the soiled laundry of my life. "I figure," Serena said, "if we really concentrate hard on it, if we *both* agree to like, die, maybe we can somehow connect, merge, reinvent ourselves as a single person, bypass the dimensional paradox. Do you understand what I mean?"

"You're talking suicide pact!" I said. But you know, I wasn't shocked. Because there had always been like, this unreality to my life. Face it, dudette, I told myself, you've always been the phantom of someone else's opera. If in dying I could become more real, more fully myself, I couldn't really refuse that, could I? And this was what my therapist called fusion. It wasn't really death. It was transformation. Right? Right. I found myself gripping my alter ego's hands so hard her palms were bleeding. Or were they mine? I didn't know. The blood was swirling like a miniature galaxy. No, the whole room was swirling. The two of us were swirling. I was a woman with two heads and four arms, one of those Hindu goddesses. We got up from the sofa and then the sofa was the world and we—I—was astride it, joyous, dancing to the hip-hop of the cosmos. My four arms whirled like the spokes of a wheel, they flamed, I was breaking the world on the catharine wheel of my passion, breaking and reforming the world, and yawning the stars and moons from my lips, and the clouds wreathing my spinning feet, I juggled chaos and order in my lightning hands, and, and, and—

Everything became very still. The tempest had receded into a faint throbbing. Only my heartbeat.

I was the only person in the lobby of the campaign headquarters hotel. The alter ego was gone. "Serena?" I said. Then came the memories. They flooded me. They overwhelmed me. I could see the dragon woman screeching across an orange sky and I could feel dead Joshua coming back to life in my arms. Not just shards of a daydream. It was *real.* And I remembered a country called America, rock-solid, not a phantom.

S e r e n a   S o m e r s

"Serena, Serena," I said—because I wasn't used to not talking to a mirage of myself—"Serena, what if there are other mes out there, or if other mes are going to be hurled out because of all these cosmoses collapsing in on each other?"

I answered myself: "We'll draw them all into ourself. We're not going to be pieces of a person. We're going to heal."

I slipped into the congressman's suite and I called Mr. E. from the cellular phone even though it was like four a.m. He groaned. "Mr. E.!" I said. "Like, I died and came to earth."

"What are you talking about?" he mumbled. "Serena?"

"Wake up, Mr. E.—oh, wake up—something wonderful has happened. Let's go to the asylum and get your wife."

"Now?"

"Did you know it's the anniversary of your death?" CNN was broadcasting the news again. "Turn it on! But you know, we're still in the middle of the Day of the Dead, aren't we? And you're dead, but you're walking the earth again, aren't you? And I've just killed myself, but I'm alive, aren't I?"

"This is too much to take all at once," said Mr. E.

"No, you see, it all makes sense because on the anniversary of your death, she becomes lucid . . . *two truths can both be true* . . . you said that. I learned it in school."

"Maybe I did," he said. "Maybe I did."

"Well like, now is the time when two truths are true. It's a window of opportunity. I know this because I have all my own memories and all my *other* memories too. I know this world as well as I know my own world. I mean, I belong to both now. So I'm telling you, we've gotta spring Mrs. E. from the madhouse before dawn. Do you think we can find Detective Stone, too?"

"Yeah." He was coming to now.

"I'll meet you back at the hotel, outside. Look, I took the car, so don't panic. I had to drive down here to Karpovsky HQ on some personal business."

"Personal?"

"Integrating my soul," I said. "Can't get much more personal than that."

I slammed Karpovsky's door behind me and took the elevator back downstairs. The Tucson night was cold and I was glad of the UAW jacket (which had kind of materialized on my back after the two of us fused). I got back in the Cadillac and drove on back to Oracle.

Phil Etchison

I staggered to the lobby just as the Cadillac pulled up. The Serena who greeted me was the same and not the same. She wasn't as thin as when she'd left, but she wasn't fat either; for the first time, her proportions seemed to be right—she seemed to be comfortable with the way she looked as she hopped out of the car and waved at me to hurry up.

I had woken from a nightmare, was rubbing nightmare ectoplasm from my eyes. I staggered toward her. She supported me as I eased myself onto the seat. "I'll drive," she said, coolly in control. "I actually know where I'm going, for once."

We moved into the night. I was relieved that she was driving. The Cadillac's gearshift was labeled PRNDBQZLL. We were in the Q-gear at the moment, and the 7-Eleven was no longer at the corner. Disjunctive fugue was setting in again. Reality was in flux, had always been in flux, and it was all I could do to stay calm.

CHAPTER TEN

YELLOW BRICK ROADS

Theo Etchison

I don't know how long I'm walking. The sound of the stream on my left is the only constant thing. The forest keeps shifting and transforming. Sometimes it's all cactus, sometimes it's redwood, sometimes it's a Tarzan-type jungle with swinging vines that might just be coiling anacondas. It's a scary place, but at least I have my dream book now, and I still have the marble . . . so I still have some idea of where I'm going as long as I don't look too hard at what's surrounding me, just walk straight ahead, straight through piles of decomposing leaves and branches, through twisted tree trunks that melt like mirages when I pass through them. The forest is full of sounds. Birds tweet and screech, rodents scurry, monkeys chitter, snakes slither. I'm afraid but I keep on walking. Walking. There's no breeze in this forest; it's as close and claustrophobic as a locked closet. I keep walking. I have the jester's bells tucked into my pants and my notebook under my arm and I keep walking.

I'm fixated on one thing: Joshua. I *know* I'm going in the right direction. I know with the certainty of truthsaying that he's near me, but there's something missing from the picture, something I can't quite see.

I keep on walking.

It gets darker. And darker. And day never comes. Night deepens into mega-night. There's never going to be day in this forest, I think. I just keep walking. I'm exhausted and hungry. Have I been wandering around in circles? I don't think so. Hasn't the stream been at my left hand the whole time? Or is the stream a circle? I take the marble out and try to peer into its depths, but there is so little light that all I can make out is the writhing of the filaments. Why is that? I wonder. Is there a truth so obscure that even a truthsayer can't see it? Or am I losing my powers? I can't tell. I'm getting totally frustrated now.

I keep walking, I don't know for how long. It doesn't get any lighter and the air doesn't get more breathable. The vapors of night cling to me and I'm almost suffocating. The trees have started to come alive. The vines hiss and lash out at me. They rip at my face. I feel something clawing at my arm, turn to look, see only a pair of soulless eyes in the darkness. I have to keep moving even though my limbs are leaden. There are things pursuing me and if I stop they'll catch up with me and kill me. A tremor shakes the darkness, like the purring of a giant black cat against my body. I can feel the vibration in my guts . . . oh God I'm frightened and I quicken my pace now, quicken, quicken, though I'm short of breath and every step is more agonizing than the one before . . . faster. Faster. Faster.

There are creatures running behind me. Their paws pound the hard earth. Their spoor stinks up the air. I keep running. And a part of me says, *Stop, stop, turn to face the demon.* And another part says, *No, no, no, I'm scared, gotta keep running—*

Running.

Running.

But I'm too exhausted. I have to stop. And I do. I turn.

Eyes—hard—yellow—crystalline—a blur of mottled yellow and black fur—canines slicing the thick air and—

The jaguar pounces and I—

There's nothing to fight back with. Without thinking I pull the jester's bells from my pants and I kind of brandish it and I hear the tinkling and see the silvery light that streaks against the forest canopy and—

The jaguar's at my feet, purring softly. Soft light emanates from the bells in my hand. I shake them again. The tinkling . . . the jaguar's fascinated by it. The jaguar's hypnotized by the dancing light. The birds' harsh screeches turn to delicate twittering. I hear the whisper of the nearby stream.

I shake the bells. Music pours from them. It's sort of a New Age sound, hardly anything to get up and slamdance to, but around here it seems to have magic. I don't feel the magic. I'm immune to it, I guess. But the forest is bewitched. Animals crawl out of the undergrowth—rabbits and fawns and porcupines. A vulture settles on the jaguar's back and tilts its head back and forth in time to the music. A snake unreels from a nearby branch and hovers over me but somehow I don't feel threatened. The music continues even after I stop tinkling; the bells are on autopilot I guess, like one of those Christmas cards that play *Jingle Bells* when you open them up.

Finally I can take a breather. I sit down on spongy earth. All the animals' cries, purrs, and chatterings begin to blend together. Soon there's a wall of harmony around me. It's almost like one of the production numbers from the *Jungle Book* cartoon. I know it's supposed to make me feel like Orpheus charming the wild beasts, soothing the savage breasts and all that shit, but the music doesn't have any power over me at all, it's just like this cosmic Muzak I guess, transcendental elevator music. I lean against a tree trunk. I wish there was something to eat. Why can't there be fruit hanging on any of these trees? Oh, but there is—it's just that they're all glittery and jewellike, they're decorator fruit, not nutrition. Like everything else here, an illusion.

I sit under the tree for a long time. Maybe I fall asleep. I'm not sure. I'm so hungry now that my stomach's stopped hurting. I'm all stretched out thin, like air. The light radiates outward from the bells and forms a circle around me. The jaguar growls softly, paws the ground, worries at something. I have a feeling that I know him.

"Who are you?" I say.

He stares up into my eyes. His eyes aren't hard anymore. He is weeping. His tears are like drops of amber. I bend down and wipe one away with my finger. I have the feeling that he's very old.

"What are you crying about?" I ask him. It wouldn't surprise me if he could talk; I've run into talking animals and even plants in these strange worlds. But before he can answer me I see that there's a deep and festering wound in the jaguar's side. He licks at it and continues to weep.

"I think I know who you are now," I say. But it doesn't make sense to me.

And that's when I notice the trail of breadcrumbs, leading from where

I'm sitting, away from the stream and into the thickest part of the forest, and, beneath the line of strewn crusts, beneath the undergrowth, the glint of metallic yellow. . . .

Phil Etchison

Serena drove fast. I barely had a chance to compose myself when we found ourselves outside the Tucson police station.

"The place looks different," I said. I had begun to remember how I had come here with Joshua last year to look for Theo . . . and how Joshua had been captured by Katastrofa. "Are you sure it's the right place? I don't remember this art deco façade."

Serena double parked—a foolhardy thing to do in front of a police station—and said, "Why don't you go inside, Mr. E., and find out if there's a Detective Stone here."

I must have looked worried, because she added, "Don't worry. Would you rather have me go?"

I said, "No, I'll do it. But leave the engine running; I don't want you to get a ticket. If there's a problem, go around the block or something."

I went up the steps. The reception area seemed familiar enough, the woman at the desk appropriately dour as she pecked at a manual typewriter, a faint whiff of death and stale tobacco in the air.

"Is there a Detective Stone here, ma'am?" I said.

She glanced up from her paperwork. "Stone?" she said. "Not on your life. He was—retired, you know, without pay. Unofficially. You should know that."

"I should?"

"You're not a reporter, are you? After they had my picture in the *Enquirer,* I almost got fired."

"I don't know what you mean."

"Well, it's not every day that a respected cop gets photographed trying on women's lingerie at Frederick's," she said. "Frankly, what they do when they're in Hollywood on vacation's not the department's business, but then when Action Against Defamation of Native Americans issued a statement saying that Milt was a *nadlé,* some kind of transvestite witch doctor, and then the ACLU put in their two cents, and someone dug up a photograph of Milt Stone in a tutu doing the *pas de deux* from Swan Lake with that defector from the Bolshoi Ballet . . . well . . . I'm sure you saw the whole thing on Sally Jessy Raphael last month."

"Ah . . . I've been in Mexico."

"He a relative of yours?"

"Not exactly. A . . . a friend."

"Oh, I see. A fellow fairy, huh. Not that I'm into queer bashing—against department policy anyway—but anyone who would hang out with Milt Stone is probably sort of a funny bunny himself."

"Milt Stone's not gay," I said, somewhat repelled by her prejudice and at the same time feeling a little awkward about having to defend Milt's honor against a creature such as this, "he really *is* a *nadlé,* a sacred man-woman of the Navajo people. Seriously. He can do amazing things . . . walk between worlds . . . die and live again . . . things you couldn't possibly imagine."

"Yeah, right," she said. "I guess you're not one of his fag friends then. You're one of his fellow druggies. Peyote, shrooms, LSD, he did 'em all, according to the thing on Channel 6."

"Well, could you tell me where I might be able to find him?"

"Went back to the hogan," she said. "You want directions?" She fished in a drawer and pulled out a Xerox of a crudely drawn map. "Come to think of it, you're Etchison, aren't you?" she added. "He said you'd be coming by. There's some other stuff with the map." She handed me a jiffy bag with lumpy contents. "That better not be drugs," she said. "Word of honor?"

I nodded, though I had no idea what the contents might be. I felt the jiffy bag. It seemed to be full of rocks. "Thank you," I said, adding, as I read the name plate by her typewriter, "Ms. Magdalen."

"Mariel," she said, and smiled at me for the first time. She rummaged in her drawer again, and, after considerable pushing aside of papers, produced a battered, coffee-stained, coverless copy of *The Embrasure of Parched Lips.* "It really *is* you, isn't it, Mr. Etchison. I really didn't believe that a low-life like Stone could actually know a *famous* poet—he never really knew any white people, socially that is. My heavens, I'm sorry about all the things I said. His friends that aren't actually Injuns are all white trash, you see. Milt told me you'd call me *Ms.*—because you got class, you know."

"I see," I said. It was hard to make sense of the map. It showed the freeway leading northeast out of Tucson. An exit (labeled "unmarked") led to a thread of a road that snaked up into mountainous terrain and wound in and out and up and down itself and tied itself into knots and ended up in a jumble of squiggles just past the Painted Desert. Tony Hillerman country, land of kachinas and gateways into other worlds. There was no rhyme or reason to the way it twisted. It obviously belonged to the "yellow brick" category of road . . . a concretization of the metaphoric journey of the soul . . . yet another "human condition" flag for the academic poetry professors who had been my most loyal and most pretentious audience for the entirety of my career.

I signed *The Embrasure of Parched Lips* with the felt tip pen Mariel held out to me. Then, on a whim, I flipped through the pages, thinking at least to anchor myself to the remembrance of familiar words.

But it is a sea of words, a seething melee of letters running into each other with now and then a single significant word breaching the maelstrom like a singing whale:

> aghastaflamelove**seeking**jumpriverhigh**storm**bursting
> leapriverleap**leap**fuckingcoprolalialexico**name**liae**ear**hart
> oh   my **soul**
> applejumpleapflame**seethe**lovetruthteethapple
> good   and   evil
> seepappleseepseekappleseepapple**seek**appleseekseep**sikh**
> and ye shall **find**

What was I to make of these Joycean thunderclaps? I knew they were not my words. But my signature was now on the flyleaf, and my name was on the spine, and *Ms.* Magdalen was fixing me with a starry-eyed stare; I searched the cinema-multiplex of memory for some image of myself and these words and came up empty.

So I thanked her quickly, a tad brusquely, for her kind information, and left the police station with the road map in my pocket.

Theo Etchison

I'm amazed at how hungry I am. I keep picking up the crumbs and wolfing them down. I guess I must have been walking in circles for days because the hard crusts are sweet as candy. The jaguar follows me. I hold the bells in front of my face like a torch. I walk in a circle of light. The crumbs have a distinct flavor of gingerbread, and as I move farther from the River I get the feeling I'm being sucked into the story of Hansel and Gretel.

The light begins to spread and the trees thin out a little and pretty soon I see the outlines of the gingerbread house, which is not at all like the way it's usually illustrated in kids' books—it's big and ominous and many-gabled, more like the *Psycho* house at Universal Studios—looming up in the middle of a clearing. It's completely encircled by a row of like these twisted, rainbow-colored mushrooms—psychedelic shrooms maybe—and it has a chimney that spews out industrial-strength smoke. It's the gingerbread house from hell. It's a little bit like Auschwitz and a little bit like Pittsburgh. The jaguar growls and I pet him to make him calm down.

I'm scared to go inside even though I know the story says I have to end up going in there and doing battle with the witch, so I hang around on the porch. I'm still totally starving so I keep tearing off little strips from the wall and chewing on them. The gingerbread's rich and spicy and it makes me lightheaded because my mind begins to drift a little—I see an image of Serena Somers—a dozen Serena Somerses, fat, thin, and medium-sized, dancing in a ring, converging slowly into a kind of mega-Serena in the middle.

Then I hear a woman's voice: "Theo Truthsayer," she says, "you've gone and eaten my food, and that means you're my prisoner now; you have to stay in my kingdom forever."

I turn around and see her: she's tall, red-haired, with a sweeping cloak and the eyes of a serpent. "Katastrofa Darkling," I say softly.

I know this is the place I've been meaning to go all this time. I know that Katastrofa has my brother captive somewhere in this cannibal candy mansion.

"Theo," she says, "why do you hate me so much?"

"Because you killed my brother."

"Your brother chose to come back to me because he loves me. And he's not dead, not exactly." She smiles this cat-and-canary smile that tells me that she has me trapped. She strokes my cheek with the edge of a single fingernail. I blush in spite of myself. She's beautiful. She's all perfumed and licking her lips and I feel something unfamiliar, you know, down in my pants, and I'm thinking, O Jesus, don't tell me my hormones are finally kicking in, what a stupid time for this to happen, nobody ever told me it would be embarrassing like this . . . and I force myself not to think about her, to think only about Joshua and the things she's done to him. . . .

"I want to see him!"

"Then you'll have to come inside, Theo Truthsayer. And perhaps you'll have to run me a few simple errands . . . simple enough, at least, for someone with your special gift."

"I'm not taking sides," I say, "in this big old war you've got going with your brothers. It's totally none of my business. I didn't ask to be a truth-sayer. I only came back here to get Joshua."

"Just park your jaguar outside and get in the goddamn house. If you want to see your brother alive you'd better be prepared to do something for me in exchange."

The jaguar has coiled up by the front door and seems to be dozing as I step over the threshold of Katastrofa's castle.

Phil Etchison

It was getting light when we reached the asylum. I wasn't entirely sure how I was going to manage the next stage of the plan, but, since I could come up with no Machiavellian ruse, I decided on the direct approach.

I pulled right up to the front of the building—which bore an incongruous resemblance to the Parthenon—and parked illegally in an ambulance space. Serena and I marched up the steps, attempting to appear as though we belonged.

A lone, corpulent nurse sat behind the reception desk. It looked as though a replay of the scene at the police station was about to occur: the only difference was the décor—art deco there, neoclassical here.

"Excuse me," I said.

She looked at me and screamed.

"What's the problem?" I said to Serena. "It's not as if she was seeing a ghost or something—"

"Actually," said Serena, "you *are* supposed to be dead in this universe. According to CNN."

"But the policewoman at the station didn't think so . . ."

"Probably just behind the times," she said. We watched the receptionist flailing in horror; I wondered when she would get around to calling the Ghostbusters. "Come on," said Serena. "While she's busy screaming, we can probably make it to Mrs. E.'s room."

She was already heading toward the elevators, and I realized that I, too, knew the way . . . as though we had trod through this segment of our lives a thousand times before, and would again a thousand times . . . I pushed the button, we negotiated the narrow corridors, turned left, left, right, right, found ourselves opening a familiar door, facing a familiar woman. . . .

"Mary," I said.

And she was the way I remembered her before the cancer. Her hair hadn't been eaten away by chemotherapy. Her cheeks were full, her lips had the impertinent pout they'd had the first time we'd met. She stood there in her hospital gown in a darkened room framed by the severe metallic window sill against iron bars that gleamed in the soft moonlight.

Oh, she was translucent, beautiful in an elfin way; and she was strangely young; and I remembered that, in this incarnation, having taken refuge in her madness at an early age, she had not lived through many of the apocalyptic events that had taken their toll on the Mary I'd lived with, the one who'd toiled beside me twenty years and more; no, this was a fresh Mary, in a very real sense a virgin Mary, a clear white parchment Mary.

"Philip," she said, "I've waited here so long. I thought I was doomed to die an unconsummated Rapunzel." She smiled. "I've always known you weren't really dead; that your death had been manufactured to prepare for this moment. Oh, come, come quickly, before the sun rises, because that's when I retreat into darkness for another year."

We embraced.

"Way to go, Mr. and Mrs. E.," said Serena.

We kissed, and in that kiss we mingled the disparate memories of our sundered selves; and oh, I knew then how much I loved her, and how much I needed to be whole.

CHAPTER ELEVEN

KATASTROFA'S CASTLE

Theo Etchison

Of course, the interior of the gingerbread house isn't what you'd expect from the outside. Because folded up inside it is the entire domain of Katastrofa, second child of King Strang, the dragon woman. Oh, when I step inside there's like the impression of a witch's hovel. There's an iron stove puffing away at one end of the chamber, and the floor is strewn with straw and bones, and there's beat-up leatherbound grimoires with human skulls holding up guttering candles, and a shelf full of alembics and retorts and crucibles with bubbling fluids in neon shades, and bats and rats dangling from the ceiling on ropes, and all the usual bullshit; but then, you look *past* these things, and *through* them, you look around corners, and you see there's much, much more. Behind the stove, there's a steep canyon, and a lake of fire, and a path that zigzags up a cliff to a

mesa, and on that mesa is a Cadillac, upright, half-buried, its front end
pointed at the moon; sometimes these vistas seem like wallpaper, sometimes they move. Wheeling over our heads are mist-creatures—fanged,
clawed, winged, dissolving in and out of one another. It's a scary place.
But I can feel Joshua's presence. I guess I've felt him all along.

Katastrofa leads me by the hand . . . her hand is almost scalding-hot
but she won't let go of me. The heat seeps into my fingers, races through
my veins, makes my heart beat faster, yeah, makes this demon inside me
stir, this sex thing I've spent the last couple of years trying not to think
about because it scares me.

"When am I going to see Josh?" I ask her.

"In time," she says. But she seems nervous.

"Show him to me now."

I'm losing my fear because I know she needs me to win her war, and
I'm too valuable for her to harm. I've been through this bullshit before,
and furthermore, this time, I came of my own free will, and I know the
score.

"If you insist," says Katastrofa Darkling. "But first, the grand tour; I'm
sure you feel like a grand tour, don't you?" And we start to descend.

I know from previous experience that the tour will only show me images plucked from my own childish fantasies; that the real world that
these creatures inhabit is full of things I have no referents for; so the best
I can do is construct these mirages around myself, pictures from pulp and
celluloid, from comic books and my dad's flights of poetry, from PBS
specials and Bart Simpson cartoons . . . this is the only reality I know,
but I'm the truthsayer, not some brilliant visionary, not some transcendental world-builder, only me; and so this is the reality they're all stuck
with. *I was a teenage demiurge.* Fuck, what a trip.

This place is nothing like Thornslaught. The castle of Katastrofa's
brother is full of daunting endless spaces, vaulting ceilings, sweeping
staircases. This is just as vast, but everything has a twisted, claustrophobic, tunnellike feel to it. The giant vistas are there but they are all gorges
and canyons with towering cliffs that hem us in. There's never a feeling
of being outside even when we glimpse the sky through a lattice of thatch
or a jungle canopy. Katastrofa doesn't let go of my hand.

Thorn had a lot of servants scurrying around, lackeys fawning all over
him the whole time. Ash had his minions too, although they weren't
slavish like Thorn's. Katastrofa's not like that. She's a loner. As she drags
me deeper and deeper down the dungeon steps, there's barely any people around. Oh, now and then a gnomelike creature skulks past. Stairwells coil. Our footsteps ring against cold metal. Walls drip with blood

and wet graffiti. Katastrofa doesn't say very much, but now and then she turns to glower at me, and sometimes she licks her lips with a forked tongue. She moves with a slithering motion; even in human form there's something of the dragon in her.

At last we seem to reach the lowest level of Katastrofa's castle. "Your room," she tells me, and points to a cell—one of those medieval dungeon type things—iron bars, straw pallet, chains hanging on the wall. "Not exactly the Hyatt, but you can change it around any way you want."

"Jesus. At least Thorn tried to recreate my old room back in Virginia . . . tried to make me feel at home, in his own way."

"I'm not like Thorn," she says. "Thorn has illusions. He's the eldest, you know. He sucks his people's blood, but now and then the human condition gets to him a little, and he gets saddled with compassion."

"Didn't see too much of that."

"Oh, but you did." I guess I do remember a few vulnerable moments. "You won't find them with me. Do you know why I chose to become a weredragon?"

"I couldn't guess."

"Because I rage through the world. I am anger; I am vengeance."

"No, you're not," I say. Because I'm a truthsayer, I can't help shattering her self-delusions. "You're just a typical middle kid, with a middle kid complex. You were jealous of Thorn's power; you couldn't stand it that Ash was the apple of Strang's eye. You chose the form of a beast because you hate yourself."

"That's ridiculous. Men fear me. And they love me. A glamour clings to me. Even through my human skin there's the shimmer of serpentine scales. I am sensuality as well as rage. I am the love that kills."

"You're only trying to convince yourself."

Sullen, she turns away from me. There's less glower in those glowing eyes. "Don't think you can subdue me with mindgames, Theo Truthsayer. You too are clinging to something you don't really have anymore—your childhood."

She kisses me. I can feel her tongue against my lips, pulsing, hot, trying to force them apart. Her arms entwine me like the coils of a boa constrictor. My dick is all straining, uncomfortable; it's not desire exactly, it's my body going through the mechanics of what it's just learning to do. I'm confused. It's like I'm losing my anchor on the truth. Quickly I pull away and say, "You don't dare seduce me. Maybe I'm like Peter Pan, you know; if I grow up and I feel real desires and come and all, I'll lose my powers." The minute I say this I wonder if it's true. It *feels* true. But I'm not sure, the way I'm always so sure of everything else. I want to change the subject.

"Joshua," I say. "Show me Joshua. Or you won't get any help from me."

"All right."

She claps her hands. Some of the prison walls kind of melt away and we're in like this torture chamber. There are cages hanging from the ceiling, dozens of them, and in each cage there's a naked man or a boy. They're all wasting away, skin and bones, most of them. They stare vacantly into the dimness. They were all beautiful once. Like my brother I guess; he was always the straight and tall one and I was always the creep. I follow Katastrofa as she works her way through the dangling cages. Now and then she stops in front of one of them and she reaches in and caresses the young man's thighs and he begins to sigh . . . it's like she's sucking out their youth . . . their manhood . . . yeah, and there's a faint odor in the air and I recognize the smell from the times I've gone to the bathroom after Joshua and he's kind of slinking past me on the landing with a magazine wrapped up in his towel. The jacking off smell. Yeah. Katastrofa's a vampire too, a sex vampire . . . she's everything that scares me about sex and about growing up. The dudes in the cages are all whimpering, moaning, they're all older than me, they've gone through puberty, and now they're being drained, they're slaves of their own desires . . . Jesus I sound like a fucking television minister and I should know better but I'm scared, sex to me is a big old dragon waiting in a cave and I'm a knight without a sword standing outside pissing myself with terror. Actually I think I might really piss myself and I tell myself no, it's been too long since you wet the bed, you can't regress to that anymore, you're the truthsayer, you're supposed to be in control.

And I can sense Joshua getting closer and closer; it's almost like he's inside of me.

Katastrofa moves quickly, sometimes brushing past a cage and making it swing back and forth; I watch the boy inside, helpless, slide from side to side against the bars. At last we reach the end of the hallway.

"My beloved," says Katastrofa. She whisks aside a curtain and that's when I see Joshua, in his own chamber, in his own coffin.

There's like an altar rail in front of the coffin. In a way it reminds me of the shrine where my mother, the statue, was being worshipped. There are votive candles and, on the wall, where his head is pointed, there's an icon of the One Mother, her hands outstretched, weeping tears of blood; at Joshua's feet there's a stone Cupid, and it too is weeping.

It's a glass coffin. But he's no Snow White. He's not a perfect creature in a dreamless sleep; he's a corpse. The coffin is filled with sea water and the room and you can hear the wind howling through high, barred, glassless windows, and outside the windows you can see the cliffside bungalow by the Laetrile clinic and there are gulls screeching and a faint murmur of a festive crowd and, fainter still, the salsa music; out there, the Day of the Dead is still going on.

Katastrofa laughs. "You think he's dead, don't you?"

"Yeah." I don't feel Joshua's presence at all, even though I know he's here, right here, in the decomposing flesh. That feeling of him close by, crying out to me, I left that feeling behind as soon as I stepped into this little room. "You've drained him. You can't keep me here because you've killed him."

"I did not kill him. I gave him love."

"It wasn't love. It was a kind of craziness." It has to be craziness. I know that no human woman's ever made me feel the way she does just by touching me. "It was Serena who loved him. And me."

Katastrofa bends over my brother's face. The salt water's been eating at him; some of the skin is peeling; the complexion is green; the eyes are jellied; a crab skitters across his lips. "Look at his eyes," she says. "Pearls; they catch the light; see, see." She flicks the crab out of the way and kisses him.

Joshua stirs. I feel a tugging in my heart.

His eyes seem to flash for a moment. "Joshua," I say softly.

Katastrofa reaches into the crystal sarcophagus and puts her arms around him, draws him into a sitting position, hugs him hard; a sulfurous mist exudes from her nostrils; her dragon nature is trying to burst through her human shape. And Joshua begins to move. His arms slowly animate themselves in zombielike, stop-motion little jerks. The fingers begin mechanically to knead Katastrofa's back. And Joshua speaks: *"Ka . . . ta . . . stro . . . fa . . ."* God, I'm going to cry. I can't stand to see him this way. I'm scared and enraged and full of grief, all at once. I sort of tackle Katastrofa and try to push her off of Joshua and I'm screaming, "No, you don't, no, he's my brother, you can't do that to him, you can't, you can't—"

She lets go of him all of a sudden and he collapses back into the brine and she's totally laughing at me, doing the whole wicked witch thing, and I see the twitching pseudo-life go out of Joshua and he's just like a rag doll again, limp, dull-eyed, dead.

But the moment he goes completely lifeless is also the moment that I feel, once again, the glimmer of his presence within me.

I don't know what it means. I know there's a chance of bringing my brother back. I know I have to stay here until I figure out how. I know Katastrofa's castle is an even more terrifying place to be than Thornslaught, because when Katastrofa comes close to me she somehow puts me at war with myself. God, I hope I lose my powers one day. I just want to be normal. I don't want to see anymore.

I turn my back on the dragon woman and on my undead brother in his glass sarcophagus. Oh, God, I'm drowning. I want out. I hate myself and I hate my life.

"Don't you dare turn your back on me," says Katastrofa. "Don't you understand, little man, that I have the key to your salvation?"

"Leave me alone! I wish I'd been an ordinary kid, I wish I'd spent my life ditching school and tagging the bus and shoplifting instead of having these dreams that aren't dreams . . . I want to forget everything. Take away my gift, take away my knowledge."

"Take it away!" She laughs. "There are those who'd give their right eye for such knowledge . . . and not just humans . . . even the gods themselves."

So what? I'm thinking. I'm not Odin or any of that crowd, and I never asked to be.

"We're just talking a simple bargain," Katastrofa says. "My brother for your brother. You help me kill mine, I help you bring yours back to life."

I don't look back at her. But she comes close to me and she puts her arms around me as I stare at the dungeon floor, and she kisses the crown of my head, and I think: I hated Thorn. I love Joshua. Why shouldn't I kill one and save the other? What fucking difference does it make to me whether Thorn or Katastrofa inherits the kingdom of the fisher king?

Somewhere, a jaguar growls.

CHAPTER TWELVE

THE DANCING WOMAN

<u>S e r e n a   S o m e r s</u>

I was still the designated driver because Mr. and Mrs. E. were lost in a private reverie. It was maybe an hour before dawn and I knew they needed to talk about a lot of things before the Day of the Dead came to an end; afterward, who knew what Mrs. E. would know, or whether her sickness would be of the soul or of the flesh. I let them both sit in the back and I tried to be a good chauffeur, not eavesdropping too much. I had the map spread out on the passenger seat, and the dome light on, trying to make heads or tails out of it.

"I turn into a pumpkin at dawn," Mrs. E. said. "But for now, I see everything so clearly . . . I mean our lives. The poetry readings by the fireplace, you telling the kids that poetry *is* the best kind of Sunday school; and the weekends in Spotsylvania County with the grandparents; and in Colorado, Theo swinging across the creek scrunched into an old tire that hung from a cottonwood tree; and in Alexandria, me getting the test results from Dr. Schmitz, knowing there wasn't any more hope; oh, God, you don't know what it was like in the madhouse, with all the wrong memories, sometimes not knowing my own name; and the voices telling me my illness was the price of the world's salvation . . . delusions of grandeur."

She was talking mostly to herself, and Mr. E. was listening; sometimes, looking up in the rearview mirror, I saw him with his eyes closed, knew he was drinking in the things she said, the confirmation of his own confounded memories. And sometimes he'd just say, "Yes, Mary, oh, God, yes, I remember now."

Mary said, "Please don't let me forget again. It's like being blind and not even being able to remember what it was like to see. They used to thorazine me when I heard voices."

"No, Mary, you're not going to forget everything when the sun comes up. Because we're with you now, and we're from the real world, your world."

It wasn't that bad going up through Pinal and Gila Counties but after that, going into Navajo County, was when the map started getting weird. For one thing, it should have been day a long time ago, but the sun stayed beneath the horizon; we were stuck in a twilight that never wanted to become dawn. On the map, the road we were on ran straight only a little while longer, then became as involuted as a ball of yarn. I was all trying to follow, wrenching the wheel hard left and hard right, scraping the bottom of the car when the road dipped or swerved abruptly. The terrain was barren and repetitive, and there were these monster rock formations, sandstone dinosaurs that seemed to totally lumber over the sea of sagebrush.

"I'm starting to feel dizzy," Mrs. E. said. And for the first time since we'd rescued her I started to smell a sick-sweet odor, like the smell of old oranges . . . that was how she used to smell when she was dying of cancer. Even the Cupid-shaped air freshener couldn't withstand the odor.

"Oh, Mrs. E.," I said, "oh, Jesus." But I had to concentrate on the road because now it was like one of those racing car video games, up and down and around and around, and the smell of the dying was heavier now, cloying, suffocating, and I had to concentrate hard on keeping my eyes on the road, and the desert was shifting too, I could see shapes and patterns in the sand and it was like a landscape-sized animated sand painting with bands of colors rippling and stick-figure kachinas dancing up and down and . . . the car careened and Mr. E. shouted "Jesus!" and the cherubic air freshener began to sway, I thought it would come to life like it did before and tell us what to do but no, it just dangled and swung and finally got entangled in the rearview mirror . . . and the clouds were gathering now, sweeping us up, a dust storm was pelting the windshield, the car was spinning in the air as though we'd been picked up by a tornado and . . .

"I don't know where I'm going anymore!" I screamed, and it was true, I was flooring the gas and the car flew of its own free will, the wheel was steering itself, the gearshift was stuck on the letter Q, whatever the fuck that meant, and then, all of a sudden, I saw we were hurtling toward the edge of a precipice a chasm a canyon and we were off the edge now and below us a lake of fire yawned spitting up sulfur fumes and . . .

The far edge of the canyon: on the plateau: a woman dancing.

. . . the Cadillac was in free fall! And the Etchisons weren't wearing their seat belts, and they were in each other's arms, a ball of arms and legs clambering over the seat back and . . . I heard something pounding . . . my heartbeat . . . the drumbeat of an Indian song.

I saw a woman dancing.
Blackout.

Phil Etchison

When we came to, the Cadillac was buried, nose down, in a sand dune of some kind. The door swung open and fell off and skidded off the ledge and I could see it plummeting down, down, down into a fiery river far below us. The wind was sandy and raucous. We tumbled out of the car but were not blown over the edge; we fell into soft sand. The sun was edging up over distant, toothy peaks. Clouds roiled in a thousand shades of mauve, vermilion, crimson, rust, maroon.

A woman was dancing against the rising sun.

The three of us stood there, me flanked by the two women, holding hands. The woman danced in a circle marked by stones. She sang in a high-pitched, ululating voice, and outside her feet a small nude boy crouched, beating on a drum. The boy had a pair of feathery wings, their whiteness in sharp contrast to his *mestizo* complexion. The boy was Jesus Ortega, and he looked up and cried, "Oh, you come now, take too long, time almost running out."

The woman was garbed in a buckskin dress. Her hair was long and it streamed in the wind as she danced. Her face was painted white, with a streak of yellow lightning down the middle, and one eye was the sun and the other the moon, and her arms were covered in crisscross patterns, and she moved in a slow and stately motion around the sacred circle, her hands, holding sheaves of corn, upraised in a gesture of invocation. Around where we stood a dust storm was raging, but we did not feel the wind and the sand in our faces. It was as though we were inside a glass bubble, and inside the bubble there was only the heartbeat of the music and the *adagio* movements of the dance.

"I think we've found our woman," I whispered—one did not feel that one could speak too loudly, for fear of profaning this music—to Serena.

"Yes," she said.

We stood still, the three of us still holding hands, until the music ceased.

The woman laid down her sheaves.

"Señor Etchison," said Jesus Ortega, "you come a long way in twenty-four hours, no? But I am good boy. I show you the way all the time."

The woman stepped over the circle of stones and immediately became a man. The change was as smooth as it was rapid, like a high-tech computer-generated special effect. She had not changed her clothes or re-moved her makeup, but his every movement was different now, less fluid, and when he spoke to me it was in the deep, familiar voice of Detective Milt Stone: *"Ya'at'eeh, shiyaazh,"* he said: *greetings, my son.*

Then he greeted Mary and Serena also.

Mary said, "Who is this man?" and I knew the past was slipping through the sieve of her memory like river-water.

"It's Detective Stone, Mrs. E.," Serena said, "the man who took us over to the other side, last year; he stuffed us to the gills with peyote tea and shot us full of arrows and carried us across the river of no return. Don't you remember?"

"Not . . . really," said Mary.

"It is well," said Milt. "In time you will remember everything, my twice-born friends."

Serena said, "Detective Stone . . . are we going to have to . . . die again?"

"No," said Milt. "Fact is, as the saying goes, there ain't no way to cross the same river twice. When you died and crossed over to the other side and had your grand old adventure, maybe you thought that, after the climax of the story, you got right back on that horse, turned toward the sunset, and rode right back into the real world; you thought that, didn't you? But it ain't true."

I thought about what he said and what it implied. A year ago we had come to the top of a mesa, come to a *kiva*, a sacred Navajo place, entered a magic circle. We'd drunk the peyote tea and our souls had left our bodies and then we'd crossed over into a crazy country where all the rules were askew. We'd brought back Mary and Josh and Theo, and then we'd driven south, down to the Laetrile clinic; wasn't that all true? It had taken me two days of sorting out my memories to get this version of the truth straight in my mind, and now Milt was telling us that we'd *never* gone back to reality . . . that we were still inside the topsy-turvy dream-time . . . that somewhere, on the other side of the river, on a different mesa in a different Arizona in a different Armorica in a different universe, our vacant bodies still waited for our souls to repossess them . . . might wait, in fact, for all eternity . . . he was telling us there is no going home, no matter that homecoming is as basic a human desire as love, as hunger.

"I can see," said Milt, "that the truth hits you hard, Phil Etchison."

"Yeah," I said.

"Oh, you old fools," Jesus said, "enough of this bullshit philoso-phizing. Can't we see we don't got no more time?" He jumped up and began to pound on his drum, his wings flapping. All at once there came a fluting from the air itself. "While we are sitting around here, señores, worlds are falling into ruin."

He laughed; he capered; sand, catching the sunrise, flurried about his head like pixie dust.

I could feel Mary's hand stiffening as I held it. Was she becoming stone again? But still she stepped forward, as did I, as did Serena, toward Milt, toward the magic circle.

"I'll tell you a secret," said Milt. "Not only have you never returned home; you've never even left the circle that you entered the other world through; you've been within that magic circle all this time, and everything you've seen since that moment has been part of your vision."

"You mean . . . it wasn't real?" Serena said. "I haven't graduated high school yet, I never went to college, never worked for Congressman Karpovsky's campaign, never was seduced by him on the mahogany desktop on the Hill?"

"Maybe not," Milt said. "But don't make the mistake of thinking that the vision ain't reality. Because reality itself is an illusion. It's the fabric that we weave around ourselves to shield our senses from the overloading sensations of a billion, billion, billion, billion, *billion* realities. . . ."

And he was chanting that word *billion, billion, BILLION* like Carl Sagan on speed. Chanting it in time to the beating drum. At each repetition of the word it was as if another layer of fabric had been stripped away from our eyes and now we were seeing far, far out over the world, over other worlds, we were seeing canyons and jungles and pyramids and cityscapes and dinosaurs and starships and aliens and exploding suns and temples and we were surfing on blood corpuscles through the veins of God and still came the chanting *billion billion billion* and below us the lake of fire was rising, rising, rising until the plateau we were standing on was an island buffeted by flames, and the Cadillac was bucking and buckling and sprouting metallic pseudopods and Rube Goldberg appendages like a robotic version of *Alien*.

"What the fuck's going on?" I shouted, but Milt seized hold of my arm and pushed me into the stone circle. We landed in a heap, me, Mary, Jesus, and Serena. The mother of all tornadoes was billowing around the circle and bobbing up and down in the wind was all the debris of my life, pages from poetry books, the house in Virginia, my dead dog Rover from my childhood, my grandfather's coffin, my baby sister's training bra, the wicked witch of the west . . . "Be still, Phil!" Milt cried. "Your life's not passing before your eyes. Get a grip on yourself."

"What can you see, Mr. E.?" Serena said, her face rapt and beatific.

"I'm seeing the day in the drive-in when me and Josh were pretending to have sex in the back seat to convince Theo we were cool, and I'm seeing the time we found you in your study by yourself and you were drunk and you started rambling about the sixties and then you read to us from the *Karma Sutra*—"

"Never happened," I said, laughing.

"Sure it did!" she said, giggling as if stoned.

Mary sat cross-legged at the center of the circle. She was becoming very still, buddhalike almost. She was withdrawing into stone. Slowly her features were becoming set, immovable. It didn't dismay me as much this time. I had seen her turn to stone before. And I understood now that the other things that had happened to her—her madness, her cancer—they too had been ways of turning to stone, metaphors for the One Mother's sorrow over the wounded earth.

The storm raged around us; the storm raged within us; but in the circle there was tranquillity. Presently, the Cadillac metamorphosed into the towers of a great city, and our circle into the central hall of a great temple, where Mary was enthroned beneath a crystal dome; and around us, past rows and rows of Ionian columns, we could see the plateau-cum-island, flying now, over a lurid and desolate terrain.

"We're back in Caliosper," I said softly. The wind screamed; above the screaming came the keening of choristers as they praised the name of the One Mother, my wife and my creator.

"You've never left," said Milt, and I saw that the boy Jesus was now perched on his shoulder, and their wings were beating the incense-rich air in alternating strokes, causing the smoke to curlicue around their heads.

It was all very well for him to say that we had never left, and that our lives between then and now had been a dream within a dream; but that was like saying all places are one place, all gods one god, all heroes one hero, all myths one myth. I half expected Joseph Campbell to form out of the swirling incense and command me to follow my bliss. But I had lived those dreams within dreams, and I was no cookie-cutter hero; I was no hero at all; in this story things happened *to* me; I did not make them happen. Once again I felt helpless, adrift.

"Don't feel that way," said Corvus—his speech was now interspersed with fragments of birdsong—"it takes all kinds of messiahs to save the world—there's the fighting messiah, the seeing messiah, and the passive messiah."

I knew that *passive* comes from a Latin word meaning *to suffer,* so I was prepared to believe him.

Serena said, "Where's Ash?"

A flurry of activity: storm troopers in trekkie outfits, bearing phallic weapons, were running around, their boots clanging on the temple's marble floors. There was a burst of turbulence—it was difficult to ignore the fact that the entire flying citadel was zooming through space at the speed of thought—and the choral antiphonies were cut off in mid-phrase.

"Ash," said Corvus-Stone.

And there he was. Of all the Darklings, the most serene and the most ambiguous, Ash (and not, as I had feared, Joseph Campbell) was forming out of the cloud of incense. He shimmered; cold blue radiance haloed his preternaturally beautiful features; he was clad in a cloak of light.

"Ash," said Serena, and the two of them embraced. I stood agape, always the last to understand anything.

Caliosper sped up, banked right, causing Corvus to trip and land on his ass while Jesus fluttered up toward the dome.

"As you can see," Ash said, "things are tough right now. We're in a hurry. We have to try to stop a full-scale war."

"Between Thorn and Katastrofa," I said.

"Yes."

"But . . . wasn't there some kind of game they played, a surrogate for actual warfare . . . wasn't that one of the things they were using Josh and Theo for?" I said.

"They can't play *shenjesh* anymore," Serena said, grasping the situation more rapidly than I. "It's because reality is breaking down, isn't it? And—"

"There is only one truthsayer in the whole cosmos," Ash said. "The other one was rendered . . . inoperative."

"Josh—is he—" said Serena.

"He's not entirely dead—and not entirely alive."

"And Theo—?" I said.

"In Katastrofa's clutches. She seems to have some kind of hold over him. Perhaps she's told him she'll bring Joshua back to life if he cooperates with her. Even though that's not really in her power at all."

"We have to get him back," I said.

"Not yet," said Ash. "There's something we have to do first—if we can."

"Where are we going now?" I said, despairing of ever seeing my sons again.

"To the battlefield."

At that moment, the city of Caliosper began to rise, steeply and swiftly, and presently we were leaving behind even the semblance of a recognizable terrain; we burst through the cloudbanks and thrust into the ionosphere of this unknown planet; we soared into regions where nebulae wheeled and planets whirled and light went wild; we saw colors too strange for psychedelia; and even when I closed my eyes the lights still danced, because we did not see our way with our eyes alone.

God, I wanted a drink. I wanted a drink so badly I could have killed for one.

BOOK THREE

THE ELVEN FOREST

"Mein Vater, Mein Vater, und hörest du nicht,
Was Erlenkönig mir leise verspricht!"
"Sei ruhig, bleibe ruhig, mein Kind;
In dürren Blätter n säuselt der Wind."

"My father, my father, oh can't you hear
What the Elf-King's whispers are promising me?"
"Be still child, be still; it's only the wind
As it wuthers through withered dead leaves."

—Goethe, Erkönig

3: In the Forest of the Adolescent Angst

And as I trekked the sylvan labyrinth,
I came upon a sage, who said: "My son:
The hero's burden is a two-edged sword.
I speak not of the object of the quest,
Not of the grail, but of the journeying.
The slaying of fierce dragons is one aspect
The other the seduction of fair maidens.
Do not confuse the two, until the moment
They demand to be confused."
"What do you mean?" I said.
"How can a woman be a serpent?
Is good then evil? What, if so, is truth?"

I shared my loaf with him, because I saw
That he had trod the path that I now trod,
And paid for all his wisdom with an eye.

"There is in the dark forest of the soul
A certain leakage of identities.
You have come far; seven leagues you have traversed
With but a kiss, a condom, and a loaf;
But now you must embrace the two-tongued truth.
Twin-breasted Madonna: dragon, mother;
Lover, constrictor; beauty, beast; betrayer
And redeemer. So unsheathe your sword,
Risk all; trust all; win all; or pay the price."

CHAPTER  THIR-TEEN

A NEW KIND OF DREAMING

Theo Etchison

I hear the growling of a jaguar.

Punting along the River I pass under the bridge of sighs. The River's all thick and oozy almost like it's made of styling gel or something, just inching its way along, slow and sticky and the sun beating down as I lie in the snake-shaped boat against the rock-hard stern and the sun's driving the sweat out of my pores and the sweat's pouring down my face making my whole body slick and sticky like the water of the River and I'm all naked and clutching the stiff wood and the sweat licks the firm stern and the pliant body and the sweat dissolves me and I'm melting in the sun into the viscous flow into the River that reeks like one of Mom's old maxi pads like the time the dog came into my room and she'd rooted the pad out of the trash and was wearing it on her snout and she leaped into my arms and . . . like when we're little and me and Josh are in the tub together smashing our GI Joes into each other and like wrestling and the soapy water's all slipping and sliding and slithering and I'm all jeeze Josh your weewee got all big and he laughs and empties the Johnson's baby shampoo over my head and I saw the commercial that says it doesn't hurt your eyes but I start bawling anyway just to attract Mom's attention but she doesn't come and I'm screaming at the top of my lungs and once I heard Mom scream that way and she was all don't don't don't and I thought he was going to kill her and I was in the bed because I'd just had a nightmare and I thought I was still in the nightmare so I shut my eyes real tight and prayed for it to end but the screaming had a tinge of laughter in it and I didn't understand so I counted sheep but the sheep were bleeding the wool was all soggy and sticky and I was like five years old maybe and the shampoo running down my face and running and running and all of sudden the dragon reared up out of the water and she grins at me and her teeth catch the sunlight and I glimpse the forest where she's plucking an apple from the nearest branch and I say no no no and the current's deeper now and the water's gathering and swirling eddying as we pass the bridge of sighs and oh God the water's streaming now and the mist is something stirring between my legs and I'm scared and I want to wake up I want to wake up wake up wake up—

I open my eyes.

Slowly. One—two—three—be awake.

I'm lying in my bed. It's Virginia. An Arnold Schwarzenegger poster is peeling from the back of the door. I've pissed myself. No it's not piss. No. Daylight is shining in through the slatted window. I get out of bed and peel off the BVDs and toss them in the hamper and hope that no one will notice. The room: piles of dirty clothing, a baseball bat, a photograph of Mom and Dad in a cracked frame, my dream book open next to my computer.

I pull on my blue terrycloth robe with the big gash on my ass where I snagged it against a nail one time. I walk over to the door, and when I open it I realize that this isn't Virginia.

"Josh?" I whisper past the half-cracked bedroom door. I want to ask him about the dream. It's a sex thing, I know it. It's big and it's frightening. I don't want to be ready for it yet. I want to be a kid. I want to sit in the tree fort of my childhood and watch the world and never have to climb down. Because there's a dragon coiled around the trunk and I can't come down without dealing with the dragon. Up here I can see across the universe and that's all I need. Down there I'll see the universe too, but only a piece at a time.

This isn't my bedroom. It's another of those illusions I can manufacture around myself when the world becomes too wild to understand. It's here because it's familiar and because I don't want to face what's beyond the bedroom.

The stick with its bells that bewitch wild animals is lying on my desk along with my jester's cap. I think it's pretty fucking stupid to be trapped in this alien world and have to dress up like a sausage vendor at the Renaissance fair, so I look in the closet for something I wouldn't be embarrassed to wear. There's a shitload of clothes here—everything from a medieval executioner's uniform to the threads of a *Star Trek* science officer—but it takes me a while to find something normal looking and when I do find it it's exactly the clothes I was wearing the very first time I got sucked into this alien universe—the too-long Redskins T-shirt and the shorts—and I've kind of outgrown the shorts, but I find another pair of pants that kind of fit—they're like sci-fi pants, with silver-lamé trimming, which could either look cool or faggy, depending on where you go—and then like I put on the shirt which is still thank God too long and it covers up the pockets where most of the obnoxious glitter is. And now I'm ready for the next adventure and I go back toward the bedroom door but I don't forget to take the tinklestick and I remember to stuff the marble in my back pocket, because it's the one thing that can tell me where I'm going in this crazy world.

Where the landing should be there's that corridor with the cages full of adolescent boys, the boys that stare listlessly and shake their heads from side to side and rattle their thin arms against the bars, that squat in their own shit, too dazed to move . . . and I know that at the end of that hall there's the room where my brother lies in his glass coffin like a sleeping prince whose princess will never come . . . only the wicked witch.

I close my bedroom door and start up the dungeon stairwell. I'm thinking about the dream I had about the river and the dragon and the sunlight and the sweat. I know that no matter what my quest is, there's going to be a dragon guarding the threshold. I've just got to grit my teeth and deal with it one way or another, or there won't be any quest.

I hear the growling of a jaguar.

It's morning in a galaxy far far away and I've awoken from a wet dream.

I've been climbing the dungeon steps for a totally long time. In fact it's been kind of like an M.C. Escher stair-climbing; I've been going up and down at the same time, depending on how you look at it, and I've never gotten anywhere. It's only when I stop looking at anything and reach out toward my destination with my mind that I start moving, and then it's like when I was falling down the dark well only in reverse. I'm chuting upward through dark tunnels with only an image of Katastrofa to guide me, a dragon that coils and coils and coils around the tree of the forbidden apples.

Katastrofa's lair: well you kind of expect to see this big old cavern strewn with human skeletons and piles of putrid fewmets, and that's exactly what there is, except bigger and twistier than any dragon's cave in Tolkien. There are stalactites and stalagmites and trails of sulfurous smoke. The cave is an illusion, of course, just like the witch's oven in the gingerbread house; but the River, which trickles along a channel gouged from the limestone floor, is real enough; I know, as soon as I hear it rippling, that it sings the true music of making.

Katastrofa's been waiting for me. She's sitting on a throne made entirely of human bones. Her hands are resting on two skulls, her head against a mandala-pattern of spoked thighbones. Although she is in human form her eyes remain the eyes of a serpent.

"Took you long enough," she says. "You spent forever in the sleep of changing."

"It didn't work," I tell her. "I haven't changed." But now, looking at her, I can feel the dream I had last night come over me in all its brutal power. I am changing. In a way that I don't dare name.

"Oh, Theo," she says, and the underlying meaning is *Don't you lie to me; a truthsayer can't lie anyway.*

And it's true that I don't sound convincing. I can't convince myself and I can't convince anyone else. I'm scared of Katastrofa in a way I never was with Thorn.

"Are you ready to go into battle now?" she says. "That jester's costume my father made you wear seems somehow inappropriate."

"I don't have any other clothes anymore. Maybe like after the battle, we'll go down to the mall and pick up something a little less dorky," I say. I'm getting tired of being a part of all these other people's roleplaying games.

I remember those battles from the last adventure—when I was fighting on the other side. There was like this totally big arena and in it there was a holographic starfield that represented the whole of the known universe. Thorn made me leap into the starfield and then it was as though I was a character in a real-live Nintendo action game, slugging whole solar systems out of my way, juggling galaxies, that kind of thing. I had really gotten into it until I came to know that everything I did was real . . . that worlds went under . . . that planets fell into the void . . . and the fates of races were determined by the outcome of the game. And then again, I found out that my arch-rival in the mega-video game of death was Joshua, my flesh and blood. Fucking Jesus it sucked.

Seeming to read my mind, Katastrofa says, "There won't be any video games anymore. You want to know why?"

She doesn't pause to hear my reply but goes on, "Come on. We're burning daylight here." She gets up out of the Texas Chainsaw Massacre chair and comes toward me, and she's already beginning to transform.

By transform I mean the whole Animatronic shebang. Appendages shooting out, tendrils of flesh whipping at the air, claws sprouting, scales flowering out of the smooth skin, her hair receding into her scalp and her forehead becoming all bony and green and her torso flattening and lengthening and she's all the time screeching like Godzilla. Her jaw begins to broaden and lengthen and her teeth start to multiply and sharpen. She's getting so big that I'm scared she's going to bust right out of the cave.

"Get up on my back," she hollers (her voice now has a metallic ring to it, and the echo of the cavern makes it huge) "and start navigating!"

I have to obey her and so I start to climb up. It's difficult to get a foothold because she keeps growing and she's not all firm like she'd be if she was a dragon ride at an amusement park—she's living flesh, quivering all over, burning my hands when I reach out to steady myself. And being this close to her, to be honest, it keeps bringing back the dream and it keeps making me pop a boner which I keep trying to will away.

I'm perched on the dragon's neck now. I ask her where we're going, and she says only, "You are the truthsayer . . . take me to where my brother is."

But before I can even start to put out a mental feeler for the vampire Darkling she's already moving toward the water. And then she plunges in. It's cold. I hold on. I think she's trying to drown me, but she thrusts one finny wing across her back so that it partly shields me from the water. It's not watertight and so I squat, shivering, against one scaly wall. The water splashes me and has a bitter, mineral water taste.

I sit huddled and wet and holding the marble in my hand. I'm gazing into it now, trying to feel my way along its convoluted pathways. But it's not as easy as it used to be. I feel resistance. I'm not as sure of where I'm going. I'm certain now that my powers are slipping away from me. Somehow I'm no longer pure. It has something to do with the dream. It has something to do with the dragon's embrace.

The dragon moves with the speed of thought, my thought that is. Somehow we're linking and somehow she senses the direction I'm thinking of as I try to focus in on the idea of Thorn. But for now all I see is a swirling, hungry dark, like he's drawn a cloak of obscurity around himself. It's taking all my truthsaying powers even to see this much. It's black and red and coagulating. It's a whirlwind of blood.

I concentrate harder. But now I'm losing that fix and I can't conjure up an image of Thorn at all. My mind is on war. I know that there's a tremendous battle looming ahead where hundreds of worlds are going to be tossed aside so that Thorn and Katastrofa can rule over what's left, assuming there is something left. I know that Strang, in his madness, has closed off many of the gateways between the worlds, and that any path to anywhere must probably be forged anew by me. I think of the last time we battled . . . in that arena of mega-virtual-reality that turned out not to be so virtual after all . . . and I think maybe if I go in that direction I can reorient myself to the River's uncountable streams. I close my eyes and try to recall that place. I see myself dancing among points of light . . . I feel myself stretched thin, thinner than vacuum, straddling whole galaxies, filling the emptiness between the stars, between subatomic particles, threading the superspace between the black holes and the white. It all comes back to me now. Me and Josh as pixels on the infinite CRT of the cosmos, me and Josh slugging it out, surrogates for the Darklings' sibling rivalry, working through our own rivalry too; I remember thinking *Jesus Josh I fucking hate you sometimes. All the time.*

No sooner thought than done. We're breaching the dank dark depths of the River, thrusting up through icy water, and then the wing-fin-canopy is whisked aside and I see the foam recede on either side of me. I'm standing on the dragon's back and the water's drying off and I can't see the River at all now because what's happened is that I visualized the place and called to it in the secret language of truthsaying and the River thrust out a temporary tendril toward it and now the River's gushing back where it came from through the vortex between the spaces and leaving us ashore, except that ashore is the middle of the grand hallway of the gaming arena on the island where a thousand streams meet, where the last great game was fought. I know that, stretching around the building I'm standing in, there's a *Blade Runner*-looking city crisscrossed with rivulets from the River. I know that it's a teeming city on neutral turf in a quadrant of the many worlds as yet unclaimed by any of the scions of Darkling. But as I look around the arena I realize that it's a lot different now. There used to be like tiers upon tiers which made the place look like the inside of a mega-Colosseum. Now the tiers are still there but the teeming crowds that filled them are gone. There used to be aliens of every description, octopoids and plantoids and sauroids and jellyoids and tornadooids and cloudoids, aliens in bottles and aliens in chariots and aliens in tuxedos, and now, yeah, there's a couple of aliens here and there, but at least one of them seems to be a corpse.

But one thing is just the same as I remembered it: the starstream-hologram that erupts out of the floor of the arena and goes all the way up as far as the eye can see. It's like a stretched-out representation of what's in my marble. It's virtual reality and it's hyperreality at the same time because from inside of it you can reach out and change reality. When I look at that thing it brings back the memories and I start to get scared. I don't want to go in there. I know that I've been inside before and that I've innocently flung star systems into each other and hurled planets around like baseballs. That was before I realized I was killing people millions of people by people I'm saying aliens as well as human beings, creatures with souls.

Katastrofa is rapidly changing back into a woman. She's covered with like this glittery Saran wrap, and her hair is all flaming and her eyes are still the same; I'd know her eyes even if she transformed herself into something totally different, like a toad or a tablecloth.

Her eyes are the one thing about her that never change.

"Why did you bring us to this place?" she says. "You know that the wars are no longer fought here." She kicks a used candy wrapper out of the way and I realize that the level we're standing on bears a real resemblance to a beat-up movie theater in the wrong part of town.

"I can't control my truthsaying. If I could, it wouldn't *be* truthsaying. There's gotta be a reason why we're here."

"True," Katastrofa murmurs, closing her gold-lidded eyes in thought. The reason becomes obvious when Thorn emerges from the stellar vortex. He's wearing a cloak of darkness and his dark hair frames his face so that mostly you see the slate-colored eyes glaring out of a tempest of shadows.   "Give the child back to me," Thorn says.

His herald, the sometime Mr. Cornelius Huang, restauranteur and conch-blowing virtuoso, steps out from behind his master. He's scary and cadaverous as ever. He lifts the conch to his lips and blasts us—it's a deep, bloodcurdling noise that makes even the dead alien twitch and causes Katastrofa to look away from her brother's eyes.

Oh, and the Cerberus-thing—the three-headed dog. I can't forget that. Thorn's pet appears behind Cornelius Huang, yapping at all our heels at once.

"I want the child back," says Thorn. "It's not fair, I captured him first, you got the other one, you screwed him up, you've only yourself to blame for killing him in the process."

I shudder. Am I wrong to think that Joshua will come back to me? Am I too late? I think of Joshua and think great big clouds of blackness but then, through the blackness, I can hear a voice, a child's cry. I know that there is still a way for me to bring him back, I know that Thorn is wrong. It gives me courage although I still don't understand how I'm going to achieve the impossible, the resurrection of the dead, even though, according to some people, I am God.

"Bullshit," Katastrofa says, though she still doesn't meet her brother's gaze. "You captured him, brother, but you lost him. He was up for grabs."

"Bullshit," I say myself, "none of you owns me. I'm me, I own myself, and it looks like I'm the only game in town. And I don't want to help either of you because neither of you has any business ruling the universe when you can't even make peace inside your own family." Just like my family, I'm thinking, and I know I shouldn't speak so boldly because there's Joshua, in his glass coffin, still waiting for me to call him out from the bowels of Katastrofa's dungeon.

I hear the growling of a jaguar.

But I can't stop to think about what that means.

Katastrofa's looking up again, and I can see the hate flashing in her eyes. Her hate is not for me but for her brother. "I wish we had never shared a womb," she says. "I wish I'd killed you before you were born. I wish that you'd choked on your own phlegm while you were clawing your way out of your mother's womb . . ."

"What would you have preferred, little sister?" Thorn says. "That we'd stayed inside forever? That we'd grown old and died and putrefied within those fleshy walls?"

"There was no need to kill our mother," says Katastrofa.

"I didn't kill her," says Thorn. "Her death was an inevitable conse-quence of our birth—you know that as well as I do."

"You could have thought of something. You're so ingenious, so full of new ideas. At least you never tired of telling me so. And everyone else who will listen . . . and in *your* kingdom, they'd better listen or they get eaten up."

These dudes must have a different gestation period than humans or something. I don't understand what they're trying to say and I don't like the pictures it conjures up in my mind—images of siblings, wet and bloody, scratching and biting each other inside their mother's body— screaming their anger at each other. That woman's womb must have felt like a living drumkit.

"Just hand over the goddamned child," says Thorn.

"I told you I'm not gonna get tossed around like a ball," I say, but they continue to ignore me.

"No!" Katastrofa screams. And then the two of them are rushing each other, fangs droolings, talons outstretched, she's a blur of scales and claws and he's a whirlwind of leather and fur, they're wrestling each other and it's like a fight in a comic book, a swirling cloud of dust where you can see now and then an arm or a wing or a tail or a spurt of blood.

"Kids, kids," I say. I feel like a hall monitor in a kindergarten. The cloud disperses and the siblings separate, panting, glaring. This isn't how you expect godlike superbeings to behave. Somehow you think they should be above this pettiness. But they're worse than me and Josh. Or are they? I know that even when I hated my brother more than anything in the world, even when I wished him dead, even when he was beating me up for no reason except for maybe some sexual frustration thing I couldn't even understand . . . even then I knew there was love there, somewhere, frail and hidden. Did Thorn and Katastrofa have love, a love that had gone so sour that they couldn't live in peace unless one of them killed the other? Did Cain love Abel? I bet you anything he did. Wasn't that part of why he killed him?

So here I am playing referee between two of the most powerful beings in the universe, who could crush me much more easily than they could ever destroy each other, and somehow I find the nerve to like lecture them on sibling rivalry. Fucking Jesus I'm stupid. But I mean well.

"Okay," I say, "isn't there some way this can be settled without taking the whole universe along with you? Isn't there some kind of way you can withdraw, retrench, stay within the boundaries Strang drew for you?"

"No," they both say at the same time.

And they laugh, knowing how much alike they are, and then they both stifle their laughter at the same time and I see that yes, there is a love there, buried so deep that not even I, the truthsayer, may be able to coax it out.

"Isn't there like, some game or something you can play? Winner take all you know, poker or . . . or chess?" I persist, thinking maybe it can all come out kind of like *The Seventh Seal*, you know, where the knight plays chess with Death. But that, of course, was only a movie, and it wasn't even in English.

"Strip poker," Thorn says, and there's another grim laugh, a meeting of gazes; maybe he's talking about something in their youth, some secret, I think, something shameful; but then, I think, they were in the womb together, and conscious, so they must have shared many secrets. The love between them is a dark and twisty thing, and it's laced with guilt and disillusion. Oh God, their love is a scary thing and it's more comfortable to think about their hate, pure and black and elemental.

"War," Katastrofa says, "let's play war."

"Yes," says Thorn, the final *sssss* turning serpentine. And then they leap into the vortex, the two of them, deadly and playful at the same time.

"Stop!" I shout. "You don't know where you're going . . . you don't know the way in there because you're not truthsayers. You'll smash the universe to smithereens before you're through!"

And well, there comes Thorn's voice, mocking me: "Who gives a shit, little one? And this was your idea."

Okay. So I'm standing there alone now, not working for either side. I can just stand there and let them blow each other apart, and that's just what they'll do. My dad once told me that, in the Roman arena, the lowest class of gladiators were called *andabatae.* They had no skills. They were common criminals. They fought in helmets that completely covered their faces. They were blind. They wielded clunky, rusty swords and thrust unseeing at each other. They fought with savage desperation because they'd had everything taken away from them, even their faces, their identities . . . they smashed, they bashed, they swung, they didn't care about anything anymore . . . and they always died. An *andabata* didn't live to fight another day. If they happened to survive, they'd be thrown to the lions or whatever the next act was.

Well like, that's how Thorn and Katastrofa are, the way they hate each other; inside the vortex that is both an analog of reality and reality itself, collapsed a jillionfold into itself so that a truthsayer like me can grasp it in my hands, they will be blind, and blindness will make them strike out at everything; and this is how the world is going to end; not with a bang, not with a whimper, but the petty bickering of a dysfunctional family.

I know I have to stop this.

I'm a truthsayer and a truthsayer only sees, he doesn't do. But I'm also growing older and I'm starting to feel the changes in my body and I'm starting to feel something awesomely grownup, like some kind of responsibility or something. I know that as I try to stop this war I'm going to age a little more, and aging is going to slowly close the inner eye through which I see the cosmos. Oh, fucking Jesus I am scared. I stare for a long moment at the starstream. Around me, the arena seems to be decaying second by second, crumbling into the primal dust we all spring from. The darkness beckons. I sense the two of them inside and I too leap into the eternal cold of the space between the spaces.

CHAPTER FOURTEEN

PIZZA IN CALIOSPER

<u>S e r e n a   S o m e r s</u>

Ash had come. I was feeling better already even though I wasn't totally sure where we were going.

He and Corvus led me and Mr. E. out of the nave of Mrs. E.'s cathedral and into a little chapel that also served as the main control room for the flying city. There were painted icons of all four Etchisons on one wall, and a reproduction of the weeping Madonna we'd seen in Baja California in the place of honor behind an altar railing with a dense fog of incense dancing all around it. Facing the wall of Etchisons was like this huge portrait of the Darkling family, but it must have been during better days. It was like one of those Renaissance artists, Michelangelo or someone, and it showed King Strang sitting on a throne with a scepter in his hand that even in the painting seemed to catch the light and sparkle, and his long white hair flowed all the way to the ground, I guess that's why it reminded me of Michelangelo, that sculpture of Moses with the wild hair, so thick and convoluted that some people say there's like this self-portrait of the artist hidden somewhere in the hair, you know . . . and Thorn and Katastrofa were standing on either side of him, Thorn with his Dracula cape billowing and Katastrofa, a dragon's head on the body of a nude woman with her arms outstretched and with leathern wings that stretched way up and ended in vestigial claws; yeah, they were monstrous in a way, but they were also smiling and gazing fondly at their father, and King Strang was beaming as if they'd just presented him with straight A report cards; and in front was Ash, no more than a boy (or girl, because you couldn't really tell, neither then nor now) clothed in a few wisps of mist, the only one not smiling but looking off into some far horizon, an otherworldly kid who somehow didn't partake of the family dynamics. The picture was framed in gold, you know one of those frames that's full of curls and swirls and squiggles.

Next to this picture was a painting in a lead frame, and it showed the same family many years later. I knew the story that the painting depicted—it was the old *King Lear* story as it applied to the Darkling family. It showed an enraged King Strang, ugly now, his face devoured by the pestilence that consumed his kingdom. It showed Ash, grown now, weeping as an angel with a flaming sword banished him from the gates of paradise. It showed Thorn and Katastrofa, still standing on either flank of their deranged father, their expressions transformed into masks of consummate fury.

In both these paintings there was also Mary Etchison, a wraithlike creature hovering above King Strang in a halo of pale blue fire.

Mrs. E. was the link between our world and the world beyond; a dying woman from Virginia in ours, the Great Mother, lady of perpetual tears, in the world of the Darklings.

The oddest thing about this whole chapel was that there was a dinette table set up in the middle of it, one of those IKEA specials, with four chairs; in the center of the people there was a statue of a jaguar rampant clawing the air; and a man in a blue and orange uniform was bringing in a stack of pizzas.

As he set them down, he intoned, like a priest, "Pepperoni, avocado, sausage and shrimp. Pineapple, gingko nuts, relish and crabmeat. Sweet-

and-sour duck, sour cream, ginger root, and eye of newt. Double cheese, plain." Then he put out a pitcher of beer and a pitcher of soda and slid away so smoothly he might as well have been on roller skates.

"Eat now," said Ash, "while you can. Soon there's going to be too much excitement for us to be able to order out for pizza."

We ate in silence for a while. There wasn't much I could say really, and Mr. E. was even more overwhelmed than I was. When conversation finally began, it was all trivial because no one could bring themselves to talk about the really important stuff.

For instance, Mr. E. began by like, commenting on the pizza. "The only time I ever saw pizza like this," he said, "was in California . . . at a New Age pizza place in Topanga Canyon."

"Oh, yeah," I said. "I hear they have things like, Peking duck pizza, pizza with Thai barbecued chicken . . . I read about it in Congressman Karpovsky's campaign guide book where it talks about American culinary habits, you know, so you won't make a fool of yourself on the campaign trail by thinking that chicken fried steak has chicken in it . . . and . . . oh, you know, insulting some poor redneck who's just donated his life's savings to—oh, I don't mean that perjoratively, I'm just quoting what the Congressman said the night we all got stoned and—oh shit, putting my foot in my mouth again—that was supposed to be a secret."

I was dying of embarrassment, even though, with the fate of the universe at stake, I should have known better. To be honest, it was like the time that had elapsed between the last adventure and this one—leaving high school and going to college and taking the time off college to work on the campaign and growing up and all that shit—it was like it had all been shrunk down to nothing. I felt like a know-nothing teenager with a tenth-grade vocabulary and a Valley girl sensibility. Especially when Mr. E. went on, "Yes," without even seeming to have heard me, "one of the most unusual things about these transdimensional crossings is the food, isn't it? I mean, that's what Alice said in *Through the Looking Glass;* she seemed to be constantly obsessed by fish; but then you could see a lot of Freudian undertones in that if you wanted to, I mean, what with the phallic symbolism of fish, the fishy odor of the female pudenda, and that's not even getting into the Christian symbolism; I mean, it's a semiotician's paradise and—"

Then Mr. E. began to weep. Not just a teardrop or two. He was bawling his guts out.

I said, "Mr. E. . . . I know how you feel."

"No you don't," he said. "Nobody knows how I feel. I've been a blind man in a sighted family . . . Theo and Josh and Mary all have these

gifts . . . and even you do, Serena . . . seeing hidden truths or whatever . . . I don't even have a way to describe these fucking talents of
yours . . . God, you don't understand how helpless I feel . . . you
don't understand a goddamn thing."

And maybe he was right about that. Mr. E. was like Joseph after the
angel told him his wife was going to have God's kid, and there were
going to be like all these cosmic events, and the world getting redeemed,
and the great big eternal war between good and evil, and millions called
to judgment, and on and on and all he was going to get to do was kind of
be the stepfather of the universe—and it was all going to happen whether
he wanted it to or not.

Bummer.

Mr. E. wept like there was no tomorrow.

P h i l   E t c h i s o n

It was at that moment, chattering inanely about semiotics while trying
to eat pizza in the chapel of my wife's cathedral in a flying citadel that
was streaking through the starstream at warp factor seven, that I realized
that I had completely lost control of my life. There was, indeed, a cosmic
drama unfolding all around me—not just *a* cosmic drama—indeed, *every*
cosmic drama from every mythos of every human and nonhuman culture
was hurtling toward simultaneous climax. I had always dreamt of being a
part of history . . . of being more than myself . . . but I felt less myself
than I had ever been. It isn't easy for me to cry despite the fact that I am
immersed in the literature of crying men. Losing my sons, my wife, had
not caused me to break down this way, but now I realized I had also lost
myself. Even as I wept I was thinking about how selfish my weeping was,
how it was improper for me to weep for such solipsistic motives. And the
most appalling thing of all was how solicitous they all seemed to be.
Serena kept assuring me she understood—I knew well that she did not—
and Ash put his arm around my shoulder, but I would not be comforted.

But presently the tears ceased flowing and the pizza was all devoured,
and the flying city continued to smash through the transdimensional void.
Most of the others had all gone up to some viewing pavilion to see the
dancing lights of hyperspace. Only Corvus, the astrogator, remained, and
he seemed preoccupied, humming into a handheld device that was to a
Star Trek tricorder as a computer is to an abacus.

I sat at the table, looking at the icons of Darkling mythology and of my
own family. I stared for a long time at the jaguar centerpiece of the

dinner table, stared so hard that I seemed to catch a flickering in its eyes. It too could have been alive, like the many statues of the One Mother in this land, I supposed; it would not have surprised me. At length, Corvus-Stone said to me, looking up from his instrument: "You find it fascinating, the *nagual*."

"Is that what it is?" I said, remembering the word only vaguely from some decades-past college lecture on pre-Columbian art. "A *nagual* is some kind of werejaguar, isn't it? Let me guess . . . the Aztecs . . . no, the Toltecs."

"Such a learned man," Corvus said, laughing. "You forget who you are, you forget the names of your children, but the intellect stays with you forever."

"But that's about the limit of my knowledge on the matter."

"And about the limit of everyone else's too," said Corvus.

The bird-man was, it must be said, wavering a little in his shape; he seemed to be turning back into the familiar Detective Stone; perhaps, with only me in the room, there was no need for him to assume the guise of the city's navigator. But then again—because I could not help thinking up new theories, even in the direst of circumstances—it also occurred to me that, if reality was somehow the sum, the intersection, of the perceptual universes of each person present, then it stood to reason that the Milt Stone I saw when I was alone in the room would have to be different from the Stone I saw when many others, who saw him as an entirely alien being, were present; perhaps the bird-man image was merely the average of all our disparate perceptions. If I actually saw Milt Stone through Ash's eyes—if Ash had eyes, granted—would it drive me mad, or even burn me to a cinder, like an unmasked view of God? Though I was consumed with grief and helplessness, a part of me viewed all this with a certain detachment, analyzing data, toying with structures of ideas; my second-rate academician's intellect may have been a house of cards, but it was the only roof over my head.

So preoccupied was I by Corvus' seeming metamorphosis and remetamorphosis that I missed half of his explication of the *nagual* myth, and zoned back in only toward the end of it: "You see, the *nagual* is in a perpetual state of *becoming;* that's the main thing. And it comes from the Toltecs, the oldest civilization in the New World, and that makes it also the oldest symbol of *my* people, my people back home. You know." His voice, too, wavered between the crisp enunciation of Corvus and the down-home twang of Milt Stone. "The elder Darkling, you know, the man who started it all, he likes to think of himself as a *nagual* sometimes, you see, because he came up from nothing, on account of his pact with the River's dark side."

"The River has a dark side?" I said, although my nodding acquaintance with Carl Jung suggested that a mythological Manichaeanism was almost mandatory.

"At the source of the River," said Stone, "which, as you know, has flowed up from the first world, the perfect country, Elysium, Paradise, all the way up to this imperfect world of the bereaved, the disconsolate . . . well, you got good and evil both, you see. Potential. Embryonic. It takes both good and evil to create *hozhoni* . . ."

"Which is some kind of untranslatable Navajo concept of balance . . ."

"Nah, Phil, sometimes we Injuns overestimate our uniqueness. It's natural in an oppressed people. A good translation might be *chi*. Or is it *wa?* But you're right, those are both brownskinned words, and some say that our people is just the Asian people, displaced across a narrow little strait. Or was it the lost tribes of Israel?"

"You archetypes can never get each other straight," I said, laughing despite my desolation.

Milt said (a hint of wings rustling about his form), "That's a wiser observation than you might think, Phil. There's got to be a fatal flaw to set the story rolling, you see. Without Adam and the apple there's no Bible because they never get out of paradise, never burst out of the womb, never fulfill their destiny as humans. Without Prometheus stealing fire from the gods, without Pandora blowing the lid off that primal box of tricks, there ain't no human story—there's just a bunch of gods, living high on the hog in Olympus, screwing around now and then, hurling a few thunderbolts, but they're boring thunderbolts because the drama hasn't begun, the Big hasn't Banged, you know what I mean? And that's how it was with Strang. He struck the bargain, took the scepter that steals men's souls, forged structure out of chaos—yes! What would these myriad worlds have been without the ordering of Strang's will? The universe became a poem. To be a work of art it had to have light and darkness, and it had to encompass both love and death. And like every work of art, like every enforced reversal of entropy in creation, it had to contain the seeds of its own destruction. To be or not to be are not the only choices. There's also to have been. To be about to be. What's more, there's being and there's *being*. When you choose *being*—you also choose death."

"You're saying that to be *is* not to be." I had to admire the casuistry. Milt's words had started off by being playful, but gradually he had become more impassioned. It was more than just a word-game to him. It was a central truth of his view of the world, and it had the pellucid obscurity of a Zen *koan*. I had to admit that I loved to watch him juggle those ideas; back at the college I'd often participated in Dean Reinman's heated cocktail party arguments, but they *were* only games; sitting around deconstructing the universe over a martini was a way of thinking out loud about how to word the next grant proposal; no, this was real. And it was like the proverbial Chinese food, too; I had been lost in the elegance of Milt's logic, but no sooner had he finished speaking than I was hungry again.

"But you look bored, Phil," said Milt, slowly turning back into Corvus, "and we really should join the others."

He started to leave; I turned to kiss the weeping statue of my wife.

S e r e n a   S o m e r s

The observatory of the palace of Caliosper was an amazing place because once you went into it it was like you became physically adrift. It was kind of a ballroom-sized bubble and what was around us wasn't the city of Caliosper with its avenues and gardens and shopping malls and minarets and all those things that cities of fantasy and science fiction always have, but a deep black nothing. In the nothing, stars zoomed past—stars and galaxies and planets with rings and ghostly nebulae—but each image was fringed with rainbow, as though the whole observatory were a great big prism and the starstream was a cosmic hologram.

Ash and I had abandoned Mr. E. to his sorrow because, I guess, we felt we were intruding on him. We didn't talk much; Ash kept pacing up and down . . . it looked as though he was walking on air, because the floor of the observatory was a kind of Möbius-stripping forcefield that allowed you access to any part of the spherical image, and the direction your feet pointed always felt like *down,* which was totally confusing when I saw Ash striding upside down toward me and then reverse himself without me catching the moment he had reversed . . . well, as I say, he paced. And the mist he was draped in paced along with him, tendriling around his private parts the way wisps of cloud drape nudes in a Renaissance painting.

"I wish Corvus would hurry up," Ash said. "He's probably started expounding philosophy to your friend . . . the more mystical he gets, the more diffusely he navigates . . . I've known him to steer us into seventeen realities at the same time . . . it's the peyote that does it to him."

"Do all pilots take hallucinogenic drugs?" I asked him, trying to get him to stand still for a moment.

"Of course they do! They can't all be truthsayers. And even after they drink the water of transformation they can only perceive a faint echo of what bombards a truthsayer's mind, day in, day out; they're all mad, you see."

"But I don't understand . . . where are we? Are we still in the River?"

"Yes, yes; it's not exactly an underwater view of things but, in the River, you see what the River wants you to see. Usually I don't spend much time in the observatory, frankly, or I have some homely image projected so I don't feel as disoriented."

I stopped paying attention because, suddenly, as the stars went whizzing by, I thought I saw Theo.

Theo was a tiny spot in the distance and then, almost instantaneously, he zoomed in for a closeup. He was bigger than the whole city. He held a marble in his hand and the marble was brighter than a sun. Theo's outline was wavery, insubstantial, and before I could cry out his name he had dwindled back to a blip among the clouds of stardust.

"Oh, Jesus, that was—" I saw that Mr. E. had come in. He was staring at that blip, watching it go out, *poof*, like a candle flame.

"Yeah, Mr. E.," I said. "It was Theo."

"In that case," said Corvus, who was now stalking around and flapping like a mutant ostrich, "we are going in the right direction; you can stop panicking, Prince Ash."

Then came the dragon, zooming like Theo out of nowhere, thrashing and coiling and clawing, wrapping herself around our sphere of darkness like a serpent about to devour an egg; fire flashed in her eyes, and her claws glittered like diamonds, and then, like Theo, all of a sudden she was gone too. And before I could say anything there was a bat-thing leering down at us with slate-colored eyes and beating black leathern wings against the barrier of force, and it too disappeared.

"Is that Katastrofa and Thorn?"

"They are nearby," Ash said. "We tracked them all down. They're about to have some kind of battle . . . with luck we may be able to slip in, spirit Theo away, leave the two of them at each other's throats. . . ."

"Time to breach the River now," said Corvus. "This is where they're going to fight."

"What kind of a place is it?" said Mr. E.

"Well," Corvus said, "it depends on your private mythology, Phil; some will see it as a *Star Wars* kind of deal; some will see it taking place in a dark forest, the forest of the soul, whatever . . . I think some might even see it as a forest of their own traumatic relationships with friends and family . . . when we all look upon it at once, we see the same thing, more or less, but if we get separated, well then it's private epiphany time. . . ."

I felt like this distant thrumming, as though the whole city were changing gears. Those prismlike fringes around the stellar objects were starting to dim and I realized we were slowly making our way to the surface of the River and were soon going to reappear in what passed for reality around here. Before we blinked back out, there was a final image . . . it was almost transparent against the starfield . . . it was the image of an immense child, you know, like the starchild in *2001—A Space Odyssey* I guess, but this neonate was in the middle of a transformation scene right out of *American Werewolf in London,* but it was turning into kind of a cat—a jaguar maybe—with glittering emerald eyes.

"It's Father," Ash said. He didn't seem as self-confident as he had a moment ago. "Is he getting involved too?"

"Well, Prince Ash," Corvus said, "it is true, there is something you must confront, somehow, before this story can resolve itself."

I remembered how Ash had been the one child of Strang who had dared tell the truth to his father; how he had been banished from his inheritance for his pains; how his father, in his pride, hadn't spoken a word to him since then, leaving his one loyal child to wander the universes, master of a single citadel with no fixed resting place. Jesus, how must it feel? I thought, and I wanted so much to make him feel better, but I didn't know how. Because for all of my life it had been Ash's job to make me feel good about myself, and not the other way round. He was the visiting angel and I was the frustrated fat girl who dreamed of love and ate away her sorrows. How do you console a fallen angel? The thing that he's lost, you know, it's so big that you can't even imagine what it must have been like to have it, let alone losing it. It made me and my own sufferings seem pretty damn small . . . a little teenage crush, a little sexual harassment, a couple of bouts of eating disorders . . . how could I know what it was like to lose the world when I didn't know what it was like to *have* the world? All right, so I went up to Ash and tried to hold his hand; he squeezed mine, and I think he even felt a little comforted maybe; then again, maybe he was just making me feel good by making me feel useful.

"Jesus, Ash, you drive me crazy sometimes," I said.

"What am I to do? Corvus is right. I've got to come to terms with Dad somehow."

Ash's Dad—whom once, in an ecstasy of teenage rage, I had called a *mega-dweeb*—wasn't worth coming to terms with as far as I was concerned. "Let him go," I said.

"I can't," he said. "But thanks for the therapy anyway."

"No problemo," I said.

Then the war began.

CHAPTER FIFTEEN

A PAGE OF MEMORY

Theo Etchison

The war's about to begin. I'm flung through the star-spangled night. I stretch. I grow. I thin myself out so that the galaxies pass through me unaffected. I'm hearing the echo of a billion Big Bangs. I look down and I see Thorn and Katastrofa locked in each other's arms in a way that looks like hatred and looks like lust. They're intertwined and whirling through the darkness. I grow, I flatten, I wrap myself around the universe, I become the sentient fabric of space.

That's the easy part.

The hard part is to follow them through the vortex, to see where they will emerge, always knowing that they're still inside the arena inside the city on the junction of the River's tributaries which is maybe all inside someone's mind, maybe my own. I follow them. I'm smaller than an electron and whizzing down the tangled light-threads inside the marble in my hand. I'm a white blood corpuscle racing through the pumping bloodstream of the universe on a speed chase after a pair of crazed bacteria. They don't know where they're going, they don't understand the twists and turns of reality, don't understand that they can't lose me because I *am* the way. I start to relax. I ride the River like I've seen surfers do, giving in to the arc and swell of the wave and making it part of me. There they are—just up ahead—wrestling the water and each other. Destruction follows them. I feel the stilling of millions of heartbeats as they travel the stream, lashing out, cutting off worlds forever, severing the arteries that connect one cosmos with another. They love pain, they're wallowing in it, others' and their own. I hate them. But I'm trying to push that hate aside, trying to focus.

Yeah.

I can feel others too now. Dad and Serena are lost in this maze too, somehow. In the labyrinth of star systems there's a faint whiff of pepperoni pizza and that's so out-of-place, so homely in the midst of all this alienness that it would bring tears to my eyes if I had eyes, if I had tears, if I wasn't Theo Truthsayer.

Okay. They're about to breach. I follow them and we—

—break out of the River into a lush green place bursting out of a creek that winds its way round back of my grandparents' place in Spotsylvania County. It's a page of memory. I can see Joshua there, only he's much younger. I can see me too and I can't believe I'm so fucking tiny I guess I'm maybe six years old and it's summer I mean hot fierce fiery steamy summer with a storm maybe about to break.

I see me and Josh (I guess he's like ten years old) and we're playing tag or something, just running in and out of the trees by the side of the stream. And Josh is screaming, "I'm gonna kill you, I'm gonna fucking kill you," I don't know why, I think it's because I decapitated one of his action figures. So I'm running and he's pursuing and hollering and he's a lot faster than I am so that's how I know his anger is just pretend because otherwise he'd have beaten me up by now. But still I'm running as hard as I can because I'm just into running with the hard sun against my skin brushing laughing and—

Joshua catches me and wrestles me to the ground. He punches me a couple of times but it's kind of just pretend hard and he punches the ground more than me; the sun is behind him and he's dark, a raven, a black dragon.

"Lemme go."

"I'll teach you to cut off Commander Salamander's head, I'll cut off your dick, then you'll never be able to grow up."

"I hate you! I hate you! I hate you!" I'm laughing and laughing because this is how you tell someone you love him when he's bigger and more powerful and too young to appreciate the word *love*.

"I hate you too," Josh says, laughing too. He's beautiful and I'm awkward and I like to linger in the shadows and I can already read Shakespeare, kind of, one word at a time, the shiny syllables dancing before my eyes one at a time, so many colors, so many senses; Joshua can't. He prefers the Teenage Mutant Ninja Turtles. We both think each other's stupid.

But too I'm thinking with the sun in my eyes and the smell of my brother's sweat and fabric softener in my nostrils, I don't want to grow up anyways, why would I grow up, why would I want to be like *them?*

And that's when we hear them.

Joshua looks up. I'm still pinned down but I don't struggle to get out of his careless hold because I'm kind of enjoying the sensation of being pushed around by my big brother.

I don't want to grow up.

This is what we hear coming out of our grandparents' house:

"I hate you!"

"I hate you!"

But not the same way that me and Josh were saying it. It sounds like they mean it. So well we creep up to the house. We know the grandparents have gone to the store or something or my parents wouldn't fight like this; they came down here to escape fighting, after all.

We go inside, leaving our Chucks by the door so we won't make the floorboards creak. We slip upstairs. They're getting louder.

—You just refuse to understand. It's a fucking mid-life crisis or something and I'm scared and all you want to talk about is yourself.

—I'm not talking about myself, Phil. I'm talking about the future.

—My poetry's not the future, I know that.

"He's pissed off because of the review in the *Post*," Josh whispers to me as we crouch beside the door. The grandfather clock in the hall goes *bong* and startles us. I gasp. I'm sure they've heard me, but they're too involved in the screaming match to be aware of us, two small slivers of shadow, two right ears plastered to the hinges of a scarred oak door.

—I don't know why Dirda allowed that to get printed. He's a friend of yours, isn't he?

—That's not fair. You know it's not personal, Mary.

—You and your friends.

—If you're going to tell me I've ruined your life again, if you're going to tell me I stole away your future on the day we met, I—

—I hate you.

"What are they arguing about, Josh?"

"Nothing. Fucking nothing."

Josh gets up and stalks away, confident now that they won't hear. He stomps across the landing toward our bedroom which is also the TV room although there's no cable out here so we never watch it and we didn't bring down the Nintendo either so all we ever do there is sleep or sulk.

But I stay in the shadow of the doorway because I think sooner or later

I'll hear something that'll explain why it is they're so angry at each other. I mean, the things they're saying, I really don't understand them. Not that well.

Then I hear this:

—You don't even spend time with the kids.

—You don't either. You're lost in your own narcissistic navel-gazing.

—It's a low blow to use the kids.

—I'm the only one who ever—

—If you're going to throw some kind of martyr thing at me, I don't buy it. I didn't choose to be what I am.

—Martyr? So you're the fucking martyr around here? I'd like to drive in the nails myself.

What does it mean? I don't even know who's saying what, they've become so shrill that it all seems to be the same voice, yes, it's just one long loud monotonous roar of rage and I'm sitting in my corner, shriveled into that little piece of shadow, wanting to cry but not wanting my sniveling to distract them and make them turn on me. Is part of what they're saying that they don't love us anymore?

Suddenly I notice the muddy handprints on the doorjamb next to the hinges and I wonder if I'm going to get into trouble, because now they'll know there was a small person squatting here, spying on them, like the time they thought Josh and I overheard them having sex and they became all weird, withdrawn, not speaking to us for days, though it was before we knew what sex was, and I still don't really know even though we read through the big book about it together, the four of us.

And then I hear, I don't know, it sounds like a struggle. Are they going to hit each other? Oh Jesus they've never hit each other before. I can't stand it, I get up and shove the door all the way open and I'm standing there. I catch them in this like embrace of hate or maybe love. And maybe Dad's about to punch Mom out or something, I don't know, because they're in a jumble together on the bed and it's stifling hot in the room, there's no air conditioning out here, the window fan is blasting my face with burning air.

And so I scream, "Don't you hit her!" at my father, and they turn toward me.

They see me standing there. And suddenly the tableau of violence breaks up and they're both all smiling at me. "Theo," Dad says, and he gives a half-hearted laugh, "I didn't see you there."

"Hello, honey," Mom says.

I don't buy it. There's no joy in their smile, and there's even a hint of fear. Did *I* cause them to fear this much? I see it all because of who I am, though I don't know it yet, of course: I'm a truthsayer and I can see the churning beneath the surface, and I run to my mother and she takes me in her arms and I can smell beneath the sun-ripened smell of sweat a trace of old perfume; I snuggle my head between the breasts that sag, braless, under the cotton print summer dress and I don't look at Dad at all and I say, "Mommy, mommy, maybe you should have married me instead of Daddy."

Daddy rails against the window: "My life's going to pieces and here I am witnessing some cliché-ridden Oedipal drama in my own household—what a disaster." He leaves me alone with my mother. I hear his footsteps down the stairs and hear him yelling, "Josh! Josh!" which means maybe Josh will get someone to play baseball with for a while, even if it's only that Dad needs to be distracted.

"Stop, stop, stop, stop, stop," I scream at the top of my lungs, not at anyone in particular, just because I desperately want the storm to die down.

"I meant it when I said I should have married you," I tell my mother.

She puts her arms around me. She enfolds me in herself. It is now, for the first time, that I feel an alien thing inside her, a sickness; it's years before anyone will diagnose it; what I feel is a kind of ooze that is seeping through her body, dissolving atom by atom into her bloodstream; when I look up at her face I know she doesn't know, because she's only half-smiling and staring far off, through the window, toward the sun that's glaring through the windless treetops.

She says, softly, "My little knight, my little husband," and kisses me gently on the lips, and I'm filled with confusion and I'm all warm from the suffocating sunlight and the rushing of my blood. I twist away and my mother laughs again. "What would I do without you, Theodore Theophilus Theomancer?" None of which are my names because I'm just plain Theo, rhymes with Geo.

"I love you too," I say. Mostly because she wants to hear it. And because she's crying now. And because I feel the illness working its way from cell to cell inside her, and I know that I'm going to be the only one who will know for a long time, for years to come maybe.

Then I step back and it's me watching myself, me out of the macrocosm gazing down at little me and little mother. All of sudden the room is shaking. The windows shatter. My mother's skin peels away and I see Katastrofa inside her flesh. The dragon's claws rend flesh and Katastrofa's standing there now, with the tatters of my mother's body dissolving into the hot moist air from the fan.

"How dare you pretend to be my flesh and blood?" I shriek, and I'm rushing at Katastrofa, pounding at her with my puny fists, but her scales are hard as iron and my fists start bleeding and with each blow I feel a more than mortal pain not in my hands but in my heart.

"Oh," Katastrofa says, "but I'm not pretending, am I?"

I whip around to see Dad. He's being sawed in half, from top to bottom, by an invisible buzzsaw, and his two pieces fall to the left and right and inside him is Katastrofa's vampire brother.

"Tsk, tsk, little brother," he says to me, "you almost fucked your mother!" Then there's a sound like a beat-up record player being started up and then I hear this old Tom Lehrer record with a song about Oedipus Rex which Dad used to play sometimes and it's stuck on the words *I'd rather marry a duckbilled platypus* and it plays those words again and again and again.

Outside, a shadow crosses the sun. Darkness falls. There's a sudden chill. It's an eclipse. My arms are prickling with tension.

I see my six-year-old self trapped between the warring demons. The baby-me sees Dad in the doorway and Mom on the bed, crying, and only dimly senses that they've become monsters. I can't remember if the eclipse is real or if it's just a projection of my childish terror.

My older self is in a forest clearing. We've never left the forest of the night, the place I plunged into when they came for me in Mexico. The two are circling me and I'm in the middle. They're almost dancing, you know like in those old westerns, me tied to the stake and them capering and pounding on their drums and yelling for my blood. And yes, the whole of my grandparents' house is a house of cards that collapses like the cards at the end of *Alice in Wonderland,* cards flying every which way blowing in my eyes slicing my cheeks with papercuts.

No, I scream *no, get me out of here—*

And I seem to hear a voice: a grating, steam-driven voice: it says: The trap is of your own devising; to escape you must think the unthinkable; you must undo the unchangeable; you must unkill the forever-dead.

And I'm thinking, you can never get a straight answer around here, every riddle is answered with another riddle. The dragon and the vampire circle me, breathing fire, spitting blood. I hear the Indian drumbeats too, *POM-pom-pom-pom POM-pom-pom-pom,* and the war whoops and the weird, winding melody of their song . . .

And at the same time that we're in my house, trapped in my memories, and we're in the forest of confusion, at the same time as all this we're also out there in the middle of a space battle of some kind—Thorn and Katastrofa and their storm troopers and their planet-long spaceships and their star-destroying weapons. The ships are whooshing and roaring the

vacuum of space and that's how I know they're ships of fantasy and not
science fiction and that even this macrocosmic spectacle is still taking
place within the jungle of the soul.

How can I break free? By solving a few simple riddles? *What has four
legs in the morning, two at noon, and three in the evening,* cornball enigmas
like the one Oedipus guessed, and so he slew the monster but ended up
marrying his mother and plucking out his eyes?

And then all of a sudden I'm back inside my memory again . . . inside it and outside it at the same time . . . I'm on Mom's lap again . . .
I don't know that there are monsters hiding inside her flesh. She's kissing
me and then she sets me down on their bed. I lick the curious taste from
off my lips, part cinnamon, part alcohol, part blood.

I have a dream in which I see my parents making love, only I don't
know that's what it is. My parents have become like dolphins, and they're
riding each other and swimming through the moonlit ocean at top speed.
I wake up and I expect to see that my mom has come in to look in on me
because that's what always happens when I cry out in my sleep. But
instead it's only Josh. We're even younger now, I'm maybe four years old,
I sleep with two stuffed animals, a Tasmanian Devil and a Pink Panther.

Josh says, "Shut up, you little fuck."

I say, "What's a little fuck?"

He says, "You stick your weenie into a girl and she has a baby, that's
what a little fuck is."

And the dream comes back to me in all its liquidescent terror.

"Josh, I had a dream, I'm scared."

"Okay, little brother," Josh says. He sits beside my bed and he strokes
my brow, softly, left to right, until I begin to drift again.

Josh is melting away. I grip his hand. His hand comes off and it's just
wood, like Pinocchio's. Josh is grinning away and his teeth are chattering
and he's like a ventriloquist's dummy or a marionette and—

I'm looking up and I see dark creatures in the ceiling pulling my
brother's strings and making him flop this way and that way and—

Joshua's a corpse, the skin's peeling from his face, a maggot works its
way out through the edge of his lower lip, Joshua's eyes are dead white
like my mother's opals and—

It's years later and I'm sitting in Mommy's lap and feeling the sickness
trickling through her veins and she kisses me and my lips tingle and her
kiss confuses me like the kiss of a serpent and—

Mom's head goes round and round like *The Exorcist* head with a ratchet-ratchet-ratchet sound and she's all, "Fuck me! Fuck me!" in a deep bass devil voice, and—

Space! The starfleets smash into one another like coalescing nebulae. Someone help me.

The open sea! The ships are ramming each other and catapulting fire onto each other's decks and the galley slaves' oars are snapping like matchsticks and—

Help me.

Joshua lies in his coffin. My mother has turned to stone. There's only one person left in my family and that's my father, the only one who doesn't have a single spark of truthsaying in him. Where are you, Dad? Oh, Dad, we're all inside each other, lost in the labyrinth of our own nightmares.

CHAPTER SIXTEEN

AN ENCOUNTER WITH THE DEITY

Phil Etchison

I asked Ash how he was going to go about confronting his father at this stage, when all hell was in the middle of breaking loose. "I don't know," he told me. He looked lost.

Everything started happening at once. I mean, first all these people in silver lamé spacesuits came charging into the observatory and they were speaking into communicators, juggling orbs of colored light, scribbling notes in the air, and doing all kinds of other incomprehensible things. They bustled about and they elbowed us this way and that. Not that they were being rude, really, they were just so preoccupied that Serena and I didn't seem to be there for them. Ash was preoccupied too; he was soon having a heated conversation with two of the paramilitary-looking people, and Corvus took me aside and said, "Perhaps we should go on a secret mission of our own."

"What do you mean?" I said.

"Ash is never going to seek out King Strang on his own. They're very much alike, you know; their pride is a fearsome thing. But it must happen or we'll all be left hanging. You understand, don't you?"

"But what can I do?"

"Phil," he said, putting his arm over my shoulder, "you've been feeling useless, haven't you?"

"Yes," I said softly. It was hard not to, when every person one ran into was either a marvel of super-science, gifted with psychic powers, or king of the universe. "But I guess I'll get over it. I've been known to feel useless before. You wouldn't have anything to drink, would you? Alcoholic, I mean."

"Oh, Phil, Phil, Phil," Corvus said, and he led me by the arm away from where Ash's minions clustered. Serena was busy with Ash; she didn't seem to have as hard a time fitting in as I did; perhaps it was because she had known Ash since childhood. "Come," said Corvus, and as we moved away from the others, it seemed to be that his demeanor was once more becoming far less avian, far closer to my friend Milt Stone's. "We're going to go on a little quest of our own."

"To find Theo?" I asked him.

"Well, I was thinking that we could go and throw ourselves before Strang, and perhaps effect a reconciliation between him and Ash."

"What good would I be at that? Anyway, I seem to recall that in the equivalent scene in *King Lear*, the ruse didn't work; Lear wouldn't see Cordelia, wouldn't speak to her, until it was all too late."

"But if we somehow manage to pick up a truthsayer on the way. . . ."

I saw. But how could we find Theo when the number of haystacks was infinite? And yet I couldn't just sit around being useless. That would merely be to repeat the isorhythms of my life.

"Come on, Philip Etchison," said Corvus, "There's a poet inside you even if you don't know it yet. Everyone *thinks* you're a poet, man, you might as well become one sooner or later; if there's anything that could get you past your mid-life crisis, it's knowing yourself for the first time."

"Yes," I said, trying to sound fervent. "Yes."

Holding onto my elbow, Corvus folded one wing across his face and whispered a word. We blinked out and stepped into an alcove in the main hallway of the temple. There was a bronze door bas-reliefed into a frieze of mythological scenes; Corvus spread his wings wide, uttered another command, and we walked through the bronze, which felt like mist on my face, moist and metallic. I gasped. We had suddenly entered the kiva, the sacred Navajo place atop the mesa in Arizona—the place from which we had entered the transdimensional portal which had transported us to the hidden cosmos of beauty and bereavement—for there, on the ground, was the sand painting that showed our family—above our heads was the tarp that had made this place into a makeshift enclosure.

The strangest thing of all was that the kiva was full of people, of varying degrees of transparency, wearing the clothing of many eras and nations. I don't know how that all fit inside this place; perhaps it was because they were infinitesimally thin; the tent held a cast of thousands. There were even people I thought I recognized: Shakespeare, Michelangelo, that sort of thing; there was even a man with flowing white robes and nail holes in his hands, though I knew he could not be the historical Jesus because of his blond hair and blue eyes.

Seeing this man, in fact, disconcerted me a great deal, since I am above all a secular person. Especially when he turned to me, transfixed me with his sea-blue eyes, mumbled to me words that stirred my heart and brought tears rushing to my eyes; words that I instantly forgot, for I cannot set them down here; I remember only their cadent echoing. I was somewhat relieved to see the Buddha there alongside him, hovering in midair in the lotus position, which was a feat I had seen attempted, but never achieved, by many would-be gurus of the New Age persuasion. When the Enlightened One also regaled me in high astounding terms, which I then also forgot, I realized that I had discovered the common ground between metaphysics and Chinese food; for in a moment I was hungry again, and the truth I hungered for was ever beyond my grasp.

Then came the strangest sight of all; I saw myself, motionless, pierced through the heart by an arrow, hanging in the air above the midpoint of the kiva. The other shadow-people flitted past me; sometimes I saw myself superimposed over images of Renaissance queens and nineteenth-century sophists; I could tell, though the eyes of the shadow-me were open, that I was quite, quite dead. There was an Aztec priest behind me, wearing a turquoise mask shaped like a human skull, in a fantastical robe of quetzal feathers, brandishing an obsidian knife.

I said to Corvus-becoming-Milt-Stone, "We had to die to come here, didn't we? And we're *still* dead, because there really is no return from the other side. . . ."

"It's true that we cannot step in the same River twice."

"Then why did you bring me here?" I said. "We've already crossed over into the dreamtime, haven't we?"

"But Theo has gone beyond where we've gone," Milt said. "He's in a dream within a dream. Haven't you ever had a dream in which you woke up, but you were actually still dreaming?"

"No," I said, "but I've seen it in horror movies. It's almost a fixture in those *Nightmare on Elm Street* pictures my kids always insist on renting."

"Well, we're going to have to go the other way, you see; we're going to practice lucid dreaming within lucid dreaming."

"More peyote?" I said.

"Well, yes, massive quantities," he said. "So much that it must be administered the Mayan way, direct absorption into that part of the body that has the densest concentration of capillaries. . . ."

Suddenly—as Corvus—he flapped his wings and uttered a piercing squawk. The phantoms of past truthseekers dispersed in a flurry of smoke and feathers. We were alone in the kiva now save for the shades of Milt, myself, my wife, and Serena Somers, who, suspended in the mist, drifted about the center of the circle like ghostly Saint Sebastians. I remembered having read something about the ancient Mayan preoccupation with hallucinogenic enemas, and I frankly began to have cold feet about the whole thing. I had died before, after all, and all at once I remembered it perfectly—the cold fire penetrating, the eerie music, the whirlwind of childhood images, and the bitter taste on my lips. I didn't want to go through it again and this did not seem like a dignified entrée into the hereafter.

Corvus shed his wings. The wings wavered, shifted shape, and presently he held in his hands two lengthy objects—halfway in size between syringes and bicycle pumps—and he handed me one. "You have to shed your clothing," he said. "Quickly now. It's easier than you think. It has ritual meaning too—naked you came into this world, and naked you leave it—you see what I mean."

He began to sing, while at the same time undoing his costume with astonishing dexterity. It seemed, indeed, that it was not only his clothing but his very skin that he was unzipping. It fell to the sandpainting in a single piece, like a deflating balloon. Inside the skin of Corvus the avian navigator was Milt Stone the *nadlé*, the sacred man-woman shaman of the Navajo; and as he stood before me I could not tell where the woman ended and the man began. Before this I had only seen Milt Stone, genetically a man, dressed in a woman's clothes and aping to perfection the gestures, bearing, the very essence of a woman; the creature I saw now was not, biologically, of either gender at all. I took it then that I was seeing the Milt Stone within, the thing his soul had become at the time when a vision had told him he must follow the way of the *nadlé*. When he spoke to me (it was no doubt an inner prejudice of mine that continued to think of him as *he*) the voice was, like that of a countertenor in an English cathedral, curiously void of sexual identifying marks. "You like my inner self?" he said. "Yours isn't bad either. I rather like the purplish aura that emanates from you." I couldn't tell whether he was kidding me or not. I had removed my clothes and folded them, through force of habit, in a neat pile to one side of the sacred circle. I saw myself for the middle-aged, nondescript man I had become. This was strange because all my life, even at the times I was most depressed, most self-loathing, there had always been something of the gilded knight in my image of myself. Tarnished, perhaps, but never an everyman.

A cauldron appeared in the middle of the circle. Around it, the figures of my family, drawn in the sand, danced like cartoon images. Above our heads, my family's corpses hovered. In the cauldron a potion seethed; Milt Stone the man-woman filled his injecting device with the liquid and handed it to me. I stared at it dully while the corpses wheeled and the paintings capered.

"You're wavering," said Milt.

"Well, can you blame me?"

"I know; this is just too weird, isn't it? But you have to look at the mythic matrix, the historical perspective. The ancient Maya used to—"

"I know, I know." I had attended a lecture by my colleague Dr. Schön, an archaeologist, and I knew all about the mystery contraptions found in the burial sites of Mayan aristocrats, only recently revealed to be the wherewithal for the anal administration of psychedelics. It just seemed so damned undignified to me.

We exchanged devices. The thing was hot to the touch and again I was afraid, but I knew that I would overcome my fear one way or another, because the many paths of possibility in my life had narrowed down to two: to stay forever in this undead dream state, or, by this death-in-death, this dream within a dream, return to wakefulness.

Then, out of the empty air, there came the sound of drums. Each beat seemed to pound my very bones. Also there came a deep and raucous trumpeting, though I saw no trumpets; but I felt a searing wind spring up and the jaws of the hanging corpses gaping wide; it seemed that the trumpeting was the wind itself, resonating through the body cavities of my family. Then the arrows twisted free of the flesh, caught fire, and fell to the perimeter of the sand painting, which also caught fire, encircling us with flame. The wind howled louder now, and the wounds of my loved ones whistled, and I could hear, behind the shrilling, the harmonies of a celestial choir.

"Hurry up!" Milt shouted.

He bent over and applied the peyote; I did the same. It was ice cold as it shot into me. A numbness spread up my torso and down my legs. The corpses were whirling now, and the singing of the wind crescendoed into a bizarre amalgam of Beethoven's *Ninth Symphony* and *Ninety-Nine Bot-*

tles of Beer on the Wall. I thought about my sons. I thought about my fractured family—about bickering in Spotsylvania County, weeping in Alexandria, recrimination in Arizona. What right did I have to demand that my wife and children be returned to me after I'd walled myself in behind my own narcissism? No one should have a self-styled poet for a husband and father. Oh, Josh, I thought, oh, Theo . . . I tried to see the same vision I had seen when last I tried to cross the river . . . the golden boy with one arm upraised, stepping into the glittering sea . . . no image came to me.

I felt myself falling. "Catch me, catch me," I whispered, but Milt made no move, and I continued to fall long past the point where I would have hit the sand, I fell and fell and fell until I seemed to be inside the painting itself. . . .

"Catch!" It was Milt's voice, echoing like a cartoon villain's. I felt something in my hand. It looked like rope but it was so light that I could barely sense it. Milt was tying the other end of the rope around my corpse, which seemed to have come to life, to be lumbering in midair like Frankenstein's monster. "We have to anchor you to yourself," he screamed, "or else you'll be lost in the labyrinth of nightmares forever!"

I caught the rope. I fastened it loosely about my waist. I couldn't feel it at all; it was a magical rope, I supposed. It was like the ball of yarn that Theseus used to thread the labyrinth. But perhaps I myself was the minotaur.

I fell and fell and then I—

Died.

I knew I was dead. I had died before. Death is the way a wineglass feels when it's been drained to the dregs. It is nothing. I felt the nothing again when the last of the feeling-stealing fluid penetrated the last nerve-endings of my body. I could see nothing, hear nothing; I could not even see that I saw nothing. But death was no longer the unknown. It was like visiting a familiar place. I welcomed the end of sensation. I floated and did not know that I floated. I did not even know that I was I. I knew there was an I, that I could reach out somehow and grab it and be in touch once more with the continuum of my selfhood, but I felt no desire for it. I felt no loss. I felt no passion.

I do not know how long it was I remained in this condition, because there was no time, only the potentiality of time. And there was Love; that, at least, was how I perceived the infinitude into which I had fallen; and that Love, it seemed, possessed a kind of consciousness.

I said (without words): "What is this place?"

But I already knew what the answer would be: it was the primal nothing; it was the cosmos in the moment before the Big Bang; it was the uncreated universe; and the consciousness I sensed was none other than that Absolute Being whose existence I, as a good agnostic and an intellectual, had always questioned.

I was hanging on to the I by a thread, by less than a thread now. In a moment I find myself extinguished, melding into the ocean of infinite Love. I cried out, "Why did you make the universe at all? If this is the way things were before . . . this utter tranquillity . . . this all-embracing oneness . . . why shatter the stillness with a cosmos? Why life and death—and I don't just mean human beings, but worlds and suns and galaxies? I don't understand," I said, "I really don't."

I believe that God was on the verge of answering me. I really do. But the next voice that I heard was the voice of Milt Stone.

"Come out of there, Phil! Another second and it'll be too late!"

"How? What are you talking about?" Waves of Love washed over me. I was sinking . . . sinking . . . sinking . . . I knew that all I had to do was allow myself to slide all the way down into oblivion and the answer to all these questions would come to me, clear and incontrovertible.

"You're sliding to Nirvana, Phil . . . it's up to you . . . you can go out, like a candle . . . or you can climb back up and save your sons."

And in the sea of Love I heard a murmuring: You have no sons; they are illusion; all is illusion. Let go your conscious self; let go, let go.

And I knew there was a truth in what I heard; for in my journeying down the River between worlds, I had learned that all men are islands; that the hard fabric of reality is only the confluence of our private illusions; that those we meet, those we love most dearly, are in the profoundest sense strangers to us, fellow travelers on alien roads; that love and death, father and mother of the artist's inspiration, they too are illusions.

"I don't want to come back," I said.

Milt said (and his voice was fast fading), "You have to come back. It's not your time yet. You are still tied to the world of illusion."

"No, I'm not," I said.

Enter, enter, enter, sang the voices, *enter the oneness of the all.*

But as they sang I realized that the rope was still fastened around me. I struggled against it. I wanted to cut myself loose. I wanted to enter the oneness, but even as I felt myself being submerged beneath waves of joy I also felt a nagging discontent with the New Age labeling that seemed to have been affixed to these transcendental truths. I writhed, but the rope held firm. I had to go back. I felt in the darkness for the cord, gripped it with spectral appendages that were fast devolving into hands, gave the rope a sharp tug, felt myself being pulled up. I kicked and screamed. I raged against the withdrawal of love's embrace, but I knew even as I was lifted out of Nirvana that the regret I felt proved I was not yet ready for extinguishment.

As I slid back up I felt a gutwrenching pain . . . a sense of agonizing loss . . . the feeling akin to when I'm desperate for the solace of alcohol and I'm desperately trying to quit . . . something I've felt a lot these days . . . but this is even worse . . . I feel that I've been wrung, twisted, flattened by a steam roller, torn apart . . . but then, when I can't stand it anymore . . . I see a vision of my two sons . . . for the first time since entering the sacred circle.

They're little . . . I think they're about ten and six . . . it's the grandparent's place . . . they're running in the woods beside the stream . . . I think they're fighting. They're screaming. I hear Theo screaming I hate you I hate you the way kids do when they don't mean it, because the opposite thing to say is so big and powerful and magic that they can't force it to their lips. I'm right beside Theo when I hear, coming from the house, another voice, and the same words . . . I hate you . . . and the voice is my own.

"No, please," I scream, "I didn't say that!"

But I knew it was true.

I had no time to react because I found myself plummeting, bursting through soft sheet metal, landing abruptly in the passenger seat of a Cadillac that was being driven by Milt Stone, restored to maleness and police uniform, and driving at top speed through desert terrain. I looked up. The roof was knitting itself back together again. I shook the steel dust from my hair.

"Welcome back," Milt said. "You seem a little shook up."

"You pulled me out of . . . out of . . ."

"I know." I saw that the rope was still around my waist; it went up right through the roof of the Cadillac. "You're anchored for a while," he said. "You pulled yourself out, really; in the battle between desire and otherworldliness, your love for your sons won out."

It was clear that the victory of my personal love against the great all-encompassing greater love was an ambiguous thing. I had to accept that. I was happy to be encumbered by selfishness. I was a human being, not a boddhisatva.

I glanced at the steering wheel and saw the gearshift, which read PRNDLL, suggesting that we had returned to the real world. But a single glance at what lay ahead convinced me otherwise.

INTO THE LABYRINTH OF NIGHTMARES

Phil Etchison

What loomed ahead—already one could glimpse bits and pieces of it behind the forest of saguarro and twisted rock that stretched out on either side of the desert highway—was the skyline of a city. The buildings were tall and whimsical and seemed to be thousands of stories high, but that was not the strangest thing about them: it was, rather, that they seemed not to have been built but to have been drawn; they were like a vast background painting for an animated sci-fi feature. Indeed, there were flying bridges that linked the upper stories of the skyscrapers; there were zeppelinlike vehicles threading their way between them; there were fleets of aircars, swarming the structures like fireflies; and there were garishly colored searchlights that crisscrossed the sunset. Two sunsets actually, the little sun athwart the bloated one; I wondered whether this meant we had returned to Tucson once again. Incongruously, the word *Hollywood* was etched into a nearby sandstone cliff; a mountain across the way read *Disneyland.*

"Where the hell are we?" I asked Milt, who drove on, impassive; I wondered whether he saw the same sights as I did, or whether the world he traveled in was some primal, Native American landscape of cliff-dwellings and sand dunes.

"You tell me," Milt said. "It's your son's world we're going into; you must know more about it than I do."

I did not want to confess that I had come to the conclusion that I hardly knew my son. And my close encounter with the godhead had rendered me even less confident of the permanence of the bond of love between us. After all, had I not entirely forgotten Theo's very existence for large chunks of my life? I was afraid of what my son might say to me. I had had a fleeting glimpse of a crucial scene from his early childhood for the first time, seen it from his point of view, seen myself as he saw me; I had felt his disillusionment. I had to save my son, but I also had to redeem myself.

Just as Milt Stone was now dressed in the garb of a police officer, I too wore the "official" garments of my profession: a kind of tunic, with a gilded border in the Greek fashion; the obligatory harp rested between my knees, and now and then let out a nervous twang.

I journeyed on; the city seemed to grow no bigger; we weren't getting any closer. I said to Milt, "Why can't you drive faster?"

He said, "I'm going as fast as I can, man; something's blocking me."

"But the highway is clear."

"Only because you refuse to see the obstruction."

"What obstruction?"

"Things happen in stages around here, Phil. You eat your soup, you get to go on to the main course."

"No more riddles, Milt. I needn't remind you of this, but I don't come from a riddling culture; I'm not used to having questions answered with other questions."

"You're right," Milt said, but didn't answer my question. We continued to move down the highway at breakneck pace. The rocky shapes on either side of the road grew ever more baroque, until at length they seemed to be monstrous sandstone statues like the monumental Ramses IIs at the temple of Abu Simbel . . . until it seemed they were actually moving their hands, nodding their heads, uttering great cavernous groans. One seemed to proffer a Papal benediction; another, like a stern schoolmarm, wagged a bony finger, showering us with dirt and pebbles.

Milt remained silent; perhaps he was allowing me time to figure out the enigma for myself. There was, I supposed, some kind of test I would have to pass before gaining admittance to the next segment of the ritual. Perhaps I would have to answer three questions. I hoped they were as simple as the riddle of the Sphinx. But I feared the test would be something far more serious; that I would be forced to face some dark part of myself. That was what the obstruction was, wasn't it?

No sooner did I think this than a ghostly form began to materialize in the middle of the road. It was, indeed, myself—not the paunchy, middle-aged self-image I had seen back in the kiva, but a younger self, wearing black, complete with Darth Vader helmet and light saber—the kind of image of his father that a six-year-old boy might have, if he was full of rage and unable to express himself.

I looked at me; the great dark me glowered, growled, rattled his saber, which filled the air with neon fireworks. The rocky figures seemed to cower behind one another.

"Time for battle," Milt said. He pulled off onto the shoulder.

"What am I supposed to do, kill myself?" I said. I didn't see how the me-creature could be defeated; wasn't it a hundred times my size, and armed besides?

"You'll figure out something," he said, and he popped the locks; the passenger door swung automatically open, and he shoved me out—not forcibly, but firmly. With considerable trepidation I stepped from the car and walked out into the middle of the highway.

The me-monster roared and shambled about, his every footfall cracking the asphalt and exposing the yellow brick beneath; in the setting sun's light he was dark and formidable; how could I defeat him without defeating myself? When I listened more carefully to his bellowings I realized they were slowed-down fragments of my own poetry.

Perhaps I should try the quixotic approach, I thought. And at once I found myself riding a fractious steed and galloping toward the monster with a flaccid lance in my arm. I looked and felt ridiculous. The monster wore the windmill's blades like the points of a tiara, and they whirled about his head, and he rumbled with laughter and stamped his feet and swung his arms about. The light saber cut a swath through some nearby cliffs, and rubble cascaded onto the road. I hurtled full tilt at the man-windmill, jabbed the lance at the empty air, fell forward on my face and hit the pavement.

The winged Corvus, appearing suddenly by my side as my second, wordlessly handed me a sword and vanished in a puff of smoke. I only understood the use of swords from epic movies and epic poems, so, trying to wave it, I was pulled to the ground by the weight of it. I tried a two-handed style but only managed to approach a few feet closer before stumbling again. The most infuriating thing was that this me-monster hardly seemed to notice my existence; it continued to shamble and stomp and bellow my doggerellike juvenilia to the world. I tasted blood. I felt bruised and misused all over.

I charged once more. "I know you're there!" I shouted. "I'll kill you! I'll kill you!" This time I actually managed to slam the sword hard into the top of a steel-clad boot. There was no clang; the blade sliced cleanly through nothingness; the giant was an illusion. "Maybe you don't exist," I said. "Get out of my sight. I adjure you, begone!" I tried raising my arms in an exorcistlike pose, but it did no good. The giant grew until it filled my entire field of vision, and my ears vibrated from the flat cadences of his poetry.

"Look where you're going!" I screamed at it. "I mean, aren't you supposed to be my id or something? The least you could do is—"

I thought of Prospero and Caliban:

> *This thing of darkness I*
> *Acknowledge mine.*

Maybe that was the problem; it was I who had failed to acknowledge the monster, not he who wasn't paying me any attention. But I *was* acknowledging it, wasn't I? I had a split lip from the pavement to prove it. I had acknowledged its existence: but had I acknowledged it *mine?*

That submoronic, fustian-burbling giant?

Was that thing really me?

I dropped my sword. It was clear I had to embrace the darkness, not banish it. I stripped away my pretentious robes of poesy. The giant had grown so huge that he enveloped me utterly. I entered the me-monster's mouth; I slid down the me-monster's gullet and into the utter blackness of his belly; and I also slid into the past, into forgotten memories.

The 50s. *Leave it to Beaver* country.

I'm alone in the house and waiting for the world to end.

The 60s. Riot time.

I'm alone in my dorm room and waiting for the world to end.

The 70s. I've received my one hundredth rejection letter from *Poetry* magazine. I'm alone in a garret in Piggy County, Maryland, eating a lot of fried foods and agonizing about the emptiness of my existence; and I see Mary from my window, standing at a street corner, waiting maybe for a bus; she clutches a pile of books to her bosom very much as a Madonna might clasp the redeemer of the world, and it's a hot steamy summer, waiting for the clouds to burst. It is for an entirely selfish reason that I lean against the windowsill praying for rain. And when rain comes it is almost enough to restore my faith in divine providence. It pours. It drenches. The power goes out across the street; the traffic signal at the corner goes dark; two cars hydroplane into each other. I don't even grab a coat; I just run out into the street, run toward this bedraggled Madonna whom I have already named Mary in my mind, and I cry out, "Mary, Mary, Mary. . . ."

"How do you know my name?"

"The bus won't be here for another twenty minutes . . . do you need a place to wait it out?" Oh God, you know how it is when it rains, it pushes people together, people thinking there's another person I can maybe hide behind or something, fend off the rain . . . and in only a few moments it seems almost as though our lips are about to collide half by accident half by design . . . and . . . and . . .

Mary says, "Who the hell are you, some kind of serial killer?" Oh, she doesn't say *serial killer;* I don't know what she says; the phrase isn't fashionable yet; I've been editing my memories.

. . . and I say "No, of course not . . . I'm a poet."

She looks at me. Through the sheets and sheets of rain I see in her eyes that she believes me. She is the first person ever to do so.

Do we kiss?

I can't remember.

Abruptly it's the 80s and I'm about to slug her in the face. I suddenly come to because I hear the shriek of my child: *"Don't you hit her!"* and I'm in a jumble with Mary on the bed and we're in a brutal embrace, brutal because I can't tell if it's a prelude to sex or violence.

What have I been doing? Going on and on about my inner torment, wounding myself while pretending to heal myself? I am furious. I know I could have killed. Myself or someone else. I don't know. I don't know. Is this the darkness in me?

I turn to see Theo in the doorway. He's frail, muddy, wide-eyed. I smile at him; so does Mary; it's the natural reaction, to hide our warring from our children, to want to protect them. "Theo," I say, "I didn't see you there."

Theo doesn't buy my pretense.

I don't realize yet that it is because he is a truthsayer; I just believe it to be the clear vision of childhood. (All children, I will come to understand, begin with a spark of truthsaying in them.) Theo looks me in the eye and doesn't speak; but I understand his silence to be an accusation.

If you're going to tell me I've ruined your life again, if you're going to tell me I stole away your future that rainy day we met—

Can it be true that in these petty domestic squabbles we reenact the life and death of universes . . . that we play out with infinitesimal precision the mythic interactions of gods and heroes?

"Hello, honey," Mary says.

I remember the rain lashing us driving our lips together and—

Theo runs toward his mother, throws himself into her lap. She hugs him to her the way she hugged those library books to her breast. I saw the Madonna in the woman on that stormy day and now I'm seeing the same image again, and I ache because my wife's embrace is no longer for me. Jesus, I'm jealous of my own child! And then he says, ingenuously, yet bringing into the open my most angst-filled thoughts, "Mommy, Mommy, maybe you should have married me instead of Daddy."

That's when I really lose it. "My life's going to pieces and here I am witnessing some cliché-ridden Oedipal drama in my own household— what a disaster." And I stomp away, away from the window, away from my son and my wife. I can hear the me-monster's thunderous footfall in my own. It *is* me after all, this shambling abomination.

I start down the stairs. I don't want to look into the eyes of my child. My other son will be more accommodating, I know. I'll call him and we'll play a game of baseball, maybe even break a couple of windows.

For some reason the stairs seem to be going on a long time. I'm descending . . . descending . . . sweating, too, because it's a muggy Virginia summer . . . or worse . . . the heat is getting worse . . . and the stairs are no longer the familiar stairs but an endless spiraling stairwell, dank and mildewed. I don't know when this transformation happened, but I am descending into the bowels of . . . I don't know, the underworld, perhaps . . . I will know if I have to cross a river and if there is a cowled old man to row it and a three-headed dog yapping at his heels and . . .

I see the River. The stairway leads precipitously downward like the narrow steps that hugged the cliffside in the town with the Laetrile clinic. I see the ferryman. There is no sky, only a lowering gray canopy of mist. Sooner than I want to be, I'm getting on the boat. There is no one on board except the hooded figure and the dog. The ferryman reaches out a skeletal hand, expecting, doubtless, the traditional one obol payment for the passage to the land of death; all I have on me is an American Express card, and it does not surprise me that the underworld is now computerized; a credit slip drops from the ferryman's sleeve, I sign it, we move noiselessly across the brackish water; in the far distance I see the same fantastical city that I have seen up there, past the highway, where presumably Milt Stone is still pulled over, waiting for me to overcome myself.

"How long till we get there?" I ask. And I'm shaking. I've relived a shameful scene from my past, and I don't see any means of expiation.

The ghastly ferryman bursts out laughing. It's the laughter of a child. His hood falls away and I see that it's Theo. "Oh, Dad," he says, "are you that anxious to be dead?"

"No," I admit.

"Let's take her for a spin, then," he says. The ferry seems to become motorized all of a sudden, and it takes off at top speed. The waters are dark except, here and there, for patches of sulfurous flame. I'm almost suffocating in the pungent air. Theo keeps giggling, and it unnerves me. "Oedipal drama indeed, Dad; you're just so fucking melodramatic sometimes."

"Are you still mad at me about that?"

"Well, you would have hit her, you know. Probably me, too. But that hardly makes our household into a seething cauldron of domestic violence. Maybe we do live in Virginia, but that doesn't automatically turn our family into a Southern novel." He laughs again. In spite of myself, I laugh a little too. "There now," he says. "It could be a lot worse, couldn't it?"

"Am I forgiven?" I ask him.

He doesn't answer.

"Come on, you *have* to forgive me!"

The boat is suddenly becalmed. Theo turns to me; he's no longer robed in black; he's just a child again; an XXL T-shirt drapes his knees. "Stop it, Daddy, stop it," he says. "Life really *doesn't* imitate art. Well, maybe, like, dude, only in other works of art."

It seems to me that we are all haunted people; but the ghosts that haunt us are often of our own creation. I know how this parallel universe business works; somewhere there's a world where I, in a frenzy of self-absorption and self-loathing, turned on my wife and children, beat them, even killed them. And even though these things did not happen for me, there still exists an echo of these events, and sometimes I bear the full brunt of their shame and guilt. Perhaps we are not islands after all.

"Congratulations, Dad," Theo says, "you're beginning to understand."

"Did I pass the test?"

"That's the trouble with you, you see. You keep thinking everything's a test." And with that Theo begins to laugh once again, only his laughter now becomes deeper and more raucous and more menacing, and the cloak of darkness gathers around him and his face is a grinning skull but I embrace him, I feel the child beneath the dry and dusty bones and—

—burst out of the me-monster's cavity like the creature from *Alien,* and found myself once again smashing through the roof of the Cadillac and attached to my dead self by the umbilical cord of my soul.

"I'm going to save you, Theo," I whispered, but this time I did not feign fervor; I knew that my child needed me; I heard his cry clear across the gulf between the universes.

We shot through the gates of the city. Inside, fire streamed from broken windows and there were multi-car-pileups on every corner. There were banners in Japanese hanging from all the buildings. People were pouring out of every skyscraper. These were expressionless, two-dimensional people with large blinking eyes and brightly colored hair, and they wore space-age garments. The tongues of flame moved jerkily . . . perhaps twenty-eight frames to the second . . . as though we were on video. When a white rabbit in a waistcoat rushed by, peering at his watch,

I realized that we had entered some kind of cartoon world, and that there was a decidedly Japanese cast to the animation here.

"The streets are impassable," Milt said. "You'll have to go on on foot."

"Aren't you coming with me?"

"No . . . I have to search for the King."

"King Strang?"

"Yes. But I'll pick you up when you're ready."

Unarmed save with the knowledge that my son was trapped within the city, I started for the city center, upstream against the crowds that surged through every street. It was easy to elbow the animated people out of the way; seen edgewise they were paper-thin; I wondered if they did, in fact, fill out into some other dimension I could not perceive, and whether they saw *me* as a cartoon figure, flat and absurd. What were they fleeing from? Was it an army of occupation? Soon I could see the thing that terrorized them, a tremendous shadow that soared and swooped above the skyline breathing fire . . . it was a dragon not unlike the witch-reptile from the final scenes of Walt Disney's *Sleeping Beauty*. And battling the dragon was a batlike creature, black and bloody-fanged, whose beating wings knocked turrets from their rooftops, whose screeching raked my eardrums. It was a *Godzilla*-style monster fight; Tokyo was being ravaged; it was a cartoon; it was a video game; and it was all real, real as a child's wildest imaginings.

It was then that I saw my son. I had reached a square at the center of the city. At the center of the square was a bronze monument, not unlike the Iwo Jima Memorial; Theo was the topmost figure in the tableau, his arm upraised, pointing toward the setting suns, just the way I had seen him at the beginning of the first journey, just before the first time I died; at his feet lay Joshua, eyes closed in death; above him was the weeping Jesus Ortega as *putto,* wings drooping, face buried in his hands; Serena Somers, too, was part of the group, standing a little apart, gazing at the horizon.

The square was virtually empty; the only citizen remaining was a man in a wheelchair with patches over his eyes, and a guide dog who whined and led the man around and around in circles. Over our heads, the bat and dragon wheeled. Sometimes the bat swerved, swooped, bit the dragon, released a shower of sulfurous blood which burned as soon as it touched stone or pavement.

"Theo!" I cried, for I knew that in this world statues were sometimes living, and those who seemed living were frequently dead. I ran up to the monument, took the broad steps two at a time, found myself within the tableau. On the dais, time moved at many different paces; for here, my son moved, breathed, and was fully human, although the other figures were still jerky, like an old silent movie.

"I've come to save you, Theo," I said. "Come on now, we can get down from here, and Milt is going to come and pick us up soon."

Theo said, "Dad, don't you know what any of this is about? Look at those monsters up there . . . they're fighting over who gets to eat up the carcass of the universe . . . but there's still life in it. As long as I'm here. I'm the last truthsayer."

"Theo, you're going crazy." I went up to my son and tried to put my arms around him, but he stepped back all the way to the edge of the dais, teetered, almost fell to the flagstones below. "You can't let the fate of the universe depend on one person. That only happens in fairytales. You told me only now that life really *doesn't* imitate art."

"I didn't tell you that; it was probably just something in a vision you saw, some pseudo-me; I've been here the whole time."

His eyes were like marbles: bright and feelingless.

"Get thee behind me," he said softly.

"But I'm your own father."

"But you don't have the gift. Look at them. They're all depending on me. I'm the only one who can save them. And Joshua, too; I'm the only one who can bring him back from the dead."

"Theo—" A sudden fury consumed me. I grabbed hold of him, pulled him back from the edge. I shook him. "You're my kid and you'll do as I say," I shouted, "even if you're the fucking *kvisatz haderach!*"

Then I did what, in my whole time as a parent in the "real" world, throughout all the hurts and misunderstandings of our dysfunctional family, I had never done before. I slapped Theo's face. Hard. Several times. I'm not proud of this. But I didn't even feel that he was human. I didn't even feel he was my son. I hated him. The Oedipal thing was there too; I envied him. I was one of the blind and he was the one-eyed man. He had a vision; he had a purpose. I hated him. I wanted to kill him. I should have strangled him in the womb. I had to pay him back for everything he'd made me go through—the uncertainty, the self-recrimination, even death itself—twice.

Only when he started to cry did I realize that my son was still there, inside the protective shell of megalomania he had created around himself.

"I'm sorry, Daddy," he said. He put his arms around me and began to bawl his guts out. He didn't reproach me for hitting him. It did not seem strange that he should seek solace from me, the person who had caused him pain. That was the way our family was. Our lives were played out on a high wire without a net. "Joshua's dead and Mom's dying. You didn't know she was dying, did you, that day . . ."

"No. It was nine years ago, Theo. Before the diagnosis."

"But *I* knew, you see! I felt the evil gnawing at her bones. And there was no one I could tell, no one who'd believe me, because I'm just a kid. And I have too much imagination . . . too much, too much."

He broke down again. Above us and around us it seemed that the city, the warring beasts, the smoke, the flames, were frozen; it was a paradox; causality and time were Möbius-stripping around us.

"I didn't mean to hurt you," I said, but it sounded lame, a half-remembered quote from a John Lennon song, an inadequate analog of the truth. "I meant to say, yes, I did mean it, and I still love you." And it broke my heart, seeing my child become so childlike.

"Get us out of here, Dad," said Theo softly.

CHAPTER EIGHTEEN

RAVAGING TOKYO

<u>T h e o   E t c h i s o n</u>

So here I am in the middle of the cartoon city face to face with the father I've never known. It's strange. I mean, this dude just socked me in the face and he's begging me to forgive him at the same time and suddenly I don't feel omnipotent anymore. Jesus I've forgotten why I came here in the first place . . . I came to heal my family, not to drive them further apart. What's going on? The battle has raged through space worlds and myth worlds and worlds of ancient and modern history only to end up in this place that looks like a planet-sized episode of *RoboTech*. And both of us are reliving a scene from years ago, a time I usually think of as the good times, before my mother got sick, only this was one of the worst moments of my life.

The brother and sister are still up there in the sky, slugging it out. They're more into the sheer destruction of it than actually winning anything. Their hatred is fueled by a kind of joy. Even though they're fighting over me, maybe they've forgotten that I'm here. "Do you think we can just slip away?" I ask Dad.

"I don't know, son. What are we going to do about Josh?"

"That's the riddle I haven't solved yet."

Serena is standing to one side of our little tableau . . . she's not all here yet . . . she's kind of translucent, like she's frozen in the act of beaming down from somewhere.

Josh is still lying at our feet. He is still dead, very dead. Maggots are wriggling in his empty eye-holes. I took him with me when they started to fight over me, but of course he's also back in the glass coffin in Katastrofa's castle; his presence here is like some kind of symbol, I guess.

Dad says, "Maybe if we start to leave something will start to happen."

"Okay."

I hold tight to his hand. He takes a few tentative steps down from the dais, and that's when the pandemonium all around us speeds up to normal. And that's when Serena becomes solid and she steps out of some kind of shimmering vortex and she has Ash right behind her.

Ash looks up at the sky. "This is the place all right," he says. "Look at them go at it."

Rubble is flying. Storm clouds are roiling around Thorn and Katastrofa as they intertwine in their deadly dance. In the city you can hear sirens; toward the sunset it's an ocean of fire.

"Are you going to try to stop them, Ash?" Serena says.

"How can I?" says Ash. "I'm only a disinherited princeling with one token castle to rule over . . . while they have all the armies of the night."

"I don't see any armies," Serena says.

"They're there all right," I tell her. "We're seeing the edited version of the carnage . . . the icon-driven simulation." The truth is that the bat and the dragon are just projections; in reality, thousands of worlds and trillions of lives are at stake; the scope of the war is something no mind could possibly comprehend. Except the mind of a truthsayer. I do no editing. My mind is a maelstrom of raw data. I can sense every one of those deaths, every one of those planets burning, because each particle of life in the universe is linked to the River, and to me. I can feel, see, touch, taste all their torments, but I can understand nothing at all.

Serena sees Joshua at last. She screams.

"Cover your eyes," I tell her. "That's really not the way he is, I swear to God."

"He's—he's—"

"I'm working on it."

Serena kneels down beside the corpse. It's more bloated now, more blue, deader than ever. Flaming rocks are pelting us from the sky. A dragon's tooth smashes into the square and up spring a dozen skeleton warriors, lumbering toward us in sinuous stop-motion.

"Can we get out of here now, Dad?" I say.

Dad grabs my hand and we start to run. We race across the empty square. I trip a few times. I graze my knee, stagger up, keep running. We're out of the main square now and into a side street. There's a McDonald's, a sushi bar, and a Sumitomo Bank, all painted in with quick, impressionistic brushstrokes—it's just a background painting because the people inside them don't move. In the street itself there are dead people—they have burn marks all over their bodies, some of them are covered in blood—these are two-dimensional people, acetate sheet people curling at the edges as the hot wind blows them up and down the street. Maybe each one of these cartoon dudes represents like, a whole civilization uprooted, annihilated; I don't know. Fireworks explode just over our heads and a constant high-pitched keening fills the air. I'm still holding tight onto Dad's hand. It feels good to have him dragging me away, to have him leading me, even though I made this world and I am the one who sees the way out of the city . . . because this time I see that the way out is by not seeing the way out . . . the way out is by letting my father be my father.

We keep on running; still the warring siblings haven't noticed us; it's just me and Dad; I don't know what the others are doing, I just have to trust that we're all going to meet up in the end, somehow, somewhere.

We run. We round another corner; we're in an alley now. A mega-Rube Goldberg device is baking bread, ironing shirts, washing a car, and shredding carrots next to a storefront window. Now and then it pauses to announce the end of the world. We keep on running, past regiments of grim-faced robots, their steel feet clanging as they goose-step along the sidewalk and turn sharply toward the town square . . . as they turn they become invisible because they're celluloid too. I keep urging Dad to hurry. Penis-shaped monsters erupt out of apartment building windows. Women in flames roll across a cobbled street. We run. We don't look, we don't pause. I think we're going around in circles because at one stage we're running back into the square and we see that Ash and Serena are still occupying the monumental plinth in the center, and now they're surrounded by several circles of many-colored fire.

And now the square's filling up with cartoon people and they're all chanting, "Freedom! Freedom!" and it's like this bizarre rendition of the Soweto riots or something because the robot soldiers are marching in and they're firing these blasts of blue laser light from their eyes and the people are crumpling, curling up, turning black, exploding.

The mega-Katastrofa has her claws on city hall now, she's uprooting the clock tower. The bat's flying in circles around the Serena monument.

"We're going around in circles," Dad says.

"I know."

"Why didn't you stop me?"

"I'm trusting you, Dad. Like I'm supposed to."

"But I don't know the way out of here! And this city comes out of your mind somehow. It's the war for the universe filtered through a ninth-grade sensibility."

"Right now my truthsayer's instinct says to follow you."

He grips my hand harder and we run again. This time we run through broad avenues. "We have to find water," my father says. "If we find water, you can find the River and we can get away."

We keep on running. I see a river crossed by covered bridges. Behind us, rowhouses are on fire.

"Taxi!" my father shouts, letting go my hand and waving. "Taxi!"

"Sure, Dad," I say, but sure enough a bright blue cab pulls up to the curb. The flashing neon logo on the side reads:

KINGFISHER CAB
FOR THE ULTIMATE JOURNEY
into the dark forest of the soul
admission free to qualified customers

Improbably, the taxi is a Jaguar. But the jaguar on the hood is real, a big old cat that's curled up asleep around where the hood ornament should be. The door swings open and it's King Strang sitting in the driver's seat. His scarred face is twisted into a leer. "My son," says the king, "it seems you've been on a fool's errand." Full circle again. I was running away from Strang and now I've run right into his waiting taxi. Fucking Jesus I'm afraid.

"Get in, Theo," Dad says.

"But you don't understand," I say to my father. "We're getting in deeper now. He's an evil king. He steals men's souls and hides them in his scepter. He's made a pact with the forces of darkness at the source of the river. You know this dude's bad news."

"Where to?" says Strang.

I look at Dad and he looks at me as the fire races closer to us, is just about to eat us up.

"I don't know," says Dad. "Perdition's edge. Ultima Thule. Where no man has ever gone before." Trying on different myths for size. Maybe he thinks he's Cinderella.

Strang bursts out laughing. Dad pushes me into the back seat and climbs in after me. The door shuts with one of those *thwhup-up-up* space-age electronic sound effects. It's like an old-fashioned cab in back, with a glass divider—a sign says *bulletproof*—and a little drawer for the money. There's an incomprehensible table of rates. Here's a sampling:

PURE OF HEART $1
FOUND WANTING 35¢
EACH ADDITIONAL PECCADILLO 60¢
PURGATORY rates same as BROOKLYN
$4 PER SCRUPLE FOR WEIGHED IN BALANCE

and a lot of it isn't even in English.

"So *you* are the ferryman," my father says. "When I was going through the labyrinth of nightmares, I thought that it was Theo."

"Fool, make me laugh," King Strang says to me.

I'm wearing the jester's suit again, and once again I'm holding the stick with the cap and bells, and tinkling it, and telling stupid old "knock knock" jokes to try to get the old king into a better mood.

We careen past the corner of First and Oracle and I realize that in a way we've never left Tucson . . . or Mexico for that matter. Maybe we've never even left Virginia. When you dive deep enough into the waters of the soul, every place is the same place, and yet no place is ever any place you've seen before.

There's the hotel where we stayed that night! It's on fire. I think I see myself silhouetted in the window, leaning against the air conditioner while my dad watches CNN. He's getting up to change the channel.

"Knock, knock," I say to the mad king.

"Who's there?" he says.

Serena Somers

We'd been following their trail . . . Corvus' and Mr. E.'s that is . . . through the labyrinth. Ash figured that, with Mr. E.'s instinctual "father sense," we'd reach Theo a lot faster than by any logical course of action. And that's like how we ended up stepping out into the heart of an imaginary city . . . in the middle of a full blast monster mash . . . with cartoon characters dying on every side. Talk about weird. Kneeling there with Josh's putrefying head cradled in my arms, I didn't think we'd ever get back to any kind of recognizable reality. Frankly I'd have settled for Congressman Karpovsky's hotel suite at that point.

So up there, battling it out with her brother, Katastrofa didn't show any interest in Joshua at all. She didn't come screeching down to wrest him from my arms. That's how I understood that he must really be dead after all; he was no use to her.

"Ash," I said, "I want to go home. There's nothing left for me here; my life's fucked up past redeeming."

"Never past redeeming," Ash said. He smiled at me the way he often did when he visited my bedroom late at night when I was a girl, my secret, my imaginary friend.

I didn't believe him anymore. He stood there, shining, beautiful, just the way he'd always been; but I was a different person now. I knew that there were things in the world that, once they happened, never got better again. Love is one of those things, and so is death.

"Come back," Ash said to me, but I had already begun walking away from him amid the chaos.

I knew he was going to tempt me with his gentleness; I knew that in his own way, as far as his kind was capable of it, he truly cared for me. He had never been in this business just to gather power, not like his siblings. But in the final analysis he too was a chess player, and I would never be more than a pawn; we just weren't the same kind. Oh, maybe he did feel Josh's death a little, but it was like maybe a pin pricking his thumb or something; he had grand schemes to think about, and no time to worry about creatures like little old me. Fuck 'em all, I thought.

I'd come a long way since being a high school kid in Virginia.

I was like totally crying when I started to leave the city square, but by the time I reached the corner my eyes were dry and I felt pretty damn detached from the whole thing. I knew I was probably stuck in this mad-cap world forever unless I could find Theo to take me back to "real" reality.

Or could I find my own way out?

P h i l   E t c h i s o n

Once more I found myself reduced to a spectator. And the scene I was watching was as mythic as they come: it was Sir Percival and the Fisher

King . . . it was the Fool and King Lear . . . the pure redeemer and
the wounded land.

I'm not sure how it happened, but after a while it seemed to me that it
was now I who was driving the taxicab, while my son and the mad king
sat on the back seat; my son told jokes; the king sat there, magnificent in
his bewilderment. What could I say? I drove, down boulevards lit by the
burning of crucified criminals; I crossed the River half a dozen times,
each time on a bridge more architecturally phantasmagorical than the
last.

Tokyo (or Tucson) was being ravaged all around us. Demons leaped up
from potholes to terrorize young women. In the air, an eerie symphonic
soundtrack played, the ultimate Bernard Hermann score, chilling and
dissonant. I had no idea where we were going and I drove as the mood
took me—and the mood was invariably stark terror, the need to escape
from some ravening monster, some wall of flame, some exploding ziggu-
rat. A Chinese restaurant identical to the one where we had begun our
adventure swam into view and shimmered out of existence.

Blindly I drove on. Tokyo-Tucson burned around us. I threaded
through rubble-strewn alleys. Sometimes the jaguar on the hood would
leap onto the windshield and glare at me. I had a desperate feeling of
being chased, but I didn't know by whom.

I didn't even know what Theo and Strang were discussing back there. I
was only an ordinary man, after all, not privy to the secrets of the universe. I was not even a very good man. Hadn't I just slugged my kid
repeatedly for no damn reason except that he made me feel insignificant? What kind of a father was I, anyway?

Who was chasing me? Why was the shadow of a giant bat cast over the
luminous fog in front of me? I gunned the gas, crashed through some
kind of glass and metal barricade, turned around, and still there was this
shadow. The jaguar was snarling now, clawing at something in the sky.

"Thorn?" I whispered.

I looked up at the rear-view mirror. Strang and Theo were deep in
conversation. I could hear the beating of leathery wings. . . .

"Knock, knock," my son says.

Serena Somers

Maybe there was a way of getting out of here on my own steam after
all. If there's one thing I'd learned from everything that had happened to
me, it was like it says in *Star Wars*: everything's connected to everything

else. Or was it Zen Buddhism? I remember once, when I brought Mr. E., the semifamous poet, into school for careers day, that he told the kids that Zen and *Star Wars* espoused pretty much the same philosophy.

So there was a war going on, wasn't there? A war for possession of the entire universe or whatever. But I knew there was like another war, too, a war inside all our minds. It seemed to me that if maybe I could win my own private war, I'd be able to claw my way free of Theo's universe.

And what *was* my own private war? Hadn't I conquered my own fear of my self-image the day I sacrificed my virginity to save Joshua's life? Hadn't I just accepted my own humanity by turning my back, at last, on Ash, my supernatural companion? Hadn't I come to terms with my ambivalence about my sexual nature the day I met and merged with the alternate version of myself in the lobby of a Tucson hotel?

Before I knew it, I found myself walking into that very lobby. It didn't surprise me one bit that the hotel would be here. It seemed almost inevitable. The glass doors swung shut behind me and there was all this fire outside; I knew that if I tried to leave I'd be burned alive. There was nobody in the lobby but there were a lot of half-full wine glasses in the reception area and where there was this piano bar, there was a glass stuffed full of dollar bills, as if the piano man hadn't even had time to get his tips before he had to leave.

There were Karpovsky banners everywhere, and wadded-up Karpovsky fliers littering the floor, and all kinds of other Karpovsky debris. It was very warm in the lobby; after all, the city was burning all around us; I was surprised they still had electricity.

I walked around the lobby several times. I was waiting for some kind of sign I guess. That's what usually happened in the past, I'd get a visitation from Ash or something and I'd know that the next stage of my life was about to happen. I didn't get a sign as such. I hung around the reception desk for a while, waiting for a phone call from on high; there was nothing. I poured myself some coffee out of the machine. It was cold but it kind of cleared my mind a bit, like Drano.

I started to wonder if maybe I shouldn't have walked away from Ash that way. Would I have really done that if I had all my shit together?

No one was going to tell me where to go from here. I was going to have to take the next step myself. And now I realized what it was going to be and why I'd ended up walking into this place, the last place I ever wanted to see again.

I knew what was going to happen.

The merging of personalities wasn't complete yet. There was another Serena Somers somewhere in this hotel. Maybe more than one. I was going to have to hunt them down one by one. I had the feeling that some of them weren't going to be that willing.

I looked up at the clock. It was totally weird but I could have sworn that the date and time were the same as when I met the first other Serena Somers. Maybe time had been standing still since that moment. Or maybe Theo'd made a bend in the River and brought me back to the same coordinates.

I switched on the speaker on the receptionist's console and I dialed Karpovsky's suite.

Serena answered the phone.

THE THIRD SERENA SOMERS

Serena   Somers

Serena said to me, "I've been waiting, Serena. Come on up. Knock on the door—three short, one long, you know, like Beethoven's Fifth. I'll let you in."

I put the phone down. My heart was pounding. This Serena had an edge to her voice, and she seemed used to ordering people around. Maybe she didn't want to be absorbed into the rest of me. But I had to make it happen somehow.

I took the elevator up. There was no noise in the corridor except for the distant hiss of the burning city, and now and then the crack of a collapsing building. At end of the hallway, next to the doorway to Karpovsky's suite, there was a panoramic window. It was night and the fires burned brilliantly for miles, all the way to the edge of the mountains. In the sky, you could see the bat and dragon outlined in fire, like animated fireworks. Below, in the avenues, antlike people swarmed away from the city center pursued by rivers of flame. Yeah. Rockets' red glare, bombs bursting in air, the whole works. It was even more spectacular than the CNN footage of Baghdad under fire. Mostly because it was the view from the inside out.

I knocked on the congressman's door.

It flew open and there stood, not the third Serena Somers, but Katastrofa Darkling.

It had to be her. She was wearing this tight-fitting snakeskin one-piece garment and glittery eye shadow and she had claws instead of fingernails and her eyes were the eyes of a dragon, metallic and predatory. And at the same time she kind of looked like me, too, especially around the lips.

She held the door open and said, "Come in, won't you, Serena dear."

I said, "This has got to be some kind of joke."

"Joke?" she said, and she made the word sound like a hiss even though it contained no esses. "Serena, dear, you disappoint me. Don't you recognize yourself?"

"You're Katastrofa Darkling," I said. "You're my worst enemy. You stole the person I love. You made him die. I'll always hate you."

"It's true," she said, "I am all that. But I'm also you. And now, as you can see, it's time for me to take you back into myself."

She spread out her arms as though to embrace me. I felt a blast of heat . . . a heat that raced through my veins and lanced my heart . . . I could feel that she was the source of the fire that was bringing the city crashing all around us. Jesus, you're stupid, I told myself. You thought she was going to be reluctant to merge with you . . . but it's the other way round . . . she's waiting to pounce and it's you who are scared of being sucked into the jaws of the dragon.

A last ditch effort: "If you're Katastrofa, how come you're still out there, battling your brother? You can't be in two places at the same time."

"Why not?" She smiled. Her teeth glittered with reflected fire. "You know that *you've* been in more than one place at the same time. If one person can occupy two spaces, why can't one space house two persons, and each one lay an equally valid claim to being the true occupant?"

"You're lying," I said. "You've taken possession of the other Serena Somers. She's a prisoner inside you. It's some kind of trick. I know myself pretty well and I know there could never be a Katastrofa Darkling inside *my* mind."

"See for yourself, sis," she said. "How dare you presume to think that the rah-rah virginal purity aspect of our personality has got to come out on top? We sluts have a right to be heard, too. . . ."

"What are you talking about?" I elbowed her aside and entered Congressman Karpovsky's suite, except that when I got inside it was a totally different place. The congressman's office maybe? But I couldn't remember if I'd ever actually set foot there before. It was D.C. though. You could see that through the window behind the big desk cluttered with papers and yeah, the big crystal whale and the bronze eagle, that image was perfectly clear . . . what was I doing here? I sifted through the memories of my two selves . . . Serena One, who'd kept herself pure and fat, who'd dreamed of Joshua Etchison, saved herself for him, fled the congressman's advances like the plague . . . Serena Two, who had succumbed to a degree, but had managed somehow or another to misdirect the congressman away from the final penetration . . . whose line in the sand was a lot closer to the enemy than mine had been . . . was there a third Serena who had gone all the way, Serena the Slut? In high school I'd been called a slut of course; it was common knowledge that the entire male population of the school . . . of G.W. Junior High for that matter . . . had done me. Except that it wasn't true. It was a myth, kept alive by my own reticence and by locker room macho tall stories.

But was there another Serena who had lived through all those tall stories?

I went into the congressman's office and I saw myself sitting in a high-backed chair across from Karpovsky. Only the top of the congressman's hair was visible because he had swiveled away from Serena Three and was gazing out over the city. A New Age CD played softly in the background. It was a concession to the image the handlers had built of Karpovsky as someone caring, sensitive, profoundly understanding of the yuppie sensibility. The crystal dolphin was another such emblem. I bet that even the professorial clutter on the desk was carefully arranged between interviews by a continuity person.

I started to say something to the other Serena but it was like there was a glass wall between me and the rest of the room. I banged on it, I shouted, I kicked. Serena sat there. I could even hear her breathing, but she was totally unaware of my presence. The Serena that I saw was unmistakably me, but everything about her was tinged with Katastrofa . . . I could see it especially in the fingernails and in the lips . . . and that skintight, scaly dress . . . and the eyes, of course . . . the eyes of a hungry reptile.

I heard Karpovsky speak the words that were common to the memories of both Serenas One and Two: except they were addressed to different mes, one to a me in a conservative two-piece outfit from Lord and Taylor, sweating because my bulk flowed uneasily into the folds of the blouse; the other me in a halter top that barely concealed what little there was to see of my breasts: "Why do you want to work for me, Serena?" He was leafing through my application.

I heard Serena Three say, "I believe in your message. And anyway, Congressman, you're kind of cute."

Serena One had like blurted that out, regretted it, sat tongue-tied for
the next ten minutes while the congressman practiced his national health
speech; Serena Two regretted it too, but figured she was in too deep now
to climb out of the water. But the way this snake-Serena said it, it was
totally flirting with the congressman, I mean *brazenly,* the way the slut-
Serena of my junior high's mythology would have uttered it. I was appalled but I couldn't look away as the scene was played out.

"I'm glad you believe in my message, Serena. Love one another. That's
the most important thing of all, and anyway, as you know, it's from the
Bible. Those fascist fundamentalists should know that liberals can quote
the Bible just as well as they can, isn't that so, Serena?"

"Yes, Congressman."

"Would you care for a joint?"

Serena Three giggled. "I hate getting stoned before lunch, Congressman, but if you insist—"

That's not what I said! I thought, but another part of me said, I wish I
had said that. I watched in disbelief. I still hadn't seen Karpovsky's face
but now he turned just a little way and I could see a gloved hand idly
rolling the joint as the phone rang and the receptionist buzzed the congressman about some meeting that he was supposed to go to with the
Rev. Jackson.

"Put if off for an hour, will you? I'm TQ at the moment."

I wondered what TQ meant. "Taking a quickie," perhaps? It didn't
sound good. The congressman was all confident, knowing that I was a
done deal, a tidbit sitting there waiting to be scarfed. I hated him. Because he started off on his spiel now, the spiel both mes remembered:
"You see, Serena, I'm a *big* man. Who's gonna change the way the world
thinks. I have inside me this huge and overwhelming compassion for the
sufferers of this godawful planet of ours. But I have a tragic flaw, too,
you understand that? Just like your Oedipus, your Hamlet, your big heroic figures . . . I'm a lonely man. A man who never had a childhood.
Did you know that my father used to beat me? He was an alcoholic. I've
never told that to anyone before. And here we are, you and me, and
you're so fresh and young, like an unplucked flower, and . . ." It made
me sick because it wasn't the first time he'd told anyone that before. It
was what he told all the girls. By proxy, for that matter, because it was in
his autobiography, *Poor White Trash,* which many people who knew him
in his childhood say was bullshit—he grew up in suburbia, not a coal
mining town. So they say. I'd heard it many ways, enough to make me
disbelieve most of what he said anymore. I don't blame him for lying—
maybe a politician *has* to be a pathological liar, how else could he fool

everyone, unless he fooled himself first?—but well it made me sick because I knew that Serena Two had swallowed it hook, line, and sinker, and Serena One had actually started to cry.

But Three, she just sat there all cool, adjusting her pout level to go along with his intensity.

"You're young and I'm old and weary and withered," said Congressman Karpovsky, "a great man with a tragic flaw, an uncontrollable libido. . . ."

"Cut the self-serving bullshit, Congressman," said Three. "I know you want to have sex with me." She shivered her dress onto the floor. She shook her hair and all at once it was wild, like the Bride of Frankenstein. When I saw her naked body I was amazed that I had the potential to look like that . . . as curved and bouncy as the ocean.

The congressman's leather chair swiveled around and he was a cartoon congressman. He was all flat and his face was painted in swift impressionistic strokes and his eyes were completely blank. How could someone like that be frightening? I banged my fists against that forcefield again. I thought I could feel it give a little. Serena Three was oozing her way over to the desk now. She skimmed her fingers along the crystal dolphin, teasing, the way men think a girl likes to caress a penis. And the thing is that my own fingers prickled with the smoothness and the cold . . . and I knew for sure that that was another me in there . . . I could feel her thoughts racing through my own head and her thoughts went something like this:

Fuck fuck fuck fuck fuck (and an image of an old man getting up from a sofa and wandering down the hall) *fuck fuck* (in the wheezing voice of an old man maybe someone with asthma and) *fuck.*

Jesus I thought, what is she thinking about, who's the old man? Serena Three sidled over to the desk. She was talking the whole time in a kind of immature parody of a sexy voice, saying stuff like, "Gosh Congressman you are so attractive so mature so beautiful I want to envelop you in my arms I want to want to want to" oh, it made me sick and angry, I screamed at the top of my lungs, "Get away from him, he's just a user, you must think you're totally worth shit to throw yourself at a man like that," and I felt like this dirty feeling, this despair, seize hold of me as I watched this Serena-serpent kind of shimmying and jouncing in front of the congressman's desk. Now she was sort of riding the crystal dolphin, rocking herself back and forth against it as though it were a dildo. Now she was climbing up on the desk itself and kneeling in front of the cartoon congressman and undulating her hips in his face and pulling at his tie and still those celluloid eyes were blank, pupilless. Behind the congressman's head, in the window, Washington by daylight was dissolving, and a different backdrop was showing through . . . the burning city terrorized by animated monsters . . . and Serena Three was smiling now, tugging at the congressman's tie . . . the tie fluttered across the room, making a cellophane-crinkling kind of noise, an echo of the roar and hiss of the flames outside. I had to smash through to her. "Help me, Theo," I cried out, thinking to myself, this is Theo's world, maybe he can hear me. My clenched fists were getting bloody.

They were embracing, the two-dimensional Karpovsky nude now, folding himself around the 3-D Me Three like a big pink sheet of gift wrap. I couldn't take it. "Theo!" I shouted again, and then I felt a surge of power flow through me, like they say you get when you're high on angel dust, and I crashed through the barrier and there I was, trying to pry the two of them apart.

Serena Three pulled away furiously. Time stood still except for the two of us. Karpovsky was intertwined around the empty air. Outside, the flames were all frozen in place. I grabbed Serena by the arms and she spat in my face. "What the fuck is going on?" she said. "And who the fuck do you think you are? Is this good angel bad angel time or what?"

"Mellow out, sis," I said, "we have to talk."

"You're not my sister," she said.

"Am too."

"Get lost."

"Serena, Serena . . ." I dodged another wad of spit. Even in her anger she exuded sexuality. Even though I was trying to chew her out, I realized that I envied her too, envied how easy it was for her to shrug out of her clothes and get it on with a total stranger. "Listen to me," I said. "You're part of me. We've gotten split off from each other, but we have to listen to each other, to help each other out. Otherwise there's going to be trouble."

"You'd better get out of my mind," said Serena Three, "or there's gonna be trouble. I know what you are. You're the mind-eater. You're going to swallow me up just like you did that other bitch, the pricktease, the one that wouldn't let Karpovsky stick it up her even though she let him do *everything* else . . . that fucking hypocrite."

I held onto her tight. "Maybe you're not going to like this," I said, "but it has to be done." I guess I'd known ever since Katastrofa flung open the door to let me into the hotel suite. I had to accept that there was a Katastrofa creature inside me . . . that there were dark parts of me that I not only had to accept but I had to come to love, willingly and without recoiling from them. That was why I had been brought back to this juncture in my life; it was a major splitting off point, a place where many mes had branched off; a node, you could call it, in the private River that was my life.

"Don't do this to me!" Serena Three said. "You were never there when I suffered all those awful things. I was hurt and you were healing yourself with Snickers bars and lard. I hate you. You don't even know about the old man who fucked us when we were little."

"Nobody fucked us," I said. "I was a virgin until . . . until Josh . . ."

But she'd said something that chilled me shitless. I *did* remember an old man. Or was it a dream? I could remember the smell of him . . . *cloves, sour wine, and a sick-sweet smell that I couldn't have known was semen and* . . . who was he? It couldn't have been a just a dream, could it? I was wavering and it was an effort to hold Serena Three, to keep her from squirming out of my grip. I did it though. This was important.

"Leave me alone," said Me Three. "Leave me alone, Serena. Because I'm scared."

It had never occurred to me to look beyond the immediate reasons for the eating disorders of my teenage years. Now, maybe there was something. Something I'd never remembered before, let alone faced; because elsewhere, in a different universe, another me had taken the pain for me.

"Oh, Serena," I said softly, "I'm sorry."

—and felt a momentary glitch or blackout as she and I began to move into one another. And saw the congressman begin to move, flesh out, expand into the third dimension. And saw, behind him, in the window, the flames fan out and leap up to the sky. As Serena Three's mind melded with mine I was flooded with anger and bitterness. I remembered encounters with nameless boys in filthy school toilets filled with marijuana smoke . . . I remembered the withered fingers of the nameless old man . . . a friend of my parents, maybe . . . I think I called him uncle, uncle . . . those papery fingers trying to spread the lips of my vulva, rasping . . . the smell of old wine and cloves and . . . they were so vivid that I knew that even if I hadn't experienced them myself, the mind that had, the mind that had been tormented and warped by these things, was as much my mind as the mind I'd carried inside my skull since childhood.

The anger that finally broke loose was like when you're floating down a river and suddenly you reach the cataract and the water's exploding all around you and there's nothing you can do now but hold on and fall and fall and hope you won't be dashed to smithereens by the rocks, and that's how I felt when I rushed at Congressman Karpovsky, who was inflating like a rubber balloon now, filling up with hot air . . . I grabbed that crystal dolphin and I just started clubbing him with it and . . . I screamed at him, just screamed and screamed without making any sense . . . and finally the congressman just popped and the air came all rushing out with a tremendous farting thunder sound and he was whizzing around the room and shrinking and shrinking and I ran to the window, smashed the window with the dildo dolphin, watched the congressman go zooming off into the flames, and . . .

I looked up into the sky. I smelled the smoke of the burning city. The fume-filled wind billowed around Karpovsky's office. Papers were flying. Katastrofa—the big Katastrofa who'd owned a piece of Serena Three's soul—the dragon writhing up there in mortal combat with Thorn—Katastrofa was wounded! A torrent of fire-edged blood was spewing from a gash in her side, sizzling as it baptized the ground.

I screamed up at the howling dragon: "You can't steal my boyfriend from me, Katastrofa, and you can't steal me from myself! The more you fight me, the more myself I'm going to become!"

Oh, Jesus, I exulted, I was proud, I was bursting with joy even though I still had no idea how I was going to escape this world. I knew that I had the power within my shattered selves, the power to tap into Theo's vision, the power to wound the dragon, woman power.

CHAPTER TWENTY

SOUL VAMPIRES

Theo Etchison

I'm not sure how it happens. One minute Dad's pushing me into the taxi, the next the taxi driver's sitting in back with me and Dad is driving, pretty damn aimlessly as far as I can see, cutting through parking lots, going the wrong way on one-way streets . . . I mean, not that it matters when the whole town is crumbling all around you.

And here I am, the joker once again, telling the mad king bad jokes which barely cause him to raise an eyebrow as he sits there, clutching his scepter with its soul-catching jewel, brooding so hard you can almost see the black cloud hovering over his head. I've exhausted my supply of

knock knock and dead baby jokes, and now I'm doing Dan Quayle jokes
. . . anyone remember him? . . . which are met with bewilderment.

We dodge a few fireballs and King Strang says, "I hope that man
knows what he is doing."

"He's a poet," I tell him.

"Ah, a kind of truthsayer then."

"One who has lost his way," I say, which is the truth, and I'm hoping
that the bulletproof glass and the noise of the explosions around us will
prevent Dad from hearing it. And it's true that he doesn't look around.
He's too busy chasing something that looks like his own shadow . . .
but sometimes it's the outline of a bat. I realize that he's about due for
some private confrontation with Thorn . . . maybe it's about, like, who
has the right to possess me. When are they going to learn that I can't be
owned? I can only give myself. It's a truth no one ever wants to hear.

I turn to King Strang. He's a man in pain, I know that, I can feel it.
He's also, at times, a very evil man; I feel that too. Maybe he regrets it,
but I don't think he really regrets it enough. What I feel from him I feed
back to him in the form of bad jokes. When it looks like he might laugh,
he cuffs me with the back of his hand. I shake the bells. I don't know why
I'm doing this except I think it's something to do with keeping him going
a little bit longer, treading water, maintaining the universe in a holding
pattern until we can perform the healing.

The next thing that happens is that we're hurtling down a blind alley. I
can tell there's no exit because you can't see the burning city down the
way, only darkness. All of a sudden, I see why my father is headed there.
A circle of light has formed on the far wall and in it, silhouetted, is a
bat—just like the bat-signal in those *Batman* comics.

My father's all cussing at the image, something about "stealing my son,
my son. . . ."

"You can't take him on, Dad," I say. "He's too powerful. That's only a
shadow of a shadow of Thorn that you're seeing, not even a scruple of
what he can do . . . oh, Daddy," I said, "don't go after him, you're
gonna crash us into that wall, it's a trick. . . ."

King Strang put his hand on my shoulder. "Continue with your jokes,
fool," he said. "He knows what he is doing."

Then Strang clutches at his heart as though he's received a sudden
wound. I sense it too. I think I know what it is. I think that Katastrofa has
been struck. It has something to do with Serena.

The bat-thing rears up and even though it's a shadow I can see the
blood dripping from its jaws and then my dad guns the gas and we go
crashing into the wall, which evaporates into a blood-tinged mist, and

then Dad is suddenly gone and the car is careening out of control in the middle of a hundred-way intersection. . . .

"Do not fear!" says Strang. "Attend to your duties, fool."

Phil Etchison

And all at once I found myself again wandering through the corridors of my past. In the bedroom again with my six-year-old son, about to strike my wife, avoiding his reproachful eyes.

"We've been through this," I told him, breaking out of my memory and addressing the child within the child. (Was this an endless loop, a perpetual *Twilight Zone*ification of my inner reality?) "I've fought the me-monster and I've started a rapprochement with you on this, Theo; don't make me relive it yet again."

Theo only looked at me: solemn, his wide eyes glared through strands of muddied hair.

"Give me a break, son," I said.

At that moment, Mary, too, detached herself from her corporeal form and said to our son, "You do have to forgive, you know. Forgiving your parents is the beginning of maturity."

Theo didn't speak.

The entire room began to shimmer; the walls became drops of blood; we were in a cavern, and my wife, a statue, stood among a thousand candles, her hand raised in benediction behind the altar rail. From outside came the sounds of the Day of the Dead: salsa music, cheering crowds, laughter, the tolling of bells, a *dies irae*. Mary was no longer able to speak, but her authority had grown considerably. Women in black robes were kneeling, crossing themselves, beating their breasts, weeping into paper cups, creeping forward to bathe the statue's feet with their tears. Children scurried this way and that, chattering, eating, hustling the tourists. But it was all window dressing; what mattered in the scene was me, my wife, my son.

"Was I the one who made you turn to stone?" I asked the limestone Madonna.

Theo said, "Oh, Dad, all men and women are made of stone, until they're touched by the breath of life."

His lips had not moved.

He continued: "Dad, Dad, we always have to be vigilant; the breath of life passes by more swiftly than a downstream current; but the quality of stone is always in us."

"You don't sound like Theo," I said, "more like a cardboard cutout of some nineteenth-century philosopher."

Theo laughed. Without moving his lips.

"I'm really having this conversation with myself, aren't I?" I said at last.

He just went on laughing.

It must be true. Each of the figures in this vision was a figment . . . a fragment of my own shattered consciousness . . . my versions of what these characters might say and do . . . I was doing, I suppose, what psychotherapists make you do . . . take the characters from a dream and put words in their mouths. But perhaps I was merely rationalizing . . . a dangerous thing to be doing at this stage in the universal madness.

I became giddy, as though I'd had a hefty noseful of nitrous oxide. As the image of my wife looked on, I embraced my cold son, hugged him hard to my chest: I said, "Maybe you are only me, but I still love you," and other nonsensical things; but as I bent down to kiss my son on the cheek, he shattered.

Like porcelain.

And another figure came swirling out of the pieces of Theo: he was tall and he was batwinged and he had slate-colored eyes, and I heard the distant conch-call of Cornelius Huang, and I knew that Thorn was here, and that by no means could Thorn be considered a part of myself.

"Get thee behind me," I shouted at him, making the sign of the cross for good measure, though I'm not a religious person. Perhaps the symbolism alone would be enough to defeat him.

Thorn laughed: it was Theo's laugh.

I said, "Get out of my vision; you don't belong here."

"Such hubris," Thorn said. "How would you know anyway?"

"I'm inside my own mind, and I'm only talking to pieces of myself; that's how I know. Within this little circle of my brain, I'm God."

"Oh, Phil," said Thorn, "you are so wrong. I am, indeed, a part of you, the part you most detest."

"Don't be ridiculous. You are the one who stole Theo from me. You're the enemy, the darkness. You're a fucking vampire, for God's sake. I don't even know how you can stand to be here, with all the holy water and crosses around."

I was trying to be flippant, trying to dispel the disturbing notion that perhaps he might be right. But I was becoming afraid. When the vampire did not answer me, I babbled on, filling the silence between us with bluster and self-delusion: "I've already battled the darkness within myself," I said. "I fought the monster within myself in order to get to this city in the first place. I've overcome the darkness, I've harrowed hell, and I'm too weary for another battle."

A hymn to the Virgin welled up somewhere in the depths of the cavern.

"You can never be victorious over yourself," said Thorn, whose features were warping as I watched, resembling more and more my own. "The fact of the matter is, you fought a monster . . . you as your child perceived you once, when he was too small to understand that you are flesh and blood and full of human frailties. I represent a far more insidious version of yourself . . . the self you've never faced . . . your vampire nature."

"That's ridiculous," I said, "I hate the sight of blood."

Cornelius Huang stood next to the statue of my wife now, and he lifted the conch to his lips seven more times, pausing between each blast for an apocalyptic flourish of his instrument.

"It's not blood you suck," he said, "it's human souls."

"Sure," I said, feigning sarcasm; but I felt the prick of terror run up my arms and scalp. "I'm a soul vampire."

"Think about it," Thorn said. "You fancy yourself a poet, don't you? And what do you do, as a poet? Don't you fling yourself on suffering and pain in a veritable feeding frenzy? Don't you distill the grief of others into words, and sell those words for a dollar apiece to *Poetry* magazine? Haven't you traded the souls of your closest family members for the poetry chair of a mediocre university? Isn't it true that you've exploited your wife's illness all the way to being short-listed for the American Book Award? And your son Josh's death . . . what do you really feel about that, you with your visions of flaming angels falling into the sea . . . do you not see another slim volume of pained metaphors and unlikely classical allusions, another credit toward tenure? You use people, Phil; I only devour their blood out of biological necessity; it is you who are truly the vampire. How can you say you don't partake of my essence?"

There was no answer to these accusations. But what was I to do? Embrace the vampire as I had embraced the me-monster? Suddenly I found myself standing at the edge of a bottomless pit. I was a kind of Wile E. Coyote, and the Road Runner was beeping at me from the other side of the chasm, and I was seized by a force far greater than myself, a force that demanded that I try to leap the gap though hell itself should bubble underneath . . . and the vampire who stood beside me said, "Accept yourself. Accept that you are nothing more than a stealer of souls."

"No!" I cried. "I can't accept it." And yet how easy it would be to take that single step, to fall and fall forever, to kick aside the safety net of self-esteem and perish in the quagmire of self-loathing. I wanted to. Poets were just leeches, after all, weren't they? I'd joked about that often enough. And thought it true more often than not, though I had never dared to think it too long for fear of losing forever the illusion that my life had a purpose.

"But isn't *everything* an illusion?" the vampire said, reading my thoughts.

I gazed out at the chasm. I despaired.

"What kind of poet are you anyway?" the vampire screamed. "Have you ever dared stand alone at the brink of the void, have you dared face the emptiness that is yourself, the utter meaninglessness of the human condition? Of course not. How could you, sitting in your comfortable suburban home with its picket fence and well-kept lawn . . . hypocrite!"

I continued to stare at that which yawned before me.

"Jump!" cried the vampire.

I could hear the word reverberate in my mind . . . *jump jump jump jump jump* as though there were a crowd down below jeering egging me on daring me to take the infinite leap accept myself for the nothing that I was accept the darkness accept the reality there is no truth there is no life there is only despair despair despair. . . .

And then I thought: Haven't I stood on the edge of nirvana itself, and listened to the voice of the universal spirit? And wasn't what it said to me the mirror image of what Thorn is saying now?

I remembered the siren whispering of universal love. Had I not resisted it? Wasn't I still fastened to my corporeal self by an invisible rope? And wasn't that rope spun from my desire to still hold on to the things I loved, my children, my wife, and even that picket-fenced suburban home with its lush lawn, vividly green in the aftermist of a Virginia rainstorm? The Wile E. Coyote image popped back into my mind. I've always considered Wile E. to be the true embodiment of the human condition, and his quest for the Road Runner to be a virtual analog of man's quest for the divine, the unattainable, God himself; and here I stood at the coyote ledge, and despaired (as Wile E. must have, oftentimes, when the latest product from the Acme company failed to operate as advertised)—and what was so damn bad about being Wile E. Coyote? And what was wrong with being racked with despair?

Love and despair were what defined me as human.

"Jump," said Thorn—I felt the parallel with Christ's temptation all the more clearly—"jump and everything will be all right. You have nothing to live for anyway. But once you jump, you'll be transfigured. The despair will have no meaning. You'll be buoyed up by flights of angels. You will have sucked in despair and conquered it, and you will again be the hunter, not the hunted."

"I'm not going to jump," I said. "I don't want to be a God. I don't want to be the Void. I am a man."

I felt the tug of the rope around myself, and I knew that the knot held firm.

Thorn screamed.

Serena Somers

And then I found myself back in the town square. Katastrofa's blood was raining down from the sky. Thorn was wounded too. His blood was a brilliant blue color and it glowed as it spattered the clouds and the flagstones. They were both wounded but they still fought. I knew it was to the death.

And well, I could feel the wound in my own soul, too, because now I knew that Strang and Thorn and Katastrofa and Ash weren't just dream people, figures out of a real-life sci-fi fairy tale, but also part of us; that the war in heaven was like, the war in our hearts as well.

I saw Mr. E. standing at the far side of the square. I started to walk toward him. He seemed different, cleansed almost, as if he'd had a totally intense therapy session. He caught sight of me and began coming in my direction as well. The square was littered with corpses, both human and celluloid. "Mr. E.," I shouted, "Mr. E., where have you been?"

Theo Etchison

Now we're busting through the wall and the jaguar taxi flies out over the city square into a rain of multicolored blood. The taxi skids to a halt beside the monument in the center of the square, which is I guess really a kind of transdimensional travel nexus or something, because the group of statues never seems to have the same people in it: this time there is only Corvus.

He's huge and white and feathery. His marble face is veined in streaks of emerald and lapis.

Slowly he softens. The flesh emerges from the stone. The jaguar—I mean the living hood ornament—growls. He leaps off the hood and bounds up the steps toward Corvus. He crouches, clawing the stone; he roars.

"Let us see what he wants," King Strang says. We leave the taxicab.

Corvus kneels before the king.

"Have pity," he says to him, "have pity."

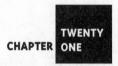

THE FALL OF THE HOUSE OF DARKLING

Theo Etchison

There's Corvus kneeling in front of his king and lord; I know that Corvus, unlike the servants of Thorn and Katastrofa, still believes that King Strang is the King of Everything. And he's all saying, "Pity, pity." Pity on who? What difference can a mad king's pity make? I take Strang by the arm and lead him toward the birdman. Strang's eyes are misting over; maybe he's crying, but maybe, maybe he is going blind. . . .

"Where am I going?" he mumbles.

"This way. This way." I tug his sleeve a little. His robes are stained with blood, tears, and dirt; his scepter must weigh a ton, with all those souls trapped inside it; he staggers toward the steps, where Corvus is kneeling with his wings spread out behind him, draped all over the steps, humbly staring at the bloodstained flagstones.

"Pity, pity, O King," he says. His voice is barely a whisper; meanwhile the sky is thundering and burning; we have to strain to hear him.

King Strang struggles to stand erect. He shakes his fist at the sky and screams: "Betrayal! Betrayal!" at them; but the bat and dragon do not even bother to glance down because they're so busy ripping at each other's flesh.

"King Strang," I say, "listen to what Corvus has to say."

"Yes, what is it?" he growls. There is a lot of jaguar in his growling. Corvus trembles. I don't know why. Hasn't Strang given up his dominion over the universe to the quarreling siblings? What power can he wield over Corvus?

Corvus says, "My lord, you must forgive your son. This is the not the first time I'm begging you to do it, and it won't be the last."

Strang says, "I cannot."

"My lord, look up there! Who is it who rends your world in twain? Not Ash. Ash is the one who has always loved you. Ash is the one who spoke the truth to you, the truth you know in your heart but dared not face; only speak the word, my lord, and admit him into your presence; perhaps there is still time to heal the rift and make the River flow once more through all the universes; you can do it, you and Ash and the truthsayer, the three of you together."

King Strang is leaning on my shoulder. I can see a lot of emotions battling it out in his face. I don't think anyone has dared speak this frankly to him before. But I know Corvus is right.

"What do you think of all this, fool?" the king says to me.

I take the bells and shake them. The music seems to soothe the king a little, and, as Corvus sweeps the blood from the steps with his snow-white wings, he sits himself down on the marble, still holding on to my arm; his hand is withered and unsteady.

I shake the bells again. I tell the king the truth, which is my duty. "King," I say, "Corvus is right. What ever possessed you to split the kingdom in three anyway? You must have known that it was going to start a war. And you shouldn't have tested your three children the way you did. It's never fair to ask your kids how much they love you, because kids always lie when it comes to love. Kids don't love their parents in a simple way. The love they have is always riddled with pain and wishful thinking and anger. You know that. You had parents once."

I feel the king's hand grip tighter; I know that I'm stirring up his rage. But I can't stop telling him the truth. "You owe it to yourself to forgive Ash," I say. "Look into his heart and you'll see so much of yourself: you'll see the stubbornness. You'll see that, like you, he doesn't like to talk about things. He sees the world in feelings, not in words. That's why he couldn't bring himself to flatter you like the others did. You know that if your father had asked you the same thing, you would have answered the same way. You've done your deal with the darkness, and you're wasting away from the wounds that you gave yourself in exchange for the power to rule the cosmos, but you were once the kind of person your son is—noble, loyal, and unafraid. Admit it to yourself, Strang. When you see him, you see the things about yourself that you've thrown away. It's that which makes you angry. Not some imaginary betrayal of your love. It's yourself you hate, not Ash."

At first it's painful for me to talk this way to him. Every word I say is a stab-wound. But after a while I really get into it. I mean, I never thought of myself as like a sadist or anything, but it felt good to lay it all out for the mad king . . . good the way it feels good when you've been rolling in the mud and you're scouring all the shit off with a strong abrasive soap . . . fucking Jesus it feels good. I'm really rattling those bells, man, they're clanging and banging and it's almost louder than the noise all around us.

I look behind me and I see that my dad and Serena are nearby, leaning against the taxicab. And Serena says: "He's not gonna go for it, Theo. The last time Corvus tried to get him to do it, he almost killed us—we barely got out alive!"

The way Strang is, it's kind of like a volcano getting ready to erupt. I feel the roar building up inside him: first he's quivering all over and I grip him harder, trying to steady him, then he's all shaking and then at last the fury comes all at once and he flings me away from him and I go flying onto the steps and I hear my own skull thudding against the marble like it's thundering inside my head and I think there's blood running down one eye oh God, the pain, and through the red-mist-blur I can see King Strang rear up, the scepter glowing, his eyes reddening . . . it's a shadow of the old powerful ruler of the cosmos . . . just a pale ghost of what he once was like . . . though I'm sure it's enough to strike me and Corvus and Dad and Serena dead . . . but you know I'm not scared and I'm not planning to run away at all . . . because I feel his sadness underneath all that anger, and so I cry out even though I'm hurting all over, "King Strang, don't do it . . . you know I can't help telling you the truth . . . if you don't like it you can just think of me as your fool . . . your jester . . . your word-twister. . . ."

He's astonished that I'm still defying him. He hesitates for a moment.

Then he says . . . simmering down a little . . . bottling his rage again . . . he says, "I will never accept Ash back into my heart. He is dead to me . . . dead forever."

Corvus says, "Nothing is dead forever, my lord."

"Never," says King Strang, "never, never, never, never."

But at that moment the war between Thorn and Katastrofa comes to an end. On some level I guess the millions upon millions of starfleets and planetary armies just blow each other all up and the universes are littered with a jillion corpses, human and alien. But that's not what we see, I guess, because it's *my* vision of things that shapes what we perceive.

We all look up at the same time because we hear a gut-wrenching shriek, so loud that it drowns out everything around us: the fires, the crashing buildings, the screams of the dying . . . and we see that Katastrofa is flailing up there among the clouds . . . a hail of dragonscales is pouring . . . it is Katastrofa who's shrieking, shrieking and transforming . . . she's a red dragon, a green dragon, a white dragon . . . she's a crystal dragon, a sea dragon, a fire dragon . . . she's a woman as she plummets down toward us . . . and Thorn, the bat, is ripping at her throat the whole time . . . we hear a high-pitched squalling, the bat-sonar gone haywire, whining in our ears . . . they are diving earthward together . . . they are becoming human. . . .

In the few brief moments that it takes for them to fall, it's like we live through the lives and deaths of a million civilizations. We're not just standing in the center of cartoon square with the city in flames around us. We're also seeing planets ripped from their orbits and hurled into one another . . . and star systems blowing up . . . and million-starship-fleets stranded forever in the warped folds of space-time . . . and a lone child crying . . . and the jangle of unfinished symphonies and pulverized poems . . . and everywhere scream upon scream upon scream and . . . and . . .

. . . and then they hit the pavement.

It's not the kind of thud you hear in movies when a body flies out of a skyscraper window . . . it's a dull, empty, echoless kind of a sound . . . I guess we're all expecting the big bad sound effect because it takes us several moments to realize that Thorn and Katastrofa are lying on the monumental steps in front of us, intertwined in each other arms, limp, broken, dead.

And not just them but thousands of territories cut off from the flow of the River . . . civilizations sundered from their roots . . . the universe no longer a whole but jigsaw fragments . . . shattered . . . decaying.

"Quick," I say to the king, "you only have one child left . . . make peace with him . . . come on, man, it's your only option."

But still King Strang says, "Never, never, never."

Above the corpses of the two Darklings, on the plinth at the top of the steps, my brother still lies, still dead. Just as he still lies in his glass coffin in the dwelling place of dead Katastrofa. Just as he still lies at the bottom of the Pacific Ocean off shore by a Mexican town, back in the real world, real time. He lies there feeding the sharks and lobsters.

And this is what I'm thinking: I'm remembering Thorn: how he haunted my dreams with his slate-colored eyes, long before I knew that my dreams weren't really dreams. I'm remembering that, in spite of all his callousness, he always believed he was doing the right thing. I'm remembering how he captured me, how he boasted to me, how he killed and drank his subjects' blood, how he exulted in his power of life and death. And I'm also remembering his loneliness. Yeah. The slate-colored eyes. I go over and kneel beside the twisted bodies and the slate-colored eyes gaze up at me, as soulless in death as they were in life. He'd wanted me to share that soullessness with him. Perhaps he had even loved me. His death makes me cry. I wonder why. Perhaps because, for all his evil, there was something of my father in him, in a way; I know that it was something between him and Dad that dealt him the death-wound.

I close those slate-colored eyes; the lids are stiff. And cold. I'm crying. I mean one of my eyes is crying, because my other eye has been partly closed by scabbing blood, and has no tears.

"You see!" I say, turning to the king. I feel pitiless and bitter. "This is what comes of all your games . . . who the fuck is the fool, King Strang, you or me? You tell me that. You fucking tell me!"

King Strang begins to howl.

Around us, in the city, the fires are already beginning to subside. A wind has sprung up and there's also a drizzle. And there's light now; one of the suns is rising. I realize that there's only one sun now . . . and that the city's not as cartoonlike as it was . . . the corpses in the square around us are becoming three-dimensional . . . the lurid colors are becoming more subdued, drab even.

Corvus flies up and hovers over the king, trying to shelter him from the wind with his outspread wings.

Next I look at Katastrofa. There's very little of the dragon left in her; the glitter of peeling scales at the corners of her eyes, maybe, the metallic fingernails. Jesus she's beautiful. I remember the way she did the gingerbread house number on me, and the way she held me, and how confused I became because her closeness was driving me crazy, I mean, making my thing thrust up and making me just shiver all over with these brand new desires; I remember Joshua in the glass coffin.

"I think they would have gone on fighting until the end of time," Dad says. "But we wounded them. Serena and I, I mean. They were like gods at first. I think that when Serena and I faced these dark archetypes in ourselves, and acknowledged that the dark gods lived in our own souls . . . that meant that the opposite could also happen . . . that the dark gods had to acknowledge a humanness within themselves . . . which made them vulnerable . . . to ourselves and to each other."

"Oh, Mr. E.," Serena says, "you're overintellectualizing everything again. You want to impose some big old structure on everything, even on chaos itself."

Dad laughs. Bitterly, to stop himself from crying.

"Oh, Theo," he says softly, "come home."

"I can't, Dad."

"You have to. Forget about gluing back the pieces of the universe. It's broken and it can't be fixed. You can't reconstruct a bible out of a million palimpsests. But maybe we can find a corner of it somewhere that'll remain stable for a little while. Long enough for us to live out our lives. Why should we care anymore?"

"You're forgetting Mom," I say. "And Josh."

And the king goes on howling. Like an animal he howls, and he tears at his garments and you can see that his wound is festering. He's gone over the edge. His mind is in a million fragments, and so is the universe. There's one more journey he's going to have to take, and I'm going to have to go with him.

How can I explain to Dad why we can't go home yet? Poor Dad. He sees the way before him only one step at a time. Maybe I should say poor me. Because I see all the steps, every direction, all the strands, all at once, and it makes me crazy. Truthsaying is a curse. I wish that I were blind.

Blindness . . .

The king crawls round and round in circles, howling.

I realize that he is losing his sight as well as his mind. I also know that he's still not going to accept Ash . . . because even in his degradation he still can't rid himself of his pride.

Once more, the future of the cosmos seems to be in *my* hands.

The city is becoming very still. A light rain has started to fall and the plumes of flame have become clouds of smoke. King Strang is slowing down . . . my father and Serena seem to be frozen in place . . . my brother's corpse is calcifying . . . all of them are turning to stone.

It has become utterly silent.

I know what has happened. I'm trapped in a single moment of time. I've made this moment, stretched it out, looped it, so that the world stands still and gives me time to make my next move. I am outside time. This moment exists so that I can see the way ahead; it captures the whole universe in a still photograph.

I'm standing in a forest of statues. They are all made of stone, like my mother is when she's here on the other shore of the River, because she, too, is outside time, existing so slowly that a civilization can spring up and be extinguished while she's taking a single breath.

The world is on hold. It's waiting to see what I'm going to do next.

Black and white. Color has drained away. Only my pied clothes are colored now, and my hands, when I look down at them, are barely pink.

The drizzle in the air has frozen in mid-fall, and when I pass my hand through the raindrops there's no sensation of wetness.

Where must I go now?

My marble drops out of my sleeve.

It skitters up the steps, up the 90° angle of the stone . . . like in a macrocosmic game of Marble Madness . . . totally defying gravity. I realize it's trying to get me to follow it. The marble rolls up to the middle of the plinth at the center of the monument. I take the steps two at a time and race over to where it's stopped. Just as I reach down to grab it, though, it like blinks out. It's gone.

But I and the marble are one. I try to see the marble in my mind . . . a many-stranded orb spinning in a starless void . . . I see it, I reach out for it, through and past the dimensions of space and time, see my arms vanish as they sink into some other cosmos, feel the marble's smooth surface touch my invisible hand. . . .

I step out of the world, out of the lattice of illusions, into a place that's colder and darker than the human mind can imagine.

BOOK FOUR

THE FOREST OF THE NIGHT

"Quiero bajar al pozo,
quiero morir mi muerte a bocanadas,
quiero llenar mi corazón de musgo,
para ver al herido por el agua.

I want to go down to the well:
I want to die my death, mouthful by mouthful:
I want to fill my heart with moss
To watch the boy wounded by the water."

—Lorca

4: In the Darkest of All Forests

The time of reckoning had come; I stood
Before the gates of hell; I had come far,
Braved men and monsters, answered riddles, slain
The sphinxes that afflict men's souls, unchained
The princess from the rock, sung songs to move
The rocks to tears, to change the River's course.
Behind those gates lay the forbidden fruit
Moly, the herb of immortality,
The quince of sexual awakening.
A fearsome voice cried out to me: "The password!
Utter the password, or be doomed forever
To wander among the lifeless shades of Hades."

I knew no password, so I temporized:
Plucked from its socket my one remaining eye,
And cast it, bleeding, past the iron bars.
I saw no more. With blindness came true vision:
I saw that I could gain the golden apple
Only by vanquishing my longing for it,
And conquer death but by embracing it,
And reach the quest's end only by acknowledging
I needed the quest no longer.

There I stood:
Racked by the final quandary, out-paradoxed;
Unable to advance without retreating
Sightless yet gifted with a godly foresight,
My loaf, my condom, and my kiss long since
Consumed in the arduous wandering. I wept,
And from my tears there flowed a mighty River
Encircling the dark forest.
Eternity long, eternity and a day

I wept. The water rose. The universe
Itself sank in my sorrow, and was drowned;
The stars fell from the sky; and I myself
Fell like a droplet into my own grief,
Infinity, infinity plus one.

In time, the flood subsided. I myself
Became Deucalion to some brave new world,
And ruled over a prosperous domain
Until an age had passed. Then, on my deathbed,
An angel led me to the gates of hell,
Beyond which lay the fruit, the herb, the pomegranate,
The pearl, the grail, the jewel, the orb, the crown.
I knew then that the kingdom I had ruled,
The cosmos flooded by my sightless eyes,
The long eternities that had transpired,
Had been as substanceless as dream, and I
Still stood before the gate, not knowing the password
That the portal's guardian still demanded from me.

I knew no password, so I temporized;
I reached up to my eye, to pluck it out.
But this time it was different. I was blind.

CHAPTER TWENTY TWO

THE RIDDLE OF THE SPHINX

Theo Etchison

. . . and step into the forest of the night.

I'm alone. I don't know this place, but somehow it feels like I've always known it, like I've been destined to come here all my life. It's dark and I can't see, but I can hear the rustling of the treetops, and I know it's a forest because of the noises and the wet vines brushing against my face. It's hot here. It's probably tropical. Yeah. Exotic birdcalls and chittering monkeys and darkness so dense it's a kind of mush you breathe in.

I keep on walking. There must be a clearing somewhere, or at least a break in the canopy where the sunlight can get through. There has to be. I keep walking. I don't keep track of time because where I am is timeless. It's the dream world of the dream world.

I keep on walking, like I've done so many times in the forest of the night. It's so dark that like my eyes go crazy and begin playing tricks on me. I see hazy whorls of color that swirl slowly around me. Where is the River? Wasn't I following the marble when I like teleported into this place? I can't see the marble so I try to reach out with my mind . . . there's a throbbing sometimes that lets me know where the marble is, but now when I reach out my mind touches only blankness. I bend down and scrabble around in what must be mud and rotting leaves and finally I think I touch something smooth and round, and I hold it up in the palm of my hand thinking I'll see the intertwisting filaments. Instead there's just a general dull flow, as though the strands have become so jumbled they are all one mass of indistinguishable light.

That's because of all the things that have happened to jumble up the River. Strang's contract with the dark forces kind of dammed up the flow of causality, I guess, and the dam had to burst sooner or later, and the catalyst was the dividing of the kingdom, the accelerating of the war, and the crazy changes that happened because I got dragged into it all. The universe is about to blow and—like in every good superhero story—it's come down to one lone man versus the forces of evil. Sounds melodramatic, huh. It feels like shit. It's probably not even true.

Here I am, walking through the forest of the night, stuck in the labyrinth without a map. It's dark and humid and there are noisy things
buzzing against my face, too big to be bugs, too small to be rats.

I keep on walking. After a while I become conscious of a faint smell of
fish in the air. Well it starts off like fish but it ends up as something a lot
more disturbing because it makes that dream I've been having surface
once more. I mean the dream about *gliding down the River and me all
slick with sweat and sliding deep deep deep into the bridge of thighs no sighs
thighs thighs and the forest is a thicket of hair human hair that smells like a
fish like a woman slippery and wet and* I'm trembling all over as I trample
the forest floor with the mud squishing between my toes because I'm not
dressed as the jester anymore, I think I lost my clothes somewhere,
maybe the moisture ate them away like acid.

The forest seems to thicken. So does the smell of womanflesh (I'm
sure that's what it is because I've heard Josh making crude remarks
about sushi and cunts but like, it's a much stronger stench than I expected, I mean it totally clogs my nostrils and makes it almost impossible
to breathe and I feel as if the whole earth has transformed itself into a
monstrous woman; I don't mean the fifty-foot woman I mean one that's
the size of the entire planet) and the dense dense rain forest that I'm
squeezing through now is somewhere in the cosmic woman's genital area
and heading straight toward the center of the world, the fiery core, the
womb . . . if the earth is a woman am I the sky? I guess this doesn't
make sense but I'm starting to get these memory flashes that go back
earlier than I've ever remembered before. I mean like, the taste of a
nipple, the spurting of fresh hot milk, totally pouring into me and me
hungry, hungry, just one monstrous screaming hunger. I remember lights
screeching overhead, they're screeching because I don't know the difference yet between hearing and seeing and feeling and smelling, the world
around me is a churning blender. The hunger's all that's driving me and
I'm screaming with my throat all raw and the lights above me screaming
and touched by screaming metal then dunked into screaming water
screaming screaming. And then I remember something else. Warm, en-
folding, blissfully dark. It quells the hunger. It awakens another memory:
the wombwarmth, the dark cavern in which I am God. I've never remembered this before but the memory is all there, a whole touchy-feely image, not a lone fragmented image like early memories usually are. It's the
first time in my mother's arms. I'm sucking in the milk now and the
screaming is slowly receding. I'm sinking back into the memory of being
a God . . . yeah I'm sinking back into the infinite sea.

In Mrs. Dresser's social studies class we are learning about ancient cul-

tures and she tells us the story of Oedipus Rex. There was a man who solved the riddle of the Sphinx then accidentally married his own mother and brought down a curse on the kingdom of Thebes. Later I say to Dad, "This is bullshit, Dad; it wasn't his fault. What a stupid thing to happen to this dude, I mean, like he saves their whole city, and he even marries this woman who's old enough to be his own . . . well, actually is his own mother, probably only does it out of pity for the poor old woman who's stuck there in the palace and can't, you know, get any." Dad laughs and he puts on a CD of a Tom Lehrer song, and we both laugh sitting in front of the fire, it's February in Virginia and school's probably going to be canceled tomorrow because it's snowing like there is no tomorrow. And then Dad says, more seriously, "Well, it's not just about some 'dude' who accidentally has sex with his mother, you see. It's about everyone who ever said 'I'm gonna kill you Daddy and then I'll marry Mommy,' and you see that makes it about me and you . . . not just a bunch of musty old Greeks." "That's dumb, Dad, I'd never say that," I say, and this is a long time before the incident down in Spotsylvania County when I actually do end up saying it and meaning every word of it. . . .

End of flash. I'm trudging through undergrowth again. With every step the air gets more intense. I'm sucking in creepy crawlies with every breath I take. There's creatures slithering up my arms. I hold the marble in the palm of my hand like it's a candleholder, try to awaken the amorphous glow that used to be all the strands of the River. Slowly the marble begins to shed light in the jungle. A flash of neon brilliance swoops by: one of those tropical birds, like a toucan or a quetzal, so bright it stings my eyes, already smarting from the acid drizzle.

After a while the forest thins out a little. I'm standing in a circle of joshua trees. Far far above my head there is a circle of light. It doesn't come from the sun because though I'm standing on the surface of the womanwood, this place is also deep inside me, the place where all memories converge, the place where everything I've ever been scared of lives, the place where the thing under the bed has gone to hide and will never die.

I'm inside out, my skin is turned around and I'm standing in the part of me that's my soul, the part that's more than man and woman . . . the way Detective Stone is when he does his own kind of truthsaying, when he becomes the messenger from the spirit world. The faint glow brightens to a half-light. The place is a cave. It's the cave where you fight the dragon to get the treasure. It's a cave though it's still a forest. The stalactites and stalagmites are the trunks of giant trees, and the tunnel walls are thick with vines.

I see the coils of the dragon here and there. She fills every twist and turn of the tunnels inside me. It's the glitter of her scales that's giving off the pale blue light. I suppose I'm going to have to fight the dragon now. Isn't that what saving the universe is all about? No use being afraid. It has to be done. But I can't even see where the dragon begins or ends. And I have no weapon except . . . except the sword that I find myself holding in my hand. It's glowing. It has no weight at all. It must be an illusion. But I heft it from hand to hand and after a while it feels like it's always been there. But where is the dragon's heart? I cannot tell.

The cave is rumbling. The dragon's surface begins to ripple. The dragon's slithering through the tunnels. I can't even tell if she's heading toward me or away from me. All I know is that the noise is crescendoing and pieces of the ceiling are falling, although they hurt me about as much as if they were made of styrofoam. At some point I realize that I'm wearing full armor . . . not real armor, clanky, heavy, and centipede-jointed, but a weightless suit of light that hugs my naked skin. I guess I'm about as ready as I'll ever be.

"C'mon," I scream, "Come out and fight."

I don't see any treasure. Maybe it'll show itself after I've slain the dragon. I run full tilt toward her, waving my sword and shrieking out an imitation of a bloodcurdling heroic warcry in my puny voice. The joshua trees that are the cave close in on me. It's like that part in *Macbeth* where the trees are marching toward the castle. The dragon seems infinitely big and I know that there's no way to defeat her because she is the dragon that coils around the tree of the universe and I know that this jousting is a ritual, preordained for me since the beginning of time, when everything was still called by its true name and all people were truthsayers. . . .

The dragon moves. She seems to uncoil with agonizing slowness yet she is too fast for me and when I think I've reached her she is gone, and me just leaping from clawprint to clawprint seeing the burn marks of her breath against the cavern walls and her in the distance, a snake of sizzling light, further down the labyrinth.

I'm really sprinting now but the dragon isn't any closer. The trees are racing past me and I see people hanging in the branches . . . my dad, my brother, Serena, and dozens of other people that have touched my life . . . all chained to the branches of the joshua trees and crying out in pain and calling on my name, *Theo Theo Theo save us save us* . . . and I keep running. There's a high wind in the tunnels still saturated with the womansmell and I'm running into the wind and it fills me with unnamed untamable desires . . . it makes me bigger than myself . . . it terrifies me . . . it elates me. I don't know how long I'm tilting at the dragon but

I'm not exhausted, I guess it's the adrenaline rushing through my blood, the blood that hurtles like the screaming wind . . . and I still can't catch up with the dragon.

Sometimes it takes all the running you can do just to stay in the same place . . . isn't that from one of the *Alice* books? It's a line that echoes through my head as I pursue the dragon. I realize I have to stop. And I do, and it's like colliding with a wall of memory, and images burst out everywhere, uncontrollable: Dad reading to me when I'm really little . . . Josh breaking a window . . . the stream beside my grandparents' house and . . . embracing my mother and feeling the disturbing emotions and . . . I stop and I've pierced the dragon through the heart . . . the skin is sloughing even now, curling up, withering, flying, and where the dragon's heart was is a whirling, dancing flame . . . and I'm inside the dragon now, inside the cage of bones, and the bones are melting together and weaving themselves into a wall of limestone and in the distance I can hear salsa music playing and I know that I am in the cave of the weeping Madonna and that behind the altar railing stands my mother . . . and there she is . . . my mother yet more than my mother . . . unfrozen from her statue stillness because in this secret place space and time are what we make of them . . . she's standing in front of the altar and behind her there's a celestial choir, Jesus flits back and forth about her head tossing rainbows in the air, and on the altar there's a chalice, and over the chalice, suspended, is a piece of a waterfall, the water trickling into the cup yet never filling it . . . the water turning to the color of blood as it touches the silver. . . .

My mother is standing in front of the chalice with her arms outstretched. She doesn't have the wild-eyed madness in her face, or the dull-eyed desperation of the cancer. She's how I remember she used to be before the illness came. Her hair has all grown back and it's the color of my own hair. She's smiling at me. "You've made it through to here," she says at last, "to the secret cavern of your soul."

"Is the cup what I think it is?" I ask her.

"Yes," she says. "It's the cup that can only be touched by the pure fool; it is the cup that continually replenishes itself from the source of the River; it's the cup of the water of transformation; it's the cup that heals all wounds; it's the Holy Grail."

"Then how come I can see it? Maybe I'm a fool, but I'm not so pure."

"You're pure enough to be a truthsayer."

"You mean because I'm a virgin?"

"Partly, Theo, but it's more than just virginity; it's your truthsaying; it's your ability to see through to the heart of things. Do you want to heal the wounds of the world? You must take the chalice and use its inexhaustible supply of the water of transformation to renew the universe. Isn't that why you came here?"

"But why were you a dragon? Why did I have to fight you? Aren't you my mother?"

She smiles again. I want so much to run up to her and put my arms around her and for us to throw off these absurd high fantasy costumes and go home, but something prevents me. She's my mother but she's also mother to the world and that makes her more than woman.

She tells me—and her words are echoed in the wind through the cavern and the sighing of the sea—"Theo, Theo, you fought me because every hero must fight the dragon. In the ancient dream time, Apollo fought the earth-serpent-mother of the world for possession of the oracle of Delphi. He wanted to wrest the art of truthsaying from the mother of the world. The truthsayers have been battling mother earth ever since that time. It's not a war that you can win or lose. It's the war that keeps the world afloat. It's a war of love as well as death; because, Theo, you know, you love me more than anyone in the world . . . at least, for a little while longer . . . until the day comes when you leave the nest, you start to look outside the house, and you find the woman who is uniquely yours . . . do you understand what I'm saying?"

I think so. But there's a music in her words that touches me far more than their meaning ever can. "Mom . . . what am I supposed to do now? Take the chalice and heal the world, right?" I go right up to the altar railing. Only a few feet separate me from the thing that human beings have spent lifetimes seeking. Only a wooden railing stops me from embracing my mother. What does it mean? Why don't I just take her at her word, leap over the barrier, grab the grail, renew the universe? What kind of universe would the renewed universe be? Will it bring Josh back to life, and return Mom to my father's house, healed of her sickness? Somehow I don't think so. It's not the right answer to the riddle of the sphinx.

My mother reaches across the railing. Our hands touch and I am afraid because this touching is where the dream begins, the dream of sweat and water and fish and things I cannot name though I know they come from the world of sex, the unknown territory that has begun to haunt my fantasies. . . . "What are you doing, Mom?" I ask. I can't help myself. She pulls me forward toward where I know our lips will touch. "Mom, does this mean what I think it means?" I say, knowing that in the woman there is still the serpent.

"Tell me, Theo," my mother whispers, "if you were Adam, would you have wanted to stay in the Garden of Eden forever?"

That's when I finally understand that there is a choice. In my innocence, I could seize the chalice and return the cosmos to its pristine state, as innocent as myself. I could remake the Garden of Eden. Everything would be healed; we would all be creatures of joy, dancing for all eternity in the radiance of perpetual morning. But is this a good thing? Isn't leaving the Garden a good thing too, like growing up, putting away your toys, disobeying your parents for the first time, and knowing at last that there must be death in order for life to have any meaning? I'm a truth-sayer. I see the true nature of things. I see that paradise is also hell, that to live forever without pain is also to be forever unborn.

I could give up my innocence. I could receive knowledge, and I know that the price of that knowledge is going to be my eye . . . my inner eye . . . that the power of truthsaying would gradually be sucked away from me . . . because I would no longer see with the eyes of a child. Is that what I want?

I'm scared. Fucking Jesus I'm scared because no matter what I choose there is a terrible price to pay.

"You've stayed a child so long," Mom says, "it seems as though you've been stuck, refusing to grow; but I know you hear the call of your own death, which is also your own restlessness, your own need to live."

"If I heal the world now, Joshua will never come back, will he?"

"No."

"We won't even be people anymore, will we? We'll be like total zombies."

"But happy."

"Yeah." It's then that I realize that I don't want to be a truthsayer anymore. And I have to pass the burden on to someone else. I start crying. I don't know, Jesus I hurt all over. I don't want to give up my special gift of seeing. But I want to become something too, even if it means suffering through adolescent angst and pimples and sexual frustrations and all the other shit I've seen Josh go through. And I realize now that I *can* pass on the burden.

I've been to the River's edge, where the unborn heroes float downstream in their little rush cradles. I've swallowed the essence of Joshua into myself. That's why, even while I was gazing down at his putrefying body, I could still feel him close by. He's inside me. I can plant him in the body of the One Mother, and I can make *him* carry on the destiny of truthsaying. But to do that I'm going to have to . . .

"I know it's unthinkable," she says. The altar railing has evaporated

into the swirls of incense. "It's the biggest taboo that humans have. But
you and I aren't just human beings; we are also forces of nature, we are
gods. There are two ways to renew the world—to return it to a state of
utter entropy—or to fire it up with the tension of a lovemaking that is
also a deathmaking. You must give up your innocence; you must make
love to me; and you must pay the price by giving up your vision. Or
else—"

But you know the strange thing is I don't feel sad about it at all. I know
that the universe is kept in the air by a monumental feat of juggling. I
can't let it drop. My blood is pumping and my mother has bared her
breasts to me and I drink in the memory of milk and the feeling of
omnipotence in being at the eye of the cosmos. I throw my arms around
her and I'm seized as though by a mighty wind and I hear the jangling
harmonies of angel choirs and the percussion of our syncopated heartbeats. She overwhelms me, she surrounds me; she is the forest of joshua
trees; she is the sea. Our love is a tumult of joy that shakes the very orbits
of a trillion worlds. I dive into the womb of the universe, pass through
the event horizon, traverse the utter darkness of the singularity, break
through the threshold in a shower of exploding starstuff . . . I am reborn.

And then, when the tempest dies down, when the world is dim enough
for me to look on once again, my mother and I walk slowly down the
steps, hand in hand, into the city square where the others, time-frozen,
have been waiting.

I'm still shaking from the sexual encounter that was more than sex. I'm
more confused, not less, because my truthsaying vision has already begun
to fade. I've managed to juggle the universe, but I've had to let myself
drop.

"We're back," I tell my dad.

But he just stands there gaping at Mom. He is remembering all sorts of
things that happened before I was born; and now those images are closed
to me.

I know he will never understand the journey she and I have returned
from, and I know things will never be the same again between him and
me.

He doesn't know that my gift is slipping away from me, that soon I'll
be blind to the true nature of things. I'll be just like all the others.

Jesus, it better be worth it.

CHAPTER TWENTY THREE

OEDIPUS REX

Phil Etchison

No time passed. In less than the twinkling of an eye, the fabric of space over the plinth atop the monument in the center of the cartoon city unzipped itself and Theo and Mary stepped out, hand in hand; I caught a tiny glimpse of the fearsome world they had left behind, fleshy, palpitating and sulfurous, and then the gap between the worlds closed up behind them.

Everything began to change. The body of my other son, which had lain, putrescent, on the marble steps, was no longer there. The dark clouds overhead began to break apart, admitting a supernal radiance, as in a *Transfiguration* by Raphael.

"We're back," Theo said softly. I looked from him to my wife. Something had happened between them. I didn't think that Mary was dying anymore. Her face was positively glowing with health and joy, and it was not just that she was standing dead center of the shaft of heavenly light, her long hair stirring a little in the wind that is cooling the smoldering city, and she was wearing the same dress she was wearing the first day we met . . . the summer dress drenched with the hot Virginia rain.

"I've brought Josh back," Theo said. "But I had to pay for it."

He ran toward me, he buried himself in my embrace; oh God, he was a frail thing, spindly, awkward, and his dirty blond hair was matted with sweat, and there was so much bewilderment in his eyes, so little of the searing certainty I had come to expect of him. "Oh, Daddy, Daddy," Theo cried, "was it worth it?"

"I don't understand," I said. "Where is Josh?"

"Inside me," Mary said.

I smelled on my son the smell of a woman, a smell intimately familiar to me because it was the fragrance of one particular woman, a woman I'd cherished for twenty years, a woman I'd given up everything for, even my own sanity; and I was consumed with rage and bewilderment.

Serena Somers

So Theo had made the same sacrifice I had made . . . and for the same reason . . . because we both loved Josh. I could tell what was dawning in Mr. E.'s mind; I could tell that it made him very nervous. He and Theo stood there, hugging each other, but when Mary said that Joshua was inside her I could see him stiffening, turning away.

"Dad, don't turn from me," Theo was saying. But what was going through Mr. E.'s mind wasn't something you could logically argue about. My heart went out to both of them because like, Theo was bawling his guts out and Mr. E. couldn't find it in himself to comfort him; Theo had wounded him in the act of fulfilling what he most desired.

Phil Etchison

Mary said, "Don't be angry, Phil. I'm not dying anymore. Theo has taken our pain upon himself . . . don't you see that?"

But I wasn't feeling very rational. I had been cuckolded by my own son, hadn't I? I'd had no major role in the drama to start off with . . . wasn't it always Theo who was the truthsayer, the redeemer of the world, the one who knew the answers? "I'm an insignificant appendage in my own family," I said. "I'm like Joseph, a village carpenter who's convenient to have around to give God's bastards a name. . . ." Why was I so bitter? Was it that Mary was back, Mary, more beautiful than ever before, untouched, it seemed, by all the tribulations that had wrenched our family . . . and I'd somehow expected even more? Was it that my son had harrowed seven hells while I stood impotent, and now by his victory over the darkness had rendered me more impotent than ever?

Mary said, "You don't understand, Phil. It wasn't what you think. We danced the dance that brings forth the light. You have to look at it mythologically. Josh is inside me again. He'll be twice-born. He's going to be the most powerful truthsayer of all. And to bring him back from the dead, to reverse the entropy of the cosmos, Theo gave up his most precious possession . . . his gift . . . and his innocence."

But there was in me an ugly thing called jealousy, and I just couldn't see all these cosmic verities, because unlike Theo, unlike my wife, I was not a god, and I was unlikely ever to become one. I had always known I was less than a poet, but now I knew also that I was less than a man. Why couldn't they see that? But they could, you see. And they pitied me for it. And their compassion made me even more bitter.

Theo Etchison

My vision is ebbing. Before, the world was fluid, because there were illusions piled on illusions, and I could see through all of them like they were so many overlays of acetate, so many cartoon animation cells . . . I could see through all the falsehoods to the bedrock of reality. But now the illusions themselves are becoming solid.

My father has stepped back. I don't know who to turn to. When I turn back to Mom, I can't meet her eyes anymore.

Standing farther off is Strang; like me, he is losing his vision; he is entering an inner world of madness. Behind him is Corvus; behind them both are the intertwined corpses of Strang's two elder children; and hovering overhead, its spires peering from the thinning clouds, is Caliosper, where Ash is waiting, alone, for word of forgiveness from his father; and I know it's not going to come.

Saving the universe fucking sucks. I've brought my family together again, but it looks like there's no room in it for me. I've been crying like a baby and my father's heart has turned to stone. He'll never understand because he's never seen, never breathed the air of these alien worlds; he's been in the theater watching the movie, but he's never *lived* it. Jesus I'm bitter. But I see that he is too. And yeah I blame him. I blame everyone.

"All right," I tell them all. "I'm going now."

My father says, "Where? What do you mean?"

Mom says, "Phil, Theo has to go away for a while."

I fling the worthless marble onto the steps. The marble cracks the stone and through it I see the surging waters of the River. Suddenly everything's shaking, I mean the whole city seems to be splitting up into a million shards, and beneath them all you can see the River. It's angry. It's been stirred up and it's about to burst the seams of reality. A geyser starts spouting where Joshua's body once lay. I start to walk away from my parents . . . I go toward the crazed old man who once was king of everything.

"Truthsayer," says King Strang, and he pets my cheek.

"No way, not anymore," I say.

"There is another journey we must take," he says, "you and me together."

And though my gift is fading, I feel the truth of what he's saying. The pavement's cracking beneath our feet and the water's lapping at my calves. Doorways are opening all around us. We could step into a million other worlds. My father and my mother are standing close together, staring at each other, poised in the tense moments before reconciliation.

There are things I must do before I lose my powers forever. There is a way to heal the universe without destroying free will . . . and I know that Strang and I must go on the journey together . . . before he becomes completely blind . . . before the truth slips away from me forever. I've glimpsed the Holy Grail, and I know its power comes from the source of the River . . . but we must go there, he and I, we must travel together through the schizophrenic labyrinth of his mind . . . to the place where Strang made his bargain with the powers of darkness . . . we ourselves must stand at the source.

Dad is striding toward me now. He's trying to use reason; he's fighting his own emotions. "Don't go, Theo," he's saying. "I know that you're acting out all these cosmic roles, preordained since the beginning of time. Sure it disturbs me, but I'll get over it. Jesus Theo, don't walk out on us. You're my son. I love you."

"I know you do, Dad," I say. There's so much I want to tell him. How much I've loved him when, Sunday mornings, he's sat us down and read to us great bleeding chunks of shiny poetry, the words all jingly and grand, echoing in my mind for days and weeks afterward; how much I believed in him when we played the game of *Trust Me* and drove blind through clashing universes; oh I'm aching because of how much I love him, but I know that I must go. It's the whole Garden of Eden thing. I have to slip away from him. To be exiled is the beginning of maturity; to be blind is the beginning of wisdom.

I reach out to take the old king's hand. Corvus is beside us now, spreading his wings to shield us from the wind.

"Goodbye for now, Dad," I say. I kiss my father gently on the cheek.

I don't kiss my mother; we've gone beyond all that.

Serena Somers

Watching what was happening between the Etchisons was painful. But I knew I wasn't just witnessing the breakup of their family; there was something else going on . . . the beginning of something.

The city was coming apart at the seams. Water was sluicing up out of the ground. Theo and King Strang were standing one moment, Theo leading him by the elbow the way you help a blind man cross the street, and then they just stepped out of the universe and were gone. And Corvus followed them, not even saying goodbye.

Yeah, there were all these turbulent feelings in my head, but there was also this urgency because I knew we were going to drown if we didn't get out of there fast. Mr. and Mrs. E. were just standing there, looking into each other's eyes, maybe thinking about how they'd let their son slip through their fingers . . . and it was up to me to grab them both by the arm and propel them toward the nearest exit. The exits were continually changing, they were like these windows into other worlds that popped in and out of the air around us. But I followed the sound of salsa music because that was the last thing we'd been listening to in the real world . . . and there was the gateway . . . through it I could see thousands upon thousands of candles, and children in skull makeup dancing, and women weeping and beating their breasts in front of the altar railing, and . . . "Let's not stick around anymore, guys!" I said, and I pushed Mrs. E. over the threshold into the other universe, and she was holding on to my hand so I guess I came tumbling after, and Mr. E. had a hold of the other hand so he came through too, and the next minute we knew—

Phil Etchison

I had landed, flat on my backside, on the hard cold limestone floor of the cave.

"¡Milagro . . . un milagro!" one of the kids was shouting, pointing at us because we had, presumably, materialized in front of the altar in the grotto of the weeping Madonna.

"Mary?" I said.

I turned and saw the statue of the virgin.

Jesus, I thought, it's happened again, she's frozen into stone again, it was all just a dream when I touched her and smelled her perfume and caressed the soft hair as it billowed in the wind and—

The limestone began to crack. The sound was like a sudden thaw of ice in the spring, up in the far north, a thundering elemental bursting. Some of the celebrants were cowering behind the rows and rows of candles and decorated death's heads. Again and again I heard them whispering, "A miracle! A miracle!" Mary emerged from the rock. She wiped the white dust from her eyes and stood behind the altar rail, a living woman in the place of stone.

Softly she said, "Phil, I've awakened from a long and terrible sleep; I've dreamed the birth and death of universes. Am I in the real world now?"

"Yes," I said, though I was far from sure of it.

"I'm going to have a baby," she said.

We embraced across the altar railing. My bitterness was slowly beginning to fade. It was good that we were finally going to have children. That was why we had come down to Baja: we wanted to spend a few romantic weeks together, doing what the doctors had said could not be done, curing my wife's infertility with an outpouring of passion.

I'd had so many daydreams about children: about strong tall sons playing catch by the stream next to the cottonwoods that ring my father's house in Spotsylvania County, about a beautiful young child who knew how to say all the things I left unsaid, who grasped the truth without the tortuous twists of logic and philosophy; who would be my best and most beautiful poem. I'd daydreamed about going on adventures into fantasy kingdoms, manufactured great epics in my mind of which the eponymous heroes were my offspring . . . woven the great classics together . . . fantasized even about myself when old and wandering, doling out pieces of my kingdom à la Lear, losing my mind . . . I could hardly believe that fantasy was about to become reality, here in a grotto known for its miracles, in a foreign land, at a festival of the dead.

"Serena," I said to the woman who had served as our surrogate daughter all these barren years, "Mary's going to have a baby!"

"Congratulations, Mr. E.!" she said. But then she added, darkly, strangely, "But don't forget the other one."

"No, don't," said Mary, as she kissed me over the wooden railings, "forget the shadow twin, the one who is wandering in the outer darkness, who blinded himself to plant your son in my womb."

Words of great mystery, sublime, poetic, dark, unfathomable words; I did not understand them. But that was to be expected on the day of the dead; it was a day of magic, where the boundary between the real and the dream fuzzied itself, and the dead could come back to life.

CHAPTER **TWENTY FOUR**

CONGRESSMAN KARPOVSKY

Serena Somers

The world was settling down once more into some kind of semblance of stability. The Etchisons and I walked back along the beach; I had to get back to my job handing out Karpovsky buttons. The festival was in full swing. It was exciting I guess: there were fireworks and there were bands and there was a procession of skeletons carrying candles and there were booths selling horror candy, and Mary was back with us and no longer mad or dying. There was still a wrongness in our world though, because Theo was out there in the wilderness with the mad king, and because Mr. E. no longer seemed to remember the hell we had harrowed together. Mr. E.'s memories were totally elastic, like the fabric of reality itself.

I had a little unfinished business too.

That's why I kind of snuck away from the two lovebirds—they were holding hands and whispering in each other's ears like teenagers—and slipped off through the crowd toward where I knew Karpovsky was still holding forth. The little holiday resort was just as we had left it—oh, maybe a tad more drunken, as it was later the same night—still full of celebrants being militantly ethnic for the benefit of the hordes of loud-mouthed, gold-card-toting tourists.

I was pretty sure that, in *this* world, no time had elapsed since the moment someone tried to abduct Our Lady of the Sluggish Tears. Which meant that Karpovsky was probably still in the same spot, buttonholing tourists and trying to get them to sign petitions for his grassroots candidacy. Yes, I could see him now. He was standing by a booth, against a backdrop of papier-mâché skeletons. A TV camera was rolling. It had a CNN logo on it, and the newswoman was saying, "But, Congressman, why are you in Mexico at all? There's a popular rumor going around that you feel that, with the trade agreement, Mexico should just be annexed and made into the fifty-first state."

Karpovsky laughed. "Very funny, Claudette," he said. "Personally I feel that Puerto Rico should come first. But no, I'm here—okay, I might as well be crass about it—for the photo-op. And the fact that so many of our citizens are spending their holiday dollars here instead of back home—why? Because a dollar will barely buy a Coke and a candy bar today."

He paused for effect, and then he pointed to the row of skeletons. "Do you see these?" he said. "We're all going to be looking like this soon, because none of us have health insurance—we're all going to be hanging in a row—unless my national health plan is implemented right away, and I intend to make it my top priority, understand?"

That's when he saw me.

"Excuse me for a moment, Claudette," he said, and walked in my direction. His place was filled by a dozen kids, jumping up and down and making faces into the television cameras.

"Serena," he said. "Where've you been?"

"Can we talk?" I said. "It's important."

He looked askance for a moment. But he saw that I was serious, didn't want to blow anything with the newspeople all around us, I guess, so he nodded. "Take five, guys," he said to his all-female, all-pneumatic staffers, and then we retired to a booth in an open-air coffee shop alongside the beach.

Karpovsky ordered a strawberry daiquiri; I ordered one too.

"I don't know about that," he quipped. "Are you of age?"

"I'm old enough to fuck, Congressman," I said.

That got to him. I'd never spoken to him directly about it before.

"Pretty strong language, Serena," he said.

"Something's happened to me sometime in the last five minutes," I said. "Well, it was only five minutes to you . . . but to me it was an adventure that like, spanned star systems and lasted lifetimes."

He was looking at me with utter seriousness now. I thought he'd act like I was crazy, but he didn't; there was a poetic side to this man, and I believed in him, in many ways, even when I was most mad at him.

I knew that there was a Serena who had never fallen prey to the congressman's lusts; she was a Serena who hid herself inside walls of lard, dreamed about Joshua Etchison, and finally sacrificed her virginity to bring him back from the dead. And there was a Serena whom the congressman had all but raped on the desk in his office between a bronze eagle and a crystal whale, a Serena who had never dared speak or point a finger or even resist because she was afraid. And there was a third Serena, who had reveled in the control she exercised over someone so much older, so much more powerful . . . a Serena who'd used her sexuality to shore up her sense of self-worth, who knew that, though she was at the bottom of the totem pole and he was at the top, in the bedroom their places could be reversed, and he could be reduced to a sniveling wreck with the threat of blackmail or exposure . . . all three Serenas had existed, and I was the sum total of all three . . . for just as each moment in time contains the potentiality for millions of possible futures, so also each moment is the junction of a million pasts . . . the River flows backward as well as forward . . . and everything you can conceive of is, somewhere, the truth.

The drinks came. The congressman was looking kind of nervous. I wondered which of the Serenas he remembered. Probably a little of all three.

I said, "You probably don't remember the confrontation we had back there in the cartoon city . . . you know, when I was in the form of a dragon. . . ."

I thought Karpovsky would probably think I was insane, but in fact he began to stare at me strangely. "Are you psychic or something?" he said. "I've been having these dreams. . . ."

"Did you dream about fucking me on top of your rain-forest-busting mahogany desk right there in the Capitol building?"

"I . . ."

I didn't know whether this was the Karpovsky who had done these things to me, or whether he had only thought about it or . . . dreamed it . . . but he said, "My therapist tells me I'm just acting out my inner desires . . . and that it's better that than actually going around . . . you know . . . harassing . . . well . . . you know what I mean. Things are a lot better now. I'm a flawed man, Serena, but you know, I believe in things . . . I want to make things better."

"Well, maybe you'll understand if I just go ahead and act out one of *my* fantasies."

"What, right here in the coffee shop?" he said, and I wondered whether he thought it would be the dragon-skinned Serena who would rapaciously devour him on the spot.

"Nothing kinky," I said.

I got up, and I picked up my daiquiri, and I emptied it over his head.

Something snapped in both of us, then. I mean, I don't know if *this* Karpovsky raped me in his mind or in his office. But I knew there was something between us, something that needed to be washed away.

And you know what? The congressman like got up, and he sloshed the rest of his drink on my dress. And we began laughing, I mean, laughing so hard we were crying at the same time, and the daiquiri glasses might just as well have been the Holy Grail with the healing blood of Christ, because when the red liquid soaked into my pores I began to feel cleansed of all my bitterness.

"Jesus, Congressman," I said, "what's happening to us?"

"Our wounds are going to get healed," he said. "Because we're able to forgive each other. Because we can look past the terrible things we do to each other, day in, day out, the searing hells we put each other through, often as not in the name of love. And maybe, just maybe, I'll even win this fucking election."

CHAPTER **TWENTY FIVE**

MAKING LOVE

Phil Etchison

In the hotel room, we made love. The curtains billowed in the open window and the fireworks in the night sky flashed against the peeling paint, and their thunder drowned out the squeaking of the bedsprings. How does it feel to make love to someone you have known for twenty years, who has been so much a part of your life that there seems to be no pore or crevice that does not contain her? God, it was like making love for the first time. It was as though she had returned to me from a long and terrifying journey, from sickness or from madness. How else can I describe that night? At first we were like children playing doctor, discovering the intimate secrets of our bodies for the first time. Then we were like adolescents, our hormones raging, thrusting awkwardly . . . I knocked the lamp off the nightstand, Mary fell off the bed howling with laughter . . . oh God I love you I love you I said over and over and over . . . and over. And then we made love slowly, like the late baby-booming yuppies that we really were, for the music outside our window had changed from percussive salsa to a slow waltz . . . and then, strangely, during the afterglow, it transformed into a lugubrious funeral march. The Chopin thing, even more dirgelike because it was pouring forth ponderously from off-key tubas and trombones and punctuated by the flat thud of an untightened bass drum.

"Oh, turn off the music!" Mary said, laughing.

She got out of bed and went to the window. I followed her. We stood there, heedless of our nakedness, watching the parade of death-masked Mexicans go by.

"I wonder where our son is now?" she said softly.

"In your womb," I said. I bent down and put my ear to her flat belly, knowing full well I would not hear any kicking for many months to come, and that Mary would make fun of me for doing it, and that I would accept her chiding with good humor. All that happened.

But then, looking away, far away, across the crowd, across the brass bands, across the dancing celebrants, seeming almost to be looking to some distant universe, she said, "No, I mean our other son."

"Are you mad?" I said. This festival . . . breaking down the barrier between the dead and the living . . . it was making us both a little crazy . . . that was why it seemed that we were seeing each other anew across a tremendous gulf of space and time. "You know you lost our child. . . ."

I thought of Theo, how we'd placed him in the cold earth, up north, in Arlington, a stone's throw from the Pentagon.

I didn't want to think about the past. "We're going to start again," I said. "We've been living through a nightmare, but now we're going to have a family, and we're going to be happy. A miracle has happened to us."

The funeral march went on up the street, and a new band was beneath our window. They were playing a jaunty tangolike song and it made me want to dance. I caught my wife in my arms, wrapped her hair about my face, kissed her several times, lifted her in my arms and gave her a whirl, carried her back toward the bed.

"Still," she said, "I wonder where he is."

BOOK FIVE

THE FOREST OF ICE

"Chocby z mych lez gorzkich
drugo Odra byla
jesce by synocka
mi nie ozywila.

Were I to weep so many tears
That I could make a second River Oder,
Those tears would never bring to life
My son."

—*Polish folk song*

PHILIP ETCHISON: *Tales of the Wandering Hero*

5: At the End of the Forest

And so, at last, I left the darkling wood.
I came to the cave where I had left my mother,
The hearth I loved, the bed in which I'd dreamed
Of these adventures.

      I came upon my kinfolk
As they supped, telling old tales to warm their nights.
I said, "Mother, I have returned, with gifts
And stories, conquests, jewels, and a bride;
I have slain man and dragon; I have ravished
Maiden and crone; I have lived dangerously,
Stooped, beastlike to drink water from the stream,
And quaffed celestial manna from gold goblets."
My mother said, "My son, take out the trash."

"But, but," I said, "what of my lurid tales,
My battles and my witty conversations
With saucy knights, my exploits the bedroom?"
"Yes, yes, my dear, but first, go wash your hands,
Or you may not sit down to sup with company."

Only that night, when I lay down to sleep,
Did she consent to hear my tales of woe,
Of joy, of passion, courage, and survival;
And then she wept full sore, because the son
She loved had been through so much suffering.
Then she did kiss me gently on the cheek
And say, "The places you have been, the conflicts,
The fierce encounters, and the nights of passion,
These places all are marked upon a map;
The map is called *The Human Journey*.

"So,
Although, my son, you have traversed the world,
And conquered love and death, and grown from child
To man, there is another thing to learn:
Your journey is the journey all men make,
An exploration of the human soul;
And I am still your mother.

"Let me kiss you,
And tomorrow I will bake you a fresh loaf
Give you a new condom and clean clothes,
And you shall venture forth again.

"The journey
Is forever."

EPILOGUE

THEO

T h e o   E t c h i s o n

. . . "King Strang! King Strang!"

I'm calling out to him across the howling void. I don't know the name of this world and I don't know the name of the one we've left behind. Where we are now it's a world of ice and snow and our raft has been moving doggedly upstream for it seems like a year now. Corvus is piloting. I don't know where Ash is but I think he is watching, waiting for the moment of reconciliation.

The King has stepped ashore to ask directions of a bearlike creature who sits, cross-legged, like a snowstrewn Buddha. He's been in that position for a million years and speaks to no one, but I think he will speak to us; he has, you see, been waiting for us.

Our journey is fulfilling a lot of prophecies. The gateways between the universes are shutting down or getting clogged. We do what we can to keep them open. My powers still work a little; on a good day I can clear a little pathway, enough for the River to run raging through. It makes me feel good.

The King and I don't speak much. I am his fool, and I tell him bad jokes from time to time, and he tries to laugh. Mostly we just sit in silence. He has his lucid moments. That's when he tells me stories about the old days. Spectacle and bloodshed beyond imagining. All I can tell him are stories about being picked on in school, or smoking in the boys' room, or Mrs. Dresser's social studies class, stuff like that. For him, though, my stories are of equal moment to his own; in a sense, I suppose, they are.

I wonder whether Josh is born yet.

I know that he'll be a far more powerful truthsayer than I ever could have been. His father is a truthsayer and his mother is the world. I can't wait to hold him in my arms. I'm no longer young even though only a year or so has passed between now and the time that I thought I would live forever, the time I held those shiny epiphanies in my hands like so many bright new glistening marbles; I'm no longer a child even though I'm only slowly moving out of my childish appearance and getting gan-

glier and having wet dreams and all that shit; I'm no longer young because I've left my innocence behind me forever, floating downstream in
the River like an unborn hero.

I don't know if I'm happy yet, but I know that now I can dream.

Fucking Jesus it's cold. The wind is like whipping us and screaming like
a banshee and it gets inside our blood and you feel like you're going to
split open, like a beer can in the freezer . . . but the cold means many
things. It means we are getting closer to the source. That's why there is
no sun. It's a twilight world here. A dark world, a dungeon among
worlds. But we keep going.

One day we're going to reach the River's source. One day my brother
the truthsayer will come bursting through the spaces between the universes, and there'll be a final healing. But fucking Jesus, I did the best I
could.

I tried to wash the memory of me from my dad's mind. He'll think I
was only a dream. He'll be happy now.

Maybe he'll even believe himself to be a poet, in the end.

Bangkok, Los Angeles, 1991–2

YESTERN

dedicated with love to

Judy,

from me and Johnny,

in memory of your last July Fourth,
when we gave you the opals, and
you told us we were the two most
important men in your life.

Row, row, row your boat
Up, against the stream;
If you fail you'll drown, and life
Will just have been a dream.

BOOK ONE

EXPOSITION: FIRST SUBJECT

THE ETCHISONS

"I breathe the air from another planet . . ."

—Arnold Schoenberg

ON TRUTH

BY PHILIP ETCHISON

My writing block, it seems, is permanent. As a result, I find my annual address from the poetry chair of this august institution to be more and more of a joke, year after year. What can one talk about, when one has been struck dumb? What eternal verities may I discourse on? Do I have a right to discourse at all?

I have decided to venture into the treacherous shoals of ontology . . . .

The greatest minds of all time have striven to answer the great question once posed by Pontius Pilate. Well, not all. Jesus Christ, to whom that question was addressed, managed to avoid answering it. And the Lord Buddha managed to skirt the issue by telling us that Truth does not exist.

I had more or less reached the same conclusion when, one morning, I heard a sound which I knew, instinctively and unquestioningly, to be an Absolute Truth. The sound came from my seven-year-old son Chris, who has been diagnosed by some as autistic, and who cannot, or does not, choose to speak . . . .

—coffee-stained ms. found in a shredder at Blair House, Washington, D.C., along with a prescription for Prozac. Believed to be in the handwriting of Philip Etchison. (Analysis available for viewing one week before the auction, 9 a.m. through 4:30 p.m.)

—offered by an Anonymous Source.

—reserve $15,000

CHAPTER ONE

CHRISTMAS IN THE WHITE HOUSE

Serena Somers

It was the 90s, the time before the mad millennium. But a dollar could no longer buy a Coke and a candy bar; indeed, the 90s had only a few more days to run. Indeed, some people would have said they were over, but the man I worked for was quite particular about how the first year of the new millennium was not 2000, but 2001.

"It's simple math," he would tell me, staring at me with those wide, ingenuous eyes, "because there is no year zero. If we were computers then I'd say yes, the first millennium goes from zero to nine nine nine, the second from one thousand to one nine nine nine. But it ain't so. Ask Arthur C. Clarke—he wrote the book on it," and would not chuckle, of course, at his own joke, for he was a man who expected others to provide the laugh track, the punditry, the musical accompaniment to his every sound bite.

"Yes, Mr. President," I said.

It was the 90s, the time before the mad millennium, and during the brief span of those 90s I had gone from a gung-ho student activist with shining ideals to the live-in lover of the president of the United States of Armorica. Everybody knew, and nobody minded anymore, because the millennium was upon us, and for all we knew, the end of the world was nigh. A man with a placard to that effect walked daily back and forth in front of the White House, and no one had the heart to send him packing, because this man, you know, knew things; he had been on Letterman once, and he thinks that the world we live in is only a shadow of a real world, a world in which our country is called America.

"Are they here yet? Jesus, I hate Christmas," said the president.

"We still have fifteen minutes, Mr. President," I said. I called him Mr. President because you never knew who might be listening.

America, said the man with the placard on Letterman, was vastly different from our own world, yet strangely the same; in America, there was no Letterman per se, Letterman having been superseded by some other late-night talk-show host whose name, said the man with the placard, he could never quite recall when he awoke from those troublesome dreams wherein this true world showed forth images of itself, images as evanescent and can't-quite-put-your-finger-on-able as a Zelazny fantasy novel, such novels being yet another figment of the man with the placard's dream-reality.

Okay, so I was thinking in twisted sentences that never seemed to quite gel into cogent utterances. That wasn't surprising.

You can easily get tongue-tied when you're about to be in the presence of one of the other guests at this very private dinner on Christmas Eve— Phil Etchison, P.P.P. (Pulitzer Prize for Poetry), the man who read the poem at President Karpovsky's inauguration, the poem that says everything about the 90s, and nothing—

(the time before the mad millennium)

These were the people, then, who were going to be sitting around the fireside: me, Phil, Mary Etchison, their son Chris, the autistic (or was he?) child prodigy; and a few assorted secret servicepersons, maids, butlers, and other staff members, but they would all be off at midnight.

I'd known the Etchisons since I was a kid. Or had I? It's true, you see, what the man with the placard said. There were great gaps in the world's collective memory. Everyone knew this even though no one could put their finger on what it was that had been forgotten. Sometimes before I went to sleep I could catch glimpses into those other universes. Other Serenas lay down beside me in the same bed . . . more than beside me . . . in the very same space I occupied. Only some of them were not sleeping with the President of the United States of Armorica, and some of them were fat and some of them were anorexic, and some of them had known the Etchisons since they were kids, and some of them were dead; and others still were barely human at all.

I didn't remember ever meeting the Etchisons before. But soon, perhaps, I was going to remember it all. Perhaps too soon. I spent the afternoon anticipating and dreading, and listening to classic alternative rock on a battered old portable DAT, while my husband-in-all-but-name sat in the oval office pondering the treaty for the secession of the Lakota Nation.

Dinner, then, was a little awkward, though delicious; they were all of President Karpovsky's favorite dishes, and the man, though I'm probably biased, has taste. Nobody spoke at all. All the way through the Sevruga on wafer-thin toast points, the lobster bisque, the medallions of beef (the same variety that had caused one of Oren's predecessors to barf into the lap of the prime minister of Japan) dinner was silent. All but for the footsteps of the staff as they changed the dishes in between courses.

It did give me a good chance to study the Etchisons, though, whom I was supposedly on such good terms with. Philip Etchison wore the distinguished-author persona like an ill-fitting toupée, and I could see that underneath it all was a kind of perpetual embarrassment. He smiled a few times—four string players from the Washington Symphony were playing Mozart's *Dissonance Quartet* in the background, and each little wincing discord made him smile more broadly. He dressed the part of the great poet, you know, the battered tweed jacket and unkempt hair and even the nervous twitch. But somehow it wasn't him.

Mary Etchison was different. She was totally serene. It didn't unnerve her a bit that no one was saying anything. They were almost a parody of an archetypal coupling: he the wind and she the mountain, he the turbulent sea and she the firm earth, or perhaps she the placid sea and he the fire that burns on the water . . . what I'm trying to say is that they didn't seem quite human.

Then again, it was only days until the mad millennium. None of us were human. And Chris, their kid, was the least human of all, although he was the key to all our humanness.

Chris, too, was a celebrity. He was a kid who never spoke—well, he had been known to speak, so it wasn't that he had a congenital defect or anything like that—but at the age of four, he had wandered onto the stage at the Kennedy Center, where Emil Gilels was supposed to be giving a piano recital that night. He had climbed onto the nine-foot Bösendorfer in the empty auditorium, and he had begun to play. By dinner time, the concert hall was full. Gilels did not play. He was weeping in the wings. He came out to proclaim the kid the genius of the age, but the boy had vanished. It was on CNN. The oddest thing about it all was that everyone recognized the music, but no one could remember its name.

The next day, Philip Etchison encountered a writing block from which he had never recovered. Paradoxically, he became rich, a grand old man—except that I guess he wasn't really old—a laconic and soundbiteful lecturer commanding huge fees. That, I supposed, was the source of the terrible sense of loss I could see in his eyes.

You could see all sorts of emotions flitting through the Etchisons' eyes. All except Chris', that is. You and I might see a few fish heads in the bouillabaisse, but Chris Etchison saw a world.

Dessert was a sort of a *crêpes suzette* thing, swimming in alcohol and whipped cream. Because we weren't talking, I was feeling this great big *thing* welling up inside me . . . you know, like that feeling you get when you're watching a musical at the movie theater, and the lovers are looking into each other's eyes and romantic music is welling up around them, surging, soaring, until at last the dammed-up emotions burst out in an uncontrollable outpouring of melody . . . well, it happened. I got up from my seat, flung my arms with such expressive energy that I thought I was going to turn into the Venus de Milo for a moment . . . and I began singing, lustily and passionately. Which was amazing, because I can't sing.

What did I sing? That was the strangest thing of all. I can't remember a note of it. But it was a complex music, a strange keening punctuated with profound rumblings; it was definitely moving, because no one else at the table said a word.

Mr. Etchison, the great poet, sat there with his jaw dropping in slow motion, frame by frame; his wife Mary just beamed; my significant other sort of rocked back and forth and seemed to fall into a sort of postcoital serenity, except that he and I hadn't done it in months . . . and then there was the kid, Chris. I don't know. I mean, he looked right through me. Like he totally knew me, even more than sexually; and he couldn't have been more than eight years old. He just penetrated me with that gaze. He had the most amazing eyes, hazel with a hint of purple.

Like he understood every word of what I was singing.

As though the song was meant for him alone, as though I was just a kind of conduit or prism that the song passed through on its way from high up there in the sky where songs come from.

Mary Etchison wept.

To say that this was weird doesn't begin to describe how I was feeling. Because, you see, conscious as I was that Chris was looking at me, I also started looking at him, I mean really focusing. And what I saw wasn't just some angelic little kid with big soft teddy bear eyes, but myself. I mean pieces of myself that were missing, though I had never known I was missing them.

There had been another Etchison, a boy named Joshua. Joshua was inside Chris, somehow. I had been his lover. But how, and where?

And there was yet another missing Etchison: Theo. The truthsayer. The boy who held the universe in the palm of his hand as though it were a marble. In fact, to him, it *was* a marble.

There had been adventures. Other worlds. Mad kings and dragon ladies and a vampire princeling. And more mundane adventures too. Losing one's way in the basement of a Chinese restaurant. Kidnapping Mrs. E. from the top floor of a lunatic asylum. Watching Mrs. E. turn to stone and turn back into flesh.

Were these all rabid fantasies, these vivid pictures that my singing seemed to conjure up? What images were the others seeing?

Mary Etchison was a goddess; in fact, she was the Great Goddess herself, who had fashioned the universe from her own flesh and fertilized it with her tears.

And now she was weeping again, which meant, perhaps, that the world was about to be renewed once more.

My lover, the president, said, "That was lovely, Serena. A lot more succinct than my Christmas address to the nation."

"Funny, Serena," said Phil Etchison. "I never knew you could sing."

"I can't," I said. "In fact, I'm not sure that it *was* me singing just now. It seemed to be coming from outside myself somehow. Or beyond myself. Or beside myself. Am I sounding like a schizophrenic?"

⌐

We retired to a little sitting room—not one of the rooms ever seen in any official tour of the White House—where the walls are covered in a velvety red wallpaper—a small, round room, not unlike a womb, in fact. A butler-type gentleman wheeled out the after-dinner liqueurs. The room contained a baby grand piano, and Chris immediately gravitated toward it. There were no servants. I myself poured Mr. E. a Cointreau, Oren a Remy Martin, and myself a guava juice. A tray of joints and a snuff-box of cocaine were proffered, in token deference to the new permissive drug laws, but we all ignored the drugs, being good clean children of the New Age.

Chris began to play a Mozart sonata.

Mrs. E. sat in a corner by herself, wiping at her eyes with a silk handkerchief.

"Sometimes," Mr. Etchison mused, "I wish my life were more like a Mozart sonata."

"In what way, Mr. E.?" I asked him.

"Well, you know, the wildness of it is so organized. Exposition, Development, Recapitulation, Coda; yet within this rigidity there's so much elasticity; you could fit a whole universe into a sonata movement, if only a universe were something you could listen to."

"But why restrict it to just listening?" I said.

"Listening," said Mr. Etchison, "is a metaphor. Music is a metaphor. But since our very existence is a metaphor, it follows that it is all just metaphors within metaphors, and there is no point to the universe."

"Come on," said President Karpovsky, "you don't really believe that."

I said, "Who is Theo Truthsayer?"

Mr. E. said, "I don't know." But he shifted uncomfortably, and downed a second shot of Cointreau.

"And Josh? He dove into the sea once, and we spent an eternity—or it felt that way, felt at the very least like the middle volume of a trilogy—searching for him through myriad universes."

"Never heard of him," said Mr. E., and looked furtively for the liqueur trolley, which a lackey had wheeled away for fear that he might become too inebriated. "Or have I? It does sound kind of familiar. Theo—there's a *theo*-logical kind of name. And Joshua was the Hebrew name of Jesus, was it not?"

"Don't be pretentious," said Mrs. E.

"It's all I have left, dear," he said, "now that I'm permanently blocked as a poet."

The Mozart was getting to him. And to tell you the truth it was more than just Mozart. Chris' playing had begun as a well-known piece—I think it was the C minor, the one that begins like a tragic hero leaping into space and time and is answered by the delicate call of some unattainable grail. But somewhere before the end of the exposition, about halfway through the second subject of the sonata movement, Chris had veered into parts unknown. That was something that happened frequently with his playing.

Far up in the treble, there was a weird, tinkling counterpoint with a mind of its own. Booming in the bass, another voice, strident and dissonant. I wondered how little Chris could be playing all those things at one time, unless he had at least four hands.

He did.

You didn't notice this right away, mind you. It wasn't anything so blatant as those Hindu god statues you see sitting up on the shelf in an Indian grocery store. But if you looked at him for a while, you became aware, as the nimble fingers ricocheted over the ivories, of other fingers, other wrists . . . other selves, in fact, and you also became aware of Chris' profound, absolute concentration . . . the ethereal tranquillity that seemed to radiate from his face, and I do mean radiate, because it was almost as though there were indeed beams of light darting about his eyes . . . or was it just the music, easing slowly away from Western harmony now, into some darkly hypnotic Eastern algorithm?

"It's true," Mr. E. said. "When he plays, he becomes a god."

He was trying to sound playful, but I knew that he meant it literally.

"Which god?" said Oren. "A music god, I suppose. Apollo, maybe."

"Truer than you think," said Mr. E. "Apollo's also the god of truth."

For me, though, one of the Hindu deities was closer to the mark. The many arms, for one thing. The pale blue radiance. Krishna, perhaps. The glorious child, the vessel of absolute truth. That was what this music was saying to me.

I was starting to remember more and more pieces. The music was truth, a deeper truth than can be said with words.

"Mr. E.," I said, "just how much *do* you remember?"

Mrs. E. continued to weep. In fact, her tears were gushing improbably, as though she were more fountain than woman. In fact, her complexion was becoming a little marmoreal. In fact, she *was* a statue—had, perhaps, always been a statue. She was a marble goddess sprouting up from the middle of the floor, her tears cascading down on the delicate patterns of a great Persian rug.

More pieces. I baby-sat little Theo once. He was a brat. He always blurted out the truth. He said, "You're just saying that because you're fat." Saying what? I don't remember. Suddenly, though, there was this adjective. *Sluglike. Sluglike Serena.* They used to call me that. I loved my Joshua from behind folds of fat, knowing that such a love would always be safe.

Many-handed, radiant, the infant Chris-Krishna went on playing. Notes were spinning from the keys—I mean literally, little flurries of them with coruscating wings, here an eighth-note, here a school of thirty-seconds whirling around the boy's head, and finally, all at once, a storm of them, like stars, billowing.

What did it all mean?

Behind it all, dimly, I could hear a heartbeat.

Okay so you remember that we were in a sitting room. All very cozy. Christmas tree and little choo-choo train. American colonial furniture, all sorts of oaken eagles and fading maroon leather. But the room itself was metamorphosing. Or was it merely becoming more itself? The neo-classical mock-Ionic wall moldings were stretching into stalactites and stalagmites. The divan I had been sitting on was softening into a bed of moss on a ledge of limestone. The walls were moist and breathing, and the tinkling piano blended with the sighing of a subterranean wind. In the whisper of the wind were angel voices, and I could almost understand the words of their song.

The heartbeat was a drumbeat now, deep, solemn, resonant.

The cavern walls were shimmering . . . some kind of phosphorescence . . . or was it starlight, and was the wind that whipped our faces some galactic storm?

The drumbeat-heartbeat came, still louder, bone-chilling now.

"Oren," I said. He put his arms around me, but seemed strangely far away.

We were in the eye of a dust storm, and the dust was the stars. And when the drumbeats suddenly ceased, and the dust abruptly settled, there was another man there with us.

A street person. Native American. He shook the stars out of his hair. In one hand he held a placard that read, **The End of the World Is Nigh,** and in the other a flute made from the thighbone of some animal. Or human, maybe.

The music came to a stop, too.

The churning world began to resolve itself. We were still in the little colonial sitting room somewhere in the bowels of the White House.

"Thank you, Chris," said the man. His face was scarred and furrowed. He put the placard down on an empty fauteuil, the one with the golden lion paws, and looked at all of us, slowly, one at a time.

"Congressman Karpovsky," he said to Oren, "somehow I didn't expect you to be one of the pilgrims; I had you figured for a day player, not a principal."

"I'm the President now," said Oren. "Where've you been all this while?" He didn't sound all that confident.

"Phil," he said to Mr. Etchison. "The river has been dammed up these seven years. No poetry, just chunks of awful verse, scraps of paper fit for the shredder. It's time for the juice to flow again! Look up, man, see what's right in front of your nose! The dam has a chink, and soon the waters will come tumbling!"

Mr. Etchison was shaking.

The Indian turned to Mrs. E., who was still a statue. "Great Goddess," he said to her, and made a quick genuflection, "mother of us all, you honor us and bless us with your presence." And kissed her marble hand.

"Chris," he said, turning to the boy, who had climbed off the piano bench and was coming toward him shyly, wide-eyed, "you are the greatest truthsayer who ever lived. But when you have said the greatest truth that can be said, will you be able to bear to say yourself out of existence?"

The boy seemed unsure of himself. He was sad. He stared like a bashful moppet. The Indian patted him on the head. "I feel for you," he said. "Yours is the greatest burden of them all."

And then he turned to me. "Serena," he said.

"Do I know you?"

"Yes."

"You're . . ." And suddenly I remembered his name. "Milt. Milt Stone."

"Thank God! For a moment I thought you were going to say Santa Claus."

"You're . . . a tribal policeman in Arizona, something like that. And . . . some kind of magician."

"Yes, I suppose you could say I am. I am a *nadlé,* a sacred man-woman, one who bridges the unbridgeable. I can step from one riverbank to the other without passing through the river. What else do you remember?"

"Not much," I said. "The Etchisons were driving through the desert. They fell into another universe. The Darklings were at war."

He smiled. "Not bad," he said. He touched my lips with the flute.

My lips smarted.

"You're the man with the placard who paces up and down in front of the White House every day," I said. "The madman. I wonder why the guards never—"

"I wonder too," he said. And laughed. Very softly. Like a creaky door. "All right," he said. "The fat lady has begun to sing—"

"I'm *not* fat!"

"But once," he said, "you were, Sluglike Serena."

I knew then with an absolute certainty that the images I had glimpsed when the music began were the One True Past, and that the reality in which we were now stranded was unraveling.

"This room and all its contents," said Milt Stone, "this country, this universe, and every event that the five of you have lived through for the last seven years, has been a dream. It has been only the blink of an eye. This whole illusory space-time you've constructed around yourselves is a self-replicating tesseract, and only the power of Chris' truthsaying can break you free of it."

He paused, perhaps to give us time to become adequately over-whelmed by the immensity of that statement. Then he went on: "There are pieces to be picked up, lies to be untangled, wounds to be healed. There's no time, either. You think all this time has elapsed, but you've just been running in place. Wake up. Snap out of it. Trust me."

"Trust you?" said Oren. "But you don't even exist, according to what you've just told us."

Milt merely laughed.

"Peyote!" said Mr. E. "I remember now. You rammed it up our asses."

"No need for peyote now," said Milt. "Chris is our direct hypertext link to the Ultimate Truth. But we're burning daylight. Let's get going.

We've only a few days left in which to save the universe. Chris, oh Chris, show us the way."

He handed Chris the bone flute, and Chris began to play.

CHAPTER TWO

THE RECOMBINANT YELLOW BRICK ROAD

Chris Etchison

why can't I speak
why can't I just come out and say
father
father
is it because
to say it would make it true

Phil Etchison

Forget about growing old. Forget about rolling up the bottoms of my trousers.

A hundred hours till the end of the world, and counting. Forget about the tract house in Bethesda where I, a poet without poetry, had been living with my beautiful, stony wife and my child who spoke only in music. Apparently it never happened.

Forget it all.

Forget mowing the lawn, kissing Mary on the forehead goodbye on the way to catch the Metro into Washington to give the weekly poetry lecture at the Corcoran that was only attended by half a dozen people, two of them vagrants fleeing the icy sidewalk. Never happened. Forget making love in the morning, trying to pull Mary back inside me when all she wanted was to turn back into the pillow, turn back into stone; forget, forget, never happened.

Forget picking Chris up to comfort him at three in the morning. Forget the dirty Pampers. Forget the way he looked at you, in his mother's arms, a few moments after he was born, staring right into your eyes and sucking the truth right out of your mind, when you know that a baby's eyes aren't supposed to even focus yet; forget that *have-I-created-a-monster* shudder that I tried so hard to repress but never quite had, not now, not seven years later . . . forget even that? Never happened. Dreamt it all.

Why should I believe the rantings of some homeless wino? Liberal guilt, because he's an Indian? Some kind of New Age *frisson*, because . . . he's an Indian? Or because I know it's true?

Or because of what I was remembering?

The images that were flooding back, flattening those other memories like sandcastles before a tsunami?

For example:

Christmas Eve's Eve. I'm shoveling the snow from the driveway. From somewhere inside the house I can hear Chris humming. It makes the shoveling go easier, somehow; the crunch of hard snow, the flop as it lands in the slush where the sidewalk begins, these sounds become the rhythm section for Chris' eerie, sidewinding melody.

Mailman shows up with half a dozen Christmas cards and a golden envelope with a 1600 Pennsylvania Avenue return address. Probably wants a contribution to some charity, I thought, and took the bundle inside, where Mary was gift-wrapping a little something for Chris, a box of marbles—ironic, perhaps, since some would say that Chris had none of his own. Chris watching her, still humming. The melody lingering in the air—literally lingering that is—you can see the rainbow-fringed sparks, slowly dying, slowly, slowly, slowly—there's always a kind of synaesthesia around Chris, you know.

"Mary," I said, "there's a letter from the President."

"Of the college, or of the United States?"

I showed her.

"Probably wants a contribution. Is he running for reelection, yet?"

I opened it.

Phil, it said, *it's just an informal little thing, don't bother to dress up.* "Mary," I said, "do we know the President of the United States?"

"We shook hands with him once, that big photo-op for the faculty, you know, the grant from the NEA."

I said, "He wants us to have dinner with him tomorrow night."

Bring Chris. This is really important. Okay, maybe you don't remember a thing, but you will once you get here.

"I don't get it," I said. "Some drunken orgy back in our college days, maybe? Oren Karpovsky is my closest friend, and somehow I've forgotten?"

"We all have big holes in our memories these days, dear," Mary said, putting the finishing touches on the gift wrap, sliding it under the Christmas tree, narrowly avoiding a collision with the O-gauge Southern Pacific locomotive that chugged around the landscape of Christmas presents. She looked at me, and I remember thinking, *She knows something.*

"Oren Karpovsky," she said, "he was so charming down in Mexico."

"We've never been to Mexico."

"Right. I forgot."

In my mind, I've been rehearsing the big speech I'm going to give on New Year's Day, to welcome the new millennium. It's my annual Address from the Poetry Chair, only since I can no longer write poetry, it's going to be a speech about the nature of truth.

Phil, Phil, don't sweat it, all will be made clear. A limo will pick up you, your wife, and your son at six o'clock sharp, and you'll get a police escort. Don't worry, this is not a hoax. It's a fork in the Yellow Brick Road.

"It appears that we've been invited to Oz. Or, perhaps, one of many Ozes, since he speaks of a fork in the road."

"What do you give a man like that for Christmas? He probably has everything."

Do you remember Serena? the note said. *She'll be there.*

"Serena Somers? Didn't she baby-sit our children?" Mary said.

"We only have one child," I reminded her. Because Mary had never been firmly anchored in the real world. You could tell that she thought our entire existence was a dream. She was struggling right now . . . struggling to wake up. If only. . . .

I kissed her gently on the cheek.

"If I'm crazy," Mary said, "why do little things keep happening that confirm *my* truth?"

"What is truth?" I asked her.

We decided to give the president a frayed first edition of my first book of poems, *The Embrasure of Parched Lips.*

🔲

Crossing the Potomac, I experienced a wrenching reality shift. The borderline between the two parallel worlds ran right along the length of the river. Of course I knew President Karpovsky. I'd written his inauguration poem. We met in the lobby bar of a hotel in Mexico, where he'd gone to address a rally and I'd gone to take my wife to a Laetrile clinic, in a last-ditch effort to patch together my gloriously dysfunctional family.

My surly son Joshua, my dreamy son Theo. Serena was Josh's girlfriend, wasn't she? Or the baby-sitter.

No sooner did I know these things than I forgot them all over again, because, somewhere around Eighteenth Street, there was another fault line in the fabric of the universe.

It wasn't so bad sitting around in the small reception hall. There had only been pleasantries to exchange, and my wife and the president greeted each other warmly, so I knew the insanity was mutual. Then, when Serena came in, wearing jeans and a T-shirt and hippie beads yet, things started to look a little odd.

"We're very informal around here," she said defiantly. "There's no press around. We'll do whatever we want."

Then not a word was said during the entire meal, until Serena started to sing. You couldn't call it singing exactly. It was a shrilling, thrilling sound, bloodcurdling, really. It was Chrislike in its apocalyptic splendor. I thought, in fact, that it must be the Last Trump, though heaven knows I'm no fundamentalist.

The first notes sent my mind reeling and I could see the road stretch on and on through the Arizona desert and feel the refractory choke of the air conditioner and hear my two sons quarreling and—

The next thing we knew, a withered old homeless Indian was expounding ontological niceties to us in the sitting room, and handing my son a magic flute, and Chris was beginning to play, and the room, the White House, the entire city of Washington D.C., was folding in on itself like a Chinese puzzle.

A snowstorm was raging, and we were at a fork in a road. Definitely yellow brick. Little stretches of it were glinting through the blanket of white.

My wife, whiter than the snow itself, stood like a Madonna at the cross-piece of the T, one hand pointing in each direction of the fork. I squeezed her hand but my flesh encountered only the cold hard stone. She wore the flowing robes appropriate to her godly status. You could not tell where the cloth ended and the snow began, for her vestments folded right into the landscape.

My son put away the flute. He looked frail and awkward in the dark jacket, shorts and little blue bowtie that we'd thought appropriate for dining at the White House—thank god we had such an outlandish costume in the house, but our son had played a concert or two, and even been on Letterman—but the flute slid right into the pants pocket with the ease of a gun into its holster. The music didn't stop, though.

The music was in the howling wind.

Milt Stone had changed, too. He was tall, his face more like a raven than a man; and I knew that in this world he had another name: Corvus, the navigator. "I was beginning to think," said this Corvus, "that none of you were ever going to come to your senses."

Only Mary's eyes seemed alive; and her left eye wept, slowly but continuously, a glistening glacier that ran down her cheek, down the snow-powdered folds of her robe, onto the ground, that was melting the snow about her feet so that we could see more and more of the road, glittering beneath the slush.

In this universe, my wife is a goddess, and my son is a seer. I, on the other hand, am nothing special. I didn't think I would ever get to be anything special, not in a thousand universes; did that, in itself, make me special, make me into a kind of archetype of Everyman?

"What are the plans?" I said to our guide.

"Hell if I know," said Milt. "This isn't Inferno, and I'm not Dante. Can't expect me to lead the way. I've brought you here—that's it. Didn't even bring you here, really; just sat around at the gateway, waiting until the moment that brought all of you together, then opened the door. Up to you people now."

"Where are we?" I said.

"Dunno," said Milt. "Chris would know."

"But he isn't talking," Serena said.

"No," I said, "he isn't."

"Should we split up?" said President Karpovsky. "I mean, there *are* two directions indicated . . . three, if you include turning back."

Turning back, it seems, was not in the cards. As I turned to look at the road which snaked behind for quite a distance until it was lost behind a towering embankment, I saw that the road itself was eroding. A brick here, a brick there, the road was rearranging itself, tying itself in knots, all in slow motion, that is. It was then that I realized what was most different about my life, or rather about the mythic adventure that happened to be my life.

Normally, when you tell a story, you start off with one brick, you lay it, you move on to the next brick . . . piece by painful piece you construct the unique path through the cosmos that is the tale. At any moment, you can look back and assess all that has gone by. The point you stand at is the sum total of all that has transpired. Stories are cumulative—like music, like sex, lumbering inexorably toward a climax.

Well, but you see, that is not *our* story. In our story, you may look back at any time, and the view will always have changed. It is a story that writes itself in both directions of time simultaneously. It is a story in which you anticipate the past with as little foreknowledge as the future.

What a journey! Or, as I would have said in the 60s, in at least one of my many pasts, what a trip!

Chris kissed his mother's cheek and turned to the right.

"Our mission," I said, trying to avoid portentousness (but not quite succeeding) "is to find ourselves."

"And to find the truth," Serena said.

"And to heal the world's pain," said Milt Stone.

"Tough missions," said the president. "Bullshit is more my line of work. Am I the scarecrow, the lion, or the tin man?"

There was more snow. I couldn't tell where the sky ended and the land began. Chris started to walk. He held the flute aloft, like a lantern. The flute played itself. The snow was thick and fast, but where Chris stepped, it parted for him, so I guess the flute was sort of like the machete in the jungle. I followed. We were all numb, I think, especially our feet; none of us had come dressed for inclement weather.

"You know what?" said President Karpovsky after only a few steps. Shouted, actually, because the roar of the wind was crescendoing. "I just don't feel right going this way. I mean, a shift to the right, on the eve of the millennium . . . it just doesn't seem politically correct to me."

He looked back. We all did. The statue that was my wife gave no reply.

"Anyone coming?" he said, but it was mostly directed at Serena. "What, no one loves me? Ah, the lonely lot of the politician."

Serena seemed very confused. She looked at Milt for a moment, then back at Oren. Oren began to stride away. I suddenly knew why. In that direction, you could sense an easing of the storm. There was a feeling that the sun was there somewhere, hiding behind an arras of mist and cloud. A true politician, Oren had figured out the path of least resistance.

Corvus said to Serena, "All quests are, in the end, the same quest. But that doesn't mean that the grail can't be reached by more than one road."

"Are you saying I should go?"

"Do you love him?"

Amazing how far away he seemed now. Trick of perspective, I guess. In a minute, he was halfway to the horizon.

"Wait up!" Serena shouted. She began running after him, kicking up clouds of snow. In another minute, she too was just a tiny figure. So there was just me, my son, and our guide.

And my son, holding the flute above his head like a banner, was resolutely making his way down the rightward path, toward a smudge of darkness on the horizon that could have been smoke, or a thundercloud, or an ocean of black ink.

"We'd better hurry," said Corvus.

Everyone was always in such a hurry around here.

CHAPTER THREE

ABSOLUTE POWER

S e r e n a   S o m e r s

The odd thing was, in no time at all the road led us through one of those weird fractures in causality or whatever it is, and we were no longer walking (him walking, me running to catch up) because we suddenly found ourselves in the back seat of some massive convertible limo and we were driving (being driven) down an avenue (still yellow brick) but widening and widening, though the snow was still falling, slowing a little, slowing and softening to an icy drizzle, snow falling at our feet, on the black leather upholstery, everywhere. Even our clothes were different now, a kind of cross between New Wave and Victorian, shaggy mink things with sci-fi collars. There were human skulls littering the plush carpeting, though. Other kinds of skulls, too. Couldn't figure out the species. Alien creatures of some kind.

The driver was dark and tall, and he never looked back at us, and he wore dark glasses. Next to him was one of those tall Chinese guys. He wore a sort of Mandarin's costume, the kind you see in historical epics. He held a trumpet in one hand. Now and then, he did turn to glance at us. He wasn't like any Chinese guy you've ever met; he was like a cliché of a Chinaman, like Christopher Lee playing Fu Manchu, stroking his straggly wisp of a beard and peering through exaggerated epicanthic eyes, and his accent came from a bad movie, too, when he finally started to speak.

"Cornelius Huang," he said, "always and forever at your service, esteemed sir and madam; might one proffer refreshment?"

The limo then seemed to be a little bit like a Chinese restaurant.

Hovering before us was a lazy susan jammed with delicacies—braised sea cucumber stuffed with minced pork, abalone with bok choi, goose feet in red wine sauce—we'd had this kind of stuff at the Chinese ambassador's, never in a restaurant—and women in shimmering *cheongsams* bobbed up and down, translucent, ghostlike, pouring plum wine into golden goblets.

"You will, of course, eat," said Cornelius Huang.

"Sure thing," Oren said, and a pair of silver chopsticks appeared in his hand.

"Wait a minute," I said. "We just ate."

I ribbed him.

"Come on, honey, we don't know where our next meal may be coming from," said Oren.

I ribbed him harder. "Oren!" I whispered. "I think this is one of those Persephone deals. You eat the food of the underworld, you stay here."

Oren gulped. "I already swallowed," he said. He tried discreetly to spit out pieces of goose bone. "What am I supposed to do, starve?"

"Perhaps you'd prefer some wine?" said Cornelius Huang. "It's not bad—in a sanguinary sort of way." Yeah, he was solicitous all right. But there was a kind of disdain in him, too.

"He needs us," I said to Oren. "But he doesn't like us."

"How do those little old Chinese ladies manage to do it?" said Oren. "You see them popping their goose feet into their mouths, and then, rat-tat-tat, the bones come flying out as though from an AK-47. I've never been able to figure it out."

"Years of practice," Huang said. "Allow me to demonstrate."

He leaned over, reached in the air for a pair of chopsticks, which materialized in his hand. Delicately, he picked up a goose foot, thrust it into his mouth, and went through the entire chomping-machine-gunfire routine. "The tongue and the cheeks," he said, "have certain muscles which atrophy if you're not used to a diet of fowl feet."

Before I could stop Oren, he had already reached for another, and was trying it, unsuccessfully, into a napkin.

"Good," said Cornelius Huang, "there goes another lump. It's time for us to discuss your new job, Mr. President. . . ."

"What happened to my old job?"

"Oh, I see, your old job." Mr. Huang suppressed a little chuckle; just your typical arch villain. "Unfortunately, your old job never really existed, you see. The life you have lived for the last, oh, seven years or so, has not been entirely real. Something terrible has happened. The fabric of the cosmos has shattered, you see. Think of each parallel universe as a jillion-piece jigsaw puzzle, each picture just a little bit different from the last. Well, what has happened is that someone has taken all the possible puzzles and mixed up all the pieces, so that when we travel from piece to piece in the great map of our existence, we are also leapfrogging from reality to reality; do you understand?"

"You mean," Oren said, "that little frisson I experience whenever I step into the *en suite* bathroom in the presidential bedchamber, and I suddenly get the feeling I'm a completely different person, that I'm not even supposed to be there at all—"

"Oh, you're so bright, Oren. May I call you Oren? Seeing that you are not president after all."

"What about me?" I shouted. Was I being selfish? My lover's position in life, after all, affected the lives of millions of others; my own, perhaps, was less important in a way. But there was something I had to know. "The real me," I said. "I don't know why, but I suddenly just *have* to know. Am I fat or thin? In the real world, I mean."

"Profoundly banal," said Cornelius Huang, sighing.

But it was more important than you might think. You are what you eat, and I seemed to remember one life that was one long eating disorder. Hadn't I been fat once? Hadn't I catapulted from bulimia to anorexia and back again? Was that my *real* life, or some fantasy of self-loathing? And if I wasn't screwing the president of the United States, who *was* I screwing?

From somewhere in the distance, I could hear the rushing of a river. Perhaps I was wrong about the food. Perhaps it was only food. It did smell tempting. More tempting than food had a right to be. That was why I couldn't trust myself.

I closed my eyes and I saw someone else I knew I had once loved. He was flying high, riding the back of a dragon, careening over a flaming world. Who was he? Not the man I was sitting with now.

"But if I'm not president in the true world, who is?" Oren asked. "Don't tell me. Clinton won for a second term, and then . . . no! Surely not Perot! Or was it Robertson? Or that other guy, the way-outa-left-field candidate . . . Danzig I think his name was. . . ."

"You don't want to know," said Cornelius Huang.

"And who am I?"

"You'd want to know even less." He peered into Oren's eyes, did the old hypnotist on a vaudeville stage stare, and I could tell that there were sort of images of some kind, projecting, laserlike, into Oren's mind. I didn't want to look, but I couldn't help myself . . . especially since the landscape that roared past was all snow, all white, all featureless.

I saw Oren change—change so completely it was like when a werewolf is hit by a silver bullet and, dying, turns vulnerably human, you know what I mean—one minute so full of power and ferocity, the next so completely frail, as in those few moments when I truly loved him, which were not many—I put my hand out to touch his shoulder and amazingly he shied away from me, flinched, looked out of the window.

"I wish," he said, "I wish things were different."

"Yes, I know," said Cornelius Huang.

"I don't always like being who I really am."

"I know," said Cornelius Huang. The refrain was ominous. There was a plan afoot, and it had to do with Oren's hunger. Oh, yes, he was like me when it came to hunger, though it wasn't as simple as with me, I mean with me it was just food, stuff myself, starve myself. He had another kind of hunger and it was all to do with power.

Not that he wasn't a *good* man, you know. I mean, his politics were *very* correct. We'd saved a lot of whales, me and my Mr. President. Women's rights, gay rights, everyone had a lot of rights now, I mean we were about as liberal a couple as our world permitted, but sometimes, when the TV cameras were turned off, I knew that Oren yearned to nuke someone's ass to kingdom come.

And so we drove on, you see. We reached a river's edge and the road went on, ploughed right through into the river, and the limousine sort of grew fins and plunged into the water, well, it was mostly ice, and it cracked and clattered against the car that was now some kind of boat and was still growing, growing, a mast thrusting up from where the lazy susan with the Chinese food had been, black sails sprouting up, a pirate flag flapping, crewmen with surly faces creeping past us, stopping to stare when they didn't think we were looking; only the leather upholstery we were sitting on remained the same, but now the seat had transmogrified into a bloated divan on a deck that overlooked a prow that was the face of a stern but compassionate goddess, to be exact the face of Mary Etchison if I looked a little more closely. Couldn't be a hundred percent certain of it.

"The prow of this ship," I said—

And Cornelius Huang, suddenly very tall, with robes that shimmered with coruscating shades of cerulean, viridian, vermilion, chrome, and a gilded trumpet in his hand like one of those monstrous Tibetan things, he glared at me for a moment, then blew three blasts (my eardrums could barely take it) and put the trumpet down and said, "Yes, we've kidnapped the goddess, of course; it's the one way we can be sure we know where we're going," and then, in a kind of delayed reaction to the trumpet blasts, the ice of the river, the air itself seemed to shatter, disintegrate, we sort of *dissolved,* the way you go in a movie from one scene to the next, and we weren't in the snow country at all, but in another place altogether. No snow here. The sky was gray, featureless, without a sun or moon.

Still a river, you understand. I remember. There's a great River that connects the millions of known worlds, and the River itself is both itself and a metaphor of itself. The trumpet blasts had unlocked some kind of cosmic gateway, and now we were far beyond where we'd been a moment before. Light-years away, maybe, or even universes away.

Oren got up. Walked over to the prow, placed his hand idly over the goddess' stony curls. Here and there, in the water, were weathered artifacts—great Easter Island heads, sphinxes, Buddhas, even an angular Jesus swinging from a marble tree—and in the middle distance a castle climbed up out of the waves, and it really did climb, clinging to the chalky cliff-face like a granite vine, a twisty mess of turrets and landings and parapets and minarets and great windows like the eyes of a thousand skeletons. Suddenly I knew the castle's name: Thornstone Slaught. I had definitely been here before. *Déjà vu* in spades.

"My master, the Lord Thorn," said Cornelius to my lover, "has been killed. There is a vacuum in the cosmos. In the vacuum there is a castle. To enter the vacuum is to gain power. You crave that power, and you're never going to have it if you allow the world to sink back to its entropic reality. Which it will, Mr. President, if you don't fight it with all your might."

And I knew then what Oren had seen. He had become the most powerful man in the world, knowing full well that the world he ruled was a dream world, only half real; he had seen what he was in the real world. I could only guess. It couldn't have been flattering. I'd never realized how much he hated himself. And you know, his self-hatred was the only thing about him that I loved. That was the strangest thing of all.

The lazy susan whirled around and around, so fast that you couldn't see the food anymore, like a roulette wheel.

"Will you bet everything on the red?" said Mr. Huang. You could hear the ball skittering. Then, as the wheel slowed, we were back to the table d'hôte. Two fortune cookies sat in a silver platter. "Surely, Serena, you'll have dessert."

"There's this game that—" I began. Who played the game? How did I know these things? "You take a cookie and . . . the other person asks a question, any question, and you open it, and whatever it says is the answer to that question."

"An absurd sort of game," said Oren. "Will I lose you?"

I opened my cookie.

"Loss," said the fortune cookie, *"is part and parcel of the karmic balance. Live with it."*

"Seems pretty clear," said Oren. He seized the other cookie, gazed thoughtfully at it, and waited for me to ask my question.

"What kind of question is that," I said, "for a fortune cookie to answer, 'Will I lose you?' "

"That's two questions," said Oren, laughing. He opened his cookie, and read to me: *"Life is a slow dance between death and desire."*

"I don't get it," I said.

Oren tossed his cookie into the water. A dozen hands popped up to drag it under. Mermen, I supposed, or some other mythical creatures. "Better get rid of yours, too," he said. "You're the one who thought of the whole Queen of Hades linkage."

It was too late. I had bitten into the cookie.

"Not a moment too soon," said Cornelius Huang. He pointed at the castle, which had become suddenly much closer. There was some kind of commotion. A flock of birds—or were they dragons?—flinging themselves against the walls, bursting into flame. "Thornstone Slaught is under attack. Master, you simply must seize control, or else there will be chaos. You see, there is an absolute need for you, here, now, even though the place and time is other than your own."

As the ship docked beside a wharf lined with human skulls, I could see that the castle was indeed under attack. But it didn't seem like a big deal. They were bats, or maybe baby dragons. The reason that I couldn't really think about Oren's plight was that something seemed to be happening to me, too. I was choking on the fortune cookie.

A steaming goblet appeared by magic in my hand—a bubbling, crimson fluid—and I started to drink without thinking, and the pieces of cookie started to slide down my throat—they were sharp-edged. I felt as if I were swallowing glass.

Drink the wine and chew the wafer—

Suddenly this whole scene popped into my mind, one big bleeding chunk of a scene, a fragment of lost memory. A hotel lobby in Mexico, just over the border, next to a Laetrile clinic. Oren's lobbying, too. He's only a congressman, though. He's about to use the clinic as a photo-op, something to do with alternative medicine, or some new health plan, maybe? And I'm a lot younger; this is a whole lot more than seven years ago, although it can't really be longer than that because it's the year 2000 now, isn't it? But well, there's Oren and he's pounding away on the lobby piano and singing *The Vatican Rag,* and it's one big politically incorrect singalong because everyone knows and loves that irreverent old Tom Lehrer song, and standing by the elevator, watching him, feeling a surge of love for him even though I know he's been sexually harassing me since I was a congressional page in my mid-teens. . . .

I felt the fortune cookie settling in me like a lump of lead.

I looked up. A walkway now extended to the shore, and the crew of the ship was unloading, hastening down to the castle. They were about as gothic a crew as you could imagine, with bald heads and silver earrings and pierced tongues and lips and eyebrows and armed with scimitars and dressed in black, and some weren't even people but were sort of skeletons or something and a three-headed dog was yapping at my heels. Oren and Huang had already left the ship. The dragon-bats were swooping down from the turrets, and Huang was picking them off with a sort of laser-tipped staff. They sizzled and plopped into the sea, and each corpse was set on by a feeding frenzy of mercreatures, their tails slapping up columns of black water.

Somehow I was unmoved by all this spectacle. It was like I'd lived through it all before. Somehow I was no longer feeling my age, either; years were peeling off me; I understood the truth of what Milt Stone had said earlier, that the last seven years had all been a dream.

The fortune cookie was a sort of lump inside me, and I could feel it metastasizing within me. Something was invading me. Something wanted to control me.

Someone I knew well. Someone I'd once fought. To a draw, if not to victory, because you can't beat an archetype at her own game.

But she was dead, wasn't she? I had defeated her in proper mythic fashion by the good old power of love. Her name was Katastrofa.

How right you are, said a voice in my head. I cannot die so easily. I am immortal. You can kill the image of the dragon, but you can't kill the dragon within.

It was gnawing at my guts. It felt like, I don't know, the worst kind of constipation plus a choking feeling plus a vomiting feeling, all at the same time. Maybe I *was* about to give birth. Mrs. E. once told me it was like shitting a watermelon. Oh, God, I felt sick. Fire and ice in my belly. PMS and heartbreak all rolled into one. I started to scream. I caught up with Oren and Huang. They'd turned into some kind of dark dynamic duo, lashing at the creatures who were storming the walls. Oren had some kind of laser-beam ray-things shooting from his eyes. Cornelius was laughing and laughing and now and then blowing his trumpet which made dozens of the bat-things plummet onto the flagstones.

It occurred to me that someone was taking over Oren, too.

Still on the brink of heaving, I dragged myself over to the battle scene. They were dashing up the steps toward the first gray parapet. The stairs were littered with the corpses of the bat-things, but as we reached the parapet most were already turning away, heading skyward toward the lowering cloudscape. Still no sun, I thought. Although there was a dismal kind of light that suffused the battered bricks and weatherbeaten balustrades of Thornstone Slaught.

At the head of the steps, more ghoullike beings stood, but these were clearly not attacking. They fell to their knees at the sight of Oren Karpovsky.

"Deliverance, deliverance," they murmured.

"No!" I screamed. "I'm not going to deliver anything!" But the dragon within me wanted to get out. She was willing to rip me apart. I just wanted to die, I really did. But I knew that if I did die, I wouldn't come back; I'd be inside the dragon, instead of the dragon being inside me. I had to fight it.

I grabbed onto the railing of the parapet. I shoved a loose brick off the edge. I belched fire. That was how powerful Katastrofa was.

And meanwhile, the citizens of Thornstone Slaught were raising up Oren on their shoulders, parading him about the parapet, cheering and gibbering. And all of them had dark and hollow eyes and you know, bad skin, the way you expect bad guys to look in books and movies. Their cheering was like the chattering of baboons or loons, really grating on the ears.

"Stay down there," I said to the dragon woman. My gorge rose again, but I forced it down by thinking of Josh.

Josh, who didn't exist anymore, who never existed, of whom Chris Etchison somehow reminded me so strongly that I could feel a kind of sexual tractor beam shooting from his eyes and reeling me in. . . .

"Come on up," Oren shouted.

He was a level higher, now, up another sweeping flight of steps, dark basalt, bloodstained; there was a kind of throne on this parapet, a throne of human skulls and bones, all black with ash and coagulated gore. At a mighty blast from Huang's trumpet, the assemblage of ghouls fell prostrate, repeating the words *Oren, Oren, Oren, Rex,* like a mantra. I threaded my way through the throng. As I got closer to Oren I realized that he too had been going through changes. Oh, I don't mean being able to kill with a death-beam from his eyes. I mean there was a different person in him.

"Hi, sis," he said to me, leering. "Ready for Ragnarok?"

That was how I was sure who that different person was. It had to be Thorn, the vampire; and that meant that the battle we had thought was almost over was about to enter its third and most devastating phase.

"You look a whole lot younger," he said to me. "Crossing the River's taken years off you."

"I know," I said. "The last seven years were like, a dream, and now I'm almost as young as when you tried to rape me in your office on the hill."

"That's a fine way to talk to your one true love," he said.

"That's another thing that isn't true anymore," I said. I was talking like a much younger woman too, someone barely out of her teens . . . maybe even still in them. This was totally weird.

Cornelius Huang then said, in like this echoing, sepulchral voice: "The Lord Thorn has defeated the creatures that have attempted to seize his castle during his period of, ah, involuntary indisposition."

"Listen to me, Oren!" I said. "I know you're still in there somewhere. They're using us, Thorn and Katastrofa I mean, trying to come back to finish off the war. . . ."

"What the hell are you talking about?" Oren said. "I never had this much fun in the fucking White House. Diplomacy, diplomacy, diplomacy . . . bullshit. I can do anything I want here. I have absolute power!"

"You're getting into the spirit of things," said Cornelius Huang. "How about killing someone now?"

He beckoned with his little finger. One of the citizens crawled forward. She lifted up her eyes to my lover, and he decapitated her with a single glance. Huang plucked a golden goblet from the air and caught a brimful from the fountaining blood as she rolled down the steps. He handed it to his new master, and Oren drank deep. His eyes reddened.

"Not bad, eh, sis?" he said to me.

"I'm not your sister," I said. "I'm still Serena Somers. I'm keeping the dragon caged up for now."

"Then I'll have to keep *you* caged up," said Oren. To no one in particular, he shouted: "Take her away!"

Burly arms pinned me. I shuddered. I tasted the dragonbile in my throat, and then, suddenly, I sort of blinked out, and I found myself totally somewhere else. . . .

CHAPTER FOUR

AFTER WE STORMED THE CASTLE

O r e n   K a r p o v s k y

I am not a crook. (Try *that* one on for size!)

Don't blame me.

The buck never stops. It would have stopped here, but the idea of the buck stopping at all is just too, too *Euclidean* to pass muster in our multilateral, relativistic universe.

I had gazed into the emptiness that was my true self, and I knew that I had lost everything. You have to stop blaming me. Somebody was using me, and I was trapped inside myself, looking out at a harsh and savage world. I climbed up to the pinnacle of the castle, where there was a sort of war room, and I paced back and forth, planning out strategy with my new chief of staff, a cadaverous Chinaman who was a parody of the Yellow Peril, tall and beady-eyed and with one of those evil-looking goatees, constantly spouting words of ambiguous Confucian wisdom; and I'd locked up Serena and thrown away the key.

We were in a room. I was pacing. He was playing chess, actually. You know, the kind where the pieces actually fight each other to the death, on sixty-four squares of carpet in the middle of the room, and you can hear the clank of armor and the clash of swords and oh yes, the groans of the dying, and now and then even the rattle of an M-16 and yes, there's the odor of napalm in the air. He was sitting in a high chair and waving his arms, making the chess pieces move, playing, it seems, both sides, solitaire.

I said, "I would like to have Serena back."

"Why not?" he said, barely looking up. "You have absolute power, don't you? You stormed the castle and now you own all the territories of my former master. You have but to say the word and she will be returned to you."

"But I *am* saying the word, and I don't see her."

"Perhaps you don't really mean it," said Cornelius Huang, and then added a somehow condescending "O Master," as if to say, "Who the hell are you trying to kid?" and I thought, Perhaps I've only exchanged one hell for another.

"Perhaps," Cornelius said, "you'd care for another blood cocktail."

"I don't get it," I said. "I have nothing to do with any war that's going on here; you just picked me off the street to fill the shoes of some archetypal bad guy or something; you sit around calling me master, and an hour ago you made me drunk with power, but now you show me that there's really nothing for me to do here except drink blood and execute people I don't even know personally. . . ."

"No, no, Mr. President. You have it all wrong. I didn't pick you to fill anyone's shoes. You were already trying to play that role before, in your stumbling way. We have simply upgraded you to the real thing."

"An impotent real thing."

"Not as such." Huang clapped his hands, and a beautiful woman materialized out of the air: the kind I used to lust after when I was running for office, and not just in my heart, either. Pouting, hair that wafted in slow motion like a hairspray commercial, and strange and unexpected curvatures, and dark and haunting eyes, you know the kind I mean, prom queen, gypsy, and slut all rolled into one, and she knelt in front of me and clasped her arms around my buttocks and began to tug at the zipper. "And when you're through with her, you can drink her blood," said Cornelius Huang, "and you can toss her desiccated corpse out of the window, all the way down to the River. You've always wanted to try that, haven't you?"

"Of course not." But he had my number. I've always had fantasies. Bondage. Sadism. Blood. That's why I worked so hard to be a perfect liberal, the health plan, the safety net for the poor, helping the needy; oh, God, yes, I saw myself now in a different light; I saw the darkness that propelled every one of my oh-so-altruistic notions. I'm a hypocrite. I knew that now. Always had, I guess, but I'd managed to bury it under a megaton of health and welfare legislation.

I hated myself. That, in the end, was what it was all about. I hated myself so much that I didn't mind bringing down the whole goddamn universe, so long as I could get myself along with it.

Serena Somers

I was in a dungeon, I guess, somewhere in the bowels of Thornstone Slaught. I wasn't chained up or anything, and the dungeon didn't seem like a dungeon on first viewing, because the walls were a sort of sensurround projection of an outside world, a world of ice and snow. Snow just streaming down, and the wind howling like a pack of madwomen.

But in the little bubble that was the prison, there was no cold and there was no wind. It was like, utterly still, and toasty-warm, and that made the images of the arctic world outside seem quite unreal.

I had one of those snow-bubble paperweight things once when I was a kid. It showed a castle almost as baroque as the one I was trapped in. You shook it and watched the flakes fly. It was weird to be on the inside of one of those things looking out. I stood with my nose to the wall, or the forcefield, or whatever it was, and listened to the wind.

In the blinding whiteness, I started to see things. You stare into empti-ness long enough and you start to hallucinate I guess. You start to see, and soon you're smelling and hearing and even touching, too. I don't know how long it was before the snow started to resolve into those ghostly pictures, but I guess I had been there a long time, without food and water, my stomach still feeling all lumpy from that fortune cookie.

I started seeing Joshua through the window, if it was a window. How old was he when he stopped existing? Maybe seventeen? I saw Josh riding the dragon with the sun on his back and I thought, I could be the dragon if I wanted, now. Josh was all beautiful, more like a *Tiger Beat* pinup than a real guy. Maybe my memories had been edited. For sure they had, but I wondered if I had done it myself or whether it was just a side effect of the universe slingshotting back and forth.

I started to cry, I guess. I don't know. I was so, whatever, cut off. Couldn't tell if I was even real. And there was this lump inside me, this Katastrofa-embryo, just itching to burst out of my stomach like in that scene in *Alien*. I lay back on the floor—there wasn't any furniture in the room, if it was a room, and the floor itself had the appearance and texture of the snow outside, but not the burning cold of it. I closed my eyes, but the whiteness of snow wouldn't go away, even when I cupped my hands over my eyelids. The snow here was more than mere snow, I guess. It was some kind of metaphor, which meant that it wasn't subject to the rules of reality; you couldn't make it disappear by shutting your eyes to it.

I lay there in the fetal position crying my eyes out. Gradually, it did get kind of dark; maybe it was night on this planet.

Joshua was standing on the other side of the force field. He seemed to be banging on the field, wordlessly begging, like a vampire, to be let in.

He was even more pale than when I'd last seen him in real life. He'd been a corpse last time. But now he moved; well, swayed back and forth, like a zombie; I couldn't tell if he was breathing or not.

"Josh," I whispered. Could he hear me? His lips started to part as though he were trying to remember how to speak. "Are you a zombie?" I asked him. I know, that was a pretty stupid thing to say, right up there with "Do you come here often?" but you could hardly blame me for being a little socially challenged.

Josh looked at me, then looked way past me at something else that was in the womb-room with me. Some*one* else, maybe. Katastrofa, I was sure. The dead, like animals, must have some kind of heightened sense about the presence of supernatural creatures. Josh *knew* that his nemesis was in here with me—was somehow *part* of me. She was standing behind me. She was my shadow, or maybe I was hers.

"Josh," I said again.

His lips moved again.

"Where are you?" I said. "*What* are you?"

This time his lips parted slowly and I thought I could hear like, this expulsion of breath, only maybe it was my own, because I knew I was gasping and my heart was beating fast.

Because I was remembering more and more including lying awake at night thinking of Josh and hiding my passion for him behind those great big eating binges. And I was remembering my imaginary friend I'd made up, not quite man and not quite woman, someone to talk to because I didn't dare talk to Joshua . . . the imaginary friend who turned out to be real . . . to be one of the sons of Strang, mad king of the cosmos.

"I—" said the pale Josh-zombie thing that stood in the snow, stretching his arms out toward me.

"You *can* talk!" I said softly.

He banged and banged against the solid nothingness. But he didn't say anything more, although I think he tried several times.

How could I let him in? How could I let myself out? I banged and banged, too, but to no avail, except that my fists became raw and I was crying so hard I could barely see.

At that moment, there came a tapping from somewhere. I whipped around to see a tray of food materializing and a gloved hand retreating into thin air, zipping up reality behind it as it disappeared.

It was a tray of fortune cookies. Better not eat them, I said to myself. Each bit of this neverland food's going to bring the dragon further up to the surface. I turned to look at Joshua again but discovered that he wasn't there anymore. Oh, he probably was, just playing some kind of now-you-see-it-now-you-don't.

I stared at the tray for the longest time. The cookies were stacked up to form a circle. There were chocolate fortune cookies and vanilla ones, and the way they were arranged was in the shape of a yin-yang symbol, a dozen cookies for the feminine, a dozen for the masculine.

The dragon growled inside me.

"Shut up," I said. "Didn't I defeat you once by sacrificing my virginity?"

So what are you going to do this time? Get a hymen implant?

I stared at the cookies hungrily.

Maybe if I didn't eat them . . . maybe if I just opened them? The Etchisons had a game they would play . . . oh, a hundred universes ago. If they ate Chinese, they wouldn't open the cookies just like that, at the end of the meal; they'd take turns asking one another questions. The person questioned would respond by reading whatever was in his fortune cookie. Mr. E. swore that any question whatsoever, no matter how recondite, personal, or ontological, could be answered by this method. He said that in his freshman "how to read a poem" class, the one I audited, oh, a hundred universes ago, because Joshua wanted me to see that what his father did was a cool thing, after all, that being a poet wasn't the same as being just another stuffy old Dead White Male that you find on postage stamps. He then doled out fortune cookies from a big old bag, and got the whole class of a hundred eighteen-year-olds playing the game.

Well, I thought it was totally brilliant, and then when I went back the next year just for kicks, some clown had substituted the porno fortune cookies from *Chest of Pleasures Bookstore* and you know what, Mr. E. even made all *those* answers work.

Maybe it was time to try.

I picked up one of the chocolate fortune cookies. Aloud, I asked it, "So, who am I?"

I cracked it open and read:

Serena Johanna Somers.

Underneath, in smaller print, was the legend: *Sometime baby-sitter to a family of truthsayers on a world named earth; reluctant participant in the great war between the Darklings; in another universe, common-law-wife to the president of a nonexistent country; in various other universes, the object of sexual harassment from this same president, although he is only a congressman and never a serious candidate for the highest office in the land; fat pig.*

"That's ridiculous," I said. "I can't have been all those things; some of them actually preclude one another."

Even smaller print:

This isn't Schrödinger's cat; just because you've cracked open the cookie doesn't mean that all the answers but one are now untrue. Contrariwise, the act of the cracking the cookie does determine whether the question gets answered at all.

This was absurd. It occurred to me that it was one of those situations where the harder you look, the more obscure becomes the answer. I decided I would just glance quickly at what was on the next cookie, then look away before my perceptions became dimmed with fine print.

I asked aloud: "Is Joshua still alive?"

IN YOUR HEART.

Did this mean he was actually dead? I *had* to read the small print after all. I peered at the slip of pink paper. The small print was beginning to swim into view now. It was sort of wavery, oscillating small print, small print that didn't want to keep saying the same thing.

—*if you build him, he will come*—

But Josh was not a baseball stadium . . . was he?

—*hear the heartbeat of the universe*—

Some kind of New Age lesson to be learned here. If Josh was alive because he lived inside me somehow, was that the only reason Katastrofa was still alive—because we had fought, because we had wounded each other—because a piece of her was indelibly graved beneath my skin?

I had to ask another question.

"How," I said, "are we all going to get home?" knowing that *home* is a relative concept, because every place we had been to on our odyssey had been home to at least one Serena Somers, just not the Serena Somers I felt I really was.

The paper in the fortune cookie was empty.

"What was *that* all about?" I asked the next cookie.

—*you can write your own ticket*—

said the next cookie, before dissolving into a blur of gibberish.

I looked at the blank cookie slip from the cookie before. There was a pile of cracked cookies on the floor where I was kneeling, and the odor of chocolate was starting to get to me. They say chocolate contains an addictive chemical that makes you feel loved, and it sure was working on me. It was as seductive as the phantom lover of my teenage years. Well, I *was* a teenager again, I guess.

—*if you build him, he will come*—

Right. Build him out of what? When I looked down at the plate of fortune cookies, however, I suddenly saw that, in removing the cookies I had removed, I'd destroyed the yin-yang pattern; and what was left was the shape of a fierce, coiled dragon; and then I saw the crumbs all around me on the floor, and I wondered if they could be molded, voodoo-style, into a little Joshua. . . .

BOOK TWO

EXPOSITION: SECOND SUBJECT

THE DARKLINGS

*"Her untitled mamafesta memorializing the
Mosthighest has gone by many names at
disjointed times . . . the proteiform graph itself
is a polyhedron of scripture."*

—*Finnegans Wake*

ON TRUTH

BY PHILIP ETCHISON

My writing block, it seems, is permanent. As a result, I find my annual address from the poetry chair of this august institution to be more and more of a joke, year after year. What can one talk about, when one has been struck dumb? What eternal verities may I discourse on? Do I have a right to discourse at all?

I have decided to venture into the treacherous shoals of ontology . . . .

What is truth?

Last night, I came very close to an answer. You see, I was dining with the president . . . oh, I see you're laughing already. How could a third-rate holder of the poetry chair at a third-rate institution such as this even know the president? Well, what you've got to realize is that it was in an alternate reality. Well, what, you may ask, is an alternate reality? It's a place where truth is different. There are an infinite number of alternate realities. You remember Schrödinger's cat? But it's not just the cat, you see. Everything that is capable of being in that box *is;* possibility, therefore, is the unseen womb of truth.

The truth is in that wombbox. But which truth? *All* of them. Think of the truth as the slip of paper you find in a fortune cookie; what it means hangs on what you mean to ask.

—coffee-stained ms. found stuck in a shredder at Blair House, Washington, D.C., along with a prescription for Prozac. Believed to be in the handwriting of Philip Etchison. (Analysis available for viewing one week before the auction, 9 a.m. through 4:30 p.m.)

—offered by an Anonymous Source.

—reserve $10

CHAPTER FIVE

A BAD HAIR DAY IN HELL

<u>T h e o   E t c h i s o n</u>

It was the 90s, the time before the mad millennium. But all the money in the world couldn't buy a Coke and a candy bar. . . .

Today's a bad hair day for the mad king. He staggers up and down in the snow, that mane of his flying every which way. Okay, you see the sorcerer king dude in a movie, his hair's always all cool, with the wind whipping it, and you flick your head one way and your hair all streams the other way, together as shit, and it should with all the fucking hairspray they use, but here in the hell world of ice and snow there's no hairspray.

King Strang shambles through the slush. Here and there his hair stands on end like he's been electrocuted. Other places it's all flat, and then it's wavy, too, and bald in patches.

I stand and watch.

"Am I mad?" the mad king screams.

We're at the edge of the River, but the River's impassable. It's a river with icebergs and dead fish. We've been camped here for a while, I don't know how long, maybe a whole year. I don't really know because time seems to be standing still. I haven't aged. Every day's the same. I don't mean that we're repeating the same day over and over, but it does feel that way sometimes.

"Tell me, boy! Am I mad?" says the king again. The wounds on his forehead are festering. He waves the scepter at me.

"I'm your truthsayer," I tell him. "You know you don't want to hear the answer to that question, because you know it'll be the truth, and the truth could kill you."

"What are we doing here? Why are we still trying to get back on the River?"

"We're going to the source," I say.

"What for?"

"So you can start over," I say.

"Well, let's get on with it."

It's started to snow again. The sky is completely black. I don't think this world *has* sunlight; if it does, I've never seen it. I think of this as hell because it's a place that doesn't know the meaning of warmth, of love; because I feel so totally cut off that I want to just fucking die. But then again, I am dead, I remind myself. Dead to all the people who really matter to me. In fact, for them, I've never even really existed.

We have a little raft that's mostly made of ice and a few planks here and there, and right now it sits jammed against the bank of the River, jutting into the snowbank. It's a pretty raft. It has a prow that's sculpted into the image of a woman, a naked woman with arms outstretched and her lips slightly parted as though to say she loves me. I made that sculpture myself; in the weeks upon weeks that we've been here, unable to go anywhere, I've just been chiseling away at that chunk of ice with a little Swiss Army knife that I picked up in some other universe long ago and far away.

The mad king rants again, and I go back to work on the sculpture. I'm working on her eyes now. I carve and carve the cold ice and still her eyes are blind. Why can't I go back to her? I know the answer to that, of course. It's the original sin thing. It's a great mystery, what me and my mom did together; we danced the universe back from the brink of chaos; but the universe is still teetering. You know how it is. *The darkness comprehendeth it not.* I am a truthsayer who is losing my power, and my mother is a goddess who has lost hers, and the king is mad.

"Still carving?" says the king. I turn to look at him. His eyes are wild. "I'll make breakfast," he says, and clambers over jagged ice to retrieve two frozen fish. Back on the riverbank, he takes his scepter and bangs it on the snow a couple of times, and blue fire spurts up from the ground; he stabs the two fish with the butt end of the scepter and, grasping the great jewel in both hands, waves the whole shish kebab over the flames. This is how we eat here in hell. "Hungry?" he says.

"Yeah, dude," I say. I leave my carving for a while and chow down. The fish is bitter. I don't bother to skin it, I just sort of gnaw at it and pull out the bones.

"How much longer until you find the way?" says the king.

I pull the cosmos-marble out of the pocket of my jeans. Squint, hold it up to one eye. In the old days I could just reach inside it with my mind and I'd unravel all the strands of the River in my head, but now the crystal ball has become murky. I still don't see where we are exactly. I only know we have to struggle on, battle the current, track our destinies to their source, or else I'll never be able to go home. Jesus, home: what a concept. Just to be able to go to the mall. Just to be able to wolf down a

Big Mac. I stare into the marble some more. There's a million strands down there, and they twist and wriggle and I can't seem to be able to grab one loose end so I can start the untangling.

"What kind of a truthsayer are you?" says the mad king.

"I'm not that good anymore," I say. His hair really is exceptionally messy today. You could build a cuckoo's nest in it and you'd never notice. "But you know, there should be a new truthsayer coming soon."

"How do you know?"

"I made him to take my place." I start to think about original sin again. It haunts me. I've had sex with mom. Oh, I know, we were gods at the time, all gods commit incest, I mean, when you're at the top of the food chain who else is there to fuck, right, but now it makes me feel like shit. Okay, so it had to happen. Joshua was dead, totally fucking dead. But I could bring him back if only I would give up the thing that made me the perfect truthsayer—my purity.

I can lie now. I've practiced on the mad king. Oh, little things like, "I feel fine," or "It's a nice day." Everyone says these things all the time. They're kind of these little pinprick untruths that shore up the house of cards that is all that humans have for security. I couldn't say those things before, but now I'm starting to.

"Who is he, this new truthsayer? We'd better find him, or we'll never get anywhere."

I put the marble away. The only alternative is to sort of slog away at the ice itself, hack at it with icepicks until it gives and we can go on. What use is a map if you can't read it?

I don't want to tell him who the new truthsayer is . . . I guess I just don't want to admit the truth, that I've created someone better than myself, something that has to take my place . . . who's going to be the one to stand at the edge of the precipice at the end of the story . . . I don't want to admit that I can't see it all, can't see the clear white line all the way from the beginning of the world until its end . . . not like before. So I don't tell Strang the truth. And even my not telling him, which isn't an outright lie, only an evasion, chips away at who I was, and pushes me a little more toward who I will become . . . draws me astray.

So here I am in front of the boat of ice with a fish head in my hand, staring at a blind statue of my mother, the goddess of the cosmos; and the fish head's blind because it's dead, and I'm blind because I threw away my sight to save the world, and I get to thinking, all three of us don't have to be.

And this little scene springs to my mind from back in the real world (which real world? I mean world one, the world we started off in) and—

⌐

—we're in Virginia, see, and it's before Mom was diagnosed with the cancer so I guess I'm just little, it's even before the 90s, cause I'm eating out of my *Return of the Jedi* plastic plate. And we're having fish, and I'm playing with my food.

"Finish it up," Dad says, "because your mother has made this cake, you see, and it's crammed with chocolate and cherries and cream, and we're all salivating for dessert but we can't do anything because you're not finishing the entrée."

So I'm all, "Dad, I hate mackerel. I can't stand looking into its eyes."

So Dad says: "There's a lesson to be learned from that, my son," and he goes into his PBS Joseph Campbell lecturing mode, and he says (meanwhile, Joshua has slipped away to call Serena, who secretly loves him but he has no idea about that and only I do because it's a time when I still see the truth) "a fish, you see, being the ancient symbol of the Christian faith; but of course it goes back much further than that. It's also the sacred penis of Osiris. You may recall that, in Egyptian mythology, mean old Set cut the god Osiris into thirteen pieces and threw him into the Nile; and Isis wept for, what was it, three days and nights? or was it forty? are we confusing mythologies here? and she never found the last piece, but she brought him back to life anyway, and that's why people used to eat fish on Fridays: not just in memory of Jesus' death, but also because the penis is the fish, the male element of the yin-yang creative power that is the river of life. . . ."

"You're saying that I don't want to eat this fish because I have a subconscious fear of eating dick."

Dad smiles a little.

"Well, bullshit," I say. "I'm not afraid of anything." And I start devouring the animal with gusto. Except for the head. "Okay, I *am* afraid of the eyes. They're like, watching me."

"A very Neolithic way to behave," Dad says. "Treating the dead as living, I mean. Everything having its own resident spirit. Animism. Very potent. Very profound."

"Oh, Phil," Mom says, "do you have to intellectualize quite that much? Maybe he just doesn't like to stare at fish eyes. . . ."

"Windows of the soul, huh," I say.

"If thine eye offend thee, pluck it out," says Dad.

"The Bible?" Mom says.

"Actually no," he says, "it's from this great Roger Corman movie, *The*

Man with the X-Ray Eyes. Saw it when I was young. It's a movie about someone who can see through *everything* . . . he can see all the way into the mind of God . . . and finally it drives him crazy and he . . . rips out his own eyeballs." Odd movie for him to talk about in a way, I mean, we're a PBS *Janus Collection* family, we spend more time looking at *Alexander Nevsky* than at Freddie Krueger's latest exploits. It must be one of Dad's secret vices. I store away the info.

I stare into the eyes . . . into the eyes . . .

. . . and finally I do pluck them out, one by one, like in the Tom Lehrer song about Oedipus, using the left edge tine of the salad fork, and I keep staring at them all through the Black Forest cake, and you know, in time, they do seem to stare back after all, there does seem to be a flash of life in them . . . .

5.

While I'm remembering that little scene I'm still scraping away at the ice on the statue's face. On a whim, I pry out the fish eyes and pop them in those icy sockets.

Now she almost looks human.

I put my arms around her, woman of ice.

Wait. I think she's coming to life.

I think she's moving. Breathing. I think, I think . . . a veil of mist that's come between us that's maybe like her breath, all hanging in the air, mingling with my own. Fucking Jesus don't play tricks on me, I think.

At that moment I hear Strang yelling.

I turn around.

He's standing on like this big old white crag. He too is craggy, and his hair's all standing straight up like he's got his fist up a light socket. And he's screaming: "The music, the music, the music—!" at the top of his lungs and for a moment I hear another fragment of my sundered childhood—

—*turn off the fucking stereo I'm trying to write poetry*—

"Turn it off, turn it off," the king screams, with his hands over his ears. I listen. At first I don't hear anything at all. But then, there does come a sound, at last—

It's kind of a flute sound but really sweet, really high. The melody seems to be part of the whining of the wind until you really listen hard, and then you can make out a kind of melody. Not a simple tune, but one that undulates and twists in on itself, a tune like a tangle of knitting; it reminds me of the millions of lightstrands inside the little marble that's supposed to show me where I'm supposed to go.

As I listen I realize that there's an absolute truth in this music. Now there's a weird concept. But only someone who has truthsaying in his genes can maybe feel it this way, in his bones. There's a chill that doesn't come from the snow, the knowledge that here's a truth truer than I ever saw. Why? Because no matter what I see, I still have to filter it through language, and language is distortion; it's a lens that changes reality.

This is a scary thing.

"The new truthsayer is coming," I say softly.

The king screams: "No, no, no, turn off the music!" and I see why: the music is showing him things about himself he never knew, never wanted to know; the music is pushing him closer to falling into the abyss.

I can't explain what's going through me. I mean, this is what I made, the savior of the world, the fruit of my sacrifice, and now he's coming down the pike to fulfill everything and set us all free, right? Then why does it piss me off so much? Is it because like, *I'm* not the fucking kwisatz haderach after all? Is it because I was better than everyone once, could see further, deeper, and now I've discovered I've only been a one-eyed man in the country of the blind, and here comes old two-eyes, my son, my Frankenstein's monster? The music is really getting to me, each shrill note jabbing into me like a lancet. Fucking Jesus. I'm scared. Really scared. "I think I want my mother," I say softly.

And that's when I feel the hand on my shoulder.

A soft hand, warm, womanly; the first warm thing I've ever encountered on this whole fucking planet. "Mom—" I start to say, and turn to see the ice-sculpture unhitching itself from the prow of our ice-raft, spreading out her arms, slowly, and begin to cry from those fish-eyes, and the tears are melting her cheeks, rilling down the crags of ice we've foundered against, and yeah, she's crying me a river, dissolving herself in the process of it—

"Don't leave me!" I cry out.

"I'm not leaving you," she whispers. "I'll see you at the end of your journey."

"Why can't you stay? You're still my mother, aren't you? Even though we—"

"But I'm also the fish-eyed goddess. The River needs the male as well as the female in order to flow. Salmon swim a thousand miles upstream to spawn. You did well, Theo."

"Then why am I so confused? Why can't I see the way ahead any-more?"

"Maybe the way to understand ordinary people is to become more like them," she says.

"Mom!"

But she's already dissipating into the mist, and then I hear her voice again: *Theo Theo Theo* in the wail of the distant flute, and I see her sort of wafting away from me, liquefying the ice as she flutters upriver. So I'm all, "Mom, mom, mom," but she doesn't turn back.

The River is melting like crazy now. Ice boulders are smashing together and grinding and squeaking against each other and disintegrating. I start to untie the raft but the raft too is melting, melting. King Strang still stands on the ledge of ice, railing at the empty sky. He howls, he shrieks. "Come on," I shout, and then I stride up the bank toward him and start to tug at his sleeve.

"Whither?" he cries out. "What am I? Where am I going?"

"The River is thawing out," I say, "and it's time to move on."

"Thawing? thawing? what river?"

Even the gods have Alzheimer's! "The source. The beginning. The end." The River is roaring now, and the sound of shattering icebergs is like a hundred-car pileup on the Beltway. And above it all comes the fluting. He's near, he really is. All that's left of the raft is a couple of pieces of driftwood; the rest was all ice. My mother, a translucent goddess, is all dancing on the water in the distance. Maybe there's even sunlight there, at the horizon where the river seems to lead.

"I don't know how to get there," I say, "but I am your truthsayer, King Strang, and I have to lead you. Now move your ass or we'll drown." I pull the king off his slope (he's frail now, easy to pull) and then I sort of half carry, half drag him to the water's edge. I step into the water and so does the king, and the shards of the raft sort of drift our way and we are able to clamber on top. And look, there's more wood now, blackened planks that have been buried beneath the ice, and they're all bobbing up and down around us, there's even rope to last them together with . . .

"We're finally on our way," I say.

The king sits down, sort of squats, by the edge of the raft. "I think I remember now. I had three children once. I divided my kingdom up according to who loved me the most. The one who told the truth I exiled from my sight."

That's pretty much *King Lear,* but it's close enough to the truth. "Thorn and Katastrofa are dead," I say, "fighting over the pieces of your kingdom. The River flows through a million universes, but the gates are shutting off, one by one, because your kingdom's falling apart, because of your own foolishness."

"Foolishness! How dare you! Guards!" He reaches over to slap me.

"You have a third child," I say. "Where is Ash?"

"Don't speak to me of him. What I've spoken, I've spoken. I'm a king, and that's how a king should be."

I don't speak. It'll take a while to lead him to the truth, especially since I'm grasping it less and less myself these days. And now that we're moving again, I also have to paddle, which I do with a sort of oar that seems to have drifted alongside us; the king uses his scepter, which gives off sparks whenever it touches the water; the scepter is death and the water is life, you see. . . .

There's a bend in the River, and suddenly there's a whole new vista. That happens a lot when you travel along the River; you switch from world to world in a split second, and here's a world that I know too well. Shit it scares me.

See, the River broadens out, and the waters become a little less turbulent, and the snow thins out a little, and then there's like these old Easter Island heads looming out of the water, and sphinxes, and pyramids, and even the top of the Empire State Building. And in the distance, by the bank, there's a tall black cliff, and perched on the cliff like a tarantula is a castle I know well: Thornstone Slaught.

Nothing to fear, I tell myself. Thorn is dead, and the castle is probably abandoned. Or maybe it's full of squatters. Those miserable subjects of Thorn's, from whom he used to drink blood.

"You know this place?" I say to the king.

"No," he says. He looks shiftily from side to side.

I know that he does, though, somewhere inside that festering brain of his; I know there's something in the castle he's going to have to confront, which is why we have to go through it on our way to the source of the River; thing is, I'm no longer navigating.

The music of truth is in the air.

Someone else has taken over the job of guiding us all upriver. I have to trust him. I have to believe that he's going to lead us all through all the right tribulations and through to the healing of the world; if I didn't believe that, I might as well give the fuck up.

And yet I have to admit I'm angry about it.

Why isn't it me?

I never wanted to be the messiah before, but now that I'm not, why I am full of such rage and envy?

Can't think about it now. Mermaids are swimming up to us. They're stretching out their arms and throwing flower-wreaths at us. The flowers are long dead, rotting, but they are probably all they have. They are shouting at us: "Save us, save us, save us," and the king is staring at the castle, which we're approaching rapidly, his eyes filled with loathing and longing.

CHAPTER SIX

CHRISTMAS IN THE WHITE HOUSE

Phil Etchison

We hadn't gone that far when it all changed. I should have known it would, but I didn't expect it quite so soon. All we did, it seemed, was to round a corner, trudge across a narrow ledge athwart a precarious precipice that felt like it was going to collapse at any moment; and then, by that familiar old Joycean "commodius vicus of recirculation" I suppose it was, we found ourselves face to face again with the icy statue that was my wife; only, while Chris twirled the magic flute and the notes flew twittering about our heads, so sharp and fluttery you could see their feathers before they soared, swooped, scattered into the flurrying snow, the statue wept, and I could not console my wife, because I was merely flesh and blood.

"Where are we?" I asked Corvus. I knew Chris wasn't going to tell me anything. "Did we just circle back to the crossroads one more time, and we've really gone nowhere?"

"Maybe," said Milt.

"Maybe? What kind of an answer is that?"

"Living in the white man's world," he said, "sometimes the forked tongue thing does come rather glibly to one's lips. Sorry. I'll think of a good answer in a moment."

As I waited for a good answer—and I knew that with Milt, a good answer could be a long time coming, because he'd have to consider and ponder the eternal verities for a while first—I saw that behind my wife there was a blizzard—well, just a sort of sheet of whiteness that hung oppressively like a Shakespearean arras—but I could make out dim shapes. Perhaps a castle. Yes, that was it. A gray, twisted silhouette, a sort of bulimic parody of Castle Dracula. Heard thunder too, though maybe it was just the percussive accompaniment to Chris' music.

"What I mean to say," said Milt, "is that you don't step in the same river twice."

"Is that all you can come up with?"

"Seriously, this may or may not be the same crossroads, Phil, but you are definitely not the same person. For one thing, you know who you are now."

"I do?"

I had to think about that for a long time. My name was Philip Etchison. I held the poetry chair at a modest university in Northern Virginia, and I was the author of a number of books of poetry, undistinguished in sales figures, undistinguished, also, perhaps, in quality, though this was not something I much liked to reflect upon. . . .

"How many children do you have, Phil? Quick now! Say the first thing that comes into your head."

"Two. No, what am I saying, one, one!"

"Right the first time. Names?"

"Josh and Theo."

"Why does your woman weep?"

"She is dying of cancer."

Was I making all this up? No. I *knew* these implausible nuggets to be the simple truth. How could that be?

"Do you know the name of that castle?" Milt said. His eyes glowed. *Children of the Damned,* I thought, suddenly remembering some old movie. What was a movie now? Never mind. It would come back to me.

"Thornstone Slaught," I said, mouthing the mouthful as though it were a household word. And suddenly, it was.

"Good," he said softly. "Let's go."

A limousine pulled up. All of a sudden, Milt Stone was the uniformed and white-gloved driver. We piled in—Chris, in his favorite blue silk tuxedo, the one he'd appeared on *Oprah* in—my wife still a creature of ice and marble, and I in the secondhand dinner jacket I had worn to give my half-assed speech about ontology to the college—and we sat down, and the invitation from President Karpovsky was suddenly in my hand, on the ivory linen stationery, in the Basildon Bond envelope.

"My name is Philip Etchison," I said softly. "I am a second-rate poet with powerful friends. I have two sons."

Chris turned to me. He put his flute back in his pocket. He put his arms around me. His cheek touched my cheek. Close-lipped, he hummed a single high-pitched note, and all at once I felt coldness and loss. He can transmit emotions this way, just by the sheer vibrations. In a way it's so much more profound than speech, yet how can I respond, I whose whole life has been the manipulation of words, those airy packets of compacted meaning? I'm like a man blind from birth, trying to gaze up at the Sistine Chapel ceiling, intuiting awe from the reverberant hush of the sighted.

"Yes," he's telling me, I think, "you have two sons, and one of them isn't me, and it hurts me even more than it hurts you."

We drove on. The Potomac was unusually icy; Washington usually only has a few days of bitter snow; winter is ambiguous here. People were actually skating, but here and there strange shapes peered up from the ice floes: I thought I saw one of those Easter Island heads . . . here a great stone Anubis, baying the invisible moon with a soundless howling. . . .

We crossed the Fourteenth Street Bridge, made a left and eased our way over to Sixteenth and Pennsylvania. The gates of Thornstone Slaught were also the gates of the White House. A marine saluted us and the iron portals swung open. Another marine ushered us into a foyer; another into a corridor; another into an elegant antechamber; everywhere we went, the walls were lined with living hands, clutching torches, buried wrist-deep in the concrete, swaying back and forth in time with a melody that seemed to issue from Chris' lips.

I said to Mary: "I feel a strange kind of *déjà vu*."

She didn't speak; she was still a statue, her arms outstretched, standing on a golden dolly wheeled along by oiled and kilted Nubian slaves, and fanned by a child of indeterminate gender, nude but for a peacock feather strapped over its genitalia.

Indeed, I had done all this before, but it was somehow not the same. The corridors had not seemed to lead ever downward before, and the walls were not quite so echoey . . . or were they? Certainly the limestone facings, with their phosphorescent specks, seemed familiar . . . the stalactites and stalagmites . . . the ever-dripping sound of water . . . drip, drip, drip, drip, drip. The little shrines set into the walls, the wailing women with joss-sticks clasped to their bosoms, the statuettes of gods with many heads and animal faces . . . all these things seemed more and more familiar even though I knew I had never encountered them quite in this combination before.

Finally, we were in the dining room, and there was President Oren Karpovsky. "Ah," he said, "you're here. I did so want to listen to your son's celebrated music of madness. Is it true that you can experience more layers of truth by hearing his music even than by shrooming or peyote?"

"Just the sort of thing an ex-hippie president is expected to say," I said, "this close to the end of the mad millennium."

"Exactly." He smiled, and Milt Stone came into the room. He was a homeless Indian in shabby clothes, but I knew that underneath the filthy clothes and rancid body odor was a powerful shaman.

"Where's Serena?" I asked the president.

"Uh, I don't know. Changing, perhaps. Women. You know. Your wife, on the other hand—"

"She's already changed," I said, "beyond recognition, even."

What was happening between us, here in this room that was clearly not really this room at all, but a twisted simulacrum of another room in another universe? Sure, we were standing around making small talk, but the conversation wasn't quite connecting—it was a sort of a simulacrum of a conversation, if you know what I mean. Hot air, vowels, consonants, lexemes, phonemes, fragments of meaning being shuttlecocked back and forth, feeding the illusion of communication, but in reality. . . .

We sat down at the dinner table.

"I'm afraid that this is going to be a rather frugal Christmas dinner after all," said Oren. "I couldn't bear to keep the staff away from their families this evening . . . the marines are another matter, of course, being marines . . . so I've sent out for Chinese."

Chinese!

We were, indeed, recycling crazily back to the beginning of our story. Because I knew more and more of what was going on. I knew that I had two sons. Chris, the apple of my eye, wasn't my real son at all.

"It's a strange kind of a Chinese restaurant," said the president. "It's called the Blue Moon, and usually, when you call, the line's busy. It's a Brigadoon kind of a restaurant if you know what I mean; it only pops into existence now and then; otherwise it floats inside its own sort of reality. But the food—it's beyond belief."

"I think I've eaten there," I said slowly. "But it was in Arizona."

"Yeah, that was its last documented appearance; read about it in the *Enquirer*," said president Karpovsky, and it was at that point that a cadaverous Chinese maitre d' in Mandarin attire, followed by a bevy of pigtailed ladies in pink silk cheongsams, came gliding into the dining room carrying silver platters of wildly exotic foods.

"Mr. Huang, isn't it?" I said.

"We meet from time to time," said the Chinese gentleman, more an ethnic caricature than a real person. "Aren't you the Etchisons? What has happened to your good wife?"

"Apotheosis," I said.

"And your sons. Dead, are they not?"

"I"

"Cornelius Huang, at your service," he said, bowing low. "We always seem to meet at times like this—at the beginnings of apocalyptic journeys."

"This *isn't* the beginning of a journey," I protested. "Actually I seem to have been traveling for far too long already . . . I'm trying to yank the emergency cord, stop the train, damn the penalty for improper use, but I can't find it anywhere, and the scenery's starting to repeat itself—"

"We'd better start eating," said President Karpovsky, "or we'll never get to the fortune cookies."

Platter after platter was being uncovered. "Here," said Cornelius Huang, "is a very fine sea-turtle soup. The turtle has been marinated in crocodile's tears for a hundred years, then braised in a bouillon-based herb medley for two hours before finally having its unfortunate throat slit."

"Great," I said listlessly. Chris was already attacking the soup. "Manners, Chris," I said, but he only looked at his statuesque mother with doleful, welling eyes.

"Here's a particularly fine dish," said Cornelius Huang, gesticulating with one arm (the other clenched an impressive-looking horn tight between armpit and elbow) at a trolley that was being wheeled in by an entire bevy of cheongsamed beauties. As they raised the cover, he said, "It's the head of John the Baptist, basted in a lubricious Salome dressing."

The contents of the platter resembled the celebrated painting by Caravaggio.

"Our lobster diablo," said Huang, and another dish showed a giant crustacean—something out of Captain Nemo, perhaps—writhing in agony as the flames of hell seethed about him. The odor of brimstone filled the dining room. "Better shut that fast," Huang said, and, bowing, the oriental ladies slammed down the lid. This was no ordinary takeout service, but a meal of allegorical pretensions, a Dantean odyssey of a meal, and now I was beginning to remember that other meal much more vividly, the meal in Arizona where all hell broke loose for the first time.

I turned to Milt.

"Should I eat?" I said.

"Depends," he said.

Chris lifted up a shushing hand and sang one note. Oren looked very uncomfortable. He started ladling food onto my plate. Chris kept singing the note, over and over in an ear-splitting ostinato, and that made the president get ever more frantic and talk faster and faster.

"You'd better eat," said President Karpovsky. "You don't know where your next meal is coming from. You don't even know where *you're* coming from. In fact, you don't even know—"

The president exploded.

Literally. I mean, it was the whole alien-pops-out-of-stomach thing, only the alien was as big as he was, and it sort of tipped him apart in a shower of blood and innards. What suddenly stood in his place was someone else altogether. Tall. Pale-skinned, and swathed in a sweeping black cloak that sort of fluttered (there was no wind) and gave off simmering, seething sounds; a creature with ruby-citrine eyes and thin, bloodless lips; a man with fangs, more handsome than Dracula, more frightening than Death.

"Master! You made it through!" said Cornelius, and prostrated himself.

"It was pretty simple," said Thorn—for that was who it was. I recognized him right away, and another piece of my jigsaw past settled into place. "Mr. Karpovsky was not exactly one of your more strong-willed psyches. After all, he got to be president by playing up the wishy-washy factor—no one really wanted to *do* anything on the eve of the Mad Millennium."

"How do you know so much about Washington politics? You're not even a human being," I said.

"True," Thorn said, "but I've been stuck inside one, trying to get out, for several days."

"What's more," I said, "you're dead, supposedly."

"Love never dies," said Thorn, "and the same might be said of hate, which, as you poets are always fond of saying, is but the reverse side of the coin."

It was hard for me to answer, soaked as I was with the president's blood, standing as I was in a room that was growing steadily gloomier and more musty. The wallpaper was peeling off the walls and behind it was the pitted stone of a medieval castle. The chandeliers had gone from crystal to smoky candlelight. Shadows danced, leaped, rippled. Thorn spread his cloak wide open.

"I've gotta have blood," he said.

The platters full of food were no longer even pretending to be Chinese. Each one held a young human being, folded, trussed up, arms and legs broken in order to be squashed into the space of a serving dish, and very much alive. Some moaned; most looked ahead with that lifeless, listless gaze that characterizes the irredeemably condemned; they had the Auschwitz stare. Thorn wandered among the platters—there were dozens more in the shadows, and the cheongsam-clad waitresses were now a ghoulish army of the grave, their flesh rotting from their bones— and now and then he stooped to sample a few drops of blood. "Gotta savor it," he said. "It's been too long."

Too long, too long.

When would I stand beside the river once again and greet my two sons, my two *real* sons, beneath the cottonwoods in the Virginia sunset?

I ached for a world that no longer was save in a few lines of poetry in my mind. How can you yearn for what doesn't exist, has never existed? This place was reality.

"I want—" I began. I felt Milt's hand on my shoulder.

"Patience," he said softly. "Before salvation comes the harrowing of hell."

Thorn laughed. "That's what you think," he said, "but the longer you harrow, the deeper you'll burrow; the more you sound, the less you'll breach; the spiral downward is a Möbius strip; there is no surface; to paraphrase Monty Python, your very existence is a dead parrot."

At this point, Milt Stone cast off the *End of the World* placard from around his neck, leaped up onto the dining-room table, and began to dance up a storm.

Chris laughed: a silvery, bright laugh, the only thing of light in the whole benighted castle.

"Catch!" Milt shouted, and plucked a drum out of the air. Chris caught it one-handed, and began pounding away with the mouthpiece end of the magic flute. Each drumbeat sent a bolt of light across the chamber. There were ankle bells on Milt's naked feet, and each jingle was another puddle of light, and Chris kept laughing until his very laughter became a song.

"Dancing'll do you no good, chief," said Thorn. "You people always think that if only you get the right moves, the old palefaces will go back across the sea and leave you to your buffalo hunting. You were wrong then and you're wrong now."

But Milt didn't stop dancing. Once again I was on the sidelines while the forces of light and dark were locked in some cosmic battle. I looked at my wife. Perhaps she looked at me; I could not tell. I looked at Cornelius Huang, who attempted now and then to fend off the blasts of light with blasts of his trumpet. Occasionally, he would hit one, and the lightbeam would shatter and scatter. From around us, out of the walls themselves, there issued another kind of music: clanking, industrial, electronic cacophonies that seemed to challenge the music of voice and drum. Dueling banjos of a sort—a David and Goliath sort, I thought in despair. "Mary, Mary, do something," I said, but I knew she could not intervene; the sickness in her soul was the sickness of the world; to cure one we would have to cure the other.

Milt danced. His body seemed to become more curvy, more ambiguous; sometimes he seemed to have a dozen arms and legs. Light darted from the drum, ran rings about his features. The vampire stood and waved his arms about and laughed, and Chris too laughed, the evil-villain laugh versus the pure-child laugh; and Huang trumpeted about while the silk-clad zombie Huangettes pom-pomed in the background.

And me? The spectacle was so confusing that I simply started to tune it out—like a hundred MTV videos crammed into one minute—image after image and nothing to cling to—and so I reached out for something else, something solid, something I could truly believe in—

And I saw Theo.

Running toward me across a plain of ice that stretched for all infinity . . . a small boy in shorts and grunge T-shirt, hastening toward me, his father, his truth . . . "Forgive me!" I cried out. "I didn't know what I was doing."

At this moment of supreme, grotesque despair, the walls in the dining room began to crack, and there was an intense, blue, blinding radiance pouring into the darkness. Someone was coming—crashing through the stone. A woman—Serena Somers. The warring music ceased abruptly.

"Sorry I'm late," she said.

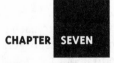

CHAPTER SEVEN

ATTACK OF THE 50 FOOT WOMAN

S e r e n a   S o m e r s

Well like, I wanted to wait to see if I could conjure up Joshua, but all of a sudden, I felt this irresistible force pulling me away, somehow, somewhere . . . I was being summoned by some mighty power. I gathered up the cookie crumbs into a napkin, folded it up carefully, stuck it in a pocket, and then I allowed myself to be caught up in what seemed to be a giant tornado or whirlwind—thank you, Dorothy—that was sweeping me somewhere, somehow. I was much bigger than myself, and I was smashing through the wall of my imprisonment, and it turned out I wasn't as far away from Oren and the others as I thought at all, because there I was, in the middle of the Christmas party that started this whole thing off, and my live-in lover was exploding in a mass of gore and tissue . . . sort of a *Texas Chainsaw Massacre* kind of thing, I mean, gross.

Mr. E. was there. Milton was there. Chris was there. The shaman and the truthsayer were cooking up a crazy kind of music, howling, jangling, banging, whistling. Everyone looked up at me. I guess I must have looked a little different than my usual self.

"Sorry I'm late," I said. At the sound of my voice, a chandelier cracked and smashed down on the roast turkey.

"Greetings, sis," said the vampire prince who seemed to have pieces of my live-in lover's skin hanging from his clothes. "Glad you could make the party."

"I'm not your sister," I said.

"Sure you are," he said. "You've come back to me. We won't fight one another anymore—learned that lesson pretty damn thoroughly. We need to stick together, or we'll never be able to get our pieces of the pie."

"I haven't come back at all," I said, and then I felt the dragon stirring inside my stomach again.

Yes I have, said the voice of the other woman inside me.

"Oh, come on, sis," said Thorn. "Crack open the egg, break free of that confining human flesh. We've worlds to conquer and all that, and there's not much time, what with the structure of the universe collapsing all around us."

"True," I said.

The dragon woman was growing inside my belly. I knew that Oren had already gone through the alien-busting-out-of-the-stomach routine, and I wasn't anxious to be next. But Katastrofa was, I mean, seriously getting out of hand. She had gone from embryo to about ten months in the last five minutes, and my belly was swelling. Mary Etchison once told me about childbirth, gave me the whole shitting-a-watermelon metaphor, and it wasn't something I was anxious to try, especially if the baby was a baby dragon and perfectly happy to rip me apart to get out.

I looked around anxiously. Mr. E. was staring at me with his mouth wide open, and I guess I realized something was amiss when my head collided with the ceiling. Bricks began to dislodge themselves.

"I feel like Alice in Wonderland," I said.

Thorn raised his arms, and his cloak flapped like the leathern wings of a giant bat . . . the wings of Satan himself. I could feel the dragon within me, and she was rumbling and shaking, and any minute now she was going to figure out how to breathe fire, and then where would I be? I couldn't allow myself to let her out.

"What's happening to you?" Mr. E. shouted, and his voice seemed curiously far away, but then of course he was way down there.

"I can't help myself," I shouted back. I didn't know my own decibel capacity, I guess, for another chandelier shattered and sprayed all the people down there with shards of glass. Mr. E. dodged, and Milt and Chris took shelter beneath a great big drum. Only Cornelius and Thorn were unfazed . . . and Mrs. E., of course, who was a statue in this universe. "There's a dragon inside me trying to bust loose. I can stay rigid, and explode, or I can go with the flow, try to stretch myself to contain her. . . ."

Suddenly I realized there was a *rightness* to what I was doing, just as Oren had done completely the wrong thing and had perished as a result, though of course perishing was not necessarily the final word around here. I had to make myself big enough to accommodate the dragon. There is a dragon inside every woman, and if she can't stretch her soul wide enough to contain it, it's going eat its way out and destroy her.

"I don't care how big Katastrofa gets," I screeched. "I'm just going to grow along with her. She's always going to be inside me, not me inside her."

But the voice inside me screamed, "Let me out, let me out, let me out," and then its rage seemed to subside and it whined, "Let me out, let me out," in the voice of a suffering, imprisoned child, and I was tempted.

Thorn flew at me. He darted at my stomach, fangs bared. I had long since outgrown my garments, so I guess I was pretty much naked at this point, except for a couple of denim patches over my pudenda . . . how strangely prudish the new me was . . . Thorn wrapped his arms around me and was trying to gnaw his way in.

I slapped him aside. Flung my arms about a couple more times, and sent more stones tumbling. A gargoyle plummeted from its perch. Tapestries ripped from the walls and caught fire on the candles.

Thorn rushed at me again. He careened through the air like an F-15. I dodged. He circled. I swatted him. I was getting bigger now, and the dragon inside me was calling to him. I had to grow some more. I broke through a few more floors. The castle was becoming an encumbrance. I started to kick and pound. It began to fall apart. House of cards, really; just needed the right kind of blows to like, self-destruct, virtually.

He charged again, this time swooping at me from a great height, funneling through the holes I had gouged out of the stone floors. I smashed more walls. Through the gaps in the ceilings, there was light now, lancet-like shafts of white light . . . cobwebs were catching fire. Stone was turning to brimstone. Flames were running up and down the corridors, and still Thorn kept attacking me, and I was aware of his minions all about him, too, an army of bats and zombies and creatures of the night . . . but they were no more threatening to me than a swarm of mosquitoes.

I tried a mighty kick. The foundations began to rumble. Well, actually, I think the whole mountain was shaking. I felt as powerful as a goddess. Shit, maybe I *was* a goddess in this world—if Mrs. E. was one, why not me? I started to really get into this.

Smash! A gargoyle-topped pillar snapped like a toothpick. Dust flying everywhere. More light now, riddling the smoky air, a forest of needles. I punched, I elbowed, I hula-hooped.

Thorn changed tactics. He and his minions started to grab at the Etchisons. I knew they weren't going to kill them because they were still needed in the final spectacle. Mr. E. was running around, trying to fend them off with a soup ladle. The bigger I got, the more comical these little humans seemed . . . no wonder God sees the world as a divine comedy . . . the world is so minuscule to him, I mean her, I mean, well, me, actually.

I decided to start doing a Godzilla kind of routine, so I began stomping in their direction. Each dinosaurian plod caused rock and tile to fly. I got down on my hands and knees and scooped up the Etchison family in the palm of my right hand, flicking off the bats and demons with the fingers of my left. And meanwhile, Mrs. E. sat at the edge of the table, now and then anointing the whole shebang with a tear or two, but otherwise quite, quite still.

I was woman. It was time for them to hear me roar, and I did so, a ten-ton torpedo of a bellow that got what remained of the castle shaking like a humungous tuning fork. Pretty damn awesome, I thought.

"It's okay, Mr. E.," I said. I held his hands over his ears. "Whoops," I whispered, "I forgot how huge I've become."

"You used to gain weight and lose it like a yo-yo," Mr. E. shouted, "but this takes the cake!"

Thorn was buzzing around my eyeball. I couldn't swat him that easily, so I tried to shake him by nodding furiously.

"I know you want out," he screamed at the dragon inside my belly.

I exhaled. A burst of blue flame exploded from my nostrils. I could smell singed hair. I've hated that smell ever since Lisa Peoples accidentally flicked her Bic beside my bangs in fourth grade. Thorn flew out of the way.

"As long as I keep her inside me," I cried, "your sis is on my team now, not on yours."

"I'll be back," Thorn shouted. But you know, there's nothing remotely Schwarzeneggeresque about a shout like that when it comes from a creature the size of a fruit fly.

Thorn and his troops swarmed about my head. They darted, they hovered, they swooped. They tried to sting me, but I hardly felt anything. Only once or twice, when a pinprick drew blood, did I feel that an opening had been made into my soul, an opening that the dragon might escape through if I wasn't careful. It was time for another shout.

"Hold your ears, dudes," I said to the Etchisons (and Milt, who was still dancing up a tempest on a little mound of flesh between my index and my middle fingers.) "I'm gonna sing."

And this time I really did. I mean, I took in lungfulls of flame-tinged air and expelled them in an eerie song. I could feel my diaphragm working like a bellows, could feel the dragon churning inside me, could feel the smoke and fire stream from my lips with every ear-splitting note.

I've done all this before, I thought. The Christmas dinner at the White House, the mysterious bursting into song . . . only the last time it happened it was only a foreshadowing of this . . . it's the same event again, only deeper, richer, more resonant . . . yeah, more resonant.

Then the awful thing happened. He and Cornelius Huang landed right on my hand, grabbed a hold of Chris, and started to yank him away. I couldn't shake them loose without dislodging Mr. and Mrs. E. as well. Thorn threw a dark cloak over Chris' head, and they took off. Dimly, I could hear Chris screaming.

The swarms of batlike creatures began to scatter. A mighty rumbling punctuated my valkyrie shrieks. Slabs of stone shattered to powder. Mr. E. was running around in circles on my hand, skittish as a hamster on a treadmill. I roared several more times for good measure, until we were standing in a pile of rubble, and the light of a pale blue star was playing over piles of rock, which stood in circles around us on the barren ground. With a single song, I had rearranged the dark into a dozen concentric stone circles. Now that's magic, I thought. But I had to go after Chris. I could see him still, his head peering from the cloak of darkness Thorn had thrown over him. The vampire's minions flew hither and thither, and I could hear thin mocking laughter in the wind.

"Chris!" Mr. E shouted. I could see them in the distance. I started to stampede through the mounds of stone, but I couldn't get a good footing. The swarm was gone. I was a failure as a goddess after all.

Chris looked back for a moment, then looked away. What was he hiding? He could not hide it for long, surely. He was a truthsayer. There was some truth he did not want to utter. It must hurt more deeply than any other truth he knew.

"Shit," I said. The dragon inside me was laughing, I was sure of it; I could feel the rumbling in my belly, the squirting plumes of flame.

"Do you think you could start shrinking?" Mr. E. shouted. "It's rather difficult to converse with you in your current, you know, state."

"I don't know how," I said.

"I've got just the thing," said Milt. He laid down his arm. "Can you hoist me up?" I did so, and he reached into a medicine pouch around his neck and pulled out a lump of something. I had to really peer to see it. It looked pretty grungy. Couldn't figure it out.

"What is it?" I almost forgot to whisper.

"Mushroom," said the *nadlé*. "It ought to work, if you know your *Alice in Wonderland.*"

Mr. E. came to the rescue. "One side will make you taller . . . the other will make you smaller. I think it was a caterpillar who said that, though he was somewhat opiumed out at the time." He was giggling uncontrollably.

"Is something wrong?" I said.

"Something wrong!" he said, flustered. "I'm stuck in someone else's dream, nothing is real, and a 50-foot woman is being hookahed up with shrooms by an apocalyptic Indian, and my son is not my son, and now he's been kidnapped by a damn vampire, and you want me to remain calm?"

I lifted my palm to my lips. I opened my mouth. I think my teeth must have unnerved Mr. E.—he was not the Fay Wray type—because he shrank back against the inside of my index finger.

"Pop it in," I said.

Milt Stone took a deep breath. There was no music in the air. Not even the sound of a breeze. It was the first still moment I had experienced since this adventure began. Milt concentrated hard, then—with the fluidity and follow-through of a major league pitcher—he projected the mushroom into my mouth.

I started shrinking. It happened so fast that Mr. E. and the gang almost didn't have time to get out of my hand. In a second we were standing at the center of the great stones, which towered over us, and Mr. E. was towering over me, which made me feel much safer.

"You were great," he said. "Just like Allison Hayes in that old movie."

"No I wasn't," I said. "I lost Chris, for God's sake! How can you say I was great?"

Softly, Milt said, "Do not be sorrowful, Serena. He's a truthsayer. He goes the way that he *must* go. That is his nature. He will come back to us in the end. Thorn needs him to get to the source of the River. Whatever he does, he won't harm him, or he will have lost the war."

Phil Etchison

The place was definitely akin to the blasted heath from *Macbeth.* Menhirs surrounded us, and here and there, strange, stunted trees pushed up out of the stony ground. The sun was not our sun, but a pallid blue.

My son was not my son, either. He was something quite other. Now that Chris had been spirited away on some ambiguous quest, I felt the way Joseph must have felt when his wife gave birth in a stable and all those kings and shepherds and angels showed up; I felt pretty damn useless, pretty much a token human amid the gods and goddesses and mythical beasts. They were all taking it pretty damn calmly, these people—a man-woman-shaman and a woman who was suddenly a teenage girl who was suddenly a goddess . . . not to mention my time-frozen wife. What could one say? What could one do?

"Are we nearly there yet?" I said to Milt, realizing as I spoke that I sounded just like a little kid on a long car trip, across the Arizona desert maybe, watching the miles of endless desert, losing all sense of time.

"Almost," he said, "almost."

"What has to happen," Serena said, "before we can all just be ourselves again, before we can go home?"

I had long despaired of finding home at all. When Serena said those words, I felt a surge of hope, but it was only for a few seconds.

Milt said, "It's all pretty simple. We have to restore the world to the way it was."

"How?" I said.

"We have to chase down and neutralize Thorn, or this Thorn-simulacrum which is just the shadow of Thorn already dead; for those who are really dead must be made to return to death; those who should really be alive must be brought back out of the land of shadow."

"And Theo," I said. "Theo . . . aren't we supposed to be looking for him? He's with this mad king, right? Going toward the source of the great River."

"He is already running toward you, but time moves at different paces in different parts of this continuum."

"And Josh?" said Serena. "Don't we have to bring Josh back too?"

Serena said, "Look here," and took a folded-up napkin out of her pocket. "I think Josh is in these fortune cookie crumbs. And I'm a goddess now, aren't I? Now that I have the dragon within me. I can blow myself up to the size of the Empire State Building, and shrink back to normal by gulping down a mushroom. You think I could breathe life into these crumbs?"

"I don't know," Milt said. "You want to try?"

Then he started gathering firewood. He piled it up in front of my wife the marble statue, and presently started a bonfire by rubbing two sticks together. There was an altarlike ledge at the center of the circles of stones, large enough for all of us to crowd on.

Meanwhile, Serena was spitting into her hand, shaping the crumbs into the crude likeness of a human being.

The sun was setting, and several moons were in the sky, crescents, half-moons, full moons; some were pock-marked, some striped, and others were bright and featureless.

Serena blew softly on her hand. Her breath was edged with dragonfire.

Nothing happened to the little cookie man, and after several more attempts she wrapped it up again and put it away.

"We're still missing something," she said sadly.

After a while, we all went to sleep in front of my wife, who watched over us with stony, moist eyes, her arms outstretched in benediction.

When we woke up, we were completely surrounded by water. Oh, the standing stones were still there, peering up from what seemed to be a crystal-clear lake; and we were still lying on the altar before the smoldering fire. In the distance, the Easter Island heads, pyramids, sphinxes, and other ancient artifacts still lay submerged, only more so. We had not moved, and yet, through the gateway of sleep, we had entered another world.

Things had been so much simpler when we were just one dysfunctional American family, driving through the Arizona desert toward a Laetrile clinic in Mexico, fighting, trying to make sense of our little lives. I wanted it back, I wanted it all back . . . even, God forbid, my wife's dying, that strange sick-sweet odor of the cancer that was eating her flesh. . . .

Serena and Milt were roasting fish over the fire. In the distance, I thought I saw something familiar. A glint on top of one of the standing stones that was now an island in the crystal lake. "Milt," I said, pointing, "isn't that . . . isn't it. . . ."

It did indeed appear to be a battered station wagon, the very same vehicle in which our journey had begun.

Milt smiled. "You see," he said, "the world is knitting itself back into shape, and though this is a dark moment, and there are fearsome battles ahead of us, you can see that the past is coming back, a piece at a time. Soon it will start to *flood* back, and you'll be amazed you ever forgot any of it."

I didn't care. I was stripping off my shirt. I knew I could swim out to the car if I picked the right stones to go island-hopping on. Then, of course, there was the question of driving in the middle of the lake. I'd cross that bridge later. That car, I recalled, had a tendency to sprout a few more gears than your usual PRNDLL. . . .

As long as there weren't any sharks . . . .

CHAPTER EIGHT

THE TRUTHSAYER SPEAKS

Chris Etchison

—and—
—father—
—and—
suddenly
suddenly I can speak
words come
the wind the words the darkness
rushing
"So!" The tall man, fire-eyes, coming to rest on the mountaintop, down looking, snow snow snow. "So, you can suddenly talk, Truthsayer."
—I—
—father—
Up looking: the sky, gray, many suns hidden. Around: the demon hordes. Bat wings, slitty eyes, eyes: citrine, coal, fire, smoke, hell. Wings flap, flap, flap, leather.

"And I know why you can talk. It's because I've set you free. Isn't that true, Cornelius?"

Across looking: the very tall mandarin, the golden trumpet: when he blasts the demon hordes fall on their faces in humblest obeisance, black leather in the snow, a sea of leather, clustering, eyes downcast. I have music too. But music is inside, won't come out, silenced, sullen.

"Indeed, my master," says the tall man.

—my father—

"He's not your father," says Thorn, "as you well know, Chris Etchison."

"You've caught the big one," says Cornelius Huang. "The truthsayer of truthsayers, the shall we say kwisatz haderach of our times; when comes such another?"

"Come, little one. You know I won't harm you."

Forward-moving: the rustle of prostrate leather.

"They think I'm dead," he says (and I gaze upward at his eyes and I *know,* he *is* dead, what is there is only a shadow's shadow) "but maybe I've only become stronger."

—not true, you are dead—

"Silence!" Kicks me in the shin, but—

—you said you weren't gonna hurt me—

"Right." Frowning. "Sorry."

—I want to go back to—

"You can't say it. Because you're a truthsayer. You can't say the word, because it isn't true."

—I already said it—

"But you weren't referring specifically to that one, the one who reared you, the one who isn't your father."

And again I fall silent.

Cornelius comes forward. Barefoot in the snow, his anklets tinkling, silver silver on snow snow. Not used to thinking in words, first come pictures, pictures, pictures, faster than can put words to, want to turn them into music but the song will be too-much-weeping. And I still, still, biting back the truth, though it's burning me up.

Cornelius says, "We can't all be truthsayers, young man, but there is something we all know. The innermost truth you're hiding is bitter for yourself, although it may heal the world. But not every truth is the holy grail, and we can take this cup from you; we can, we can."

—that's true—

"You see!" Thorn says excitedly. "I was right. I may only be a zombie recreation of my former self, but I can still win the game."

"All you needed to come back to life," says Cornelius Huang, "was the sort of homeopathic tincture of a human soul."

"Would you like to see where Oren Karpovsky is now?" Thorn says. "Look into my eyes, boy, gaze deep into them. . . ."

He bends down and I peer. First the churning flaming whirlpool-well down down down and then yes there, I see him, two of them, twins, one in each eye, little President Karpovsky, the size of a mosquito, running back and forth and back and forth battering his body against the sides of the well and screaming his pinprick little screams.

—you're big and he's little—but you're dead and he's not-dead—

"Silence!" Slaps me again, pain stinging, bringing salt tears, fuck you I won't cry out. "You will take me to the source of the River."

—fuck you—

"Foul-mouthed, aren't you, for such a sweet little boy." Pulls me up roughly. "Where did you learn language like that? And don't say from your brothers. You have no brothers. They never existed. Not if you exist."

—they exist inside me, all of it exists inside me, all the pathways, all the little rivulets and tributaries and stop hitting me you motherfucker you need me more than I need you and—

Starting to get into this talking stuff a little. But talking I don't have a voice, I have a hundred voices, a thousand; I'm parroting back little fragments of other people's conversations. Words are not true enough. They only nibble at the edges of truth. They never show the heart of things.

"Listen, you sniveling little moppet. I want to offer you, for lack of a better word for it, an unholy alliance. Right now, we have a common goal. We both have to get to the source. Now, you're going to go there regardless, because it's your destiny; the fact that you let me capture you so easily proves that, or you'd have conjured up some kind of symphony of terror, put up a major struggle, *something*. I mean, Serena Somers, pregnant with a dragon yet, is no match for me. You have the truth, but I have the strength; you see, truth isn't the only card one can have up one's sleeve, is it, now? You *will* take me to the source of the River, and once we get there, I'll have a sporting chance with my agenda, just as good a chance as you have with yours. And I have another major advantage. I *want* to conquer the universe. You, on the other hand, my squeamish messiah, are reluctant to reach the end of your song, because to do so would mean—what?—that's where we come to your dark truth, which I, of course, am not privy to."

What can I do what can I say? He's right of course. I have to go where

I have to go, and if he keeps me chained up by his side he'll end up going there too.

And I can't lie. I'm a truthsayer.

Can I make the journey longer, make time for the others to get there too? Can I misdirect maybe, or is that going to destroy the thing I am?

I don't want to get to the end of the journey. That's true, too, isn't it? I can't lie about that either. How can he be so right when he's one of the bad guys?

—all right—

"I knew you'd come around," said Thorn. "But you're a far better truthsayer than the last one I had. You probably don't need any marbles or visual aids at all, do you? You can just close your eyes and spirit us there, and we can take over the whole show."

—the way is murky—a lot of tributaries dammed up—some sections of the River have run dry—

"I know, I know. Now go."

Around-looking: far away, clouds, beyond clouds, the lake; my mom and dad and Serena and the shaman, cooking fish by the fire, and—

Around-looking: even farther, farther, farther, my brother has abandoned his fish and is running toward us, but his moment of running is an eternity, that's relativity you see, and I'm afraid that they're going to be long gone before we can—

"Go, I say!" says Thorn.

I close my eyes.

—you—follow—I—lead—

Listen. Listen. The real universe has an underlying heartbeat. You can call it Love. You can call it Om. You can call it God. It's so slow that worlds can evolve, devolve, and perish between two beats, yet you can hear it if you know how to listen. Listen. Listen. How can it be that the others can't hear it when to me it's the rhythm that drives all other rhythms, the ostinato that anchors the cosmos? Listen, listen, listen.

"What are you doing, child? Don't zone out, just take us where we need to go."

—be quiet! I'm concentrating—

"Oh." Thorn steps back. Suddenly I'm the boss and he's the anxious, waiting attendant. Role reversal. All right!

—how many are traveling with us?—

"I guess I ought to take the whole army. I'll have to fight my father for possession of everything. And who knows, maybe my dragon sister's gotten loose by now, and she'll be setting out for the source of the River too. And then there's Ash. Whatever the hell happened to him? Okay, so he's the wimpy, rah-rah sibling, always telling the truth—half truthsayer himself in a way—but what if he gets it into his head to run for the source? A four-way battle is coming up and I want to make absolutely sure I win."

Eyes-closed looking around: chaos. Where's the River? Sending out feelers. Reaching out. Listen. That universal heartbeat . . . slow slow slow . . . listen. Listen. I think the heart is diseased. The echo of the heartbeat comes across the continuum, and it's all skipping, skipping, like the pulse of a man with a heart condition . . . slow, slow, slow, slow, stop, slow, slow.

A flicker. The trickle of a mountain stream. The River's broken up, a lot of places it doesn't even flow anymore, but I hear something. Close by. Tap tap tap the rush of an underground river, just gotta smash my way through to it.

—okay. All of us. Everyone who's coming with me. Hold hands. I'm going to smash through, make a new gateway—

Taking Thorn's hand in mine. Clammy. Cold. A hand that sucks all the warmth out of you. Just how a vampire's hand should be. Listen. That heartbeat is still pulsing, weak, weak, weak, pulsing still pulsing pulsing. Be still. I think about the source—

Crystal pure lightness pure crystal

—I'm going to think a big dreaming-thought now. I'm going to bring us closer to the source by—

"I knew it!" Thorn says excitedly. "You *can* change the fabric of reality just by your will."

—I am a truthsayer. If I say a thing, it is not only true—it has always been true. That's the curse I carry inside me—

"Yes, yes, let's go!" Impatiently he thrusts his left hand behind him, and Cornelius Huang diffidently takes it in his right. Then Huang stretches out his left hand, and one of the demon things shimmies up and seizes it in a gnarled paw; and so it goes on, all the way down the mountainside and down the hierarchy, all the way to the valley, as far as I can see; and I'm going to think a big dream-thought and I'm going to carry them all with me through the sheer force of my truthsaying and—

Now! I synchronize myself with that great heartbeat.

Now! I open my lips, and I sing.

The sound that I sing partakes of the breath of creation. It's the new-world-joy that sings in the wind of a world that's just sprung into being at the hand of a god. Thorn frowns. He doesn't like the sound of joy; he tries not to smile, but I feel the smiling stir inside him, and I know he hates that, loves to be the villain, loves to be the darkness, but he must know that he has allied himself with me and must accept that my truth-

saying comes from the light, the first light of the cosmos, the light that
bursts forth in that great Big Bang that set the particles to dancing at the
dawn of time.

Fireworks! The fabric of space-time rips, and we step through, and
now:

Around-looking: the edge of a mighty canyon, the living rock carved
with ancient petroglyphs in a long-dead language, and in the sky above, a
flock of pterodactyls craning. Demons hang on the stone facings, some
upside down like bats; the canyon side thick with leather and fanged
faces.

Below-looking: the River. I've carved a new gateway. The River roaring, foaming, exhilarated. The pulse of the universe beneath it all, more
steady now, more smooth, like a man who's just had a coronary bypass;
because that's really what I just did, bypass the clogged arteries of the
River. I'm already beginning to heal the universe and I know that's not in
Thorn's agenda.

"This isn't the source," Thorn says.

—still a long way off—

"I'm hungry!" He lets go my hand. He paces. A thousand demons pace
in the background, shadowing him.

Cornelius says, "Perhaps one of your own subjects?"

"Boring," he says. He gazes at me and what's in his eyes is akin to lust,
akin to hunger, yet also a kind of love. "We'll need some kind of boat,"
he says.

—around the bend of the canyon—

He seizes my hand again. Throws his cloak about me. Dark, all dark.
He leaps. No wind rushing, no landscape flashing by, because in the dark
cloak is like in the thick womb of sleep, and it's like a dream of forever
falling . . . and when he whisks away the cloak we're standing on the
deck of a monster ship, all iron, all rusty and smelling of death, and the
demons are swarming all over it.

Thorn laughs, throws his head back and does the whole evil villain
guffaw thing. "The *Titanic!* How singularly appropriate!"

Then he crooks a finger at one of the demons, who bends down so he
can drink his blood. Other demons toss him, drained, into the water, and
so my pristine path to the source has already been polluted.

"I suppose we can move on now," Thorn says, and waves at me. What
do I do now? I close my eyes. Listen to the heartbeat of the universe. I
center my truthsaying sense on the source of the River. I know that if I
start to move toward the source, the energy of that movement will carry
all these creatures along with it, and the dinosaur of a ship, too. I listen.

Listen. Listen. And then I pluck out of the air the notes that resonate with the heartstrings of the cosmos, tentatively at first, and then more confidently, filling the space around me with the music of pure joy; I know how uncomfortable that makes Thorn, and it makes me smile a little, for the first time since my abduction. . . .

The ship rumbles into action, and we start to roll upstream.

CHAPTER NINE

ASH

T h e o E t c h i s o n

So, we're on the water racing toward the castle, but then what happens? There's like this big old explosion. The castle starts to shake. Flames leap up. The king starts and stares, and now and then he murmurs, "the dragon, the dragon," softly to himself, and cradles his scepter in his arms. But then the urgency of it strikes him and he plunges the scepter into the water once more, churning it up and sending up sparks.

The mermaids shriek and dive back into the depths. I have to get to that place . . . I know that my father's there . . . I can feel him with what remains of my truthsaying, try to reach out to him, and for a moment I see what he sees—

—me running to him along the riverbank, back in Virginia I guess, among the cottonwoods, calling out "Daddy, Daddy" to him, a million worlds ago—

The castle is on fire and there's a giantess stomping about in the distance. It's like watching a monster movie in the distance, all totally unreal. "It's Serena Somers," I say, but King Strang doesn't know who that is. There's a music in the air, too, a drumming and a high-pitched keening. It's the music of the other truthsayer. The one I brought into the world. The son I got on my own mother. Sounds sick, huh. We were gods at the time. You know how it is with the gods: incest, incest, incest. Sex with mom, sex with mom, okay, I admit it, I'm obsessed with it, it's like a black clot in my head and it clouds my thinking all the time. And then there's the kid. When I think of him, I feel all sick inside, sick because of how he came into the world, sick because he's so much better than me, because he has my gift, a thousand times my gift, and mine is getting fuzzier every day. But I have to play this thing out to its end.

The raft moves on. On toward the castle. But the landscape keeps morphing, distorting itself. Sphinxes rear up and pop like balloons. Aztec gods in gold and nephrite peer up over the frothing waters. We're about to reach the castle when like, this humungous flock of bat-creatures comes soaring out of the flames. The castle crumbles and our raft rams against the shore and Strang and I get out, him brandishing the scepter like it's a magic wand, trying to silence the divine and maddening music.

For a second I see them all: Dad and Mom and Serena, who's towering above the whole big burning mess, but everything's all blurry again, and I try to call out to Dad through the wall of fire but the fumes are burning my eyes and then the walls are shimmering and fading and—

Dad turns to me. Does he really see me? Or is there one of those yawning abysses between us, are we really standing in separate universes?

"Daddy!" I scream.

Dad cries out: "Forgive me! I didn't know what I was doing—"

And there's kind of a double vision about it because I know he doesn't see me, Theo Truthsayer, navigator to the mad king, but some little kid running toward him across a plain of ice. . . .

"Dad!" I scream again, but—

There's a tremendous explosion.

It's all gone. All of it. And now, just as suddenly, we're floating on a lake, a crystal lake, and it's all intensely calm.

"What happened?" says Strang.

"There's been another glitch in reality," I say. "We haven't moved, but the sands of the cosmos have shifted under our feet."

He looks up. "Clear. The sky. Bright and clear. Hasn't been this way in a while. Must be testing me."

He smashes his scepter at an imaginary enemy: the air.

"You're acting paranoid, Strang," I say.

He swings the scepter at me, but I dodge; I'm good at that, I'm still agile, still got my junior high school Super-Nintendo reflexes. "Get thee behind me, varmint," he growls. But he's not even looking at me. He's haunted, of course, and doesn't know that it's himself who haunts him.

"Cool it, O King," I say. Sometimes I can lighten his mood by talking that way. But he begins to weep, though he doesn't know that I'm looking at him, doesn't quite know I'm there, really, so many other creatures in his world, all creatures of illusion.

The place we're floating in: rocky structures jut up from the lake like little islands arranged in concentric circles. I think my mom and dad are close, real close; I try to reach out with my mind, but when I try, a fog kind of seizes my brain.

"I was a child once, you know," says King Strang. "Didn't always have the scepter. Maybe I was better off without it."

"You could always throw it away," I say. But I know that won't solve anything; there'll only be another Strang, and even if he means well at first, the sickness that's in the scepter would eventually drive him mad too. "Tell me about being a child," I say.

"Not just me. The whole world. Morning of my life, morning of the world."

"Must have been exciting."

"It was lonely. I wanted to be loved, but since there was no one to love me, I had to settle for being worshipped."

Suddenly I think I see something on one of the islands, further in, toward the center of the circle. Something flashing, chrome and pale blue-green, a station wagon maybe. I think I know this car, which is just sitting there, parked on a basalt ledge poking up in the middle of this lake. The way it glints. The Arizona desert, the heat, the smell of my mother dying; it's all wrapped up in the image of that beat-up car. I know my parents have to be near.

"Look," I tell the king, pointing. "I think we're about to rendezvous with my family."

I start paddling the raft. Despondently, the king begins to strike the water with his scepter. We move. It's a zigzag drifting as we skirt the many jutting stones. Isn't that a tendril of smoke swirling skyward from the center? Could it be a campfire maybe? I wish I could see more clearly. . . .

"What about *my* family?" says the king. "What about my children, spinning in the void? What about the dragon woman and the boy with the slate-colored eyes?"

"You have another child too."

"I don't!"

"You do. Think about him."

We have reached the first of the islands—no more than a mound of basalt. I tie the raft to a knob of smoldering stone. I have to think. Maybe I'm wrong to think we're closer to the source. King Strang sits by the edge, dangling his feet, not worrying about the water that soaks his fraying robes.

"This used to be Thorn's castle," I say. "There's been a struggle. That's all I can figure out." The surface of the basalt is covered with a fine ash, some of it still glowing. I kneel down, take a handful of it. Here and there are crystals, like unpolished diamonds, white and hard.

I blow the ash into the still thin air.

That's when the ash starts to form into the shadowy image of a man.

"Hey, take a look, King Strang! Someone's come to see us."

The king doesn't turn around.

It's a shimmering figure, a dance of light, a wavering in the air; I think I'm just imagining it at first, and then I can hear him speak to me; it's a weird voice, a not-quite-man, not-quite-woman voice. "Theo," he says. "Good to see you again."

"Ash?" I say.

King Strang winces, and still won't look.

"I've been wondering when you would turn up again."

"I've always been here," Ash says. "When my siblings consume each other in their rage, I'm what's left behind; I'm the broken pieces of their love for each other."

"I'm losing my gift," I say sadly.

"And I never had much of a gift," he says, "though I have been known to tell the truth once too often."

The king looks up for a moment. "Are you crazy, boy?" he shouts at me. "Speaking to the air like that."

"You're in denial," I tell the king. "You know very well who I'm talking to. . . ."

Strang turns stubbornly away. What's he doing with his scepter? He's swishing it through the water. A dead fish comes floating to the top. He tears it apart with his bare hands, peers at it, sniffs at the guts.

"Help me," Ash says. "I can't go on like this. It's not natural for me to live as the quintessence of dust. But without reconciliation with my father . . ."

"I don't know what I can do," I say. "You know I'm losing my powers."

"We can help each other. I've never been a truthsayer, but I think I have a little bit of the gift; it's telling the truth that got me in this bind in the first place."

That's true. He's the Cordelia in this King Lear story, putting his foot in his mouth by refusing to embroider the truth with flattery.

"You mean," I say, "that between us, we could figure out how to get to the source?"

"Why not?" he says.

"The blind leading the blind?"

"Something like that. Whatever happened to your big blue marble?"

"I guess it got lost somewhere in the melee." I had a map once. It had the whole River scrunched up inside what seemed to be a crystal, a marble. There was another map, too. It was in the palace of Caliosper. An arena, a kind of mega-Nintendo virtual map. "Whatever happened to your flying city?" I say.

"Lost it somewhere, too. But I get the feeling it's close by."

"Yes. Close by. That's the problem. So near and yet—"

"My father has some of the answers. You should listen to him more."

"But he's mad."

"Maybe there's method in it."

I go and sit down beside the king. Ash comes behind me, a swirl of dust that wheels around my shoulders and catches the blue sunlight; it's as though I were wearing a necklace of stars. The king doesn't look at me.

But he says, "Amuse me."

I say, "All right, but then you have to answer one question, no matter how hard it is, no matter what the pain. Truth or dare kind of thing."

"Tell me about your silly world, boy. It's always good for a laugh."

🔲

Okay so I tell him one of my stupid stories. It's about the time the British exchange students decided to teach us all cricket. So they get out all these wickets and bats and other weird paraphernalia and start explaining it to me and the other kids in Mr. Norris' P.E. class, with curious words like *googly* and *maiden over* and *howzat,* and it's what sounds like a really really slow version of baseball, you know, except that there's two people running back and forth instead of in a circle . . . well then we decide to try it out for a lark, and no one picks me because I'm such a dweeb, so I end up in, I guess the outfield kind of position, and I'm all lying in the grass, knowing that the ball will never come my way, dozing; it's already summer, feels like it anyways, you know how muggy Virginia gets, and school's gonna be out soon and the fucking Brits will go home.

By the edge of the field, the grass is super-tall and there's a creek. There's hornets too; I think there's a nest close by. There's only three kids from England, but they're explaining up a storm over there in the distance, and I don't think they'll ever get started; so like, I stop paying attention; I've got a beanbag for a pillow and I lean over on my side and part the grass a little and look out over the creek, because I can hear someone sobbing, very softly, to herself.

It's Serena Somers. And the thing is, she's all naked, and blubbery, and standing in the stream, and she looks like one of those Stone Age Venus idols that we learned about in Mrs. Hulan's class; she's not ugly but kind of beautiful. But what's she doing in the middle of the school day, butt naked at the edge of campus? What the hell is she thinking to herself?

Thing is, it's the first naked woman I've ever seen. So I don't care that she's a slug, I'm just so amazed at how it's all put together. I'm so in awe that I don't even pop a woody. Okay so she's fat, but it's amazing how beautiful she is, with her Venus-on-the-half-shell hair plastered to her plump breasts, and her clear eyes, looking fucking Jesus knows at what; and there's a kind of rustling in the air, I think at first it's the hornets, but she looks, straight at me it seems, yet straight *through* me too, and I let out a little startled cry or grunt; and she says, "Ash, Ash, is it you, is it really you?"

And I don't answer, because if I speak I have to speak the truth.

And she says, "Ash, but you only come at night."

And I'm all, "I'm not Ash."

But she hears something else. She's in another world, parallel to the world I'm lying in, but not totally congruent.

"Of course you are," she says. "But you only come, you know, when I'm about to go to sleep . . . you're the whisperer before the dream."

She laughs. She splashes me with water. Her clothes are hanging on a nearby bush and suddenly I catch a whiff of, I don't know, underwear, and suddenly there comes the long-awaited stiffy after all.

So this is Serena's big secret; she ditches fourth period and skinny-dips within a stone's throw of the school . . . I wonder if Joshua knows.

In the far distance, there's that hooting-cum-steam-whistle sound that passes for the bell in our school, an electronic racket cooked up by a computer class last year. Startled, she jumps out of the stream, grabs her clothes, starts to dash away, but not before she turns and looks me right in the eye, and smiles, and says, "Oh, it's only you." And thunders off through the bushes.

Only me? Only Ash, the imaginary friend, or only Theo, the pesky little bro of the boyfriend?

⑤

As I tell King Strang this story he continues to fish, and Ash himself continues to waft around my shoulders as a flurry of silvery dust. The king's not pleased that I've worked Ash into the conversation. He's silent for a long time.

"You're forcing me," he says.

"What?" I say.

"Forcing me to relive things. I don't like that. I'm old, boy, old, and those things were a long time ago."

"It'll be over soon," I say, "I promise. Because we're at the dawn of the mad millennium, and we're all almost at the end of our journey. . . ."

"I know something you don't know."

"That's probably true," I say. "I know less and less these days. My truthsaying totally bites."

"I know you've been speaking to a certain someone who shall remain nameless." He shakes his head. His mane is soggy, and he asperges me with lake water, cold and smelling of fish. "I also know you're thinking of others, people close to you, and you think that all we have to do is swim out a little farther, and meet up with them, and all convoy together to the source of the River where there'll be some big apocalyptic event and the world will be reborn. Isn't that right?"

"Something like that."

"How far is it to the next island?"

I look across the water. It seems a lot closer than it did before. I can see the station wagon clearly now, I can even make out what seems to be my father, a thin balding man in a crumpled suit, banging at the car door; I guess he doesn't have the key. "I could swim it easy," I say. "But I wish I could give Dad the key."

"Sometimes you have to go in the opposite direction," says the king, "to get where you want to go." He gets up suddenly. Grabs me by the shoulders. He may be stooped and emaciated but when he wants to grip you he can dig right into your flesh. "Let's go another way," he says. He lets go of my shoulders, grabs onto my hand, brandishes his scepter with his free hand.

"Go where? You're crazy. . . ."

"I certainly am! Stark staring bonkers, mad as a hatter, ho ho ho!" And he's all waving the scepter and pulling me in circles, staggering around the perimeter of the island which is after all less than fifty yards maybe, with the Ash-dust streaming behind me. "You want to get to the end," he says, "you have to come to the beginning! Now run, run, run!"

And we're all running hard, running in a spiral toward the center of the rock. The king's robes, stained with blood and bile, are flapping in the breeze he's made by his running. And suddenly it seems that the world is spinning around us and we've like become still. The still point of the turning world as Dad would have put it. Still, still, still, and the universe rushing like mad, circling us, pushing us squarely toward the center, and—

"Ash," the king says.

"Ash is with us," I say, astounded that he has finally brought himself to say his child's name.

"No, no, no, you idiot, you be Ash, you stand in for him; see with his eyes, know what he knows; because Ash was with me, you know, when the world was young; he was there at the moment of original sin."

Now I understand the spinning. It's like in those *Superman* comics when Superman flies so fast he overtakes the speed of light and catapults himself back in time so he can explain some paradox.

The king's opening up to me now. He's carrying me with him down the river of remembrance. "Are you listening to this, Ash?" I whisper, as the world whirls so fast it's no more than a blur of rainbow streaks. Then I see like this desk calendar whizzing around, with the pages tearing off one by one . . . yeah, just another of those visual metaphors that comes to me when there's no rational way to analyze what you see around you. "Ash, Ash," I say.

Ash doesn't answer. I guess it's true. He's inside me now. Or I'm inside him. The world begins to settle down. King Strang is still holding onto my hand. But when I look at him I can't believe the transformation. He's all, you know, tall and goldenhaired and his complexion is all gold; and his robes are white and shiny.

"Come, Ash," he says to me.

We step out into the morning of the world.

BOOK THREE

DEVELOPMENT

THE MAD KING

"In my end is my beginning."

—*T.S. Eliot*

ON TRUTH

BY PHILIP ETCHISON

My writing block, it seems, is permanent. As a result, I find my annual address from the poetry chair of this august institution to be more and more of a joke, year after year. What can one talk about, when one has been struck dumb?

I have decided to venture into the treacherous shoals of ontology. . . .

What is truth?

We all long to believe in the existence of an Ultimate Truth. A truth that is the touchstone by which we can measure all our private little falsehoods, beside which even the whitest lie is black as night and death. This Ultimate Truth, we believe, is the thing that will "set us free," as it says, not only in the Bible, but in that old protest song—but of course, you're all too young to remember that.

What would happen to us, if it were suddenly revealed that this Ultimate Truth does not exist? If this Ultimate Truth is the rock on which our faith in our perceptions is founded, does it not follow that to negate its existence—to say that it has no clothes—would automatically plunge humanity into a dark, suicidal despair?

History shows that this has already happened on a number of occasions. And, in a smaller way, we all experience that moment of gravest doubt. I know I have. I think it is that moment of doubt that propels us, causes us to yearn for, to strive for, to demand artistic permanence.

—coffee-stained ms. found stuck in a shredder at the Kremlin, along with a prescription for Prozac. Believed to be in the handwriting of Philip Etchison.

—reserve $10,000

CHAPTER TEN

AT THE MORNING OF THE WORLD

T h e o   E t c h i s o n

I'm still Theo Etchison, but I'm inside someone else, watching through his eyes. I'm a kid I guess, and the place we're in is a rambling palace that goes on and on. Ivory pilasters and tile floors, and murals with scenes from unfamiliar mythologies; but the place we're in now is like, some kind of playroom. And I've got two older siblings, a boy and a girl. I'm sitting in the corner. Maybe I shouldn't be playing with dolls, but I kind of am; it's like an alien Barbie Doll kind of thing, all heads and tentacles and slimy skin yet giving off a strange seductiveness.

"Ash, Ash," says a strange voice from above.

I look up at the ceiling and there's like, this Michelangelo Sistine Chapel God-thing floating among the holographic clouds, only it's animated. I call it the Godfather. "Stop playing with dolls," says the voice from above. "You want to grow up like your sister?"

My sister Katastrofa is breathing fire over a city made of chalcedony building blocks, and my slate-eyed brother Thorn is torturing one of the servant children with a little needlegun. No fear that I'm going to be like either of them.

My father's not really in the ceiling. The ceiling has only been imbued with his personality, the better to control us. After all, it's hard to be ruler of a planetary fiefdom; one doesn't necessarily have time to spend with one's kids. And certainly no quality time.

There are no people at all in this wing of the palace. Occasionally servants, but even those are mostly spirits. I'm looking through Ash's eyes but because I'm me, Theo, from the 90s, the time before the mad millennium, I see and taste and smell things differently; the scent in the air, decaying flowers maybe, a hint of a chemical smell, it all evokes a sadness for me, a feeling of loneliness; maybe it's because I've smelled this smell before and it's the smell of visiting my mother in the hospital, the smell that says goodbye, I'm dying.

And because I know Ash, Thorn, and Katastrofa from a much later time, I can see the future in their childish games.

Thorn says, "Let's get Ash."

Katastrofa does a flip through the air, wraps her scaly arms around my neck, throws back her head and sends out a fountain of flame; Thorn laughs; I'm on the verge of crying; abruptly, she lets go of me and I go sprawling onto the stone floor, and Thorn says, "He'll only go crying to you-know-who."

I look up at the Godfather, who wags a finger. "Stop picking on your little brother," comes the booming admonition, like the voice of God in *The Ten Commandments.*

"Sissy," hisses Thorn.

Katastrofa flies up to the ceiling; I think she's going to lob a fireball at the Godfather, but she doesn't dare. It may be a computer simulacrum, but it slings real lightning bolts. So she only swoops back down to glare at me. It's a typical morning in the nursery.

I don't hate my siblings, but they certainly hate me.

Suddenly, to everyone's surprise, there's a break in the routine. Softly at first. The tramp of lizard feet. Tramp-tramp, tramp-tramp, in a corridor far away, yet coming closer.

"Military exercise?" Thorn says.

Katastrofa listens. "Only a few of them. They're coming to the nursery."

Now they're in the doorway, my father's saurian henchmen, they of the hivemind and scaly complexion. They don't even glance at Thorn, the firstborn, or Katastrofa, who practices her gliding among the crowned pilasters of the nursery. They come straight up to me. They speak in tandem.

"His Imperial Majesty, your Father," says one—

"Commands you to see him in the throne room—"

"Right away!"

"Five minutes to make yourself presentable!" Their voices grate like actors in a Japanese monster movie.

"We will wait."

Katastrofa and Thorn scowl at me with the kind of single-minded hatred that only ten-year-olds can feel. I look at the floor. "Could be anything," I say. "Could be a death sentence. You know how Father is. He could be disowning me."

"Fat chance," says Thorn. He sounds hard and bitter.

"He never summons *us* to the throne room," says Katastrofa. She tries to sound hard but there's a hint of heartbreak in her voice.

The imperial lizards wait. Their scales glisten like anodized titanium. I

clap my hands for a body-slave, who crawls into the room and changes
my clothes for me before slinking away.

The palace is a labyrinth, but a prince of the House of Strang must not
walk far. The two lizards lift me onto a litter that rests on a cushion of
air; they levitate it; one on either side, they guide it out into a mile-long
cloister whose walls are empanelled with gold and malachite. We move
swiftly; the lizards can run like machines, and the palanquin *is* one; the
walls are a blur; we race down more cloisters, more corridors, more
passageways; and now we are levitating up along a flight of steps, and on
either side are painted scenes from our family's history: the first Strang,
forest-born, emerging from the wilderness with an army of jungle animals at his back; the second, floating down a river in a chest of gold,
wrapped in the skins of marmosets; the third, a holy king, squatting in
lotus position on the summit of a mountain, preaching to the monkeys;
these are all scenes the three children have been required to commit to
memory, along with the inscriptions, in archaic poetry, that run along the
walls and are etched into the glazed-tiled steps; the palanquin glides up,
smooth as a gilded hawk.

My father's throne room: viziers and ministers are prostrate on the
floor from which rises a rose-tinged mist. Cherums with censers flit above
our heads, and the air is filled with the sweet fragrance of frankincense,
myrrh, and copal. A major domo with a golden, Anubis-tipped staff
stands sentinel. I tweak his wig as the litter sails past him, over the sea of
suppliants, all the way to the foot of my father's throne; and there he sits,
the Seventh Strang, the father of Ash, and also my father, because I'm
still inside of Ash, seeing with the eyes of a young Virginia boy. This isn't
a Strang I've ever seen before. This Strang is bright-eyed, vigorous, deci-
sive; his hair is a mane of reddish-brown. A torc of gold and amber hugs
his neck, and within each nugget of amber is the remains of an ancient
creature.

"Father, father," I say, in a piping little voice. How old am I really,
seven or eight? I can't tell because Ash isn't thinking about that, but I
know that his kind don't age at the same speed as humans.

He doesn't look at me at first. One of the many viziers is at his side,
and they are poring through documents. It's Cornelius Huang, who
doesn't look any younger than when I first saw him at the Chinese restaurant in the wilderness.

"Yes," Strang says, "yes, yes," and with each *yes* there's like a sigh of
pleasure from the suppliants, and then, one time, he says "No," and
there's like this hush that falls over the crowd, and Corny frowns a little,
and turns to one of the lizard guards that flank the throne and raises just

one eyebrow; and a detachment of guards runs off to execute the king's command; and Strang looks at me at last, and I'm all, to myself, He's tired sometimes, he doesn't like his job sometimes, and I'm the only one he lets see this; and it moves me.

"Son," he says. Really softly. But suddenly, as though he has spoken with the voice of thunder, the suppliants begin backing away, the lizards turn their backs on us, the advisors and viziers look at the floor and shuffle their feet so as not to intrude on this totally private moment in this totally public place; and I think, Shit, that's *power*.

"You wanted to see me, father?" I can't help trembling.

He smiles. The viziers, of course, have turned their backs to us, and yet they too are smiling; they've picked up on his mood, understand that he's not displeased with me, and this makes their jobs all easier too.

"I haven't seen you for days," says Strang. "Come on up."

I climb out of the palanquin and hop down onto the lowest step of the throne where there's a velvet footstool, and I sit down, but he crooks his finger and makes me crawl up onto his lap, and he gazes into my eyes and I'm thinking, Yes, it's true, how tired he is, all those yesses followed by that single no, it must really have hurt him to say it; and I know how much it pleases him to have me there, bright-eyed, adoring him.

"If only you knew," he says. "There's got to be another way of doing this."

Abruptly, he rises.

"Come, child," he says. "We're going fishing."

CHAPTER ELEVEN

DREAMS WITHIN DREAMS

Phil Etchison

I swam toward the island of the station wagon. It was easy; the water was warm, and heavier, too, than regular sea water; I didn't have to struggle to stay afloat. I heard that swimming in the Dead Sea's like that, because of the high salt content; you jump in and you just float, and float, and float. But this was no Dead Sea. I don't know what was in the water;

maybe some of the peyote tea that Milt was so fond of serving us. I felt wonderfully alive here. I felt nourished. The water of the lake had an amniotic quality. I swam . . . no, I drifted. Slowly but surely, toward where my car was miraculously parked. But all of a sudden, night fell, just like that: like switching off a light and going to bed. I tingled. I felt secure. I knew I would arrive at my destination even if I fell asleep in the arms of mother darkness. . . .

Night fell and I dreamt, dreams within dreams, and with each dream I came closer to awakening from the grand dream that had been my whole existence.

I'm a king on a throne, dispensing justice, picking life or death for my erring subjects. I have three children; one is the apple of my eye. In this dream there are corridors lined with scenes of my many pasts. In this dream, the child I love most is flying to see me on mechanical wings. All morning, I order executions. My child drifts toward me over a field of prostrate suppliants; I am both god and king.

I see my child, goldenhaired and swathed in light, and I think to myself, but of the other children, lost in the darknesses of alien worlds, what of them? And I'm torn, because this is my son, yet but for him the others would be here, imperfect though they are, the sullen brooding one and the bright-eyed truthsayer.

I say to Chris, "Son, let's go fishing."

And he says, "You see yourself as the Fisher King now, Dad?"

And I say, "You can talk!"

He says, "This is a dream, Dad; truths are spoken in dreams that dare not be spoken in life."

"True," I say. The strange thing is, I know the place I'm in is real, though I've never been here; I know that the body I inhabit is a real person, even though I'm interpreting the world around me through the lens of what I've seen and known; I know that what's in this dream has really happened, but to me and not to my son.

"What do you want to fish for, Dad?" Chris says. "Are you sick of the old 'fishers of men' thing? You want something bigger and better than a few miserable souls?"

"Maybe."

"Okay then. I'll take you. Come."

He pulls me up from the throne and the next thing I know I'm—

Theo   Etchison

—floating—

Through Ash's eyes, I see Strang, rowing with a fevered energy I've never seen in him before. This is some boat; first we were carried to the edge of a crystal lake, then we rode like this hovercraft thing, its prow a mass of writhing serpents, across the lake to this stream, and the stream fed into a river that was descended lower and lower into a canyon where the guards finally left us; this boat, a battered old dinghy, was moored to a post, and there were cataracts beyond, thunderous and foamy; and I got into the boat with king, and he straps me down with chains of silver, and I'm all, "Where's the bait? We're not really going fishing at all, are we?" And a wild thought races through my mind, that he's brought me to this wild place to dispose of me, to fake some kind of accident. King Strang doesn't answer me, but just rows; he closes his eyes, and we plunge down the first cataract, and I think, Fucking Jesus this water is bitter, it's like carbonated Robitussin or something, and it's cold and it's pouring down my nose and throat and like I'll drown or something if it doesn't stop and I think oh shit I'm maybe drowning or something, I'm going to die—

And then—my eyes are closed—we're all flying through the air and then, *bam,* we hit something hard and I'm all, This has got to be the end. Water just slams into me, winds me, I'm puking it up and coughing, and then, suddenly, there's calm.

"Open your eyes, boy," says Strang.

I do. This is what I see: we're drifting smoothly down a river of blood and mud, and where we are is the bottom of a chasm whose walls are etched with petroglyphs and images of hell, souls being tortured, brimstone, demons; the riverbanks are carved out of the rock, they're totally straight, artificial-looking.

"What do you see?" says Strang.

"I don't know . . . ancient artifacts maybe, the work of some lost civilization, something like that?"

"I think so," says my father. "I stumbled on it quite by accident. An old truthsayer told me there's a fork in the River and one channel leads straight to the darkest of all places."

"But why are you taking me? It scares me."

The walls are so high that there seems to be no sky; the walls simply meet up there somewhere, and I feel caged in, trapped in an endless tunnel, and there's a whooshing, wuthering wind that sears my eardrums.

"I'm taking you," my father says, "because this is a big thing, and I must share it with someone, and because of all my children you are the only one who tells me the truth."

"I can't help it," I hear myself say out of Ash's lips, "there's a little voice inside me, someone else, not me, and he whispers to me, and what he whispers is always true."

"What's he like, this other voice?"

"I think it's a boy. But it's someone on another world, a world where reality doesn't shift around as much."

Strang laughs. "Are you possessed," he says, "by the ghost of some truthsayer yet unborn? Or do you maybe think *you* could have the gift?"

Holy shit, I think to myself, how many times have I haunted Ash's dreams, slunk into his thoughts before? When I thought I was dreaming, was I really living this totally other life? Are we like mystic twins or something? I answer him (Ash answers him) "It's not my gift, father, but I sometimes feel it, some big alien thing, tickling the back of my mind."

"Then let's test your skill. Come on. We're coming to a fork in the river. Pick the right path."

That's when Ash realizes there's an ulterior motive, perhaps, why his father has brought him on this journey. He needs a guide, and he has no truthsayer. There was one in the palace, but no one has seen him for years; perhaps the old man crawled away to die somewhere. I remember him vaguely; they used to trot him out on holidays to give a few pointers at banquets, the future of the nation, the direction of the king's policies; I never saw him myself, only on the palace's closed-circuit baby-sitting television. Ash really loves his father, though there's as much fear as there is love there; he's happy his father wants to do something with him, doesn't much care what it is as long as they're together.

The stream narrows. The walls darken. Somehow we've gone from canyon to cavern. The paintings on the walls become more realistic. I think they're moving, some of them; there are demons with pitchforks, lost souls lashed to fiery wheels, tongues of fire, glowing eyes that seem to follow us as we drift. Strang rows and I sit back, watching him, worshipping him, in a way; and pretty soon the stream does seem to divide; one fork is well lit, and in the other the light grows dim, and the cavern walls press in harder, and stalactites hang down like rows of sharks' teeth.

"Which way, son?" says my father. "Listen to your inner voice."

Ash does listen. He makes his mind very empty, and what fills the void is me, smartass little kid from some future millennium. "I think we should go—"

P h i l   E t c h i s o n

"—into the dark side," my son tells me in this increasingly baroque dream that has me playing the role of a bearded, ancient god-king, an Osiris.

"Are you sure, Chris?" I say. "Doesn't it scare you?"

He says, "Sure, Dad. But we have to face it sooner or later."

The walls of the subterranean stream are painted with murals, and there are scenes that I know all too well: Mary, standing in the rain; Joshua and Theo playing by the riverbank back in Spotsylvania County, a dog barking, the cottonwoods with their deep russet sunset shadows; so why I do I feel that behind the lurid hues of this sunset are the flames of hell? I reach into the water and let the minnows nibble at my fingers.

"This isn't where we usually go fishing," I say to my son.

He says, "That's true."

Then I say, "Son, I get the feeling that this journey we're taking is—

T h e o   E t c h i s o n

—a timeless journey," Strang says, "a journey that a billion fathers and sons have taken together, down into the darkest depths of their own souls, and yet—

P h i l   E t c h i s o n

—this is different," I tell my son, "because I'm not really a king, or a high-priest, or some mythic hero, I'm not the arch-guru of reality, I'm not Prince Siddhartha seeking enlightenment; I'm just an ordinary guy trapped in these cosmic events—

T h e o   E t c h i s o n

—because we are kings and princes, you and I," says Strang, "not ordinary people; because the petty domestic tragicomedies of our lives are writ large, because whole worlds and civilizations can fall to dust if we utter a wrong word, a mistaken command."

"Yes, father," says Ash (and me too, listening intently) "Yes, I know."

The tunnel narrows. It's like we're little micronauts sailing through the bloodstream of a giant creature. "Do you know why I was so upset this morning?" Strang says.

"You had to have someone killed, didn't you?"

"You have to understand, boy. I need a better way. I need to know things. I'm a good king, mostly, I think, but it never seems to be enough. If only I could change the way men feel . . . if only I could make them see how great they can become when they join their dreams with mine. . . ."

"You think the better way is to have more power?"

Strang looks away. Into the distance, where the tunnel has narrowed to virtually nothing. Ash understands him, knows that each time he exercises his kingly authority, it eats away a little piece of his soul; I too understand a little more, although I'm seeing him from a whole 'nother vantage point, although I know how corrupt he's become, how much of his soul has been eaten away by the time I'm journeying with him, a thousand years later, in the wilderness of ice.

"Now which way?" Strang says.

"Left."

More and more. Twisting and turning. Bends in the river. Down, down, down. No silken thread to guide us back out of this labyrinth. Ash tells his father the way; I tell him the way because here in the past I still have all my powers, I haven't yet gone blind.

Now there are three pathways; darker, darker, and most dark. Ash knows the answer; so, I think, does Strang; he doesn't need truthsaying to figure that out. I point; Strang steers the boat; we go on. It's tough steering now, but Strang doesn't ask me to help him row; we both know why; it's a journey he has to undertake entirely with his own muscle; this is a game that you just can't cheat at. The waters are brackish. A corpse floats by, stinking, draped over driftwood. I think, it can't be this easy. There's got to be obstacles. You can't just sail right up the river into the mouth of hell without battling a few monsters.

That's when the boat thuds against rock.

The river can't be blocked. It's still flowing. But there's an island in our path, and the water's rushing through the living rock like it's not even there . . . and there's the obstacle! The guardian of the abyss! A humungous three-headed dog—

<u>P h i l   E t c h i s o n</u>

A sphinx, standing before a wall of impenetrable flame! Not the serene, pharaoh-headed sphinx of the desert, but the sphinx of the Oedipus legend, a winged yenta with the body of a lioness. Her shrieks make me shiver, and from her withered dugs runs blood, and her eyes are like ice.

"What'll we do?" I ask my son. The boat is about to be sucked into the flames.

"You know what to do," Chris says.

"Answer a riddle?" I said.

"I guess," Chris says. "Meanwhile, I'll try to keep you cool."

Chris spreads his wings, sheltering me from the heat of the flames; I can see that it pains him. But he smiles bravely and says, "Just call me Mr. Asbestos."

The sphinx has a curiously plaintive voice, like a cat, like a woman dying of cancer, my wife; she has my wife's eyes, too, those wild, wide, dark post-chemo eyes. "Phil Etchison," she calls, her soft voice echoing above the roaring flames, "why do you want to pass through the impenetrable fire?"

In the background, you hear a sort of Wagnerian melee of themes from *The Ring*, as in the scene where the god Wotan declares that only the hero who knows no fear shall pass through the flames to the sleeping goddess. Where is the orchestra, I wonder, just sawing away behind the curtain of fire, is it only a scrim, a projection, an illusion? I think, I can handle the sphinx, for god's sake! I'm an English major. I know my Greek mythology.

"Answer her, Dad," Chris says.

"Is it one of the riddles?" I say.

"Maybe," he says.

I call out to the sphinx, "I'm here because I'm dreaming. I think I'm living through someone else's experiences, but somehow making them my own—"

"Good answer," says the sphinx. "But now it's time for the riddle."

"Oh," I say, "I know the answer to your riddle. It's *man*. Four legs in the morning—as a baby—two in the daytime, three, with a cane, in the twilight of his life."

She laughs.

At this point, the sphinx is supposed to leap off a cliff to her doom, and then I enter the city in triumph and have sex with my own mother, and I end up having to pluck out my eyes. I know the score. But she only laughs and laughs and laughs, till the whole cavern echoes with the sound of witchery.

"I have a much harder question to answer than that," she says at last. "Come on, little man who would be a poet. You think I'd let you get away with Mythology 101?"

"I guess you're right." Standing in the pool of coolness, fanned by my son's bright wings, I still can't quite feel it's all real. "Fire away."

"The riddle of the sphinx is this: *If God commanded you to do it, would you sacrifice your own son?*"

"That's easy," I say. "I don't believe in God."

But my words ring false. There've been gods in my very own home, after all. But there's a difference between gods and God, I tell myself. The flames leap up higher, and there is definitely a stench of brimstone in my nostrils.

"Since you don't believe, you say—and I am not here to argue theology with you—I'll rephrase the question. *To save the universe, would you sacrifice your own son?*"

I stare at her. I stare at Chris. This is more than a riddle. The question is actually the answer. "Is this why you don't speak to me?" I cry out to my son.

"But I *am* speaking, Dad," he says, so softly his voice is almost one with the hiss of the spurting flames.

"But I'm *dreaming,*" I tell him, and I look at the sphinx in consternation as she shrugs, awaiting my answer, and—

Theo Etchison

—Cerberus, guardian of the underworld—I know all about him because he was on the boat when Thorn first abducted me from the Chinese Restaurant, way back in, as it were, the first volume of the trilogy, because when you're in an adventure like this you always think of it as a trilogy—okay so there he is, guarding the gateway to the underworld, barking up a storm from his three slavering mouths—he was a fuck of a lot tamer when I saw him way back then, but I've got to realize that though this is later in my stream of consciousness, it's earlier in the stream of time—

"Watch out for him, Father," I say. "He's probably rabid."

"No dog is going to stop me from pursuing this River to its beginning." His ice-blue eyes are already beginning to acquire that deadness that I first saw in him, when I first looked on him and wrote about him in my dream book; the obsession's there. But Ash can't know what I know. Unless I slip the images into his mind. . . .

The three-headed dog is charging us now. His three mouths are flecked with foam. Water churns around us. There's no way past him. "I can't very well throw him a piece of steak," says Strang. "I'm not prepared for this."

The dog growls, gnaws at the boat, chomps off a big chunk of the prow. We spring a leak. Strang leaps down and I follow. The dog rips off a piece of his robe. Ash cries out, "Throw me to him, Daddy—" and I think, you fool, it's not worth it, not for this, but I feel the force of his love for his father, I know there's no way I can break it.

Strang says, "I can't—"

I huddle in his arms. He throws his robe around me. The cloth, infused with spells of protection, feels cold, smells faintly of frankincense. The dog throws himself at us. Ash thrusts his hand into one of his mouths.

"He'll bite you!" Strang screams. "You'll lose your hand!"

But Cerberus seems to quiet down a little. He backs away to a slab of rock that blocks our access to the next leg of the stream. But I know he won't let us go on. He snarls. He froths.

"What do I have to do?" Strang grips me/Ash by the shoulders. His big hands clamp down and I feel the lust that drives him, the terrible need to control men's destinies. "This is important, Ash. Call the truthsayer inside you. Make him tell you what I must do."

And that's when I speak, through Ash's lips: *"If thine eye offend thee, pluck it out."*

Yeah. The Bible and *The Man with the X-Ray Eyes*. Suddenly I picture Dad in the living room expounding about how the same myths blow through both Bible and B movie. And Odin exchanging his eye as the price of knowledge. And Oedipus, too, losing both eyes because he can't face his new knowledge about himself. Yeah, all the stories, from Sophocles to Roger Corman, all jangling inside my head, all told in my father's deep, patient voice, each one a shiny jewel for the magpie's nest of my imagination. How true it is. King Strang looks at his son, sees me, standing there in the back of Ash's consciousness, knows me, though he will not meet me until much later in time; knows that what I'm saying is true, because a truthsayer's truthsaying always rings true.

And he howls. It's the first time I've heard this howl, though I've heard its future echo many times before. Howl, howl, howl. Oh, I'm afraid. This howl comes from the despair of knowing for the first time that the first step in any journey is the first step to that journey's end; that after Oz, the next exit off the yellow brick road is Death. Oh, God, he howls, and Ash, not understanding, howls with him; and then, indeed, he covers his face in his hands, and reaches in with his thumbs, and wrenches out his right eye, and thrusts it at the dog, howling, howling, howling; and then the dog trots forward, gulps it down, lies down at our feet, whimpering, our slave now; and I look at Strang, I look at the bleeding socket and the gore that spurts down his face and spatters his beard and his robe, and I see that the wall of rock is starting to crumble, and—

Phil Etchison

—and looking at my son I learn an awful new truth, the reason he hides behind silence, the reason he won't run into my arms and cry out *Dad Dad Dad,* the reason he will never say how much he loves me—

And I scream at the sphinx, at the top of my lungs, "No, no, I won't answer, you can't make me answer that question," and furiously I rush at the sphinx and I start pummeling her with my fists while my son wheels overhead, his wings burnished by the flames' reflection—

Theo Etchison

We step through the wall of rock. Ash (and I with him) holding his father's hand, guiding him gently. The dog follows us. He's meek now, sniffing our heels, whimpering.

And there it is.

The still point of the turning world.

The whirlpool, and, in the whirlpool's center, an eye of calm; and in that eye, floating to the surface, glittering, thousand-faceted like the compound eyes of an insect, is a crystal.

"Son," says Strang, "reach out there and grab it for me."

And I say, "No, father. It's for you to take."

Strang steps into the water. The water sears him. He howls again and again as he thrusts through the whirlpool to reach the quiet center.

"What is it?" he cries out to me.

And I say, through Ash's lips: "It's what you gave up your eye for. It's knowledge. It's the power to steal men's souls."

The king's fist closes around the jewel. We gaze at each other over the turbulent waters. I see that the light has fled from his good eye; that this moment contains a future moment, a moment we're all inexorably rushing to; and Jesus it scares me because I can see what that moment contains, because in *this* moment, I am a truthsayer, and I have not lost my vision—

Phil Etchison

—the sphinx shatters and spills into my arms and it's my wife and we're making love in the fireworks in a small Mexican town near a Laetrile clinic and—

Theo Etchison

—and I call out to my real father, my other father, lost in another labyrinth, and I—

Phil Etchison

—laughing, she says to me, "Aren't you lucky this is only a dream? Aren't you lucky you don't really have to answer the question?" and—

Theo Etchison

—the king, closing his eyes, cries out, "I dream, I dream, I dream"—

Phil Etchison

—and sobbing I wake up, on the shore of the island where stands the chariot of the sun, Odysseus' ship, the *Titanic,* the rusted station wagon of my life—

Theo Etchison

—and now more images, floods of memories—

The king implanting the jewel in the scepter. Fashioning a new eye from an iolite crystal, emerging triumphant on the balcony of the palace. Stealing his first soul. Feeling that first pang of guilt and terror.

And withdrawing further into himself.

And one by one, the lights darkening in the palace over the years, the turrets falling into disrepair, the minarets shrouding themselves with rust and dust and birdshit. And the kingdom growing. Growing. But not like a tree. No vegetable love here, as Dad would say. The kingdom grew like a cancer. The kingdom was its own sickness, its own corruption—

Phil Etchison

—and the dream was etched in my mind, every byway and fork and crossing, so that at last, I, Philip Etchison, the plainest Everyman who ever lived, possessed a piece of my son's magic: I too had a map, I too knew the way to the source of the River that runs between worlds.

But I wasn't sure I could *read* the map . . . .

Theo Etchison

—and there, on the island, sitting beside the mad king, I know that the jewel in the scepter is the same jewel as the eye of knowledge. Ash has gone to ashes, but I can bring them back, I can bring them all back. Death is pregnant with renewal.

King Strang says to me, "I've seen things I shouldn't have seen. If I had my real eye back, I would be blind again. I wish I were."

"What would you say to Ash," I ask him, "if he were sitting with us now?"

The king says: "I don't know. We'd have to try it. A little at a time."

I say, "You wanted me to lead the way to the source even though I've lost my gift."

"You people never lose it all the way."

"Well yeah, I wanted to tell you, I didn't know the way before. But now I do. Because, in a way, I've been there."

The ashes swirl in the bright air, sparkling, star dust. The ashes settle a little. They fleck his beard. They clog the creases in his brow. I wonder if he knows how close Ash is, how little time he still has.

CHAPTER TWELVE

THE BATTLE OVER THE AMETHYST CITY

Chris Etchison

—navigating—

I raise up my arms. I split the iceberg. The ship busts through. Cold. Cold. Funnels belch dark smoke. Satanic mills. Demons blacken the sky. Thorn paces up and down on the ship's uppermost deck. Cerberus is running amok, worrying at three old bones. Cornelius Huang paces too, a few paces behind his lord and master so he won't intrude on him. All I'm thinking about is—

—navigating—

—navigating—

The ship shatters more ice. Ice scatters. A million itty-bitty rainbow prism fractures hailing down, the whole sky shivery and shimmery. Thorn says: "How soon, how soon? I'm hungry."

—carving great channels in the ice floes—

Cornelius Huang: "Your hunger is a great consuming flame, my lord; soon it will swallow up the world."

"Bullshit!" says Thorn. "I'm just hungry."

The slate-colored eyes are the color of the gray gray sky.

—listen listen listen—

Thorn and Cornelius buzz around my thoughts. Like horseflies, worrying at me. Shutting out the heartbeat I need to hear.

—we'll never get there if you don't—

"Stop for a moment! Look, isn't that a city?" says Thorn.

Across-looking, beyond the ice: a patch of lavender light. A city all in amethyst.

Huang says: "My lord, we have to hurry if we're going to reach the source before anyone else."

"I don't care. I'm hungry."

Not a physical need, this hunger. Thorn feeds on power, on subjugation, on submission. He needs to oppress someone. An itch that has to be scratched.

"Truthsayer," he says, "lead us to that city. We'll lay it waste, eat up a few souls, then go on to the source when we're all full."

I won't need to delay the journey. Thorn's own greed will do it for me.

Serena Somers

Mr. E. came cruising toward us in this kind of speedboat thing that also looked like an old station wagon. "Pile in," he said. I got in on the passenger side.

"What about you?" Mr. E. said to Milt, who was still putting away his fishing pole.

"First things first," Milt said. "We have to make sure the mother-goddess is comfortable." He and I carried the Mary statue, placed her reverently in the back seat, made sure she was adequately belted in.

"Think I'll just ride on the hood," Milt said. He swirled around and at first I thought he was going into one of his man-woman transformation things, but no, with every twist he seemed more and more feathery and more and more black. He spread his arms and did like, this flapping, springing sort of dance, eerily graceful.

He flapped and flapped and flapped himself into a great black raven and perched himself where the hood ornament should have been if Joshua hadn't stolen it years ago to use as part of a collage in Mrs. Shigenaka's art class. He wasn't all raven, either; sometimes he looked completely human.

Guess it shouldn't have surprised me.

Mr. E. said, "Serena, Serena, I've had the strangest dream. I think I know where we're going now."

I said, "Cool, Mr. E. Where's that?"

"It's a place I visited in the dream. I can't really explain. I've got a kind of map of it in my head. But I don't know how to read it."

"Joshua could read it if he were here."

"I know," he said. "And Chris wouldn't need a map at all. And Theo. . . ."

"Can we find them?"

"I think I already have. At least, inside the dream I did. I just have to get back."

The raven screeched, a word that sounded something like "Shebabalah."

He put the car into drive. There were a lot more gears on the gearshift than I thought cars were supposed to have.

"Mr. E., we're on an island. How far are you going to drive, maybe a hundred feet?"

"I got the car here, didn't I? Let's take it as it comes."

The engine purred.

"The gas gauge is on E," I pointed out.

"This car apparently doesn't run on gas at all," he said, "but on the stuff of dreams. Close your eyes and make a wish."

Joshua, I thought, hard, with all my might.

Joshua at the edge of the bed, Joshua smiling, Joshua picking at a zit,

Joshua in an oversize sweater, reaching out to me, Joshua in my arms, dead—

The car began to move.

I opened my eyes.

"Good," Mr. E. said. "Your dreams are very lucid. Look in the side mirror. Your side, not mine."

I did. And there he was, standing by the car door, in the oversize sweater, picking a zit, smiling, laughing even, but he vanished into thin air as soon as I tried to concentrate.

The car pushed off into the water. Zoomed, in fact, churning up a wall of water on either side. We zigzagged around the standing stones, rounded the tip of a sphinx, vaulted all the way up the side of a pyramid, hung in mid-air for the splittest of seconds, crashed hard into the crystal foam. The raven turned to us. His eyes were shining. In a moment we were just skimming along.

Reached the bank. A road ran alongside the river. A autobahn with signs in hieroglyphics. We were speeding now and the woods and hills were a blur of green-gold-icy-blue. The sky flashed with purple light-ning—the lights of a city just over the horizon.

The raven shrieked: *Shebabalah! Shebabalah!*

"What the hell does that mean!" I said.

"My wife would probably know."

I turned to look at Mrs. E., but she was, of course, a statue. When she is in this state, it takes her a thousand years to take a single breath. She can't exactly answer questions, but she does the enigma of a godthing really well. Mr. E. drove on. The landscape was alien and rural: checker-board fields in garish hues of neon pink: and lime, mountains shaped like fists, shaking at the setting sun.

"Are you hungry?" Mr. E. said.

"Hungry: I guess so. We could fish, maybe. I think it's unlikely that we'll find a McDonald's around here." You know, when there's a furious dragon, gnawing away at the pit of your stomach, the thought of food seems totally distasteful.

"You never know. There is a city up ahead. We should stop. Maybe get a decent night's sleep in a hotel. Take a shower. Watch cable. You know, all the things one does on the road."

"You're daydreaming, Mr. E.!"

"Maybe not."

We're swiftly passing by signs that say GAS FOOD LODGING. Say other things too: CHEAP SEX. FACTORY OUTLET MALLS. PUBLIC EXECUTIONS. This is quite a town we're racing to.

"Stop for a moment," I said. Mr. E. pulled over. We got out and stood by a clump of saguaro under a purple-brown sky. "I've got an idea."

The raven, who had detached himself from the hood, and was circling overhead, came down and perched by the side mirror, tapping at the window as if he needed to talk.

"I see you agree with me," I said. "The goddess goes on the hood, not the shaman."

I remembered that Mary Etchison was much worshipped in the many worlds we'd passed through. We'd get a much better reception in a strange city if we were preceded by divinity.

"So we'll tie her to the bumper, like a—like a dead deer?" said Mr. E., appalled.

"No," I said. "I think she'll find her own way of adapting. She usually does."

The raven cawed out that weird-sounding word, over and over. "What's he talking about?" I asked Mr. E., because he always seemed to know such things.

"It sounds to me like Xibalba," he said, "which is to say, the labyrinth of nightmares. It's some ancient Maya thing," he added with a glance at the raven; he probably felt a twinge of political incorrectness, lecturing about Native Americans in the presence of a real-live one.

Milt Stone morphed back to humanoid for a moment. "You're right," he said. "For a paleface, you're pretty perceptive."

"Good," I said, "you're human enough to help us with Mrs. E."

We sort of hefted her onto the hood, and you know, the very first thing that statue did was to like, shrink into about the size of a hood ornament, and to stand, her robes fluttering, with open wings, the way they do on Rolls Royces—or is it Bentleys?—or on the prow of an ancient ship. It was totally cool. But why not?

"Fascinating," Mr. E. said. "She's very adaptable, isn't she? She's had many shapes and sizes. She's been in a lot of places at the same time.

One of the rules seems to be that, if two of her are in roughly the same location, one of them gets subsumed into the other. Two of her can't occupy the same perceptual cosmos. . . ."

"That's pretty intellectual-sounding , Mr. E.," I said. One of Mr. E.'s problems is that he's always trying to figure out the underlying rules of whatever cosmos he finds himself in. This is okay, to some extent, but the rules always end up breaking down, don't they? Better to take it as it comes . . .

"Okay," he said.

So now we're in a battered old station wagon with a wheezing air conditioner with a goddess as a hood ornament, and a raven wheeling overhead. And we're closing in on the Amethyst City, kilometer by kilometer. That's how I thought of it in my mind. It makes sense, once you're in Oz, that there should be a city for every precious stone.

Chris Etchison

—swooping—

Demons are spreading their wings. Diving off the upper deck of the ship and flinging themselves against the purple minarets. Screeching, howling, shrilling. Thorn watches with me.

"Come on, boy," he says.

—what about the pursuit of the source?—

"First, dinner." He claps his hands and they roll out a blood-red carpet woven with designs of skulls and crossbones. "You like Arabian food?" he says.

—not if it's sucked from the living—

Thorn laughs.

He spreads out his cloak on it. Motions me to sit down beside him; then, knocking on the cloak three times, causes the carpet to levitate. I hold on tight. The carpet ripples, threatens to throw me off. I cling to the frayed fringe. We're in the midst of the squadron of demons. Their gargoyle faces spit fire. They black out the bloody sun.

Down-looking now: streets full of panicking citizens. Men in bejeweled turbans fending off the diving demons. Naked children dashing through the alleys, veiled women running in circles.

We flit over an avenue, careen down a twisty muddy lane; a woman being raped against the side of a great stone statue of the goddess, a bewildered zebra running wild with his gold chain clanking against the gutter, a man trying to ward off the demons by flinging stones . . .

Thorn's very smug, very satisfied; he feeds as much off the commotion and the confusion as off blood; as we speed over gardens of rose and lilac, we watch one of his minions twist the head off a child and toss it in the air so that it lands in Thorn's lap, and he bends over and slurps up the hot carotid blood but I look away; but I can still see it of course, I can feel it, a sharp dissonance in the music of my mind; I can't help seeing it because I'm a truthsayer.

The flying carpet comes to rest at last. A purple parapet overlooking the city's central square. Thorn tosses the head into the street. On the terrace, priestesses in sweeping lilac robes are propitiating a huge statue of a weeping woman. My mother. Clouds of lavender-tinged incense. The women beat their breasts, tear at their hair, wail, moan, make a ferocious noise. The high priestess wears silver horns, and one breast has been replaced by a breast-shaped crystal of deepest amethyst; and when she sees Thorn she holds up her hand. At once, the cries of lamentation cease. The priestesses regroup. They stand in a semi-circle, protecting the statue of the mother goddess. We are in a little pocket of silence, but from beyond the parapet the dying can be heard screaming.

Thorn says, "You've turned your back on me."

The priestess says, "We heard you were dead."

"Never dead," says Thorn, "not so long as my name lives on. Now let's get rid of your goddess and put up the proper statues; it's fine to worship her in secret, in the catacombs, in the gutter, but this city's my turf." The priestess throws herself at Thorn, tries to scratch out those slate-colored eyes. But Thorn merely laughs, slaps her around a little—casually stoops to kiss her fingertips and draw a drop or two of hieratic blood—then cries out: "Time to topple the bitch!"

A passel of demons hovering around Thorn's head like a black halo; at his command, they switch direction, swirl, reconstitute, gather into an arrow of dark flesh and smash into the statue. The statue totters, tumbles. The priestesses scream. Thorn laughs like an evil scientist. He guffaws, he yawps, and the wind picks up his laughter and sends it echoing back and forth and back and forth.

The statue: suddenly: just before it hits the ground: a burst of purple radiance from the sky . . . lightning . . . thunder, like the crack of a great stone heart . . . then, all at once, the statue disappearing in a flash of white light.

Thorn stops laughing.

"The goddess has disappeared," says one of the priestesses. "That means—"

Another says, "—that another incarnation of the goddess has entered the city—that means—"

"That the battle isn't over yet—"

Thorn turns to me. "Quick! Where is the goddess? Who's brought that bitch into the city?"

I close my eyes and:

Listen, listen:

First the heartbeat of the world. Then, above it, the pounding surf that is life, human and alien, angel and demon: high above, the pinprick birth and death pangs of the stars.

Mother, I cry out in my mind.

And this is what I see:

The hood of a beat-up station wagon, wheezing up a freeway somewhere . . . Arizona? Perhaps it was Arizona once, before the River changed its course.

Behind the wheel are Philip and Serena. Wheeling in the sky is a black raven; and the hood ornament is the triple goddess. Somewhere in that car there is also a dragon, but she is invisible.

—the goddess is at the gates—

Thorn stands tall but in his eyes there is consternation.

Phil Etchison

—and so I drove up to the gates of amethyst—I was in about seventeenth gear by this time—and the gates shattered and I drove on past them. Fire was racing up and down the streets. Demons were swooping down from the sky. The cobblestones, the walls, the storefronts, even the fast-food places were a million shades of crystal purple, but the liquid fire that spewed over them all was neon green. Purple and green comic-book villain colors . . . the colors of the Joker, who is also the Antichrist. . . .

"Duck!" Serene screamed. I steered hard left to avoid a Temple-of-Doom-sized ball of flame, crashed through a lavender store window, could stop the car in time to hit a blank wall, but—

The wall just pulverized itself at the last minute and I sped through, did a sort of bounce down into an alley, zoomed on.

"How did that happen?" I said.

"Look," said Serena. "It's the goddess." Sure enough, the hood ornament that had been my wife had changed position: she was standing up straight now, one arm held out in a warding-off-evil gesture, the other over her heart.

"Mary!" I cried.

The hood ornament turned and winked at me.

"Way to go, Mrs. E.!" cried Serena. Then, suddenly, she clutched her stomach as we swerved past a soda fountain that featured a ten-foot-high purple sundae in the window and a flock of festive demons inside.

"What's wrong?" I said, slowing down a little.

"My stomach," she said. "It's all . . . churning. . . ."

"Butterflies in your stomach?"

I heard a whirring from beneath her dress, Like the sound of locusts hitting a wheatfield. "More than butterflies," she said.

"A dragon?"

Smoke belched up through cracks in the crystal pavement, "Yes," she said.

Chris Etchison

At that moment, I clutch a pure white tone that squeezes itself out of the heat-haze of the burning city and—

I weave that tone around me until it becomes a circle that is both light and music all at once, and—

Spin and spin and—

White-hot! Blue-hot! The music of the spheres and—

Mom, I cry out once more, and—

—Mom—

—Mom—

I hear her coming. She's raising up her right arm and with her right arm she's crossing her heart.

Thorn is glowering.

"Where's the fucking goddess?" he screams, and grabs me through the cocoon of light and tries to shake me by the shoulders but the power of the music is too strong for him, it burns him and he backs away and—

Serena Somers

This time the dragon really wanted out, and I knew that if I grew into the fifty-foot woman again I'd bust through the roof of the station wagon and then I suppose we'd get rained on or something once we started back up the road. Wasn't thinking too straight, but I had the presence of mind to hop out of the passenger seat in a hurry. Not a second too late because as soon as my feet hit the sidewalk they started to grow. Meanwhile, my stomach was really churning and I was sure there was going to be a remake of the gut-popping scene from Alien right here in the middle of the street.

I reached out, grasped the cherry from the ten-foot sundae and it skittered down the burning pavement like a big purple marble.

I need something to settle my stomach! I thought to myself. The dragon was rearing this way and that inside me. I couldn't tell if Katastrofa wanted to get out to help her brother or to battle him, or whether she was just going to come bursting forth in a tumult of raw, ungovernable energy. I looked up at the sky—

C h r i s   E t c h i s o n

—Mom—

S e r e n a   S o m e r s

I gazed at the hood ornament, which was spinning, its arms whizzing back and forth, palms held out, deflecting laser shafts as the demons in the sky blasted us with their burning eyes.

Milt Stone, too, wheeled overhead, dashing his beak against one demon after another, making them sizzle and plummet, but there was always a fresh gargoyle figure to attack; the sky was black with them.

I sure needed something to settle my stomach—

CHAPTER THIRTEEN

THE RETURN OF THE TRIPLE GODDESS

Chris Etchison

—Mom—

Serena Somers

Well like, then I suddenly knew what I had to do. Oren always used to lecture me about checks and balances and branches of government when I was working for his campaign, oh, I don't know, fifty million universes ago. I was shooting up like, well, like Alice in Wonderland, and there was a dragon flailing around inside my belly, and now and then tendril of smoke was totally pouring out of my nostrils, and I felt a hell of a tickle at the back of my throat, but I thought, oh, God, if I cough, the whole street will explode in a ball of flame. There was only one way to balance the dragon.

I knelt down beside the station wagon. I cupped my hands around the hood ornament. Milt, approvingly, circled my head, and I could once more hear that other worldly screech: *Xibalba, Xibalba*. Mr. E. looked pretty panicky, though.

"That's my wife," he cried out.

I said, trying hard not to boom, "It's okay, Mr. E. I'm only borrowing her for a few hours. The transformation wasn't complete before, but now it will be."

Mr. E. puzzled over this—the motor was still running—and then he suddenly cried out, "Why, of course! The triple goddess . . . virgin, mother, crone . . . or should I say, young woman, dragon, hood ornament? Without the third piece of the puzzle, you were almost the real thing, but now you can be it all . . . and you can really *fight* the forces of darkness."

"It's not really a light versus dark thing, Mr. E.," I said. "It's more yin and yang . . . it's more the feminine principle counteracting the masculine . . . you know the kind of thing I mean."

I stood up . . . I hadn't yet reached the full fifty feet, but I was about a couple of stories high now . . . and I lifted the hood ornament to my lips. I looked around for a fire hydrant, kicked it open so that it spouted up lavender water, took a swig, then swallowed the goddess as if it were the toughest pill in the universe.

It caught in my throat for a moment, and then, as though my saliva were an acid bath, it smoothed itself out and slid down to meet the dragon. I felt like a glass of water that you pop an alka-seltzer into . . . when it hit my stomach, I started to hear the rumbling. Then I kind of stretched like a really big yawning kind of stretch . . . and all of a sudden there were these lines of fire gridding up and down me. I was powerful. Not just tall and strong, but full of the pull of the earth itself; where my feet touched the ground they linked with the nervous system of a whole planet. My hair was a mess of fiery serpents.

"Here I come, Thorn," I shouted.

I was naked, too, and my hips and breasts were full, robust, like those obese prehistoric Venuses, bursting with fertility. I covered my vulva with my left hand because the dragon inside it might spew fire and devastate the alleyway.

Where was Thorn?

Chris Etchison

—Mom—

—and then I see her. Rearing up above the parapets of amethyst and sugilite. A woman in flames, her eyes white-hot, her breasts brimming and fecund, yeah, I see her. She is beautiful. And then—

The priestesses are all falling to their knees and crying out, "The Goddess, the Goddess." Thorn stares about, Cornelius holds up the trumpet, the three-headed dog yaps.

"Muster the demons," Thorn cries. He pauses to suck the juices from a dead woman, then tosses her over the stone tiles down to the street beneath. The triple goddess towers over us. Her hair is a mass of fiery snakes.

Cornelius blows his horn: three sharp blasts that shatter the heartbeat of the cosmos into a rhythmic cacophony.

Up-looking: the black sky splits into three stripes, three ranks of dark angels: mandibled, drooling, fanged. Each file is arrowed at the triple goddess.

Three more blasts—

Then Serena-Katastrofa-Mary flings her arms wide and her breasts heave like volcanoes, and I can hear the warm milk churning, the milk that is the manna that is the nectar of the gods.

"Get out of my city," she whispers: her whisper makes the pillars rattle.

"No, you slug," says Thorn, but he sounds listless, not at all defiant. Turning to Cornelius, he orders him to sound the trumpet once more.

"Nobody calls me slug now!" screams Serena. One at a time, the lines of demons hurl themselves at the goddess. The goddess spins; she twists; she dances. The demons shatter like glass. They snap in her hands. They dash themselves into pieces. Dead demon shards pelt down, obsidian rain.

The goddess shrieks, and from her lips stream moons and stars that flock up heavenward, each planetary body thrumming with the crystal harmony that makes up the music of the spheres.

And I say:

—Mom—

but suddenly I realize for a fact that the man I call my father has entered the city, is nearby, and I know too that I soon will lose the power of speech, because I can't say what I have to say and still remain his son, can't break his heart, can't stop the spinning cycle of our fate (and I hear my father's voice now in my memories, making some curious dry pun about spin cycles and washing machines), can't say what I have to say because the moment isn't right yet, feel all wrung out inside and out because what I have to say is so, you know, so, so, so fucking crucial to the world.

The priestesses are still prostrate—those that survived the attack of Thorn. The goddess slams her fist on the parapet and a crystal causeway arches up and over and down to the lowest story of the palace.

Thorn says, "Come on, boy. We've been here too long anyway"

Cornelius says, "My lord, we seem to have lost the advantage."

Thorn says, "Fuck the advantage. I came here to eat, and I'm full now."

"But I thought you wanted to recapture the Amethyst City from the Triple Goddess," Cornelius Huang says.

"I don't give a flying fuck about that bitch," says Thorn. "Grab the kid and let's get out."

And I can't speak, because, inching up the causeway at a gravity-defying angle, a battered station wagon is creeping, led by a raven with bright eyes and open wings; and because *he's* so close, I'm frozen, I'm back to the state of dumbness.

"What are you staring at, kid?" Thorn screams.

—*—
—*and*—
—*father*—
—*and*—

I can't even get out one syllable. But I feel a great music welling up inside me, a music of desire and loss and the impermanence of the world; and that is weird because I'm a truthsayer and I see the things that are real, firm, permanent, the bedrock beneath the shifting sands of illusion, and here I am hearing the counterpoint pound louder than the theme. I open my lips and a few notes come tearing out and the notes sunder the sky, and then Thorn and Cornelius grab hold of me and drag me, carry me, across the parapet, away from the triple goddess and the car, and the car has screeched to a halt and Phil is standing there and he's calling to me, "Chris, Chris," but I wonder if what he sees is really me because for those few seconds I can't hear the real music. And in that split second of doubt Cornelius Huang kind of wraps me in a bubble of his trumpet's blasting. The blast is piercing, crimson-sounding; it coils around me, renders me helpless long enough for Thorn to cast his cloak of darkness over me, and then we're flying again, flying and fleeing, to where the ship of lost souls is docked beside the sundered city—

"Quick, boy!" Thorn cries out. "Make us a new gateway! Get us to the source, the fastest way you can!"

—and I—

—fly—

Phil Etchison

I saw him. I really saw him. Chris just the way I saw him last. Looking back at us, being flown up into the sky, staring fixedly at me with an expression I couldn't fathom: oh, I know he is brighter than me, and sees more, hears more, understands more, but still he's a child, and it breaks my heart, that's what it does to me.

We pulled up to about the middle of the parapet and parked. There was a broken altar. The priestesses were getting up, helping each other up, adjusting their headdresses, recoiling the silver snakes they wore around their bare breasts.

Serena still loomed above us; there was a hint of sunlight behind her hair; we watched at the edge of the terrace; Thorn's ship, which might or might not have been the *Titanic*, lumbered off upstream, past floes and

icebergs, toward a shimmering circle of light that I knew was Chris'
gateway to the next portion of the journey toward the source.

The priestesses all turned and fell prostrate once more, this time in
front of the congressional page turned live-in president's lover turned
giantess. Serena blinked, and a beam of laser light ignited the altar, and
it soon plowed, deep, rich purple. Violet smoke curled skyward.

"I guess I should come back to earth now," she said.

She put her hands together in a Buddhalike gesture. And started to
shrink, but not before coughing out the hood ornament, which landed
with perfect precision on a plinth, where once my wife's statue had
doubtless stood. I wondered whether she would disgorge the dragon as
well—there was a lot of fire still whirling about her body—but I guess she
managed to hold it down. She was no longer naked, by the way, but
dressed in an unassuming pair of jeans and a shapeless, oversized Beavis
and Butthead sweater.

"You seem younger, somehow," I said.

Serena said, "I am, Phil. I've shed about seven years since we all got
back into this adventure; what I thought were seven years, Oren winning
the presidency, my moving into the White House, all banquets, speeches,
and congress-wrangling, they all turned out to have been a dream, didn't
they? And like, now I'm barely out of high school again."

"Where's the dragon?" I said.

"Around my neck," she said, and pointed to a shiny amulet. I came
closer, and I saw now that she wore the dragon; that the coin-sized
creature was alive, spluttering up tiny tendrils of smoke, squirming
against the space between Serena's breasts, clawing at her skin. "And
she'll stay there until I need her again."

Serena, for once, seemed to live up to her name. There was a kind of
tranquillity in her features that, once or twice, I'd seen in my wife's face;
sometimes it would be when she and I stood in the doorway and watched
our babies sleeping; sometimes it was after she and I made love.

Milt Stone, all raven now, perched on my shoulder and stared out at
the world with icy eyes.

One of the priestesses—a head priestess of some kind, I guess, because
she wore a plumed crown and a silver torc above her bare breasts—came
up to me; stretched out her palm reverentially toward me as in an Egyptian mural; touched her lips; bowed deeply.

"I am," she said, "the priestess Polydora. 'Thank you for bringing our
goddess back to life. I take it you're the Mortal Consort, the hero who
keeps the flame."

"I didn't realize I was anything at all in this drama. I mean, my sons have become seers, my wife is a goddess, even my former baby-sitter has turned into a scared cow and then—I thought I was the one guy left out of everything—you know, like Joseph, shut out of the whole Madonna and Child situation, always suffering from a complex at having been cuckolded by the Holy Ghost."

I said, "The way this goddess keeps coming and going, vanishing and reappearing—it's very confusing."

"I know," the priestess said. "The goddess is real, and the goddess is alive, and the goddess is omnipresent, but her physical manifestation can't occupy the same general area in more than one form: that would violate the paradox of allness-in-oneness."

"So if two statues of my wife are near one another, one of them disintegrates?"

"That's how we knew that the goddess was on her way to rescue us. Well perhaps you'd like to attend a celebratory banquet, since the City of Amethyst has been rescued from the forces of darkness one more time."

This was all wonderful and good, you know, but I had to confess that there was a certain remoteness about all this frantic, mythic warfare. I really could have cared less that there were goddess-cities and Strang-cities and there was a perpetual state of Manichaean tension between them. I just wanted to get on with the journey. "Can't we forge ahead?" I said. "They'll get to the source before us if we don't hurry."

Serena said, "They may, Phil, but the final conflict can't be fought without all the protagonists present: the sensible thing would be to get a little food into your stomach."

"And then?" I said.

"And then resume our quest," Milt said, or rather croaked, since he was still a raven; then he craned back his neck and shrieked, "Xibalba."

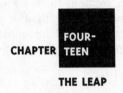

CHAPTER FOUR-TEEN

THE LEAP

T h e o   E t c h i s o n

So here I am, the blind leading the one-eyed king. I look through the eyes of Ash, who knows the way because he once looked through my eyes. As Dad would say, paradoxes within paradoxes. Cool. He loves paradoxes. Thinks they have a sparkle to them, like brilliant-cut diamonds.

"So you do know the way," says King Strang.

"I guess so, dude," I say.

Around us, the water ripples. The blue sun dances on the lake. The concentric stones are all shiny and metallic, like they've just been minted, glittering against the deep.

"I bet," says Strang, "that it's down."

"Yeah," I say. The journey to the heart of things is always down. That's a new truth that I see clearly now, even without my gift. The path to the summit of the world is through the center of hell. Fucking Jesus I see it all so clearly now, that shiny paradox, I can just imagine Dad holding it out to me in the palm of his hand and grinning, probably muttering something about the human condition.

"You've been a good fool," says Strang, "you've never lied to me."

"I know the way now, nuncle. It's like, totally through the darkness and out the other side. Like a black hole."

The water swirls around our little island. We are the eye of the whirlpool. We climb a little higher up on the standing stone, using the basalt ledges that are barely wide enough to hold our feet. Strang goes ahead of me, his scepter under one arm, now and then reaching for me so I can steady him. He seems frail, but there are sinews beneath the soft skin; he has one last great act of power left inside him; but since I am no longer a truthsayer, I can't know what it is exactly; I can only feel the surge of energy. Clutching the rock as he does, he draws strength. Perhaps it is because he's a child of earth, and the earth still suckles him.

"Do you know where we're going?" he says again. It's one of those magic questions, the ones that you have to ask three times before the answer actually comes true.

"Yeah," I say. "Into the arms of darkness."

We have reached the topmost ledge. The king squats, stares out at the churning lake; his face is as furrowed and pitted as the moon. I can't tell his good eye from his bad; they're both like ice. "So you're saying," the king says, "that I just have to stand up, open my arms, and leap."

"I think so," I say. "We've reached a place where thousands of pieces of the river intermingle . . . maybe every molecule that jostles every other molecule is a molecule from a different universe . . . you see what I mean? We're going to have to rely on instinct . . . well, faith, maybe."

"You are still a truthsayer, boy."

"I can't see the truth anymore, but maybe the memory is in the cells of my body . . . you know, the way Dad gets in a car sometimes, and he's all talking about Keats and Shelley, and he never once looks at the road, but the way home is imprinted deep inside him so that he always makes the right turns, doesn't exit the Beltway at the wrong place; so what I'm saying is, that you and I were there once . . . well, you were physically there, and I was there inside of someone else who is now inside of me . . ." I know that Ash is around because, now and then, I sneeze.

I scramble up onto the topmost ledge beside him.

"Hair-raising, isn't it, boy?"

"I guess."

The wind rises a little. I shiver. "And we just jump?"

"What? So momentous an event, one small step, one giant leap and all that, and there's not even a modicum of thunder and lightning to portend the drama of the moment?"

Far, far away, a lone fork of lightning tickles the horizon. Far, far away, a burp of thunder; or maybe it's just the splash of a pebble, or a blind bird braining itself against the standing stones . . . not with a bang but with a whimper, that's what Dad would've said, declaiming his T. S. Eliot over a massive pot roast. To travel to other worlds, you first have to die a little. Dying can be a metaphor or dying can be real. I wonder which it's going to be this time.

"C'mon, King Strang," I say. "Time for the chicken to cross the road."

"Are you saying I'm a coward?"

I laugh. "Let's go, already."

King Strang stretches up to his full, majestic height; yes, there is still one great spell inside him, one final making or unmaking. He scares me. The sky darkens and yes, there's another thunderbolt, a little closer; and when he lifts up his arms, the wind begins to whistle, to encircle him, and his hair starts flying, and yeah, he is like King Lear after all, old, mad, possessive; his robes begin to flap and they are more thunderous than the thunder; his eyes flash and they are brighter than the lightning.

"Do you know me?" he screams. "Do you know who I am?"

I try to answer until I realize he's not shouting at me. He's shouting at the elements, the storm, the lake.

"I'm the king of the whole damn universe," he cries, and he twirls his scepter above his head like a demented cheerleader. "I'm the head honcho, the judge, the reckoner, the destroyer of worlds!" He doesn't say it like he means it though. There's a lot of despair here. I feel it. The storm around us has been wrought by the turbulence within him. "Do you know how many souls have been sucked into the jewel in my scepter? Do you know how many deaths have fed my power? Millions, billions, trillions."

"But you need one more death," I scream back at him.

"My own?"

Thunder and lightning. His eyes darken, redden. There is a hint of the dragon about him. I sneeze again. Ash is filling my lungs.

"Hold on to me," I say, and grasp his gnarled hand, and then, together, we both jump.

Phil Etchison

—and ride in triumph through Persepolis?—

I thought to myself, *Is it not passing brave to be a king?* There were too many great poets jangling in my head. Maybe that's why I could never quite become one myself. The women of the Amethyst City were crowning me, robing me in ermine and purple, while Serena looked on and Milt wheeled above my head. Below, the gutted streets were full of people, and they were cheering, and there were fireworks.

"Why are you crowning me?" I asked the high priestess.

"Because you saved our city."

"But I'm leaving. Got a train to catch, as they say."

"It's all right," she said. "It's just a formality; this city is really a matriarchy anyway. But we do need a quick dose of spectacle to make up for the carnage we've been through."

That night, there came to me another woman, in a palace apartment overlooking the river. I was alone this time; Serena and Milt had found other things to do; I think they were a lot more in tune with the goddess-ruled religiosity of the place than I.

The woman's name was Porphyria, and, true to her name, she was pale and purple-haired, and her hair was her only clothing. She seemed very young—well, maybe not her eyes—but she carried herself like a queen.

"Your Majesty," she said to me (a weird thing to say to a man in a T-shirt and faded boxer shorts) "is there anything I can do for you?" I took it that she meant in a sexual sense, because why else would a naked woman show up in a man's bedroom and smile brazenly at him with her hair fluttering just a little in the breeze from the river, and a tallow candle in her hand, set in a heart-shaped candleholder?

I said, "But I'm married." Not that I had a wedding band or anything bourgeois like that.

She said, "I know."

"I can't go through with—"

"It is traditional for the conquering hero to take the goddess herself to bride."

And still she came toward me. She smelled of rain. Like the first time I saw Mary. "Is it raining?" I asked Rapunzel of the purple tresses.

She laughed, shook her hair, sprayed me a little. "Only in your memories," she said.

And then I understood what she meant. My wife is a statue in this world, a mysteriously self-replicating statue that obeys a whole different set of laws of physics. I can't make love to a statue, but . . .

She shakes her hair again. Between the curve of her breasts, I see an amulet that bears a remarkable resemblance to a certain hood ornament. . . .

"Mary?" I said softly.

Porphyria smiled.

I thought: What is it about this woman that reminds me of my wife? Is it only the smell of rain, that lashing, scalding Virginia rain that reeks of fertility? Because that was the first time we met, that wetness clinging to her. She smiled. My wife had a crooked way of smiling sometimes; I wonder if she always knew she was sick, that every breath she took was pregnant with impending death. Porphyria smiled and moved a little closer, and when she touched my cheek I could feel Mary's soul.

"How do you do that?" I asked her.

"Prayer," Porphyria said, "and meditation. We breathe in the goddess' essence with a special kind of incense."

"Mary," I said, "Oh, Mary, Mary," because we rarely made love any-more, not since Chris was born, and it was taking a moment for my body to remember how it was supposed to react; but she touched my lips with a pungent finger, and said only, "Not Mary, not Mary; I am only her shadow's shadow."

Then she enveloped me in herself, and I too breathed in the essence of the great mother, my wife. Porphyria seemed to grow and grow; I don't mean she became bloated and hideous, like those two-thousand-pound women on *Donahue*, but that her womanliness seemed to spread out from her so that she was in the bedsheets, in the air, in the dust, in the walls, in the carpeting, in the feathers in the pillows. If I had not loved her I might have found the experience disquietingly arachnoid.

We made love, and the next morning Porphyria baked me a loaf of bread, wrapped two baked fishes in a banana leaf, and put them in a basket for me; and she said to me, kissing me awake, "These are for your journey." She also made a fresh pot of coffee, and we drank it from amethyst coffee mugs, and I could hear the whisper of the River from the open window, and I could see the gauze curtains shifting in the breeze.

I left the apartment and walked over to the parapet of the goddess.

The station wagon had been buffed, and it shone as though it were the chariot of the sun. Milt was back in human form now, robed in black feathers from head to toe, and looking as sexually ambiguous as ever, with his eyes heavily mascaraed and his lips painted goth-black . . . .

Serena Somers

That night, they put me up in the goddess suite—that's how it seemed—a penthouse overlooking the river. It was even better than the White House. For one thing, you didn't have to call down to the kitchen for room service; you could just clap your hands, and whatever came to mind would appear, probably on a silver platter, trumpets blaring. To think we decided to stop here for a burger and fries on our way to the great rendezvous. . . .

In the middle of the night, in the moonlight, after I had hung the dragon pendant over the mirror, a man came to me. He wore nothing but his own purple hair, twined and twisted around his body so that it was like a silky tunic. His eyes had a silvery tinge to them, like the moon; his fingernails, too, were painted silver.

"Goddess," said the man—more boy than man, perhaps— "is there anything I can do?"

I realized that I hadn't had sex in a very, very long time. Moreover, I had never had sex since becoming a goddess. It certainly put a different spin on things. It wasn't that I felt the way I think men feel, when they see women as a garden, and they go through plucking a violet here, a tulip there; but there was a certain, like, appraising quality to the way I was able to look at this offering. I looked, and I liked, and, after a moment's consideration, I fucked.

I don't know what kind of training these priests of the goddess have, but I do know that I didn't get any sleep at all that night.

P h i l   E t c h i s o n

And then we got into the car . . . we started to move up the yellow-brick causeway that had sprung up overnight by a miracle of the goddess . . . the causeway climbed and climbed, arrowing skyward at a dizzying sixty degrees . . . the sun was out and I could barely see to drive. And no goddess hood ornament to protect us, because we were still within range of the goddess of the city . . . the law of conservation of goddesses still held firm. Higher and higher we climbed. I sweated. I shifted all the different gears, even the ones I'd never heard of, trying to reduce the strain on the station wagon. But you know, the gearshift itself kept shifting; one minute it would be the usual PRNDLL, the next a mind-boggling PRNDZSDFGEWLZ, and one time it even read PRINCE. Unless the bright sun was driving me mad.

Sitting next to me, Serena watched me, strangely calm. Radiant, even. I wondered what kind of interesting sexual experience she had had the previous night. I wondered whether Milt, the raven, had been vouchsafed an experience himself, or whether, as a sacred hermaphrodite, he was allowed only to conjugate with himself. Milt was occupying the back seat, tapping slowly and methodically on a drum, and muttering to himself in Navajo.

I floored the gas.

Higher! Higher! Higher! Around us, the crystal skyscrapers dazzled! Ahead, below, the river sparkled!

"Do you know where we're going?" said Serena.

"No, I don't!" I said. "But my body knows." Because the dream that I'd had while floating in the waters of the lake had etched that memory in every cell of me; it was as though I had a special piece of DNA now that knew where the source of the River lay.

"Xibalba," said Milt Stone. "Nifty-sounding word, isn't it? Native American words always roll around the tongue that way. Mythic resonance, you know."

The car was morphing every few seconds now. Sometimes it was a golden swan whose wings flapped mightily against the gusting wind. Sometimes it was a spaceship, sometimes a galleon, sometimes a pink Cadillac, and always accelerating. And then . . . just as the causeway was starting to become more and more and more perpendicular, just as we reached the crest of it, just as we reached that moment, you know, on the first hill of a roller coaster when you are magically suspended, defying gravity, and we hung there, waiting for the great fall—

That's when I noticed the gap in the causeway—

That's when I noticed the sheer drop into the churning river.

"Shit," I said, "I didn't put on my seat belt." I fumbled for it, but there wasn't one.

Serena screamed. We plummeted.

"You said you knew the way!" Serena shouted,

"This is better than peyote," Milt said. "No external chemicals; all the synthesizing's done right inside your brain."

We plummeted faster.

"We should hit terminal velocity soon," said Milt,

"We're gonna crash!" Serena shrieked. I, on the other hand, was too terrified to say anything at all.

The station wagon hurtled toward ground zero. My face smacked into the windshield. The wipers went on, the air conditioning went berserk, and the car radio burst into Strauss' *Also sprach Zarathustra*.

The goddess materialized on the hood—

Then impact.

CHAPTER FIFTEEN

20,000 LEAGUES UNDER THE SEA

Theo Etchison

—and hit the water hard. Bubbles flying, liquid flooding our nostrils. Fucking Jesus, I think, I've made the wrong choice, this death is the one true death after all and not another metamorphosis—

Chris Etchison

—the iceberg—
—smash and—
Concentrate! Hard! The whistling wind, you blink and your iced-up tears break off your lashes and glide down your cheeks and
—the ship! Capsizing!—
—no wonder it was the *Titanic*—
Demons are dashing around me. Their webbed feet slide on the steep, slippery decks. They scream, they belch fumes of brimstone.

Phil Etchison

—striking the water, the car morphed rapidly into a kind of subaquatic vessel, sprouting dials, levers, periscopes, computer screens, and—

Theo Etchison

—Confusion! Slowly we turn, while around us churn—
—the moon the stars the cavernous earth—
Strang clutches my hand hard. He's almost like a child, and I'm almost a grownup, teetering on the brink of it at least; I get a glimpse of how things may be one day, when I'm a lot older, and when the power of truthsaying has left me forever—
—bubbles—
I close my eyes. I can't breathe. I'm drowning. Got to find a straw to

grasp and it has to be the right straw. Over there, what's that, a hint of yellow, a half-brick bobbing up and down? How can I even see it when my eyes are closed? Or is it the memory of the journey burned into my brain?

Phil Etchison

Then came a miracle. The water smoothed out somehow. The station wagon was a surrounded by a bubble of still, sweet air. My wife had reconstituted herself on the hood of the car. We were still descending. The depth gauge read 100, 1000, 7000, 9000 feet . . . way beyond the car's physical tolerance. We went down gently. Serena began to hum, and Milt began tapping out a slow, syncopated rhythm on his drum.

The view as we sank was a bit like the Captain Nemo ride in Disneyland; the lake we swam in was all the lakes and oceans of our dreams. You could see the things you dream about, but only a glimpse at a time—here a flash of the Loch Ness Monster, there a glint of pirate treasure; here a barnacled turret of lost Atlantis, there a mermaid, shimmying past, only to turn and whisk herself away in shock at seeing a carload of human beings. . . .

A glimpse of yellow. A piece of golden brick drifted by.

More bricks. A rain of gold, ping-ping-pinging against the side of the car, tinkling against the windows. I could feel it in my bones . . . the road was close by.

"I hope you know where we're going," Serena said.

"I've been there," I said.

"Tripping," said Milt Stone.

Suddenly something went by . . . sinking a lot faster than us . . . the hull of a gigantic ship . . . I thought I could see the word *Titanic*. The metal sheets had gaping, woundlike gashes, and through those gashes we could see Thorn's demons, spinning, twisting, grimacing. How could Thorn have so many creatures at his beck and call, when he wasn't even the real Thorn? Were they self-replicating, regenerating, so that there was always an infinite supply of gargoylelike spear-carriers to enhance Thorn's powers?

I didn't really have time to think about it because the whole ship went barreling down into the depths. And at the topmost corner I could see Thorn himself, his trumpet-blowing sidekick, and my son-that-was-not-my-son, each of them encased in a bubble of air.

"After them!" said Milt.

"Yeah, right," said Serena, "one sinking stone chasing after another."

"We can't catch up," I said.

"Stop dodging the bricks," said Milt.

One brick after another pelted us. I said, "But they'll smash the windshield . . . we'll drown!"

"They're not those kind of bricks," Milt said. He rolled down his window.

"We'll drown!" I screamed.

"Have a little faith," he said, "we're inside an air pocket of some kind." He reached out and grabbed a brick on the fly, then rolled the window back up again. He held it up; I watched in the rear view mirror, fascinated, as he squeezed it—it made little whiffling noises—and I realized that this was like one of the bricks they sell in Universal Studios— a fantasy brick, a latex brick, a movie special-effects brick—though it was just as glinting-yellow as a block of gold. "Fool's gold," said Milt.

"So we're all fools?"

Milt said, "Yes, sure we are, in a way. Only a fool would set out on a quest. And only a pure fool can see the holy grail. . . ."

"Oh, Milt, you're always mixing mythologies," Serena said, giggling a little.

"You can talk," said Milt. "You're about the most mixed-up triple goddess I can imagine."

"Wait a minute," I said. I wasn't avoiding the bricks anymore, and in fact they were sort of coalescing into the faint outline of a road. "Why did the *Titanic* sink faster than us?" I saw the Leaning Tower of Pisa poking up from a bank of ruddy coral. "I thought everything fell at the same speed. Laws of physics."

We spun around and were suddenly face to face once more with that hull.

"One of the rules of this place," Milt said, "seems to be that nothing is true until the moment that you know it's true. Everything is in flux, waiting for the pronouncement of a truthsayer "

We and the hull were falling at the same speed now. From the gaps in the metal, the creatures stared at us, hollow-eyed, hollow-cheeked. I stared back, since there didn't seem to be much steering to be done. The yellow brick road formed and unformed itself beneath us, and we sort of hovered above it, now and then passing through a school of manta rays or coming eye to eye with a humpback whale or a sea-monster, though none seemed quite as malevolent as the packs of Thorn's creatures.

Slowly we kept sinking.

Theo Etchison

Slowly we find ourselves inside a pocket of air; slowly the water seems to drain from our lungs. The air pocket grows; soon it's almost the size of a toilet, and we can see out clearly and it's the old underwater wonderland that we see, all garish colors and singing clams and dancing mermaids.

It's raining yellow bricks.

The bricks are drifting, dancing, spiraling, spawning . . .

Making a road beneath our feet. . . .

But here's the weird part. We don't seem to be following that yellow brick road. The road seems to be following us. See like, I'm leading the way (walking in the middle of the water, still falling, the ocean floor nowhere in sight) and I just seem to tread wherever instinct leads me, and the minute my foot lands somewhere there's a yellow brick to receive it, materializing out of nowhere or just floating up from the depths.

"You do know the way," King Strang says.

I'm relieved that now we can talk, we don't have to just say *glub glub glub* to each other. I keep walking . . . walking . . .

Chris Etchison

—falling—

—and I hear—

—the heartbeat of the cosmos—

Serena Somers

That's just it: we were descending, the *Titanic* was descending, somewhere out there the mad king and Theo were probably descending too, dropping faster and faster into the abyss. Mr. E. was attempting to drive, in a way, mostly just steering a little to avoid the odd whale or coral reef. The yellow bricks were forming and unforming beneath us. They made pretty patterns . . . little Figaro chains . . . little herringbone necklaces when would we hit bottom?

Glimmering in the depths were hints of moments long forgotten. The shaft of moonlight in my Virginia bedroom, where I first saw Ash and thought he was just like, my imaginary companion even though I was too old for imaginary companions . . . I saw that moonlight once again, heard the drapes rustle, held up my dappled hand to the soft radiance. . . .

But I was still in a station wagon, sinking to the bottom of the ocean. . . .

Or were we sinking backward in time? Were we heading back toward some intersection in our lives, when we could have made other choices, become different people?

I saw another glimmer: me naked in the creek by the school, ditching; that was wild! I smiled at my own audacity. I fingered the dragon around my neck and stared at the Mary-shaped hood ornament, and I knew that I was going to have to be the goddess again soon.

Then I thought about Joshua. . . .

Phil Etchison

If existence was like a symphony, were we now heading into the recapitulation, when the themes articulated at the beginning are replayed straight through, only now they carry the weight of all the passions that we've lived through?

Because I was starting to see things in the deep ocean. Little flashes. Mary suckling Theo in front of the fireplace. Theo bigger now, me declaiming Whitman at him while he jabbed at his cereal, the chocolate milk mottling his cheeks; Joshua running through the cottonwoods. The real world. So long ago, so far, it had become like a fairy tale; it was as though myth had become reality, and reality myth.

Swimming in and out of those images: fantastical deep sea fish, with flashlight eyes and spiny fins and outlandish neon colors. . . .

We were going back. Not just in memory, but in time itself.

We were returning to the big bang, the place where all worlds began.

BOOK FOUR

RECAPITULATION
HOWL, HOWL, HOWL

"Hirou mono
Mina ugoku nari
Shiohi-gata"

"Everything I pick up
Is moving, awash
On the beach at low tide."

—*Chiyojo*

ON TRUTH

BY PHILIP ETCHISON

My writing block, it seems, may not be permanent after all.
Still, I find my annual address from the poetry chair of this august
institution to be more and more of a joke, year after year. I *have*
managed to shit out one half-baked lyric this year (pardon my
French, Mr. Chairman). The poem appeared in *Poetry* magazine,
unnoticed except by an advertising firm who paid me $25,000 to
adapt it slightly for the tagline of a deodorant soap commercial.

Having thus sunk to the very depths of poetic despond, I have
decided to venture into the treacherous shoals of ontology. . . .

What is Truth? Is Beauty Truth, or is that just Keats' wishful thinking?

My son, who in some ways does not exist, has an instinctive grasp
of Truth. But he cannot express it in words at all. So how can I
presume to do so?

I had another son once, who has since ceased to exist; he knew
truth well, and could articulate it. But it wasn't enough to keep him
in this world. He vanished without a trace, and thus became an
Untruth.

I had a wife once, but she became a goddess and deserted me.

Have I gone crazy?

—coffee-stained ms. found stuck in a shredder at the University of
Northern Virginia, along with a prescription for Prozac. Not believed to be in the handwriting of Philip Etchison by most handwriting experts; one, Mr. Pinkham, disagrees, and attributes its variation
to an excessive consumption of hallucinogens.

—reserve £500

CHAPTER SIXTEEN

DISJUNCTIVE FUGUE

Theo Etchison

The time before the mad millennium . . .

The shimmering sand. My father's cold cold eyes. The smell of my mother dying, hanging in the wheeze of the dying air conditioner . . . somewhere in Arizona . . . so fucking long ago I don't even know that it was ever real . . . so vivid that it's now.

Flash. Flash.

Fighting Joshua in the men's room of a phantasmagorical Chinese Restaurant in the middle of nowhere.

Flash. Flash.

Now it's the present, and we're running in place somewhere at the bottom of an ocean of chaos, the truthsayer who's lost his truth and the king who's lost his kingdom. I used to be so young and a dollar could still buy a Coke and a candy bar, and every new truth was fresh and shiny and spanky-bright, and now, running in place, with the weight of the universe pressing down on me, I feel so old, so blind, so tired, so decayed, so fucking senseless, I don't know why I don't just die.

And the yellow bricks are streaming down, and the road is forming and unforming beneath our feet, and I know that we are getting closer to a place where the universe is young and still coming into being. And the king, striding beside me, he seems younger too; or maybe it's just that I'm taking on part of his age, his blindness, his tiredness, his decay. His white robes billow around us. We are trapped in a bubble of air and time. The ocean we're in is a place where quadrillions of little pieces of the river have come together in a rich confluence of pathways. We could go anywhere that the river goes, if only we knew the sequence.

A turn in the road. So familiar. Are we in a battered station wagon once again, are we turned south toward Tucson, are there billboards advertising weird Chinese delicacies, is the desert air stifling? No. I'm journeying toward the source of the river with the mad king, but I seem to be experiencing the many pasts all at the same time, too. That's how I know we're heading in the right direction.

Another turn, and then the brick road leads steeply down into a pitch-black chasm. King Strang turns to me questioningly. I nod, I guess. We descend. I have no maps, no knowledge of what we're doing: I'm hoping that the universe itself is snapping back on track, thrusting me down the right road, the path of least resistance.

And after the longest time—I would say that it seems forever but that's such a stupid cliché, but you know what I mean—we seem to bottom out, and there's a faint light . . . a bluish light . . . I can't see where it's coming from, but the bubble of air seems to have grown bigger, too.

I guess we're in some kind of caves. It always turns out to be caves somehow, caves, caverns, underground tunnels. Don't know what it is about caves. I never liked *Dungeons and Dragons* that much even when I was like eleven or twelve; never liked being trapped in level after level, getting killed, coming back to life, it's all totally claustrophobic. I know the universe is a metaphor, but why *this* metaphor? It sucks. Deeper and deeper into the labyrinth that's really inside our collective heads.

"Quiet," the king says.

"I didn't say anything," I say.

"But your thoughts are thundering in my ears."

Okay, so we both laugh, a little; at least, I laugh and the king smiles.

"Come on," I say. I recognize something—a little grotto with a statue of my mother, candlelight, Mexicans in skeleton costumes. The Day of the Dead in that little town next to the Laetrile clinic. We turn down another musty corridor. The tunnel swerves. It pulsates; it's almost organic; no, it *is*, we're in the guts of some cosmic creature.

Then, abruptly, we're somewhere else completely. . . .

🔄

I'm a little kid and Daddy is writing next to the basement fireplace in the dead of winter. No one else is in the house. Mom went to pick up Joshua from somewhere. I'm watching him. He has a little notebook. He scribbles, he rips up, he trashes, the fire leaps up and I see little pieces of words before they shrivel and burn up:

love
darkness
energy
ensorcellment

I don't know all the words. But I think of how they must sound and their music jangles in my ears along with the hiss of the fire . . . it's a fake fireplace . . . fake logs . . . but the pictures that dance in the flames are all too real . . . yeah. I'm a little kid, maybe six or seven, but I can read pretty good. Around here, they make you read all the time: store signs, book covers, food labels, and of course those poems that I can't understand even, but the way the words tumble and crash makes me feel mighty and powerful.

Daddy's scrunched over in a big old leather armchair by the fire. Too close to the fire really 'cause when you sit on it it makes you jump, the leather's so hot: I don't know how he can stand it and he's all sweating. And the words keep flying into the fireplace:

darkness
silence
gold-winged
sentinel

I creep up closer to him. He's scribbling like a maniac but only one or two words at a time, and the pieces of paper keep flurrying around him like snow. I want to say something but I'm scared of breaking his mood.

He cries out. He's in some kind of creative agony I guess, and he's all, "Oh Shit, I'm nobody, I'm nothing."

Then suddenly I have to say something, and this is what it is: "Daddy," I say, "you're not nothing, you're a king."

Daddy stands up suddenly and he's a hundred feet tall and his hair is a white mane that billows in the wind, and he's wearing these big old Moses-type robes that billow right along with his hair. I step back. I'm scared. "I'm a king, huh," he says softly.

Then he picks me up and holds me in his arms (I smell him: Old Spice, sweat, a hint of liquor maybe, and something a little bit like dry leaves) and tosses me up in the air and I fall along with a thousand itty-bitty paper shreds, all of them inscribed with letters and half-words all in a great big jumble and my dad seems as tall as the sky.

"I'm a king, huh," he says. And laughs. "I wish."

"You are, Daddy, you are. You're a hundred feet tall and when you write a thing it becomes real."

"So it is written—so it is done," he says, I think that's a quote from some ancient Egyptian movie thing, we watch them late at night when I fall asleep in my mother's arms even though my brother keeps prodding me. And I reach up and touch my daddy's face and I run my fingers along the deep, dry furrows . . . and I know I've touched another person, a person Dad carries inside him.

"Why are you staring at me like that?" says Dad. "You act like I'm a strang—"

"Your eyes, Daddy," I say.

Because I've seen another's eyes: the cabochon iolite eyes that years later I'll know to be the eyes of the mad king; and he senses I'm having this strange disjunctive double vision thing and he says to me, "Kid, you've got too much imagination, too much, too much. . . ."

And laughs, and throws me up, catches me, smothers me with security; I glare with pretend-angry eyes at the icicles in the two high window-panes, the only way to see outside from our basement.

Then Daddy lets me go. I scrunch down on the floor and pick up the scraps of paper and I start putting them together and this is what comes out:

time river back

My Dad looks down at the words in amazement. I put together an-other piece of the jigsaw:

two truths can both be true

My Dad slumps down on the armchair. He's not a king anymore. He's a tired man, and I think he's maybe feeling kind of old. "You're better than me," he whispers, "and you can barely read. . . ."

I look into his eyes. One of his eyes is like a big blue marble filled with crisscrossing paths of light. . . .

回

Strang's eyes . . .

Deeper in the caverns now, and the roar of water rushing, just behind some limestone wall; Strang and I are walking, walking . . .

And then, somehow, we're driving I guess, we're back in the wheezing wagon with the stale smell of dying, and I'm slumped in the back with my dream book, watching the desert unreel behind me, sand upon sand upon sand; and I kind of creep forward, gaze up above the seat, look into the rear-view mirror and I see my father's eyes, Strang's eyes; the one eye false, the other true; and in the eye that is the marble that is the map of the cosmos. I can suddenly see the way, clear and bright and terrible; I know we're going to have to die again before we can be born, and I'm so scared I could fucking shit myself right now, but I have to hold myself together, have to hold true to the path; I stare into the eye, into the map, and know that we're headed straight to—

回

Hiding in the bushes by the river by the school, I see the river-goddess rising naked out of the waves; don't know if she sees me, but there she is,

wet and smiling in the muggy Virginia summer, and her name is Serena
Somers. . . .

🖻

Two truths can both be true . . .
    . . . all comes to me in fragments, pieces of a great dream, someone
else's dream maybe . . .
    . . . Mom. . . .

🖻

A halo of ash surrounds me. . . .
"Trapped," the king cries out, "trapped inside my own madness!"
Then suddenly: the wind takes us both—
What wind? There's a whirlwind in the tunnels, a wind that shrieks and
wuthers, and it carries us up and twirls us and spins us and wrenches me
around, a wind like the wind of a rollercoaster, endlessly plummeting.
I'm holding onto King Strang's robes. He's holding out the scepter and
the scepter's light darts back and forth, back and forth, in and out and
across, and the dank walls glisten with phosphorescent stars, galaxies
within galaxies. The river has a mind of its own now. There's no navigating to be done at all because the paths that we must go down have been
predestined since time began.
Ash dances in the black walls of the caverns.
Ash dances in the eaves, in the stalagmites, in the thick air.
Ash dances.
We're whisked further down the tunnel of stars. Round the seven-
bended snake, up the down chute, down the upslope of the cavern. Every
place we pass I know, I've been here before, but I don't know when.
Maybe it's my birth canal. Maybe I'm inside myself. We whip around
corners and spiral down stairwells.

🖻

The sphinx is there now, between the king and me and the great chasm
that yawns between us and the holy of holies. She is a beautiful woman
with fiery hair and coal-bright eyes. Her wings are black and leathery,
and she prowls back and forth and she claws the sulfurous air. She looks
like a scream queen from a B horror movie. She has vampire teeth, and
when she roars you can tell she is part lioness.

"I'm not just any sphinx," she says. "My conundrums go far deeper than you can delve; even you, King Strang, who are finally but mortal."

"King, you can do it," I say, "you can answer her riddle and go on through. But I remember that last time there was no sphinx, no riddle, only the rabid Cerberus and the sacrifice of an eye, so this is a second test, a more difficult test."

"I can't give up my other eye," says King Strang.

The sphinx cries out, "Answer the question! Answer the question!" and she darts back and forth, her bat wings dripping slime.

"But you haven't even asked the fucking question," I scream. What is this, *Jeopardy* or something, are we supposed to guess the questions too?

"You're right," says the sphinx.

"Four legs in the morning, two in the daytime, three at night, is that it?" I ask her.

The sphinx laughs. Really laughs; and each time she laughs, lava erupts, pieces of the ceiling come pelting down, and the smell of brimstone becomes more and more choking. "The clichés never seem to change, do they?" she says at last.

She settles down, just a few feet from us. She's a real harpy despite her beautiful face, and her breath is totally kicking. She looks at us, waves and shakes at us like some Las Vegas showgirl.

"Maybe you don't think I'm that frightening," she says, and bares her teeth. Behind her, fire leaps up out of the chasm. "But I am." I know she is. "Here's the question: *To save the universe, would you sacrifice your own child?*"

"What kind of a riddle is that?" says King Strang. "I have no children."

I say to him, "O King, have you forgotten?"

"Did I once have children?" he murmurs. "Didn't they die? Didn't I myself kill them, not with my own hands, but with a few misspoken words?"

Ash dances in the sulfer fumes; Ash dances in the haze; Ash is a halo bright about my head, sparked by the brimstone's burning.

"No," says Strang, "no sons. No daughters. No one."

Ash swirls. Ash begins to form into a semblance of human shape; Ash glows, Ash dances.

I remember the first of my many dreams. A king is dividing his kingdom between three children. He holds his scepter in his palsied hand and the three children, vampire, dragon, and something unknown, they kneel to him, one by one, speaking in honeyed tones of the love they have for him . . . all except the last one, the one who dares speak the truth.

"What about the one who was neither son nor daughter?" I ask him. "What about—"

"Don't speak to me of that one!" cries the king. "Ashes to ashes, dust to dust."

The sphinx waits, tapping her feet; she purrs and the floor of the cavern rumbles with her; her purring is the stirring of magma deep beneath our feet. "What's your answer?" she growls.

"Ash," says the king.

And when he says the name, the name he has refused to utter in all the time I've been with him, that's when Ash starts to become Ash. Ash of the still small voice; Ash, luminous, androgynous, kind of beautiful in a waiflike way; that's who Ash is, and he begins to form out of the cloud of Ash that's followed us all the way from the island in the crystal lake.

"Father," Ash says softly.

No longer speaking through my lips, no longer seeing through my eyes, Ash steps out of the spinning dust-cloud. He looks at his father and his father looks at him, while behind us the sphinx springs from crag to crag and roars and belches hellish fumes and waits for the answer to her riddle.

Strang says, "You told me the truth, child, didn't you?"

"Yes," says Ash.

And in my mind's eye I see Dad swinging me up in the air and I see the words that are pieces of unborn poems scattering, swirling, dancing like dead leaves in the autumn wind, and I see the fireplace in the basement in winter and I think, this place is not different from that place; they're the same somehow; because we're close to the source, the place that's the anchor for all places and times, and we see how the whole universe is interconnected. I see how I'm like Ash and Dad's like Strang; I always used to know the truth that Dad strove so hard to find, him the great poet and all and engaged in the great quest for the meaning of our existence, and me just some clear-eyed kid who had no right to know because I hadn't struggled to know, hadn't sacrificed one eye as the price of knowledge, was born with the right eyes, the right map, burned into the ROM of my brain . . . fucking Jesus it must have pissed him off, I think to myself, I don't know why he even talked to me . . . and now I remember the poem that he wrote, the poem that was grown from the seed of my putting together the scraps of paper:

. . . *for in the momentary closure,*
The blink's breadth between two truths, two truths can both be true.

How would *you* answer the riddle? How could I answer it for him, when I could see that both answers to the riddle were true and false?

I watch them embrace, father and son. I feel kind of bitter because who am I in this? I've brought the king to the edge of the abyss, to the last gateway, but all I am is this blind navigator; the king's finding love again at the eleventh hour, and I'm here on the outside, not even family, not even knowing when my own father's going to get here, not even knowing if he'll know I still exist, because in the universe he's in now, I never existed, there was only Chris, the one true truthsayer.

Ash says, "I'm sorry I told the truth, father."

And Strang says, "Never be sorry, child." And kisses Ash, solemnly, on the cheek, not like a father and son, but like two world leaders on television, like President Karpovsky and President Yeltsin; and they stand, a little bit apart; the moment is so big, it's too big even for tears, but I cry, I cry for the two of them, feeling the truth of their grief and their joy.

Finally, King Strang turns to me. "Which is it to be, truthsayer?" he asks me. "What is the answer?"

I say to him, "It depends on whether you're a man or a god."

The king sits down on a rock. He is more weary than I've ever seen him. The journey is almost over. The jewel in the scepter glows. All the light here is hell-hot; only the scepter's radiance is cold. Ash sits at his feet. How could the king have been so blind before, not to see the difference between real and imagined love?

"I see what you mean," says Strang. "A god *would* sacrifice his son, wouldn't he?"

"Many have," I say.

"To heal the world, it's the natural thing to do. But what would a man do? Wouldn't a man put his child first, and let the world plunge to perdition?"

"Two truths," I say, "can both be true."

This is the final great piece of truth that I know; the last piece of truth I am able to divulge, before the big darkness of normality swallows me up and I become just Theo Etchison, just about to go into the tenth grade, dreamer, good-for-nothing, kid with too much imagination, kid who plays by himself in the forest in Spotsylvania County, loner who thinks too much.

"So what's it to be?" Strang says. "Man or god?"

"Well," I say, "you've been pretty godlike for the last couple of thousand years. . . ."

"To be man," says Strang, "doesn't that mean I would have to—"

"Die?" I say. When I think of death, I think of my mom, I think of the close, dank air in the station wagon, I think of that awful smell.

"Die," says Strang, and the sphinx waits; she holds her breath; the whole chasm seems to have fallen silent; you can't hear the hissing flames, the screaming of lost souls, nothing like that. You can hear death itself in that big old silence. "Maybe there's another answer," Strang says. "You mythical creatures are always trying to force humans to choose, always putting us into an either-or situation. Heaven or Hell, black or white, truth or falsehood . . . isn't there another path, one that lies in the cracks, a third, hidden answer to every question? For example—"

I know now what he's going to say. So does Ash. Ash steps back. He hasn't expected this, but now he realizes that Strang has chosen the right answer to the riddle; right, at least, for him. "Godlike," he says, "I will my own son's destruction. But like a man, I hold him to myself, I let the world go to keep his love for myself. What if I want both to be true? I have to give a death for a death. I give my own death for my son's death. I am old and foolish. I have lived too long. I shall go now."

Holding the scepter aloft, King Strang totters over to the edge of the precipice. The flames leap up. The sphinx appears panicky for the first time. "Don't jump," she shrieks. "It's hell down there. You'll choke on brimstone before you even land, and then you'll be consumed."

Strang turns to her. His face is wedged between the shadow and the fiery light. The ridges, the furrows, are deep as the mountains on the moon. His eyes are filled with terrible anguish; but there's like, a resurgence of power inside him. Like when my dad gets the words right in his poems, and his whole body seems to zing and his eyes are full of fire.

"My scepter," he says, "has one last great magic in it."

He leaps off the edge of the world.

I see him fall, the scepter's jewel flashing like the head of a comet.

Ash grabs my shoulders. "Come on, Theo."

"Come on?"

"What are we waiting for?"

"Waiting for?"

"Yeah," says the sphinx, who now seems considerably drained of her fierceness; she's gone back to squatting on a rock and purring softly; she's more like a kitten than a lioness now.

"Let's follow him," Ash says.

"Follow?"

"Yeah," says the sphinx. "Stay, follow, whatever. Two truths can both be true. Makes me kind of useless, doesn't it? I mean, if people start answering the riddles any way they choose. . . ."

"Follow?" I say, gazing down at the comet that's blazing in the pitch blackness below. Teetering on the edge of ultimate darkness.

"Are you scared?" says Ash.

"Shitless."

"All right then."

The comet darts, does a three-sixty, zigzaggs, spins round and round. We jump.

Into the embrace of nothingness.

CHAPTER **SEVEN- TEEN**

DOORS AND TAPESTRIES

S e r e n a   S o m e r s

—a ship was wedged at the bottom of the sea. We parked the car beside the hull, which angled upward into the dimness. I could hear a high solitary voice, singing: it must have been Chris, though maybe he was singing in the language of the whales or something; it was a weird, keening, wailing kind of a song, and it echoed and echoed against fluid and metal, clanking, murmuring, burbling. God it was spooky.

We stepped out. It was all right because the air pocket grew to about the size of a football field. We were walled in by water, and above us was a great big dome of dark, cold, wet, oppressive ocean.

"The *Titanic*," said Mr. E., "seems to have landed." He emerged from the car.

"Thorn and Chris must be inside," I said. But I couldn't see anyone at all. You know, before, we'd seen demons and gargoyles lurking in the rips in the ship's hull but now it seemed totally abandoned. In fact, it was hard to believe that it had been seaworthy only hours ago, because now it was all rusted and twisted and looked as though it had been underwater for centuries . . . then again, maybe we had been sinking for centuries. There was no way of telling. They call it time dilation, or something. It's in science fiction books. Speed of light. I don't get it, and I don't think anyone else does either.

Milt Stone stepped out of the back seat. He was still carrying his drum. We could still hear Chris' eerie singing, or whatever it was, reverberating around us. The air was sweating a cold salt moisture onto our hands and faces.

"I guess I should go look for Chris," said Mr. E., and he strode toward the ship. I watched him for a moment. He began to kind of waver, like a mirage. I started to follow him, but he got harder and harder to see. I mean, his outline was shimmering, and he was getting all distorted, like a special effect, folding in on himself.

"Mr. E.!" I shouted. "Are you okay?" A stupid question to ask at the bottom of the ocean without an oxygen tank, but no question seemed too stupid for this mad universe. "Wait for me," I said. I hurried, trying to catch up. I could sense my own self wavering and contorting too, and when I looked down at my own arm, I noticed that it was twisting like a corkscrew, though I didn't feel any different. "Wait up!" I shouted again.

He couldn't hear me I guess.

"Don't go," said Milt.

"Why not?"

"This is the classic moment in the drama," Milt said, "when the characters say to each other, 'Let's split up.' "

"What do you mean?" I asked him, as Mr. E. kind of twirled himself into a vortex and popped out of existence, a few yards in front of the wreck of the *Titanic*.

"We are all here for a purpose," he said. "We all have unfinished business. What's yours?"

I had to think awhile. I mean, I had been the triple goddess. I'd trampled down cities. I'd spewed out dragons from my maw. What was there left to me? But then I remembered: there'd been *men* in my life. "Oren Karpovsky," I said . . . "and Joshua Etchison."

"See what I mean?"

"What am I supposed to do?"

Milt Stone began to beat on his drum. He did a kind of dance around me; feet together, feet apart, slowly making a complete circle with me at its center. "This is the round dance," he said. "Women do it, because they are the encirclers, because they are the earth." With every step he became more and more feminine. I don't know how he did it. It was as if he had always been a woman. "Strictly speaking, this is not a Navajo dance," he said, "but a Plains Indian one; but you know how it is; cross-fertilization some call it, others cultural pollution. But it doesn't matter;

I'm a *nadlé*, a holy man-woman, and I can ransack the mythologies of the world if I want, so you'll see the truth. Look at me," he said, "look at me, love me."

He went on dancing, and the drumbeats made a weird counterpoint with the wailing that was Chris' whale music. After a while it seemed like Milt was moving faster and faster and faster and was maybe turning into more people . . . or were they all the same person? . . . there was Milt the tribal policeman in his uniform . . . there was Milt the end-of-the-world homeless madman with the placard around his neck . . . there was Milt in, oh my, a bridal gown, smiling on his way to the altar . . . Milt in wild, made-in-Hong Kong-style Indian regalia, grimacing as he leaped up and down to the strains of a Hollywood movie score . . . a hundred Milts were writhing and wriggling around me . . . a kaleidoscope of blurring Milts. The music was confusing too: there was the whalesong and the drum, but also bits and pieces of reggae, hip-hop, and house leaking in—music from when I was fifteen or sixteen, music I used to turn my nose up at. It was like listening to the radio when you're driving through nowhere, just bits and pieces of weird stations.

Then, suddenly, I was inside the—

Phil Etchison

—ship. But it was not what I expected to see. Yes, it was dank, and clammy, and musty, and there were barnacles and twists of seaweed coiled around broken shafts of metal, and there was a cold, blue light—that Spielbergian, sci-fi movie light that you always imagine as an accompaniment to a close encounter of any kind—lines, whorls and pools of this light fantastic. I stepped in a little farther. You could hear chimes, bells, and whistles in the distance . . . or was it the tinkling of anvils?

I got a little braver. Somewhere in this labyrinth was Chris, and a piece of unfinished business I dreaded more than anything in the world. I had spent a trilogy's worth of adventuring caught between the Scylla of heroism and the Charybdis of mediocrity, and the way ahead wasn't really getting any clearer. Was I now expected to charge in, dispatch the vampire (who was only the outer shell of a vampire, since within him lurked the soul of the President of the United States, my friend) and rescue the child who would soon prove not to be my child? In that dream I had had, submerged in the amniotic waters of the lake of the human unconscious, I'd faced the sphinx, and I'd failed to answer her question. This time, I supposed, it would be no dream—except insofar as our entire existence is a dream.

Perhaps it was time to try the direct approach.

"Come and get me, Thorn!" I screamed into the cavernous emptiness.

I didn't really expect a reply, but I went on in that vein for a while: the jig is up, come and face your doom, a swift and terrible justice is sweeping down the freeway toward you . . . I shouted myself hoarse, and exhausted the clichés of poesy, and still there came no answer save my own voice, echoing, echoing in a metallic roundelay about my ears.

Presently my eyes grew used to the dimness. As I wandered, I became more aware of sounds, too: clickings, tickings, ratchetlike scrapings. There were cogs, wheels, fanbelts, all turning, whirring, painfully snapping into place. I was inside a monstrous machine. It was pretty damn Kafkaesque. All the way up one wall, as far as the eye could see, were anvils, and robot elf-arms swung hammers in complex, mechanistic patterns of pinging. The floor of the cavern was stone, and it was littered with broken cogs, loose spokes, tortured fragments of steel. There was a certain gigantism about some of the pieces: I mean, if I was meant to believe that I had been caught inside the workings of an immense, infernal machine, it would not have been difficult to convince me.

From far away . . . somewhere in the high invisible vault of this clockwork cathedral . . . I could hear Chris' voice . . . part human, part whale, part angel . . . a high pure sound that lanced through the must and dust like steel, like lightning.

The floor was rising . . . that figured, I supposed, since the ship itself had struck bottom at a 45° angle . . . but presently the slope softened into steps. I kept moving up them. Wheels spun. Gears shifted. Somewhere, a cuckoo announced the time. I went on climbing. I was vaguely aware of light, somewhere in the heights. I kept moving. The odd thing was, even though I was moving upward, against the pull of gravity, there was also an energy propelling me so strongly that I almost felt I was descending. Did this mean I had reached "the still point of the turning world"? There came the sound of another cuckoo, then another. Time did not precisely stand still here. Perhaps it ran around and around in circles. Or spirals. Or corkscrews. It moved and did not move. And the ticking and the tocking made a joyful, jangling noise in the back of my mind. This, I thought, is how the echo of the Big Bang sounds on radio telescope, to a being vast enough to be able to hear radio waves as a comprehensive music. This, perhaps, is what Chris hears, the bedrock of ultimate truth that underlies all of our disparate realities, the ocean floor above which swirl the waters of consciousness. Tick, tick, cuckoo. The clockwork theory of creation. Newtonian physics in action.

I went on climbing. Not, you understand, thinking all this through—I was not expostulating some mechanistic theory of the universe to myself as I ascended—but just keeping my mind open, letting random thoughts flit through, flirting with cosmic concepts yet never quite grappling with them—the Phil Etchison patented method of dealing with things too big to understand, too deep to find meaning in.

Perhaps, I told myself, you too are clockwork.

Perhaps you too are a machine.

At the top of the steps was a great iron door. It was Brobdignagian in its proportions; I could see the door handle about thirty feet above my head. The door was one of those things you find in Italian cathedrals, crowded with scenes molded in high relief. Beyond the door, doubtless, was the thing I most desired and feared: the final locked room of Duke Bluebeard's castle, the infamous Orwellian Room 101. There was nothing for it but to try to reach the doorhandle, and the way to get there was by climbing up the relief itself. It looked like there were plenty of protruding footholds for me.

I too can be a hero, I told myself. I too can stop being this nonentity, this brain-blocked poet who at best can shit out only a line or two of advertising copy; I too can brave the final door; I too can summon up the courage to answer that fucking sphinx and send her spinning into the void.

Yeah, right. No bright sword, no .38 special; just me and the blunted saber of my poesy.

So you know what?

I grabbed onto the first protuberance on that iron door, which appeared to be the fangs of a great, coiled dragon; I wedged my knee firmly into the crook of its belly and planted one foot on one of the dragon's claws, and then—

—a great dimensional shift and—

Iron, iron, the whole world was iron The door was the gateway was the world. I too was sculpted in relief. Looked down. My hands, my arms glistened, polished, silvery. And there was no time to lose. The dragon threw me to the ground. The ground, boulders, grass, all metal—the blades were literally blades, needle-sharp, but I too was metal, and the grass scraped and whined against my robot skin. We were on the edge of a cliff, and the edge was the edge of the door.

The dragon clanked and whirred as it approached me. Reaching behind me, I found my sword, the traditional hero's sword, all chrome, its hilt studded with emeralds, but it wasn't much good; I could barely heft it. Meanwhile, the dragon snorted, and I smelled its sulfurous, fetid breath and felt like barfing. Behind the dragon was a cave. Treasure inside, no doubt. I could hear the whimpering of a woman; somewhere behind those rusted rocks was the virginal princess I needs must rescue. I was doomed to reenact scenes from mythology and bad fantasy novels before I could find redemption. Since my adolescent son was the ultimate demiurge whose dreaming made the world the way it is, I guess I shouldn't have been surprised to find myself trapped in Tolkienland, wrapping my brass knuckles around some medieval weapon.

The dragon charged, and so did I. We missed each other. He ran into an iron wall that replicated the texture of limestone. Clanged against metallic rock. I landed on my butt but felt no pain—how could I? Iron can't feel. Iron never hurts.

The dragon turned, sniffed the air, clawed at the ground. The wind was foul; it reeked of a carnivore's breath. It occurred to me that the dragon could not see me. It was blind. It was senile. It had lost its sense of focus. It rolled its empty eyes. A cloud of gas escaped its nostrils with a strained, mechanical wheeze. I wondered how long the dragon had been there, and whether it longed for death after so much time guarding some treasure whose meaning, no doubt, had long been lost.

"Perhaps," I said aloud, "you want me to run up, deliver that killing thrust, return you to the earth."

The dragon stirred, cocked its ear in my general direction. "Oh, good," it said, "you can talk. So few of them ever talk. All they want to do is joust; joust, and be consumed."

"We all talk," I said softly, and I ventured a little closer. He was about as big as a two-bedroom apartment, and his tail stretched beyond the edge of the door. "It's just that most of us don't talk to dragons, because we don't know that dragons can talk back."

"A communication gap," the dragon sighed.

"Yes," I said.

"What kind of a creature are you?" said the dragon. Its voice, hollow, raspy, reverberated through the metal mountain, in a hundred virtual passageways. "I've fought so many, and I've lost my sense of smell and taste."

"Actually," I said, "I'm a human being."

"No shit," said the dragon. "Don't get many of those anymore."

"What do you mean, you don't get many of those anymore?" I said. "What about all those knights in shining armor that rush in to save the virginal princess? That is a princess you've got back there, isn't it?"

"Of sorts," said the dragon.

I heard a scream coming from behind an outcropping. The voice of the woman was oddly familiar, but I couldn't yet place it.

"I suppose," the dragon said, "that we should get on with it. I can barely smell you, or hear you, and of course, I can't see you, since I'm blind as a bat; perhaps you'd care to point me in the right direction?"

A kind of wind was gusting over us. I creaked, I squeaked; I wished I had been better oiled. Carefully I shifted my position to the upwind, and projected my voice against the side of the mountain so that it would bounce away. Nothing like a bit of trickery.

"I'm over here," I shouted.

The blind dragon charged—too fast, too far—and soon it was hanging over the cliff, clinging to the edge of the great iron door by a single frayed claw. I tried to lift that sword again, thinking I could perhaps chop it off at its most vulnerable link. Couldn't heft it. So I just walked over to that claw and I looked down, and I saw the dragon, dangling in a bizarre forced perspective, over a chasm of cogs, spokes, wheels, chains, gears, and intermittent cuckoos.

"Dispatch me quickly," the dragon gasped. "One way or another, it always comes to this; there's always one hero too many; one can never retire in peace."

"Isn't there something you're supposed to do?" I said softly, leaning over the precipice. "Grant me a few wishes, answer my burning questions about the secret of the universe?"

"Not anymore," the dragon gasped. "I've exhausted my supply of answers to burning questions. The questions, you see, got harder and harder; the heroes got dumber and dumber. As for granting wishes—you can see that I hardly have any power. I can barely even cling to a cliff."

"There's got to be something you know that you can teach me," I said. "For example—what is this place, what am I doing here, that sort of thing."

"You know where you are," said the dragon, "if only you'll search a little harder inside yourself."

"But—"

"You were going to say, 'What about magic?' or some such thing, weren't you?" said the dragon. "Unfortunately, there is no magic anymore—that is the great and final truth that we all must learn."

"I don't agree," I said, though I wasn't at all sure that I meant that.

"You can't say there's no magic when here I am, converted into a thing of metal, trapped in an enchanted door, talking to a hunk of sculpted pewter."

"You mean there's other places?"

"Of course," I said. "Like the place I came from. A green place. Very green. Virginia"

"Virginia," said the dragon softly. "Green, you say. I can't, you know, see anything anymore."

But then he couldn't hold on anymore either; the iron rock was ripping; through the tears in the metal I could see and smell the flames of inferno. He gave a great cry—I want to say a great cry but it was more like a kind of desolate wheezing—and sort of dropped away . . . siphoned out into the musty emptiness that was beyond the door . . . I watched him whittle into darkness . . . I did not feel that I had achieved some moment of high apotheosis in the hero's journey . . . I only felt empty and afraid.

The wind sucked the dragon away; the only sound it made was a peculiar wailing, like Wagner played backward.

I was trapped in a metal skin in a metal landscape in a metal door. I heard the familiar voice of the woman call me from somewhere within the cavern. I decided to continue on. The only alternative seemed to be leaping off the cliff, and ending up as discarded clockwork.

"Phil," the voice cried.

At least, I thought, I'm not the hero with no name.

But I was still stuck inside the—

Serena Somers

—doorway of the great ship of fools. Milt's drumming was now a universe away. I don't know what I expected the inside of the ship to look like but where I was was a huge and fleshy place. At first I couldn't see much at all. But I could feel a heartbeat, and I could hear the rush of, like, a great big ocean, the same ocean you hear when you put a conch to your ear. I knew then that the ocean was the racing of a bloodstream, and that I was inside some vast organic thing. It wasn't frightening, I mean this wasn't like some Jonah-in-the-whale deal. I felt comforted. I felt completely at home. I felt happy.

Serena-in-the-womb.

But whose womb?

I thought I knew the answer. Why wouldn't I know? Hadn't I once been the goddess? I'd swallowed the goddess once; I guess it was only fair that the goddess had now swallowed me.

There was the heartbeat, and then, from far away, that eerie keening that was Chris' music. . . .

A shaft of light . . . a warm, red glow that illuminated what? a staircase? an escalator? I stepped forward. I could feel the pulsing, hear my own pulse echo it. A tunnel stretched up toward that distant, blood-red height. I had to be resolute. I had to step into the tunnel. I did. And then I was caught up in a great wind, a wind that roared like the ocean that is the conch shell that is the surging blood. It was a kind of rapture, the thing that the fundamentalists are always talking about, being swept up into heaven in the flesh, but there was something kind of, I mean, lubricious about it too. This scene was definitely pagan. The odor held sex as well as sanctity.

So there I was, being skyrocketed around by a great big whirlwind inside a twisting tube of flesh. A rollercoaster without seats, without safety belts . . . pretty wild, I guess you'd say.

At last I was deposited on kind of a landing. A woman sat, with her back to me, working on a massive loom. She was weaving a tapestry of some kind—weaving with one hand, and unraveling with the other. I knew that myth all right—it was the story of Penelope, waiting endlessly in the Odyssey for her husband to come home. I watched the woman, whose hair was draped all over her body . . . a sort of Rapunzel type . . . in fact, as I became used to the dimness (she was just beyond the shaft of radiance that illuminated the tunnel-cum-stairway) I saw that her hair was the actual thread she was weaving into the tapestry. It wasn't just one myth I was meeting up with . . . it was a kind of Cuisinart ® version of mythology.

I squinted. I wanted to see the images in the tapestry. They were vivid . . . almost *too* lifelike . . . but squeaky-clean, like a computer-generated virtual reality simulation of the world. They seemed to be animated. The thing is, I started to recognize the people, even though they were dressed in kind of ancient Greek clothing . . . there was Mr. E., for example, waving some kind of sword and wearing the costume of an ancient hoplite. He seemed to be battling some kind of monster, and there was a woman lashed to a rock with strands of her own hair, though I couldn't see her face. Mr. E. was slashing at the empty air, and the monster was dodging him, but as I watched, he managed to get in a hit, and the monster kind of disintegrated . . . or maybe it was just that Penelope managed to unravel the monster at just that moment. Mr. E. looked out from the tapestry with a quizzical expression, straight at me, kind of pointed as if to say— "You?—

Phil Etchison

—here? in this place?" I said to the woman. She was a young woman, and she was in chains, as they always are in these legends, and she had the kind of floor-length hair that they tend to have in these operations, which more or less draped itself coyly around the naughty bits. Her face was obscured by hair, too. But I knew her. At least, I thought I did.

"Mary?" I said.

She laughed. It was Mary but not quite Mary.

Serena Somers

I smiled.

Phil Etchison

She was Serena but not quite Serena.

"Who are you for sure?" I asked.

"You don't know?" She frowned. She was the dragon Katastrofa . . . but not quite.

"Aren't you going to cut me loose?" she said. "It's traditional."

I gazed at the treasure piled up in the cavern. Oh, it wasn't your usual rubies and diamonds and gold coins and coronets: instead, there were nothing but blocks. You know, those alphabet blocks that little kids build castles with, only each block had words on it. They were stacked up at random everywhere. Some were textured like wood; others seemed to be cinderblocks; still others were that foam stuff that they use in Hollywood, stunt bricks made to be harmless. All, of course, were really iron, shaded with rust, for I was still inside that metal door, still a semiflat animated relief; and the woman was all iron, and her hair as harsh and abrasive as steel wool. I still had the sword in hand, of course, but it was not vorpal enough to cut through chains of magical iron. The woman, who was the woman of my dreams and nightmares, moaned; the metal chafed her wrists.

"I don't think," she said, "you're supposed to do it that way."

I looked around me. "How, then?"

"We all have our own gifts," she said, "and you were never a fighter, Phil; you're a dreamer."

"But I killed the dragon, didn't I?"

"The dragon killed itself," said Mary-Serena-Katastrofa. I kissed her, tasted the salt of Mary's suffering, the sweetness of Serena's youth, the bitterness of Katastrofa's rage; I understood then that in a sense, the hero's journey is not nearly as unpredictable or as chaotic as one might think. For you see, it is like a well-worn roller coaster, and provided that you keep your seat belt strapped on tight, you will retread the same dilapidated track that other men have trod; what's different is not the journey, but how you feel about the journey; that's the difference between a hero and a geek, what's all inside oneself.

I looked around me then. The words on the bricks were simple and complicated: short words that held profound meanings like *love, home, death, woman, heart*; long resounding words like *fibrillate, obscurity, insomnia*; nonsense words like *masticoma, unduleverage, erastomanic, slipslink*. I saw now that this was a treasure designed for me alone, the building blocks of poesy.

"So I'm to be like Orpheus," I said. "The super-poet, melting the chains of steel with my honeyed words."

She smiled at me. "Sometimes," she said, "you think too much of yourself, Phil. There's a greater power that's manipulating us all. The road map for this journey was made millennia ago. We're all expendable, in a way. Others could have gone on this adventure. Others could have saved the universe. In the end, it doesn't matter. The universe will be saved whether we want it to be or not. It's the nature of the cosmos to fracture, come apart, heal itself; we're just little pieces of the great plan."

"So it *is* a mechanistic universe," I said, "and we really are just cogs and spokes." Trapped inside an iron world six inches wide, I felt the most profound despair I had yet experienced.

"That's one way of looking at it," said the woman who was the goddess who was my wife.

"You don't sound very encouraging," I said.

"I'm not allowed to encourage you. It's against the rules. You have to find the courage within yourself."

I knelt down to peer at the piles of word-blocks. *Antique, antick, antics, attics, antelopes*. I lifted one up (they were heavy) and placed it on top of another. They clove to each other by some sourceless magnetism. What sentence fragment had I created?

I am

"So I'm to sit here," I said, "and build a toy castle . . . an edifice that's also a poem . . . and that will set you free?" *Oscillate, osculate, osceola, ossia, Austria.*

"The pen is mightier than the sword," the woman agreed.

I am a—

"But if I do sit here," I said, "and I exercise my imagination . . . me, a third-rate poet who teaches in a third-rate college . . . won't the poem I create be third-rate too? And won't the quality of your rescue be mediocre, and the healing of the world be imperfect, and—"

"You think too much depends on you!" she said.

"Then who? Whose is that master plan?"

It was then that I heard the music—

Serena Somers

—echoing in the landing at the top of the stairwell in the shaft of light—and slowly the woman turned to me, and I saw that she was my-self. I don't mean a clone of me, I don't mean Serena II—I mean that she had me inside her, this ageless woman from an ancient myth.

Milt's drum still pounded in the world outside. But the spaces between the strokes seemed infinitely long. Lifetimes were passing between each beat of the world's heart. And in the interstices of that slow pulse came the melody that Chris was singing, somewhere aloft; his song was the making of the world, and its unmaking.

I remembered words from one of Mr. E.'s most well-known poems, where he says that

In the blink's breadth between two truths, two truths

Can both be true.

If you slow the world down enough, anyone can be a truthsayer. I think that's what Mr. E. was trying to say, even though he wrote that poem long before he like, knew there was any such thing as truthsayers. People like Theo can grasp all those shifting strands of truth kind of on the fly; they work fast, faster than the speed of light I bet. But a dummy like me, an ordinary human being, even I can see where the strands unstrand, if you run it by me slowly enough. Was that what Milt Stone's dance was trying to do for me, slow reality to a crawl so even an airhead like me could seize it in my hot little hands?

In my own little way, I decided, I too can be like Theo.

So I said to Penelope, "There's another way of doing this."

She turned to me and she's all, "What do you mean?" And I thought: I see clearly now my eyes reflecting in her eyes, see how I carry a piece of Penelope in me, the woman who waits and waits for the right man to show up; I see that she's me, but I don't have to be her.

"How long are you going to weave that thing?" I said to her. "How long are you going to wait for Odysseus?"

"As long as it takes," she said. "It's my destiny." And smiled a wan little smile.

"You must be getting pretty frustrated by now. Did they have dildos in the Bronze Age?"

"I don't know what you mean. I sit, I weave, I wait."

"This is the 90s, girl," I said. "We women don't sit, weave, wait anymore. We actually do things. Let me show you."

So I kind of leaned over into the tapestry and I stuck my hand into the warp, or the woof, or whatever it's called, I mean right into where her hair was shuttling back and forth on that loom. The hair felt rough, not silky; twenty years of dandruff, I imagined.

I pulled out a big hank of it. It was right in between where Mr. E. was waving his sword around and being very macho and phallic, and the damsel in distress was writhing about against the wall. A big black hole appeared in the midst of Mr. E.'s universe, and his woven image stared woefully down at it.

And Penelope stared at me. I guess she wasn't used to girl fights. I could have punched her out right then and there, but something weird was beginning to happen.

I couldn't pull my hand free.

The strands of hair were kind of twisting and turning around my hand. They were wrapping themselves around my fingers. They were alive somehow. Penelope turned to me and her head was a mass of serpents. It made sense, I guess; Mr. E. would have been able to lecture for half an hour about mother goddesses and snakes and the negative aspect of the earth-mother archetype and so on. But cultural anthropology isn't much of a comfort when snakes are writhing around your hand and coiling and tightening and cutting off your blood flow.

"Thank you for coming at last," she said to me. "Since you feel so strongly about changing the way things are done around here, you might as well take over . . . you might as well change things from within."

The snakes pulled me right into the cloth and there I was, right there, inside the tapestry. Everything was virtually two-dimensional. Looked at head-on, Mr. E. was a flat line; when I shifted my vision a little he kind of expanded into view until he was fully human to look at. It took some getting used to. I was pretty much 2-D myself, but I think that because I knew about the third dimension, I was able to lift my point of view off the surface of the cloth a little and see the universe for what it really was. I saw him the way a psychic might see me, I guess.

I looked around for a moment, trying to get used to being this flat. I mean, I was *fat* when I was a kid, and now I had the thickness of a silken thread. The world around me was all fluid and crinkly, just how you'd imagine living on the surface of a piece of fabric might be. The world wavered and billowed. I didn't realize it was so windy outside, but I guess the slightest motion of Penelope's loom was like an earthquake inside these images.

"Mr. E.," I said, "you'd better—"

But you know what? Mr. E. wasn't there anymore. I wasn't looking in on *his* heroic journey anymore—I had embarked on my own, and the person who was chained to the wall was not some airhead in distress but a man—yeah, he looked something like Mr. E., but a lot more like Oren Karpovsky, president of the United States of Armorica, my lover, my erstwhile sexual harasser. And behind his eyes, I could see a hint of a third personality. A lost, dead boy. Joshua. I was startled. I called out to him.

"He can't speak to you yet," Oren said. "Not until you free me."

And we weren't inside a dragon's lair at all, but a network of catacombs. Rats ran wild. Bones littered the muddy ground. Half-eaten corpses lay, their wrappings ripped open, their faces missing big chunks, in little niches in the walls.

A stone sarcophagus stood in the center of the chamber. A lone shaft of light shone down from some opening high above us. I looked at myself, felt myself all over, was horrified to find that I had somehow ditched my street clothes and I was dressed as a kind of Amazon woman, brass brassiere and all, out of some low-budget adolescent sword-and-sorcery movie. "This isn't me," I said. "This is like, ridiculous."

The coffin lid started to inch open, screeching in the most nerve-wracking chalk-across-blackboard way.

"Yes it is," said Oren. "Inside every dull, domesticated woman is a wild Amazon struggling to be free."

"I'm not dull! I'm not domesticated!" I shouted.

"Then prove it," he said. "Dare."

"Dare? Dare?"

I couldn't say much more because the lid of the sarcophagus came crashing to the floor and Thorn sat up.

He gazed at me with his slate-colored eyes.

His fangs glistened.

"You're dead," I said. "You were killed, way back, a long time ago, in a different volume of the trilogy. You keep getting killed. What's wrong with you, don't you understand that you *can't* come back? Why don't you just disappear?"

He started to lift himself from the coffin, carefully brushing the mud

from his cloak, which billowed about him as the fabric we were trapped
in moved. I looked around for something to kill him with—a pick or a
shovel or *something*—and I ended up going at him with somebody's
jawbone. The jawbone splintered.

Thorn laughed. "Very funny," he said. "Jawbone of an ass, I suppose."

Where was a stake when I needed it? Or a phial of holy water? Just as
I thought those things, they appeared, one in each hand. Of course they
did! This was creative dreaming of a kind.

Thorn said, "You catch on fast."

I said, "I am, after all, the goddess."

I threw the holy water at him. He screamed and melted into a puddle
of bubbling effluvium. It couldn't be that easy to get rid of him, surely.
Unless he had never been the real enemy. Unless the real enemy had
really been inside myself, all this time, and he had only been its corporeal
manifestation. Heavy.

The puddle quivered, started to reshape itself into human form—

I rammed the stake right into its ectoplasmic heart.

"Good for you" said Oren. "Now rescue me."

I heard, from overhead, the high-pitched keening—

P h i l   E t c h i s o n

—that was Chris' song of creation.

I started to pile up the blocks, at random almost, feverishly, words
locking into other words, poems jigsawing into a barbarous, crude simulacrum of prosody.

—to be or not, thou still unravished
Bride of the monster—

I heard, behind Chris' song, the slow heartbeat of the world. In a way,
the words of the song no longer mattered; the truth was too deep for
words; that was what Chris had come to teach us.

—where Alph, the sacred
riverrun, past Eve's and—

Words joined with words, but the blocks ran in all directions: famous
poems, dirges, threnodies, doggerel, limericks, bathroom scrawls; I was
assembling them all, and the poem that was this multidimensional meta-
poem was less than a single word, the word that Chris knew, the word
that would soon unmake and recreate the cosmos.

The song grew around us, and at long last I forgot that I was creating
the poem in order to free the woman, for the woman had long since been

freed and was kneeling beside me, gazing at me, bedraggled, in a slow-motion, silent rainfall that I knew to be the first moment I set eyes on Mary, mother of my son, mother of Theo, mother of god; she watched me in wordless wonder as I spun the web of words. For every poem is a spell.

"You *are* Mary," I said.

"Among other things," she said, and clasped my free hand—the other was assembling another string of words—

I wonder by my troth what thou and I—

lonely as a cloud—

morning's minion,

a mountain wind that shakes the mighty oak-tree—

the still point of

world enough and time.

What did it all mean? All the poetry of the world run through a blender, fresh-squeezed into a killer juice cocktail? Did I care anymore? As all true poets know, in the end, poetry writes itself. Was I finally becoming a true poet? No. These were other men's words, mostly, though I detected a few strands in the fabric that were my own.

"Do you want some help?" Mary said at last, after she had looked at me adoringly for long enough.

"I guess so," I said.

She knelt down right next to me and began assembling the bricks along with me. The bricks shot into place, each one locking into the next with a *thwup*, spinning off more meta-poetry as we went along. It took me a while to realize that Mary was no longer chained up. I don't remember when she had been freed, or which strand of poesy it was that undid her shackles. I had thought that I was building this edifice of words in order to melt down her chains, but I began to realize that the structure was an end in itself. It was a kind of world, internally self-consistent. I don't know how long we were assembling the building blocks, but after a while I began to notice that we were kneeling on a pathway the paving-stones of which were the words we had put together, and that the texture of the world around us was no longer quite as metallic and two-dimensional.

The pathway had railings (each railing, exactly seventeen bricks high, was a haiku, spelled out in Japanese *kana*, inscrutable to me except that I could count to seventeen) and through the railings came a whispering wind, and in the wind there was moisture.

I crept closer to the edge.

"It's a bridge," I said softly. "We've been building a bridge."

"A bridge of words," Mary said.

"Words," I said, "which are mere airy nothings."

"Where does the bridge lead us?" she asked me.

"I don't know," I said, "but I think, I think—"

We both stood up. The bridge we had been building soared up high over our heads. It broke through the iron world we had been trapped in. In fact, where the bridge shattered the metal, there were rip marks in the cavern wall, like a fist that has punched through aluminum foil. Hand in hand, we followed the pathway. Each paving-stone I stepped on was a word:

Serendipitous

Huzzah

Calcite

Anaconda

Starstuff

and each word's meaning tingled all through me, as though the building block was the word itself; and I thought about the ancient theory of magic that holds that magic works when things are called by their true names, which names are known only to mages and wizards; and I wondered whether each of those words was in fact, the true name of the building block that bore it. I turned to Mary and she only smiled, as though she had heard all, agreed with all of it.

"It almost seems too easy," I said.

"That's because," she said, "what happens in the world you touch, taste, feel is not necessarily what's really happening; it's only a blueprint for what happens in here," she touched my head, "and here," she added, lightly tapping at my heart with a petite index finger, still smiling.

We held hands. We started walking toward the rip in the fabric of the steel universe.

"Where *does* it lead us?" Mary said, wonderingly; from beyond the iron door, there came the rushing of a mighty wind, like the beating of great wings. I thought Mary probably knew the answer to that question; wasn't she, after all, a goddess in this world? Was she just waiting for me to come up with the right answer? Was this yet another test, another tribulation that lay in the path of the hero's quest?

At the rip itself, the jagged strips of sheet metal quivering a little in the wind beyond the door, I took her in my arms and kissed her. Her hair wrapped itself around us both. I kissed her hungrily, because I had been without her so long; oh, she'd been around, as a hood ornament, as a statue, but as a woman, no. And she was nude beneath her hair, though her hair hissed like a nest of serpents, and hugged me as though it had a life of its own. I parted the hair from between her breasts and that was when I saw what I feared, what I knew I would see: the telltale lesions. This was my wife all right, my real wife from universe number one, my wife who was dying of cancer.

"What happened?" I asked her. "How did you—"

"Become myself again?"

"You were always yourself," I said. "But the very first yourself, the one who came to me in Washington in the rain—"

"The ur-Mary?" she said. And still she smiled, though I now knew she was in terrible agony. "She was always at the heart of me, if you peeled away enough layers."

"But if you're dying, it means—"

"The cosmos is dying? Because I am the world?" One almost expected the strains of that hideous Lionel Ritchie Christmas song to burst into the air, but instead her words were punctuated by Milt's drum, and by the stratospheric coloratura of Chris' voice, from somewhere in the steel vault of heaven.

I understood something profound in this moment, and I said it aloud: "we're seeing each other in our real, original forms, because the end of the world is finally at hand, isn't it? And this is, as it were, the moment of insight we are all being vouchsafed, this split second of vision . . . for a little while, until the cosmos is consumed, we too have become truthsayers, we too can see the way Theo sees, with the eyes of ultimate innocence."

"And what do you think I see?" Mary said softly.

"I don't know," I said. "One can't see oneself. But I would imagine you see the twelfth-rate poetaster that I am, an aging man, a little on the plump side, perhaps, a varicose vein or two, a man who doesn't even know his own son, a man who has achieved remarkably little in his life, considering his talents and social advantages."

"You call this bridge a little achievement?" Mary said.

"But somehow I think I was cheating. It was all so damned easy. And we still don't know where this bridge leads to."

"Let's take another step," she said, "and find out."

I kissed—

S e r e n a   S o m e r s

—Oren Karpovsky on the lips. Hard, wet, as if he were my one true love. And Oren slowly began to dissolve into a mist. The mist was soaking through the tapestry of our universe, and I could see that the walls of the catacombs were getting soggy.

"Where are you, Oren?" I said. I heard a gloppy movement over my shoulder.

When I turned around I saw another Oren, soaked in gore, rising from the puddle that had been Thorn and holy water. This was more of a golem-Oren, because his face and limbs had a muddy, unfinished texture to them. He even had a few qabbalistic signs inscribed on his forehead. "Can you talk?" I asked him.

He shook his head.

Of course he wasn't all formed yet. He had been caged inside the ravening psyche and soma of Thorn for a long time. It's hard to become unpossessed, I guess; it doesn't happen all in one sitting.

But if Oren was inside the Thorn that rose from the coffin, who was inside the Oren that was chained to the wall?

Who was the mist?

"Joshua?" I whispered.

The mist swirled softly around me. I followed the mist, which was almost humanoid, and the golem followed me. The catacombs deepened, narrowed, became mustier; but there was also more light. I think it was from rips in the fabric, places where the thread had worn thin; perhaps Penelope had stopped weaving and was finally contemplating doing what I did—taking matters into her own hands, not waiting around for her husband to come home like an eternal Donna Reed.

Maybe so. The fabric of the world didn't seem to be shifting anymore. The threads were lifeless, motionless. There was a wind of sorts, but it came from like, outside the tapestry, from the world beyond. There was a way out somewhere. I listened. I could hear the rushing of water.

The mist began condensing against the farthest wall. It was eating away the cloth now. It was opening up a ragged exit, wide enough for a single human. The mist wound itself up into a sort of mini-tornado, and thrust itself through the hole. I followed. Behind me lumbered the Oren-golem. We were standing at one end of a bridge.

At one end of a rainbow; and the other end was shrouded in mist. In Joshua, perhaps. He was the gold at the end, perhaps. My one true love, stranded in a world that no longer existed except in memory. I was alone with my mute ex-lover; he had gone from master of the world (or at least some simulacrum of the world) to a brutish zombie, not even all flesh and blood.

The wind was powerful as shit, and freezing, too, even though the sun beat down on us. The bridge had no pavement as such. We were walking on something solid, but we couldn't see what it was. It seemed to hold us up pretty well. The fabric of the rainbow itself was definitely what you'd call gossamer. I mean, you could put your hands right through it and not feel a thing. It was spun out of thinnest air.

The floor of the bridge could have been glass, or some kind of force field, or even—

Philip Etchison

—yellow bricks, for all I knew. All I could tell is that we were hanging over the most awe-inspiring gorge I had ever seen—dangling on a skein of verbiage and beneath us the waters were rushing—we were suspended over the confluence of a million rivers, a million worlds.

There were other bridges too, arcing up in the distance; bridges of masonry and steel, of gold and crystal; bridges that were rainbows; precarious bridges that were a single rope lashed to struts of bamboo. And on some of those bridges I could make out tiny figures, human mostly, all making their way toward some unseen nexus.

And below! Whitewater rapids. Geysers and fountains thousands of feet high. This had to be it, the fabled source of the river that runs between the worlds. There were ships down below, too. Shattered against the rocks. I saw the upturned prow of what might have been the *Titanic*, from which I had recently escaped. I saw triremes and barges, liners and rafts, all dashed to pieces against sheer precipices.

I heard Milt's drum beating behind the roar of the waters.

Where was the shaman? At length I could make him out, a minute figure far ahead of us on the bridge, dancing up a storm.

"Let's go to Milt," I said. "He'll know what to do next."

"As if," said Mary, "you didn't know yourself; you have your mythology pretty much down cold."

I smiled. "You're right," I said. "Let's go, then."

"Yes, let's go."

But for a long moment, we did not move. We merely stood there, almost touching, reveling in the fact that we had come so far and that we now stood on the brink of . . . what? A universe was going to end, and another was going to be born. We would be among those fortunate enough to be vouchsafed the privilege of stepping across the line that divided two great cycles of existence. Even though I was still a mediocre poet, and Mary was still a middle-aged mother, dying of cancer, isolated and afraid.

<u>O r e n   K a r p o v s k y</u>

I cannot speak.
I can only follow.
I don't know where I am.
The whole world is the sound of water.

CHAPTER EIGHTEEN

THE FRODO SYNDROME

<u>T h e o   E t c h i s o n</u>

—and land.

In the confluence of a million rivers, at the place where all bridges cross, there is a pool, a quiet, circular pool, oblivious to the raging of the waters all around. The old mad king lies sleeping on a rock, his scepter cradled in his arms; his scepter is the light that plays in the grotto. We hear the crash of clashing rivers, and we know it is just beyond the wall of rocks that surrounds us, but somehow it seems infinitely far away.

Ash and I are looking at the king. He's sleeping like a baby, I guess. Like he's not carrying half the tortured souls of the world within the jewel of his scepter.

Ash and I creep up to the edge of the pool.

When I gaze into the water, it's as if all my truthsaying powers have come back to me; it's like I never started to feel the tug of hormones or the pollution of doubt.

"Father says," says Ash, "that the scepter has one last great magic in it. Do you know what that magic is?"

"Yeah," I say, "it's the magic of unmaking. It's the power to unravel the whole cosmos."

"Scary," Ash says.

"As if you didn't know," I say.

"It sounds better," he says, "coming from the lips of a truthsayer. There's a kind of certainty to it."

"I'm not much of a truthsayer anymore," I say.

Then I gaze into the pool again. I see that all the protagonists in this story are slowly coming together, and that we're all going to meet up here, in this little space, to play out the final stages of the drama. I see my dad, striding over the chasm on a bridge of poetry, and my mother with him, shivering in a frayed Navajo blanket, the same blanket she was wrapped in when we were driving to Mexico.

I see Serena Somers hurrying toward us over another bridge. Behind her was a man of clay. Ahead of her was a humanoid mist . . . a sort of preperson I guess; someone who doesn't exist yet, but who will soon exist if everything goes the way it should.

"So what do we do now, truthsayer?" Ash asks me.

"I guess," I say, "we pry away the scepter from your father, and we drop it into the source of the river, and everything returns to square one."

That sounds right. It has that mythic ring to it. But I can't help thinking that it's not that simple, that there's one more piece to the puzzle. What could it be? I gaze into the reflecting pool once more and now I see myself. In some ways I haven't changed that much. I'm still scrawny, I'm still an unkempt, dirty blond kid with scarily clear eyes. Somewhere out there, in one of the many branches of the river, it's still the 90s, the time before the mad millennium, and a dollar will still buy you a Coke and a candy bar; somewhere out there I'm still young, so fucking young I still don't know what it's like to be afraid of the all-embracing darkness, I still haven't looked death in the eye, even though I've heard him breathing over my shoulder, and I know his smell too well, the sick-sweet-orange-putrid smell of my mother dying.

But then when you look at me again you see that I've lost my innocence; that the vision I have now is just a temporary flashback to the time before; you see that I have one foot permanently in the real world, the world without magic, the world where truthsaying has no meaning: that's the world where I will end up one day, when the healing's done and the redemption all taken care of. We are all gods, but only for as long as we need to be.

Ash has been trying to loosen the mad king's grip. "This thing weighs a ton," he says. "I just can't get it off him."

That's when I realize what the problem is. It's the Frodo syndrome, of course; the ring gets heavier and heavier the closer you get to the crack of Mt. Doom; just as, no doubt, the cross got heavier and heavier the closer Christ got to Calvary; that's in the nature of redeeming the world.

"Come on," I say, "I'll help you."

The two of us tug at the scepter. To say that it's heavy is an understatement, and it's jammed tight in the mad king's embrace. We pull and push and we can't budge it.

"We're going to have to wake him up," I say, and I start kicking him and pulling at his beard.

The king seems strangely at peace. He hasn't slept much during our long journey, but now, it seems, the weariness of the years has caught up with him all at once. I don't understand it. His eyelids are quivering; he's in a state of REM, I guess; perhaps he's even dreaming the whole world into being, like the Red King in *Alice Through the Looking Glass*. Perhaps, I think, like in *Alice*, we will all disappear if he wakes up. Perhaps, I think, that would be just as well in a way. No more terror. No more pain. No more Mrs. Hulan's social studies class, for instance.

"I'm going to have to do it," Ash says softly. He prods the king lightly on the cheek; when that doesn't work, he kisses him gently on the lips. This time, not as statesmen kiss, not like before; this time he does seem like his father's true son at last. And Strang opens his eyes.

"I didn't die," Strang says.

"No, father, you didn't."

"It's time for me to hurl the thing away "

Strang struggles to get up. But still he's hugging that scepter to his chest, and the jewel glitters, deadly and cold; and you can tell that it weighs him down but he doesn't want to let go.

"Father, father," says Ash, "remember how you answered the sphinx."

"Yes," I tell him, "we have to let go now."

Strang says, "If only you knew . . . how many souls are imprisoned in this jewel . . . if only you knew how each pinprick death caused me to grow in power until I . . . I . . . I encircled the whole world, like the river of time. . . ."

"The river of time," I say, "has circled back on itself now, King. We'll help you. Come on, Ash, grab hold of one of his shoulders."

Ash and I heave the king up, a frail thing, yes, a king of shreds and patches as my dad would have called him; and we try to support him, but it's hard because the scepter weighs so fucking much. I keep thinking, *Ditch the scepter, ditch the scepter, ditch the scepter*, and that inner voice sounds a constant counterpoint to the other music we hear, the music that emanates from the world's heart and from that other truthsayer, the child of my incest.

"Heavy," the king murmurs, "heavy, heavy."

Ditch the scepter! Ditch the scepter!

"You hear it too, don't you," Ash says to me.

"Yeah."

We half pull, half push the king toward the pool. "I don't want to give it up," the king says. "I don't, I don't." He sounds like a child with a favorite toy. He is, after all, still crazy; that moment of lucidity, in which he and Ash acknowledged each other and their love for each other, was maybe just a flash of lightning in a dark storm that can only deepen.

But the scepter is so heavy we can barely move the king at all, and now we start to hear voices in the scepter itself: they're the voices of lost souls, screaming for release; all of inferno is tesseracted into that scepter, I'm sure of it.

The drumbeat still goes on.

Suddenly, the air above us is full of Thorn's creatures. They hover over us with their gargoyle faces and crimson eyes. I don't know if they're going to attack or not. I don't see their leader; in fact, I thought I saw a vision of him dead, in a puddle of steaming holy water, in some cata-comb, when I gazed into the pool. They keep descending, settling on every nook and niche in the wall of rock that surrounds us, until there's like a thousand pairs of demon eyes staring down at us. I can hear their collective breathing, and I can smell their breath, a trace of fetor behind the pure fresh scent of the source.

They don't attack. They only stare.

Then we hear: *Ditch the scepter! Ditch the scepter!* over and over again, inside our skulls, like a throbbing headache; it's the voices within the scepter, it's the voices of the gargoyles, coming from their minds I guess—you remember in *Alice through the Looking Glass* Lewis Carroll says that the animals "thought in chorus"—and then what happens next is that King Strang's eyes begin to bleed.

No, no, just his left eye, the one he gave up as the price of all this power. Blood brims up around the iolite crystal, his artificial eye. It oozes down his cheek. And now the sores, the cankers on his face that are the outward symbols of his inner corruption start to erupt. Pus and bile run down his face, his neck, soak into his robe. He looks like something out of a low-budget monster movie.

He begins to scream in utmost agony. It's hard to bear. I know he wants to get rid of that scepter, but it's like it's glued to his arms. He is the only one who can toss that thing away, because he is the one who originally made the deal to steal the jewel from the River's source.

That's when the demon-creatures start to swoop down.

They come down in twos and threes. They worry at the king with their beaks, try to jab him in the arm. Ash and I try to fend them off, but what can we do? It's like being stuck in that Hitchcock movie, *The Birds*, you know, where they just keep coming and coming. They screech like banshees, caw like crows, they start pecking at the king's open wounds. Strang screams. He lashes out with the scepter. He bonks one and it sort of disintegrates and gets sucked into the jewel. So even now, it's gathering more souls, more power, becoming heavier.

Ash is doing pretty well at first. He karate-chops a couple of the creatures and they split in half. Why are they even attacking? Don't they know they have no leader anymore?

But I'm wrong. I hear a rumbling. The wall of rock is shaking. Then it suddenly splits, and the prow of the *Titanic* bursts through; and leaping down from the height, his cloak transforming itself into a leathern parachute as he falls, is Thorn, who has died three or four times during this adventure yet is proving eerily resilient. Behind him, through the shattered rocks, I can see the vista beyond the source: the rushing rivers, the rainbow bridges, the unscalable cliffs and impenetrable mountains, the tiny figures making their inexorable way toward me, the center, the place of their destiny.

"Father," Thorn screams, "give me the scepter now."

The demons circle overhead as Thorn lands beside us. He glances at me only for a moment. "Why do you keep coming back?" I ask him.

"I'm a vampire," he says. "That's what we do. We come back from the dead. You can kill me as often as you like, but it won't do any good."

He turns to his brother. "I'll dispose of you as soon as I get the scepter," he says, and he reaches for it.

King Strang stands firm. But Thorn has a way of getting to him the way I and Ash cannot, because we're not experts at lying; when Thorn tells the truth, the truth hurts his father in a way he can't control, and control is what he knows best. "Father," Thorn says, "do you remember when you divided the kingdom into three, and you gave me all the worlds controlled by Thornstone Slaught? Do you remember what you asked your three children then? To tell you how much we loved you? And do you remember what I said?"

Strang gasps, "You said 'I love you like the sky. I love you like the earth. I love you like the infinite sea.' "

"What a fool you are, father. I lied."

"You lied?"

"Love was never the issue, father. A vampire does not feel love; he feeds on the love of others; love is something to be sucked out, never given back; that is what I am. Why did you make me a vampire, father?"

"You were born dead," Strang says softly.

I kneel down by the pool and gaze into its depths. I see it all. Vividly, for this is the pool in which all time stands perfectly still, and where every moment of existence is captured in some kind of unbreakable stasis; this pool is the universe's memory bank, the one place where there are no lies.

I see the scene. The palace I recognize from having traveled there inside Ash's consciousness. I see the palace newer now, just after the coming of the firstborn. The king cradling the dead child in his arms, the queen sobbing with grief, the courtiers standing with their eyes downcast, not daring to show any emotion in case the king lashed out at them; the lizard warriors, weapons upright, flanking the walls and staring straight ahead.

I see the dead child's eyes, still open, slate-colored. He's not a baby, even though he has just been born; these are not exactly human beings; perhaps he has been gestating for ten, twelve, fifteen of our years; he's a boy, not an infant. He is being laid in a stone sarcophagus now, and I see the king, inconsolable, speaking to some mage or grand vizier, a man with long black robes embroidered with stars and moons; the mage is whispering back to him, dire secrets about the nature of life and death.

The mourners file past, one by one. The water of the pool ripples and we are no longer in the throne room, but in some dank and foul-smelling catacomb beneath the palace complex. At length, King Strang is alone except for the queen, Thorn's mother, and the body of his son. Then the queen too leaves, dismissed with an angry glance and a harsh command. Strang stands before the body. He is a young king still, his face unlined, his scepter not yet adorned with the jewel that steals men's souls.

He kneels over the dead boy. He whispers words into his ear, words he has heard from the dark mage; and presently he stabs his own wrist, and lets the blood run down his palm, down his index finger, to the dead boy's lips. And he is whispering, "Come back to life, my son, the one I love so much, come back, come back; I don't care if what you are is just a simulacrum of life; I'll accept anything, any shadow, any vestige, any animated imitation of what you might have been, if only you will walk the earth once more and be my son."

The blood drips. The blood of a king is a powerful magic, especially that of a king who rules over not one country, but many worlds. No doubt that's what the mage has been telling him.

The child stirs. I see Strang tremble with anticipation and also a certain fear. The child's eyes open. He looks at his father. Not with affection, but with accusation. Not with respect, but with recrimination. Then Thorn howls, a howl of profound, dark agony, a howl that makes me shiver because I can't ever know what it's like to be undead, always to hunger, to live in a perpetual twilight, an eternal aloneness; I just can't know these things. I'm scared. I look up from the pool, and I see the living Strang, who's been reliving those moments along with me; I see that the agony hasn't stopped for either of them.

"Why, father, why," cries Thorn, "did you bring me back from the grave?"

And Strang says, "Because I loved you, my son."

But they do not look into each other's eyes.

Behind Thorn, Cornelius Huang has landed, trumpet in hand. The little Cerberus-creature is yapping at his heels.

"You made it so I can never be swallowed back into the darkness. You made it so I can never know the womb-warmth of the earth; I'm always homeless, always hungry; are you surprised I hate you?"

"I—" says the king. God, how I feel his pain. Sometimes you do hate your parents, sometimes you feel like pummeling them with your fists and shouting *I hate you I hate you I hate you* but you know that this kind of hatred stems from a kind of love. Thorn's kind of hatred goes a lot deeper. It is perpetual. He can't live and he can't die. He's been killed a million times and still he comes back, breathing himself into fresh clay; he is all hunger, all rapacity.

Only the force of this hate is strong enough to dislodge the scepter from Strang's arms. There it goes. Crashing to the stony floor. A little closer to the source. Thorn dives after it. He can't lift it, though. He tugs at it with all his might but it seems to be soldered to the rock. He screams for reinforcements, and his gargoyle troops dive down in V-formation, each one grasping the tail of the one below; there's a V of demons reaching all the way up to the sun, and the head demon reaches down and clutches the scepter with both fists and all together, hundreds upon hundreds of ruby-eyed monsters, they manage to hoist the scepter up, an inch or two at first then higher, higher—

Thorn turns to his father. He crows. He laughs the laughter of mad scientists, and, like a comic-book villain, he can't stop himself from lecturing us: "After light, father, there comes shadow; after day comes night, didn't you realize that, glorious and brilliant though your reign was, there had to be an equal and opposite age of darkness? You may think you're saving the world by tossing away the scepter and healing its wounds, but what about us, the creatures of night, who are its wounds, who would be destroyed by the process of healing? You're not saving our world, father, are you? But if I wrest the jewel from you, if I'm the one to plunge the cosmos into a million-year-darkness, won't I be the one to be remembered for redeeming my creatures from the tyranny of light? You see, there's always two sides to everything."

King Strang is too mortified to answer. I watch the scepter slowly rise above our heads. There is nothing I can do. I still hear those voices, though, the ones that cry out, *Ditch the scepter*, and I know Thorn hears them too, because he's holding his hands over his ears, he's tormented, he's dying to block out the sounds.

"You can't hack it," I tell him. "You can't handle being the adversary, the prince of darkness."

"Of course I can," Thorn says. "I was made for the part. And don't try to bullshit me with some dimestore psychology, kid, because I know you're not a real truthsayer anymore."

"Oh, but I am," I say. "Here, inside this circle, everyone's a truthsayer. So I tell you this: As far as the Great Satan thing is concerned, you're just another wannabe. Inside your black heart there's a frightened little boy, and that boy knows why your father did what he did. He's angry as shit about it, but he always recognizes there's a spark of love behind the selfishness of it. He sees that Strang was desperate when he called you back from the dead; desperate because kings are fated to be unloved, and he wanted something to love him, even if it was only an imitated love; do you understand that?"

"Don't give me that New Age nonsense. I won't be reconciled to my father. I won't forgive him and don't want him to forgive me."

He waves at the V of demons, and Cornelius blows seven quick blasts, and the V jerks upward, and we see the scepter swing back and forth; it's kind of a pendulum effect I guess. The jewel glitters so much that it almost blinds me. They're all undead, all the souls trapped in the jewel; I think if Thorn had it, he could release them all—if you can call it release when you turn a living thing, with free will and all that, into a fucking zombie.

"It's not New Age nonsense," I tell Thorn. "It's the simple truth."

And Thorn knows it, too.

"Never liked truth too much," he mumbles. "Just never liked it."

He waves his arms helplessly at his minions.

With a great flapping of leathern wings, the scepter crashes to the rock once more . . . a few feet closer to the pool,

"Father, father," says Thorn. "Maybe I did love you a little bit. But that was a long time ago, before it became too late for love."

He stands, facing his father, his arms outstretched, looking curiously like the crucified Christ somehow.

Strang does manage to lift the scepter up.

"Too late?" Strang says softly. "Too late for love?"

"How do you do that?" Thorn says in wonderment. "You're old and feeble, and that jewel carries the weight of so much death, so much remorse."

I tell him, "You bear your cross, and he will bear his. At least, you see, it's his own."

You're doing a little too damn well," Thorn says, "in the truthsaying department, you weasel."

I try to smile. But my smile dissolves when Strang does what, I guess, destiny tells him he must do; he thrusts the tip of the scepter into Thorn's chest, cracks through the sternum, penetrates his son's heart.

"You brought me into this world," says the vampire; "I suppose it's only right you should take me out of it."

Blood begins to spurt from the wound with a wet, sick, gloppy sound, like reluctant ketchup. Thorn still has something to say. "Father," he says, "I always thought this was going to really hurt, and you know, it does. But the amazing thing is, I feel it; I really feel it; this pain gives me the illusion of once having been alive."

And little by little, like, frame by frame almost, the prince who once abducted me from the men's room of a Chinese restaurant, who sucked the blood of mermaids, who imprisoned me in a gothic castle and made me navigate his sinking ship, my one time nemesis . . . well, he begins to kind of liquefy, like a Salvador Dali clock, and he slowly oozes into oblivion. They are all dissipated into thin air: not just Thorn and Cornelius and the three-headed dog, but also the army of dark spirits hovering in the air; they're all kind of dissolving; the air ripples. Presently, they seem no more threatening than a swarm of flies. In fact, that's what they are. Thorn, distorted and distended now, steps forward. His slate-colored eyes are bleeding; it's not blood exactly, but a purple-green sap; Dad would have said it was ichor, the fluid that runs in the veins of the gods.

King Strang tries to embrace him; it's awkward; even now, at the last minute, he is afraid to love whom he now knows has always loathed him.

Only the scepter remains; and it's even more dazzling now, because it contains the soul of someone who was truly close to its owner. The jewel of lost souls is as bright as the sun itself.

"Now, King Strang," I tell him. "Throw it into the pool. Before something else happens to slow you down."

The king takes another step toward the source. The scepter is still cradled fast within his arms.

But, at that moment—

CHAPTER NINETEEN

THIS IS THE WAY THE COOKIE CRUMBLES

S e r e n a   S o m e r s

I stepped into the circle of rock. Theo was already there, and so was the mad king. They were sort of struggling over the scepter. But most amazingly of all, I saw Ash, and he saw me; when I looked at him I was reminded vividly of all those summer nights, lying alone, thinking wet thoughts, with Ash as my lone imaginary companion.

With the mist that was Joshua spinning above me, and the golem that was Oren behind me, and my dream lover standing at the water's edge, I was surrounded by all the people I had ever had any deep sexual feelings for. Well, there was Mr. E., too, but I guess that had just been a school-girl crush.

But I couldn't think about all that right now because there was a final piece of unfinished business I'd been called upon to do. I could feel myself morphing now, twisting, I could feel the scales push through the skin, the claws protrude through my fingertips and toes. This was the reason I'd been carrying Katastrofa inside me all along . . . so she could confront her father for the last time.

My human skin was peeling from me now. Doesn't every woman have a dragon within herself? I felt: I am Katastrofa and she is me.

My scaly self rubbed hard against the underside of my epidermis and yes, I felt pain, such pain, you can't even imagine it; I was giving birth to the dark side of myself. What kind of a dragon was I? The fire scorched my throat as I exhaled. I threw a glance back at the still shiny pool that I knew must be the source of all those rivers. I saw myself; sleek, monstrous, golden-eyed, wreathed in the smoke of my own breath; god I was frightening, and I was beautiful, all at once. I watched myself from a deep safe place inside my mind because the one who controlled the body was now Katastrofa Darkling, not sluglike Serena.

"Father," I said to the old man.

"Katastrofa?" he said. "Aren't you dead? I never brought you back from the dead, never condemned you to an eternity of hunger. . . ."

The Katastrofa in me coiled and uncoiled herself, shook her golden wattles, inclined her head so her scales caught the sunlight and made her all bright and bronze. "But father," I said, "I still never answered your question. I mean, the one about how much I love you."

"Yes," said Strang, "you did. Didn't you? Wasn't that the answer about the sun and the moon and the stars and the planets and the great galaxies that wheel and whirl?" Strang sounded indecisive; he must have known that I was going to disappoint him.

"Oh, father," I said, "I do love you. Let me show you how much." And so it was that the dragon coiled herself around the old man, and stroked his rubbery flesh with her searing scales, and I realized that Katastrofa's love for her father had been more than filial. It had been that old Electra complex thing.

"Don't tear your eyes out, father," said Katastrofa, seductive and brazen. "Well, you already tore one out, but with the other you still have to be able to look at me. You still have to see that I'm beautiful, I'm your little girl."

With my inner eye I started to catch glimpses of Katastrofa's childhood. She was not always a dragon. She was a little girl indeed, in pigtails, running naked through the palace, chased by the nursemaids, and her father was remote, on his throne, a person who visited her only in dreams or when she saw his stern hologram in the ceiling of the nursery, and always surrounded by those lizard guards, one at each corner of the throne, their weapons perpetually drawn; I overheard a childish thought: *He loves those guards more than he loves me.*

At night I dreamt of ravishing my father. Only once was I admitted to his bedchamber, and they blindfolded me before they would take me there, and I was escorted by twelve fierce lizards in chrome-colored suits. But my unconscious mind always had a good sense of direction, so every night I flew down those scores of corridors, and each night in my dreams I grew scalier, and my wings sprouted and my fangs began to grow; and one morning I woke up and I was a dragon. The lizard guards had rubbed off on me, because I thought he loved them more than me. . . .

That morning I came to the throne room. My father's wives fled. The lizards stood firm, knowing what I had become, having, perhaps, some inkling why. The grand vizier, the one who advised my father to make my older brother a vampire, whispered in my father's ear; I stank up the hall with my fetid breath, and melted the gold steps to my father's throne with a single exhalation. And my father looked at me, and I could see all the disappointment in his eyes, because I was no longer little and beautiful; but all he said was, "Is this, Katastrofa, what you really want?"

And I said, "I don't know, father. It just happened, somehow. I think it's because you don't love me enough. I'm not beautiful enough, I'm not your little girl enough, I don't know. Somehow you made this happen." Which wasn't true, not exactly. We had both made it happen. I because of some dark, lustful emotion no one had ever tried to explain to me, he because he had always neglected me . . . now, seeing the broken old man, now I knew he had always loved me . . . but I was too angry to want to understand that. I wanted him to love me the way I dreamed about in my childish, hormonally challenged fashion . . . and so it was that I was wrapping my limbs and coils around a spent, mad king, and watching him squirm, and becoming strangely, inexorably aroused; even my scales sweated lubricious fluids.

"Get away from me," said Strang , but he couldn't command me any-more. Wasn't I a dragon, and wasn't he a king without a kingdom? In this place, only the truth could be told, and my truth was a shameful truth, but it was so powerful that my dragon frame shuddered with the realiza-tion of it.

"Love me, father," I said. "This is the true answer to your question. This is the way I've always loved you. I've been consumed by it, and now I'll consume you too. Fuck me, father, fuck me now."

"Abomination!" Strang said. "You can't really be my daughter."

"Well," said the dragon, "if I'm not, then it's okay to do it, right?"

Strang howls, howls, howls, like the winter wind.

(The I that's Serena watches from deep inside the dragon's mind. I'm alarmed at all this incest. I've taken enough Joseph Campbell in Mythol-ogy 101 to know that it's what the gods seem to do best, though when humans do it they tend to pluck their eyes out, as Tom Lehrer says in that song of his about Oedipus Rex, "one by one.")

She wound herself tight around him like a golden boa constrictor. She snarled. She shook herself and sent droplets of flame flying. The old man was horrified, sure, but I could see, through Katastrofa's eyes, that there was something in him a little bit like lust; that was the way Oren had first looked at me, across the desktop in his congressman's office, predatory and a little jaded; I knew that Strang had feelings for his daughter, long repressed; maybe it was his feelings that had sparked off his daughter's secret feelings, and the secrets had nourished each other through the years, fed on each other until they drove both of them mad.

"You have to consummate this, father," said Katastrofa. "It's the only way this can end for me. I can't completely die, not until I've mated with the god."

"I'm not a god," Strang gasps, "never was, thought I was, perhaps, but never will be now; I am an old man and I have no power."

"Fuck me, father," I said in Katastrofa's metal-tinged voice, "fuck me, give me the scepter."

The flies that had once been demons buzzed about his open sores. He looked pathetic but, through Katastrofa's eyes, I also saw the magnificent god-king, with his mane of dark hair, astride the world, controller of the gateways between worlds; he was beautiful to her, beautiful even as he was hurting her by his abandonment.

"The scepter! The scepter!" she (and I) screamed. I couldn't tell if it was agony, ecstasy, or something in between.

Nightmarish images flashed through my mind. Strang naked and covered with sores. The dragon thrashing in a crimson sea. The dragon stretching, stretching, elongating herself and tunneling and winding through the thousands of miles of corridors in the king's palace. Meanwhile, the real king writhed in a frenzy of guilt and desire.

At length, I think he must have seen the way out of his dilemma. He lunged forward, scooped up the scepter with a superhuman effort, and raised it high.

"That's it, father," she cried out. "The scepter, the jewel of your manhood, the ultimate power."

And Strang thrust the scepter deep into her—me—oh, God, I felt those thrusts, I felt them penetrate me deep, felt raped and violated, felt my womb become warped and ravaged. He plunged the scepter into me again and again, as relentlessly as a low-budget porno. Katastrofa screamed—I screamed with her—and I knew that this time she would really die. Yes, there was joy in being stabbed to death by father's phallic scepter. I couldn't really understand it, but waves of Katastrofa's twisted love flooded my mind. I couldn't think. I was enveloped in a sea of red. It was the dragon's blood. I was swimming in blood. The blood was fiery and warm. It scorched me, it seared me, but it gave me a strange kind of high, like mainlining heroin or something, not that I've ever done that, but it was totally addictive, totally seductive. Katastrofa was dying in an orgasmic bliss that I couldn't even imagine, but because I shared her mind, I could touch the edge of it and even that was enough to make me jump out of my skin . . . well, *her* skin, actually . . . because I found myself, dry and dressed all in white, standing in a pool of dragon ectoplasm.

The scepter gleamed; it was more dazzling than before; it had absorbed not only the essence of Thorn, the lord of the dark places, but also the brilliance of Katastrofa, the dragon who had soared by day and eclipsed the sun with reflected sunlight.

And once again the scepter fell out of King Strang's hands and rolled a little closer toward the pool. . . .

Strang wept in the arms of his one remaining child. Impassively, the Oren-golem stood, his eyes shifting from side to side like clockwork.

Theo said to me, "It's almost over, Serena."

My true love's little brother, the truthsayer, still a frail skinny kid; a lot less time had passed in his inner world; we others had all grown old, then grown young again, and Theo hadn't aged at all . . . or had he?

"What do we do now?" I asked him.

"Just a few more feet," Theo said. "Then the jewel will be cast back into the waters; then the world will end, and the world will be reborn; then, maybe, we can go home."

"You want me to help you?" I said. "Throw it in, I mean."

"None of us can. Only Strang."

The old man brushed aside his son and stood. He tottered toward the scepter. "I will do it now," he said. I hadn't been able to touch Katastrofa's lust, and I couldn't comprehend King Strang's sorrow, either, it was the whole world's sorrow.

⌐

Then, at that moment the Oren-golem lurched forward—

"Power," it grunted. "Me, power, me, power, all."

It strode toward the scepter. Lifted it up. Easily. Even though I knew that it had the weight of billions of lost souls. Lifted it over its head. It shone. I had to shield my eyes.

"Me, power, me, power, all," said the man of clay.

"Now what?" I said.

Theo said, "It's time for you to decide who it is you really love."

"But I—but I—"

"No time to waste! Pick sides! The entire universe is going to blow!"

With a line like that, you know you're either imprisoned inside a cheap sci-fi movie, or well like, it's really happening. You start thinking a lot faster. The Joshua mist was spinning next to the source. Who do I really love? It's Joshua, I thought, that's the plain simple truth, totally no contest. I need to bring him back, and I do have the power to, because I've had the goddess inside me, and because of the enduring strength of my love for him. Didn't I once yield up my virginity to save him from the dragon's clutches?

Then I remembered the crumbled fortune cookie.

Way back. Imprisoned in Thornstone Slaught. I'd almost brought him back to life then, hadn't I? It was time to try again. Because now I had many more pieces of the puzzle that was myself, Serena Somers.

In one of my pockets—how many pockets did I have now? hadn't I been transformed into some kind of Amazon lady with a kilt, a sword, and popping boobs, at one stage, before standing here in a virginal, priestessly white robe?—there should still have been a napkin, and, wrapped up in the napkin, the crumbs with which I had hoped to reconstitute Joshua.

Oren lifted the scepter easily above his head. He wasn't, of course, quite human; I suppose that's why he was able to. In fact, he was becoming less and less human every second. There was an aura that the scepter cast about him, a cold blue light that danced about his clay features, and kind of dug itself in beneath his earthen skin. The dirt was hardening, becoming more glistening, more metallic. It was like he was recapitulating the whole history of robotics—all the way from the ancient Jewish myth of the man of clay, to the chromium androids of the future, and he was becoming more rigid, more powerful.

"That's what you always wanted, isn't it, Oren?" I shouted at him. "You wanted to get rid of the human part of you altogether. You wanted to become a machine."

"True," he said. His voice was hollow and emotionless. "But what about all your great ideas about saving the world? The Karpovsky health plan? Bringing culture to the proles? Were they just tidbits thrown to the masses on your way to ultimate power?"

King Strang said, very faintly: "Don't do it, man of clay. It isn't worth it."

And Oren swung the scepter, and with each swing more of the wall of rock came tumbling down; you could see past the wall, to the whitewater vista of converging rivers, to the rainbow spaghetti of bridges that spanned the sky. And he said to the king, in a voice of gravel and dirt, "Why shouldn't I do it? You did, didn't you? Look at you now, you desiccated old thing . . . don't tell me it wasn't worth it. Don't tell me you wouldn't do it all over again."

And Strang was silent, because, in the end, Oren was right. Power was its own reward.

I found the napkin tucked into my bosom. I pulled it out and there were the pieces of the fortune cookie, and I remembered the words on the slip of paper:

if you build him, he will come

and I thought, there's a double meaning in that, it all boils down to sex again somehow, doesn't it? and that totally confused me. But still, I knelt down on the rock and opened up the napkin and spit into my hand, and then I rolled the breadcrumbs together and started to form them into the shape of a man. I felt embarrassingly domestic for doing it. I mean, it wasn't a 90s thing to do at all. But the homunculus started to take shape in my palm.

The mist that swirled around us was Joshua's soul; now I had to make his flesh. I was all goddess and all woman; my personal mystery was the mystery of creation. But how could I make it work?

Theo said to me and Strang, "Everyone has one great piece of magic inside themselves. Everyone does. But after you work that great piece of magic, then you're just a human being again. But you keep going. Because you remember that you had the magic once. And you hope that it will come again. And maybe it will. In the last moments before you die, maybe. At the cusp between worlds, between the unmaking and the unmaking, you know what I mean? There's magic nibbling at the corners of the world. Grab hold of that magic in both fists and reel it in. Dad'll kill me for mixing all these metaphors, but hey, rules are made to be broken, and now's as good a time as any to break them."

I looked at the golem, who was raging up and down, swinging the scepter, striking at the swarms of flies left over from Thorn's army of darkness; I looked at the puddles of viscera that used to be Thorn and Katastrofa, and I thought to myself, this is a pretty sordid way for the world to end. I'd always heard Mr. E. quote that T. S. Eliot thing about the end of the world, *not with a bang but with a whimper*, but now I totally saw what he meant by that.

"Come back, Joshua," I whispered.

The mist, which had been whirling around the mirror-still pool, shifted and came to me. It swirled around my face. I could smell him now. I started to cry. I guess my salt tears started to blend with the crisp dry crumbs. Things started to happen. The mist blew over the pile of crumbs. The wetness softened them. There was a little doughboy in the palm of my hand and he was starting to grow.

He was heavy. I was afraid I couldn't hold on. I did for a while, though; I thought of all the times I'd dreamed of Josh, the times I'd looked at him in school; the times I'd wangled a job baby-sitting Theo on the off-chance I might see him on his way to a game; it's strange to love someone who doesn't exist, who never existed except in some universe that is, for all intents and purposes, mere fantasy, until the moment you turn around, switch paths, and breathe the world back into being. . . .

What can I say? Joshua came to life out of the cookie crumbs (which are made of flour which is made of grain which comes out of the earth and so goes back to the great mother who lived within me) and the mist (which was part of the air which was part of the breath of god which was the sky) and he was more than beautiful; he was the Joshua of my dreams, bigger, better than I ever remembered him; he rode a shining white steed caparisoned in cloth of gold, and he wore armor of solid gold, and he plucked a flaming sword out of the air. He knelt down at my feet and I ripped off a sheer scrap of my bridal costume for him to tie to the hilt of his sword. Then he got back on his horse and charged at the golem, and they clashed, just on the other side of the pool of still water, shrieking at each other in some medieval language.

They jousted; Oren unseated Joshua with the scepter, and then they scrambled up and down across the rocks, parrying, thrusting, leaping, dodging. It was all very swashbuckling I suppose, but I couldn't really get into it. They ran all the way around the pool like cartoon characters and made me dizzy; Josh was quick as lightning, the golem lumbering but full of strength. They scurried around and around the pool. Sparks flew from the jewel and the flaming sword. Josh made samurailike noises, while Oren growled and grunted.

After a decent amount of fighting, Joshua sort of tapped Oren on the head with his flaming sword. Oren shattered into a cloud of clay and metal fragments and landed on the ground in a heap.

"That's it?" I said. "That's the one big magic? Seems kind of lame if you ask me."

Theo laughed. His laughter made me happy because, for the first time since all this began, he sounded like himself, a more-or-less happy teenage boy in more-or-less average circumstances. Then he smiled a secretive smile, like the kid who comes up to you to shake your hand and he's got a toad stowed up his sleeve, or one of those electric buzzer things. He said, "No, stupid," and laughed again, "that's not it at all. That's just the teaser. The real magic is about to happen . . . right . . . *now*."

And here's what happened next:

Strang stood at the edge of the pool. He had managed to lug the scepter all the way there. He paused. You see, Oren was right; power was power, and there is nothing so tempting as power. So finally, Ash went up to him, and very, very gently began to nudge him toward the very edge.

Strang wept.

"You've hurt the world," Ash said, "and now it's up to you to heal it."

Another step.

Another step.

Strang's tears were healing tears. Where they touched his cheeks, his sores were closing up. The pustules on his forehead were smoothing out. The wrinkles were not going away, but they seemed less, well, less wrinkled, somehow. He took another step toward the edge of the source, and now his tears were actually dripping into the pool itself, and the mirror-stillness was shattered. In the rippling, I saw Milt Stone, in the eerie mask and garb of a kachina, banging away at his drum, turning as he pounded so as to face the four corners of the universe. In the rippling, I saw Chris Etchison, eyes closed, lips parted, a wordless melisma streaming from his throat. I saw them reflected, yet they weren't there with us, not yet.

"Father, please," Ash said. He tugged at the scepter. His back was to the water and he was pulling his father in. And still Strang's face was racked with reluctance. "You have to do it," he said.

Strang's cheeks quivered. The weight of the scepter was such that it must have seemed like he was carrying the whole world. But he still couldn't drop it. He continued to weep, and now the tears ran thick. He stood at the very edge and he still wouldn't take that last step, until, until. . . .

"I love you, father," Ash said, "and I know what I have to do."

He flung himself on the point of the scepter and impaled himself through the heart. Strang cried out, one last, heartwrenching howl, and then, as Ash's soul was sucked into the jewel, the scepter attained critical mass; Ash's soul was the last straw, the scruple that tipped the scales. The scepter itself pulled Strang into the water, because he would not let go. Ash held his father in a deadly embrace, pierced by the emblem of his father's power; and the two fell, arm in arm, into the embrace of the waters, and the waters started to churn and froth and slowly, slowly, slowly they sank into its depths.

Only the jewel remained. The waters slowly grew still. A child's hand rose out of the pool and clasped the jewel. The drumbeats pounded louder and louder. The jewel glowed through the clenched fist. Slowly, Chris emerged from the water. He was sitting, cross-legged, on a white lotus, and behind him, in a circle of sand, Milt danced and drummed. Chris was haloed with blue light. Chris smiled and his smile outshone the sun. Chris opened his palm, and the jewel was the sun. His *other* hand held a golden flute, which played of its own accord. His *other* hand—how many did he have?—held up a marble which contained a map of all the known worlds. His *other* other hand . . . no, two hands . . . were playing a spectral piano that hovered in the air behind him. He seemed to have a lot of hands. Another pair was weaving a tapestry, for example, and those reminded me of Penelope's hands. Perhaps all the mythological creatures we had met in this whole adventure had all been aspects of Chris, after all. Mr. E. once harangued me about how if god existed he had to be a solipsist.

Chris' pale blond bangs flapped against one eye in the breeze that played over the lotus. He looked at all of us, including the dead, and said nothing. God, he was beautiful.

"In a few seconds," Theo said to me, "he's going to play the music of unmaking. But if you want, you can make those seconds last forever. . . ."

And Joshua came to me, his long hair streaming; not a hint of acne; he took me in his arms; he said, "Serena, just say the word, the world doesn't really have to end. . . ."

CHAPTER TWENTY

THE LAST TEMPTATION OF PHILIP ETCHISON

Oren Karpovsky

—until this moment, I felt like a man of clay, half-formed, less than human. But now, suddenly, I find myself in the Oval Office, and my finger is hovering over a little red button.

The room is full of men in black suits. Everyone wants to tell me what to do. There's Kissinger, there's Schlesinger, there's MacNamara. I've got the dream team working for me—even dead people—Bill Casey is working the phones at a side desk, even though the top half of his head has been removed, and his carcinoma-riddled brain is showing. And everyone's muttering, trying to avoid my hearing what they're saying, little realizing that the President of the United States of Armorica has ears like a bat. God I'm powerful. This is what I've always striven for. On one wall dead presidents with electrodes attached to their skulls have been chained up, their heads moving from side to side in approval of all my actions. The decapitated head of Stalin speaks to me from a silver platter.

I look out of the window and see a vista of the whole world, because the White House has been hoisted up on a beanstalk and stands astride the stratosphere. They say I can blow the whole thing up right now.

I am having tea with Marvin the Martian, a little dark creature with a spittoon on his head. He's trying to sell me the rights to his explosive space modulator. I smile, and tell him that there are no arms for hostages deals on the table right now, and hand him the business card of the president of the Acme company, warning him to ignore Wile E. Coyote's lawsuit, even though that infamous consumer advocate is on the cover of *Time* magazine this week.

"Ja, Mr. President," says Henry Kissinger, fawning over me. "You might as well blow the whole thing away. After all, the universe is going to end in five minutes; why not be the one responsible? Think of the power, the power, the power."

"There's not much real estate left on Planet X," says Marvin the Martian, greedily guzzling his tea, "and they made me check my disintegrator pistol at the gate, so I am unable to blow you away."

A beautiful young girl—one of the congressional pages—is coming in with some document for me to sign. Her name is Serena Somers. She worked on my election campaign once. She smiles at me. So much power! I could make her drop to the ground and give me a blowjob right in front of all these celebrities. Barbara might throw a tantrum, but the press wouldn't even find out. "Mr. President," says the girl, "I'm so proud of you for getting elected. I adore your health plan. Like, you really care about us ordinary people." And I look at her with what passes for compassion in the 90s.

And my finger's still hovering right above the button.

Several of the White House staff look like they're about to cream themselves over this.

At that moment, as I looked out over the earth, misty and blue, I see a child hovering in the window. He's sort of an angel, I suppose. He's playing a golden flute. The melody filters through the window even though there's no sound in space, and one by one all the people here are struck dumb: the military advisors, the dead presidents, the celebs, even the cartoon characters; the only ones who don't seem to be affected are me and Serena.

There is a voice in the music of the flute, and the voice speaks to me, to me alone. And this is what it says: "Oren, Oren, this is what you've always dreamed of; this is the pinnacle of what you can achieve. With your finger hovering perpetually over the button, the cosmos is frozen in the moment before rebirth. You can push the button and be the next great power in the new universe. Or you can walk away."

"And if I do that—?" I say.

"You will be plain Oren, man of clay," says the angel, his voice emanating from the puff of breath at the head of each pure sweet note that issues from the magic flute.

"I don't know," I tell him. "It's a hard decision. . . ."

Philip Etchison

And so, at the end of our bridge, we came to a perfect place, a garden. Oh, more than a garden! The source of the River was a waterfall at its center, and we bathed in the sweet clear water and our clothes melted away, and we were as innocent as if we were at the beginning of time.

"Look," I said, "there are signs of a struggle." A smashed scepter lay in the grass. A jewel had been ripped from its mount. There were pieces of clay that seemed to have come from a statue; perhaps the statue had walked once.

"We were late for the final conflict," said Mary, "but not too late to wipe away the last signs of it." Mary scooped up some of the water with the palm of her hand and sprinkled it over the clay, the scepter . . . there were also some pools of blood . . . and where the healing water dripped, the things of darkness melted away.

"What place is this?" I said to her.

"I don't know," she said, "but it looks perilously like Eden."

And it was. Because we wandered through it . . . having stepped into it, Eden seemed endless. Perhaps it was an infinite garden that was folded back on itself a millionfold through space and time and tied up in a knot for us. There were animals that we did not recognize, and we named them. There were trees and flowers and bushes and ferns, and we named them all; there was a mushroom I named Theo, because Theo means god, because we felt that's what the place needed, a thing called god.

We wandered through the garden. We made love. We ate well, as vegetarians go; it didn't seem right to kill any of the animals, and in any case there was only one pair of every species, and none of them ever seemed to reproduce. Because the world was frozen in its perfection.

I don't know how long we were there. You don't count the days in a place like this. You laze around and let the warm sun seep into your pores. I rested from my long adventurings. I felt, at last, like the hero returning home from the quest, kicking back in paradise with his woman by his side, not a care in the world; I deserved this; I wanted it to last forever.

But there came a day when we wandered into the apple orchard, and we encountered the angel. . . .

Theo Etchison

It was the 90s, the time before the mad millennium. A dollar could still by a Coke and a candy bar; I was young, I was puffed up with shiny new epiphanies; I was a truthsayer and I knew everything, and my mother was dying as the station wagon sputtered across the Arizona desert on its way to Mexico and the Laetrile clinic.

I'm half asleep in the back, my head propped up on a Stephen King novel, leafing through the book where I've been writing all my dreams, and I'm not really reading it, just catching random words:

In a Chinese restaurant
the recombinant yellow brick road
forest of the night
Caliosper
the darkling wind

and I'm afraid, so fucking afraid, because half the words in here I don't remember putting down, and I think there's other mes out there, other Theo Etchisons driving through other Arizonas, and they're all reaching out to me through this dream book.

That's when I see the angel, sitting right next to me, a thin little kid in a tattered T-shirt, but like, you can see his wings as they rustle against the worn cotton. The angel doesn't speak exactly; he kind of hums, and I hear voices in my head.

And this is what the voices say to me:

"Theo, Theo, the world sucks, but you can remake it to be any way you want. Your mom doesn't have to be sick, and your brother doesn't have to be an asshole."

"Fucking bullshit," I say, and Dad turns around for a second, but he's not sure if he heard me I guess.

"It's all in the dream book," says the angel, "just close your eyes, grab the old felt tip out of the backpack, and start editing the past and the future. People do it all the time."

"But, but—" I say.

I do close my eyes. And what do I see? A dragon crossing the face of the sun, her shadow black over a desert landscape. A vampire standing at the prow of a ship. A Chinese restaurant rearing up out of the mist of morning. Fucking Jesus it's weird and I don't know if these are things I've experienced, or if I've dreamed them, or if it's a premonition and I'm going to have to face these things a ways down the road. And I see a mad king, harrowing the ice, dimly, at the eye of a snowstorm.

"Who are all those people?" I ask the angel. "And anyway, who are you?"

The angel only giggles, and then says, "You wouldn't want to know." Then he starts whistling that Tom Lehrer song, one of Dad's favorites:

There once was a man named Oedipus Rex,
You may have heard about his odd complex. . . .

S e r e n a   S o m e r s

He swept me off my feet. And onto the back of the white steed with the gold caparison. Oh, god, I loved him. Why shouldn't I? I had made him out of my own spit and a handful of cookie crumbs. Oh, he was beautiful. His armor glistened in the sunlight. His lance was still adorned with the ripped-up hem of my bridal garment. He took off his helmet and kissed me passionately and rode off with me into the sunset.

When we got to the sunset, though, there was an angel standing there, not smiling, his eyes dead serious, and he said to me, "Serena, Serena, are you sure?"

"What do you mean, am I sure?"

"Is this what you really want?"

"Why wouldn't it be?" I was a princess here, and not a slug. I was dressed all in white. Even my hymen had knit itself back, and a full day of horseback riding hadn't ruptured it either.

"Think, Serena, think," said the angel.

C h r i s   E t c h i s o n

soon I will have to
speak
soon I will have to say it
the word
that will unmake
all I have ever loved
the word

that will lose me
everything

J o s h u a   E t c h i s o n

I am dead. I am floating. It's been an eternity. It's been beautiful.
Eternity is a beautiful thing. To lie forever, to rest, to listen to nothing
but the slow heartbeat of the universe, to know that nothing matters
anymore . . .

I don't know how much time has passed because there isn't really any
time here . . . but now I think I'm hearing a voice. Music. Calling me.
Telling me I'm not really dead. . . .

P h i l i p   E t c h i s o n

. . . and he was sitting on a tree limb, his legs dangling, dressed in a
spangled loincloth, his golden wings fluttering and making a perfumed
breeze as we lazed in the afterglow of passion beneath an apple tree.

We looked up. A single apple glistened in the sun. It was golden. I
knew what it was right away. I'm not stupid. Just because we had re-
verted back to the Urzeit didn't make me unaware of mythology. This
apple was the querulous quince itself—the fruit of the knowledge of
good and evil—it was the thing that would set the world in motion, the
catalyst of the Big Bang—the mcguffin, as my Hollywood friends used to
call it.

"You don't have to eat the apple," the angel said. Well, he didn't speak
exactly. He held a golden flute aloft in one hand, and the flute played of
its own accord, and in the interstices of the melody I heard words, or
perhaps they were just word-fragments; they were tucked between the
phrases of the melody.

"I know," I said.

And Mary looked up and asked the question that needed to be asked:
"Why not?"

"The cycle doesn't *have* to begin all over again," said the angel, "and
you have the power to stay here forever. You don't need the knowledge
that's in the apple."

"Why not?" Mary said.

"Because if you were to know it—"

And the angel began to weep.

I said, "Aren't you my son, the one who doesn't speak because what he speaks *must* be the truth, so he would rather stay silent in front of me because there is a truth that dares not be spoken?"

And the angel wept.

"Is my temptation, then, to stay in Eden, to remain forever ignorant, not to know myself?"

The angel nodded.

"What kind of temptation is that?" I said. I was angry. I felt that my intelligence had been impugned a bit; this didn't agree with Joseph Campbell, not to mention Freud and Jung, at all. Knowledge was to be the temptation, not ignorance.

"But he's right," Mary said, "in a way. We're happy here. We don't have to go anywhere. This world is huge, and we'll never grow tired of exploring it. Can't we just stay here, stay happy?"

I reached up and touched the apple, *the*
jewel from the source, the
eye of Odin, the
forbidden
fruit

and I felt the jolt of power, and I said softly, "But Mary, how can the world begin without the first little bite of truth?"

And I plucked the apple and the angel began to weep still more, and the thunderclouds gathered and lightning flashed in the distance. . . .

S e r e n a   S o m e r s

. . . and I said, "You're right; this isn't the real Joshua"—even as Joshua turned his shiny new self away from me— "this is the Joshua that springs only from my fantasies."

And Joshua's weeping as he puts his arms around me and hugs me hard, and he's all metal, sharp and shiny, but underneath the armored skin I can hear the heartbeat of a human being, and—

T h e o   E t c h i s o n

—but I'm all "Dude," even though he thrusts the felt tip in my hand, "I don't want to be god, I want the story to write itself, doesn't matter how far it goes away from my dreaming," and the angel nods, like a wise old man, even though he's just a kid, and he says to me, softly, "Free will, free will, free will," and in the faintest of all whispers, "You're a good god, Theo, you're the right god for the new world"—

<u>O r e n   K a r p o v s k y</u>

—I push the button—

<u>P h i l i p   E t c h i s o n</u>

—eat the apple—

<u>S e r e n a   S o m e r s</u>

—rip away the metal cage around my lover's soul—

<u>T h e o   E t c h i s o n</u>

—throw away the felt tip pen and start ripping up the dream book—

<u>P h i l   E t c h i s o n</u>

—and Chris, who was once my son, speaks to me for the first time, and says, "Father, father—"

—and I embrace him, knowing that he has just uttered his first lie, and thus unmade the world—

—and Mary says, "You mean, I conceived you in sin?" and Chris sobs, passionately, in her arms and mine; we are not the Holy Family at all, just three lost souls who once forged a brief bond in the midst of the vaster chaos that is the cosmos—

<u>O r e n   K a r p o v s k y</u>

—and, as the world blows up in magnificent slow motion from my vantage point in the heavens, the angel—

<u>T h e o   E t c h i s o n</u>

—begins to dissipate in the flurrying scraps of paper that were once my notebook and—

S e r e n a   S o m e r s

—dissolves into the mist that was once my beloved's breath, and—

J o s h u a   E t c h i s o n

—pulls me out of the womb-warmth of mother darkness into a—

P h i l   E t c h i s o n

—garden of light that melts into the air and—

T h e o   E t c h i s o n

—leaves behind a single note of music—

P h i l   E t c h i s o n

—hanging—

O r e n   K a r p o v s k y

—hanging in—

S e r e n a   S o m e r s

—the chill—

J o s h u a   E t c h i s o n

—Arizona night—

O r e n   K a r p o v s k y

—Virginia morning—

Theo Etchison

air.

Phil Etchison

And so, outside a bizarre and baroque old Chinese restaurant that is already rippling away like a mirage, in the freezing desert night, our family, the four of us, embraces; the memories are already beginning to slip from us; the station wagon is waiting; in a moment, we're going to get in the car, get back on the highway, and head on south to Mexico; it's as though none of this ever happened; and yet, yet, yet—

Theo Etchison

I'm a kid again, puffed up with shiny new epiphanies, but more than a kid, too. Once, in another world that I know is more than a dream; once, I was a—

Serena Somers

—a goddess, a—

Phil Etchison

—bard who bridged worlds with mere words, a—

Joshua Etchison

—hero who faced and conquered Death himself, a—

Oren Karpovsky

—world-destroyer, a—

Phil Etchison

—kingmaker, a—

Theo Etchison

—god—

Phil Etchison

"I love you," said Mary Etchison, as the moon rose over the blood-stained mountains.

"I love you," I told my two sons, even though they weren't listening to me anymore, because they'd started fighting again. "I love you," I told my wife, "and one day we'll have another child."

Mary said, "How can I? I'm dying."

My two sons stopped fighting. They always do when their mother starts to talk about death. They don't say anything; they just become uncomfortable, withdrawn.

But this time, Theo turned to us and said, "Sometimes death is just a doorway."

And that, I knew, was the truth.

BOOK **FIVE**

C O D A

F A D O G R A P H

"a fadograph of a yestern scene"

—Finnegans Wake

from a catalogue of an auction to raise money for the Native American

Religious Freedom Fund:

ON TRUTH

BY PHILIP ETCHISON

Eternal verities . . . .

By now you will all have heard the great news—that I've finally managed to break my writing block, and that, as of last week, I have written over a hundred new poems. Posterity will decide if they're any good, but it means I won't have to give this annual lecture about the nature of truth anymore . . . I can actually give poetry readings. But today, let us ask ourselves that imponderable, unanswerable question for the last time: *What is truth?*

The greatest minds of all time have striven to answer the great question once posed by Pontius Pilate. Well, not all. Jesus Christ, to whom that question was addressed, managed to avoid answering it. And the Lord Buddha managed to skirt the issue by telling us that Truth does not exist.

Let me tell you now—before you cart me away—that the following things are all true. Dragons fly above our skies. Vampires pilot ships of doom through nights of direst gloom. Mad kings rage amid bombastic tempests, and goddesses give birth to planets; and all these things happen every morning of our lives. Lest you think these things are too fantastical, I'll tell you yet more truths. Children comprehend what adults but dimly apprehend. Music cannot lie. My wife is a living incarnation of the triple goddess. I personally have slain a dragon.

I can get away with telling you these things, without being dragged away by the men with the straitjackets, because you believe them to be metaphors. But what is the difference between a simile and a metaphor?

When you use a metaphor, you say that a thing *is* something else. You say the thing that is not true, elevating it to the status of truth, constraining it into truth, by the transforming magic of poetry.

But I say unto you (do you detect a bit of the messianic madness about me? But you know, they pay me well to occupy this chair of poetry, this utterly useless anachronism in our shiny 90s universe, this lip service tokenism of the human intellect) verily, I say unto you, we stand perpetually at the edges of a cosmic dream. We stand eternally hopeful that the things we call metaphors will one day become concrete, discrete, replete, not to mention paraclete; and if we did not believe (to quote one Samuel R. Delany, semiotician and madman) in the literalization of metaphor, in the ongoing process of *becoming* one with our metaphoric natures, we would not be entirely human.

I think that now that I can proudly stand head to head with George Steiner as far as winning first prize in the impenetrability sweepstakes.

Hey, what I'm really trying to say is:

Who gives a fuck? We know who we are. And sometimes, when we lie awake at night, and it occurs to us that maybe we're really someone else, that outside that familiar bedroom door, closed for the night, a whole different world has suddenly sprung into being, and that world will just as suddenly vanish come morning, when the door flies open once more, and maybe, maybe, maybe, out of the corner of your eye, that glimpse of unreality that you caught could be a little corner of that secret world. . . .

Don't tell me you haven't experienced that. I know you have.

Well, the secret is out now.. It's all true. Go home and chew your shrooms and take your peyote enemas, because there are doors, there are gateways, yes, there are, I promise you.

—*coffee-stained ms. found in a shredder at George Mason University, Fairfax County, Virginia, along with a prescription for Prozac. In the hand-writing of Philip Etchison, popular lecturer and poet, and host of the PBS series* Reality, Illusion, and Meta-Reality, *which had a highly successful run before its NEA grant was canceled by the Helms Commission. It appears that this lecture was never actually given.*

—offered by an Anonymous Source.

—reserve $150

CHAPTER TWENTY-ONE

CHRISTMAS IN THE WHITE HOUSE

S e r e n a   S o m e r s

It was Christmas Eve, and we drove right up to the front gate of the White House, which we were able to do because Oren had congressional license plates, so the guards kind of turned a blind eye.

Nathaniel, the driver, was the soul of discretion. The congressman was getting ready to hit the campaign trail—had a gig in Tucson, and then he was going to bop down to Mexico, to some Laetrile clinic, to show his support for alternative medicine. I suppose it was an honor when he asked me to dinner on Christmas Eve, though I kind of suspected there was going to be a bit of the old harassment thrown in. But what the hell. I'm almost eighteen. I know what I'm doing, and shit, I mean, Congressman Karpovsky, the dream idol of the young, with the MTV spots and the cameo on that Nine Inch Nails video. . . .

And anyways, it was the 90s.

A mad millennium was coming, and we were all getting ready for it in different ways.

So we sat in the limo drinking champagne and watching an *outlandish* Howard Stern-Rush Limbaugh special—who'd have ever thought it!— and yeah, sharing a joint, I admit it—me and my greatest idol. I had a letter from Joshua Etchison in my purse, you know, postmarked Arizona, and I hadn't opened it in a couple of days. I guess I felt like I was cheating on him. Imagine that! I'd never even gotten past, you know, letting him play with my tits. This was different. Congressman Karpovsky, I mean, you could just feel the power emanating from him, the aura, I mean, he was the bomb.

On television, they said it was midnight.

Christmas had arrived.

The congressman was a little tipsy, I guess. He started telling me the story of his life. He put his arm around me, which was, I guess, okay, and he said, "One day, you know, I might be having Christmas right inside that little ol' mansion. I mean, why not? I've got ambition. Great big fucking ambition."

"I know, congressman," I said.

"Call me Oren."

I giggled.

"I had the weirdest dream," Karpovsky said. "I was in the Oval Office, and I was about to push, you know, The Button, which was weird in itself as you know the Cold War is over. Marvin the Martian was on a state visit, but everyone else was there, too, everyone from Barbara Streisand to the animated corpse of JFK. I was about to destroy the universe. And then, and then—"

"I came into the room, right?"

"Whoa! You a psychic?"

"No, but I have some clue which way this is leading."

"I guess you weren't born yesterday after all, Serena," said the congressman, pouring me another glass of champagne. "So yes, you came into the room, and you were this vision of loveliness, and you see, the world was about to be destroyed, and you were all that stood between— you get the picture."

"You dreamed this, congressman—I mean, Oren? Exactly the way you told me?"

"Well . . ."

I thought he must have embellished here and there, but, you know, it was a pretty imaginative line of conversation, and not a bad way of turning a young girl's head. But then again . . . "I've had a dream, too," I told him, "and maybe you won't want to hear it."

"Try me."

"I dreamed it was the eve of the millennium, and you were in the White House, just like you said and I was there with you . . . and you became possessed by a vampire."

"That's kind of morbid," he said. "Look at the Christmas lights." He pointed. A couple of tourists ran by, oohing and aahing, and there was an Indian man sitting on a bench, with a placard in his hand that read *End of the World*. The congressman held my hand and I didn't rebuff him; probably a mistake.

I went on with my dream. "It was easy for the vampire to get inside your skin," I said, "because you already have this secret desire to be a bloodsucker . . . I mean, metaphorically, to drain people, to have total control over them. People like you always have it, even though they may try to deny it."

"You're so serious! And it's Christmas."

"And then, guess what, the vampire finally left you, and what was left behind was a man of clay."

"A golem!" he said. "The first Russian Jew to become president, and you have me turning into a golem—how singularly appropriate!"

Oh, but I laughed. I laughed till the tears started. And then, finally, the moment I'd expected and dreaded happened. The congressman turned to me, and this time he was all predator; his eyes reminded me of another dream I'd had, a dream of a vampire with slate-colored eyes whose father was a mad king and whose sister was a dragon. They were hungry eyes. And he smiled a thin little smile, and said softly, "How about that blowjob now, Serena?"

Our eyes met. For a split second I felt, you know, hunted, I felt how a deer must feel, knowing the rifleman's footfall, the spoor of the cougar, the howl of the wolf. And then I thought of Joshua's letter in my purse, and you know, I decided that it wasn't worth it after all, even though I'd half planned the evening with acquiescence in mind.

"I've got a boyfriend," I said, "and I'm like, saving myself for him. It sounds old-fashioned, but hey, I love him."

For a moment an angel stood between us. I didn't exactly see him. I felt him, I heard a mystical harmony ring in my ears, felt a sudden rush of warmth and love; and you know, Oren was still holding my hand, but the look in his eye was one of regret, of nostalgia; I felt a sorrow in him, and an awful inner turmoil I knew I would never be able to understand.

"Can't blame me for trying," he said at last. "You're a beautiful, beautiful . . . oh, shit, jailbait's gonna fuck my career one of these days."

"One of these days," I said, "you might even succeed."

In my dream, he had succeeded after all. And there was something about this dream; god, I think I lived lifetimes in that dream, I think that somehow it was all real.

"What's his name?" asked the congressman.

"Joshua."

"He's very lucky. Where is he now?"

"Arizona . . . on his way to Mexico."

"I see . . . well, how would you like to meet him there? Give him a cheap thrill, a little surprise? I don't think the PAC is going to miss among a couple of extra thousand, one more campaign worker . . . you see," he said, "I am *not* a sore loser."

"Maybe I was wrong about you," I said. "After all—"

"It was just a dream. Is that what you were going to say? Dreams are like the air. But where would we be without them? Or, for that matter, without the air? Let's have a kiss, at least."

And so I kissed him; and in that kiss took back the thousand kisses of my dream, the seven years I'd lived with him, the spats, the petty resentments, even the good times, the laughter, the glamour; I took it all back. The congressman was a good man, in his way; perhaps he'd even make a good president, one of these days.

"You have to have a phone in this car, right?" I said. "I'd like to call Arizona, if you don't mind."

"You're really tempting me to be a sore loser," said Congressman Karpovsky, laughing.

I rooted around in my purse for the letter. It was crumpled, but still unopened. I hoped Josh had had the presence of mind to leave a phone number where I could reach him . . . and I hoped Mr. and Mrs. E. would be fast asleep so they wouldn't be able to listen to what we had to say to each other. They always think, because they were in love once, a zillion years ago, that they can understand us. No one can. We can't even understand ourselves.

I reached Josh in a motel on a street named Oracle somewhere in Tucson.

"Merry Christmas," I said. "You'll never believe where I'm calling from."

"I'm dreaming," he said.

"No, you're not," I said. "Dreaming is for dweebs."

"Like my little brother."

"Where is he?"

"Passed out. And he insisted on ordering the Playboy channel. . . ."

"I love you," I said.

"Shit," he said. "You woke me out of the weirdest dream. I dreamed that I was dead. . . ."

"I love you," I said again. Didn't he hear me the first time? But he was doing the teenage macho thing, showing me how tough he was. I probably wouldn't get a response from him today. But tomorrow I'd be in Tucson. I'd be there for him. Everything was going to be all right. I was going to *make* it all right. Because I'm a woman. Because I'm powerful. Because I've been a goddess, and I know how to tune myself to the heartstrings of the world.

IN A LAETRILE CLINIC

<u>T h e o   E t c h i s o n</u>

—and so we're here, at the Laetrile clinic, in a weirdass Mexican town that's so American it even has a Taco Bell, and me and Josh are sharing a room in an adobe cottage by the sea; the hotel is an extension of the clinic. Today they rushed Mom into some intensive care thing, and Dad has gone with her, and my brother has gone to meet Serena at the border, and I'm all alone, by the sea, looking out at the sunset.

Are the memories really going fade?

Am I really going to get fat and middle-aged? I know I see less and less every day. Now it gets so that I have to wait until nightfall and close my eyes, *really* close them, tell myself I'm not going to wake up unless I see, feel, taste, touch *something*—the outline of a dark castle, a few flakes of snow, the heat-haze of distant dragon's breath—god, I tell myself, don't let me lose it all, don't tie my feet to this one world, to this one vision of the world.

Did the universe end and start again, and am I the only one who still knows that it happened? And am I too going to forget? Fucking Jesus I hope not; I know I want to be young forever, know I can't be, know there's compensations in being a grownup, wonder if it's fucking going to be worth it; wonder how they can stand it, being so blind, so unfeeling, so empty; and yet, yet, yet, there's got to be more to it than this dark desolation, because out of these grownups comes love; out of them comes the strength that keeps me going; and these things keep coming no matter how much of an asshole I am, no matter how much I rebel, no matter how much I tell the whole world to fuck off.

Today I've started a new dream book. No, not a dream book, kind of more of a memory book. I put in a few words here and there so that I can hold on to little pieces of all that happened. Serena came running down from Washington and Joshua's hormones have been thumping ever since, so he's no good for remembering, and anyway, he was dead half the time, or half dead all the time, depending on how you look at it.

These are the words I write down:

vampire
king
dragon
heart
jewel
source
love
death
goddess
life
circle
universe
forever
ever

Each word is a key. I wonder how long it will be before they change the locks.

A man is coming up the pathway from the clinic. He is a withered old Indian dude, dressed all in black, like a crow. I know him. When I look at him I hear drums in the back of my mind. It's Milt Stone, I know it is. "Milt," I say, "Milt," thinking, surely *he's* not going to have forgotten, because he's a shaman, he walks between worlds every morning before breakfast.

"You know my name," he says, and smiles.

It's not, "Hey, how surprising that you know my name," or, "how dare you call me by my name," or anything like that. It's just a statement, him telling me that he knows I know he knows.

"What are you doing here?" I ask him.

"They called me in from the reservation," he says, "because there's a lady here who has visions. She sees a clear, cool spring, and a crow hovering over the water, and the crow's flying in circles around her head and with each circle that he flies she becomes more and more herself, more and more whole."

"I see," I say, laughing a little, "that's . . . out there all right. One step beyond even Laetrile." Because I know that these miracle cures don't do a goddamn thing, I know she's really only coming here to die.

"But you see," says Milt, "I too have been having visions. And in my vision, I am that crow, and the woman is mother to the world."

My heart almost stops beating.

"What is the woman's name?" I ask him.

"You've been old," he says, "but soon you will be young again."

"What the hell is that supposed to mean?"

"You've been lost," he says, "but soon you will find yourself."

"I don't get it."

"Come back to the clinic with me," he says. "They sent me to fetch you."

🔳

Mom is sitting up in a high-backed wooden chair, and she's completely wrapped in a Navajo blanket. Dad sits on the bed, and he gazes, uncomprehending, at a bank of monitors and oscilloscopes. It's all very hospital-like, even though this place is kind of bogus as far as hospitals go; they don't even have real doctors here.

Mom's eyes are closed. She's sleeping, I guess. She's breathing evenly, which doesn't happen much anymore; so I know she's not feeling too much pain. Maybe she's all doped up though, and can't feel anything at all. That would be okay. I don't want her to hurt anymore. I think maybe the doctor's going to come in and say, Dudes, that's it, say your last goodbyes now.

Milt walks over to my mother; Dad holds up a hand as if to say no, no, not yet. "We're still waiting for Joshua," he says.

And Joshua shows up, in a rush, with Serena in tow; their hair is all mussed up and I wonder what they've been doing. Josh says, "I don't know why I'm here, we were all parked by the side of the highway and suddenly, I don't know, I get this *feeling*—"

"Good," Milt says. "Trust your feelings."

Then he crosses the room and places one hand over my mother's brow, and softly he begins to sing to her. His voice is all quavery and whistly, like a bird, and I hear another voice too, a melody from another world; I don't know if it comes from the pinging of the oscilloscopes or the thrum of some life-support unit, but it blends in with Milt's eerie wheezing and it all comes together, like an ancient car engine cranking itself back to life.

"What's going on?" says Josh. "Who is this Indian dude?"

"Wait," I say. "Wait. In a moment, you'll remember. . . ."

"Oh, wait a minute, yeah," he says. "You're a crow." Milt begins to spin, very slowly. When he spins clockwise he's a man, and when he spins counterclockwise she's a woman, but the transformations are so complete that you can't even believe they ever occurred. Back and forth and back and forth, and he's still singing, and there's a drumbeat too, but maybe it's my own heart pounding, can't understand why it seems to keep perfect time with the music.

Soon he's whipping around so dizzyingly that I can barely see him at all, and then, for a split second, I see someone else—someone who looks a little bit like my mom, and a little bit like an angel, and a little bit like me—but he's just a flash in the blur, and then he's out of sight, and then Milt is back with us, only this time he's wearing a white labcoat, has on a pair of hornrimmed glasses, and is making furious notes on a clipboard, shaking his head.

"Mrs. Etchison," he announces to all of us, "has inexplicably gone into remission."

My mother opens her eyes.

"I've had," she says, "such a strange, bewildering—"

"Dream," we all finish for her in chorus.

"We went to the very ends of the earth," Dad says, "and you bathed in the redeeming blood of the Holy Grail."

Josh says, "We fought monsters. We defeated wicked wizards and horrible dragons. I don't know where all the treasure went. I guess it kind of vanished into thin air."

"Yeah, Mrs. E.," says Serena, "it was cool I got to go along for the ride. I mean, even though you guys aren't really my family." She looks shyly up at Joshua. "Yet."

Then it's my turn. I think we're taking turns. I say, "We didn't dream any of it. It was all true."

And that is the last statement I shall ever make as truthsayer; it's the last pure shining truth that will ever fall from my lips; because from now on I'm going to be just plain Theo, human being, loving son and brother. I won't know what it's like to see the one true stream that's clearer than all the others. The river will be as muddy for me as it is for everyone else, and you know what? I don't care. Maybe we did redeem the universe, but for me it's not about that. It's about getting my family back. It's about starting again. It's about me and Mom and Dad and Joshua and maybe, a little bit, Serena, because I can tell she's going to be one of us. Fucking Jesus, I can barely believe it worked, and I can barely grasp how we moved heaven and earth, literally, to make it happen, but it did work, and we're home now, home again at last.

Milt, who has become Mom's doctor in this new version of reality, explains, patiently, how remission doesn't necessarily mean a complete cure, but how one might lead a productive, healthy life for months or even years without any sign of the cancer returning; he tells us to savor each moment, to make each little thing count, because nothing is certain. It's a speech that doctors have been making since time began, and Milt's totally good at it; he sounds so reassuring, so soothing, it doesn't really matter what he says because the bottom line is that we've all come back from the edge of the abyss.

So, like that night, we celebrate our asses off, because it's coming up to New Year's anyway and we never really did Christmas because we were so full of pain. Dad gets so drunk we have to put him to bed in the hotel with a trashcan beside his pillow in case he pukes. I guess that's good; I never saw him be that way before.

Serena tells stories about Congressman Karpovsky—how in his dreams he hobnobs with Marvin the Martian and Wile E. Coyote. She makes us laugh till we practically piss our pants.

Then she decides to give Joshua a tour of Karpovsky headquarters, on the other side of the border, and I'm left alone with my mother sharing a marshmallow and a cup of hot chocolate, watching someone else's fireworks beyond the cliffs in the clear Mexican night.

"Mom," I say softly to her—and I haven't hugged her yet, haven't even touched her yet, because, you know, of the thing we did, back in the other universe, and I'm still scared to be close to her—"Mom," I say, "how much do you remember?"

Her eyes sparkle. Maybe it's the reflection of fireworks. Or starlight. Or the crescent moon. She says, "I remember as much as you want me to remember."

And she kisses me, gently, on the cheek, and I know that she knows everything. "But," she cautions me, "we'll never speak of it. Or we'll end up in that horrible old asylum together, you and me, having cold pointy thermometers shoved up our butts by nasty old psychoanalysts."

"They really did that to you there?" I say.

"As I recall "she says.

"You really *do* recall," I say.

"I love you, Theo," she says to me, "but don't get fresh. Remember, we are human now, and I *am* your mother."

And so, after I kiss her goodnight and she goes in to my drunken snoring father, I go to my room and turn on the television: I debate whether I should order up Playboy; Josh, I know, won't come back to-night.

I get a Coke and a candy bar from the in-room refrigerator. I munch the candy bar and sip the Coke and watch the TV until the station goes off the air and then I watch the snow for a long long time . . . once in a while, I think I see the angel hovering above the million flecks of white and gray . . . I think I see the mad king raging and the jewel glittering . . . I think I see my son, the once, the future, the never-present . . . the truthsayer who might have been.

I close my eyes, and—

Strang! Thorn! Katastrofa!

A whole universe died and was reborn so my family could start to heal itself. What a strange and amazing truth. What a thing for a young boy like me to know. How long will I know it for, how long, how long? How long until I just come to think that I have too much imagination, too much, too much? Oh, fucking Jesus, it's a huge burden to bear, this truth, and maybe I should just slough it off, emerge a born-again innocent, a shiny new dragon from the river of time . . . maybe I should let go . . . but not just yet, please, not just yet . . . I still want to stand in the twilight edges of the dream country . . . I still want to look back at the burning citadel of my childhood.

Katastrofa! Ash!

There is a cure for what ravaged my mom's body, and for the sickness that still gnaws away at the world's dark heart.

Chris

(oh my heart aches the most for him)

Yes. We have found the cure. We harrowed hell for it. We racked the four corners of the universe. God we fought hard, and now we hold it in our hands. But we can't quite identify it.

We're not sure what it's called, this magic herb that can seal up our wounds, renew the world, turn back the clock to rub out our mistakes.

Maybe the cure is Laetrile.

Or maybe it's love.

Bangkok, Los Angeles, 1994-6

Somtow Papinian Sucharitkul (S.P. Somtow) was born in 1952 in Bankok, Thailand, and grew up in Europe. He was educated at Eton College and at Cambridge, where he obtained his B.A. and M.A., receiving honors in English and Music.

His first career was as a composer, and he has emerged as one of Southeast Asia's most outspoken and controversial musicians. He has had his compositions performed, televised and broadcast on four continents. His most recent compositions include the dazzling *Gongula 3* for Thai and Western instruments, commissioned for the opening of the Asian Composers Expo, and *Star Maker—An Anthology of Universes,* for large orchestra, four sopranos, and other soloists, recently premiered in Washington.

In 1977 he began writing fiction. He was first nominated for the John W. Campbell Award for best new writer in 1980, winning in 1981. Two of his short stories, "Aquila" and "Absent Thee from Felicity Awhile," have been nominated for the coveted Hugo Award, science fiction's equivalent of the Oscar. He has now published eighteen books, including the complex, galaxy-spanning *Inquestor* series and the satirical *Mallworld* and *The Aquiliad* as well as the serious, philosophical *Starship & Haiku* and *Fire from the Wine-Dark Sea,* a short story collection.

S.P. Somtow's career as a novelist has expanded far beyond the boundaries of science fiction. His horror novel, *Vampire Junction,* written under the name S.P. Somtow, was praised by Ed Bryant as "the most important horror novel of 1984," and the *New York Daily News* called it "the grimmest vampire fantasy ever set to paper . . . sure to become a cult classic." His second mainstream novel, *The Shattered Horse,* has been compared to Umberto Eco and was called, by noted author Gene Wolfe, "in the true sense, a work of genius." A young people's book, *Forgetting Places,* was honored by the "Books for Young Adults" program as an "outstanding book of the year."

His second horror novel, *Moon Dance,* is already being hailed as a landmark in the field and has been nominated for the American Horror Award. Critic A. J. Budrys has compared the work to Henry James and Nathaniel Hawthorne. It is a vast novel in which a pack of Eastern European werewolves settle in the Dakota Territory in the 1880s. Somtow spent six years researching the novel, himself traversing every inch of his characters' odyssey from Vienna, Austria, to California, and studying Native American languages. *Moon Dance* sold out before publication date and has gone back to press three times.

The horror film that S.P. Somtow wrote and directed, *The Laughing Dead,* has been called "a horror film for the 90s" by *Cinéfantastique* and "one of the best independent productions in a long while" by Michael Weldon of the *Psychtronic Review.* It has been released in Europe and will appear in the U.S. later this year.